FAMILY OF THE EMPIRE

Sheelagh Kelly was born in York in 1948. She attended
Knavesmire Secondary School for Girls, left at the age
of fifteen and went to work as a book-keeper. She has
written for pleasure since she was a small child, but
not until 1980 were the seeds for her first novel, *A
Long Way from Heaven*, sown when she developed an
interest in genealogy and local history and she decided to
trace her ancestors' story, thereby acquiring an abiding
fascination with the quirks of human nature. *A Long
Way from Heaven* was followed by *For My Brother's
Sins*, *Erin's Child*, *My Father*, *My Son*, *Dickie*, *Shoddy
Prince* and *A Complicated Woman*. *Family of the Empire*
is the second novel of a new three-book series about the
Kilmaster family.

SHEELAGH KELLY

Family of the Empire

HarperCollins*Publishers*

HarperCollins*Publishers*
77–85 Fulham Palace Road,
Hammersmith, London W6 8JB

www.fireandwater.com

This paperback edition 2002
1

First published in Great Britain by
HarperCollins*Publishers* 2000

Copyright © Sheelagh Kelly 2001

The Author asserts the moral right to
be identified as the author of this work

A catalogue record for this book
is available from the British Library

ISBN 978-0-00-787979-3

Typeset in Ehrhardt by Palimpsest Book Production Limited,
Polmont, Stirlingshire

Printed and bound in Great Britain by
Clays Ltd, St Ives plc

ACKNOWLEDGEMENTS

I would like to thank the following people for their assistance in my research: Briony Hudson of Pontefract Museum; Guy Kilminster and the staff of the York and Lancaster Regimental Museum at Rotherham; the staff of the National Army Museum; the staff of the Public Record Office; the lady at Birr Library whose name I unfortunately omitted to ask; Ian Winstanley of the Coal Mining History Resource Centre.

My thanks, too, for the expert writings on military history of Lord Baden-Powell (*The Matabele Campaign*), Thomas Pakenham (*The Scramble For Africa; The Boer War*), Lawrence James (*The Savage Wars*) and the journalistic eye of Donald Macdonald (*How We Kept the Flag Flying*).

Finally, my gratitude to the soldiers of the York and Lancaster Regiment whose memoirs provided me with valuable information, in particular I.W.O. Davies and E. Buffey, but most of all to Regimental Sergeant-Major P. J. Wilcox.

For my dear husband, James.

There were others in the wooden cage besides him. Suspended in pitch blackness, he could not see them, but could smell their tense mood mixed with yesterday's sweat and pipe tobacco, shared their apprehension in the knowledge that any moment all could be plunged to eternity. Deeper, the cage and its mute occupants descended into the chasm. Now came the scent of wet earth, the trickle of water, the reek of explosive. He wondered, as he sank deeper still, if they would get him today. So far he had managed to avoid them but one could not fight the inevitable.

A jolt signified that the cage had reached the bottom. Here were flickering tallow candles, yet to his uninitiated eyes the figures around him remained amorphous. Trying to avoid contact with anyone, he stumbled through the murk to the deputy's boxhole to receive instruction. Then, equipped with orders, he embarked upon a tunnel, tripping occasionally over the ropes and pulleys underfoot, grazing his head as overhead timbers suddenly dropped in height.

After rambling seemingly for miles he finally located the ventilation doors he had been seeking, and crouched down to wait. Away from the shaft, the air was hot and uncomfortable. There came faint groans and rumblings from the earth; his vivid imagination compared it to being trapped in giant intestines. Wrapped in darkness the mind played tricks. Averse to being up at such an hour he fought the tendency to yield to his sluggardly nature. Only the fear of what might be lurking kept him awake.

Gradually, though, the weight of the darkness forced his eyelids to sag. His head began to droop – and that was when they made their move, swooping silently like barn owls. Jerked awake, he found each limb clamped by rough talons, yelled and tried to kick out to prevent his trousers being hauled to his ankles, voiced even louder protest as his manhood was laid bare for inspection.

'Eh, not bad for a young un!' The gasp held admiration.

There was a snigger. 'What's tha talking about, it's bigger than thine!'

A bout of scuffling and laughter ensued.

Alarmed further, that his attackers could obviously see him whilst he could make out no human form, he opened his eyes to their utmost aperture but encountered only a solid wall of pitch. To struggle was useless; they continued to pinion his limbs and made closer examination, their comments becoming even more lewd, until one of them grabbed a handful of coal dust, applying it with deft intimacy. Deeply embarrassed at having such attention paid to him he begged to be released, his melodic Irish brogue contrasting with their gruff Yorkshire tones.

'Dat's enough, fellas! Aw, will ye please have a heart!'

Friendlier now, warm even, the hands and voices invited freedom, but the rumble of wheels and the jingle of harness interrupted further ado. Another had joined the audience. 'Bring him over here and gi' us a look at him!'

He felt the sudden change in mood, real danger threatened now.

'We've done him,' said one of his attackers, though in wary tone.

'Is tha deaf? I said, fetch him over here!'

After some hesitation, he was bundled to another place, calling in vain for them to let him go. Still, he could see little, but his nostrils detected the musky whiff of pony, and the persistent draught on his skin told him he was under fresh review.

A crude oath preceded the statement. 'I've seen bigger on me two-year-old nephew.'

Beyond his discomfort, he sensed that others shared his humiliation. One of them even spoke in his defence, albeit subduedly. 'Nay, it's all reet.'

Another tried to lighten the situation. 'Bill thought it were like one of his dad's prize carrots. Mindst, he would, the scratty thing he's got.' There was the dull thud of flesh being pummelled, and nervous laughter.

'Carrot, eh? Let's see if t'hoss thinks so.' The dangerous one yanked on his pony's bridle, attempting to bring its muzzle into contact with the victim's flesh. 'Away you gormless sods, hold him up! Come on, Prince, have a bite o' this.'

Terrified at the thought of being emasculated by equine teeth, his scream echoed down the tunnel.

'Let him go!' came the vain order from one of his erstwhile assailants.

More swearing and jingling of harness. Unsettled by its rough treatment, the pit pony whinnied and tossed its head.

Probyn Kilmaster did not mind a joke but this was beyond endurance. Reaching into a cubby-hole for a hidden candle – no safety lamps at this pit – he shed light on the tense proceedings. 'Leave him alone, Judson! Lad's taken his whack.'

Still gripped, the fearful victim saw for the first time his attackers, one of them now apparently his saviour, a youth with the family name of Kilmaster whose members were well known in the village for their various shades of red hair. In the eerie glow he recognized one or two of the others also, though only by sight, for they were outside his circle.

All of them, though, were familiar with Judson, a notorious, sixteen-year-old thug, who was now wrenching viciously at his pony's harness to force its compliance.

Probyn knew the victim Michael Melody by sight but, coming from a staunch Wesleyan enclave, had been forbidden to associate with Catholics. He had only joined the initiation team because this was what happened to every new boy.

However, a light-hearted prank had now become intimidation, and Kilmaster detested any form of bullying. So, instinct overriding indoctrination, he spoke up for Melody, telling his friends: 'Let him go, lads.'

Judson was having trouble controlling the stocky Welsh pony and hurled a vile epithet at the other. 'I haven't finished with him yet!'

'Well, we have,' said Probyn, in his brave, rational manner. Though he himself might let slip the rare curse in anger, he abhorred such violent crudity as offered by Judson. However, with such a thug one was forced to apply restraint if not wishing to induce physical assault. 'Old Wilson'll skelp us if he finds we've been larkin'. Here's your cap, young un.' Nonchalantly, he helped the victim to his feet, speaking as man to boy, though he was only seventeen and Melody barely two years his junior.

Judson shot a look of venom, but was distracted by the obstreperous pony. Launching into a bout of expletives he began to thrash it about the head with a switch. There was a high-pitched whinny of pain, the animal lurched backwards and with a great din the tub attached to its harness was derailed.

'Serve him right, cruel swine,' came the rash utterance from one of the former attackers, courageous amongst number. 'Aw look, Probe, he's cut poor divil's face open.'

Melody wondered how they could see so much whilst he remained blind. Would he ever achieve his pit eyesight? But he was too busy struggling to cover his own nakedness to worry about an animal.

Judson's gravelly voice spat derision, and he merely scooped up a handful of coal dust to staunch the wound, daubing it roughly on the pony's nose. 'He'll live! Come and help us get this corf back on t'rail.'

'Toss off,' came the impudent reply, and all bar Melody pelted off down the tunnel.

'Bastards, I'll do for thee!' bawled Judson, and was about to

4

pursue them, when out of the blackness loomed the deputy, Wilson, his face resembling a wild, limestone crag.

'What's all this foul language about? Judson, you dozy little –!' He would have sworn himself had not the manager, a stalwart of the chapel, been in the pit, but instead he had to suffice with brandishing his yardstick. 'Get this back on track before Mr Lewis sees it!' The manager's random visit intensified Wilson's ire at finding such incompetence – as if it wasn't bad enough being Christmas week, everyone in a hurry to be done, safety precautions ignored in the rush to earn extra money.

'It's this unruly bloody hoss,' grumbled Judson.

'Less of your cussing and get on with it!' Wilson turned to inspect the trembling pony.

Melody shrank back into position by the air doors, hoping to be unnoticed. With the others gone, Judson would doubtless vent his spleen on the only one left behind.

But the furious Wilson spotted him. 'Don't just sit there! Help this naff-head.'

Caked in black dust, scuttling like a rodent, Melody grasped one side of the heavy tub and, straining and grimacing alongside Judson, managed to heave it back onto the rails, all the while his heart praying to Wilson, please don't leave me alone with this lunatic!

Alas, it looked as if this was to be his fate. Having checked that the pony was satisfactorily hitched to the tub, Wilson barked one last comment and turned on his heel.

Melody battled with his natural shyness. 'Em, begging your pardon, sir!' His musical brogue danced along the tunnel.

A gruff voice came back through the darkness. 'What's to do now?'

The anxious boy wrung his hands. 'I know how busy ye are with Christmas, Mr Lewis being here an' all, so I was wondering if I could take a bit of the strain off your shoulders by doing something more useful? Seems an awful waste, paying me to sit and open and shut dese air doors –'

'If you're after more money –'

A pained cry. 'That's not my intention, sir! I just want to feel I'm earning it fairly.' Melody tried to sound enthusiastic, though hard work was something he normally avoided. 'Sure most of the ponies are so bright they can open the doors demselves – and ye did say once I'd got me pit eyesight ye might give me more responsibility.'

'You can see all right now, then?' asked the disembodied voice.

'Indeed I can, sir!' The lie tripped out without a quaver.

'Do you know Eddie Redfearn, pony driver?'

'I do.' Another lie.

Wilson did not prevaricate further. 'Go swap places with him, he's been like a slug in a trance this morning. You'll find him on Pearson's road.' With this he strode off. Melody too beat a hasty departure, putting as much distance as possible between himself and Judson.

Unable to locate Pearson's road amongst the warren of other haulage tunnels that ran off the coalface, he eventually found himself at the stables on the pit-bottom, and was regarding it as a comfortable place to sneak a nap when the horse keeper pounced on him. Driven out with fresh instructions, he finally came upon Redfearn and wasted no further time in relaying Wilson's order. Though, after this burst of alacrity, he adopted a snail's pace in delivering his tubs, much of this being due to the pony who refused to obey his commands. It turned out to be harder work than he'd anticipated, the tubs having to be shoved part of the way by brute strength before being hitched to the pony. After this he spent most of his time imploring the animal to move.

It was in such a vein that Probyn Kilmaster happened upon him again. About to trundle past with his own train of corves, he saw who it was and, with a call to his pony to 'Whey!', he applied a wooden chock to the wheels, remarking on Melody's change of fortune. 'By heck, you land on your feet don't you!'

6

'I'm not so sure,' wailed the lad, indicating his stubborn companion.

'Eh, come out, I'll show thee.' The more experienced youth took charge, holding his flattened palm under a velvety muzzle. Not seeming to mind that the offered lump of turnip was tainted by coal dust, the pony became instantly accommodating. There was an awful crunching noise at which Melody grimaced. 'They all have their own personalities same as us,' explained Probyn. 'You just have to get to know 'em. General here only responds to bribery. Here, I've found a bit in t'other pocket. Give it him later.'

Extending his hand through the gloom, Melody felt the lump of vegetable upon his palm and transferred it to his own pocket. The animal observed this, its ears pricked in compliance. 'Seems to have worked – tanks.'

Even as he gave assistance, Probyn could not empathize, having a low opinion of one who had to be nannied. He straightened his cap. 'Don't know how long he'll stay sweet with only one bit o' tunnip, but that's thy concern.' Without further ado he turned to go.

'I might be calling on your help again!' blurted Mick.

'Not after today you won't. I'm off to be a filler after Christmas.' Probyn had only remained driving for so long because he liked the ponies, but lately his father had insisted he apply for a man's job. Removing the brake, he and his train of corves melted into the darkness.

Eager to maintain the link with this approachable ally, Melody called out – 'I'm Mick by the way!' – and received a ghostly response.

After this, the Irish youth found his passage a little easier. Eventually, he reached his first delivery point, lured to the collier by the tap-tapping sound of pick against coal. Here the roof dropped to a height of four feet, prohibiting the entry of the pony. Crouching, he moved as far as he could into the stall, then studied the full tub that awaited him, wondering how he was going to shift it. To his great surprise he found that he had begun to see things more clearly now and for a moment he paused to watch the two men at work. Stripped to their shorts, their torsos gleamed with black rivulets of sweat. One broke off to take a long swig from his water bottle, his jutting Adam's apple bobbing up and down beneath the glistening skin. The other turned from his awkward kneeling position to observe the onlooker, and issued instruction to the boy he had not seen before.

'Don't take that corf yet, love, we've another nigh on ready for thee. What's tha name?'

A shy utterance. 'Mick.'

The collier used the back of his arm to wipe black sweat from his forehead. 'Well, Mick, you might as well start polishing top layer of t'other one while you're waiting, it'll save time later.' At the boy's confusion, he added lightly, 'You've heard Mr Lewis's here? Then you must've been told he likes to see every tub immaculate, won't let it out of t'pit unless there's a nice, neat, polished surface he can see his face in. Will he, Fred?'

His thirst slaked, Fred's lips broke suction with the glass bottle in a satisfied gasp and he rammed the cork home. 'Just do the top layer, mindst. It doesn't matter what it looks like underneath.' He resumed work, his dour face an image of the rugged black wall before him.

Though this was only his third day underground Michael Melody had worked two years on the surface and was wise to such tricks. He grinned. 'Would dat be after I clean the windows or before?'

'Eh, I can see there's no fooling this un,' sighed the first hewer, and continued sounding the coal with his pick, testing how difficult it would be to remove.

His partner hacked at the big lumps of coal that the first had hewn, splitting off the muck with hammer and wedge. Happy for this restful interlude, Mick watched in admiration of these men. Once the lumps were the required size, the man seized a shovel and set to topping up the half-filled tub, grunting and wheezing for, with less than a foot between the top of the tub and the roof, his body was hunched and deformed. Once finished he told Mick to drag both tubs away. Pausing for breath, his ribcage undergoing a rapid rise and fall beneath the wiry body, he leaned on his calloused knees and asked, 'How many corves are you leaving us?'

'Em, three,' came Mick's quiet reply.

'Any chance of you bringing us a few extra? We've nearly got enough to fill another now and by the time you get round to us again we'll be sat twiddling our diddlers. We'll make it worth your while with a few bob when we get paid.'

Delighted at the prospect of a bonus, Mick agreed and with great effort began to manoeuvre each of the full tubs back to the pony, then hooked them up to the chain at its rear. Finding it once again necessary to apply bribery, he gave the solitary piece of turnip to General, hoping its effects would be lasting, then it was off to the next haulage road.

His return with five empty tubs provoked much gratitude from the colliers, who promised a florin each from their Christmas wages, though they failed to mention that his action might make him unpopular with others.

Pleased with himself, and imagining what this bonus would buy, Mick was travelling back to off-load his full corves, when he came across Probyn Kilmaster again. The road was badly laid here and one of Probyn's tubs had come off the rail. The auburn-haired youth had enlisted the help of two colliers to get it back on the track and was being castigated for taking them away from their livelihoods.

'If you laid your road a bit better this wouldn't have happened,' Mick heard Probyn's breathless grumble.

This provoked anger from the colliers. 'You clever little snot, you can do it thissen!' And they abandoned him struggling to keep the full tub upright.

'Oh, get back in your bloomin' 'oile,' muttered Probyn under his breath.

Seizing the opportunity to repay a favour, Mick left his pony and rushed forth to help the older youth.

After lengthy exertion, the two managed to get the tub back on the rail, then stood back to catch their breath, appraising each other.

Probyn ballooned his cheeks and offered a grudging, 'Thanks.'

'Don't mention it,' replied Mick, and was about to return to his pony when an oath pierced the gloom and Judson came striding towards him.

'You little shit, you pinched my frigging corves!'

Mick stared into his assailant's face – a mindless, ill-bred hooligan, obviously possessing not one scruple – and saw that to reason was useless. There was little to be gained except the small satisfaction of having offered defiance. 'Em, I didn't see your name on them.'

'You cheeky –!' Judson repaid the other's audacity with a blow, sending the younger boy tumbling to the floor, his lip split open. He was about to swing a kick when Probyn launched himself forth and pushed him off balance, giving the dazed Mick a chance to totter to his feet and make his escape into the nearest stall. Judson swore and, telling Probyn he would have him next, dashed after Mick.

Crouching beside the two colliers whose stall it was, Mick threw a pleading glance for assistance, but, loath to lose money, they ignored his swollen bloody face and continued to hack at the seam with their picks.

Probyn scrambled in after Judson who voiced obscenity and threatened violence. One of the colliers did intervene then, but only to tell all three youths to, 'Sling your hook! If tha wants to fight do it somewheer else!'

Judson glared threateningly for a while with his ice-blue eyes, before backing out slowly with an arrogant look on his face that told the other two this was not surrender.

Thoroughly irritated that Melody had got him into two scrapes with Judson today, Probyn gritted his teeth and moved out to confront the bully. Mick lingered anxiously, holding his throbbing, bloody mouth and waiting to see what would happen to Kilmaster.

Then suddenly there came a groaning sound, props began to crack and splinter like matchsticks. The whites of their eyes portraying terror, the colliers scrambled for all they were worth towards the exit, urging Mick ahead of them with frantic shoves at his back as the roof began to cave in: 'Get out get out get out!' First into the main roadway, sprawling headlong under their violent shoves, Mick saw the look of horror on Probyn Kilmaster's face, on Judson's too, could tell that something awful had occurred behind him but did not stop and turn until the thunderous noise had ceased and the roof no longer moved.

Through the choking cloud of dust came an agonized moan. One of the colliers had escaped, the other's leg was imprisoned by a heap of stone and timber.

Whilst Judson stood there indecisively, Probyn delivered a thump to Mick's arm. 'Go fetch help!' Coughing, he himself fell to his knees and began to aid the uninjured man in freeing his partner, the latter beginning to scream.

'Oh, Christ, get me out!'

'Your leg's stuck, John!' cried his friend, grubbling amongst the debris, frantically trying to release him, blood mingling with the coal dust.

Another tormented shriek. 'Chop it off! For God's sake I can't stand it!'

Hypnotized, Mick had not moved from the spot. Probyn yelled at him again to fetch help and he at last sprang to action, but had no need to run far. Hearing the telltale rumble men came dashing to the site with shovels, began to seize boulders and pit props, hurling them aside, others shoring up the roof to avert another fall.

Finally the mutilated collier was dragged out. Hearts still thumping with shock, Probyn and Mick watched him being borne away to the surgeon's house.

Without delay came the furious inquiry. 'Cutting corners

again!' panted the deputy, making a random guess. 'You're that concerned trying to make a few extra bob for Christmas you risk everybody else's lives!'

The hewer whose partner had been injured took great offence. 'Eh! It were nowt to do wi' me! It were that little bugger who wrought it!'

Mick was aghast to find the finger pointed at him but before he could offer any defence Wilson began to lay about his shoulders with his yardstick.

Hating injustice, Probyn came to his aid for the third time that day. 'He didn't do owt, Mr Wilson! He only ran in there to get away from yon fella.' Even as he indicated Judson he knew it was madness.

Wilson ceased beating Mick and turned his ire on Judson. 'Right! Manager's office, sharp. Everybody else back to work. And I'll be having words with your father!' Probyn was dismayed to find the latter threat addressed to him, and was even more disturbed by Judson's parting caveat – 'Make the most o' your Christmas, Ginger' – for it held not genuine goodwill but the promise of retribution after the holiday.

Whilst everyone moved back to their various positions in the workings, Mick found his limbs were still trembling. Cautiously dabbing the back of his hand against his gashed lip, he winced, then donated a sigh of gratitude to the sandy-haired youth. 'I'm much obliged to ye.'

Probyn had been momentarily distracted by the sight of the injured miner's clothes, still hanging neatly outside the stall where they had been put a few hours ago, his snap tin complete with uneaten sandwiches. How terrifying that a mere thirty seconds could wreak such havoc. He tore his eyes away, stooped angrily to retrieve his fallen cap, bashed it on his thigh and rammed it back on his head. 'Aye well, don't think it makes us lifelong friends, I'd do it for anybody.' And he strode off.

On reflection he took issue with himself for being so harsh. He was not unkind by nature, it was just the thought of what Judson would mete out to him that had caused the bad-tempered utterance; not to mention his father's reaction. However, he decided not to apologize as he might have done had it been anyone else. Melody might get the wrong impression, and Probyn had no wish to encourage fraternization with a Catholic.

Hours later, the exhausting toil finally came to an end. Awaiting the signal to pass between the banksman and the winding-engine man, Probyn Kilmaster gave an inwards hallelujah at the jerk that signified his resurrection, as the cageful of weary pitmen moved heavenward. Never was he so glad.

At last the merciful earth released them for another day. Spilling forth amongst his comrades – more talkative now at the thought of the Christmas holiday – he enjoyed only momentary banter then handed in his numbered disc, collected his pay and set off home. It had been dark when he had gone down the pit this morning, and it was dark now although it was barely four hours past noon. Only by reason of the festive sojourn would he see daylight tomorrow.

But Probyn was not thinking about Christmas. Life was no different in the Kilmaster household even at this time of year, other than a good spread. No, he was keeping his eyes peeled for Judson. They would inevitably meet at some point, but he would try to delay that collision until the pit re-opened.

A call made him jump. Upon turning quickly he spotted the Irish youth trotting after him. With an inward lament, he continued his brisk march. Against the gunmetal sky rose the outline of railway wagons, stacks of timber props, slag heaps, locomotive sheds, winding gear, chimneys and brickyards. A steady flow of miners wended their tired passage from the colliery. He moved to overtake them all, bent on escape.

'Hang on, Probe!'

Probe! Anyone'd think he'd known me years, thought the other crossly, marvelling that Melody appeared undeterred by the earlier rebuff. God preserve us from the thick-skinned.

Mick's snap tin rattled noisily as he caught up with the

13

Kilmaster boy and fell in beside him, his sparkling blue eyes illuminating the sooty face. 'Tanks again for fighting my corner!'

Tanks! Probyn enjoyed an inward laugh at the Irish accent. 'Don't mention it,' he said, but forced himself to remain grim-faced. However, this did not appear to discourage Melody.

'I haven't that many friends,' explained Mick.

Probyn's heart sank. Please Lord, don't lumber me with this teague.

Mick checked himself with a self-conscious laugh. 'Not underground I mean. All me muckers are up top.' He hurried to keep pace with the other, hopping across a railway line as if performing a jig, thought Probyn. 'Been working on the surface for two years cleaning tubs. Would've stayed there too but me father said it was time I earned more money. Me mammy didn't really want me to go down ye see.'

Unaware that the barrage of chatter was a disguise for shyness, Probyn saw only an empty vessel, and tried to discourage it by remaining silent.

But Mick seemed oblivious that his informative prattle was not wholly welcomed, perhaps because the folk in this village were not given to facial animation. He had known them to display both anguish and pleasure with a similar detached mien. One never quite knew what they were thinking. 'Not dat she's bothered for my safety y'understand, she wanted me to join the Christian Brothers. Well, ideally she wanted me to be a priest but the church is not for me. Truth be told I don't really know what I want out o' life.' He took off his cap to enjoy a vigorous scratching of his head. 'How about yourself?'

Probyn's blue-grey eyes shot an irritated glance.

Blackened digits raked through their owner's curls. 'Do you like working down the pit?'

'Are you soft?' Probyn tore his eyes off the other's con-spicuous widow's peak and marched on, weaving around another bunch of weary silhouettes and embarking upon the lane that led to the village of Ralph Royd. To either side of the hedge now lay soggy winter fields.

Mick replaced his scruffy cap. 'Ah well, you're obviously keen to get home. Jesus, ye walk awful fast for a little bloke!'

Sensitive about his lack of height, Probyn gritted his teeth.

Unaware that he had caused offence, Mick clutched his side and maintained both his pace and his chatter, apparently unhindered by the swollen mouth. 'I'm the only one left at home now. The eldest, Joe, he's away working down south somewhere. The other one, John, he's married, works on the railways, can afford to eat chocolate for breakfast if he wants to. Imagine dat!' Mick's voice held deep admiration. 'Me mother says she doesn't know where she went wrong with me.' He discounted this with a happy shrug.

Probyn formed a tight smile, hoping this would not encourage further confidences. His late mother had possessed a deep aversion to the Irish, so out of respect for her he chose not to mix with them; though in truth, her placid, thoughtful son had never been able to see what religion had to do with someone's character and Melody seemed a decent enough sort – for a Catholic.

Apart from this not insubstantial drawback, Probyn had noted from a sideways glance that Mick seemed to have every advantage over himself. Skinny, maybe, but taller and more attractive even under the layer of coal dust. Not classically beautiful but good-looking in an impudent sort of way. The sort of way that counted, came the resentful thought. That was, with females. And to a seventeen-year-old youth desperate for sexual knowledge this was all that mattered. He, who had never had much luck attracting girls for anything other than friendship, and had been rejected in favour of a similar thatch of luxuriant brown hair, could only marvel at how easily females could be taken in. 'Ooh, hasn't he got lovely wavy hair,' they'd say, squirming round the chosen one like maggots; as if a mop of curls had some sort of bearing on his integrity. Irritated that Melody was still at his shoulder, he increased his gait.

But Mick clung like a limpet, glad to have made a new friend. He liked what he saw in that good strong face with its well-defined features. 'How many brothers and sisters have ye got?'

'No brothers, five sisters,' came the reluctant murmur. Thank goodness his home was now close by. 'I had six but one died.'

'Jesus, a veritable army! Dere's only four of us. Did I mention I've a sister too?'

'Your mam must have lost lots of babbies then.' It just slipped out.

The curly-headed youth frowned. 'Not dat I know of. Why d'ye say dat?'

Unthinkingly, Probyn repeated his mother's opinion. 'Well, Catholics usually have loads o' bairns.'

The other became suddenly aloof, his reaction mocking. 'Do dey now? Den I shall have to tell me mother and father to buck der ideas up, dey're letting the side down. Christ almighty! Dat's a fine observation from somebody with a family of seven. What has everybody got against the Catholic Church dat's what I'd like to know?'

Probyn disapproved of the blasphemous exclamation and it showed in his tone of voice. 'Maybe they're scared your lot're going to take over. That's what me mam always said. You have lots of kids so you can populate the world.'

Mick was starting to be really offended. 'Your mother talks rot.'

Probyn wheeled to a sudden halt and became a different character. His eyes glittered with intensity and he knocked Melody's cap off his head. 'Take that back!'

In danger of losing this valuable ally, Mick immediately backed down. 'I'm sure she's a very nice woman but –'

'She's dead,' snapped Probyn.

'Ah.' Mick's sharp gaze was softened by a look of contrition. 'Well den, I take it all back.' In a trice, though, his widow's peak descended in a frown. 'But I've seen your father with –'

'That's my stepmother!' cut in Probyn, then turned and strode on, leaving the other to pick up his cap.

Without hesitation Mick tripped after him, his tone appeasing. 'I'd no wish to cause offence! But see, 'tis wrong for folk to say tings like that when dey don't even know us. I don't want to rule the world. God knows, I'd just like to get through a day's work without getting me head kicked in. Jesus, I tink dat bastard's knocked one o'me teeth loose.' He wiggled the molar gingerly.

Probyn chose not to respond. They were at the top of the lane. Here now was the main street, the glimmer of lantern and the whitewashed inn that neighboured his own cottage. In moments he would be able to shake this wretch off. But just as he was about to do this, something else took his attention. The door of the Robin Hood's Well opened. Emerging on a waft of beery fumes stepped a military figure, who paused under a lamp to adjust his pillbox hat. The buttons on his scarlet tunic glittered alluringly. Probyn's eyes lit up too. Ignoring Melody, he slowed his pace right down, in order to imbibe the wonderful sight.

Mick's face took on similar interest, but for a different reason. Grateful to have this opportunity to catch his breath and also to change the subject, he expanded his narrow chest and remarked upon the uniform. 'Well now, wouldn't I look great in dat! 'Twould get me out o' Judson's clutches, and no bloody coal dust to wash off every night.'

Of a nobler mind, Probyn tried to forget the other was there, concentrating on the recruiting sergeant who had spotted the blackened young pitmen and now strode smartly towards them.

'I tink I'll join,' declared Mick capriciously.

Probyn could not help displaying shock at such impulse. 'What'll your parents say?'

The response was light-hearted. 'Sure, as long as I send money home won't dey be glad to get rid o' me.'

Gripped by silent fury, Probyn could not speak. That this

ignoramus with his *dis* and *dat* and *tink* and *tings* could achieve in seconds what had been his own lifetime's ambition! Without a care for the morality of the situation – glad to get rid of him, he'd said, as if the army were some kind of midden tip! What sort of parents were they? How shallow was Melody whose only interest in the handsome military garb was that it would spare him from washing on a night!

In truth, Probyn admired the scarlet tunic too, but it went much, much deeper than that, entailed dreams of honour and chivalry and valour . . . all impossible to fulfil. His fantasy petered out on a note of utter despair. It wasn't simply that his father had always referred to the army as being composed of riff-raff and forbade his son to enlist, but that Probyn's mother, whom he had always revered and missed dreadfully, had held the same view. He could not go against her memory.

'Join with me!' urged Mick.

Probyn deliberately ignored him. Watching the sergeant's majestic approach, he was consumed by fury that he would never wear that magnificent uniform, that this . . . this *Catholic* could achieve it on a mere whim.

'Good evening to you, lads!' The grandly-attired personage halted before them, imposingly erect, his chest adorned with medal ribbons. 'Sergeant Brown at your service. Could I interest either of you in the honour of accepting Her Majesty's shilling?'

'You can, sir,' announced Mick.

A note of surprised pleasure. 'Good lad! But it's not *sir*, it's Sergeant.' The eyes above the moustache instantly narrowed at the sight of Mick's blood-encrusted lip. 'I hope you haven't been a-fighting?'

'Indeed not, Sergeant! I don't yet have my pit eyesight and I walked into a prop.'

'Good, 'cause the army likes its men to reserve their fighting inclinations for the enemy. And how old are you?'

'Oh, em, sixteen.' Mick would not be sixteen until the spring but it sounded better.

However, the sergeant affected to clear his throat, its staccato rattle obliterating Mick's answer. 'I beg your pardon, that was eighteen you said, wasn't it?'

'Ah, so it was, Sergeant!'

'Good lad! That's what I like to see, a quick learner. You're just what the York and Lancasters are looking for, and might I say you are similarly fortunate, for a finer infantry regiment you could not hope to serve. Well now, I'll just take a few more particulars then we'll see you again, clean and smartly dressed, at Pontefract Barracks after you've enjoyed your Christmas holiday.'

Despite his loathing of the situation, Probyn was riveted to the spot by envy as the sergeant gave Mick a date and time to present himself, entering his details in a notebook. The uniformed hero then turned to him and enquired if he was of the same mind. He had just opened his mouth to issue reluctant negation when a rude voice pre-empted him.

''Ee can cross this one's name off thy list right now!' Monty Kilmaster was outwardly composed, though the restoration of his native Somerset burr conveyed to his son that he was livid. It was always more pronounced when he was angry.

'Father, I weren't –!' His attempt to explain was lopped by another terse response.

'I know what 'ee were at! 'Ee shameful, sneaking varmint!' Monty stabbed a coal-black finger in the direction of home, obviously expecting to be obeyed.

Probyn was compelled to move, averting a face that was crimson with shame – thank goodness for the layer of coal dust – but nothing could shield him from the eyes of Melody and the sergeant as he was chivvied like an infant. 'I were just watching Mick sign up, that's all!'

'Mick!' A contemptuous bark from an irate father. 'How long have 'ee been consorting with the likes of him? Long enough to be tainted by his bad ways. Thank the Lord your mother bain't alive to witness your shameful behaviour! Not just trying to sneak off to the army behind my back but in the company of Catholics!'

What thought did you ever spare for my mother's feelings? Probyn wanted to yell. Marrying another woman before Mother was even cold in her grave! But no one would ever offer such rude retort to Father. There was no argument at all in the Kilmaster household: Father's word was law.

Nevertheless, the boy was upset enough to persist with his explanation. 'I only met him today! He kept hanging around me 'cause I protected him from Judson.'

'Huh!' Monty jerked his blackened chin skywards in a gesture of derision. 'A fine soldier he'll make if he needs the likes of you to fight his battles, and if you're hoping to follow suit you don't set foot in my house again.'

'Father, I weren't signing up!' Thoroughly humiliated, Probyn tried to speed ahead of his oppressor. Notwithstanding the stooped posture, his father was a lofty man, six inches taller than he, making Probyn appear even more of a child; the image this must portray to onlookers would make him a laughing stock for weeks. Without knowing why, he'd always imagined he was something of a disappointment to his father: this confirmed it. They had nothing whatsoever in common.

'Better not've been! I already seen my name blackened once today!' Monty had been told by the deputy of his son's involvement in the roof fall incident. 'There's a man lying half dead because o' you!'

Probyn was mortified. 'No!'

'You were larking I'm told!' His father delivered a hefty shove between his shoulder blades. 'Larking at your age!'

'I weren't! Judson was after Mick, I was –'

'Mick this, Mick that! Well I hope you think your protection of him was worth the loss of John Cox's livelihood.'

'That were just an accident!' came the humiliated gasp, the injustice of it all making Probyn rash. 'He should have propped his roof up better, we could all have been killed.'

'Why you –!' On the verge of losing his temper, Monty

fought to restrain the outburst. 'I'll tell you which one would've been most missed if you had all been killed! He was a fine collier, John Cox, but he won't be going down there again will he? Won't grow another leg! Well, you can kiss farewell to any pocket money this week. I already promised it to his kin.'

Of all the indignities heaped on Probyn this was surely the worst. After such hazardous occupation a man should be entitled to keep what he had earned.

But things were to grow even more dire. As he was prodded along the street, the assault was witnessed by a smirking Judson who, before disappearing into the taproom, offered the taunting reminder: 'See you after Christmas, Ginge!'

Monty paid him little heed, now focusing his attention on the sight of a horse and cart outside his house and groaning, 'Oh no, that's all I need.' His youngest sister and her husband were here – and Kit usually brought trouble.

Taking some small comfort in this distraction, Probyn swerved in at the cottage gate and, trained not to enter the house until rid of his layer of coal dust, hurried round the back. In contrast to his father he welcomed a visit from the kind and jolly Aunt Kit. At least she breathed warmth into the place, so empty these days. In fact it was due to his aunt's generosity that they lived here at all; the cottage had once been hers, but upon marriage she had bequeathed it to her brother, little guessing at the time what financial misfortune was about to befall her.

Her nephew showed delight at seeing her in the back garden when he rounded the corner of the cottage. She was chatting to his nineteen-year-old sister Meredith who waited with towels and water.

Both women noticed that his greeting masked another emotion, and when he was closely followed by his father's annoyed face they understood the reason why. No comment was made on the obvious bad feeling though.

'Probe!' Kit greeted him with a fond smile and a West Riding accent like his own, but did not hug him for he was covered in grime. 'Here give us your coat, if there's two of us on t'job we'll get done quicker.'

Meredith objected. 'Nay! You'll mucky your clothes.' Whilst she herself was modestly clad in black wool, Aunt Kit, a fine seamstress, always wore beautiful gowns. 'I've got it down to a fine art now. Just stand there and talk to us.' She was a large-boned and well-fleshed girl, a good-natured sort like her aunt, possessing a similar shade of auburn hair, though not quite so tall.

Handing over his coat Probyn had to look up to both women, which never ceased to irk him, much as he loved them. What cruel joke had made him, the only boy amongst six girls, the shortest of them all?

At Meredith's prompting he handed over his wages which, along with her father's contribution, she put in her apron pocket. Probyn took off his cap, feeling the solitary curl at his brow spring to attention. That was another perversity: why had he been the only one to inherit his mother's short stature, yet was denied her dark good looks? True, all the Kilmaster children had red hair but whilst his sisters' ranged from deep auburn to copper his was an insipid sandy colour and dead straight, except for that ridiculous forelock. Concealing his bad humour, he took off his trousers.

Wondering what had caused the upset between father and son, Kit hugged her unnaturally small waist. To the north and south of this restricted circumference ballooned great domes of flounced and satin-clad flesh. Only on special occasions these days did Kit lace her corset so tightly and she was beginning to regret it today for who was there here to appreciate her effort? Nevertheless she passed warm greeting to her brother who was also disrobing.

'Your better half inside, is he?' asked Monty, trying to relax the lines of bad temper from his brow as he handed each garment to his daughter.

Kit's crystal clear blue eyes shone with affection. 'Yes, Worthy's inside talking to Ann. Er, by the way, will you please not leave boxes of Pomfret cakes by the side of your chair? Our Toby's been into them, must've crammed a dozen in before we noticed. Goodness knows what sort of Christmas we're going to have.'

Monty gave a theatrical wince. Probyn forced himself to grin too. Stripped to their shorts, both underwent a quick wash in the enamel bowl on its old wooden stand. Whilst they scooped hot water over their heads Meredith hurried further along the garden and proceeded to beat the clothes with a stick, removing as much dust as she could before returning to scrub her father's back, her brother waiting for the same treatment. Crossing her plump arms under a voluptuous bosom, Kit remained to watch the steamy ritual, occasionally passing jugs of water to her niece who tipped them to order, two lathered backs slowly turning white again, save for the coal scars that were a tattoo of their trade and the pink weals from an enthusiastic scrubbing brush.

It was too cold and damp to linger over ablutions today and, leaving a black scum on the water, they were soon towelling themselves dry and pulling on fresh clothing. Then, rosy-cheeked, all went indoors, where only a pathetic sprig of holly on the mantel betrayed that it was Christmas, though the blazing fire was sufficiently cheerful. In a cage by the window a canary hopped from perch to perch. Worthy, a colossal man even when seated, was chatting to Monty's wife Ann, keeping tight hold of Toby's dress lest he delve into prohibited areas, unaware that his baby son was gnawing on a chair leg to relieve the pain in his gums.

'Oh, blooming heck he's eating the furniture now!' Kit swept the baby up and held him out to her brother to show how big he'd grown. 'Nine months old. Bless me, this last year's really flown.'

Monty paid due interest, then ran a comb through his remaining wisps of damp red hair and sat at the table, massaging his knees that were swollen and painful from years of bending at the coalface.

Averse to sitting alongside the man who had just humiliated him, Probyn fabricated interest in his nephew who sat chewing his fist and slavering. 'He's a big lad for his age, isn't he?'

'Is there any wonder?' Kit shared a laugh with her ox of a husband who, never one for grand gestures, merely nodded.

Clamping one hand to his wet, disobedient forelock in the vain hope that this might flatten it, Probyn continued to chat to the visitors.

Ann, a neat, dark-eyed woman, attractive despite the house-wife's pinafore, came to her husband's side with a knife and a fork and a quiet smile. Married into the Kilmaster family for only a couple of years, she still felt out of place, especially when Kit came to visit. Nice and kind as the latter might be, the sheer presence of her made Ann feel somewhat awkward, not to mention the way her husband felt about his sister's reputation.

'I suppose they'll be stopping for tea,' he murmured, below the level of others' babble. 'I shall have to take out a loan to cover the cost.'

'Ssh!' Keeping her voice low Ann Kilmaster replied, 'It's no hardship, I've done plenty of veg.'

'Wonder what trouble she's brought with her today,' grumbled Monty.

But Kit had not brought trouble, replied his wife, only a leg of ham and two jars of preserves. 'You don't expect me to take their gifts and not offer them a crumb,' came her scolding whisper. 'Anyway, what's up with Probe? Have you been having words?'

'Oh, I'll tell later,' he promised, without enthusiasm. 'Don't want to spoil tea.'

Holding one ear to his father's mutterings in case they were about him, Probyn conversed with the visitors. 'Will you be staying the night, Aunt?'

'Pray the Lord she's not,' mumbled Monty, receiving a nudge from his wife.

'We'd love to, Probe, but there's haminals to be fed.' Since selling their house in York – her husband unhappy with city dwelling – they were now settled on a smallholding a few miles east of there. 'A neighbour's lad's taking care of them this evening but we must be back before bedtime.'

'I shall have to come and see you when I get me new bicycle,' promised Meredith. Having finished rinsing the men's stockings she put them by the fire to dry.

'Oh, you're not wasting your hard-earned money on one o' them are you?' Kit touched her huge frilly bosom in concern.

'Yes! I've nearly saved up enough.' Whilst her stepmother laid out more cutlery for the guests Meredith put a slab of Yorkshire pudding onto her father's plate and doused it in gravy.

'Ooh, don't get one, lass,' begged her aunt.

Meredith chuckled. 'Why on earth not?' With Father served, she put a similar plateful before her brother.

'Well . . .' Kit seemed loath to reply, glancing at Probyn, who looked away and started to eat. 'It can't be good for . . . you *know*.' When Meredith looked mystified she mouthed as best she could, 'Your *works*, love. Women aren't built to ride machines. I thought you were keen on getting married and having bairns?'

'I am,' declared Meredith with a laugh for her aunt's oddly old-fashioned stance on this. Kit had always acted outrageously in her own youth. 'But I'll never even get to see my sweetheart without transport. He's had to move to Huddersfield, been promoted.'

Kit showed a keen interest. 'You never mentioned anything about a sweetheart last time I came.'

'It was what you might call a whirlwind affair.' Ann Kilmaster smiled demurely.

'Ooh, what's his name?' Kit thrived on romance.

The big girl turned coy, primping her fringe of red curls. 'Mr Clegg.'

Her aunt pulled her chin into her neck and shivered,

25

creating rolls of fat. 'What a name to be called! Couldn't you find anybody with a better one? It always makes me think of a horsefly. Doesn't he have a first name then?'

Probyn raised a smirk but said nothing as he devoured the delicious pudding, dribbling gravy.

'I'm not telling you. You'll only make fun, like this lot did,' said Merry, but there were laughter lines around her blue eyes. Then, at Kit's insistence, she mumbled. 'If you must know, it's Christmas.'

Kit could not help a cry of glee. 'Merry and Christmas! Aw, dear – no I'm not laughing really I'm not!'

'Yes you are!' accused Merry, but was chuckling herself as she waved her aunt to the table.

'Well, I suppose you can be thankful it's not his surname,' finished Kit, and prepared to dine, the chubby babe on her lap.

'Sit next to me, Uncle Worthy,' invited Probyn. For such a big fellow he never seemed obtrusive, an unsophisticated country man who was happy to remain in the background whilst his dear wife took centre stage. Probyn liked his uncle, though it was not simply this that had caused the invitation. If Worthy sat opposite then Probyn would not be able to take his eyes off the mangled ear that was the result of a shotgun accident. He found it horribly fascinating. In this way it was out of his view.

There was a hiatus then whilst the family consumed their meal of roast pork and vegetables, all of which had been raised on the family allotment.

Afterwards, though, there was more talk of matrimony. Kit noted with pleasure that Monty did not seem so averse to his daughter leaving home now that he himself had remarried and, hence, had someone to take care of him. Questioning Meredith on her sweetheart's occupation, she learned that Merry, like her sisters before her, was to be the wife of a non-manual worker, and commented, 'Your mother'll be up there wearing a proud smile.' Sarah Kilmaster had made a great effort in encouraging her girls to look further than the colliery village for their husbands.

'A smile for her daughters, maybe.'

Kit sensed an underlying sarcasm to Monty's remark and sprang, as she always did, to Probyn's defence. 'Well, there isn't much choice of employment round here for lads.' She turned to her nephew. 'Eh, next time I come you might be the only one left at home, Probe. We'll have to see if we can find you a nice chapel girl.'

'Oh, this one's too busy dallying with papists,' came Monty's sour utterance.

Kit's expression changed. 'What? Eh, never!'

Monty nodded. 'Fallen in with the wrong type.'

Annoyed to be in the line of fire again, Probyn tutted. 'May I leave the table please, Father?' Granted permission, he went to sit on the fender.

But there was no escape; to his greater indignation his father, unable to contain himself any longer, relayed the episode of John Cox being trapped by his leg, told of his own shame upon hearing that his son had been involved – and with an Irishman of all creatures – after all his parents had warned him about folk like the Melodys! Ear lobes burning red, Probyn should have been grateful his father had chosen not to mention the business with the recruiting sergeant too, but with everyone in the room except Worthy heaping their bigoted opinions upon him, it was no relief. Prejudice ran deep in the Kilmaster abode. Even the liberal Kit looked down on the Irish. They might live in the same street and the same kind of house but morally they were poles apart. No insult was made to their faces of course. Oh no, Monty's creed was to treat everyone with courtesy, as low as they might be; but one did not have to socialize with them.

'Well, I'm surprised at you, Probe,' scolded his aunt. 'You're usually such a sensible lad.'

Whilst others continued to discuss the shortcomings of their neighbours, Probyn cupped his chin in his hand and sulked, becoming nostalgic for the old days when he had a family; a real one. Since his eldest sister had died, he had watched that family disintegrate as, year by year, the others went off to form their own lives. Since Mother passed away things had grown even bleaker. Sister number five, anxious not to be burdened by an ageing father, had deliberately got herself with child in order to be allowed to wed. Now it looked as if Merry would be going too, leaving him to play cuckoo in the nest.

Despite the strictness, for Monty was no stricter than others in the village, Probyn loved and respected his father but there was no great comradeship between them. He, a calm, intuitive youth, always able to see the other side in any disagreement, would seldom explode unless pushed beyond endurance. His father rarely lost his temper either, yet Probyn sensed that this was only achieved by years of self-discipline. Should one dare to differ one would immediately sense a menacing glow of lava bubbling beneath the artificial crust.

Probyn had noticed, though, that his father had seemed more contented in the years since his mother's death. To one whose sense of loss was as fresh as ever, the boy was unable to understand this attitude. However, there was one area of the relationship that was unequivocal. Monty despised his son's ambition to enter the army. Soldiers were drunken, uneducated riff-raff. That was that.

His eyes strayed to the map of the world on the wall. It had been in the family's ownership for as long as he could remember. With age and sunlight the vast expanse of deep pink that signified British territory had now faded to a shell-like hue, yet in reality Queen Victoria's glorious Empire remained unconquerable. Probyn knew every inch of it, longed to play a bigger role in its upkeep, to hold the savages at bay with musket and derring do, rather than simply wave a Union flag and eat buns at a celebration party.

Love of Empire was one of the few things he and his father did have in common, and about which they could meet in friendly conversation. All this rot about Home Rule for Ireland, Father had told him, start lopping bits off here and bits off there and before you knew it centuries of achievement would have vanished. Nobody was foolish enough to suggest the Indians or Africans could rule themselves, why then should otherwise intelligent people think the likes of Michael Melody were fit to rule? And if Ireland was so good why were half its inhabitants living over here? No, it was imperative that the Empire be upheld at all costs. This was fine, Probyn had dared to put forth during one of these lessons, but who exactly had the job of maintaining the Empire? Why, Her Majesty's army! He had been told to shut up then, that he did not know what he was talking about, soldiers were rabble, only kept in order by their officers and if this was his way of wheedling a favourable response out of his father about him joining the army then he could jolly well think again.

Whilst others droned on, the map continued to hold his eye. Africa, India, Mauritius, the West Indies, Hong Kong . . . Michael Melody would be going to all those exotic places soon. The wretch.

'Well, we'll have to be making a move if we're to get home tonight,' sighed Kit, easing her corseted spine. 'We've got to call on Owen yet.'

The unspeakable one. Monty felt all eyes turn on him, as if to gauge his reaction. Deliberately he made no comment.

'Would anyone like to come with us?' Kit knew there was no point asking her elder brother, merely addressing his offspring.

Probyn wordlessly consulted his father who had not spoken to his younger brother in over five years, nor mentioned his name, save for one brief skirmish when their sisters had foolishly brought them together in an attempted reconciliation. In this he was not abnormal; many families had been fractured during the bitter miners' strike of 1885, and there were those in the village who still refused to speak to Monty for his part in breaking the deadlock. That didn't make it any less difficult for those such as Probyn who could not help admiring the reviled one over his adherence to principle.

Monty was terse. 'They can please themselves.'

His daughter was apologetic. 'I'd love to but I promised Mother I'd see to preparations for tomorrow's dinner while she's out.' Wednesday was Mothers' Night at chapel.

'Oh, you don't have to,' permitted Ann, eager not to sound a domineering stepmother.

'Yes I do! Make the most of it, there's nobody else here who'll help you when I'm gone.' Merry and her stepmother had become firm friends since Ann Kilmaster had persuaded Father to see sense over his youngest daughter's intended.

No such amity occurred between Ann and Probyn. He would certainly never call her Mother. None would take the place of his own. Though a nice enough woman, she would always be Mrs Carr to him. Relieved at being able to escape this atmosphere, he jumped to his feet, helped his aunt into her coat, then put on his jacket.

Passing Toby to her husband, who held him with incongruously delicate hands, Kit donned her flamboyant ostrich feathered hat and inserted a marcasite pin. Then, she and Worthy wished everyone merry Christmas and, with their little son, went out into the night followed by Probyn. In no time they were all seated behind a shaggy, plodding mare and on their way to Garborough Junction.

Responding to the knock on his door, Owen's dark, billy-goat face peered warily round the edge of it. The astrakhan eyebrows remained lowered for a suspicious moment, before their owner saw who it was and bade his visitors enter. Outlined by the glow of a lamp was a thin, but not puny man, whose handshake implied a determination of character.

'I weren't aware there was an eclipse due to take place this year,' came his dry utterance upon Kit and Worthy entering his parlour, their large bodies blocking out the lamp light. 'Good Lord, when the two o' thee get in a room –'

'Eh, he's that rude!' scolded his wife, Meg, and shoved him out of the way. But seeing that Kit was laughing the motherly woman laughed too and paid court to their baby son. 'Oh, hasn't he grown! The little cherub, eh, who could hurt 'em? Well sit down. Now then, Probe! We've just had us teas but I'll gladly make you something.'

Owen's eyes perused Worthy's massive bulk. 'Aye, this lad hasn't been fed in ages, judging by the look of him. Careful how the pair of you sit down, don't go breaking me furniture.'

Probyn always felt uncomfortable when Uncle Owen made such rude fun of Aunt Kit and her husband. If Owen had a clever remark to make he didn't care who he hurt only that his audience laughed, but then Kit did not seem to mind.

'Eh, he's always predictable, isn't he?' With droll expression, she lowered herself on a battered sofa, settling the drowsy babe on her lap. 'Thanks, Meg, but we've already eaten.'

'Oh aye, at t'other fella's house.' With a sage nod, Owen sat down too, offering Worthy a clay pipe which was politely declined. Settling back to smoke his own, he sniffed huffily and addressed his wife. 'Funny, how they allus leave poor relations till last.'

'Behave!' ordered Meg. Although it was meant as a jest, there was a genuine rift between Owen and his brother and she feared his words might give offence to Probyn. However, her apology was directed at Worthy, a comparative newcomer to Owen's idiosyncrasies. 'You'll have to excuse him he's only kidding.'

Worthy knew this, and performed his characteristic twitch of a smile. Despite all the insulting banter there was a happy atmosphere in this house. 'Think yourself lucky we're not imposing ourselves on thee for Christmas dinner.'

Worried that he might have overstepped the mark, Owen was immediately generous. 'Eh, you can stay t'night if you want, tha knows! We've got family and t'grandbairns coming tomorrow, two more won't make much difference. We'd be glad –'

'Nay, we have to get back,' chuckled Kit, kissing the top of her baby's head. 'But thank you anyway.' He was a dry stick, her brother, but kind in his own way.

Owen relaxed amongst a cloud of tobacco smoke, his small pointed chin held at an interested tilt, the dark features turned on his nephew. 'And how's our Probe?'

Accepting a cup of tea and a bun, Probyn said, 'I'm very well, Uncle, thank you.'

'Hope you've been going to your union meetings.' Owen had always been heavily involved in the union which to him was as much a religious occasion as attending chapel.

Whilst not so staunchly supportive of either, viewing the monetary subscriptions as one less treat for himself, Probyn told his uncle what he wished to hear. 'Never miss.'

Owen looked knowing. 'Eh, wash thy mouth out with soap an' water.'

Probyn's grin marked the start of an hour that was a good deal lighter than he had enjoyed at home. Aunt Kit had always been a great entertainer. Owen, too, could be relied upon to provide a certain dry humour, even if it was a little cruel, felt Probyn. But then much of his uncle's humour was a reflection on life, and life in a mining village could oft be cruel, as was testified in Owen's left hand, minus two of its fingers.

Fired by the jocular atmosphere, Probyn was lured into making his own contribution, and divulged the scene with the recruiting officer, using gross exaggeration to bestow a comic air that helped to remove some of the humiliation. 'I'm just standing there all innocent and I feel this big hand grab me collar and shake me half to death, almost lifted me off me feet! I'm dangling like a bloomin' puppet!' He performed a contorted jig, mimicking Monty's Somerset burr and making his aunts and uncles giggle. 'I tried to tell him I were only watching but you know what he's like. I thought he were gonna flatten the sergeant an' all.'

The mirth was tinged with sympathy. Everyone knew how

much he wanted to be a soldier and it must be hard to tell the story at his own expense.

'Aw, poor lad.' Kit wiped the moisture from her eyes, then soothed Toby who had begun to fall asleep before being roused by the sudden laughter. 'You'll have to stay away from that Irish chap in future.'

Probyn displayed frustration. 'That's the whole trouble, Aunt! I'd been trying to get rid of him all day. He stuck to me like pig muck.' Loath for her to retain the misapprehension that he had purposely befriended Melody, he risked rebuke from his uncle to reveal the whole story. 'You know the roof fall that me father was on about?'

'What's all this?' Owen became alert. 'Was anybody hurt?'

'Aye, John Cox lost his leg,' said Probyn, adding quickly, 'Me dad thinks it were my fault but it weren't. The Irish lad were running away from Judson –'

'I don't think I know him,' frowned Kit.

'Dreadful family,' provided Meg. 'Lives in Fenton Row, next to that woman who stabbed her husband.'

'Ah, yes,' Kit nodded.

'I had to help him, he would've got a pasting. Anyroad all we did was run into John Cox's stall and at same time his roof caved in. I could've been the one who lost me leg, worse even. It were just an accident but me dad blames me, and all because I were sticking up for somebody.'

'I'm sorry I jumped to conclusions, love.' Kit's honest face showed remorse. 'I should've known you wouldn't be involved in owt daft.'

'And now that blinkin' Melody has caused all this trouble he's off to join t'army! Lucky blighter. I wish it were me.' Probyn sighed and flopped back in his chair. 'I hate it down t'pit.' Catching Owen's eye, he sought to add, 'Oh, I like t'lads and that, but . . .'

He didn't need to finish. In total agreement, Owen bestowed a cognitive nod, puffing away on his pipe.

'Well, most o' the lads anyroad.' Probyn gripped the oaken

arms of his chair. 'I can't say I'm looking forward to seeing Judson when I get back to work.'

Owen removed his pipe to voice concern. 'Tha's not freetened o' going back 'cause o' that yahoo? I'll have a word –'

'Nay!' Probyn didn't want to appear any more foolish than he had already been made to look. 'I'm not scared of him. I just think fighting's daft.'

Owen gave a barely perceptible wink at Worthy. 'Does this augur well for a military career?'

'Nay, I mean fighting for the sake of fighting,' Probyn explained to the gathering. 'I can't see t'point of scrapping with anybody unless you're trying to kill 'em, for Queen and country, like.'

Meg had once witnessed Judson's cruelty to animals. 'Well, make sure you give him a real good braying. It's long over-due.'

Owen took a sip from his cup, addressing Worthy again. 'I always think compassion's a fine quality in a woman, don't you?'

Fired by the memory of that sergeant in his glorious scarlet tunic, Probyn barely heard the quip, offering more argument as to why he should be allowed to enlist.

But in this Owen shared his brother's viewpoint, added to which was a distaste for imperialism. 'You might change your opinion next time there's a lock-out and the troops are called in. They're hard cruel men.'

Probyn knew when to curb his tongue. He pulled out a rag and trumpeted into it, dislodging the black dust that perpetually coated his nostrils.

'I'll agree, no man should be forced to grovel in t'bowels o' the earth like some parasitic worm to earn his living,' continued Owen. 'But coal's got to be dug and somebody's got to do it. And in the main you couldn't ask for braver comrades than you've already got.'

Shoving the rag back into his trousers, Probyn gave a mature nod. Even in his few years down the mine he had witnessed acts of outstanding heroism. It was also true that there was a certain beauty in the gleaming black coalface. Yet he longed, *yearned*, to be free of it.

On the way home, he gave further vent to his yearnings, conscious that there was no way his aunt could help, but desirous of at least one sympathetic voice in the darkness. After rambling on for perhaps a mile, he had the feeling that his words were evaporating unheard into the cold night air, and tested Kit by asking her advice; not for the first time. 'What would you do if you were me, Aunt?'

The only response was the steady clip-clop of hoofs upon the country lane.

Kit felt a nudge from her husband and came to life. 'What was that, love?'

Probyn gave an inward sigh. Nice as it was to see his favourite aunt, she was different these days. You might be chatting away quite happily to her and she'd be nodding and smiling, but then you would notice a faraway look in her eye and you'd know she wasn't really listening, and that had always been the nice thing about Kit, she had always listened even to a three-year-old's babblings. He repeated his request.

Kit tried to shake off the image of the tiny grave she had visited this afternoon, that of her firstborn baby, then hazarded a guess as to her nephew's topic. 'About the army, you mean?'

'Yes. Do you think Father's being unreasonable?'

At first she refused to oblige. 'Never interfere in other folk's lives, Probe, that's my motto. I only ever did it once and it ended in tragedy.' She envisioned another dead baby and just as quickly thrust it aside, enfolding her own little son in a protective hug. 'A person must make up their own mind.'

'It's not really Father's view that worries me so much' – though the thought of a good hiding at his age did concern

Probyn very deeply – 'I'm more bothered about what me mam'd say.'

Kit made quiet utterance. 'It's good that you respect her wishes, Probe, but then you can't live your life for other people.'

This in its own way was the advice Probyn had been seeking. He came alert. 'Aye, you're right, Aunt! I'm going to do it.' But within seconds his firm decision waned and his pose relaxed into despondency again. 'Me father'll go mad, though.'

Kit gave a tired shrug. The motion of the cart was almost sending her to sleep. 'Well, to my mind, if a lad's old enough to work he's old enough to make his own decisions.'

Worthy cringed, but voiced no judgement of his wife's assertion, holding the reins and looking straight ahead, relying on the mare to steer him through the darkness. He tended to detach himself from the Kilmaster family's affairs. Life had been very dull before his marriage to Katherine, but during the last year it had been turned completely upside down. Still, the deep love she inspired in him decreed that he would change it for nothing.

Probyn leaned on his knees, swaying with the rhythm of the cart, trying to reach a final resolution. 'I shan't be going anywhere this week. Father confiscated me bit o' brass.'

'Oh that's not right.' Holding Toby with one plump arm, Kit delved into her coat pocket. 'Here's half a crown. Go on, it's Christmas.'

Though a refusal was the last thing on his mind, Probyn delayed his acceptance, not wanting to look as if he only viewed his favourite aunt as a source of funds. After respectable hesitation, he received the coin in exchange for deep gratitude. 'Eh, you've always spoiled us, Aunt.'

'You can't spoil quality, Probe,' she issued fondly. 'And if I had more to give you'd have it. You're going to have to sit up straighter than that though if you're off for a sodjer!'

He sat bolt upright then. 'I am! I've decided, I'm definitely off!'

'Bravo!' Kit displayed the smiling urge to help. 'Do you want us to come in as moral support while you tell your father?' They had almost reached the fork in the road where they would drop him off.

Probyn shook his head rapidly. 'No, you were right, it's my decision and I have to do it me own way.' And he had finally decided how this way was going to be: he could not, would not, risk a beating from his father. He would simply go without saying anything. It wasn't cowardice, just expediency. There was a vast difference between running away and running *to*.

Responding to the soft tug on her bit, the mare clip-clopped to a halt.

'Thanks anyway, Aunt. Enjoy your Christmas. You too, Uncle Worthy.' Patting little Toby on his bonneted head, Probyn jumped down from the cart, then stood at the roadside to wave them off, face bright as a soldier's buttons.

Adding her endearments to the resonance of hoofs, Kit waved back over her shoulder until her nephew's figure melted into the darkness, then she faced the road ahead. Despite the fact that her husband had offered no opinion, she read his mind and, as the cart proceeded on its homewards journey, she tendered, 'I'm going to cop the blame for this, aren't I?'

The mere turn of his ox-like head was enough to convey that Worthy agreed.

'Oh well,' Kit pulled the baby's shawl up under his chin and cuddled him closer, kissing the top of his head. 'That'll be nowt new, will it, Toby Treasure?'

2

On Christmas morning they went to chapel where, to Probyn's chagrin, his stepmother took the liberty of inviting the minister, Mr Lund, for tea at the weekend. That would mean he'd be kept in check even more, sighed Probyn. Mrs Carr was a fervent chapel goer. Some days she was there morning, noon and night. If she wanted to see the minister so much, why hadn't she married him and not Monty Kilmaster?

Though wet, the rest of Christmas was enjoyable enough with sisters Rhoda, Alice, Ethel and Wyn coming to visit.

However, by the Sunday afternoon before the pit was due to reopen his nerves at the thought of his daring plan had begun to affect him physically and it did not go unnoticed that he vanished to the privy for long spells.

'I wonder if that stuffing's to blame,' worried Ann. 'It was very rich.'

'It were beautiful,' corrected her husband, others in agreement. 'Stop worrying your head about that little so-and-so.' Monty detested the way his son acted towards Ann who was the most inoffensive person and had shown him nothing but kindness. Oh, the lad was neither ill-mannered nor blatant enough to come right out with it, but the polite *thank yous* and *may I pleases* ill disguised that fundamental air of resentment. Monty could tell, for much of it was directed at himself. For pity's sake, it wasn't as if Sarah had hardly been cold when he'd remarried. If the lad only knew what it was like being wed for almost thirty years to someone totally unsuitable he wouldn't be so quick to judge. After dutifully bringing up six siblings plus seven children of his own, wasn't a man allowed a little joy before he died?

Probyn re-entered wearing a look of discomfort and sat on the fender, all the chairs being taken. Mrs Carr's adult son and daughter were here with their respective spouses and offspring. Probyn bore no personal grudge for any of them; he was always relegated to the fender whenever there were visitors, and at least they offered sympathy for his plight.

'Well, I've no sympathy for 'ee,' reproved his father, massaging his painful swollen knees. 'You made a pig of yourself at dinner. Get some o' that jollop down you before Mr Lund arrives. I don't want you hopping to the farleymelow every five minutes while he's here.'

Obediently Probyn opened his mouth for the spoonful of chalky liquid offered by his stepmother, knowing full well it would not ease his nerves. He found himself actually praying for the minister's arrival, though only to get the episode over and done with. How he wished it was tomorrow morning and he was on his way.

Whilst his father, stepmother and sister chatted happily to their visitors, Probyn suffered torment. Clad in his best navy-blue suit, starched collar and tie, he shifted nervously on the fender, going over his plan.

Eventually, the minister made his appearance. Probyn had never cared for Mr Lund without really knowing why. Nevertheless, he jumped up and responded with a courteous smile when Mr Lund deigned to address him, though the minister was obviously more interested in the feast that awaited him on the table. Barely had six words of grace emerged from his mouth than he was cramming it with pork pie and pickles.

Probyn would have enjoyed it too had his father not issued a warning cough, instructing him not to over-indulge, whilst the ravenous guest polished off one delicacy after another, including an array of iced buns that Probyn loved so well.

Gauging her stepson's disappointment over the empty plate,

a smiling Ann began to rise. 'There're more cakes if anyone wants them. Probe, what about you?'

'He's had enough for everybody.' Monty wagged a finger. 'You're not here to run about after him.'

No, she's here to run about after you, sulked Probyn; or that greedy old codger, or anyone else who might be deemed more important, which included just about everybody except him. It had been the same at dinner time, with the visitors receiving the choicest cuts of meat whilst he was left with the fatty stuff. A desire to be free and the current resentment made his memory selective. Never during his entire lifetime could he recall one single word of praise from his father. He was nothing in this house. If he had suffered any indecision about running away it vanished at this moment.

But there was just one more thing to be done before his plan could take effect. 'Please may I leave the table?'

'Where are your manners?' asked his father. 'The minister's not finished yet.'

Forced to wait whilst the minister extended his teacup for a refill, Probyn turned his attention to what must inevitably come. Though worried at the thought of confronting Judson, he could not be seen to be running away. Probyn Kilmaster had never run away from anything. Finer by far that he seek the thug out than be labelled a coward. Nothing must hamper his intended getaway tomorrow morning, he must meet Judson tonight, if only the wretched minister would finish quaffing.

At last, the elderly man smacked his lips, raked a currant from between his teeth and mopped his white-bristled chin. Paying compliment to his hosts, he duly took his leave.

Probyn jumped up to help the man into his coat. 'I'll walk you back, Mr Lund!' Thus did he finally manage to escape the house, bent on confrontation.

After accompanying the minister far enough through the drizzling rain along Main Street, he made as if for home, but instead of keeping to the highway he turned off between the church and the post office and headed up an incline. Passing the allotments and Savile Row where he had been born, he strode on up the hill to the very top where a row of houses overlooked the dark expanse of Coney Moor. It was the boldest move he could make, going directly to the enemy's door, yet the move was not without apprehension. Judson was well known for using the dirtiest methods when fighting, even resorting to knives. Unable to reciprocate such vile practice, Probyn envisioned himself lying injured and bleeding, felt the sting of imaginary wounds. By the time he had reached Judson's home his stride was somewhat less confident. Nevertheless, he injected a false boldness into his knock and waited to face his enemy.

But the door was opened by a listless slattern.

Even to a thug's mother one must be polite. 'Hello, Mrs Judson, is your Clarence in?'

There was little animation in the reply. 'He's locked up, love. Got nabbed poaching last night.'

A huge rush of relief flooded Probyn's breast – he could have laughed aloud – though he tried to sound sympathetic in his response to Mrs Judson. 'Oh dear, then would you please tell him, when you see him, that I called?'

'Aye, I will.' She made to close the door.

'You won't forget will you?' It was vital that Judson knew Probyn was not intimidated.

With Mrs Judson's promise, he returned down the hill oblivious to the drizzle, a new buoyancy marking his homewards passage. He had faced up to the threat of violence. No matter that it had not occurred, he had gone there just the same. He was now at liberty to fulfil his ambition with a lighter heart.

Normally, Probyn would be roused by the sound of his father's coughing, but this Monday morning he was awake hours before anyone. In fact he had hardly slept for excitement. However, it was not his intention to slope away now: far better to set off for work as usual. That way they would not know he was missing until this evening. He couldn't leave a note: it might be found too early and give the game away. He would write from Pontefract and tell them he was safe. Amidst his machinations there had been a slight worry that, when he did not return, Father might think he had been involved in an underground accident, but he had dismissed this. Upon enquiry Father would ascertain that Probyn's numbered disc had never been taken out that morning. Lacking a corpse they would know he had gone of his own volition.

He stared up through the darkness, wondering over their reaction. Certainly they would be angry, but would they miss him too? More rational now than the night before, he recalled all the nice times: himself as a three-year-old standing by his father's knee waiting to receive the top of his boiled egg; the songs and stories Monty had recited . . . Yes, he supposed he would miss them in a way, though nothing would make him change his mind which was fired with all manner of exciting images. Unable to lay there any longer, he rose and used his chamber pot. Then, dragging a haversack from the cupboard, he stole down the chilly staircase to the kitchen. His pit clothes had been left on the hearth overnight. He struggled into them, grateful to be encased in their warmth. Once into his clogs, he rushed outside to stow his haversack in the shed, then scuttled back into the cottage and rammed a poker into the banked-up fire. By the time everyone else came down at five o'clock the flames were flickering merrily.

'Stomach trouble again?' asked his father, thumping his chest to ease the overnight congestion and expectorating a gobbet of grey phlegm at the fire.

Ignoring the cynical tone Probyn merely nodded, then, at the sound of the milk cart, went outside with a jug.

'Without even being asked!' remarked an impressed Merry, laying the table.

When he came back his stepmother had a pan of oatmeal on the stove. Father had never taken breakfast so early in the old days, preferring to eat his snap later on down the pit, but Mrs Carr insisted he needed something inside him especially on cold mornings, and today Probyn was glad of it too, devouring a large bowl of porridge. Who knew when he would get fed again?

It was not unusual for father and son to set off independently to the pit. So, when Probyn dawdled over a cup of tea Monty saw nothing odd and went off to work. 'See you this evening, the Lord willing.'

Upon hearing this invocation, and watching his sister bustle around happily with her housework, Probyn felt a twinge of guilt for deceiving them both; which was why he delayed his exit until Meredith had gone upstairs to strip the beds, for how could he take his leave face to face?

When she had gone he rose as casually as possible and said without looking at his stepmother, 'Well, I'd better be off. So long.'

'Yes, see you tonight, Probe,' murmured Ann quite innocently, and bent over to light a fire under the copper in preparation for washing day.

Once outside he crept into the shed and retrieved the haversack packed with his best suit and other necessary items. Hefting it over his shoulder he paused for a few nervous seconds then, glad for once of the December darkness, he made hastily away from the sordid grime of Ralph Royd.

Upon reaching the bridge over the Calder, he hurriedly took off his pit clogs, then exchanged his garments for the ones in his haversack. Creased and cold from their stay in the shed, they came as a shock to his skin. Bundling up his working clothes he hid them under the bridge. He would tell his father in the letter where to find them. They might be of use to someone else.

Best boots laced, he sprang to his feet and set off on the three mile walk. The air was damp but at least the rain had stopped. Depending on how tired he was upon arrival in Castleford, he might use the money Aunt Kit had given him to buy a

43

train ticket to complete his journey. At this stage, though, his exhilarated spirit would have carried him to the ends of the earth.

For one accustomed to walking miles underground, the first leg of his expedition proved no difficulty and as it was still very early by the time he reached Castleford he decided to go the next three miles on foot too, saving his half-crown for emergencies.

Given much time to ponder, his excitement burgeoned further still, every corner of his mind crammed with matters military. Images of comradeship, of daring acts and foreign climes, of valiant deed and glorious battle, the invincibility of youth obliterating any thought of his own death. Oh, there would be injury, yes, but Probyn Kilmaster would bear every wound with fortitude. At last, at long last he was going to achieve his dream!

On arrival at the market town of Pontefract he was tired but not excessively so and when he stopped it was only to get his bearings and to buy a bottle of lemonade from one of the few shops that were open. It was not yet light. Apart from those who worked in the local coal industry most folk were still in bed and many of the windows remained shuttered. He glugged thirstily at the bottle until it was empty, the fizzy liquid burning a passage to his stomach where it mingled with the juices of excitement. Too agitated to linger, he was soon bouncing onwards for his ultimate goal, the barracks.

On a stretch of high ground above the road leading to Wakefield was an imposing red brick fortress. Gaining access, he was directed to an office wherein resided a Corporal White who unsmilingly informed the auburn-headed lad that he was late.

'The rest of 'em arrived yesterday. Where've you been?'

Cap in hand, Probyn gave hasty explanation. 'Oh, I'm not expected! I just decided to come on the spur of the moment.'

'Must be mad,' responded the other. 'I can't wait to get out of here. Roll on my pontoon. Which regiment are you for, then?'

Taking great interest in everything military, Probyn knew that two regiments shared the barracks. Wishing to avoid Michael Melody who had signed up for the York and Lancasters, he had intended to say that he wished to join the King's Own Yorkshire Light Infantry, but the man to whom he spoke now was wearing the former regiment's emblem, the Tiger and Rose, and so not daring to offend he changed his mind. 'The York and Lancasters.'

'You address me as Corporal,' corrected the other, though not in unpleasant manner.

'Sorry, Corporal.'

'Never mind, you can't be expected to know all the rules. That's what we're here for, to pass on our knowledge. But you'll only be told once, so take heed.'

'Yes, Corporal.' Probyn displayed an eagerness to learn.

'So, you want to join the Young and Lovelies do you?' The corporal looked up and down Probyn's sturdy frame, noted the toughness of his jaw. 'What did you do before – miner?'

'Yes, Corporal.'

'Thought so.' The corporal rose and set paper and pencil on the table. 'Well, we'll expect a bit more of you here than digging coal.'

Somewhat concerned over what appeared to be a sheet of arithmetical questions, Probyn was relieved to find upon closer inspection that these were very simple and could have been done by an infant. He had them finished in seconds.

The corporal merely glanced at the completed page without comment, then demanded, 'Right, open your bag!'

Probyn unbuckled his haversack, displaying the few garments and the razor within.

These did not appear to be of interest to Corporal White who sniffed and asked, 'Anything valuable you want me to take care of? A watch?'

'I haven't got one, Corporal.'

'Any cash at all?'

Probyn dipped into his pocket and displayed the money Aunt Kit had given him.

A kindly gleam lit the other's eye. 'Ooh, better let me look after that for you.'

Watching his coins disappear into the man's pocket Probyn felt he might have made an error, but before he could object he received another order.

'Right, young man, follow me!'

Stuffing his few belongings back into the haversack he put on his cap and hared after the swift-footed corporal. It was light now. There was activity on the tree-lined parade ground, a sergeant barking commands to scarlet-clad ranks. Erstwhile, Probyn had been at ease in his best suit, but now he felt horribly conspicuous, shoddy even, beside these skilled and polished individuals. However, he had little time to observe for the corporal had entered a hut and he was compelled to follow.

'Wait in 'ere!' Offhandedly, the corporal shoved him into a room and closed the door behind him.

In keeping with the rest of the garrison the room was very modern, but as regards to furniture had only a row of beds down either side, upon which sat fifty or more young men in civilian garb, all of whom turned to gawk at the new man.

Clutching his haversack, Probyn's eyes toured the inquisitive assembly, his lips muttering a cursory, 'How do.'

'Why, if it isn't me old marrow!' One of the group leaped up to approach him, hands outstretched, his face bearing the open friendliness of a young animal.

Probyn's heart sank as he returned Michael Melody's greeting. He had hoped that amongst such a large assembly of men the risk of bumping into the Irish youth would be minimal.

'So ye took my advice!'

Probyn was offended. 'It was always my intention to join!'

'Was it?' Mick seemed genuinely pleased to see him, pumping his fist as if this were their first encounter in years. 'And how the divil did ye manage to get round your ould fella?'

'Oh, it's a long story.' As diplomatically as he could, Probyn disengaged himself and regarded the other occupants who were still gaping at him.

Mick gave a sly laugh and nudged him. 'He doesn't know you're here, does he? I suppose the thought of a pasting from Judson had nothing to do wid you running away?'

Probyn clung to his temper. 'Who said anything about running away? I'm me own man, I go where I please. As a matter of fact I went to sort Judson out last night.'

A cry of incredulity. 'You're mad!'

'Aye well, turns out he's in clink.'

'Best place for him.' Judging by Probyn's curt reaction, Mick had the idea he might have upset him in some way. To compensate he told him smilingly, 'Well sure, 'tis grand to see you anyhow,' and for the next few moments he stood there looking awkward until he realized that Probyn expected to be introduced to the others. 'Oh, em, can't remember all the names, but this here is Billy, Fred – sorry, Charlie – Joe, Alf and Sid. This is my pal Probe.'

'Probyn,' the newcomer corrected. After nodding to each of those named he looked around for somewhere to sit. There were no vacant beds.

'Sit yourself next to me!' Eyes smiling, Mick watched Probyn's every move, as usual over-compensating for his shyness by jabbering non-stop. 'Well now, isn't dis a turn up? Yes, yes indeed.'

Balanced on the edge of the bed, rubbing his cold hands and feeling ill at ease, Probyn felt he ought to say something. 'So, how long have you lads been here?'

Mick was first to speak, apparently not suffering any handicap from last week's split lip which had almost healed. 'Most of us arrived yesterday tea-time, and a nice tea it was that they gave us, wasn't it, lads?' This instigated a short but animated discussion between him and the others.

'Bit different this morning, though,' grumbled the big, raw-boned youth whom Melody had called Joe. 'Lump o' rooty and a swill o' coffee.'

'Rooty?' Probyn frowned.

'That's what you call bread in the army,' explained Joe, assuming the role of old soldier. 'They give you your ration in the morning and you have to make it last all day.'

In the short silence that followed Mick laughed at the gurgling noise that emerged from the newcomer's intestines. 'Sounds like ye left before breakfast.'

Probyn laid a hand over his churning stomach. 'Nay, it's just excitement.'

'Good, 'cause I'm not sharing my rooty with anybody,' muttered Joe. 'And soon as we get our Queen's shilling I'm off to buy some butter to put on it from t'canteen.'

'Bring any money with ye, Probe?'

Probyn wished Melody would stop calling him that. 'Aye, but the corporal's looking after it. Seems a good sort of bloke, doesn't he?'

In agreement, the other recruits said he was guarding their valuables too, then went on to discuss various aspects of garrison life as they had found it, all of them obviously conversant with the rules and regulations. It transpired that much of their knowledge had been gleaned from an introductory speech by the colonel last night. A very nice gent by all accounts. The non-commissioned officers seemed decent enough too, giving the recruits a guided tour of the barracks and explaining various bugle calls to them.

The prevailing accent was that of South Yorkshire, however, Probyn was surprised to find other parts of the country represented too; lads from Middlesex, Kent and Buckinghamshire who had enlisted in London, originally intending to join a cavalry regiment but these being up to strength they had been coaxed into joining the infantry. Others hailed from

Lincolnshire and Derbyshire. All seemed to have made themselves at home here.

Feeling the odd one out, he was compelled to ask, 'What happens now, then?'

'We're waiting to see the doctor and get sworn in,' said Mick. 'Tell me, Probe, would ye be thinking of putting your name down for foreign service?'

Probyn gave a keen nod. 'Aye, it's a few years since I've been anywhere interesting.'

One of his fellow northerners scoffed. 'Where was that, Leeds?'

Probyn levelled a glittering eye at his detractor. 'Spain as a matter of fact.'

'Gosh, how come ye went there?' Mick and others were instantly in awe.

Probyn tried not to sound boastful. 'Oh, me Aunty Kit wanted somebody to keep her company.' He glanced away as the door opened and a fierce-looking man with three chevrons on his arm snapped an order.

All jumped to their feet and lined up, Probyn inserting himself between Melody and the big one called Joe. In procession they accompanied the sergeant to another room as unadorned as the one they had left, save for an alphabetic chart on the wall, some scales and a device for measuring height. Here they were told to disrobe.

One by one they shivered and shuffled across the bare floorboards to undergo physical examination. Surreptitiously inspecting the others' unhealthy physiques, Probyn drew consolation from his own, what he lacked in height being compensated by muscularity. It was also encouraging to find that there were others shorter than himself, the youth currently being measured was only five foot four.

Standing directly behind Melody's undernourished frame, he listened alertly as the Irish youth's statistics were shouted out. 'Height, five foot seven and a half. Get on the scales. One hundred and twenty-eight pounds. Lift your arms, lad! Chest

'– don't inflate it until I tell you to! Complexion, ruddy. Eyes, blue. Hair, light brown . . .'

Then came Probyn's turn. Just as the Irish youth had done before him he lied about his age, though with his eighteenth birthday only six months away it was not so blatant a fabrication as Melody's. His details were subsequently entered on the service record. 'Height, five foot six inches. Weight, one hundred and thirty-one pounds. Chest, thirty-four. Complexion, fresh. Eyes, blue-grey. Hair, auburn. Any scars or marks?' After a few seconds' thought, Probyn held out his left hand to reveal the distinctive blue coal scar between forefinger and thumb.

With his heart and lungs pronounced sound, he gave a sigh of relief, for others had come to grief at this point, some of them even being found to have tuberculosis. Unfortunately Melody was not amongst those rejected and was now just ahead of Probyn in the queue for eyesight examination. Perhaps he might fall at this hurdle. The youth in front was certainly experiencing trouble.

'It's not *War and Peace* we're asking you to read, laddy, come along, hurry!' A heavy sigh from the examiner. 'Oh, Lord give me strength, another failure.'

'Aw, please don't chuck me out, sir!' begged the lumpish youth whom Mick had called Billy but his superiors called Ingham. 'I can see t'words well enough, I just can't read 'em.'

'That's hardly surprising! They're not meant to be words but a collection of letters. Ah, you mean you can't read at all?' The examiner's pained expression was eased somewhat. 'Then it's a different matter, we've an excellent fellow who can remedy that. A few trips to the schoolroom and you'll be up to scratch.'

Mick turned and murmured to Probyn with a look half of pity, half scorn. 'Chroist, and they accuse the Irish of being thick.'

Probyn wished the other would stop using the Lord's name

in such a manner, and showed his displeasure by giving Melody a shove to indicate that it was his turn.

The majority of the recruits having passed the obligatory standards, they put on their clothes and stood in a ragged line before the sergeant, who asked, 'Would it be dangerous for me to assume that, apart from Ingham, the rest of you have got your school certificates?'

All muttered that they had.

The sergeant cocked his ear. 'I didn't catch that. Lift your chin up when you speak! You're not talking to the floorboards.'

The answer was repeated more smartly. Mick caught Probyn studying him as if he were lying, and adopted a defensive attitude. 'So I have! 'Tis here in my pocket if ye want to see it.' To the other's astonishment he presented written proof of his intelligence.

'Thank you, Melody,' said the sergeant, with a long-suffering attitude, 'you can put it away now, we can all recognize a superior brain when we see one.'

The next few moments were spent with the recruits handing over details of their former occupation, religion and next of kin. Upon completion of this chore, the sergeant told them, 'Right, fall in!'

At the ensuing shambolic efforts he sighed. 'I can see we're going to have our work cut out with you lot.' Separating those who had already been sworn in elsewhere, he told Probyn and the rest, 'Just try to march in as straight a line as possible to the colonel's office. By the left, quick march!'

Probyn could hardly believe he was moments away from achieving his lifetime ambition. As if in a dream he marched as competently as he could with the other potential infantrymen, hoping that it would not be too long before he was clad in more appropriate garb. Please God, military apparel might improve the others' behaviour too, came his annoyed thought, for at present they seemed not to be attempting any formation at all, their arms and legs swinging wildly at different rates, their ranks all higgledy-piggledy. A frown leapt to his brow as Melody, trying to get into step, performed an ungainly dance, causing others to laugh and the sergeant to glare. Idiot! If he wanted to play the fool why had he not gone on the stage instead of degrading such a serious occupation?

Whilst they waited to go before the colonel, the sergeant told the recruits that upon attestation they would be split up and handed over to their different companies. At this news Probyn was struck by a bolt of joy. For one exquisite moment it appeared his future was about to turn rosy . . .

Until Melody piped up. 'Em, begging your pardon, Sergeant, but me and your man here are comrades from the same pit. It'd be absolutely great if we could stay together.'

'Oh well, we don't want to spoil any nice little friendships,' came the lightly sarcastic riposte.

Probyn was alarmed and embarrassed. 'Don't put yourself to any trouble, Sergeant!'

'It's no trouble at all, son! Tell me, would you care for a pot of tea with your morning call?' The sergeant made a violent gesture as a door opened and the regimental sergeant-major appeared. 'Squad 'shun!'

Deeply in awe of the occasion, the recruits were escorted into the colonel's office. Seconds away from voicing his oath of allegiance, Probyn underwent terrible indecision. After all these years of waiting, was his chosen career about to be ruined by some Irish oaf with delusions of comradeship? Might it be more expedient to back out now and reapply to some other regiment?

Too late! He found his lips chanting the words that would bind him, and a silver shilling pressed into his hand. He was no longer a civilian, but number 2893, Private Probyn Montague Kilmaster of the York and Lancaster Regiment.

Upon exit from the colonel's sanctum, Probyn's worst fears were confirmed: he was to be in the same platoon as Melody. However, things could have been worse for the haircut he duly received could not match Mick's in severity, the barber seeming to take exception to such curly locks and shaving them to resemble a prison cut. Moreover his excitement was soon to be revitalized as he was marched off to be measured for his dress tunic, then supplied with undress uniform with which he rapidly adorned himself.

Unable to credit that he was really a soldier, he fastened the last brass button then grinned down at his metamorphosed figure, tugging the scarlet tunic across a chest that swelled with pride. The legs of the dark blue trousers were a shade too long, but his upper half felt perfect. He could feel his entire figure blooming in stature. With no mirror, he could only imagine how magnificent he must appear. He should have his photograph taken as soon as possible and send it to his family!

'Jesus, that red coat don't half clash with your hair.' Melody's casual utterance instantly exploded the myth.

Jaw twitching, Probyn wondered what sentence might be incurred from killing a member of one's own side, and quickly shielded the offending thatch with a glengarry. 'At least I've still got hair! You look like a shorn old ewe.' A plague on Melody for spoiling his moment!

There followed an inspection, the first of many, by their platoon commander Lieutenant Fitzroy whose critical eye picked out the deficiencies in their regulation garb and ordered these to be amended.

After drawing their kit and equipment, the recruits were instructed by their platoon sergeant to return to the hut where they had spent the night and collect their biscuits.

'Kilmaster,' Sergeant Faulkner was consulting a list, 'you only arrived this morning so you won't have had a biscuit. Get over to the quartermaster's store and he'll give you one. Fetch it back here and you'll be shown where to go next.'

With an expression of restrained delight at the prospect of this mid-morning refreshment, Probyn made his exit.

'Biscuits? I didn't expect such treats in t'army. I hardly ever get them at home.'

But there was to be disappointment. The biscuit turned out to be a mattress. Added to this, upon his return, there was mockery from his companions. 'Sure, ye'd be hard pressed to dip that in your tea,' laughed Mick, almost splitting his sides at the sight of Probyn's disgruntled face over the mound of bedding.

Fortunately his discomfiture was soon curtailed as the recruits were sent along to another store where each was given a rifle. This gave rise to a lot of boyish horseplay, which was frowned upon by Probyn who, taking everything in deadly serious vein, set himself apart so as not to incur the wrath that would surely come. Whilst others were bawled to order he tried to familiarize himself with the numerous items of kit. But there was to be little chance of accumulating knowledge at the moment for they were on the move again.

Laden with their respective burdens, he and Melody, the oafish Ingham and a host of others with whom he had yet to make proper acquaintance were marched to another barrack block. This one was more populated and divided into sections, all of which buzzed with masculine voices. Deposited in another stark room with beds down either side, the recruits were left to their own devices and told that someone would be along in a while to give them instruction. Waiting until Melody had dumped his kit, Probyn selected the bed that was furthest away from this pest.

A period of further introduction occurred between the recruits. Trying to remember their names Probyn seized on physical defects to aid his memory: Barnes had a face that was big and square and rather wooden, like a barn door; Bumby's round cheeks were like a pair of buttocks; Chambers and Gover were both average-looking chaps with no obvious blemish, he would probably forget them; Havron . . . well that sounded a bit like chevron and as his forehead was perpetually striped in a frown it was a good enough aid;

Queen had a London twang and London was where the queen lived, Rook was dark and watchful as his name would suggest . . .

Throughout the swapping of yarns, it became clear that many of them had come here via a shared act of rebellion. Against tradition they had refused to follow their fathers down the coal mine. Yet this was where the similarity ended for, unlike Probyn, they had joined the army not from love of Empire but simply as a means of escaping a wretched existence. Others like Ingham were quite obviously from much more deprived backgrounds. Worse, their dullard expressions were far from being skin deep.

Whilst not highly-educated himself Probyn did not lack intelligence and he was dismayed as to the high proportion of inarticulacy and dim-wittedness, the majority of their stories being of gang fights and trouble with the police – not the sort with whom this well-brought-up young man would have associated in civilian life. Still, they were friendly enough and he made an effort to get on with them.

But after twenty minutes or so when still nobody had come to offer instruction, and concerned that certain members had started to act the fool again, Probyn addressed the squad. 'Hadn't one of us better go and ask what we're supposed to be doing?'

'Ah, you go if you're bothered,' yawned Melody, obviously happy to lie on his cot and do nothing.

Annoyed at the lack of enthusiasm, Probyn wandered out into a corridor and followed the sound of voices to a room nearby, intending to seek guidance. However, it was doubtful he would find it here. Hovering in the doorway, presented with the men who were to be his comrades in arms, his heart sank lower still, for many of those before him were characteristic of the riff-raff portrayed by his father.

Even down the pit he had never heard such language as was bandied here, the majority of their words beginning with f and b and c. Riven by disgust, the young idealist wondered how the wearers of so dashing a uniform could bring themselves to sully it thus. The content of their discourse was even more vile, centring on the local womenfolk and what sexual favours they had granted at the weekend, most of which Probyn could not believe even the lowest type of woman would contemplate. To make matters worse a couple of the redcoats appeared nearly as old as his father – more than old enough to know better. Many were in stockinged feet and shirt sleeves, their braces dangling in a slovenly manner. To compound everything, one of them was openly farting. The room reeked like a sewer.

Unsure of his reception, the youngster stood there aghast, wanting to turn his back on the whole degraded crew but pinned to the spot by fascinated horror. In the centre of the lofty whitewashed barrack room were a number of tables and wooden forms where men variously sat cleaning kit and other chores, all performed in an unenthusiastic method. Others warmed their hands at a fuel stove, apparently doing nothing.

As yet, no one in the room had spared so much as a nod for the newcomer. Uncertain what to do, Probyn cast a forlorn glance around the walls, the sight of a withered sprig of holly making him even more demoralized.

'Do you want something, shit-stick?'

Shocked and insulted, Probyn shot to attention. 'We were told somebody'd come and show us what to do but nobody's come.'

Twisting his words, the man who had made the enquiry voiced an obscene comment which Probyn felt it better to ignore, though his cheeks flamed red under the coarse laughter.

'Oilbederwhenoivedonedesefecknboots!' A wiry, middle-aged twig of a man, in the act of blacking his footwear, paused to direct this comment at the new boy but spoke so rapidly that Probyn failed to comprehend.

'I beg your pardon?'

It was delivered more coherently, though with exaggerated patience. 'I said, I'll be along to help yese in a while.'

Dismayed by the Irish accent, Probyn hurried away to inform the others what they could expect.

In a short matter of time, true to his promise, the old soldier came to assist. The stringy-looking man was accompanied by two others, both of whom had caught Probyn's eye earlier and both earning his contempt. One, who introduced himself as Jessop, was no more than twenty but was the possessor of a luxuriant moustache and a cocksure, swaggering manner; the other, Oliver, was a florid-cheeked man, somewhat older, stocky, confident, and despite being the possessor of a foul mouth, much more amiable than Jessop who was now standing over Melody in threatening pose.

'Shift your arse off my cot.' He was carrying a mattress, as were the others.

Melody's lips parted in silent protest as he glanced enquiringly at other unoccupied beds in the room.

'If I'm stuck in here helping you babbies learn the ropes,' growled Jessop, 'I'm having a decent cot, now shift!'

With all eyes keen for his reaction, a good-natured Mick treated it as a joke and, clumsily folding up his mattress and belongings, vacated the bed by the window for one in shadow. 'Ah well, I'm sure this one'll be fine enough.' He dumped his equipment on the cot beside Probyn's.

The eldest soldier appeared not to be so selective, throwing his mattress onto the bedstead to Probyn's left flank. Oliver took the bed that was furthest away, which was a relief to Probyn for the man appeared to be suffering from unremitting flatulence, making this room smell as rank as the one he had just left.

For a time, no more exchange was made between new and old. The recruits, completely in awe of the three experienced soldiers, merely watched them on their several journeys back and forth, transferring their kit from the other room, the two Yorkshiremen occasionally throwing a question at the

Irishman who would reply with a bout of rapid fire. Probyn was amazed at their powers of interpretation for the entire speech was unintelligible to him. It was as if all the words were joined together, though amid the swift delivery he did detect the liberal use of the word fuck which seemed to be employed as a means of punctuation.

After his final journey, the weather-beaten private, aware of Probyn's close interest as he stacked his items of kit on the shelf above his cot, addressed him again.

'I'm sorry,' replied Probyn. 'I didn't catch what you said.'

The Irishman sighed and rattled off a further incomprehensible speech before repeating in more measured terms. 'I said, we'd better acquaint ourselves if we're to be cot mates. What the divil's up with yese can't y'understand the Queen's English for Christ's sake?' His skull resembled an ancient sea shell, gnarled and discoloured by the tide of life. 'I'm Felix Lennon.'

Increasingly disillusioned by events and characters, Probyn was somewhat lacklustre in his response, merely divulging his name.

Mick in his usual amiable fashion, and encouraged by the Irish accent, sprang up and leaned over Probyn's cot to introduce himself. 'And what part of the old country are you from, sir?'

Faced with much heckling from his companions, Lennon's leathery face creased in a grin and he advised Mick not to call him that.

'He's not sir, he's Grandma,' explained Private Oliver, his rough-looking face transformed by a smile. ''Cause he mollycoddles all the new recruits.' He emitted another blast of wind at which Private Queen giggled, infecting others.

'I beg yese don't encourage him.' Lennon picked up a boot and resumed the chore that had been interrupted earlier, as he did so answering Mick's question. 'I hail from Rathkeale in Limerick. And yourself?'

Even with ears keenly pricked, Probyn still found it hard

to grasp the man's speech and was forced to rely on Melody's response as a means of enlightenment.

'Galway city,' said Mick. 'And how long have you been with the regiment?'

'My pontoon comes up next summer,' replied Lennon, indicating the long service stripe on his cuff.

Not conversant with the term, the recruits were told it signified twenty-one years of service. Good gracious, thought Probyn contemptuously, still a private after almost a quarter of a century!

As if reading his expression, Lennon gave a wry smile, but said nothing, just spat on his boot and performed circular motions upon the leather with the bone handle of a knife. The recruits had begun to gather round him.

'Twenty-one years!' breathed Mick.

'Well, aren't you planning to stay that long?' sniped Probyn, inordinately annoyed with everyone for ruining what should have been an auspicious occasion.

'Jesus, I don't know if I'll even last the seven,' answered Mick, embracing others in his friendly smile. 'Sure, I don't normally plan further than the morrow.'

'Don't have to do any planning at all now,' offered Oliver, with another of his crude appellations. 'Not even a trip to the bog. You go where you're told.'

Lennon agreed, polishing stolidly at his boots. 'And 'tis somewhere unpleasant you'll be going if ye don't get all that kit off the bed before Corporal Wedlock spies it.' His seasoned head jerked towards the shelf over his bedspace where items of kit were neatly arranged, his only other storage area being three pegs. 'Look and learn.'

'Wedlock? Sure, that's a funny name.' Mick's ruddy face creased in laughter as he tried to make sense of all the military paraphernalia spread on his mattress, the others doing likewise, aided by Jessop and Oliver.

'Ah, he's a very funny chap is our Corporal Wedlock,' came the rapid reply.

'Otherwise known as Out-of,' provided Oliver.

'Why's that?' Probyn frowned innocently, but was not to be enlightened, receiving only a cynical glance.

He sighed and took great care in stacking his kit on the shelf, he and his fellow recruits referring occasionally to Lennon's methods and placing their own belongings in similar mode. During this period of absorption there was another burst from the bugler.

'That'd be mail,' Lennon anticipated the question whilst examining his gleaming boot. 'Ye'll soon get used to the different calls.'

Perhaps, came Probyn's dismal thought, but will I ever get used to you and these other scoundrels? Glancing miserably round the barrack room he could find not one occupant to admire. But the mention of mail had reminded him; he must write home at the first opportunity to inform his father he was safe. Maintaining his diligent placement, he went on filling the shelves.

Lennon, Oliver and Jessop continued to answer a barrage of questions, none of which came from Private Kilmaster. Probyn would not lower himself to show ignorance before these disappointing specimens. However, he was most anxious to learn and, without seeming to, made careful note of the answers.

'Eh, Gingernut!'

Probyn clenched his teeth. How often had this annoying sobriquet been hung on him. Now in the act of folding his blankets in the required manner, he half turned to address Jessop who had hailed him, though did not look him in the eye, averse to confrontation at this early stage. 'My name's Kilmaster, actually.'

'Oh, Mr Double-barrel are we? Well, Kilmaster-Actually, get thy bloody arse down to the dry canteen and fetch me a can o' button brass.'

The man's expression brooked no argument. Probyn affected willingness to comply yet was bound to ask in astonished manner, 'Do we have to buy our own? In that case I'd better go to the office and ask Corporal White for my money. He's looking after it for me.' Others echoed his intention.

Placing his boots in meticulous juxtaposition, Lennon gave a mirthless chuckle. 'Sure and ye won't see that again, my boy.'

Upon interpretation, Probyn suffered renewed shock. 'But there was nigh on half-a-crown! I've only got the bob they gimme when I signed!'

'And they'll have most o' that back off ye too,' warned Lennon, his jabbered reply punctuated by the usual obscenities.

Growing more disaffected by the second, Probyn had an awful thought. 'We don't have to pay for food, do we?'

'Ye do if ye want any more than bread and meat.' Lennon examined Probyn's shelf and nodded approvingly at his effort. 'Threepence a day for vegetables and other non-essentials. A ha'penny a day for your laundry.'

Aghast, Probyn determined to save money by taking his own washing home whenever possible.

'Mother o' God, how will we afford all the polish for our kit and boots?' wailed Mick, clamping a hand to his shorn scalp.

'How much have you got?' Jessop interjected.

'Same as everybody else, no more than a shilling.'

'Right chuck us it over here! Away, I'm not gonna diddle you. You two an' all.'

Reluctantly, Probyn and the lumbering Ingham handed over their coins to the older man who spread them on his palm in informative manner.

'There we are! See what you can do with co-operation? You've got three shillings. That's more than enough to buy brass polish, boot blacking, all the stuff you need for cleaning.'

'Ah true enough!' Mick grinned at his two pals. 'Share and share alike.'

'That's very generous of you!' Jessop handed the coins to Probyn. 'So fuck off and get it then.'

* * *

61

If Probyn had thought things were grim enough, they were to grow steadily worse. He and the others had just nicely begun to achieve some semblance of order with their kit and equipment when a cry of, 'Stand by your beds!' went up and the infamous Corporal Wedlock finally appeared. Still unable to decipher the nickname, Out-of, Probyn was nevertheless made all too aware of the reason for the communal dislike for he strutted amongst them like a bantam cock intent on a fight, his grey eyes displaying an assertiveness that overcame any lack of stature. After ordering each man to recite his name, rank and number, Wedlock passed briskly between the two rows of beds, flicking and tossing each recruit's carefully placed kit into disarray until the barrack room looked as if a hurricane had visited, his language no better than those in his charge.

'A bloody disgrace! I send you three good swaddies to show you the way and do you follow their example? No! You've got ten minutes to get it picked up and into proper order!' With this the aggressive bantam turned on his heel and marched out leaving the panicked recruits to sort out the mess and their disgruntled helpers with extra work.

'Dlittleshoite,' mumbled Lennon to Jessop and Oliver, then swiftly addressed the baffled youngsters, 'Well, what did y'expect in the army? Your mother's not here to make your bed now. Come on, get it done – and do it properly this time.'

Wedlock's return proved not so violent, yet he was still unimpressed with their efforts. 'Does *this* resemble *that*?' he demanded, pointing first to Melody's shelf and then to Private Lennon's. 'Does it?'

Mick compared both shelves and could not see the difference. Neither could Probyn. The Irish youth might be idle but his attempt was quite neat. However, it was no good trying to argue with one who was obviously intent on finding a flaw.

'Em, maybe not, Corporal,' conceded Mick.

Wedlock thrust his snub nose into the other's face and squawked, 'Then make sure it does!' Eyes like rivets, he stood over Melody whilst he brought his kit to order, then began to strut up and down the room, picking fault, imaginary or genuine.

'Right, fall in for drill!'

At the confused reaction, Wedlock swore, 'Bloody useless buggers!' Then he turned to Lennon and his cohorts. 'You three, show them how a swaddy gets fell in!'

With a short series of regimented movements, the trio carried out the order, coming together and standing smartly to attention at the corporal's further command. Probyn was rather amazed at the metamorphosis in the men's attitude.

'In future, when I give you the order to fall in that is what you will do!' Wedlock encompassed the recruits with a challenging scowl. 'Now fall in!'

Probyn performed what he assumed was a close imitation of Lennon's action, irritated that others had not paid such close attention. He was therefore mortified to be included in Corporal Wedlock's scornful mockery.

'What a bunch of tossers! Not a brain between them – I have not told you to stand easy, stand to attention when I'm talking to you!' Again he turned to address the experienced soldier. 'Private Lennon, show these lumpen louts how to march. At the double, left-right left-right left-right. See how it's done, you useless cretins? Outside! That man, stop flapping, you're not a bloody goose!'

Harried at the double to the square and reunited with their fellow recruits, all were to be further upbraided in the most offensive terms.

'Right! While we're waiting for Sergeant Lockwood to arrive and put you through your drill we'll give you an intelligence test. You, what's your name?'

'Kilmaster, Corporal!'

'Kilmaster! Give me another name for privates.'

Heart still thudding from his stressful treatment, desperate to impress, Probyn racked his brain but was forced to blurt a nonplussed reply. 'I don't know, Corporal.'

Wedlock assumed a childish mimic. 'Don't know, Corporal! Well, I'll tell you. It's genitalia! A bunch of pricks is what you are, and floppy ones at that.'

Immersed in the very depths of despair, Probyn lowered his gaze.

'Eyes front, you piece of shit!'

From somewhere came a disgusted mutter. 'Isn't he the gentleman.'

Wedlock darted up to Melody and bawled at him. 'Gentleman? What would you know about fucking gentlemen?'

There was a giggle from Queen on the back row, but under the corporal's violent outburst this was soon quelled, Mick and the rest of the squad grimly standing to attention. ''Twasn't me who said it, Corporal!'

'Who was it then?' Wedlock's eyes were devoid of any humanity. 'Come on, out with it!'

Standing close enough to attract a glob of the furious corporal's spittle Probyn reminded himself to put others between him and Melody in future.

Unwilling to betray a comrade, Mick tried to endear himself with a smile, but it wavered round the edges.

'Dumb insolence is it? Any more and I'll have you on a charge! Take that look off your face!'

Amazed, Mick stammered, 'Sure, I can't help the cut of me face, Corporal, 'tis the way God made me.'

Derision from Wedlock, his bellowing mouth so close that Mick could see down his throat. 'God wouldn't waste His talents on the likes of you! You came out of somebody's arse!'

Probyn closed his eyes, a gesture of abhorrence.

'Oh, I seem to have offended Mr Namby-pamby 'ere!' Wedlock shifted his focus to the shortest recruit, strutting up and down before him. 'However can that be?'

Trying to keep his head and shoulders erect whilst at the same time avoiding the corporal's challenging stare, Probyn thought it wiser to remain mute.

Another spray of spittle dotted the victim's red tunic. 'The captain's going to be very busy isn't he! What with all these charges of dumb insolence to attend to!'

Alarmed by the threat, Probyn attempted to explain. 'It's just that we don't swear in our house, Corporal.'

Wedlock grew more melodramatic. 'Oh, I'm *so* terribly sorry. Private Ingham, go fetch the carbolic and I'll scrub my foul mouth out. Stay where you are, you stupid pillock!' Ingham had seemed about to move.

'God give me strength!' Wedlock held supplicating hands to the wintry sky. 'It'll need a bleedin' miracle to turn this bunch o' fannies into soldiers.' After a moment of theatrical sobbing, he caught sight of the drill sergeant approaching and gave a final address to the recruits, this time with an icy determination in his eye and threat in his voice. 'But we *are* going to turn you into soldiers or see you bleed to sodding death.'

Sweating profusely despite the cold weather in the two torturous hours that followed, Probyn feared this was no empty threat. He was used to hard labour, yet the word exhaustion took on a new meaning as he was drilled and harried, insulted and threatened. The lack of sleep last night had already begun to tell and there was still twelve hours to go before bed time. How would he survive? Joints and muscles that had seemed so adequate in normal life now began to fail him, screaming under the effort as his stamina was tested to breaking point. Stinging rivulets of salt ran into his eyes; barely could he find the power to raise his arm and dash it away. A tired glance showed that for a shirker like Melody this was inflicting even more hardship. Having taken instant dislike to the Irish youth, Corporal Wedlock had warned the drill sergeant of his predisposition, thus Lockwood drove him harder than any of the others until, finally, Mick collapsed in a panting heap, unable to go on, unable even to speak. Only the aroma of cooking on the air forced the tyrant to curtail his sadistic proceedings, with the vow that there would be more of the same this afternoon.

Supporting Mick between them, Probyn and an equally exhausted Ingham limped back to their barrack room with the rest of the squad, faces as red as their sweat-drenched tunics, and after dropping him on his cot, fell onto their respective mattresses, thoroughly sapped of energy.

About to slide into unconsciousness, Probyn was roused by the bugler sounding the arrival of dinner. Dragging his feet to the dining hall, he sat there with heavy-lidded eyes, passing a grateful nod to Lennon who had, unceremoniously, slammed the meal before him. The other recruits joined the assembly, then, like automata, proceeded to shovel the meagre helping of mashed potato and sinewy meat into their mouths. No word was shared between them, though an occasional impolite comment passed amongst the old soldiers amidst their piggish slurping and chomping.

Hampered as he was by weariness and disrelish, many of the others finished long before Probyn. Having finally taken his fill, and mechanically following example, he rinsed his mug, knife and fork in an iron bath placed by the door. The water had grown cold and had a layer of greasy scum that adhered to his utensils, coating them not only with his own mess but other people's too. Without drying facilities he shook off the moisture as best he could, returned to his barrack room and put the implements back on his shelf, then tried to relax on his bed.

Alas, before the meal could be digested there came another shrill command from Corporal Wedlock who ordered the recruits outside for a further two hours of drilling under the indefatigable Sergeant Lockwood. Thence, amid more vile threats, followed more marching, about-turning, left-righting, saluting and incessant abasement.

Other than the fact that punishment stopped for tea, there was nothing further to inspire joy. Probyn had always been well fed at home, his father's allotment providing fresh vegetables, an abundance of brambles and elderberries for home-made jam, and plenty of rhubarb. Here it was bread, the attitude being take it or leave it.

Probyn ate the scanty meal in the customary daze – though now it had grown from a dream to a veritable nightmare. This was only his first day; how would he endure seven years of this treatment? For he had quickly dismissed the idea of staying for the full twelve – and the thought of twenty-one was preposterous!

After this, the last meal of the day, whilst he and the other recruits lay on their cots attempting to recover their strength, the old hands prepared for an evening in the wet canteen. Best boots were dug out, tunics pressed, moustaches tweaked and waxed.

Attending to his toilet, braces dangling, Private Lennon warned the new boys not to fall asleep before they prepared their kit for morning, and offered to show them what to do.

'Stuff that,' griped Mick, his thin limbs draped misshapenly over his bed like a swatted cranefly.

'Ah, come on now, play de game,' insisted Lennon, standing over him. 'Ye don't want to get on the wrong side of the corporal.'

'You're not trying to cod me he has a right side?' Summoning great effort, Mick rolled off the bed.

Ingham complied too, falling easily into barrack vernacular. 'He's such a twat that Corporal Wedlock.'

Probyn winced at the language.

'Ah that's true enough.' Lennon was sick of the corporal too. 'He just got his second stripe last week and wants to make sure everybody knows it. So don't give him any more cause for complaint than ye have to.'

Resentfully, the recruits set about doing as the experienced soldiers taught them. Whilst the likes of Melody and Ingham showed hesitance over the chore, Probyn launched straight in with an air of confidence, paying scant heed to what Lennon was saying, for there seemed little to be learned from one who had never earned promotion in twenty-one years.

'Don't go clarting your pipeclay in too thick else you'll be here till Tattoo – oh, what an atrocious mess!'

Shrugging off all attempts of help, Probyn continued doggedly applying the pipeclay to leather, but only accomplished a greater bungle, even managing to get the stuff in his hair.

Glancing round to see how everyone was coping, Jessop cackled. 'Eh, Kilmaster-Actually, are you a plasterer by trade?'

Probyn was offended at being made fun of, and hoped this appellation would not stick.

Turning to see what the laughter was about, Lennon gave a sigh at Probyn's lack of skill and peppered him with abuse. 'Ye won't be told, will ye?' Arms akimbo, he stood over the culprit. 'Think ye can't learn anything from the likes of me, is that it?'

Probyn blushed and didn't know what to say.

'All right you're so wise, consider this.' Lennon presented the bedevilled recruit with an anecdote. 'You're in a cell, the walls of which are twelve inches thick. There's a window but it has iron bars on it. The only items in the room are a stone slab for a bed and a bucket to piss in. How do ye get out?'

Trying to rid his fingers of pipeclay, Probyn struggled to contain his irritation. 'They'd feed me wouldn't they? I'd use the knife or fork to scrape the cement away from the bars, so's I could remove one and squeeze through.'

'Take a long time,' mused the old soldier. 'Why don't ye just use the door? Didn't say it was locked, did I?'

Made to appear foolish, Probyn groaned under subsequent taunts.

'Always look for the easy way first, son, and pay heed to them as'll take the time to show ye.'

'Sorry.' Probyn looked suitably ashamed.

'Here now, let Felix sort it out.'

Conceding that there was much to learn, Probyn gratefully

observed Lennon's advice, even venturing a question as he laboured. 'Does your wife live near by, Private Lennon?'

'Never married,' said Felix, adding some unintelligible remark that Probyn decided not to question, for he did not want to irritate the man by his constant demands for repetition. Merely nodding, he threw himself into his task and, after a series of short cuts, had cleaned enough of his kit to stand him in good stead for morning.

Itching to go out, Jessop showed a sudden disinclination to help the recruits any longer and abandoned them in favour of the wet canteen. 'Away, Grandma, that's enough, you'll be breastfeeding them in a minute.'

Lennon hooked his arm through his braces and donned his scarlet tunic, his lips rattling out a final burst of advice. 'Mind you boys have all that kit cleaned and put away before ye get your heads down.' With this he and the two others departed.

Absorbed in their tasks, the recruits continued to polish and clean and iron for some hours afterwards, but eventually exhaustion began to claim them. Mick was first to succumb, making down his bed, flopping onto his back and groaning that he needed a rest before continuing. Within moments he was asleep. Havron and Ingham proceeded for a while longer, complaining throughout of their hunger, then they too surrendered to weariness. Fearful of Corporal Wedlock's wrath, Barnes and Bumby, Queen, Rook and the others stuck at their chores, though their eyelids were heavy and their muscles ached.

The rest of the barrack block appeared to have joined Private Lennon at the wet canteen for there was not the usual row in the corridor. In the comparative silence, Probyn glanced up occasionally to check on Melody. Worried that the bane of his life seemed to have fallen into a deep sleep, he cleared his throat noisily in an attempt to wake him, but to no effect. With so much else to concern him he decided to let him lie, and continued beavering until everything was spotless and in its place, ready for morning.

Only then did he allow himself to get ready for bed, others following suit. At home there would be cocoa at bedtime and perhaps a slice of bread. Here there was just a parched mouth and an empty belly.

It seemed like only a moment ago that Lennon and his pals had gone out yet here they were back again, some of them the worse for drink and making enough din to wake even a sloth like Melody.

Face creased and bewildered, Mick sat bolt upright at the soldiers' noisy entrance.

'I told you they'd be slacking,' Oliver told Lennon, examining the scene.

Dressed only in his shirt, about to get into bed, Probyn looked offended and indicated his neatly placed kit. 'I can't see owt wrong with mine.'

'And what're dese strides doing here?' Felix Lennon directed an arthritic digit at the pair of trousers draped over the foot of Probyn's bed. 'And dem and dose.' One after another he pointed to similarly placed garments. 'Come on now, get your arses up.'

A bleary-eyed Melody conformed with the others.

Probyn followed Lennon's instructions too, applying soap to the creases of his trousers, though not without a mutinous grumble to his cot mate. 'If he doesn't shut up with his dis, dat and de udder I'm going to stick them up his –'

'Em! Would you be making fun of my accent, Private Kilmaster?' came the Irishman's narrow-eyed query.

'Not me.' Aching for sleep, his face grim, Probyn carefully arranged the trousers under his mattress and, finally, climbed in on top of them.

It transpired that they were not to gain respite from Corporal Wedlock even now, for as the bugler sounded Tattoo in he pranced, surveying the cowed recruits with a baleful eye and ordering one or two of them out of bed to complete an unfinished task, before finally taking to his cot in the warmest corner of the room.

Ill-at-ease, his mouth as dry as a bone, Probyn closed his eyes. Normally before getting into bed he would have said his prayers, but tonight he offered only the silent hope that tomorrow would see an improvement in his situation. Even before the lights had all gone out he yielded to exhaustion, the last thought on his mind one of utter disillusionment.

Probyn was roused early, though not by yesterday's thrill. Reveille was accompanied by the same sense of pessimism with which he had finally dropped off to sleep, seemingly minutes ago. Exhausted and hollow, aching to his very bones, he rolled into a sitting position on the edge of his mattress. For a second, as he experienced the bare floorboards under his feet, he imagined himself at home, but the impression was soon dashed.

The dark room stirred with animal grunts and the other bodily noises he had come to expect of its occupants. Spending a gloomy interlude kneading his face, he finally stood, retrieved his trousers from under the mattress and shoved his legs into them. Others were doing likewise. Now, only Melody was still a-bed.

The last note of reveille faded away. Over in the corner Corporal Wedlock sat bolt upright, reached onto his shelf for an object, took aim and let the missile fly.

With an agonized yelp Mick propped himself up in bed, dazed not just with sleep but by the wooden club that had skimmed his head. Had it been any more accurate, thought a horrified Probyn, it would have killed the youth. As it was, the side of his scalp had been laid open.

Wedlock leapt smartly out of bed and without further preamble charged up to Mick's cot, grabbed the edge of the mattress and tipped its bleeding occupant onto the floor. Whilst others went about making their beds, terrified of similar retribution, Probyn hovered to watch. The man was an outright hooligan!

Wedlock had started to kick his victim, shouting at him to get up. Bare feet or no, Probyn could not allow this to go on. He stepped forth to intervene, but was immediately rewarded with an upraised fist.

'Want to find yourself on a charge, Kilmaster?' came the threatening hiss.

'No, Corporal!' Reluctantly, Probyn stood down.

'Then make up your bed!'

Probyn hurriedly complied. Always looked after by his sisters, he had never made a bed in his life until shown how to yesterday and now could not recall what to do. Snatching frequent glances at the old soldiers for reference, he dragged every item from the cot then attempted to fold each in the required manner, bringing the edges of the sheets together, tugging and smoothing, until they were of a precise size and displaying them neatly on his mattress. During the time this took he was relieved to see Mick clamber to his feet, and whilst not exactly upright he was at least living.

'Right!' Wedlock was saying, 'Me-lody, Mel-ody or whatever way you bloody pronounce it –'

'You can say it whichever way ye like, Corp,' offered the dazed Mick, a trickle of blood running down his neck.

The snub nose adopted an arrogant tilt. 'So if it takes my fancy to pronounce it turd you wouldn't object?'

'Not at all, Corp.'

'Good! And when you hear reveille tomorrow morning, what are you going to do, turd?'

'I'm going to get up, Corp.'

'Correct. Now make your frigging bed and get this floor scrubbed!'

Smoothing the last wrinkle out of his folded blanket and placing his pillow just so, Probyn joined others in sweeping and scrubbing the floorboards. Then it was off to ablutions. Normally, he would shave only every three days, but not wishing to appear childish, he took up his razor and scraped at imaginary whiskers, though it was an extremely unpleasant task with only cold water at his disposal. Trying to staunch his nicked chin, he glanced at Melody who had just staggered in, the bloody wound on his head beginning to congeal.

In passing, Lennon undertook brief examination and pronounced in his speedy brogue, 'Dat's a nasty scratch, an' all, son, here, let me see to it for yese.'

'Oh, leave it be.' Lacking his normally ruddiness, a pain-faced Mick extricated himself. 'I've no wish to invite more injury from Corporal Wedlock if he comes in and catches me doing naught. Sure, the man's a raving lunatic.' He had a swift if delicate wash and, with only a downy growth on his cheeks he had no need of a razor and was soon able to catch up. When the others were dressed in their red serge and polished boots and mustered for inspection, he was amongst them, though looking none too happy.

As on the day before, there was a period of bullying from Wedlock who picked fault with everyone's appearance and made them do things again and again before finally handing the recruits over to a different corporal who took them to the gymnasium. Here they exchanged their tunics and caps for canvas shoes and belts. After inspection by a sergeant, they were ordered to complete twenty laps of the gym, then it was on to dumbbells and parallel bars, during which period of exertion Mick collapsed in a faint.

'How did he get that cut to his head?' demanded Staff Sergeant Milner, testing Melody for consciousness with a few prods of his foot.

Probyn exchanged a glance with Rook who seemed equally unwilling to make a worse enemy of Wedlock. 'I think he fell out of bed, Staff Sergeant.'

The flicker of one stony eye told Probyn that Milner did not believe him, but thankfully there was to be no repercussion. An order was given to Ingham and Havron. 'Right, you two, carry him to hospital!' And the injured party was removed from the scene.

Far from being sympathetic, Probyn was vastly relieved to have this burden removed, and hoped Melody's sojourn might be extended so as to allow others to keep a lower profile.

An hour or so later, proud of himself for surviving the latest ordeal, he and an equally exhausted squad went to eat breakfast. After washing a chunk of his daily bread ration down with some foul tasting coffee, he stored the remainder on his shelf. In no time at all, it was back to work.

There were tables to scrub and equipment to clean, then, with the coming of light, they were driven by Milner around a muddy field with press-ups along the way until everyone was the colour of chocolate. After a change of clothing came a lecture, then rifle exercise, and more drill until noon, and after another unpalatable dinner there followed another two hours of exertion. With hardly a moment to draw breath or even to visit the latrine, the day seemed more arduous than the one before.

To Probyn's annoyance, Melody rejoined the platoon at tea-time, though he was gratified to note that the latter was rather more subdued than normal and paid much more care to the cleaning of his equipment than he had yesterday. Hopefully his efforts would pay dividends for all with Corporal Wedlock.

Adhering to his own scruples, Probyn passed the hours as on the foregoing evening by vigilantly polishing, folding and ironing, wondering whether tonight he would get time to write that letter of explanation to his father.

But no, Privates Lennon, Jessop and Oliver were already returning from their night out at the wet canteen signifying that it was time for lights out. The letter would have to wait yet again.

Once more an exhausted Private Kilmaster found himself shrouded in a musty blanket, trying desperately not to think of the horrible future that lay ahead.

*　　*　　*

Within seconds, it seemed, of Tattoo being played the bugler was sounding reveille. It was immediately obvious to Probyn that he had never moved his leaden limbs all night for they were still in the same position in which he had fallen asleep and were excruciatingly painful. The barrack room hummed with its usual malodorous stench. Grimacing, he hauled himself into a sitting position, then forced his eyes open and peered through sandy lashes to gauge others' movements. Whilst many were already up Melody was still fast asleep. Anxious to avoid a replay of yesterday's episode, not only for Melody's sake but because it reflected on him too, Probyn breached the eighteen inches between their cots and dealt the Irish youth a sharp jab in the back that had him up in seconds, gibbering and dancing into his trousers before he realized who it was that had awoken him. This time when the last note of reveille died out the cudgel remained harmlessly on Wedlock's shelf.

Not that this indicated any weakening on his part though, nor that of the physical training instructor either who drove them as mercilessly as ever around the gymnasium, likewise the drill sergeant who persistently yelled and abused them for one misdemeanour after another and, oh, the constant marching! Probyn was used to walking long distances but not in such ill-fitting boots as these. It was obvious without looking that the continual rubbing had caused dreadful damage to his heels and toes. When, with the utmost relief, he tugged off his boots at noon he found that his feet resembled items on a butcher's slab.

Blisters had burst and disintegrated, exposing raw flesh. Following an all too short interlude during dinner when he left his feet bare, he took the rags normally used as handkerchiefs and tore them into bandages. Alas, any relief these might have given was quickly undone the moment he donned the offending footwear. He could hardly endure the weight of stockings, let alone boots. Angered by the callousness of Jessop's mocking laughter, he limped stiff-legged towards another gruelling afternoon of drill, each step sheer agony.

Between then and tea-time the shreds of linen worked their way into his lacerated flesh, becoming so firmly embedded that, when came the merciful return to his barrack room, he discovered it was impossible to dislodge them without soaking. Even then, the pain of removal brought him close to tears.

And the worst thing of all as he climbed into bed at night was the knowledge that in the morning it would all begin again.

The hours between dawn and dusk melted into a blur of pain, the recruits undergoing various forms of torture, rewarded only by the smallest amounts of food, and robbed of their precious spare time by old sweats who bullied them into running errands. Forced to show outwards deference or take the violent consequences, Probyn was nevertheless inwardly contemptuous, not least of their smutty talk and activities. He was not putting himself through all this just to emerge like them. Should he survive the training he was determined to rise above their rank and make something of himself, though just what that would be he was at a loss to say, for there was not one here to admire.

Notwithstanding this, Felix Lennon had emerged as a kind enough soul, lending him ointment that worked wonders on his feet and helping him make his boots more supple, also taking the time to interpret the various bugle calls, another army ritual of which Probyn was becoming heartily sick; it was bugle to breakfast, bugle to bed, and countless other bugles in between. At times he wanted to ram the wretched thing up the bugler's fundament. Now, though, towards the end of his first week that felt more like a month he was at least able to distinguish the calls which were relevant to him, and to ignore the others. He had also begun to be acclimatized to his surroundings, now familiar with the location of the dry canteen, though he had neither the time nor the money to go there very often. Even if granted the funds he would not be visiting the wet canteen which seemed to be the haunt of every other soldier in the block, save for the recruits who were too exhausted to go anywhere.

However, on Saturday evening it appeared there was to be a different venue. Private Lennon and his friends were venturing beyond the garrison walls and into town. Moreover, the recruits were invited to accompany them.

'Who's coming for a jar of neck-oil with us?'

There came a roar of mass approval from the young soldiers, Melody being the first to leap to his feet despite his exhaustion.

'Ye'll have to clean your kit first though,' warned Lennon.

'Aw, in God's name why?' demanded Mick, amid the unified groan. 'Is it not Sunday tomorrow?'

'Sunday might be a day of rest in your house,' rattled Lennon. 'But in the army . . . ?' He shook his head with an exaggerated tutting noise. 'I don't think. Ye've got Church Parade for a start –'

'Oh, Mother wouldn't like me to attend anything other than the real church,' butted in Mick.

'Don't bother trying to wriggle out of it, son,' advised Lennon. 'They've got churches to suit every one of yese, real or no. Come on now, get those buttons polished, the sooner we can be on our way.'

A period of intensive buffing occurred. Probyn noted to his disgust that he had never seen any of them work so hard when there wasn't a drink at the end of it. With no intention of being an accessory to this, he himself took his time, making sure he hadn't missed any smudges or blobs of mud, for Wedlock could detect one the size of a gnat's dropping.

Having anticipated some respite from the stringent discipline Mick was stunned to find that even outside there were rules to be observed. Many respectable establishments, said Lennon, would not serve anyone in uniform, and as common soldiers were not permitted to be seen without it, this tended to limit their choice of watering hole, but at least it would be a change of scenery.

'Sure, I'm all for a change of scenery,' agreed Mick, his elbow working furiously back and forth. 'Preferably a distant one. Tell me, Private Lennon, how many foreign countries have you been to?'

Felix mused. 'Mm, Africa, India, Mauritius, the West Indies, New Zealand. Oh, about a dozen I'd say.'

'I can't wait to see Africa,' grinned Mick, happier now in his polishing. 'Would there be elephants?'

Continuing to work, Felix nodded. 'Sure there's all kinds o' marvellous creatures.'

'What are the niggers like?' asked Ingham.

'Oh terrible brutes. Beware they don't catch ye or they'll slit your lips like tomatoes and cut off your ears and your nose.'

'And your goolies,' added Oliver, enjoying the look of horror he had created. 'Jessop lost his that way, he's lucky to be alive, aren't you, Jess?'

'Toss off,' muttered Jessop, shoving his feet into his boots.

Mick swallowed. 'What're goolies?'

Probyn smirked with the others at this display of innocence, though he could only hazard a guess as to the identity of the referred items.

Felix kindly explained.

'They'd really do that?' Mick was aghast.

'They would,' affirmed Felix. 'But 'tis the Dutchmen ye really want to watch – sly, bombastic creatures. And if they don't get you the enteric will, or the scorpions or the snakes, or the little wriggly fellas that live in the water.' With the listeners enthralled, he spent the next few minutes relating his experiences in foreign lands, and would have gone on all night had not his companions announced that they were ready to leave.

'Eh, Kilmaster-Actually, are you coming?' bawled Oliver.

'What with?' They had not yet received any wages, but it was merely a convenient excuse for Probyn. Moving stiffly, he began to return the cleaned articles of kit to his shelf.

'We'll give you a sub till you get paid,' said the swaggering

79

Jessop, preening his moustache. 'We're lending your mates some.'

'Thank you, but no.'

Jessop detected an air of aloofness and challenged him. 'What's up, aren't we good enough for you?'

Living cheek by jowl with these oafs, Probyn had no wish to make things worse by offending them, nevertheless he refused to be intimidated. 'I'm very grateful for the offer but I don't want to get into debt. Besides I don't take strong liquor.'

'Good, 'cause they don't serve it at the Black Boy, it's like gnat's piss,' this from Private Oliver. 'But it's the only pub that'll let us in after the ruction we had last month. Away, you maungy bugger.'

'Aye, come on, Probe, do,' begged Mick, other voices joining his. 'Aw, come on, come on, now! God knows, ye've worked hard enough for it.'

It was a quirk of Probyn's nature that, the more folk applied pressure, the further he dug his heels in. Now, he merely used another tack to fob them off. 'I've got an important letter to write. Can you tell me where I can get some paper?' The change of topic was directed at Private Lennon.

Before the other could answer there came mockery from Jessop. 'Doesn't swear, doesn't drink, writes letters. You're in the wrong place, pal, there's a monastery up t'road.'

Havron sneered. 'Must be a bloody poof.'

'What's a poof?' whispered Mick to the man beside him.

On a resentful sigh, Probyn explained, 'I just need to write and tell me father where I am while I've got the chance, that's all. My head's spinning enough without alcohol.'

Lennon offered solace. 'Don't worry, you'll soon find your feet.'

Queen made giggling observance on Probyn's short legs. 'Won't have to look far for them.'

'Take no notice,' slurred Lennon mildly, then remarked on the youngster's angry blush. 'Ah now, ye won't last long here, sonny, if ye can't take a joke.'

Probyn manufactured a smile, but inside his heart was awash with disappointment that his high ideals were not met by others.

'C'mon now!' With the exodus begun, Lennon crooked a finger at the outsider. 'Ye'll find what ye need at the soldiers' club. I'll show ye where it is.'

The temperance centre with its reading and writing room, its innocent games of chess and its tea and coffee bars, provided great relief to one seeking respite from the evils of his fellows.

Finding pen and paper and mercifully some quietude at last, Probyn seated himself at a desk, dipped his nib into an inkwell and scratched out his new address, then pondered over the date and suddenly realized that the old year had passed without him even noticing. It was now 1891.

Having sought out a calendar to check the date, he wrote, *Dear Father . . .*

Several minutes elapsed before he could think of anything else to say. Should he offer apology? No, because he wasn't genuinely sorry; he had been driven to this by his father's obduracy. There would certainly not be the slightest admittance that Father had been right all along. Regardless of the terrible disappointment Probyn had suffered he did not regret that he had chosen to make the discovery for himself. However . . . he should atone for the method of his leaving. Yes, that was the way to begin.

A dip into the inkwell and the nib made scratchy contact again. *I am sorry if you have been worried about my disappearance. I have put pen to paper at the first opportunity to let you know that I am safe and well. By now you must have guessed where I am. Doubtless you will think I planned it all along but it was a spur of the moment decision over Christmas that led me to coming here. By the way, I left my pit clothes under the bridge. They might come in useful for someone.*

After a further interlude of reflection, he fought his disconsolate mood to inject a note of enthusiasm. *I have passed all the
entrance requirements and am now kitted out and looking like a real
soldier. Don't know what happens next, nor where I shall be going,
but I will be thinking of you and . . .* he was about to write Merry,
but Father would be offended if he didn't include Mrs Carr so
he changed it to, *everyone at home. I promise to send you some
money as soon as I get paid. My regimental number and address
are at the top of this letter if you care to write. I should be pleased
to hear from you. Wishing you a very happy New Year. Yours
respectfully, Probyn.*

After depositing the letter for despatch, he was loath to swap
his peaceful sojourn for the barrack room and hence extended
his stay amongst the sober occupants of the Wesleyan centre.
Though their number was few, it was a relief to find that
there were, after all, people of like mind in the garrison.
More relaxed now, he nodded amiably at those who caught
his eye, and looked for a place to sit, then, as an afterthought
he approached a bookshelf. Browsing for a while amongst
interesting tomes, he finally selected one about the regiment's
history and sat down to read.

Some chapters later, in danger of nodding off, he was alerted
by the bugler calling Retreat. Stretching, he enjoyed the first
genuine sensation of pleasure since he had arrived. The regime
might be harsh and his fellows lacking in gallantry, but here
at least was an oasis to which he could escape every night.
Deciding there was just time to finish his chapter he lowered
his eyes back to the page, but it took longer than he had
thought and when he glanced up again everyone had gone.
A mahogany wall clock showed it was almost time for lights
out. Thoroughly reluctant to return to the den of iniquity,
he nevertheless hurriedly replaced the book on the shelf, and
loped back to his barrack room.

Den of iniquity had he called it? Bowels of Hades would
be more apt. Taking shallow inhalations, he cut a disgusted
passage through the haze of alcoholic and bodily fumes,

and made for his bed. Instantaneous to his arrival, Ingham deposited a pool of vomit on the floor, spattering Probyn's boots as he tried to dodge past. With an exclamation of revulsion, he sat on his cot and unlaced the soiled articles as quickly as possible, seeking a rag with which to clean them. To his greater repugnance, he noticed that his dark blue trousers were also contaminated.

'Ingham, you filthy –!' With an angry gasp he wrenched them off and dabbed at them frantically with another edge of the rag, trying to dislodge vomit from the weave.

Only Private Lennon came to his aid, handing over a damp cloth which eventually did the trick, though a disgusted sniff told Probyn further work would be needed. It was more than he could do to resist descending into foul language, comforting himself with the knowledge that at least his oath was justifiable and not issued in the casual manner of this scum. Hands trembling with rage, he soaped the creases of his trousers and duly got into bed, but how he would sleep with his head so utterly consumed by fury he did not know.

Apologizing to the Lord for his inappropriate method of communication, he prayed only for the lights to be turned out, so that he would no longer be tormented by these reprobates who had ruined his dream.

Melody, his blue eyes like glass, was serenading Ingham who was trying in drunken fashion to brush the puddle of vomit onto a shovel, but kept losing it along the way.

'Better sober up before the corp catches yese,' Lennon cautioned the pair. 'Or ye'll be answering a charge on Monday morning.'

Had Probyn been in command he would have had the whole block on a charge for such lack of decorum. Men who should have known better paraded their nakedness without shame, undergoing all manner of lewdness as they made ready for bed, exchanging graphic details about their female consorts. Trying to block out the dreadful vision, Probyn squeezed his eyes tightly shut and begged the Lord that it would not always be thus.

Amid more swearing, belching, staggering, the rabble continued to annoy him. Only when Corporal Wedlock bawled at them did they finally settle down.

The lights went out. The corporal climbed into his own bed. Some semblance of calm was achieved as one by one the lazy, undisciplined, beer-sodden, foul-mouthed womanizers fell asleep. Yet the rage in Private Kilmaster's head was not so easily extinguished.

4

On Sunday after breakfast there was a stampede to turn out
in full dress at ten o'clock. Though Probyn and the others
were not deemed proficient enough to join Church Parade,
they were nevertheless compelled to march afterwards in
their various denominations to their own places of worship,
and at this point Probyn found himself astounded yet again
by another fact of army life. Whilst the beeswaxed pews of
his own Methodist establishment were amply filled by scarlet
uniforms – for in the mining community this religion was very
strong – he was unnerved at the large number who patronized
the Catholic church: not just men and NCOs but officers too!
It was a sobering thought, one upon which to ponder as he
waited for the service to begin. In all his romantic dreams
he had never envisaged that the army he so admired would
harbour papists.

After worship the padre welcomed the new members of his
flock, speaking to them about love of regiment and offering
encouragement, telling them that he understood how difficult
this transition must be for them but to remember that every
man had suffered identical hardship in their early career and
they must not consider themselves victimized if they received
punishment for violating an order. It was a soldier's duty to
obey. It was also his duty to avoid the evils of alcohol or any
other temptation of the flesh that might be laid before him,
for this had been the downfall of many a good man. If only
the rest of his platoon could be made to heed the padre's

lecture, thought Probyn, for surely he was ministering to the converted here. Finding the speech uplifting, he delivered an inward rebuke, putting to rout any tinge of self-pity and resolving to start the week afresh with a different attitude.

Sad to say his mood was short-lived for on being reunited with the platoon at dinner he found them conversing on such topics of evil that had been denounced by the padre. As soon as the meal was over, desperate to escape his uncouth companions, he decided to go for a walk, avoiding any bid by Melody to accompany him.

After a damp and dirty week it was refreshing to experience the nip of frost on one's cheeks and to see a clear blue sky. Undecided where to go, happy just to be alone, Probyn took the downhill slope towards a town of great antiquity. Black coal, black liquorice, both had left their mark. The stone Butter Cross, the octagonal tower of St Giles, Ionic portico and eighteenth-century hovel, every building had been tainted by the dust and smoke of industry, and in its crooked narrow lanes and wide elegant marketplace there were more public houses than he could count, yet Pontefract endeared itself to his sense of history, particularly its ancient castle, and it was towards this crumbling relic that he now found himself heading.

Standing amid the ruin on its elevated rock, Probyn shielded his eyes against the January sun and stared into the distance. With the air as clear as crystal, every outline sharply defined by the frosty atmosphere, he could see for miles, could even make out the towers of York Minster, which came as an instant reminder of Aunt Kit. The edges of his mouth turned up in fond remembrance. It was on such days as this that she had taken him and his sisters on picnic walks. Inevitably, Beata, his dear departed eldest sister, wandered into his mind's eye, causing a tinge of sadness. But though his eyes burned with a sentimental tear Probyn was not given to melancholia and for the most part his memories were pleasant ones.

The view took on a different perspective. Out of the past

sprang a massive army, ten thousand men intent on battle. He heard their blood-curdling yells as they charged upon his stronghold, the whinny of armour-clad steeds thundering towards him, saw and felt the glint of sword and spear, rallied his doughty band of northern men to defend the ramparts that had never yet been breached, except by the ravages of time . . .

Battle was interrupted by a girlish titter. He wheeled around and saw that he was being observed by two young women. Instinctively he went to raise his glengarry, then, unsure whether this breached army etiquette, he merely touched it instead and turned back to the view.

Almost immediately he found the girls at his side. They appeared to be of similar age to himself.

'Lovely day, isn't it?' said the bolder of the pair, a friendly manner compensating for any lack of prettiness.

'Grand! Particularly after so much rain.' Having so many sisters, Probyn was at ease in the company of girls, especially ones whose plaid shawls and out-dated hats betrayed that they were of modest status.

'I hope we didn't disturb you?'

He responded happily. 'No! I was just standing here thinking.'

His coquettish, dark-eyed inquisitor leaned against the ruined wall. 'Thinking of your sweetheart? You seemed to be miles away.'

Probyn laughed as if this were ridiculous. 'I haven't got a sweetheart! No, I was just . . .' he broke off at the thought that they might mock his soldierly fantasies, and changed tack, 'just remembering the picnics my Aunt Kit used to take us on when we were young.'

'That's my name too!' smiled the bold one. 'At least it's Kitty.'

Probyn nodded respectfully. 'Private Probyn Kilmaster.'

'I love picnics,' enthused the girl who had not yet spoken.

'Oh, this is me friend, Fanny,' exclaimed Kitty.

After another series of smiles and nods, the girls appeared to become lost for words and it was left to Probyn to maintain the conversation. Considering it impolite to speak about himself he asked if they lived in Pontefract, though their accent which differed from his own had already told him this. Replying in the affirmative, they informed him that they worked at one of the liquorice factories, and in turn asked if he liked being a soldier which gave him a chance to shine without being boastful.

'You look very dashing,' commented Fanny, her eyes running admiringly over his red tunic.

Only then, in his enjoyment of this unaccustomed praise, did Probyn become rather tongue-tied and made a joke of her words. 'Oh, er, thank you! I don't know about dashing but I'm going to have to dash soon, I've lost track of the time. May I escort you young ladies back down the hill?'

They appeared to find it amusing that he addressed them as young ladies, but snatched his offer and accompanied him back into town. Shoulders back, head erect, he strutted like a peacock between the two duller hens. Disappointingly, the townsfolk being accustomed to the presence of soldiers, his uniform drew barely a glance, but at least the girls seemed taken with him.

'Let's go dahn here,' said Kitty, steering him out of his way, though he was quite happy to be led, thinking that his luck had surely changed. Then, 'Oh, look!' she cried, stopping to read a poster. 'There's a concert on Saturday.'

'Well, you won't be off,' said her friend pretending to sulk. 'And neither will I.'

Kitty groaned, then turned to explain to their soldier companion, 'We have to pay a neighbour for his broken window.' Emitting a sudden giggle, she told Probyn, 'We were laiking with me brother's football. Didn't do it on purpose.'

Eyes glued to the poster, Fanny gave an exaggerated sigh. 'What a rotten shame.'

Probyn smiled to himself. They must think he was green

to be so taken in. It was quite obvious they had led him past the billboard deliberately. But what young man would pass up the chance to go to a concert with a girl on either arm? 'You could come with me if you like. My treat.'

The girls beheld each other in glee, then turned on him excitedly, Kitty grasping his arm. 'Really? You're such a gem!'

'Ooh, I love a concert,' gushed Fanny, hugging her shawl about her, 'but I can't afford to go very often.'

'Why, because you're always breaking windows?' teased Probyn.

They cackled in a rather unladylike fashion, then Kitty made sure he was serious about paying for them. 'It is a shilling to get in, are you sure . . . ?'

'Perfectly,' he replied with confidence, hoping the veneer of nonchalance would conceal his boyish excitement.

Equipped with details of where to meet on Saturday, their gratitude ringing in his ears, he parted company with his new-found friends and returned to the barracks in uplifted mood.

Somehow in his short absence the garrison had taken on a different, more welcoming appearance, or maybe it was just that he had more time to study his surroundings this afternoon. Apart from the barrack blocks around the square there were married quarters to which mothers and fathers and little children were now returning from their Sunday outings. The sight of these respectably dressed women caused him to wonder how they could bear to live amongst such dregs as were in his own barrack block. He wouldn't like to bring a wife here.

An officer was approaching. Deep in thought, Probyn saluted him, surprising himself at how naturally the action had come to him, he had not realized how acclimatized to army life he had become, though he hoped he would never grow acclimatized to the filthy language that greeted his return to the barrack room.

Melody was still sleeping off his dinner, Ingham, Rook and

half a dozen others were playing cards and invited him to join them but Probyn declined and instead set to cleaning and ironing and polishing his uniform and kit in preparation for the morning. Only after tea, when everything had been put in meticulous order, did he permit himself some leisure, and visited the reading room, seeking comfort in the educational tome that had given such enjoyment the night before.

Unfortunately, the mood inspired by the padre's speech and his meeting with the girls was not to last. In fact Probyn found it even harder during that second week of training not to abandon his cherished career and throw himself on his father's mercy, for the tests were to become even more strenuous. Discipline, too, was stepped up and inspections by the sergeant were now occurring daily. Whilst the recruits stood to attention like frightened hares, Sergeant Faulkner and Corporal Wedlock took the part of lurchers, worrying and ripping their victims limb from limb. Prowling from bed to bed, Faulkner would seize upon something out of place and, yelping in sadistic glee, would toss it high in the air, be it fabric or metal, not caring a jot if it fell upon some unfortunate skull, whilst the corporal would enter the misdemeanour in a book for future reference – and it was often grossly unfair, sulked Probyn to his comrades, for he should be the last person brought to book; only an idiot could pick fault with his standards of neatness for he had done nothing but clean since he had arrived.

It was unfortunate that Sergeant Faulkner happened to be passing at the time of complaint and Private Kilmaster was ordered to, 'Get outside the bloody office now!' and after the beasting received therein he was slow to complain again. Yet he had made a grave mistake in drawing attention to himself and for the next few days on the parade ground it was not Melody who was singled out for harassment, but himself.

'Why haven't you shaved this morning?' demanded Staff Sergeant Quigley on Tuesday.

Probyn faltered, 'I have, Staff Sergeant.'

'Then what are all these bits of bum fluff?' Quigley nipped the golden hair on Probyn's cheeks, making him wince. 'You are going the right way to making me angry, Kilmaster!'

On Wednesday it was fluff on the back of his tunic and Probyn was certain he had brushed it thoroughly, though his protest cut no ice with Quigley. 'Do it again, boy, and you'll be on a bloody charge!'

Yes, there were times during that first fortnight when he would gladly have turned his back on the whole caboodle. Only a stubborn, determined nature and the thought of being ridiculed caused him to stand firm. He could not, *would* not allow any of these oafish bullies to completely ruin his dream.

Thursday brought a response to his letter. Seizing on this comforting link with home Probyn ripped open the envelope and pored over it anxiously, but was immediately tipped into fresh despair. Evidently despatched on an impulse of anger, the single page consisted of only a few lines and came not from his father but from Merry, its content terse.

Dear Brother,

I rescued your letter before Father could throw it on the fire . . .

Probyn's heart sank.

He does not know I am writing to you and if he did he would be furious. He says he will never speak to you again, and I can't say I blame him. How could you be so wilful? Running away like that. You must have known how worried we would be. What a mercy that Mother isn't here. After all her encouragement for us to better ourselves she would be so sad that you have descended to this. I have only taken the trouble to write back to let you know how your shameful behaviour has upset everyone. Father says you are no longer welcome in his house. He may come round in time, but I suggest you do not write for a while. It will only inflame matters.

Your sister, Meredith.

As an afterthought, she had inserted an arrow before the word sister and above it had written *loving*, obviously deciding to bestow a morsel of pity.

But a postscript was to endorse her disapproval: *PS Don't send any money. Father would never touch it from such a source.*

Lower in spirit than he had been all week, Probyn folded the letter into his pocket. It was no empty threat, he knew. A man who had not spoken to his brother in five years would have little qualm about disinheriting his son. Any thoughts he might have harboured about escaping from this desperate mess were now abandoned, for with his home barred to him there was nowhere else to go. Bitterly disappointing or no, the army was his only family now.

The torturous regime continued with no let up, the only thing keeping him afloat being the thought of foreign service in some exotic location. Only now did he begin to see what he had given up to be here, to stop and think who had put his clothes to warm on the hearth overnight and lay out clean underwear for him, and he felt sorry that he had treated Mrs Carr with such indifference. Much as he condemned his father for not lifting a finger in the house he saw now that he had been guilty of it too. As the youngest child there had always been sisters to look after him. But no more.

On Friday morning, still sulking over the letter, Probyn was even more nettled than usual by the sight of Melody slumbering through reveille, and decided that it was not his job to wake this feckless hound. Hence, the Irish youth was to make further acquaintance with Wedlock's cudgel. Albeit on the shoulder this time, the blow was no less painful. Nor was the look on Mick's face as he confronted his erstwhile bodyguard whilst they were scrubbing the barrack room floor prior to a spell in the gymnasium.

'How could ye be so mean as to let me lie there?' he asked reproachfully, grinding away at the floorboards with a stiff brush. 'I'm destroyed.'

Probyn broke off his chore to give aggravated response. 'It's not my fault you're an idle so and so! You can look out for yourself in future.'

'My, my, what happened to Lord Protector of the Weak?' goaded Havron.

'He gave notice to quit!'

'God forgive ye,' accused Mick.

'Now, now, boys, play nicely,' Lennon advised the squabblers.

'Why don't you ask Grandma or one of the others to wake you up?' spat Probyn.

''Tisn't a bloody nursery,' Lennon reminded him. 'And 'tis Private Lennon if you're taking that tone.'

'Sorry,' Probyn showed contrition. 'It's just this useless lollard who's got me mad.' He went back to scrubbing.

Mick continued to look hurt, his arm moving listlessly in its task. 'You're supposed to be my pal. I could've been kilt by that bloody club.'

'Same goes for any other lazy article in here,' countered Probyn, anger making him scrub all the harder, bringing sweat to his brow. 'If I slept in I'd say it was me own fault, not blame other folk.'

Whilst others beavered, Mick sat back on his heels, stared into space, then conceded above the grating noise, 'Ah, I suppose you're right. I've never been good at getting up on a morn, 'tis like a sickness with me. I genuinely don't hear a thing.' He touched his injured shoulder and winced before returning to work.

'How can you not hear that b-lithering trumpet?' Irritated beyond endurance by the said instrument and by Melody, Probyn found it hard not to swear.

It took little for Mick to break off again. ''Tis that bloody letter ye got yesterday, isn't it?' he demanded. 'Got a good telling off from your ould fella, did ye? Jesus, you've been as arsey as hell since ye got it.'

'Will you stop using such blasphemous language,' ordered Probyn through gritted teeth. 'If I'm annoyed it's nowt to do with any letter but that you're a lazy pig! I'm sick of having to carry you, you're just going to have to fend for yourself in future.'

'Sure, I can't believe you're such a hard man, Probyn Kilmaster,' reproved Mick. 'I know you, you won't let a pal down.'

For some reason this made Probyn all the more furious, but any response was to be interrupted.

'Get a move on, Melody! You've got fifteen minutes before Colour-Sergeant Doyle gets here.' Wedlock had poked his head in to see how things were progressing. An inspection imminent, his eyes darted about the room, checking for slackers.

Doyle! Another wretched Irishman, thought Probyn, scrubbing frenziedly. Even if most of those with Irish names spoke with a Yorkshire accent it made no difference, they were still Celts. How could he have dreamed the British Army would be so contaminated?

'Melody, come 'ere!' Wedlock was now beside the stove, his expression ominous.

Mick groaned into his chest, but jumped to his feet and, hopping between the network of scrubbing arms, hurried to obey.

'I thought I told you to clean this coal bucket!'

'I did, Corp.'

'So what's this?' Wedlock displayed a black fingertip.

'Em –'

'And why can't I see my face in it?'

'I thought I'd got it clean, Corp.'

'Look. Come on, look a bit closer.' Wedlock held his finger

nearer to Mick's face, then formed his hand into a fist and rapped his victim's nose, causing Mick to reel backwards in hurt surprise.

'Is that what you call burnished? *Is it?*'

'No, Corp,' admitted Mick, examining his hand which had blood on it.

'Why – leave that bloody neb alone and listen to me! Why did you disobey an order?'

'I thought it was a joke, Corp!' Unstaunched, the trickle of red oozed over Mick's lips.

'A joke? What do you think this is, the bloody music hall? Haven't you learned by now that I don't tell jokes? Get the fucking thing polished!' While Mick scuttled to obey, Wedlock stalked around the stove examining it for a sign of ash. Finding none he glared and gave one last comment. 'If you can't get it right for the Colour-Sergeant how you gonna satisfy Sergeant-Major Mars and the CO? Get a bloody move on!' He strode out.

Mick sagged with despair and pulled out a rag to dab his gory nose.

Feeling rather sorry for him now, though still deeply irritated, Probyn took a break from his scrubbing. 'Why don't you just get out now while you still can?'

'And do what?' came the nasal demand. 'Go back down the pit and get walloped by the likes of Judson?'

'Well, you're not really cut out for this life.'

'And you are?' Made angry by his sore nose, Mick took offence. 'Who says you're the better man than me?'

'Nobody's saying that,' answered Probyn. 'But this is all I ever wanted to do.'

'What, be insulted by a little shit of a corporal? Can't say I admire your ambition.' Grabbing cloth and polish, Mick attended to the coal bucket.

'I meant,' said Probyn, his annoyance threatening to get the better of him, 'being a soldier. You can't honestly make the same claim. You just thought you'd look good in uniform.'

'And so I do,' boasted Mick. 'Ye can't dispute that. Know what I think? Ye want rid of me so's ye won't have to play second fiddle.'

Probyn scoffed. 'Have you looked in a mirror lately? Your teeth are green.'

'Well he is Irish,' chipped in Queen.

Probyn ignored this and resumed his scrubbing. 'Don't you ever clean them? And all them cuts and bruises aren't exactly flattering. You'll end up as one big bruise if you continue to get Wedlock's back up. I seem to remember you saying that all you wanted was to get through the day without getting your head kicked in.'

'You're talking to someone who was educated by the Christian Brothers.' But Mick soon abandoned his air of bravado and sighed, picking self-consciously at his teeth. 'Ah sure, it wouldn't matter where I went, there'd always be a bully-boy. I seem to attract them. Always have. Must be jealous, the lot of them.'

Probyn grew exasperated. 'Jealous? This is the army, Wedlock's trying to turn you into a soldier!'

'And how long have you been an admirer of his?' grumbled Mick. 'Anyhow, I'm doing well enough.'

'When you're out of bed maybe! I'd like to lozzock in bed on a morning an' all but a man has to have discipline. You can't keep relying on others to wake you up.'

Recognizing his friend's past assistance, Mick acquiesced. 'I know, and don't think I'm not grateful for what ye've done.'

'I'd do it for anybody, I just want you to make an effort on your own!'

'I've tried really hard,' wailed Mick. 'I tell me brain, you must wake up at five o'clock, but it doesn't work. I don't hear a thing. Me mother says, 'tis the sign of a clear conscience.'

''Tis the sign of a blinking half-wit! How can you stand all the bashings?'

'Ah, he'll tire of it eventually. They always do. Anyways, as I said, where else would I go? I get fed and clothed here, money to send home to me ma and enough left over for a few beers on Saturday.'

Probyn shook his head. 'Is that all the army means to you? Have you ever thought you might have to die for it?'

The pain in his nose subsiding, Mick reverted to his normal cheery self. 'I'll face that when I come to it. No point worrying yourself to death beforehand. Anyhow, I've got me trusty weapon to protect me, and me trusty pals too.'

'This trusty pal is going to kick your backside if you don't get that scuttle done and Wedlock takes it out on me,' warned Probyn.

'For God's sake, will you two shut up!' shouted Havron. 'You're like a couple of old women, witter, witter, witter.'

'Shut up yourself,' said Mick, and set to polishing the scuttle.

Wearing his habitual bad-tempered frown, Havron abandoned his chore and made towards the Irish youth. 'I'll shut you up permanently!'

Probyn flicked his hand dismissively. 'Oh, get back to work, Havron!'

Havron immediately altered course, with Probyn now his target. 'Who the hell d'you think you are ordering me about, short-arse?'

Probyn dropped his scrubbing brush and jumped to his feet, holding the other with glittering eyes. 'If this room isn't in order when Wedlock comes back we're in for another rocket and I'm damned if I'm taking the blame for you not pulling your weight, you haven't even had a shave yet!'

Havron leaped for Probyn but before they could engage they were wrenched apart by Jessop and Oliver, each delivering a good shaking and telling them to get back to work. Only under threat from the two older men did the room succeed in passing inspection by Colour-Sergeant Doyle.

No amount of threat, however, could extinguish the mood of rivalry and resentment that had sprung up between Havron and Probyn and this grew steadily more unpleasant until by Saturday night Probyn felt such misery that was only assuaged by the thought of his trip to the concert with Fanny and Kitty.

Prior to his intended night out, the rabble again tried to lure him into bad ways, inviting him on a tour of local hostelries, to which they had recently gained readmittance on the promise of good behaviour. But he demurred, concentrating on polishing his equipment, refusing to be hurried, diligently rubbing with his rag and polish, deaf to their goading.

Seated close by, lacing his boots, Felix Lennon demanded in his rapid, barely decipherable manner, 'So, you're going to sit in again all night are ye? I'm beginning to worry about you.'

Having tutored himself to disregard Lennon's foul punctuation, Probyn had come to like the man and decided to confide, leaning across the gap between their beds and lowering his voice accordingly. 'I am going out as a matter of fact, but don't tell that lot.'

A conspiratorial gleam lit Lennon's blue eyes and he leaned closer. 'Ah, with a bibbi – a woman?'

Probyn tried not to look smug. 'Two.'

'Ye greedy little piggy.' But Lennon was impressed. 'Will ye not share them with your pal?'

Probyn looked awkward.

'I don't mean me, ye daft eejit! I mean himself.' Lennon cocked his head at Melody.

Probyn glanced at Mick, even with the prison haircut winsome in his scarlet uniform, and immediately shook his head. 'Once they see him neither of them will want to know me.'

'Ah, don't I know what ye mean,' nodded Felix. 'He's a bonny lad, but sure, don't be selling yourself short.'

'I am short,' grumbled Probyn. 'Anyway, I can't think Melody will care much for a concert at the Town Hall, which is where I've promised to take 'em.'

An odd expression overtook the older man's face.

Thinking that it represented derision Probyn took umbrage. 'Why, is there something wrong with that?'

Distracted by the calls from his fellows, Felix donned his glengarry and made to leave, replying lightly, 'No, no, nothing at all! I trust you'll have a very fine evening.'

Keeping his eyes alert for other recruits, who would no doubt spoil his pleasant outing, Probyn hurried through the darkened streets towards the Town Hall clock under which he had arranged to meet the girls. Smiling widely at their pretty demeanours, he escorted them into the neighbouring assembly room, pleased that his was the only uniform in sight, not least because he stood out magnificently from the crowd.

Whilst not lacking confidence, he found himself quite nervous, for this was his first adult liaison with one female, let alone two. However, he was representing the regiment and must set a good example. Approaching a desk, he asked the woman seated behind it for three tickets.

'Sorry,' came her unsmiling reply.

'You're full?' enquired Probyn politely, money in hand.

She stared him coldly in the eye. 'No, I'm not permitted to let soldiers in.'

Taken off guard, he reddened and immediately stepped aside feeling extremely foolish.

The two girls remained by the desk, looking cross. 'Well, I don't see why we should be disappointed!' complained Fanny, addressing no one in particular. 'We were expecting an evening out. Got all dressed up an' all.' Kitty tossed her head in agreement.

'Oh!' Feeling incredibly naive, Probyn looked at the coins in his hand then immediately shoved a florin across the desk. 'I'll just pay for the young ladies then.'

Stern-faced, the woman passed two tickets to the girls who, with a smiling shrug of commiseration, disappeared into the concert hall, leaving him standing there open to derision from the queue, though not for long. Feeling utterly humiliated he dashed outside and began walking, walking anywhere in an attempt to escape the awful situation.

After a time, though, mortification was displaced by fury. It had taken him two days of arduous labour to purchase those tickets and what thanks had he got? None! They hadn't even had the decency to make other arrangements to meet him – not that he ever wanted to see them again. Anyone with an ounce of virtue would have stood up for him, would have refused to enter if their friend had been barred, which just went to show what sort of women they were. He should count himself lucky he had found out in time before they had fleeced him of everything.

But it didn't make him feel any better, for apart from those mannerless females he could not rid himself of the one who had barred him, her prim, supercilious face refusing to leave his mind. How dare she deny him entry? No soldiers indeed! Who did she think was going to defend her in time of war?

After much angry, directionless marching around the undulating gaslit streets and much self-castigation for not standing his ground, he came to an abrupt halt to get his bearings. He was in the Corn Market, surrounded by public houses. Groups of people travelled between one hostelry and another; people enjoying themselves. Staring through a window of the timber-framed building by which he stood, he caught a glimpse of red tunics and listened to the soldierly merriment for a while, wondering whether to go in and seek a friendly face, for apparently this was the only venue in town where he would find one.

But no, his father would disapprove. With his bladder aching to be emptied, he merely wandered into the dark mouth of an archway that led into the courtyard of the Blackamoor's Head and made use of the privy therein. On his way back he felt himself under observation. Two short-legged terriers were tethered in a pool of lamplight by the rear entrance to the pub.

'Hello,' he said, without much enthusiasm.

One of the mud-caked animals wagged its tail. Grateful for any friendly gesture, Probyn made a detour and dropped to his hunkers to stroke both dogs, at the same time noticing the collier's shovel propped against the wall and the sack nearby. As he patted the dogs he saw the sack move. Curious, he stared at it for a moment, then gave it a poke. The creature inside made a noise that signified pain. Tentatively, he unfastened the string that tied the neck of the sack, the terriers became excited then and strained at their ropes, tails wagging furiously. Hardly had Probyn loosed the string than the creature leapt out at him, causing him to stagger back with a cry and allowing it to escape. In a trice the maimed young badger was dragging itself into the night with the berserk terriers straining to be after it.

In response to the frantic yapping, two figures stepped from the rear door of the inn and, upon seeing Probyn with the empty sack, rushed up to confront him.

'You meddling bastard!'

Probyn's heart leaped in anger as Judson grabbed two handfuls of his tunic and shook him violently. Knowing what was to come he dealt the first blow, considering this to be justified as there were two of them. But these were vicious opponents. Made even more violent by the pain in his nose Judson retaliated with a thump to the stomach that took Probyn's breath away and whilst he was bent double proceeded to rain more blows upon him. The other youth lost no time in joining the attack, the two of them using both fists and clogs in an effort to fell their victim. Inside the pub a sing-song had arisen. No one came to help. All the while the terriers were in a frenzy. Struggling to keep his balance and to ward off the blows Probyn could issue none of his own, his arms pinned to his sides to protect his belly, his hands covering his head, his mind seething with fury and praying that they would tire before inflicting too much damage so that he could deliver retribution to these cowardly pigs.

But the battery was taking effect, he felt his head bang up against the wall, became suddenly disorientated, felt his legs begin to buckle. The terriers' delirious yelping was growing fainter.

'Eh!' Someone else had appeared on the scene.

Sliding down the wall, Probyn saw through dazed eyes a man in red uniform. Momentarily distracted by the shout, Judson and his counterpart stopped beating their victim and turned. Corporal Wedlock strode up as he might to a platoon of recruits, stared at the two for a mere second, then, before either of them could act he dealt two swift jabs, each landing with a sickening crack and sending the assassins crumpling.

Stupefied by violence and shock, Probyn leaned against the wall and gaped at the two unconscious bodies beside him, then rested his head on one knee in an effort to recapture his breath. The dogs sat down too, panting and lolling, their barking stilled.

Face set in its usual grim mask, Wedlock rubbed at his knuckles for a moment then pulled the young soldier to his feet, yanking Probyn's clothes to order as if he were carrying out an inspection. Then, satisfied, he tugged at his own white cuffs and stood to attention.

Still fighting his amazement and the effects of the beating, Probyn managed to stutter his thanks.

Wedlock fixed him with a cold eye. 'Get this clear, Kilmaster. That wasn't for you, that was for the uniform. I won't have anyone, least of all scum like these two, defiling that scarlet frock, got that?'

'Yes, Corp! Thank you, Corp!' Probyn tried to recoup some of his pride and stood tall, though his body was hurting dreadfully.

'As you were.' Without further ado Wedlock strutted smartly over the recumbent figures, both of whom were still out cold, and headed for the privy which had been his initial objective.

For the moment, the only thing which registered on Probyn's dazed brain was the trickle of urine from the darkness. Then, taking as deep a breath as his cracked ribs would allow, he brushed himself off. A glance at Judson and his pal showed they were coming round and, deeming it wise, he proceeded to leave the scene, still shaken and amazed – but just as he was about to disappear under the archway Wedlock emerged from the privy to accost him again.

'Where do you think you're going, Kilmaster?'

Probyn spun round. 'Er, back to barracks, Corp.'

'Not before you've bought me a jar for saving your hide you're not. Inside!'

Probyn dealt an anxious glance at his two attackers who were sitting up now, though looking groggy.

Recognizing the youth's concern, Wedlock demanded of the pair, 'Are you still here?' He gave each a vicious kick in the back, causing them to scramble up, grab their dogs and make away. 'Now,' the corporal said to Probyn, opening the door and releasing a gust of alcoholic fumes, 'jump to it!'

Reluctantly, Probyn entered the tavern. The beery emissions were even stronger now. He had never been in a saloon bar, though he had glimpsed the interior of the Robin Hood's Well whenever he had been sent by his parents to fetch a medicinal brandy from the out sales lobby. This one was little different in its rowdiness, and in its choking pall of smoke from pipe and cigarette, yet instead of miners with blackened faces the room was frequented by military personnel and the kind of women as might be expected.

At his dazed appearance a shout went up from those who knew him. 'Why, if it isn't –' Mick broke off as he saw who accompanied his pal, and was even more astounded when, instead of approaching his friends, Kilmaster went to the bar and subsequently handed over a pint of beer to the hated corporal.

Only then, after Wedlock had dismissed him, did Probyn weave his way around the crowded tables to join the bemused watchers.

Mick was in the act of lighting a cigarette, having recently taken up the habit. 'Jesus! I must've had a drop too much,' he declared on a puff of smoke. 'I swear I saw you buy the corporal a beer – and what in God's name have ye done to yourself?'

Probyn made light of his bruised face, looking ruefully at the occupants of the table, all of whom had the same question on their lips. 'You won't believe this: Wedlock just saved my skin from a good hiding.'

'Fuck me,' breathed Ingham.

'Do you have to blinkin' swear like that?' scolded Probyn. 'There are females present.' He did not care for the look of these females, but deemed it his duty to shield them.

But the only effect of his words was to draw forth hilarity and a fresh nickname for the speaker. 'Sorry, Padre!'

Angered, he made as if to go but, urged to sit with them he relented and sat down to recount the episode, his companions no less amazed than he about Wedlock's intervention.

Only the older ones seemed unmoved, Lennon explaining that Wedlock was a champion boxer, then further amazing them by saying, 'Sure, and any of you'd do the same.'

Mick guffawed, almost falling off his chair. 'What? If I saw Corporal Wedlock getting pulverized I'd join in!' His oath was enveloped by a roar of agreement from other recruits.

'Anyways,' said Felix, handing over his glass to Probyn, 'seeing as you're in benevolent mood, Padre, ye can fill that up.'

With more glasses waggled under his nose Probyn displayed grazed knuckles. 'I can't carry all those!'

'Any excuse!' Trying to act older than his fifteen years, Mick directed an expert blast of cigarette smoke at the other. 'C'mon, we'll help yese.' With the assistance of Bumby and Queen he transported Probyn to the bar where the latter was to see more of his hard earned money disappear into the till. However, with Judson still somewhere out there he deemed it safer to remain for a while.

'Wasn't the concert any good?' enquired Lennon when they had struggled back to the table with a tray of full glasses.

'What?' Probyn, who had been staring into his ale, now took a hesitant sip at the forbidden beverage. Although he had enjoyed a clandestine taste before today it had not been in such copious amounts as others seemed to be putting away here. At Lennon's repetition he frowned. 'Oh . . . no. It wasn't much fun, I came away early.' Having temporarily forgotten about the mercenary girls he was annoyed to be reminded.

'You've been to a concert?' Mick lifted his face from his beer, upper lip outlined in froth. 'And ye didn't tell me? I'd have kept ye company.'

'Oh, but your man had company,' grinned Lennon, tilting his glass. 'Female company.'

Swamped by a tide of barracking, Probyn was thoroughly embarrassed and took a long gulp of beer, self-consciously wiping his mouth. 'Well . . . as a matter of fact they wouldn't let me in.'

'The dogs!' Melody slammed down his glass, his face even ruddier than usual. 'Let's go teach them a lesson.'

'You won't say that when I tell ye the whole story.' Felix's weathered face was even more creased in laughter.

'Eh, there's no need –' began Probyn.

'He didn't just go with one girl but two!'

Amid catcalls, Mick dealt him a thump. 'Lord a'mercy, what poltroonery is this? I'm deeply hurt. Well, I trust 'twas worth it.'

Probyn stilled the rude and noisy conjecture by admitting that it was only himself who had been turned away, the girls had chosen to attend the concert.

There were cries of, 'Shame!'

Probyn smirked and made further bashful disclosure. 'That's not all, I was daft enough to pay for them!'

This brought howls of laughter, and the fact that he had provoked it at his own expense endeared him to companions who had hitherto dubbed Kilmaster a bit of a prig. Even Havron temporarily removed his bad-tempered frown.

'Serve ye right ye greedy little demon for not wanting to share your good fortune,' but Lennon's mockery was warmly delivered.

'You knew they wouldn't let me in, didn't you?' Only now did Probyn recognize this.

Lennon shrugged. 'Some men have to find out for themselves that scarlet isn't the most popular of colours. Oh, if there's a war to be won 'tis heroes we are, but in peacetime we revert to being scum of the earth.' He sounded philosophical.

Probyn tried to adopt the same lack of bitterness. 'Oh well, I'm not bothered. I'm enjoying meself more here than with those two money-grubbing biddies.'

'Well said, Padre!' Oliver smacked him on the back with such violence that it dislodged the youth's glengarry. 'Get that down you.'

Accepting the friendly blow without complaint, though it hurt dreadfully, Probyn took another long pull of the beer, enjoying its taste. 'Good riddance to them.'

'Aye, there's plenty of generous girlies here,' said Jessop, patting a female rump, then pulling his willing victim onto his lap and sinking his moustache to her bosom.

Though rather disturbed at this treatment, Probyn noted that the girl made no struggle to escape, and therefore he withheld his intended stricture, burying any embarrassment in his glass, and somewhere in the next ten minutes or so it ceased to matter. In his new-found state of relaxation he found himself almost recovered from his ordeal with Judson, and it was undoubtedly due to this wonderful beverage. He was quite disappointed when the last drop of beer had been drained.

Rubbing his knees, he began lamely, 'Well, I suppose I'd better –'

'Here have one on me,' invited Mick, placing another glass before him, he himself clutching a tot of whisky and lighting another cigarette. 'In thanks for getting Judson bashed up.'

Probyn gave a smiling frown, flapping his hands as a form of refusal, but his argument was short-lived. Considering that he had already broken his father's rule in being here at all he decided he might as well enjoy himself.

And enjoy himself he did. No sooner had he emptied a glass than it magically appeared refilled before him, nor was this the only pleasure. Out of sympathy for his ejection from the concert his friends decided to hold an impromptu one of their own, one after another jumping up to perform monologue, song and verse, Melody proving to be the most talented of all. The drink removing any trace of shyness, he performed a wonderful ballad that drew uproarious applause and calls for encore, even from Probyn who slapped him on the back and called Melody his good friend.

'You are all my dear good friends!' he shouted, swaying merrily between two of them, his face flushed with happiness and his eyes like glass marbles. 'Stuff the bloody rest! Stuff and bugger and damn them!'

'I think dis boy's had enough,' opined Lennon, his own eyes slightly glazed. 'C'mon, let's get him home.'

'No! Bring me more!'

But Lennon was firm, downing the last of his ale and rising. 'Beddy-byes.'

'It's my round!' All despondency vanished, Probyn's merry state led him to throw caution to the wind. Who better to spend his money on but his comrades? With much fumbling he rammed his hands deep in his pockets, sending an array of coins clattering over the table and onto the floor. In an attempt to pick it up he toppled off his stool.

'Aw Christ, now we're going to have to carry him,' complained Havron, once again wearing his characteristic scowl. 'How can you get this slewed on only four pints?'

Amid much protestation, swearing and staggering, Probyn was lifted to his feet and half dragged towards the door.

'How are we gonna get him past the bloody guard?' The question was passed around the group, none of them very sober.

But before they could exit there was to be further upset. A

customer cleared his throat, aimed at the spittoon but missed and a horrified Mick saw the gob of mucus land in someone's whisky.

'Ah God, no! I'll never drink whisky again!' And he was immediately sick all over the floor.

With the landlord's wail of wrath there was added impetus to escape, but as they rushed for the door their outlet was blocked by the arrival of the Garrison Military Police.

'Every man back to barracks!'

'Weren't we just off, Sergeant,' replied Lennon calmly and tried to force Probyn towards the door but it was no easy feat, for Probyn's legs kept buckling and he was giggling like an imbecile.

So practised were Lennon and his peers at escaping punishment over the years that they might have succeeded in getting Probyn out of danger too, had he not decided at the moment of exit to shout an uninhibited farewell.

The sergeant of the guard, unappreciative of being addressed as shite-hawk, promptly relieved the companions of their drunken friend, walloped Private Kilmaster over the head and clapped him in the cells overnight.

He was roused in the morning with a splitting headache, eventually allowed to get medical attention for his injuries, and ordered to appear outside the company commander's office on Monday morning with the additional warning that he could be passed on to the CO for his crime. Unsure of how he had come to be in this situation, but deeply ashamed, Probyn slunk back to his barrack room.

There was to be no quiet entry. 'Oh, welcome back, Padre!'

Everyone gathered round for details of his imprisonment. There was laughter from some, apology from others. Aware that his barrack mates were somehow to blame for his incarceration, Probyn waved aside their attempts to relive the incident. Wanting to forget the whole matter the embarrassed young man went directly to his bed, intending to make a start on getting his kit into good order for his appearance before Major Lousada, but everything appeared to be in its rightful place. Frowning, he sought explanation.

'We found out Ingham slipped a large whisky in your beer,' said Lennon, 'so we made him see to your kit as well as his own. You've only got to clean the stuff you're wearing.'

This was little consolation to Probyn, who was extremely worried as to what would befall him on Monday morning. He turned angrily on Ingham. 'You blasted clot, you could've killed me giving me that whisky when I'm not used to it!'

'Ah well, here's another who won't be touching it again,' vouched Mick, and told Probyn of his disgust at seeing the man spit in the whisky glass.

Almost sick himself at the lurid description, Probyn begged him to shut up, grumbling accusingly, 'I wondered why I'd got such a rotten headache.'

'Ah no, that'd be the guard,' said Lennon mildly. 'He's no sense of humour.'

Upon learning what he had called the man Probyn bit his lip. 'Oh, my goodness, who else did I insult?'

'No one that matters,' replied Lennon. Then, despite Probyn not really wanting to hear it, the old soldier informed him of the previous night's events, though he already vaguely recalled the episodes of the concert and Judson's violence.

'Haven't you something to say to Padre, Ingham?' Lennon prompted the culprit then.

'Sorry, Pa,' mumbled Ingham, still busy cleaning and looking suitably ashamed.

'Oh well,' Probyn tried to sound magnanimous though his head was banging. 'You never forced me to drink it, did you? I've only meself to blame, but don't any of you dare accuse me of being unsociable if I stay away from the Blackamoor's for a while.'

'You and the rest of us,' sighed Lennon. 'We've been barred

again.' Then he sensed the youngster's apprehension. 'Ah sure, it'll all blow over, son. Don't worry.'

But Probyn did worry, throughout the rest of the day. Many recruits had gone into the major's office for such an offence as his and had been banished from the garrison forever. There had to be good reason for the army to want to retain him. Hence, he ensured that no fault could be found with either kit or uniform, redoing many articles, for Ingham was not fastidious enough for his liking. The only items that might present a problem were his socks which had sprouted holes. The pair he had on were hidden by boots, but what of those on his shelf? He held his throbbing head in his hands, wondering what on earth to do about them. It was pointless sending them home for darning, Meredith was quite obviously still angry with him.

A spark of genius pierced his despondency. Aunt Kit was a seamstress! Why had he not thought of her before? Good old Kit had never let him down. After a mad search for some brown paper and string he triumphantly wrapped up the socks with a little note and went out, the parcel under his arm.

As he was crossing the square, however, his journey was interrupted by a blood-curdling sound, somewhere between a scream and a bellow, that had the immediate effect of stopping him in his tracks. Wide-eyed, he gaped at the regimental sergeant-major in full regalia who now beckoned him none too politely, and realized to his horror that he had committed the ultimate sin. He had trodden upon hallowed ground.

Feeling physically sick, he gave rapid response to the summons, setting off at a trot towards the RSM and the two officers who accompanied him, both much less intimidating characters.

'*Around!*' bawled Sergeant-Major Mars, again stopping the boy in his tracks.

Changing direction, he ran to the edge of the square, hurrying around its perimeter until he reached the RSM whereupon he stamped to attention and recited his name and number. He now noticed that one of the officers was the colonel, yet it was Sergeant-Major Mars who had the greater presence. Possessed of a terrible nobility, he towered over the hapless young infantryman, bedecked in scarlet, gold braid and brass that glittered dauntingly in the sunshine.

Quaking before this god-like figure, Probyn glanced at the young second-lieutenant who made up the quartet and who was obviously as in awe of Sergeant-Major Mars as was the recruit.

'How long have you been in the army, soldier?' screamed the RSM, eyes like burning coals.

Through lips that were dried with nerves Probyn stammered a reply. 'A fortnight, sir!'

'Then you must surely know that you do not set foot upon that square unless you are on parade!'

'Yes, sir! Sorry, sir!'

'You will be after you've done ten laps of it! Put that bloody parcel down and run!'

Probyn set off, wondering after the first lap how he was possibly going to manage ten of them, and there would be no getting out of it, for, although the officers went on their way, the RSM stayed to watch, obviously enjoying this brief spell of winter sunshine.

However, just when Probyn felt he was about to collapse, the RSM called him in.

'I have not told you to stop! Mark time! Knees up! Left-right-left-right-left!'

Heart and head thumping, face like a beetroot, Probyn continued to run up and down on the spot until finally, after much yelling, the RSM rested his hand on the pommel of his sword and told him that was enough. 'Right, laddy! Pick up your parcel and get out of my sight – hang on! What's in it anyway?'

'Socks, sir,' heaved Probyn, tucking the parcel under an arm that dripped with sweat. 'I'm sending them home to be darned.'

'*Darned?*' Freshly aroused, the RSM emitted his oxen bawl, the power of his voice drowning out all other sound. 'Why do you think you've been issued with a housewife's kit?'

Hardly daring to look at Sergeant-Major Mars, Probyn found that his legs were trembling. Yet oddly the encounter inspired not just fear, but hope. Here was a man one could truly respect, a pillar of the glorious British Empire that Probyn held so dear. This was what he wanted to be! Not the nervous young lieutenant, nor the colonel – he was not of the right class for these posts anyway – but *this*, this magnificent specimen of manhood before him, to this he could aspire. In that instant his former attitude towards the army was resurrected. It became imperative that he was not discharged over his shameful drunkenness. For, granted a second chance, he would strive to emulate this man, to wear that coveted emblem upon his sleeve!

The minotaur emitted a final scream. 'Get back in there and darn them yourself!'

And Probyn fled for all he was worth, but there was the glimmer of a smile upon his face and hope in his heart. For he had been handed back his dream, and this time he was determined not to let go of it.

After a nervous period of waiting on Monday morning, he was escorted by Sergeant Faulkner at the double to the major's office where he was compelled to listen to an account of his drunken behaviour. His platoon commander, Lieutenant Fitzroy, was also in attendance, a tall, handsome, athletic-looking gentleman, some thirty years of age. Having formerly suffered a brief but disapproving tongue-lashing from the lieutenant, Probyn was well aware of his opinion on the misdemeanour. However, in the major's presence, Fitzroy's well-bred features were now smoothed into an emotion-less mask.

Major Lousada, too, was also straight-faced. 'Very well, Private Kilmaster, what explanation have you for this?'

Humbled before these two career officers, the major a courageous veteran of the Ashante Campaign, Probyn swallowed and, with his tongue sticking to the roof of his mouth, offered, 'I wish to apologize, sir. I'm not accustomed to dealing with alcohol, sir, it's forbidden at home.'

An inscrutable blink from the major. 'Then may one enquire what you were doing in the Blackamoor's Head?'

Probyn had been asking himself this same question. He could hardly condemn Corporal Wedlock who had saved him from a beating, nor could he blame Ingham for adulterating his beer. No one had tied him to a chair and poured it down his throat. 'It was a bad mistake, sir, but I vouch on my honour I'll never touch another drop!'

'I have nothing against alcohol nor the public house,' replied the major. 'Indeed, I enjoy a brandy myself, in moderation. That is the word for you to remember, Private Kilmaster, moderation.'

'Yes, sir!'

'And what of those abrasions on your face? I take a dim view of my men brawling.'

'Oh, never, sir!' Probyn sounded hurt. 'I was attacked outside the public house by two civilians, without provocation. Corporal Wedlock came along and saved my skin.'

'Did he indeed?' The major looked interested.

Content that he had slandered no one, Probyn finished his explanation. 'That was the only reason I entered the public house, in order to buy the corporal a drink in return for his gallant assistance.'

After a moment's rumination, the major turned to Lieutenant Fitzroy. 'Platoon commander, what sort of a man is Private Kilmaster?'

Lieutenant Fitzroy ran his candid blue gaze over the accused. 'He's normally of very sober habit, sir, even a little aloof from the spirited antics of the rest of the platoon. I suspect perhaps that his foray into the Blackamoor's Head was just a way of trying to fit in with his fellows.'

No! A deeply insulted Probyn wanted to shout, I don't want to fit in with those louts – I'm not like them!

But he was to be quickly recompensed by the lieutenant's next words. 'He is always well turned out, the best in his platoon in fact. He performs well at foot drill. A lot of work to be done on rifle drill but he keeps his weapon in good order and in general he is an enthusiastic and valuable member of the platoon. He will make an excellent soldier.'

Probyn almost fell over with shock and pride. After a fortnight of degradation here was someone telling him he was an excellent soldier!

'I hope you will heed those words from Lieutenant Fitzroy, Private Kilmaster, and not throw it all away?'

'Yes, sir, thank you, sir!' *An excellent soldier!* He had not known that Lieutenant Fitzroy had been watching him so assiduously. A wave of warmth swept over him, such as he had never felt for his father.

The major cast aside his stern cloak and took on a more paternal role. 'You see the thing about drink, Private Kilmaster, is that some men know when to stop whilst others do not. A pint or two never did anyone any harm but if you are to maintain this agreeable recreation you should get to know your limits.'

Probyn shook his head adamantly. 'Oh, I won't be drinking again, sir.'

'I should not like this to deter your admirable efforts to fit in with your fellows, that is what the army is all about, but you know there are many other ways in which a man can integrate. The regiment has a very fine football team. Do you play any sport, Private Kilmaster?'

'Yes, sir, I like football and rugby.'

'Splendid! Then I would encourage you to sign up for one of the teams. Naturally I understand that military training takes up most of your time at present, but once you have made the grade things will become more enjoyable. I can assure you of that.'

'Yes, sir.' Still basking in the lieutenant's compliment, Probyn felt as if he were reborn. *An excellent soldier*!

'Very well, Private Kilmaster, I am disinclined to allow this isolated incident to blight your record. You may consider this a caution. Any similar misdemeanour will occasion a fine.'

Probyn could hardly believe there was to be no harsher punishment. 'Sir! Does that mean I can stay in the army, sir?'

The major nodded. 'If that is your wish.'

'Oh, it is, sir! I intend to make the army my life.' It was such a wonderful relief.

Major Lousada's lips twitched at the youthful earnestness. 'And you'll find that there is no better life, Private Kilmaster. Thank you, Sarnt Faulkner!'

And with that Probyn found himself marched at the double out of the office, his heart singing with joy to be granted this second chance.

However, it was not to be his only piece of good fortune that day: upon his return to the barrack room with his news he found himself presented with a letter from his sister. Tearing this open, he was soon beaming even more widely for, although Meredith was quick to say that their father had not forgiven him, she herself had, and what was more she had asked Father if Probyn could come to her wedding on Easter Sunday, and he had said she must invite who she liked.

He was quick to relay her words to his pals. '"So I would like it if you could be there," she says here!'

'Ah, good for you, Pa,' nodded Mick, then saw the other's face drop. 'Oh no, what's the catch?'

'"But please don't wear your uniform,"' Probyn read out loud. '"You'll only inflame matters and spoil my day" – the cheeky monkey!' Immensely proud of his uniform, he was most put out. Besides which, it was an offence not to wear it. 'Let her turn me away if she wants. I'm not going to deny what I am.'

But this sour note was soon put aside as he devoured the rest of Meredith's letter. All in all it was excellent news and in accepting the invitation Probyn saw a chance to mend the rift between him and his father. 'Well then,' he finished cheerily, 'I'd better go and ask permission to attend. If nowt else it'll mean a good feed!'

5

It was with this same good heart that, throughout the two months which followed, he marched and drilled in rain and snow, gave everything that was demanded of him by Wedlock and Faulkner who worried the recruits even more savagely between them in preparation of the ultimate test: drill on the square before Sergeant-Major Mars.

When the sergeant and corporal were not harrying his fellow recruits then Probyn was. Having come to know the weak links in the platoon he set about forging them, his keen eyes forever inspecting the kit of his brothers-in-arms, pointing out a speck of soot here, a strand of cotton there – 'It sticks out like a chapel hat-peg on that red tunic you sloppy 'a'porth!' – and leaving everyone in no doubt that he was not about to be dubbed a failure by their inadequacy. This penchant for taking charge remained an area of contention between him and Havron, and there would be outbursts and quarrels for supremacy between the pair, but these were quickly stamped upon by the older hands Lennon or Jessop and hence no real violence was committed. Besides, after months of withstanding Wedlock's vicious treatment, Probyn was not intimidated by the likes of Havron.

Even so, it was with trepidation that he stood to attention before the sergeant-major on a bright March morning after a long and complicated sequence of drill, awaiting the reaction of this inspirational figure. However keenly he himself had strived, one wrong move from Melody or one of the less able recruits, and the entire platoon would be condemned as useless. And Probyn just could not bear that. If Melody spoiled this for him today he would personally thrash the fool!

The wait seemed endless as the magnificent Sergeant-Major Mars prowled along each row, stopping occasionally for closer inspection, the one thing maintaining Probyn's optimism being Lieutenant Fitzroy's statement of confidence in him.

Having finished his inspection the RSM was now standing before them, gimlet eyes moving constantly, though his lips said naught. The silence was excruciating. Probyn hardly dared to breathe.

And then with one curt nod the raw recruits who had started out only a matter of weeks before were miraculously transformed into professional infantrymen. The rigorous training had all been worth it as, to a roar of approval, the platoon was deemed fit to parade with the ranks on Sunday.

Overjoyed, Probyn shared a victorious cheer with his comrades, his eyes sweeping their laughing faces and seeing not ruffians nor drunkards. Oh, they may revert to drunkards in celebrating their achievement on Saturday night, thought a grinning Probyn, but who on earth would blame them? Certainly not he! He was thrilled to be one of their number. Not the scruffy mob of layabouts who had started out but ranks of fit and dashing young men. Soldiers of the Queen.

And on Sunday when he marched with his regiment through town before admiring crowds, behind a band in full regalia, the thunderous boom of the big drum striking him full in the chest and making the hair on the back of his neck stand to attention, it was surely the proudest moment of his life.

Now, three months into his career, though the training remained arduous and his whole life was subject to regulation, Probyn was well able to cope, equipped with a new self-discipline and stamina. There was a confidence in his stride and in his eye that refused to be dimmed, no matter what rejection he might suffer outside the garrison, although this was infrequent, for he had learned that there was no better place to be than amongst his comrades. There might still be the odd lapse of inexperience, but Probyn was man enough to admit it.

During that period of self-discovery there were naturally still endless chores to be done, days of repetition and routine, kit and weapons to clean and tables to scrub, hours on sentry duty, but by now it came as second nature and Probyn found time for the athletic amusement that the major had prescribed. Others in his platoon had joined the rugby team too, Melody turning out to be an outstanding player. More tolerant of the Irish youth now, Probyn numbered him amongst his circle of allies, these being mainly the ones who annoyed him the least, who ate and spoke quietly, unlike the oafish Ingham. He still abhorred the way Mick blasphemed – how could he reconcile this with a regular attendance at Mass? And he still frowned on the Irishman's drunken carousing at weekends. Rejecting the latter course, he himself had decided to stick to the reading room in order to improve his chances of promotion, and, although others might tease him about this there was no malice intended in his nickname of Padre. In fact, even Ingham was making great headway in becoming literate with his regular attendances in the school room. Collectively, the platoon had gradually been moulded into an institution in whom he could place his trust, as far as military backing was concerned. And yet, there was none of like mind with whom he could really share his thoughts and ideas, no one with whom he would want to spend time outside army life . . . but then the army *was* his life.

Whether or not Corporal Wedlock was any less violent or whether the recruits were simply more able to comply with his demands was difficult to say, though his dislike of Private Melody was never in question. Mick's name seemed never to be off the defaulters' list. Much of this was due to his incompetency in getting out of bed, yet Wedlock unquestionably singled out failings that he might overlook in another soldier and often these were punished with violence. It took every effort from Probyn, his self-appointed keeper, to protect the Irish youth from serious injury.

If anyone above the rank of sergeant had noticed that Private Melody spent more time at the hospital than any other man in the garrison it was never mentioned. As if this were not bad enough, Melody appeared to be accident-prone too, forever pulling muscles or spraining ankles.

Even today as Probyn prepared to go to his sister's wedding, Melody was over at the hospital having his foot strapped up for some clumsy self-inflicted injury.

'Oh, here you are, you hoppity-elf!' On his way out, Probyn bumped into Mick in the corridor. 'I thought they might have had to amputate, the time you've been gone.'

'I was just making the most of it,' smiled Mick, resting on his good leg. 'Ye've never enjoyed a stay over there have ye? Oh, ye should see the rooms those medical orderlies have, the Savoy's got nothing on them. And they've hardly anything to do, talk about kooshi. Going to your wedding are yese? Well, have a good time.' He patted his friend on the back.

'I will. See you tonight!' Probyn set off.

'If you're not too drunk!' called Mick before hobbling away.

It took a few hours to reach Ralph Royd. Without a watch he was unsure just what time it was when he arrived but he had made good pace and was not worried about being late for the event. What did concern him was his reception. Guessing that he wouldn't be welcome at home, he pondered whether to go straight to chapel where he might have a long wait, or for a glass of Dutch courage at the Robin Hood's Well, for alcohol would not be available at the wedding. He chose the latter course, using the lame excuse that there would be a clock at the pub.

Knowing that Judson might be in the saloon he entered the best room, wherein was a host of Sunday suits, starched white collars, gold watch chains and polished brass. A collection of typically dour Yorkshire faces followed the soldier's approach to the bar. Their eyes remained on him as he waited to be served.

'Eh up, it's young Probe!' With the aid of a crutch, Peggo Wilcox, an elderly ex-miner, limped up to serve the young soldier.

'I'm a bit early for our lass's wedding,' explained Probyn, indicating the clock. 'So I thought I'd come and have a chat and a pint with you, Mr Wilcox. Am I all right in here?' He had seen men in uniform come out of the pub but under the disconcerting gaze of those now present he began to wonder if he might be relegated to the saloon.

The landlord's reply was civil. 'You can sit where you like, son, although I don't think your father'd be too pleased at you being here at all.'

Probyn nodded sourly, viewing it as hypocritical that Monty regarded this purveyor of alcohol as a friend of the family yet would not allow any member of that family to patronize his establishment. 'Him and a dozen others.'

'Well, we're glad to have you. Marion get this lad a pint!' An avuncular man, Peggo called to the middle-aged barmaid who, in friendly manner, supplied the ale and joined the landlord in asking about Probyn's new way of life.

'Doesn't he look all grown-up in his uniform?' she said admiringly in her deep soft voice, and to Probyn himself, 'Eh, I can remember you being born. In fact I remember your Meredith being born! And here she is getting wed.'

Glad of the amicable welcome, Probyn enquired if they would be attending. He was told they would not miss such an occasion and would be going along after closing-time. 'I'll walk down to the chapel with you,' he told them, 'if you don't mind being seen with me.'

Marion smiled kindly and said of course she did not.

Taking his pint slowly, so as not to become inebriated, he chatted intimately for the next half hour with the landlord and barmaid, almost forgetting from the natural way he was able to converse with the latter that she was in fact a man.

When the time finally came to enter the chapel he was glad of their moral support, for the moment he encountered his relatives he knew it was not to be the pleasant afternoon he had hoped for. If not openly hostile they were far from welcoming either. A few acknowledged him with brief nods as he edged along the aisle looking for a sympathetic face by which to sit, but he was left in no doubt as to their disapproval. His father would not even look at him. Only Aunt Kit extended compassion. Responding to her smile he left Peggo, Mrs Wilcox and Marion with a few grateful words and hurried to seat himself beside his favourite aunt and uncle and their baby.

'You look very smart,' whispered Kit, trying to control her wriggling son.

He thanked her. 'Me dad apparently doesn't think so.'

Towering above him, Kit bent to murmur her response, which had a rueful edge. 'Aye well, we're both in his bad books. He sent me a stinking letter saying I encouraged you to run off. I tried to put your side but you know what he's like.'

Probyn apologized and thanked Kit for her support, yet even as he spoke he could hear another more elderly aunt, Gwen, slandering him from behind. 'Look at the brazen little varmint! Coming here in his uniform bold as brass, spoiling his sister's wedding – and I can smell drink on him.'

His cheeks flushed to the colour of his tunic and he looked at his feet. The last thing he wanted was to embarrass his sister.

'Looks like he's come empty-handed an' all,' sniffed Gwen.

More embarrassment! He had not even contemplated buying a gift for Meredith.

Kit threw a reproachful glare over her shoulder at Gwen which had little effect. Her eldest sister had never been shy to air her opinions.

'Oh look, here comes the bride!' Kit's plump elbow nudged

her nephew, trying to distract from his abashment. 'What do you think of her gown? I made it.' Just as she had done for each of her other nieces.

Probyn would not normally pay much heed to women's fashions but grateful for this one line of support he said it was lovely. Then there was no more time for talking as the marriage ceremony began.

Afterwards, though, even this slender thread of assistance was broken, for Aunt Kit with her husband and son was ushered away to a distant table whilst he was seated with his sisters and their husbands who shared his father's disapproval – it was as if it had been done on purpose – and his favourite aunt could only make contact by throwing the odd sympathetic smile whenever he met her gaze. Normally a Kilmaster wedding, whilst not a roisterous occasion, was an enjoyable get-together for its family members but today's proceedings were extremely stilted. No one at the table had, so far, uttered anything more than hello.

Meredith was annoyed with him too; she hadn't said so and had introduced him to her groom quite civilly, but he only had to look at her face whenever she set eyes on him to know that all was not well. Waylaying her after the meal was over as she and her groom, Christmas Clegg, went from table to table, sharing niceties with their guests, he tried to explain.

'Merry,' he blurted, 'I hope you don't think I've worn me uniform deliberately to upset you. I'm not allowed out without it, it's a serious offence.'

'Mmm.' Meredith looked down on him, her tight smile showing she was not convinced. 'Well, if you must you must I suppose. Have you had enough to eat?'

'Oh ample!' In truth he had not felt like eating anything.

'Good, well, I'd better move on I've a lot of guests to speak to.' And with that she left him.

'Best of luck!' Probyn sank back against the hard frame of his chair, feeling utterly despondent.

Whereupon those amongst whom he was seated appeared

to take this as a signal for releasing their own observations, until now suppressed.

'Well, you'd better not turn up at my house wearing that outfit,' warned Rhoda, regarding him over her imperious beak of a nose. 'I won't answer the door.'

'I won't come if I'm not welcome,' he murmured resentfully. Mother must have thought she was doing good by encouraging her daughters to elevate themselves from the pit community but in reality she had created a family of snobs, all of them looking at him disdainfully down their large noses.

'She didn't say you wouldn't be welcome,' scolded Ethel, the eldest and the only one unmarried. 'Just that uniform. And don't be making out that it's all of us who are out of step when it's you who's the villain. You've really upset Father.'

Alice added her contribution. 'I don't know what's got into you, Probyn. You've become really wilful.'

'He always was a pampered little devil,' muttered Wyn to her husband who, trying to stay neutral, exchanged uncomfortable looks with his brothers-in-law, none of whom came to Probyn's aid. 'We were all expected to put him first.'

Rhoda was shaking her head and looking him up and down. 'I can't seem to recognize you somehow.'

All his sisters were of this same opinion: their little brother had changed, which was odd because he had been thinking along the same lines. It was almost like being amongst strangers. It wasn't just that they were cool towards him, regarding him like a naughty child for running off, but that he himself was different. With some irony he found himself longing to get back to his platoon.

After the condemnations had been aired he was left sitting on his own as his sisters went off to mingle. Being strict chapel goers, there was no dancing at the wedding and consequently nothing to take his mind off his troubles, and, with Kit otherwise engaged and no one else apparently keen to speak to him, he sat there looking more and more uncomfortable. Even the old tyrant Gwen began to feel sorry for him and signalled for him to come over. Alert to her summons Probyn approached self-consciously, tugging at his tunic.

'Well, I suppose you must've learned your lesson, nobody inclined to speak to you all afternoon! You won't be wearing them wretched clothes again on your next visit home I dare say.'

In view of this terrible insult to his regiment, Probyn controlled his feelings well. 'It isn't a matter of choice, Aunt Gwen.'

'And I suppose it wasn't a matter of choice you running away and not letting your family know where you'd gone for over a week! I hope you're repentant for all the trouble you caused?'

'I am.' He looked suitably apologetic, a quite genuine sentiment, for he accepted he was in the wrong.

'Well, I suppose what's done is done.' Gwen was more amenable now, and though her face had its habitual expression of misery her voice offered encouragement. 'Sit down and tell me how you've been faring. I'll wager the army was a horrible shock after the good upbringing you've had.'

Though he had never liked the eldest of his father's sisters with her old-fashioned clothes smelling of camphor and her bossy manner, he was relieved that someone other than Kit was talking to him and he began to tell Gwen about his training, though his eyes kept darting across to where his father was sitting, face deliberately averted.

'Do you think Father will ever forgive me?' he asked suddenly.

Gwen looked across the hall at her brother. 'Shouldn't think so, the stubborn fool.' Then returning her attention to Probyn she felt immediate regret. Despite his grand airs in that uniform he looked so young and forlorn, the same way he had looked at his mother's funeral, trying so hard to be a man.

Clasping his knee, she used it to pull herself out of her chair, saying she would not be a minute. Probyn watched her make a beeline for his father, and waited alertly for the outcome.

'All right, you've made your disapproval plain!' Gwen told her brother without preamble. 'Sort it out.'

Immediately, the guests nearby began to withdraw to a discreet distance, leaving only Ann seated at the table with her husband.

'Mind your own business, Gwen.' Monty turned his eyes away.

Noticing that battle lines were about to be drawn, Kit disengaged herself from the conversation she'd formerly been enjoying and sidled over to check what was going on.

Gwen persisted. 'Don't you remember the way our parents died, walked out the door one morning and never came ba –'

'How could I forget?' came Monty's annoyed interjection, ''twere left to me to bring you up and all the thanks I got was a deal of grumbling and interference!'

Taking immediate huff, Gwen gathered her frumpy skirts. 'Right then! If you lose your only son don't blame me!'

Noting that Kit's lips were about to form a subscription Monty held up his hand. 'Save your breath! You're the last person to give advice.'

'I wasn't going to.' Kit remained dignified, her clear blue eyes holding his. 'If you want to see all your efforts wasted again that's up to you.' At his look of angry confusion, she enlarged, 'Did you spend your whole life looking after your brother and sisters, keeping the family together, just so you could cut Owen off and never speak to him again? Seems a daft waste to me. Are you going to do the same with Probe?'

'If I do then you're to blame!' Monty did not grant Kit time to put voice to her expression of amazement. 'Ever since you gave him that wretched box of tin soldiers he's been obsessed by the idea. Now go away, Kit,' he finished tersely. 'You're spoiling my daughter's wedding.'

As usual, Kit complied with her elder brother's demand,

though her expression said all as she made her way over to Probyn.

Mouth set in an angry line, Monty only fractured it to grumble to his wife. 'What gives them the right to gang up on me with the troubled lives they've had? I'd like to see Gwen's face if either of her lads wanted to be soldiers.'

Ann was in wholehearted agreement, offering a consoling pat to his forearm. 'And Kit's got that dubious pleasure still to come; her Toby's only a year old. People are always quick to advise others how to bring up their children.' After a further period of censuring others' shortcomings, she asked with casual interest, 'Tell me, dear, how did you envisage Probe's future?'

Monty opened his mouth to give immediate reply, then looked rather lame and was forced to yield a foolish smile. 'A life down the pit – doesn't sound very auspicious, does it?' He stared thoughtfully into mid air. 'But it wasn't as if I forced him to go down, Ann, I'd have been glad for him to do anything he chose, but the stubborn little tyke said if he couldn't go soldiering he might as well choose the pit. Certainly his mother had big ideas for him but he didn't have the brains, if he did he wouldn't have joined the army. Well, so much for her big ideas now.' He groaned and squirmed in his smart wedding attire. 'Oh, it's not just that he's defied me, Ann, it's the whole thing between us, our personal differences. I remember so well the afternoon he was born – I were that proud!' His expression fleetingly mirrored the joy he had felt at the arrival of a boy after so many girls. 'I thought we'd do things together, man to man, you know.' His joyful visage faded and he sighed, rubbing unconsciously at his painful knees. 'But he always seemed to prefer his mother's company to mine. Well, that was inevitable. Sarah had more influence on him, him being with her all day and every day till he went to school. I only saw him for an hour before bedtime or on a weekend, or when he needed a thrashing. Perhaps if I'd been allowed to spend more time with the lad . . .' His voice trailed away. With a hint of petulance he seized a lone currant from his plate and nibbled on it. Then, feelings of guilt brought an addendum. 'I suppose that's not really fair: even as a tiny chap he was so different to me.'

'Yes, completely different,' nodded Ann. 'You always got on with your father didn't you.' A gentle smile showed she was teasing.

Monty searched her face. 'You think I should be the one to repair the damage?' He became awkward. 'Well . . . I might, if only he'd show some sort of contrition for his wilful behaviour.'

Ann looked apologetic at having to correct her husband. 'Well, he did write and say he was sorry –'

'Not face to face though!'

'He seems embarrassed,' Ann pressed forth. 'Pushed into a bit of a corner what with Gwen and the rest of them putting their two pennorth in.' She could not abide the eldest of Monty's sisters but had to side with her now. 'Give him a chance, dear. I know he was wrong to go against you but you can only force your children to do so much, and in the end wouldn't you rather they be happy?'

Monty's mind was reluctantly drawn to his thirty years of unhappiness with Sarah. Life with her had been one constant verbal assault. 'What gives him the right to be happy? I had to do as I was told.'

She became concerned for her own wifely powers. 'But you're happy now, aren't you?'

'Oh, of course! Of course.' In the absence of eavesdroppers he squeezed her knee under the table. Ann was so different to his first wife. 'With you at any rate.' He sighed again. 'I can't make up my mind what to do about the boy.'

Ann was distracted. 'Looks like he's going.'

Having considered that he had done his duty and to stay longer would be pointless, Probyn was taking his leave of those who would speak to him.

The grip on Monty's arm had an urgency to it. 'If you want

to patch things up you'd better do it now – I'm not trying to interfere, I just mean you don't know when you might see him again.'

Fighting indecision, Monty leaned forward on his chair. It seemed to his wife that he was about to rise.

But pride got the better of him. When the young soldier turned questioning eyes on his father, seeking permission to approach, Monty glanced away. When he looked back, his son had left the hall.

After the hostile atmosphere of the wedding, Probyn had never felt so glad to get back to barracks and a sense of value. Putting the episode behind him, he concentrated instead on nurturing the feeling of comradeship that was beginning to manifest itself in the platoon, determined to make it into a family he could be proud of.

There was more reason to be glad that week too, for he was excited to learn of his posting to the 1st Battalion.

'Where will we be stationed, Corp?' he enquired of Wedlock eagerly.

'Kings County,' replied Corporal Wedlock.

'Ireland!' Mick looked delighted.

'Ireland?' Probyn's echo was more one of horror. 'But I put down for foreign service, I thought we'd be going somewhere like Africa!'

Wedlock offered a half derisive smirk. 'You don't think they're going to let you loose on the niggers until you know which end of a rifle to point at 'em? You've got months of home service ahead of you yet.'

Brought back to earth, Probyn looked decidedly unimpressed. 'When are we going, Corp?'

'Twenty-first of this month, so you've got seven days' leave starting this weekend.'

Whilst others shouted approval, Probyn continued to grumble. 'And where will I go for seven whole days? Nobody'll give me houseroom.'

'What about this favourite aunt you're always talking about?' Mick reminded him.

'Aye, that's an idea.' Probyn nodded firmly. 'I'll go to York.'

'York is it?' Mick seemed interested. 'I've got kin there myself, I could come with yese. I haven't seen them in ages.'

Fearing that the Irishman would bring him into disrepute with the only relative who was on his side, Probyn replied quickly, 'She doesn't actually live in York, but in a village outside. I have a long walk when I get off the train.'

Mick was quick to interpret the reluctant tone. 'I wasn't asking for a free bed –'

Probyn interrupted. 'Oh I know, I didn't mean –!'

The other smiled, but to rather sad effect. 'I just thought ye might like the company that's all. Still . . .'

'I would! I just didn't want you to trail all that way thinking . . . I mean, Aunt Kit hasn't got very much room and I don't think she'd take kindly to me landing her with . . . what I mean is, I'd be happy to meet you in York as long as you've got somewhere to stay.'

Mick retained his smile, though it was obvious he was conversant with the true reason for Probyn's reluctance and was hurt by it. 'Oh yes, I'll have no trouble finding a bed – but ye must say if ye don't want me to come, I won't mind, I just thought –'

Probe was ashamed of his own bigotry. 'I do!' He tried to project interest. 'Where do your relatives live? Write down the address and we'll arrange a day to meet.' He hoped his babbling attempts to make amends did not sound as stupid as they made him feel.

However, Mick agreed to meet him on the Tuesday afternoon of their vacation. 'And will we travel to York together on Saturday?'

'Fine!' smiled Probyn. 'I'll be glad of the company.'

An early morning train ensured that Probyn would reach his destination in time for lunch. Grateful for an uneventful journey, he parted company with Melody at York station and went the rest of the way on foot.

Arriving at Kit's smallholding an hour and a half later, he had no sooner picked his way through the clucking hens in her front garden than he found himself immediately clutched to her sumptuous bosom and made most welcome. 'What a lovely surprise. How did you get here?'

Probyn was both charmed and embarrassed by her exuberance; the Kilmasters were not great huggers. 'By train to York, then walked the rest.'

Kit released him. 'Eh, your feet must be killing you!'

He laughed dismissively. 'It's nowt compared to the miles I've marched.'

'Come in then. Oh but you're even thinner than the last time I saw you! They can't be feeding you. Worthy, bring more taties!' Her husband had been in the process of rifling his potato store for luncheon. 'This lad needs building up before he goes back. How long are you here for, Probe?'

'A week if that's all right, Aunt?' Her delighted smile showed him it was. Uncle Worthy too seemed pleased at this intrusion as he followed them into the kitchen, his arms cradling muddy potatoes. 'They've allowed us time off before our posting.'

Fond of travel, Kit was swift to ask, 'Ooh, where are they sending you, anywhere exotic?'

Probyn gave a rueful laugh. 'Ireland!'

'Oh you poor soul!' Kit's repugnance of Catholics was undiminished. 'How long for?' She began to peel the potatoes.

He shrugged. 'I don't know. Anyway it won't be that much different to Pontefract barracks – Hibernia Place, I've taken to calling it. I'd no idea the army took so many Irishmen. I mean, they don't all talk Irish but they've got the names. You should hear roll call: it's Boylan, Casey, Cahill, Donovan, Fennesy,' he chanted it in gay manner, his head going from side to side, 'Gormon, Kelly, Lenagan, Mel –' he broke off at this point with a laugh, it wouldn't do for Aunt Kit to remember Michael Melody. 'Oh, I won't go on!'

Kit threw a horrified joke at her husband. 'Eh, it's a wonder the army can march to order with so many left-footers. If it's that bad, Probe, maybe we could help to buy you ou –'

'No, it's not really! I'm only kidding. They're good enough fellows, and they're far outnumbered by Yorkshire lads.' Smiling, he re-familiarized himself with his aunt's kitchen which he had visited only a couple of times before. On one of the walls, somewhat concealed in shadow, was a painting of his sister Beata. In actuality it was a composite made after her death using the features of his other sisters, and in no way portrayed her the way he remembered. He suspected that Kit hated its artificiality as much as he did, that was why it had been given such a discreet position. The only reason it was here at all was that it had been bequeathed to Kit by his mother. 'Where shall I put me bag, Aunt?'

'Just sit there and talk to me while I get the taties on.' Kit reached for a pan. 'You can't afford to lose any more weight.'

Brushing the soil from his hands, Worthy took the haversack off his nephew and carried it upstairs, allowing Probyn to sink into a comfortable fireside chair. Hauling Toby on his knee, the young man told his aunt how glad he was to be here – not least for the mouth-watering smell of mutton from Kit's oven.

Later, after grace, Probyn watched his plate being laden with the succulent meat. It was quite obvious why everyone in this house was so large. 'Eh, steady on, Aunt! I won't be able to manage all that.'

'Course you will! Don't worry you're not costing us anything, we grow it all ourselves.'

The plate now in front of him, Probyn added a spoonful of mashed potatoes and one of carrots. Thinking he was only being polite, Kit grabbed the ladle and added more. 'Come on, we've got to build you up! I don't know what the army's feeding you but there can't be much of it.'

Alarmed that he would be unable to eat it he held up his

palm. 'Ooh, that's enough, Aunt, honestly, it'll only spoil me for going back to army fodder.'

'Well, it's there if you want it.' Kit filled the baby's plate to its outer edges and fed him mouthfuls in between eating her own meal.

To the clinking of knives and forks, she asked to hear all about her nephew's experiences, Worthy showing a quiet interest. Making light of the bad parts, Probyn said that he was very happy and proud to be a soldier.

'It would have been nice if you could have made it up with your dad at the wedding,' said Kit, munching. 'I did try . . .'

'I know.' Probyn had always enjoyed his aunt's support. Not wanting to pursue the subject he filled his mouth, then said, 'Eh, this mutton's absolutely luscious!'

There were to be more luscious meals in store over the weekend, though this was not the only form of entertainment, for Aunt Kit had always been an amusing performer, ready with a song and a joke, and thoroughly enjoying an audience however small.

Probyn almost hated telling her at Tuesday luncheon – another gargantuan offering – that he would be going into York for the afternoon and so would not be in for tea.

This did not have the effect he had imagined. Assuming that her nephew was travelling alone, she exclaimed, 'I'll come with you! Uncle Worthy will get the cart out and take the pair of us. I only ever get in occasionally on market days and that isn't very exciting. We could go to the matinee at the theatre!'

Detesting having to upset her, he blurted apologetically, 'Actually, Aunt, I'm meeting a pal!'

Kit's eager expression melted into disappointment, but it soon passed. 'From the army? Oh, you should have brought him here, we wouldn't have minded.'

You would, thought Probyn, and hoped that his aunt would not ask to meet Mick nor ask his name. 'He's staying with relatives, we just arranged to meet up for the day.' He gave a forced laugh. 'I don't know why I'm bothering, you'd think I see enough of him at the barracks.'

'Aw well, it's nice that you've made a pal. Tell you what, bring him home for tea, your Uncle Worthy will take him home on the cart.'

'Oh no, that's all right! I've been invited to his relations' house for tea.' He had the grace to blush.

Kit nodded thoughtfully for a moment. 'Then the next time you both come to York we must return the invitation. Don't forget now, will you?'

Probyn said he wouldn't and, refusing Worthy's offer to take him, went on his way, relieved that no more questions were asked.

But Kit, being a more practised liar herself, recognized a bad one when she saw it. 'He must think I'm daft.' She cast a smile at Worthy, and watched her nephew hurry down the path. 'He's off to meet a lass.'

Walmgate was a rough area of the city. Probyn had heard his aunt speak scathingly of its occupants and he was more than a little apprehensive as he made his way along its decrepit route, his scarlet uniform an obvious target for hatred.

However, he arrived at Melody's address unharmed and his knock was answered immediately. 'Mrs Melody? I'm –'

'Private Kilmaster, come in, come in! Michael told us to expect ye. No, I'm not called Melody, I'm a Lanigan.'

'Oh, sorry I just assumed you'd have the same name!' The fervour of her welcome took Probyn by surprise; he half expected the woman to embrace him but was glad when she made do with a smile as she ushered him into the best parlour.

'I'm Michael's Aunt Louisa on his mother's side,' explained Mrs Lanigan, under the threadbare clothes a lithe and attractive woman. 'He's just having a wash. Make yourself comfortable while he comes. Could I get you a cup of tea, Private Kilmaster?'

Probyn thanked her but refused the offer, waiting for her to sit down before joining her. It was as if he were in a church, though like none he had been in himself, with a statue of the Virgin Mary at one end of the mantel, a depiction of the Sacred Heart at the other and all manner of religious pictures looking at him from every wall. It rather unnerved him and to cover this he threw a smile at Melody's aunt.

'Nice weather for your holiday,' she observed warmly, her gaze falling on the shaft of spring sunshine that fell upon the hearth rug. 'And will you be looking forward to going to Ireland afterwards?'

'Oh, yes,' lied Probyn. 'It'll be . . . a change.' Glancing about him again, amongst the many religious icons he spotted a wooden box, its lid painted with a galleon on rolling waves. 'That's nice.'

'Your man did that for my birthday last year,' said Louisa proudly.

Probyn was stunned. 'You mean Mick?' He stood to take a closer look, and was still admiring it when the artist came in.

'Sorry, Pa! I slept in.'

'That's unusual for you,' said Probyn, then indicated the box. 'Your aunt tells me you made this!'

'I only did the painting.' Mick was still shrugging himself into his military garb and fastening buttons.

'Still, it's . . . remarkable.' Probyn, who had not one creative bone in his body, could not disguise that he was impressed.

Mick seemed amused at the praise.

'Will ye be staying for tea, Private Kilmaster? We'll be having a special one. 'Tis Michael's birthday. I don't suppose he'll tell you that himself.'

'Oh don't, you're showing me up!' Mick begged his aunt, but nevertheless reiterated her invitation to his friend.

Glad to accept, for this would transform his lie to Aunt Kit into a truth, Probyn tore himself away from the box he had admired so much. 'I'd love to stay, Mrs Lanigan, if it's no trouble.'

'We'll be going into town first though,' Mick told his aunt, comb in hand.

'And what will you boys be up to? Anything I should report back to your mother – oh by the way!' Louisa hurried over to the sideboard. 'Have ye finished this library book ye borrowed?'

Mick seemed at once embarrassed and merely nodded into the mirror. The haircut looked less severe now, fresh curls beginning to form.

'Well ye can take it back. I know you, you'll be trotting off at the end of the week and leaving me to pay the fine.'

Obviously uncomfortable at having this mentioned, Mick mumbled that he would take it back tomorrow and tried to change the subject, but his aunt insisted he take it back right now and held it out to him.

With Melody's hands occupied in arranging his glengarry, Probyn took quick possession of the volume. Melody, reading a book? Whatever next! Intrigued, he sneaked a look inside the cover but the text was unfamiliar. In fact he was taken aback by the intricately worded content, and began to see Melody in a new light. If he were truly able to decipher this sort of thing then the hail fellow well met attitude, the carousing and drinking, was all an act. There was more to him than met the eye.

Snatching the book from his pal, Mick shoved it under his arm, still looking self-conscious. 'Away with ye then, Pa!'

'I didn't know you enjoyed reading,' said Probyn as they went first to the library.

Mick was dismissive. 'No well, 'tis not the sort o' thing to brag about at the garrison. A man likes to fit in doesn't he?'

After returning the library book, the two young soldiers wandered around town looking for adventure, and were not slow in finding it. Having stopped to buy some mussels at a market stall, Probyn felt someone poke him in the back and turned to find himself accosted by a man in a dangerous state of inebriation. What was more, his assailant was brandishing a revolver.

'You lobby-lobsters!' The man swayed. 'Think you're brave?'

With Mick open-mouthed and paralysed by shock, Probyn held up his hands, trying to look fearless, though his heart was thumping. 'Steady now, we're unarmed!' He looked around, seeking assistance. The man who owned the fish stall had run off, and though there were plenty of onlookers no one seemed keen to help the soldiers. Never dreaming he would be required to put his military training into action so soon, he had no option but to handle this himself.

'Stay back!' warned the drunkard as Probyn made a move towards him and he discharged the revolver.

Women screamed as Probyn staggered back holding his body. Aghast, he looked down expecting to find blood, but a swift inspection told him that he was unhurt and, furious now, he lashed out automatically, knocking the revolver out of the man's hands. Whereupon both he and Mick seized their would-be assassin and bundled him to the greasy cobblestones where they continued to pin him struggling and bawling.

Once the man was disarmed, the crowd tightened its circle, murmuring admiration for the heroes as the stall holder returned with a policeman who immediately took charge and placed the villain under arrest. Volunteering their regimental details, the soldiers were informed that they might be required to give evidence in court. Finally, the drunkard was hauled away to the cells and the crowd began to disperse.

Heaving a joint sigh of relief, their ears ringing with praise, Probyn and Mick brushed themselves off, but could not so easily remove the tremble of excitement at their first taste of danger.

'I hope I'm a better shot than he is,' breathed Mick. 'Standing two inches away and he didn't even nick ye.'

'Don't sound so disappointed about it!' But Probyn felt exceedingly pleased with himself. 'Do you think it'll be in the papers?' No sooner had he said it than a horrible thought wiped the grin from his face. If Aunt Kit read of his association with Melody there would be ructions. He had intended to tell her all about this heroic escapade when he got home but now decided to keep quiet.

'What's up?' Mick had seen his pal's face drop.

'I were just thinking our involvement might not go down too well with the CO. Let's get a move on before a reporter comes nosing round.' Probyn was about to move off when he noticed that two female members of the crowd had lingered and were staring quite openly in adoration. He nudged his companion. 'Eh, I think we've got some admirers!'

Pretending to attend to his uniform, brushing and flicking with a hand, Mick gave a sly glance at the pair who smiled invitingly.

After a series of coy exchanges, Probyn murmured, 'Shall I go ask if they want to come for a walk?'

Mick fell prey to his natural inhibitions. 'Oh no, I couldn't!'

'Go on!' Wiser after the episode with the factory girls and the concert, Probyn would make sure he was not similarly duped again. 'A walk won't cost us owt.' Despite being paid before coming on leave their wages had been riddled by barrack damages and replacement of lost kit; he was determined to hang on to the rest of it.

Mick gnawed his lip. ''Tis terrible trouble I'll be in if me mother finds out.'

But his argument was to become academic, for it was the girls who forced the issue.

'Me sister and I think you're really brave!' Close up, the speaker was not so demure as she had seemed at first.

But Probyn did not mind, smiling at the compliment. 'Oh, not really. He wasn't a very good shot. We were just about to ask if you wanted to come for a walk? We're in York on holiday and we thought you might show us the sights.'

'Our pleasure!' Both girls wasted no further time and linked arms with the soldiers without even being invited, giving their names as Mabel and Ruby. 'Then afterwards you might like to come home with us for a cup of tea? Our mam isn't in.'

Without daring to look at his friend, Probyn said he would look forward to that.

However, the tour of York's ancient landmarks was cut short by one of the girls saying that the soldiers must be gasping for refreshment. Fearing this meant an expensive visit to a café, Probyn was reassured to be led to the girls' home where a pot of tea was duly brewed and consumed.

'You've got lovely curly hair,' Mick's companion told him, to Probyn's disgust. 'Just like our dad's isn't it, Ruby?'

Mick, primarily flustered by the compliment, now looked alarmed. 'Em, your father won't mind us being here?'

'Oh no, he's dead,' she replied. 'You're ever so like him. There's a picture of him in the parlour, do you want to come and look?' Giving him no choice she removed the empty cup and saucer behind which he had been hiding and led him from the room.

Alone with Ruby, Probyn was happily nervous, voluntarily putting his cup aside. It was obvious that her sister had sought privacy in order to kiss Mick, but was he to be as lucky? He had never done this before.

His concern was needless for Ruby took the initiative, sitting on his knee and pressing her warm lips to his quite boldly.

More kisses followed. Then, in an act of the utmost aud-acity, she took his hand and placed it under her clothes. Immediately something leapt inside him. He had heard of girls like this but had not quite believed it. The kisses became harder. So did something else. He felt deeply embarrassed but did not want it to stop, nor did he know what to do next. He had always been inquisitive about sex but no information of that nature would ever pass his father's lips and his meagre knowledge of it had only been gleaned outside the home, from youths at work and from Aunt Kit's *News of the World* when he could sneak a look at it.

But now his crude perception was apparently going to

be widened. The girl was removing articles of her clothing and inviting him to do likewise. He was not silly enough to refuse.

After Ruby's seduction of him they dressed straightaway for she said her mother would soon be home. She then went to tap on the parlour door to alert her sister who reappeared almost immediately with Mick.

Feeling thoroughly delighted with himself, if slightly shameful at the rapidity of his departure, Probyn made his way home with Mick, the latter quietly thoughtful.

For a while nothing was said, until Probyn could bear the suspense no longer. 'Did anything happen with whatsername in the parlour?'

'No!' blurted Mick immediately, then frowned inquisitively. 'What sort of thing would ye be meaning?'

Probyn shrugged and affected to reach into his pocket for something. 'Well . . . kissing and stuff.'

Mick scratched the back of his neck and looked embarrassed. 'All right, I confess she did kiss me. But then she – oh, I daren't say it!' He covered his mouth. 'The most outrageous hussy, not the type a man would want to introduce to his mother. Well, I told her, I wasn't having any of it!'

At the affronted tone, Probyn was made to feel even more scandalous that he himself had yielded to lust. 'You mean she was going to – and you said no?'

'Of course I did!' Mick's look of outrage turned to suspicion. 'Did yours –'

'No!' Probyn denied it vigorously. 'I wouldn't do anything like that. Just kissing and cuddling, you know.'

'Well, there's nothing sinful in that.' Mick's curly head gave an adamant nod. Yet he became silently thoughtful as they walked, looking up at the sky and performing a tuneless whistle. Lighting a cigarette, he eventually asked, 'D'ye think it's true that a girl can have a baby just by kissing?'

Probyn experienced a jolt. Not once had he thought of that!

What if he had to marry Ruby? He didn't even like her! He stroked his lips in worried fashion.

Mick immediately interpreted that look of thoughtfulness, exclaiming, 'You dirty dog! Ye did, didn't ye?'

With a guilty grin Probyn was forced to confess.

'Me too!' Mick covered his mouth, then whispered, 'Oh I shouldn't say this, but wasn't it great!'

His co-conspirator chuckled heartily with him. 'I still can't believe my luck!' Then Probyn tried to look guilty, which was difficult wearing so broad a grin. 'Oh, but what if they get in the pudding club and come looking for us? I don't even like mine!'

'Me neither!' Mick was chortling now. 'Chroist I don't know why I'm laughing. Whatever will I say in confession?'

'Why bother saying anything?' Having become quite familiar with Melody's religion, Probyn still could not come to grips with the Catholic's hypocritical habit of confessing all sins on a Saturday only to commit those same offences again the next day.

''Tis easy for you to say that! You're going to hell anyway, being a Protestant.'

Thinking this was a jest Probyn laughed, but then saw that Mick was deadly serious. 'Do you really have to tell the priest everything?'

'Every single detail,' wailed Mick. 'And I only went out to return a library book.'

When Probyn got home that evening it was dark and, hearing the dog bark, Kit was at the door to light his way down the path with a paraffin lamp. 'Did you have a nice time? What did you have for your tea?'

'Oh, er, we had a little party.' Ears pink from the cold, Probyn fell onto a sofa and smiled at Uncle Worthy in his chair by the fire. 'It was me pal's birthday.'

'Fancy!' Kit lowered herself beside him. 'What did you say they call him by the way?'

Rubbing his hands to warm them, her nephew stumbled over his answer but was saved by Kit herself who laughed uproariously and patted his knee, including Worthy in the joke. 'Oh, don't get yourself all het up, lad! We won't tell your father.'

Probyn was shocked. He was sure he had not let Mick's name slip. 'You mean, you know?'

'That you've been meeting a lass? Well, it didn't take much working out when you didn't want me to come with you! He's a she, isn't she? What's she called?'

Half relieved that Kit remained ignorant of his association with a Catholic, half guilty for deceiving his favourite aunt, Probyn mumbled an answer, trying to muster some truism. 'It's nowt serious! We didn't arrange to meet again.'

'Aw!' Kit shared what she saw as his disappointment. 'Never mind, there won't be any shortage of lasses for a good looking lad like you, will there, Worthy?' With a last pat of his leg she stood briefly in order to fetch an orange which she began to peel into her lap. 'Eh, it's been grand having you here. I'll be sad to see you go.'

He smiled, watching her fingers disrobe the fruit, nostrils twitching as little explosions of juice scented the air. 'I'll be sad to go too, Aunt, though I can't say I'll be sorry to be rid of all this clucking and grunting that wakes me up every morning.'

Kit looked apologetic. 'I know, it's dreadful. I've had your Uncle Worthy to the doctor's but they can't seem to do anything for him.'

Probyn laughed at the big man's remonstrance and at the jocular exchange that followed between husband and wife. Theirs was such a nice, loving household, and even more so tonight.

Kit's clear blue eyes remained locked with her husband's for a moment, sharing their secret; they were to have another child in autumn. However, this was not a fitting subject to tell a youngster. Instead she handed him a skein of orange and one to her husband. 'Well, now your secret's out, Probe, you're more than welcome to invite your young lady here.'

'Thank you, Aunt, but I prefer to spend the rest of my time here with you.' Though disappointed that there was not to be further sexual adventure that week, Probyn could afford to be philosophical as he bit into the juicy skein. Now, at last, he knew the full extent of what it meant to be a man.

Chopping sticks for kindling, collecting eggs and cleaning out the henhouse to earn his keep, the rest of that week passed quietly, save for one awful moment when Aunt Kit saw the shooting incident reported in the police court proceedings column of the *Yorkshire Evening Press*. Luckily no names were mentioned, apart from the defendant's, for the man had pleaded guilty and so the soldiers' evidence would not be required. For Probyn it was rather disappointing in one respect, that such heroism could not be recognized: if only he had not been accompanied by an Irishman he would have gladly confessed his involvement. As it was, he would just have to remain anonymous.

On Saturday morning, Kit wrapped a parcel of food for Probyn to take back to barracks. Moreover, she and Worthy insisted on driving their nephew to the railway station. Fearful of colliding with Mick Melody, he begged them not to hang around, they must surely have things to do, but to his alarm they escorted him right to the platform and waited for the train to arrive.

Fortunately, by the time the train arrived there was still no sign of Melody. Grateful for this, the young soldier quickly boarded and, opening the narrow window of his compartment, urged his aunt and uncle to leave now. 'I don't want to be responsible for Toby catching a chill,' he told them when they continued to linger. 'You must all be freezing on that platform.'

'Nay, we've got enough fat on us!' joked Kit. 'Another minute or two won't make a difference. Oh, it looks like you're off anyway.' There came the sound of doors being slammed. She held Toby's little hand aloft. 'Wave bye-bye to your cousin, Tobe!'

Probyn was much relieved to see the guard making ready with his green flag and whistle. Sinking onto the moquette seat he waved cheerily to the infant.

But just when it looked as if departure was imminent a screaming horde descended on the platform, yelling at the train – 'Stop! There's someone wants to get on!' – and that someone was Private Melody, encircled by the type of people whom his aunt had always warned him to stay away from.

'There's Pa!' Spotting his pal's face at the window, Melody made a beeline, wrenching frantically at the carriage door and flopping down in relief on the seat beside him, then instantly bounding up again to wave at his aunt, uncle and numerous cousins who were now standing next to a disgusted Kit on the platform waving and hollering their goodbyes as the whistle shrilled and the train finally did start to move.

'Is that your aunt and uncle?' demanded Melody and, at Probyn's sickly nod, included Kit and Worthy in his wave, shouting through the small open window, 'Hello there! I'm Probe's friend. Pleased to meet yese! Dat's my aunty there next to yese!'

The look on Kit's face as the train slowly chugged away was sufficient to convey her annoyance to her devastated nephew. And if it were not enough, Probyn saw her lips move in further condemnation as she mouthed her opinion to Uncle Worthy. 'That lying little toad!'

6

The moment he arrived back at the depot Probyn scribbled an apology to Kit. It was not, he said, that he had intentionally deceived her, but simply that he knew she would be upset with his choice of companion and he did not really have any alternative for these were his comrades in arms. Besides, he wrote, the Irish boys are not such bad chaps you know, Aunt Kit . . .

Whether it had the desired effect he was not to learn, for within hours he was being handed a travel warrant and told to form up in readiness to march to the station, thence to entrain for Liverpool. There were also goodbyes to be made.

Though not sorry to see the back of his drill instructors Probyn was taken aback when the grizzled Felix Lennon came to extend good wishes. 'I thought you'd be coming with us, Grandma!'

'Not with my time expiring in summer,' replied Felix. 'I doubt I'll be here when ye get back to depot, so here's wishing ye luck.' The sentiment was peppered with the usual expletives.

'And to you too. Where will you go?' asked Probyn. 'Have you any family?'

'Not at all, no. I'll probably take lodgings round here. Find a little labouring job to supplement my pension.'

Probyn considered this an ignoble end for one who had served his country, and mentally vowed it would never happen to him. 'Tell me, Felix, did you never fancy going for promotion?'

There was the hint of derision on the weathered face. 'Lose my good conduct pay in exchange for ordering a few swaddies around? Ask me that again when ye've got six rooty-gongs yourself.'

Probyn was respectful. 'Mm, I think I might go for the exam as soon as I'm able.'

Felix had already recognized the other's ambition. 'Ah well, if that's your choice I wish ye success. I'm sure you'll go far, so long as ye listen to good advice and don't crack on ye know everything already.' He beckoned the youngster to come closer, as if about to bestow a last favour, but instead displayed the contents of his shelf. 'I'll be selling me kit when I go, you can take first choice, whatever ye fancy.'

Probyn was bemused. 'But you'll still need it until summer.'

'No, I've accumulated extra bits and pieces over the years so I have a spare set that I keep for inspections, so's I don't have to be cleaning all the time do you see.'

'That's a good idea.' Probyn stroked his chin and scanned the shelf, looking for items that might be of most use.

Felix sensed a lack of enthusiasm. 'Sure, I know you're careful with your money and ye must have plenty put by. Never was there a greater opportunity to put it to good use. How about these boots here? You're the same size as meself. They'll be a godsend when ye come in dripping wet – and I'll throw the tin of blacking in.'

Probyn accepted the well-worn boots. Though reluctant to encumber himself he recognized the old soldier's need for cash, and selected what other items he could afford.

Felix was duly grateful. After pocketing the coins he gripped Probyn's hand with bony digits. It was obvious he liked the younger man. 'Goodbye to ye now, Padre. Enjoy the Old Country.'

Though wondering what on earth there was to be enjoyed

about Ireland, Probyn nevertheless returned the handshake warmly and thanked Felix again for all his assistance.

However, some hours later, once on the dock about to embark, the young man revised his opinion of his destination and decided he was excited after all. There might not be an exotic location at the end of the voyage, but there was the promise of much accomplishment. Up until now he had only used his rifle for drill; soon he would be allowed to fire it. Then at last he would be a fully-fledged soldier.

In the odd moment that he was not consumed by thoughts of soldiering he was engrossed by images of sex. Shameful though it might be, he could not help wanting it again. They had not discussed it since that afternoon but he guessed from the preoccupied look on Melody's face now that he harboured a similar longing. Perhaps between musketry practices the opportunity would arise for more sensual application.

Once aboard, though, there were other distractions, new and interesting people to meet and, the weather being unusually clement, Probyn thoroughly enjoyed every minute of his crossing.

They arrived in Ireland to a downpour and were billeted overnight in Dublin, in parts a most elegant aristocratic town yet spoilt by abundant beggars, even its finer quarters possessing that air of indolence which Probyn attributed to all Irishmen.

In the morning they were crammed onto another train that was to take them away deep into the heart of the country. And what a wild and ancient heart it was, decided Probyn, watching through the constant drizzle a succession of ruined churches, untamed heath and forbidding purple hills flit by his carriage window. Under this grey sky, the landscape was unlike any he had seen in England, making him aware that this was home service in name only. The deeper their incursion the grimmer it became, flat plains of rugged grassland broken only by dark patches of bog and a lonely wading bird, and occasionally a tumble-down cottage. No wonder, he thought, that much of the population had chosen to live abroad.

Stiff and bored after miles of sitting still, their only source of amusement a farting competition won by Private Oliver whose expertise none could surpass, the infantrymen heaved a mass sigh of approval when the train finally arrived at Birr, although the rain made for a miserable welcome. Nonetheless, as they jostled to alight, a military band struck a rousing welcome, serving to lift their spirits considerably. Probyn and his companions were happy to be escorted by trombones and drums along the rain-drenched route into town, the attention they received along the way making the youngsters feel akin to royalty.

Apart from the fact that this was a small market town, as was Pontefract, there were few other similarities. Probyn noted that the air was fresher here, untainted by coal dust, and there was a very different character to the streets and buildings. The magnificent Georgian mall past which he marched now bespoke great affluence.

As at home, a number of the local populace had gathered to watch the soldiers parade, but here it seemed that every one of them had black hair and pink cheeks. In small groups they gathered around a square that had as its centrepiece a tall Doric column surmounted by a statue. Whom it represented Probyn did not care, having more interest in the flesh and blood creatures who emerged from Dooly's Hotel to stand and watch, glass in hand. Glancing briefly at them to examine the mood, he observed that though some might look odd, their expressions were for the most part benign. It was also comforting to note that there were a number of pretty girls amongst the crowd.

Called to a halt and paraded in the square, he took further stock, glancing at each of the streets that branched off it. In contrast to the subtle Georgian edifices around the corner this part of town held rows of shops and public houses. Nary a brick in sight, the stone frontages were painted in every garish colour imaginable, emerald green, puce and purple, custard yellow being a particular favourite.

Then, with the band playing, it was off again, marching along another street, taking a left wheel at St Brendan's – the second church of this name he had seen – and along yet another elegant Georgian mall.

Again, as in Pontefract, Birr had its castle, but this one was obviously lived in, its well-kept outer walls extending all along this road.

The band played on, more people came out of the shops and houses to watch. After passing a third church called St Brendan's the troops came to a little stone bridge over the river and yet another St Brendan's which Probyn now recognized as the starting point, realizing that he had completed a circuit of the town and was now heading out of it the way he had come. Upon reaching the barracks a mile up the road it came as something of an annoyance to find that these were situated only five minutes from the railway station and the purpose of their march had simply been to exhibit them before the townspeople. But still, he had been pleasantly surprised to find such an air of gentility instead of the mud hovels he had been expecting.

The garrison, too, was far larger than he had imagined, its limestone fortress accommodating two thousand men, besides a considerable amount of land outside for reviews and such. It boasted, too, excellent entertainment facilities, a library and reading room and, Probyn was to learn, dances were often held in the gymnasium, the rest of the soldiers' needs being met in the village of Crinkle just outside the gates which had several pubs and shops. At first impression, the people had a quiet way about them – indeed he had not noticed just how loudly-spoken were his Yorkshire friends until measured against different folk – but this was not to be mistaken for aloofness. From the outset they were exceptionally friendly and welcoming, many of them letting a room in their homes to soldiers' families, and forcing Probyn quickly to revise his opinion of the Irish.

Once settled in at Crinkle Barracks he found he was to be posted to a new company. Any hope that this meant an end to his association with Melody was quickly dashed – he seemed fated to have the Irish youth forever at his side – but having grown used to Mick's ways this did not displease him too much. Neither did he grumble that the rest of the platoon remained virtually unaltered, with Wedlock still its corporal. Better the devils one knew. One beneficial change was that Jessop and Oliver, who had erstwhile cramped Probyn's style, were no longer amongst them, allowing him to assume a more dominant role. Havron did not like this one bit, though as yet had made no move to overthrow his rival. It was doubtful that he ever would, for over the months Probyn had come to read the characters in his platoon very well and recognized that, despite vociferous grumblings, Havron was a posturer who had never carried out one single threat. Hence Probyn continued to practise his leadership skills on his roommates, adapting to his new status with relish, and hoping Lieutenant Fitzroy would be suitably impressed.

Though far from delighted to be presented almost immediately with another boring round of gymnastics and drill, within days he was uplifted to have the serious business of musketry added to his schedule, welcoming the opportunity to draw praise from his officer.

To get to the range involved a two mile march through the rain which had remained constant since they arrived on Irish soil, though today there was little grumbling to be heard, all keen to learn how to put their rifles to good use. The intense quietude of the Irish countryside, broken only by the cawing of jackdaws, was now invaded by two hundred thudding boots and boyish exclamations.

In high spirits, the Londoner Queen called out as they marched, 'Permission to sing, Corp!' One had to seek Wedlock's consent over anything, however trivial.

Wedlock threw a morose answer over his shoulder. 'Your singing is like a duck farting.'

'I was only arstin,' muttered Queen, highly offended.

'Arse tin. Would that be a receptacle you put your bum in?' quipped Probyn, incurring a ripple of laughter.

Rook piped up. 'Melody's a good singer, Corp! Can he start us off?'

'I hope he's a better singer than he is a soldier,' replied Wedlock, which served as permission.

Melody looked self-conscious but, after brief decision, broke into a marching song, the others joining in quickly, their lusty voices carrying over the fields of newborn lambs.

From a village church a bell tolled; drowned out by the choristers it went unheeded. Their tempo unbroken, the soldiers proceeded along the road, maintaining their sturdy theme. Up ahead was an elderly woman, bent and beshawled, a basket over her arm. From his position in one of the front ranks, Probyn had been aware of her for some time as, due to her painful slowness, the company made great strides in closing the gap that separated them. She was now only thirty yards ahead. Suddenly, at the tolling of the bell, she came to a halt and, to his amazement, lowered herself to her knees in the middle of the wet road and began to pray! So taken aback was he by this that it affected the rhythm of his marching, causing the man behind to tread on his heel, and consequently throwing those in subsequent ranks out of step. Their chorus fractured, there was much swearing. Just as quickly, Probyn righted himself but was unsure what to do. The old lady was directly in their path! He cast an anxious glance at Wedlock but it was apparent the corporal was uncertain what to do either for he looked back at the musketry sergeant who was leading the company behind. Some of the rear ranks were still singing, unaware of the obstacle. Only just in time did Wedlock scream an order for them to cease forthwith and in the same breath gave instruction for them to 'Halt!' thereby sparing the devout matriarch from being trampled asunder.

Mere feet away from her kneeling form, Probyn stood and

gaped as the old lady, seemingly oblivious to the intruding army behind her, continued to pray, a rosary gripped between her hands.

''Tis the Angelus,' explained Mick under his breath at Probyn's look of incomprehension.

Even his whisper, thought Probyn, came as too loud an encroachment on this intensely religious moment. With the singers silenced, their boots motionless, the countryside was once more as quiet as the grave, but for the uncomfortable shuffling behind him and the patter of rain on their hats.

Eventually the woman finished her prayers and, with discomforted movements, struggled to her feet. Wedlock rushed forth to lend a hand. From the folds of the black shawl that was draped about her ancient head she thanked him with a silent dignified nod, then moved leisurely aside leaving the road clear for them to pass. An order was shouted and the embarrassed soldiers were once again on their way, leaving as quietly as their boots allowed.

For some moments Probyn remained affected by the spirituality of the moment, and indeed of the countryside around him. Only when others had spoken first did he add his voice to theirs, asking Melody, 'What did you mean, the Angelus?'

'Here in Ireland, when ye hear the bell ye drop everything and pray,' replied Mick.

Probyn remained thoughtful, others were less civil.

'We'd better thank heaven you're not so holy then, Melody,' remarked Corporal Wedlock. 'You'd never get anything bloody done at all if you were always on your knees.'

However moved he had been by the episode, Probyn was quick to put it aside on arrival at the rifle range, concentrating instead on mechanical matters. After illustrating how to load the ammunition, the sergeant instructor came along the line showing each how to hold their guns correctly, shifting and tugging them into the correct firing position. Eager to excel, Probyn pre-empted any instruction, brought the rifle up to his chin, narrowed his eyes and stared along the barrel to the target beyond, anticipating a word of commendation as the sergeant passed him by. He was therefore much chastened to receive worse treatment than many of the others, the sergeant roughly altering every aspect of his pose and chivvying him with the comment: 'It's not a bloody pea-shooter, laddy! Fire it like that and you'll smash all your teeth out.'

Once satisfied that every man was holding his gun correctly, the sergeant instructed them to fire individually, starting with Melody. Mick aimed at the target and squeezed the trigger. Nothing happened. He squeezed again, harder. There was a loud report and the recoil sent him staggering backwards which everyone treated as a huge joke. Determined to do better when it came to his turn, Probyn braced himself, held the rifle as firmly as he could, fixed his eye on the target and pulled the trigger – and was amazed at the intensity of the blow that was delivered to his shoulder.

Such shame! But he was not to stand alone in this. One by one the would-be sharp-shooters were to undergo identical disgrace, apart from Havron who, amazingly, was the only one to hit the target first time round, and by the end of that first session every man's shoulder was aching and bruised from the constant recoil and no one in the platoon except Havron had managed to puncture a bullseye.

Back in barracks, everyone demanded to know the secret of Havron's success. This, it transpired, was as a result of a temporary job with a gamekeeper which had lasted only until the employer had discovered his assistant's inclination for poaching the stock he was meant to be guarding.

Irked with his own lacklustre performance, Probyn sat apart, directing his anger into removing mud from his uniform, and trying to ignore the bouquets that were heaped on one so undeserving. In the end though his vexation got the better of him. 'Well I suppose it's just as well he's good at summat because he sure as heck doesn't know how to clean his boots!'

There were jeers at such an obvious display of envy.

Probyn tried to defend himself against the accusation of sour grapes. 'Look at the mud on 'em! You won't be so quick to congratulate him when he gets us all a beasting for him being dirty on parade. Get 'em cleaned, Havron!'

'Go bugger yourself,' said Havron.

Queen delivered a smiling rebuke. 'Praise where it's due, Pa.'

'I'll give him praise when he deserves some!' retorted the other, brushing furiously.

'You mean, when I get the award for best shot in the company?' goaded Havron.

Probyn tried to adopt a temperate air. 'If you win best shot, Havron, I'll be the first to congratulate you, so long as you pay the same diligence to your boots!'

However, he was determined that there would be no need for any grovelling congratulation, for he himself was going to win the accolade.

From then on every ounce of determination was channelled into winning the trophy. By the end of the week, the musketry instructor had begun to knock them into some sort of shape and Probyn had become much more confident, and proficient enough, he hoped, to win the badge for best shot in the company when that time came.

Apart from musketry and bayonet practice, there was more marching – five, ten, fifteen miles a day – which meant that every night Probyn went to bed exhausted. Nevertheless it did not prevent this virile young man from wondering, in the brief seconds before he fell asleep, when he was to be granted an opportunity for the extra-curricular activities he craved.

But alas it seemed unlikely that he would be allowed to investigate the town's female populace in the foreseeable future as during his second week in Ireland the company, plus three others, was on the march again to be quartered at Portumna, County Galway. Set at the northern end of a huge lough, it was a charming little town with fragments of a Dominican priory and a castle, and the countryside was most picturesque, the hedgerows bright with yellow gorse and white blossom. Notwithstanding this, it was a difficult march, the road rising most of the way and terminating in a large hill which had first to be got up before coming down the other side. Furthermore, there were to be similar marches throughout their stay here. With so much demanded of them it was inevitable that grumbles of exploitation should arise.

''Tis atrocious the way they're treating us!' complained Mick as, after another round trip of twenty miles along the banks of the Shannon and only a cup of tea and a biscuit for refreshment, they were ordered to set up firing positions. 'How can I be expected to hit a target with my arms like jelly after lugging this pack around all day?'

'Shush, Corp's coming,' warned a breathless Probyn, fighting his own weariness and wafting at the cloud of midges that encircled his head.

'To hell with him!' Mick scratched uncomfortably at his crotch, looking a picture of misery. 'I don't give a shit whether he hears me or not.'

'I did hear you, Melody,' barked Wedlock. 'And if you're not careful you'll be travelling another twenty miles on the end of my boot. What did you expect to be doing, having a bloody picnic? Do you think in a war the enemy's going to say, oh, hang on don't fire yet 'cause that chappie's just having a rest before he fires his gun? Jump to it!'

Amid much bad feeling, the soldiers did all that was asked of them, grovelling on their bellies over flood plains dotted with bulrushes, seeking out an imaginary enemy, but as firing practice came to an end and they were instructed to march immediately back to their quarters there were rumblings of dissension, men vowing that they would refuse to move an inch until they had had some relaxation.

'Well, moaning will do us no good at all!' Shoving the last item into his pack, Probyn stood with a look of resolution on his face. 'I'm off to get permission to stay here and do some fishing.'

'Fat chance!' scoffed Havron.

'We'll see.' Probyn strode off towards Corporal Wedlock. He was back amongst them within thirty seconds.

'Told you!' Havron, his face dark with mutiny, began to prepare for the homewards trek.

'Off, are you?' said Probyn lightly. 'Oh well, we'll bring you some fish back.'

'You mean you talked him round?' Mick was amazed at his friend's powers. 'What the devil did ye say to him?'

Probyn adopted a grim expression. 'I said, listen to me, Wedlock, if you don't stop driving these men like slaves you're going to have a mutiny on your hands. He said, you really think so? I said, I do, and what's more I'll be first in line to smack you in the gob –'

'You never!' Bumby's jaw dropped.

Mick dealt him a disparaging shove. 'He's codding yese, ye soft arse.'

Bumby shoved him back. 'I knew that – and stop scratching your balls!'

Probyn laughed. 'I hardly had to say a word, the corp beat me to it and said we can stay for two hours as long as we fetch him a salmon. I nearly dropped!'

Thumping the messenger on the back, the young soldiers wasted no further time and pelted off to hire fishing boats and tackle. All of a sudden their exhaustion appeared completely to have vanished.

Happy at his success, Probyn called for others to accompany him.

Instead, Mick lay back on the damp grass. 'I think I'll just catch up on some sleep, if ye don't mind.'

Probyn scoffed. 'I thought it was too good to be true you getting yourself up on a morning.' Melody had risen before anyone else all this week; the lack of sleep showed in his looks.

'If only you knew,' murmured Mick out of earshot and, with a testy slap at the midge that hovered whining around his ear, closed his eyes in despair.

Probyn and others set off to wander leisurely across a lush sprawl of meadow carpeted in dandelions and on towards a bay where sand martins dived and swooped above glittering water, skimming the surface for mayflies. Today, washed in sunlight, its trees and hedgerows bursting into leaf, the landscape gleamed like an emerald. A far cry from the wild forbidding country he had witnessed from the train window.

The remainder of the afternoon was pronounced absolutely splendid and the entire mood had been transformed by the time they made their way back to their quarters with bagsful of freshwater mussels and a respectable haul of fish. But the crowning moment was yet to come. Ever on the look out, Probyn was first to spot the three girls who stood chatting by a horse-drawn cart some way ahead. Tapping Mick on the arm he began to walk more briskly twixt the blackthorn hedgerows, eager to be first to reach the quarry. But others had seen the colleens now and in a mad rush they charged up the road in pursuit. Alarmed, Probyn strove to beat them.

Hearing the rapid thud of boots one of the girls turned and, her face portraying fright, alerted her companions and all tried to scramble into the cart, but it was too late for they were instantly encompassed by a host of red tunics and muddy leering faces.

Not as swift as some, Probyn had to fight and jostle his way to the centre of the pack. 'Eh, don't frighten poor lasses, give them room. Look, you're scaring t'hoss too!'

But his plea was taken as a ruse and he was persistently shoved aside.

'Push off, I saw 'em first. Eh, do you want to come behind that bush wi' me, sweetheart?' Ingham certainly knew how to court a lady.

'No, she wants me, don't you?' Havron elbowed him out of the way.

'They'll not be going with any of yese!' Three wild-looking youths came dashing out from behind a hedgerow where they had been answering the call of nature.

'Keep your neb out, Paddy!' warned the hulking Ingham. 'They're ours.'

'Saxon brutes!' returned the aggrieved spokesman. 'We came for a quiet day out with our girls and this is what we get. Take your filthy hands off them! Why, 'tis animals you are! Coming here and pawing decent womenfolk –'

'Eh, we meant no harm!' Probyn was quick to see that, if allowed to develop, this could become nasty. The girls were becoming increasingly anxious and the horse looked ready to bolt at all the noise, tossing its head and jingling its harness. 'We were just admiring the lasses, that's all –'

'Well don't!' Another of the youths, with jet-black hair and a sallow complexion, lunged forward and began to pull at the arms of those who imprisoned the girls. In a medley of choice words, the soldiers resisted.

'Eh, eh!' Probyn took charge of the situation, trying to calm matters. 'There's no need for rough stuff.' Turning to his fellows he displayed a conciliatory air. 'Come on, lads, ease off and let the girls free. You can see they belong to these fellows.'

Havron was most unwilling. 'Shove your bloody orders!' Queen and Bumby too echoed his objections. Only Mick held back.

Probyn remained calm. 'See sense! The lasses are frightened of you, they don't want to know.'

But still there was resistance and, with the girls trying frantically to disentangle themselves from the writhing mass of red-serged arms, the Irish youths launched an attack, showering the soldiers with kicks and punches in an attempt to break the circle. Bumped and elbowed, the horse began to lash out.

Envisaging a terrible accident, Probyn was quick to act. Unslinging his rifle he directed it at the Irish fellows, hoping they would not call his bluff for it was unloaded. 'Right, get into the cart and sling your hook or I'll blow your heads off!'

Things were brought to an abrupt halt, although the one with the jet-black hair and sallow complexion still squared up to his adversaries, unmindful that the soldier brandishing the weapon was trying to prevent worse injury. 'Oh 'tis brave lads you are when you're holding a gun!'

'Go on, Pa, give it to him!' exhorted Ingham.

Furious at Ingham's stupidity, Probyn dared not take his eyes off the Irish youths. 'I'm warning you, get in the cart now!'

It proved effective, even if the three defeated youths did manage to hurl plenty of abuse as they boarded the vehicle.

An hurrah arose from the soldiers.

'Don't blinkin' cheer me, Ingham!' Probyn was angry. 'I've told you to let them lasses go and I mean it.' He was still holding his rifle, his posture threatening.

Amid much grumbling, the girls were released and were immediately helped into the cart by their countrymen whereupon the driver lashed the reins and set the vehicle into motion, though not without a few departing curses. 'We know where you're from! Don't think you've heard the last of it!'

'Aw blimey, d'you fink they'll report us?' asked Queen worriedly, stooping to gather mussels that had been distributed all over the road in the skirmish.

Out of sexual frustration and annoyance that the pleasant afternoon had been tainted, Probyn snapped back, 'I don't know and I don't bloody care!'

'Ooh! Did ye hear that, boys?' Hating discord, Mick injected a note of jocularity, his attitude changing to one of mock horror. 'Your man *swore*. Right that's it, you're on a charge, Kilmaster! Outside my office now!'

'Behave you barmy clot!' Probyn elbowed him away and began to walk.

But Mick would not desist, and began to walk alongside him,

poking and jabbing him tormentatively in the ribs. 'Never dare to tell us about our language ye filthy crayture.'

'You'd drive a man to owt you would!' Probe was laughing now but tried to maintain his dignity under Mick's teasing assault by marching on ahead.

Undeterred, Mick followed and began to aim shellfish at him.

Offering loud complaint, Probyn stooped to pick up a mussel and returned it with more vigour.

Eager to inflict his own revenge, Havron aimed a missile too. This became the signal for all-out war with Probyn as the target, everyone pouncing on the shellfish for ammunition, mussels whizzing to and fro, bouncing off the victim's unfortunate skull, even fish being used to slap Probyn round the head as he made a run for it with the rest of the squad flying after him down the road, everyone blaming him, albeit laughingly, for ruining their chances with the women.

For a few days the squad remained wary, awaiting repercussions for their conflict with the locals that might have brought the regiment into disrepute. Thankfully, there was nothing at all, except a constant barrage of marching and musketry and drill and at the end of the week when they returned to Crinkle they relaxed and forgot all about the incident.

The mood was especially happy on Sunday, for they were allowed to go beyond the village for their entertainment, though no further than Birr. Probyn's instinctive reaction was that here was another opportunity to look for females. 'But whatever you do,' he whispered to Melody, 'don't mention it to any of the others. I don't want them ruining my chances again.'

'Women is it?' Mick seemed less than enthusiastic.

Probyn took this attitude as fabrication, and grinned. 'Don't play the innocent with me! I know you too well.' It was not out of any sense of fellowship that he included Melody in his plan, but that Mick with his curly hair would serve to attract the females where he himself could not hope to.

It was some irritation then, after lunch, to find certain members of his platoon tagging on behind as he and Melody wandered into town and congregated in the square. He would have to think of some way to shake them off, for he had just spotted two likely candidates for romance. Wondering how to orchestrate this, he slowed down, waiting for the others to overtake him.

For once, Ingham was to be of assistance. 'I wonder if they give free samples at the brewery,' he said as he and the rest drew alongside.

'Shouldn't think it'll be open on a Sunday,' Bumby pointed out. Every shop was closed, the streets very quiet and few people about.

'Worth a look though,' said Ingham, Queen agreeing. 'Are you two coming with us?'

Probyn grabbed hold of Mick's sleeve to prevent him following. 'No we're off to see that giant telescope at the castle. It's fifty-six feet long I've heard.'

'Nearly as long as my rod then,' said Ingham. 'Get your priorities right, Pa. We can all go and have a look at it together after we've sniffed out this brewery – away!'

'Nay, we've had enough of drinking,' said Probyn. There were half a dozen pubs just outside the barrack wall. 'We fancy doing something else.'

'I told you, they're bloody pooves,' said Havron to Rook.

'Grow up,' Probyn told him, trying to remain casual whilst holding onto Mick's arm, and saying to the others, 'All right, we'll come, but we just want to find out who this statue's of. We'll follow on.' Ignoring the catcalls from those departing he stood by the iron palings that encircled the statue of the Duke of Cumberland, affecting to be studying it with interest.

His arm still imprisoned, a thoroughly perplexed Mick beheld his friend.

'Aw, blast! They've gone.' Voice full of disappointment, Probyn swivelled and cast frantic glances around the quiet square.

'Who's gone?' Mick frowned.

'There were two bonny-looking lasses over there a minute ago!' A quick look over his shoulder showed that their army companions were out of range. 'They must've gone down that way – away, let's see!' Dragging Mick after him, Probyn made for one of the streets off the square. With so few people about it should not be so difficult to find them. Alas, all his agitated searching was in vain; there was no sign of his quarry anywhere.

Wrenching his sleeve from the other's grasp, Mick seemed overly annoyed at being dragged about so. 'I don't know why you're working yourself into such a lather over these colleens, ye won't get what ye think ye'll be getting, not from the good Catholic girls round these parts.' He tugged his distorted tunic to order, unusually ill-tempered.

Taking little heed, Probyn wore a thwarted scowl. 'There must be more than two of 'em round here. Come on!' He set off with a reluctant Melody in tow.

Standing once more in Cumberland Square, he allowed his eyes to rove, ostensibly studying architecture but alert for other attractions. After a while, though, he was forced to accept that the afternoon was going to be a failure. Casting his frustrated gaze to the leaden sky he cursed the country. 'Haven't they ever heard of the colour blue in Ireland? What a miserable bloomin' place.'

And then as if by some miracle, that which he sought was delivered into his hands.

'Good afternoon to you, sirs!' The driver of a jaunting car pulled up alongside them, doffing his bowler as he spoke. 'Could I be interesting you in a bit of a drive away to the Slieve Bloom Mountains? I'm already taking these young ladies but I need two more to make it worth my while.'

A delighted Probyn beheld the girls he had seen earlier,

one fair and pink-cheeked, the other dark and exotic like the signoritas he had admired in Spain. Without forethought he made eagerly to board.

'Em, hold on there!' Mick held back. 'How much is it?'

'Does it matter?' growled Probyn and urged him to comply.

'Sixpence each,' said the jarvey cheerfully.

'There you are, it's cheap!' hissed Probyn.

Still Mick remained wary. 'Oh, I don't know. 'Tis looking a bit black up there.' He pointed at the overcast sky. 'And how far is it you're taking us? We have to be back in barracks by four and 'tis half-past two already.'

'For heaven's sake what's up with you?' Probyn thrust his face into Melody's.

'I just don't feel like going,' whined Mick.

'Well I do!' Probyn was not going to allow anyone to jeopardize his chance of a sexual encounter. 'And I'm always doing stuff for you so you can do summat for me, sithee, I'll pay for us both if you're that narrow-nosed!' Forbidding any more refusal, he took a shilling from his pocket and paid both fares, then without further delay shoved Mick at the carriage and climbed up after him.

As the jaunting car set off on its tour, Probyn twisted round in his seat and made introductions with the girls who sat back to back with him and Melody. That the latter seemed very subdued made him irritated but not unduly concerned and, as the vehicle made its way out of town and into the countryside, he managed single-handedly to initiate a conversation with the girls who, though quietly spoken, responded with pleasant smiles to all he said. This was going to be a wonderful afternoon.

The mountains towards which they were heading were hardly more than gentle curves, the pony having to make little effort in its ascent along the winding road.

Engrossed in his pursuit of the colleens, Probyn hardly noticed that they had been travelling for miles when Melody tapped him and suggested they had better turn round as the weather was decidedly taking a turn for the worse and it surely must be close to four o'clock.

Having coaxed one of the girls into becoming more talkative, Probyn barely acknowledged him, nor did he heed the ruined churches, their graveyards crammed with celtic crosses, nor the gambolling lambs, his mind engrossed with baser images.

Further into the mountain range they rolled, their vehicle rising steadily. Mick began to feel increasingly threatened and not simply due to the leaden sky. There was an air of desolation about their surroundings now. They had not passed an inhabited building for miles and save for the ever-present jackdaws the landscape was divest of animals. Some while ago, the driver had branched off the main road onto a narrow track. The route was becoming exceedingly bumpy, he wondered how this could go unnoticed to his friend, but then Pa was so sickeningly pleased under the female attention that an earthquake would not have distracted him. With spots of rain beginning to dapple his blue trousers, Mick decided he had had enough, and called out, 'Em, would ye be able for taking us back now, jarvey?'

'Best to take shelter,' came the cheerful reply. 'There's a place just up yonder that will do.'

Temporarily diverted, Probyn examined his surroundings and suddenly began to share his comrade's misgivings. The rain was becoming heavier, his tunic would be ruined if they did not find shelter. But just then he saw that the driver had spoken the truth, there was indeed a stone cottage ahead. It looked rather derelict but its roof was still intact. His predatory instincts rose again to the fore – surely fate had stepped in to lend a hand! Perhaps within those walls he and the Spanish-looking beauty would enjoy an erotic interlude to while away a rainy half-hour.

With the drizzle now appearing like a mist over the bleak expanses of grassland, the occupants of the cart were glad to reach the cottage. Jumping down, Probyn helped the girls to alight, escorting them to the rickety pile of stones, a wary Melody lagging at the rear.

Just as they reached the door, however, it was dragged open by a youth with jet-black hair whose sallow visage Probyn recognized immediately. It was one of those with whom they had traded insults last week after musketry practice, and what was worse, the two others from that day appeared behind him.

Instantly robbed of libido, he glanced at Melody who obviously shared his worry.

Steering the females past him and into the cottage, the youth with the black hair barred Probyn's way. 'Thought you were going to have a nice little get together with the girls, did ye? Sorry to disappoint yese but they were only bait – and it didn't take you eejits long to snap, did it? Back on the car with yese!'

Again Probyn silently consulted with Mick, alarm on both their faces. 'We don't want any trouble.' He began slowly to retreat.

'Then ye shouldn't be invading another man's country,' came the dark reply, the youths following Probyn on his backwards route to the jaunting car.

He could go no further, an iron wheel against his back. He tried to reason. 'Invading? I thought we were all British.' But from the looks on their faces he knew he could have said nothing worse. Preparing for flight, he inhaled sharply as a knife was thrust at his neck, forcing him to lean backwards over the wheel.

'Confound you, we're *Irish*,' came the menacing rebuttal of the one who stood over him.

Stunned, Probyn blinked the rain from his eyes but tried to avoid meeting the other's confrontational gaze, instead fixing his sights on the lock of black hair that was only inches away from his nose and saying as evenly as he could with a blade at his throat, 'So is my friend! You've no argument with him.'

'On the contrary,' sneered his abductor, removing his gaze

only to flick a withering glance at Mick. 'Your johneen here is even lower scum than you. No true Irishman would stoop to wear that bloody tunic.'

Eyes back on Probyn, he stared into his captive's face for a moment longer. 'Not so brave without your gun, are ye, soldier boy?' Then he straightened abruptly and reiterated his demand, 'On board!'

The relief at having the hard wheel rim removed from his back did not reflect itself in Probyn's expression, for he noticed that the other two had produced cudgels. 'Where are you taking us?'

'Somewhere you'll be taught a lesson.'

'Oh, you're not man enough to do it yourself?' asked Probyn.

The youth did not react. ''Tis just that I know someone who'll take even greater pleasure in it than I.'

Probyn's face took on a look of obstinacy, but this was soon displaced by one of shock as the knife blade performed a rapid movement and he looked down to see a large rent in his tunic.

'That'll be your neck if you don't do as you're told right now!'

'Pa, do as the man says!' Mick urged his friend, then cried at his kidnapper, 'We're going, we're going!'

With a mocking smile, the black-haired youth asked, 'You've brought your rosary with ye?' Then he signalled for his companions to assist their prisoners on board. For Probyn and Mick there was no other option than to yield.

The vehicle was on its way again, two of the youths seated next to the captives, their black-haired companion squeezed next to the driver who had obviously been in on the plot all along. Though the knife had been withdrawn from its dangerous position it continued to present a threat. There would be little chance of escape.

It was still raining and the light was failing rapidly now. Trying to bolster himself, Probyn decided that this was an advantage, for if the men could be distracted he and Mick could leap unseen into the gloom. The one important thing was to keep calm. The chilling thought recurred that he might be going to die, but he would not allow it to fester. He must keep his mind clear if there were to be any chance of escape.

The journey seemed to take forever, taking them deeper into the mountain range, mile after bumpy mile was covered, rain trickling down their faces, clothes becoming sodden, until suddenly ahead appeared the dark outline of a building, this one inhabited, for a ribbon of smoke curled from its chimney. For Probyn and Mick there was a mixture of emotions as the jaunting car finally halted and they were ordered to get down. Every muscle tense in anticipation and at the mercy of their captors, they were bundled into the cottage.

The sole occupant, a much older man, seemed totally unprepared for this intrusion. A moment ago, lulled by the sweet scent of a peat fire and the contents of the black cooking pot upon it, he had been dozing. Now his startled visage flushed in anger and he jumped from his fireside chair, his pipe falling to the floor as he berated them in Gaelic. 'What in God's . . . is it mad you are, bringing soldiers here?'

Probyn glanced at Mick to see if he understood what was being said, though it was obvious that the man's anger was not directed solely at the infantrymen. The youths seemed not quite so menacing now, one of them offering apology as the man slapped each around the head and herded them outside demanding an explanation, all conducted in Gaelic. The pipesmoke had a ridiculously comforting effect on Probyn – he might well have been in his Uncle Owen's cottage were it not for the murderous mutterings outside. Alert to any opportunity of escape, he strained to hear what was afoot. Even in the foreign tongue it was evident that no one was sure what to do with their captives. Through the open door came much heated exchange, the man seeming to have the upper hand; for one exciting moment it appeared that there was to be salvation, until they overheard the forceful suggestion in English from the black-haired youth, obviously for their benefit – 'I want them dead!' – thereby robbing them of all hope.

'Oh, Jesus Christ!' Mick could not prevent a frightened exclamation and began to pace and mutter dementedly.

Afraid as he was, Probyn became furious at these craven antics as Mick prayed and muttered and paced the bare floor. If he were going to die he would die like a soldier. *Keep calm!* he urged himself, trying to sustain his courage, yet it was almost impossible not to be affected by Mick's demented gibberish. Sweat sprang to his armpits, his gut felt twisted inside out. In horror of his own demise, he was about to furiously castigate the other for doing this to him when he realized that, between the lines of invocation, Mick was trying to tell him something.

'Be ready to run!' whispered Mick, interspersing his words with more prayer. 'Hail Mary full of grace . . .'

Through the open doorway the older man cast a sharp glance at the soldiers who appeared to be hatching some mischief. Aware of the enemy's observance Mick began to jabber more loudly, 'Blessed be the fruit of thy womb –'

The plotters had finished their angry discussion and were coming back inside. Chanting even more loudly, Mick danced agitatedly on the spot, his rain-streaked face even ruddier than normal, his back to the glowing turf fire. Praying that his friend was about to make some relevant move, Probyn waited heart in mouth, every nerve tingling, saw Mick's hand move behind his back and cast something upon the fire before moving quickly aside . . .

He did not have long to wait for the outcome. Within seconds the room exploded with noise, bullets whizzing all over the place, shattering the window panes, ricocheting off the walls. Assuming they were under an infantry attack, each would-be assassin leapt for the nearest stick of furniture, crouching behind it, arms wrapped tightly around their heads as the bullets zinged dangerously close.

The pandemonium lasted only an instant but in that brief

glorious diversion Mick lurched for the open door with Probyn immediately at his heels and before anyone could realize what had happened they were away and running for their lives down the wild rain-lashed slope. Ignoring the jaunting car for it could not offer the speed they required, they instead relied on the sheets of rain to hide them, their aim to put as much distance as they could between them and their attackers, stumbling and tripping and barging into each other as they tried to avoid tussocks of grass and gorse, running, running, running . . .

Glancing feverishly over his shoulder to see if they were being pursued, Probyn was encouraged that there was no sign and, legs furiously pumping, ran on, immediately falling headlong, rolling over and over down the slope before picking himself up again and with Mick's help dashing onwards.

They ran until they could run no more, whence, lungs rasping, they fell heavily upon a springy mound of grass, ears cocked for any sound other than their own laboured panting and the pitter-patter of rain on their backs. Finally, to their great joy, it became clear that their liberty was won.

Even then they dared not so much as whisper, their only communication being a joint gasp of relief as they locked eyes, each silently thanking the Lord for their deliverance.

His heartbeat beginning to return to normality, Probyn allowed his tensed muscles to unfurl, sitting upright and massaging his aching shoulders. His clothes were smeared with black peat, his tunic ruined. Still, he was alive. For now.

After a period of silent contemplation, he finally spoke. 'Can you see a track anywhere?'

A worried Mick narrowed his eyes against the drizzle. 'Not a thing.'

Probyn felt the desperate urge to relieve his bowels. 'No point trying to find our way back in this lot – we could get even more lost or run into those blokes again.'

'Ye mean spend the night out here?' Mick sounded incredulous. 'Jesus, we've hours ahead of us, and 'tis terrible cold.'

'Keep your voice down!' hissed Probyn. 'It'll carry for miles out here.' Despite the shroud of drizzle their red tunics acted as beacons on this wasteland. 'You want to think yourself lucky you're not permanently cold.'

'Oh, and who have we got to thank for that?' Mick studied him quizzically.

Probyn stared back for a moment, then looked suitably grateful. 'Aye, well . . . thanks, it was a good bit of thinking. Where did you get the ammo?'

'Snuck ten rounds in me pocket after musketry practice the other day. I was going to play a trick on Ingham but never got the chance.'

'Thank God.' Probyn eased his painful joints, marvelling that they could discuss this as if it were nothing. They had almost been *murdered!* 'Come on, we'll get some shelter under that big rock over there while we decide what to do.' Checking to ensure they were unobserved, he and Mick darted for the cover of a huge boulder and, using grass to cushion their rears, leaned heavily against it. Thankfully, in its overhang the ground beneath was relatively dry. 'I wonder what time it is.' It was hard to tell, being prematurely dark because of the rain, but he guessed it was about seven o'clock. 'They're bound to have noticed we're missing by now – they might already be looking for us. Best if we stay put. If they haven't come by the time it gets light we'll set off.' He closed his eyes as if for sleep.

Mick affected to settle down too, but kept scratching and fidgeting, and besides it was impossible for either of them to relax, not simply due to cold but from what they had just encountered. Their mouths were dry with fear that the men might suddenly pounce. Even the mere thought of the cold wet hours ahead of them was enough to deter any form of rest.

'God, I need a pony and trap!' Mick jumped up and went around the other side of the rock.

Temporarily alone, Probyn huddled into himself for warmth, and when Mick finally came back he suggested, 'We should sit as close as we can, keep each other warm.'

Grimacing as if in pain, Mick shuffled his buttocks until his hip came into contact with the other's, pulled his elbows into his sides and curled into his damp tunic. Again he tried to sleep, but the monotonous patter of rain drove him to distraction.

'D'ye think they'd really have killed us?' he asked eventually.

'I wouldn't put it past the treacherous dogs, and will you keep bloody still!' Probyn's fear was now being overtaken by anger. 'Lord, if I could meet them one to one – and those blasted politicians who talk about Home Rule!' He shook his head in disgust. 'They've obviously never even been here. I ask you, who in their right mind would suggest giving these thugs power? Well, if that's going to be the case I hope they throw out all the teagues in England who're enjoying the benefits of a civilized country!'

Suddenly aware of the tension in his companion's shoulder he sought to qualify his rantings. 'Sorry, Mick I'm not including you, just the ones who cause trouble. It makes me bloody furious.'

'I'd never have guessed.'

'Well, what do you make of all this Home Rule business then?' demanded Probyn.

'Ah well,' sighed Mick. 'Ye can't blame people for wanting a say in the way their country's run.'

There was instant retort. 'Aye, but you can't think much to the place if you chose to live in England.'

Mick was shivering. 'I didn't exactly choose it, I just went where my father told me to go. There's no work here.'

'That's exactly what I mean! You lot are happy enough to be British when it suits you.'

'Have ye ever imagined how ye'd feel if the boot was on the other foot?'

Probyn was silently thoughtful for a while, then conceded, 'Aye, well, maybe. Let's agree to differ.'

Mick became more vociferous. 'Oh, 'tis not to say I don't

agree with yese about those murderous hooligans though! I'll make jam with their goolies if I catch up with them.'

Probyn winced. 'Don't mention goolies. It was following mine that got us in this trouble. Well, there's nowt so sure as I shan't be led astray by another lass in a hurry.'

Mick was even more adamant. 'Huh! Never again for me. The last one was enough to finish me for good.'

Sensing more to this than met the eye, Probyn delved beneath the surface. 'I got the feeling you weren't keen on joining the girls in the first place. Is summat up?'

'Ye could say that!' After the initial outburst, Mick appeared hesitant to say more, merely tendering, 'Have you . . . ah, don't let it bother ye.'

'Go on!' Probyn sounded irritated. 'I've nowt else to do but listen.'

'Well, em, I don't know how to put this.' The rain still falling around them, Mick hugged his legs and rested his chin on a damp knee. 'Have you encountered any ailment since you were in York?'

'What sort of ailment?'

'If ye'd had it you'd know what sort of ailment I mean.' For a second Mick prayed to the heavens, then blurted, 'Oh God, ye might as well know, I'll have to tell someone or I'll go mad! Ever since those two in York . . . I've had trouble with me rod.' He did not look at Probyn as he explained the symptoms of his malady.

'Aw no, it sounds like you've copped a packet!' breathed Probyn.

'That's what I feared,' moaned the other, clutching his legs tighter. 'And 'tis getting worse by the day. Me goolies feel like lead. Oh Jesus, whatever am I going to do?'

'Well you'll have to see the doc for a start.'

'Oh, I couldn't!' Mick emerged like a jack-in-a-box from his huddle. 'He'll put me in the dirty hospital!'

Probyn was firm and fatherly. 'You'll have to do summat or it'll drop off.'

Mick groaned, rived frantically at his crotch, then hugged himself again. 'The shame of it. And you've been perfectly all right you say?'

'Aye.' Probyn was thoughtful. 'If I were going to get it I'd have had it by now.' Still, this episode had taught him to be more discerning about his women in future – in more ways than one.

Gratified by his own rude health, he sought to put Melody at ease. 'Don't worry, they can cure it.'

''Tis the cure that worries me,' wailed Mick. 'I've heard they stick something up it.'

Probyn's stomach lurched in horror. 'That's rubbish!'

Laying great store by his friend's knowledge, Mick sounded encouraged. 'Ye've had it yourself then?'

'Nay!' It was said with a growl of disgust. 'But I'm sure it can't be right.'

A sigh in the dark. 'They say ye can get stuff from the chemist but I daren't go in and ask for it.' He underwent a hopeful pause.

'Best leave it to the experts,' advised Probyn.

Mick's disappointment and shame was almost palpable. 'Ye won't let on to anyone?'

''Course not.' Probyn was rather thankful that Mick's predicament had served to divert his mind from what had just happened, but within seconds of this realization the fear came flooding back and he struggled to channel his thoughts along a different route.

A period of silence followed.

'What're you thinking about?' asked Mick.

Probyn chuckled and shifted position against the rock to ease his muddy, aching limbs. 'Oh, I were just eating one of Aunt Kit's dinners. I'm famished.'

Mick forced a smile, and after a thoughtful moment said, 'Your aunt doesn't like Irish folk very much does she?'

Probyn could not see his friend's face but sensed his hurt. 'Oh, I don't think –'

'I saw her expression at the station,' said Mick.

Probyn could not pretend otherwise. 'Well, she's really nice and kind, I'm sure if she knew you personally she would hate to think she'd offended you, it's just that my whole family has this prejudice towards Catholics.' Feeling comradeship towards Mick for rescuing him and sympathizing with him over his ailment, he felt the need to offer some token of intimacy. 'In my view, it's all a bit hypocritical – all right, I know what I said about Home Rule but that's a political matter, and I've learned enough to know that not all Irish people are the same. I really like Aunt Kit but she's hardly one to throw stones when she had two children before she was married.' In response to Mick's gasp of amazement he added, 'I was too young to know how it happened then, I just knew it was shameful from the way folk behaved towards her. So you see my family's got no cause to look down on anybody.'

Urging his companion to divulge more, Mick listened assiduously without interruption. Probyn was happy to talk. What else was there to do in order to while away the hours until morning? Eventually, though, he suggested they make a supreme effort to get some sleep for they would have a very long walk in the morning. Balanced uncomfortably on their tussock, backs to the unyielding rock, they closed their eyes, each tense body trying to leech heat from the other, and eventually they dozed.

Their awakening gave birth to apprehension that their assailants might return to finish the job, but the landscape was completely deserted, at least it was as far as they could see, for a layer of fog made it almost impossible to navigate. Ravenous with hunger, they eased their aching bodies upright and wandering down the slope began to search for a track, a task that seemed nigh impossible in this bleak half-light. They could be wandering around in circles for days, could die of starvation or tumble into a bog and no one would be the wiser. But no! Graced by fortune they finally stumbled instead on a road, whereupon they set off eagerly in what they hoped to be the right direction.

The fog had begun to lift, yet this was no signal to relax for without any signpost their location was still unclear. But just when the exhausted young men were at their wits' end they heard the sound of wheels and through the mist materialized an elderly man leading a donkey cart.

Certain that such a cheery face could offer no violence, Probyn rushed forward. 'Excuse me, sir, could you tell us the way to Birr?'

Taken by surprise, the man studied the two forlorn faces for a moment before pointing. 'Well now, if you go down here a few miles you'll come to a sign that says Birr, I should think that would take you to Birr.'

Thanking him, the pair set off eagerly, this surge of optimism to be reinforced some half an hour later when, a few miles after seeing the signpost, there also appeared a band of men in red tunics, one of whom let out a whoop to his superior.

'Found 'em, Sarge!' Seizing credit, Ingham rushed forth.

Enveloped by their peers, who laughingly reproached them for getting lost and hooted over their mud-caked appearance, Probyn and Mick were quick to set the record straight, especially when the sergeant began to dole out reprimands for their stupidity.

'Sergeant, it wasn't lost we were but kidnapped!' revealed an earnest-looking Mick.

Initially this was treated by Sergeant Faulkner as an attempt to escape punishment. 'Melody, who in their right mind would want to kidnap thee?'

But when Kilmaster, who was known to be a sensible chap, gave confirmation, a whole new light was cast on the matter. Angry murmurs rapidly displaced the merriment as the swaddies listened to their comrades' tale, vowing to get even.

'There'll be none of that talk!' The sergeant called his men to order, warning of the repercussions this could have. 'We'd better get back to the garrison. Fall in!'

Faced with another lengthy walk, Mick fell in with a marked lack of enthusiasm.

Though similarly tired, Probyn offered an encouraging grin at the one who had suddenly attained kudos. 'Never mind, chum, think of the medal that awaits you – you're a hero!'

7

'Right,' said the sergeant, upon their grateful entry to the barracks. 'I've managed to wangle you a bacon sandwich. Soon as you've wolfed it, get yourselves bathed and your uniforms cleaned up – you'll have to get yourself a new tunic, Kilmaster – then I want to see you both outside my office.' He went off to visit the company commander.

Never had bacon tasted so good, the happy heroes helping it down with mugs of tea whilst being badgered by their pals for details of their extraordinary adventure.

Enjoyment of this celebrity was not to last for, arriving at the quartermaster's store, Probyn learned that it would cost him a month's pay to replace his ruined tunic. The injustice of it! But there was little time to grouse for he was soon having to rush off for a bath.

Cleansed and refitted, he and Mick hurriedly presented themselves at the sergeant's office, from whence they were taken before Major Kirkpatrick. With their section commander present, they were asked to give the whole story, which Kilmaster provided, it having been agreed between the two of them that Mick would say as little as possible. At this stage it was unnecessary to lie, but when asked by the major if there had been any precursor to the abduction, any situation that might have caused it, Probyn was to suffer guilt. Monty Kilmaster had raised his children to face the consequences of their actions and detested any form of untruth, he would surely despair of his son now.

'I'd never met either the driver of the carriage nor the girls before, sir.' This at least was the truth. 'There was no hint of danger when we set out on the trip.'

A note of rebuke. 'You were aware, Kilmaster, that you were meant to stay within a mile of the garrison?'

Probyn looked contrite. 'Yes, I was aware, sir, and I regret my laxity.'

'Could you recall the location of the cottage to which you were taken?'

'No sir.' This too was honest. 'It was just somewhere amongst those Slieve Bloom mountains, but I'd recognize those involved if I saw them again.'

After further stringent interrogation by the major, they were told that due to their ordeal they would escape any punishment for straying out of bounds. Even though it was assumed that the culprits would probably be long gone by now a warrant was to be put out for their arrest, and Melody and Kilmaster might be required to give evidence.

Only then were the exhausted pair allowed to return to their barrack room for some rest, although there was not much of the latter to be had, their comrades refusing to let go of the subject and teasing them over the whereabouts of their medals.

Weary as he was, Probyn dismissed any idea of getting some sleep and instead began to clean his kit, but found he had run out of brass polish.

Bumby lent him some and came to sit on the cot beside his, watching him work. 'Eh, Melody tells us this Aunt Kit of yours is a bit of a goer.'

Probyn's mouth fell open. He stopped polishing and immediately looked at Mick who a moment ago had been laughing but now turned sheepish.

'You bloody arse, Melody, that was private!'

Mick wailed his innocence. 'But ye told me!'

'In confidence!' Such was the vehemence of Probyn's expression that Bumby immediately made himself scarce; others too looked uncomfortable.

'How was I to know?' beseeched Mick. 'I'm sorry but ye should've said it was a secret!'

'I didn't think you were that much of a half-wit!' Both furious and guilty with himself for betraying Kit who had been so good to him, Probyn warned himself not to make the same mistake again, should have trusted his original judgement of Melody who was faithless and shallow. They could never be true friends. 'I'll bet you haven't told them your own little secret!'

At once their roommates were eager to interpret the look of horror that spread over Mick's face and demanded details.

'He's got clap!' Spite was a rare visitor, but Probyn felt extremely let down.

With only himself to blame, Mick donned a fatalistic expression, whilst others roared with laughter and told him that even a hero could expect to be put on a charge for this self-inflicted wound. Glancing over at Probyn he saw that the latter had set to polishing furiously, and wondered bemusedly how Pa could have been so malicious.

The erstwhile heroes were to say little to each other for the rest of the day which was to end on an even sourer note when it was announced that everyone was confined to barracks until the risk of further ambush was deemed to be over.

After almost a week, Probyn had just begun to think the episode was closed, that his abductors had answered his prayers and vanished, when Corporal Wedlock singled him out.

'Kilmaster, Lieutenant Fitzroy's office now!'

Alarm prickled his scalp. Checking his appearance, he hurriedly answered the summons.

But when he arrived in the office, Lieutenant Fitzroy seemed amiable enough. 'At ease, Private Kilmaster. You must be wondering whether we've apprehended those fellows . . .'

Probyn held his breath.

'I'm afraid to say it looks as if they're long gone.'

Probyn tried not to sound relieved. 'Sorry I couldn't be of more help, sir.'

'Never mind, you conducted yourself well, but that's not the reason why I wish to speak to you, or rather it is indirectly. I'm instructed to extend an invitation to tea tomorrow with a Mr and Mrs O'Neil.'

Probyn gaped. 'To me, sir?' Glancing at the corporal he observed a similar expression of surprise, though Wedlock's rapidly turned to disgust.

'To you, Private Kilmaster, and the Major and myself and Private Melody – but the less said about him the better. Mr O'Neil is a very important member of the community. Upon learning of the harm inflicted upon you and Private Melody by local men he was appalled and has made this gesture as an act of goodwill in order that our soldiers may continue to enjoy the same cordial relations we have always held with the people of Birr. May I take it that you accept his kind invitation?'

Probyn replied simply. 'Yes, sir.'

There seemed to be insufficient gratitude in his manner for the lieutenant. 'I hope you understand that this is a highly unusual occurrence, Private Kilmaster, and a great honour?'

'Oh yes indeed, sir!'

'Good!' After his sharp reminder Lieutenant Fitzroy became more affable. 'Now, the major fully appreciates that such sophistication is beyond the realms of your experience; he has therefore asked me to instruct you on the way to behave. I would not expect you to let the regiment down intentionally but of course there are social nuances of which you will be totally ignorant. Corporal Wedlock did you organize that tray of tea?'

'Yes sir, it's a-waiting!' Teeth set in a disapproving grid, Wedlock marched stiff-legged to the door.

Unsure what was expected of him, Probyn remained mute as the corporal summoned in a private with a tea tray bearing cups and saucers. It soon became evident that this was to be a rehearsal, with the lieutenant showing him the correct way to hold his cup and saucer and how to respond to any of his host's questions. Stunned by the unusual social occurrence, Probyn was quite glad of any tips, though in fact he had already been taught very well by his mother. What was most enjoyable about this, though, was the look on Wedlock's face as he was forced to stand there without benefit of cup whilst his minion took refreshment with the lieutenant. Why, he was almost foaming at the mouth.

After fifteen minutes or so, thankful that there had been no slurping of the tea, Lieutenant Fitzroy congratulated his protégé on having grasped this so quickly and without further ado told Kilmaster at what time to present himself outside the major's office on the morrow.

Probyn returned to his barrack room, answering his comrades' queries truthfully but with such nonchalance that he gave the impression he was fully accustomed to dining with gentry and, thus, was teased unmercifully for hours afterwards.

There was no such nonchalance the following afternoon. Seated with the major and lieutenant in the carriage that had been sent to collect them, he felt much more intimidated than at his rehearsal, and even more so upon ascending the wide stone staircase of the Georgian mansion, passing beyond its gracious portico with its spider's web fanlight, into massive gentrified rooms smelling of polish. And yet within moments the overwhelming hospitality of his host and hostess and their three maidenly daughters and two adolescent sons, all extremely courteous and friendly, had served to put him at ease.

'We were most upset to hear that your friend is indisposed and cannot join us.' Mrs O'Neil, an Irish version of his Aunt Kit but substantially smaller and quieter, directed her sympathies to Probyn now that her guests were seated in the drawing room. 'I did so wish to make amends for the terrible ordeal you both suffered. And how is the poor boy coping with his malady?'

Just beginning to relax, Probyn stiffened and looked to his superiors for assistance. The major jumped in smartly. 'Private Melody is recovering well, ma'am. We hope to have him back with us in a few weeks.'

'Bronchitis has such debilitating effects,' Mrs O'Neil showed genuine compassion. 'I do hope you will extend our good wishes to the young man.'

The major said he was sure Lieutenant Fitzroy would oblige.

'I will, ma'am,' smiled Fitzroy.

'Well now, shall we have tea?' A beaming Mrs O'Neil gestured for one of her daughters to ring for the maid who duly arrived with a companion, both laden with tasty-looking refreshments.

Whilst this was being served, the conversation was maintained by Mr O'Neil, a handsome, tweedy man with a red face and an avuncular manner, who asked Probyn if he enjoyed any sport.

'I play in the rugby team, sir.'

'Ah really? And have you enjoyed our local sport yet?' enquired his host.

'Mr O'Neil refers to hurling,' the major explained.

Probyn confessed to his ignorance but showed great interest and was given a short description of the game, Mr O'Neil proposing that Probyn and his fellow soldiers take it up and thereby enjoy a friendly match with the local team.

During tea, with Probyn conducting himself admirably, the younger O'Neils joined in the solicitation of Private Kilmaster, the boys seeking details of his abduction, which was quickly hushed up by their mother, the girls wanting to know if he had any sisters and what were their names. Despite the difference in status it was all very reminiscent of home, or at least of home in the old days, and not being of a shy nature, and their questions being in no way impertinent, he warmed towards his interrogators, even relaxing enough to entertain them with a joke.

At the end of the afternoon Probyn could honestly state that he had thoroughly enjoyed himself. Both his host and hostess had been genuinely warm and interested in all he had had to say, which had not been up to much at all, but had been delivered with honesty and politeness and his hosts had responded in kind. In no way had it been some artificial undertaking of appeasement as, prior to arrival, he had feared.

'Thank you for having me, sir, ma'am,' said Probyn, as he had been taught to by his mother and, making ready to leave with his superiors, decided a compliments would not be out of order. 'I hope you won't think me impertinent when I say that was the best chocolate cake I've ever tasted.'

Both Mr and Mrs O'Neil laughed at such simple gratitude. 'Oh, then you must take some with you, Private Kilmaster!' said his hostess and immediately instructed one of her daughters to wrap some cakes in a napkin and give them to their guest. 'You have a splendid chap there, Major,' complimented Mr O'Neil as the soldiers departed.

The major obviously agreed, lauding Kilmaster's performance as they made their return to barracks.

Lieutenant Fitzroy too was delighted that the youngster had behaved so impeccably. 'You're a sterling good fellow, Private Kilmaster!' he congratulated Probyn when they were back in his office and the major had gone. 'I knew you wouldn't let me down.'

Thriving on such compliment, Probyn returned warm reply. 'Thank you, sir, it was an honour.'

'Stand easy.' Fitzroy sat down.

'Thank you sir.' It was hard to sustain military bearing when holding onto a bundle of cakes. 'And may I say, sir, I really enjoyed myself.'

The lieutenant assumed a smile of admonishment which was not entirely without substance. 'Yes, I noticed the warmth of your behaviour towards the Misses O'Neil! I have to warn you that you must not expect anything to come of it.'

Probyn was most offended, all previous compliments annihilated by this needless remark. To him the girls were asexual, holding not the slightest allure save to remind him of his sisters. How could the lieutenant praise him in one breath and in the next damn him with such low regard?

The answer came, its tone shrewd. 'I'm fully aware of how fond you are of the ladies, Private Kilmaster, which was how you came to be in the mess that started all this, if my memory does not desert me.'

Subdued by this truism, Probyn could only answer, 'Yes, sir.' Trained not to show emotion, his annoyance remained deep within.

'Apart from that your conduct was beyond reproach.'

'Thank you, sir.' Expecting to be dismissed now, Probyn came to attention again.

But Lieutenant Fitzroy leaned back in his chair, seemingly in no rush to part company with his protégé. 'At ease, at ease. So, tell me, what does the army hold for Private Kilmaster?'

Preoccupied by the napkin full of cakes and a bladder that was filled to explosion point from copious tea at the O'Neils', Probyn looked bewildered.

'To what rank do you aspire?'

'Oh! I'd like to be sergeant-major, sir.'

'Then you'd better maintain an unblemished record,' advised Fitzroy. 'There are one or two men taking corporal's exam next week, why not join them?'

Forgetting all about his bladder, Probyn brightened. 'If you think I'm up to it, sir.'

'I'd hardly have made the suggestion if I did not.' Abruptly the lieutenant came out of his relaxed pose and looked at his watch. 'Now you'd better be running along, and once again, congratulations on this afternoon's behaviour. You're a credit to the platoon.'

His mood rejuvenated, Probyn snapped to attention,

performed an enthusiastic salute and thence departed, eager to establish himself on that first rung of the ladder.

Acting on the lieutenant's recommendation, Private Kilmaster was quick to add his name to those taking the corporal's exam. This done, it was back to a daily round of drill and musketry and marching, that brief spell of gentility a thing of the past, a lovely cameo to be brought out and looked at during those punishing hours, but never to be enjoyed again.

It was of no great importance. He was living the life he had chosen, a hard but rewarding life, and those outside the garrison were of little interest to him – although he had been pleasantly surprised, now that he was allowed out and about again, by the number of folk who had extended their apologies for what had happened to him, shopkeepers murmuring their regrets in that quiet Irish way of theirs, hoping it had not coloured his judgement of the people of Birr. And indeed it had not, far from it, for apart from that one incident, everyone he encountered was exceedingly kind and he had come to respect the majority for what they were: an hospitable and deeply religious people . . . if occasionally given to unpredictable violence.

Save for those fleeting encounters in the street with apologetic housewives, he stayed well away from the womenfolk. It was difficult sometimes, being without female company, but he had learned his lesson and would suppress his appetites for safer shores, preferring to focus all energy on his imminent improvement in rank.

He was to pass the exam quite effortlessly, and not wanting to appear boastful, kept it to himself for a few days before his roommates found out. Havron was miffed of course.

'Must be a bloody easy exam then,' he belittled Probyn's achievement.

'Why don't you take it then, big gob?' challenged Bumby, others adding their support for Kilmaster.

Finding himself a lone objector, Havron was forced to

recant, though did not go so far as to offer congratulations with the rest of the platoon, most of whom seemed genuinely pleased.

It was they who told Melody of Kilmaster's achievement when he finally came out of hospital after three weeks' duration, for Probyn had not spoken to him since his treacherous disclosure and showed no sign of wanting to do so now.

Mick extended a hesitant hand. 'Congratulations, Pa.'

Probyn's blue-grey eyes held him sternly.

The hand remained outstretched. 'I'm no longer contagious.'

'You're still a rat.' But Probyn finally breached the gap with a handshake and the rift was on its way to being healed.

'I'm sorry.' Mick hung his head. 'I never meant –'

'All right, all right.' Probyn swiftly dismissed the episode. 'So, what did they do to you, then?'

'Ye don't want to know!' But Mick told him anyway, horrifying him and others with his gruesome descriptions. 'Anyhow, I'm all cleared up now and that's the way 'tis going to stay. No more women for Michael. Now, tell me what this corporal's exam was like, for I might want to do it myself.'

There were sniggers from Queen and Bumby. 'You?'

'If your man here can do it so can I!' Mick viewed the promotion rather differently to his friend: as a means of escaping fatigues.

Aware that this was not an empty boast, for he knew from Melody's reading matter that he was brighter than might be construed from his foolish behaviour, Probyn decided there and then to go and apply for the post of corporal. It would not do for Melody to gain advancement before him. Telling Mick, 'I'll give you the details later, I've just got to visit the lat,' on this pretext he hurried from the room.

Having assumed that the paper qualification made his quest straightforward, he was not anticipating any difficulty when he approached Corporal Wedlock, and was therefore utterly stunned to receive a snub.

'Just 'cause you once quaffed tea with the major and them gentrified paddies, don't get too big for your boots,' sneered Wedlock. 'You'll have to get a few years in before they give you a stripe.'

Assuming he had been misunderstood, Probyn explained, 'But I passed the exam, Corp.'

Wedlock was unmoved. 'You can pass twenty exams and paint your arse blue but you're not up to being a corporal's snot rag.'

A flicker of panic. 'But Lieutenant Fitzroy told me –'

'And I'm telling you,' feathers fluffed, the bantam leaned towards him, glaring, 'that it's two years at least in the ranks. Now hop it!'

Furious and impotent at Wedlock's cavalier dictate, Probyn strode back to his barrack room trying to maintain his self-discipline. It would have been very easy to bang about and throw his kit all over the place but instead he sat down and immediately began to polish his boots, rubbing and buffing at the leather for all he was worth though it had no need of improvement, being already gleaming.

However, living so intimately for so many months, everyone recognized this needless polishing.

'Oh dear, somebody's upset him,' observed Bumby. 'What's up, Pa?'

'Nothing!' Probyn maintained his grim-faced task, his arm working like a beam engine. Then abruptly he stopped. 'If you must know I've just been refused my stripes and told I have to wait two flaming years!'

Mick sympathized, but immediately ruined it with a note of self-interest. 'Jesus, I'm glad ye told me before I took the exam. No point wasting me time now.'

'Oh well, it did some good then!' Probyn launched into another bout of polishing.

Rook emerged from his usual taciturn state to enquire, 'Who did you ask?'

'Wedlock.' A sweat was forming on Probyn's brow.

Rook gave a quiet knowing smile. 'Oh well then . . .'

'Sure, you're not going to take Beelzebub's word are ye?' demanded Mick. 'Go over his head.'

With others exhorting him to do likewise, Probyn abruptly broke off his polishing and marched off to consult Sergeant Faulkner. Unfortunately, the answer was not reassuring: he would indeed have to gain experience in the ranks before promotion.

Infuriated at yet another petty rule, he returned to convey the news that Wedlock had spoken the truth.

'Aye, but I'll wager he took great pleasure in telling you,' said Bumby.

A miserable Probyn agreed. After the month had opened with such promise, it was such a massive disappointment.

His hopes pinned on gaining eminence in another sphere, Probyn was to face further setback later in the summer. Despite all his best efforts it was Havron who emerged as marksman of the company. Of all the people it could have been! Still, not for Probyn the babyish antics that Havron might have employed had the tables been turned. Conjuring magnanimity, he was the first to shake his rival's hand after the competition, turning a deaf ear to the champion's conceited boast that he had been bound to win, and treating such insult with a smiling shrug. It was hard, though, to remain cheerful in the face of such defeat, and there was a barb in his sunny response to those who insisted on reminding him throughout the afternoon of Havron's superiority. 'Yes, but can you see your face in his boots?'

There was some small consolation to be had, though, for upon return to barracks he found a parcel from Aunt Kit. As this was the first response he had had to his letter, he ripped it open eagerly, seizing upon the note inside. After the first line he gave a sigh of relief. Her delay in writing back was not, as he had supposed, because his aunt was still angry with him, but that she had been ill. Upon reading this he felt another twinge of guilt at revealing her intimate secret to Melody who had broadcast it to less sensitive beings. Nevertheless his eyes could not help straying to the parcel that accompanied the letter and it was not long before his curiosity got the better of him.

Inside the cardboard box was a selection of food and a card that invited him to enjoy his birthday. A murmur of revelation emerged from his lips. He had completely forgotten until now. 'Eh, I've got a birthday coming up!'

Ingham and Bumby were quick to investigate the hamper. 'We'll be having a party then!'

'Keep your grubby hands off!' Probyn snatched it back protectively, hugging it to his chest as others swooped like vultures.

Mick was too well-mannered to join in the scrimmage but asked plaintively, 'You're not going to sit there and eat it all yourself?'

'I might throw you a crumb after I've taken me fill.' Probyn remained aloof for a while, then made great play of relenting. 'Oh go on then! You might as well share it, I'll never get round to eating all that and it'll only go off.'

'His generosity knows no bounds!' chaffed Mick.

There was much high spirits as Probyn doled out the contents, fighting to keep his favourite titbits.

'How old are you now then, Pa?' asked one of the partici- pants, munching.

Remembering he was supposed to be eighteen already, Probyn had no wish to advertise his age and, with his mouth full of pie, the reply he gave was incoherent. Nor did he give a true answer to the next question.

'Who sent you the grub?'

'Lord Salisbury,' came his quip.

Everyone was instantly impressed, Ingham displaying the contents of his mouth. 'How come you know royalty?'

Probyn laughed, then saw that most of them took him literally. With Uncle Owen heavily involved in the union and Aunt Kit once romantically linked with a cabinet minister, the subject of politics was often discussed in his house, in one form or another. But it seemed that few here had even heard this name. 'He's the Prime Minister, you daft clot!'

'You know the Prime Minister?'

'I was joking! It's just a relative who sent it.' He did not enlarge, for any mention of Kit might spark comment about her dubious past and he would then have to defend her. Silently though, he thanked his aunt for this homely reminder; it was nice to know she had forgiven him.

The taste of crumbling pastry generated childhood memories and, inevitably, thoughts of his father. One of them must make an effort to build bridges. The concept that it might have to be him was rather daunting, but the trials he had faced in army life had made him resilient. He decided there and then that on his next furlough he would visit Ralph Royd. It was a pity he would have no stripe to mark his achievements, nor even the award for best shot in the company. It would have been helpful to have something to make his father proud of him.

The opportunity to build bridges with his father did not come until Christmas and by that time he had changed his mind again. The prospect of seven days' leave seemed not so thrilling when one would be going home empty-handed. Robbed of the chance to impress, there seemed little point in subjecting himself to confrontation. Should he simply go directly to Aunt Kit's where he would be assured of a welcome? Whatever the venue he would be going there alone, for Mick had decided to look up his relatives in Galway and even those without Irish connections had plumped to spend their entire holiday in Dublin rather than waste it in travelling.

Untrammelled by kit and rifle which had been left behind in the sergeants' storeroom, he journeyed with his pals as far as the Soldiers' Home opposite the gates of Phoenix Park, he himself enjoying only one night there before going to catch a boat to Liverpool the next day.

Waiting to board, the young soldier's eyes flitted about the quay, singling out the female form. Appetites which had been suppressed now began to fire anew. It had been the best part of a year since his sexual enlightenment, and hardly a day had gone by when he had not been obsessed by the thought of experiencing it again. He must have it, he must or he would explode, was almost exploding now at the mere thought. But, presented with only wide-eyed innocents, nuns and schoolgirls, matrons and black-shawled crones, his frustration was to continue and he urged himself to try and think of other issues. Once embarked there was no difficulty in doing this, for the crossing was much rougher today and, at the mercy of grey waves, he was soon unable to think of anything except his own nausea.

On reaching Liverpool he was still undecided whether to go straight to Aunt Kit's but, forced to make a choice of which train to catch or dither forever on the platform, he reverted to his original plan of making peace with his father. First though, he would test the lay of the land with his sisters, for their welcome, or lack of it, would be good indication of what to expect at Ralph Royd.

His favourite, Meredith, lived in Huddersfield which would mean breaking his journey, so, as most of the others lived within walking distance of Pontefract and this was on a direct route from Liverpool, he decided that the easiest option was to catch a train there. It would also mean he could call in at the depot and say hello.

With half an hour to wait for the train he began to think about sex again, eyes constantly roving over breasts and buttocks. In mid-thought he tensed. A likely candidate had wandered into range. She was hard-faced, with no redeeming features, but this was the only type of girl who would do as he craved. Scrotum tightening, he dallied for a moment to watch her, remembering Melody's infection. The thought terrified him but was eventually overthrown by frustration and, catching the girl's eye, he was soon heading off in quest of privacy.

She appeared to know where she was going so he allowed her to lead. Smiling, she beckoned him into a dim recess behind some pipes. He wasted no time but hoisted her dress and began to emulate the activity he had enjoyed with the girl in York. It was only as he pulled away to unbutton his trousers that he sensed her lack of enthusiasm, and glanced into her face. Her eyes were full of tears.

'Can't you even be bothered to kiss me?' Despite the hardness of her face and voice, it was apparent she was deeply hurt.

Blood still pounding for sexual gratification, he blurted, 'I'm sorry I've got a train to catch.'

'Oh, thanks!' Even more tearful, she pushed him away. 'What do you think I am?'

He didn't know how to answer, his basic urges fast being overwhelmed by shame.

'I'm not one of them, I don't take money!'

He tried to sound apologetic. 'I didn't think you were!'

'No, you're the sort who'd want it for nothing!'

Afraid someone would hear the altercation and come to investigate Probyn hurriedly re-buttoned his trousers, fumbling in panic. 'I'm sorry I didn't mean –'

'And even if I was a pro they're human beings you know!'

'I know, I'm sorry!' Ridden with guilt he tried to extract himself. 'I'm really sorry!' And, shamefaced, he hurried back to the platform, brushing incriminating cobwebs from his tunic and praying that the train would be there.

During his long, bleak journey over the Pennines he was to see those tears bulge from her eyes again and again. What a rat he was! The sheer thought of it caused him to blush. He had been so intent on slaking his appetite that he hadn't even bothered to ask her name. For the first time in his life he compelled himself to imagine his sisters as sexual beings – a horrible image but a necessary one. What if someone had treated Merry or Alice as simply objects of lust? He would be the first to rail against such caddishness yet he had been about to use that poor girl as if she were less than human. Just because one hard-faced trollop in York had given her favours freely he should not assume that because this one was of similar visage she would perform in a like manner. Women were individuals, just like men, only much more difficult to understand. He sighed. It was another lesson well learnt, and gave him much to ponder during his rattling journey.

Hours later when he reached Pontefract he was very subdued, alternately berating himself for his cavalier attitude whilst still heavily burdened by sexual frustration. He was also in desperate need of refreshment. The latter he acquired at the depot canteen, though he was not to tarry here long for it was mostly filled with new faces, youngsters in their first months of training, who seemed incredibly boyish, and as he had no wish to protract a reunion with his former drill instructors he was soon on his way again. His departure coincided with the arrival of a dray wagon conveying barrels of Christmas ale for the garrison which raised a lusty cheer from those within. Probyn hoped there would be similar welcome at his sister's house.

Wyn had never been his favourite sibling, he found her particularly selfish, but she lived closest to the barracks and so it was to her abode he went first.

Upon hearing the knock, Wyn halted the conversation with her sister Rhoda who had also come to visit and glanced out of the window, but immediately sprang away. 'Oh my goodness it's our Probe, and he's in uniform!'

Sharing her annoyance, Rhoda gestured for Wyn to return to her chair. 'Pretend you're not in!'

Ignoring a second knock, Wyn continued to peep from behind the curtains, complaining, 'Why doesn't he just go! I don't want the neighbours coming out to ask who he is. I've told them our brother's a minister.'

Outside, Probyn stepped back from the door and glanced at the window. Catching a movement beyond the pristine lace he went to investigate, thrusting his nose to the pane.

Wyn jumped back and flattened herself against the flowered wallpaper as her brother's eyes tried to pierce the lace barrier. Rhoda leapt behind a red moquette armchair to crouch grim and unmoving whilst Probyn's outline blocked out the light. When his shadow was removed each gave an expression of relief, but this was premature for, creeping back to the window, Wyn uttered a squeak as she saw her brother raise the knocker of the house next door. 'Oh, the embarrassment of it!'

Tormented by the sight of a uniformed Probyn undergoing conversation with her neighbour, and awaiting his inevitable return to knock again, both Wyn and Rhoda were extremely relieved to see him instead turn smartly and make his way back down the street.

Certain that he had been snubbed, Probyn felt angry and upset. If this treatment were typical of what he could expect from the rest of the family then there seemed little point wasting any more of his furlough by trailing from house to house. Christmas Eve was already looming, two days after that and he would have to be making his way back to Ireland; only an idiot would not spend it where he was assured of a welcome. Hence he returned immediately to the station and caught the next train to York.

Yet throughout the journey he remained troubled. Why had his sister pretended not to be in when he was certain he had seen her? Surely she could not be so ashamed of him?

Normally, an encounter with Aunt Kit would make things instantly brighter, but today upon their meeting at the gate he felt that her greeting was superficial. Behind her smiling exterior there was an emptiness to her eye. She had also put on a great deal of weight in the months since he had seen her. Naturally, he made no comment on either point as his Aunt Gwen would doubtless have done, but merely told her how good it was to be back amongst his own kind.

'It's nice to have you, lad.'

At such lacklustre reply, Probyn feared that she had not

really forgiven him at all for the episode with Melody and thought perhaps that he should reiterate his original written apology.

'I'm sorry, Aunt, for not telling you about Melody . . .'

This seemed to jerk Kit out of her trance. 'Oh, we've forgotten all about that!' The poor lad, how could she tell him of her heartache at losing yet another baby? Putting her arm around his shoulder in a conspiratorial manner she affected subterfuge. 'I'm just keeping me eye out for Uncle Worthy, he's over in the shed plucking geese and he'll have us both roped in if we aren't careful. I'm sure that's not what you'd choose to do on your Christmas leave.'

Reassured, Probyn smilingly said he would like to help and followed her towards the house. 'It's good just to be back in Yorkshire. You'll be glad to learn I'm on me own this time, no bog-trotters in tow.'

Any further such comment was forestalled by Kit who puckered up her mouth to hiss a warning *shush*, at the same time giving a confidential tilt of her head towards the cottage where Probyn now saw a female figure waiting just inside the doorway. Glancing at his aunt he read upon her lips the silently uttered information: *Catholic*.

Changing the subject completely, Probyn bent swiftly to the little boy who toddled up the path to meet him. 'By, look at our Toby, he's grown twelve inches since last I saw him!' And, picking up the child, he followed his aunt who was now handing over payment.

'Thank you very much, Mrs O'Brien, I'll see you again next week!' A business-like smile accompanied Kit's words.

Donating a beaming nod in return, the Irish woman pocketed the money and, with another smile for Probyn and Toby, consequently left.

'I'm sorry about jumping down your throat,' Kit guiltily explained to her nephew when Mrs O'Brien was out of earshot. 'I didn't want you saying something you might be embarrassed about. Not to mention losing my washerwoman.'

Intrigued at this apparent change of heart over the employment of a breed so formerly despised, Probyn laughed and asked for an explanation.

Picking Toby up, his sturdy little thighs straddling her hip, Kit retained her somewhat guilty expression. 'Well, when I got your letter it made me think long and hard: if Irish lads are prepared to risk their lives to defend this country alongside my nephew who am I to tar them all with the same brush?'

Probyn wondered what his aunt would say were he to tell her of his abduction by Fenians, but he had no intention of marring her new-found tolerance.

Kit set a wriggling Toby on his feet. 'I'm not saying I approve of their religion mind, but they can't all be bad. So, when my usual washerwoman had to leave and recommended Mrs O'Brien I decided to give her a chance. She's nothing like the Irish minx I had in London. Your father would no doubt see me as mad to even let one of them over the threshold, but she gets my linen sparkling and that's good enough for me.'

'Does me father have a good word for anybody?' sighed Probyn, only half joking.

Kit gave an empty laugh. 'Now you come to mention it, I'm not sure he does.'

'Certainly not for me.' Probyn gave a sad smile. 'But then he isn't alone in that.'

Kit echoed his sigh. 'Eh dear, sounds as if you need a cup of tea.' Ordering him to sit down, she began to clatter cups into saucers then opened a tin. 'Here, you can be the first to sample this Christmas cake. Away then, tell me what's amiss.'

Probyn accepted a wedge of cake and broke off a crumb for Toby. 'I thought I'd visit our Wyn first, seeing as she's a bit closer to the depot than you, but she wouldn't come to the door.'

'She might not have been in.'

'She might not but somebody was.' Probyn was terse. 'I saw t'curtain move, and her neighbour told me she'd seen a visitor arrive not long before I did so she must have been there.' Sounding deeply insulted, he added, 'Well, it's the last time I bother with her.' He bit into the slab of cake. 'By this is tasty, Aunt. Oh, thanks for the hamper by the way! It went down a treat. I were king for a week with the lads.'

Kit said she was glad. 'Would you like some Wensleydale with that?'

'Aye grand. Sit still, I'll get it!' Familiar with Kit's pantry, Probyn went directly there and cut himself a thick wad of cheese, placing it with reverence atop his cake and consuming the two with relish. Toby sat at his feet, waiting to receive the occasional titbit.

After a brief interval, the conversation returned to Wyn's underhanded treatment of him. Probyn had never shown much interest in his distant relatives before, but now, being ostracised by his father and sisters, to have friendly kin suddenly assumed great importance. He knew that his maternal grandparents lived in Wales, but what of Father's kinfolk? 'Tell me, Aunt,' he said as he licked the last crumb of cake from his lips, and raised his cup, 'do we have any other relations anywhere?'

'Haven't you got enough of them badgering you without wanting to find more?' joked Kit. Then after a mouthful of tea she spoke seriously, 'Oh, I believe there are some folk in Gloucester but I've never met them myself.' After a pensive moment, she sighed. 'Eh dear, what a family, and none of them have cause to throw the first stone, certainly not your father when he did the self same thing. I don't mean ran off to the army but ran off to get wed. I don't recall any details, I was too young, although I do remember vividly the row when he said he intended to marry your mother. A right ding-dong of an argument it was.' She had issued it quite matter-of-factly but saw by her nephew's startled expression that this required further explanation. 'Eh, I'm sorry, lad. I know what it's like being the youngest in the family, nobody tells you anything, they all assume you just know, but you must have heard that your dad brought us all up, surely?'

Probyn knew vaguely that his father had raised his siblings, but that had all been in the distant past by the time he'd been born, he'd never spared it much thought. Still overwhelmed that his father had even entertained such romantic thoughts of elopement, it was all he could do to issue a dumb nod.

'Well, that was because our own parents died, just a few days after Monty was married.' Kit told him briefly of her parents' catastrophic death. 'Luckily they'd forgiven him and came to the wedding after all.'

'How tragic,' breathed Probyn, then curiosity overlapped his concern. 'Why didn't they want him to get married, Aunt?'

'Oh, I don't really know.' Gwen had told Kit that their mother had not been pleased by Monty's choice of a bride, but this was not something one could say to his son. 'As I said, I was too young. I think your father's always been stubborn. Didn't get on with his father either.' She echoed Probyn's astounded laugh. 'Yes, I know, it's rich, the way he's behaving towards you, isn't it?' Nevertheless, she sought to give Monty his due. 'I can't fault him in the way he raised us, though. It must have been an almighty struggle. He wasn't much older than you are now, and as I said newly wed, but he took us all in and brought us up as his own, he and your mother. The poor little things, when I look back and see how much I took for granted, it must've been dreadful for them, not much more than children themselves. Then the babies started being born, one almost every year, your mother and father never stood a chance.'

Probyn felt a deeper understanding now. Equipped with the extent of his parents' sacrifice he wanted to know more, and he wanted his father to be the one to tell him.

'You know,' his blue-grey eyes beheld her informatively over his raised cup, 'I'd go and see him if I thought he'd open the door to me.'

Kit smiled broadly. The past half an hour with her favourite nephew had acted as a tonic and diverted her mind from her own sadness. 'He'll open it if he sees two battering rams on either side of you. I were just saying to your Uncle Worthy last night we should pay our Monty a visit over Christmas. The trip'll do me good. If we can get somebody to look after the beasts we'll go tomorrow shall we?'

Everything in the village seemed as it was when he had left, yet somehow it felt completely different. The pit stood grim and quiet for the Christmas holiday. Wassailers travelled through the streets, heralding the coming of Christ as they had done since his childhood. Old neighbours waved to him and Kit and Worthy as they passed on their cart. Someone was cleaning bird droppings off a window pane and Aunt Kit called to her, 'You can come and do mine when you've finished!' Yes, everything and everyone was the same. It was he who was different. He didn't fit in here any more.

'Nervous?' smiled Kit as he helped her and Toby down from the cart, Worthy tethering the mare and fitting her nosebag.

Unable to deny it, Probyn merely nodded and took his bag of belongings from the cart. His aunt had insisted he fetch it though he doubted he would be staying long enough to need anything in it. Robbed for a moment of his soldierly confidence, he allowed Kit and Worthy to go down the path ahead of him, and waited apprehensively for the door to open.

His father was obviously taken aback to see him. For one awful moment Probyn thought he was going to be spurned again. Then Monty stepped aside and directed all the guests to come in.

'Look who we've brought with us!' Kit smiled at Ann, her eyes holding a plea for assistance.

Without hesitation, the neat dark-haired woman drew her stepson into the warmth. 'How lovely to see you, Probe, welcome home! Let me take your hats and coats, every-body!'

Probyn snatched off his glengarry and handed it to his

stepmother who examined the badge on it briefly. 'You're looking well, Probe.'

Kit disagreed. 'I've told him he needs fattening up. There's more meat on our Toby here.'

Ann laughed. 'Aw, but he still looks well, doesn't he, Father?'

Probyn threw an awkward smile at Monty who nodded amiably and told them all, 'Sit yourselves down then.'

Encouraged, Probyn waited for everyone else to seat themselves first and was even more encouraged at being directed to one of the better chairs by his father, but then perversely he realized the significance of this. He was being treated not like a member of the family but as a guest.

A smiling Ann investigated the contents of the teapot. 'I think this is stewed, I'll mash some more. You're stopping for your teas?'

All said they would if it was no trouble. 'It's no trouble,' smiled Ann. 'Good to see you back on your feet, Kit. How are you feeling now?'

Kit replied that she was much better and, with that, all reference to her miscarriage was ended.

It was all surprisingly pleasant, if a little stilted, and Probyn considered it fortunate that Toby was here to draw attention away from him, everyone smiling at the little boy's antics. But eventually there came a need to widen the discourse. For want of anything else to say Monty talked about the pit, but spoke as if to a stranger who had no knowledge of its workings. Whilst glad to be included in the dialogue, Probyn couldn't help thinking how peculiar it was that he felt more ill-at-ease in this his own home than he'd been at the grand O'Neil residence, and he was grateful to Aunt Kit for filling the silences.

After tea, though, Kit and Worthy made ready to depart, saying they must call on Owen before returning to York. 'But you don't have to come, Probe,' Kit told him. 'We can pick you up on the way back.'

Probyn became uncomfortable again, and glanced at his father.

'Don't have to rush off,' Monty told him calmly. 'Unless you want to.'

'Oh no, I'll stay then!' Probyn was quick to respond. 'What time shall I be at the end of the lane, Aunt Kit?'

But Monty answered first. 'Stay overnight, longer if you like. Your old bed's still there.'

This precipitated a quandary for his son. 'I'll have to start making my way back to Ireland on Boxing Day. The holiday seems over before it's begun what with all that distance to travel. I only arrived up here yesterday – but I'd like to stay tonight,' came the hasty addition. 'Thank you.'

Once Kit and Worthy and their little boy had gone it was much more difficult. How did one begin to mend such a breach?

His father appeared to feel as lost, judging by the needless question. 'They give you time off for Christmas then?'

'Yes, seven days.'

'Seven days eh?'

'I would have come sooner but –' Probyn shrugged uncomfortably.

'Don't matter, we're pleased to have you any time, aren't we, Mother?'

Probyn looked grateful. Then racked his brain for something else to say. 'Will the girls be coming to visit?'

Monty nodded. 'We had Wyn and Rhoda yesterday, Merry's coming tomorrow and Ethel on Boxing Day.'

'I went to call on Wyn myself yesterday,' revealed Probyn. 'But she didn't appear to be in.' Catching the look that passed between his father and stepmother he knew he had been right and his annoyance with his sister returned, especially in the knowledge that her visitor must have been Rhoda.

'No, she was here most of the day,' nodded Ann. 'What a pity you didn't come here first.'

In the awkward hiatus that followed she rose and started to

move around the room, collecting various items. 'Well, don't mind me, I'm just going to get things ready for morning, then later I'll make us all some cocoa. I know it's a bit early yet but would you like a hot-water bottle in your bed, Probe?'

He burst into genuine laughter. 'I'd forgotten there were such things. Yes please!'

Smiling, she began to organize her kitchen for the Christmas onslaught, peeling and slicing and mixing, filling the room with pungent aromas, whilst the two males sat one on either side of the hearth staring into the fire, discussing everything save that which was important.

Towards eight o'clock, when the scent of cocoa was added to that of sage and onion, Ann said she would take her mug up to bed. 'I'm just a bit tired. Don't feel you have to rush, Monty, there's no work tomorrow, you must have lots to chat about with Probe.'

But they were to be even less talkative in her absence. Father and son sat for a long time gazing into the embers before a relevant comment was finally issued.

'I'm sorry I left the way I did,' murmured Probyn.

Eyes still on the fire, his father simply nodded, then reached for a box of Pomfret cakes. 'Here, have one o' these.'

'Thank you.' Probyn delved into the box. 'Oh sorry, I've got two by mistake.' When his father waved for him to keep both he peeled the liquorice discs apart and put one into his mouth. Then, chewing, he stared at the other black disc in his hand, studying the castle imprinted upon it. 'Aunty Kit's been telling me a bit about how you eloped with Mother.'

That had the effect of injecting some life into the discourse. 'Did she indeed?' Monty tossed a Pomfret cake into his mouth and chewed testily. 'What else of my private life has she been airing to all and sundry?'

'Oh, nothing untoward! She was just explaining to me how you had to raise all your sisters and Uncle Owen when you were newly married. I never really knew.'

'There's a lot you don't know.'

Probyn's nod conveyed admittance. 'It must've been difficult.'

''Tweren't easy.' Monty had never spoken to his son on an intimate level. It was no different now. 'But then I'm just the same as anyone else in that situation.' He was reluctant to depict himself a saint.

Even so, Probyn had gained a new admiration for him. 'I couldn't have done it.'

'You would if you had to,' replied Monty.

Grateful for this note of faith, Probyn put the second liquorice disc into his mouth, waiting till it was gone before speaking in his own defence. 'You know, they're not all riff-raff, Father – soldiers I mean.'

'Not now they've had an injection of good stock.' It was the nearest Monty would come to a compliment. 'Let's hope they don't pollute your decent upbringing . . . still, they don't seem to have done that so far.'

Probyn decided it was safe enough to climb down from his defensive position. 'Well, I grant you there are a few who I wouldn't dream of bringing home, but then there are in any walk of life, and if I had to choose who'd fight beside me in a war and protect my kin and other people's kin I wouldn't change any of them. They're good lads.'

Monty simply shrugged and nodded in a bluff kind of way as he handed his son another Pomfret cake, but Probyn sensed that an understanding had been forged between them.

With the absence of recrimination, he felt at liberty to fill the next half an hour with details of his accomplishments. When he went to bed it was in a much happier mood than he could ever have expected.

Whilst there were not the boisterous games he might have enjoyed at Aunt Kit's, Probyn thoroughly enjoyed Christmas at Ralph Royd. The relaxation of his father's iron ruling, the feasting, the laughter, Meredith's obvious delight at seeing her brother and the fact that she had totally forgiven him, all made for a wonderful holiday.

How sad, then, that other relatives could not be so forgiving. On Boxing Day, faced with the persistent coolness of his eldest sister Ethel, Probyn decided to leave immediately after lunch, saying he would put up at the depot in order to catch the first available train tomorrow to Liverpool. The thought crossed his mind that he should make a financial contribution to cover his stay, but he decided against it; it might cause offence and demolish the still-wet cement on the bridge he had managed to erect. And, as uplifting as it had been to make up with his father, there would always be the feeling that he did not fit in here any more, the impression that he was only a guest; he had no wish to endorse that by handing over money.

Valise on his back, he was heading down the path when his father hailed him and came hurrying up with a box of Pomfret cakes. 'Here! Put these in your bag to eat on the train.'

'Nay, I don't want to pinch your favourite goodies!'

'Go arn!' A hint of old Somerset. 'They'll only rot my teeth.'

Thanking his father, a grinning Probyn allowed the other to shove the box into his valise, then continued his departure, the older man accompanying him to the gate, where both stopped and faced each other.

Monty extended a hand. 'Well, it was good to see you, Probe.'

'You too, Father.' Probyn returned the handshake warmly.

'Come again, won't you?'

'I will.' With a gesture resembling a salute, Probyn marched away.

8

The battalion had been in Ireland for a year and, after their arduous training, Probyn and his friends were now competent for war – had there been one, came his bored complaint. It was good that there had been no more dangerous incidents between soldiers and locals but with nothing else happening either, save for the occasional dance or garden fête, he began to despair of ever setting sight on a foreign foe. Every day, month after month he had assiduously studied Battalion Orders for information on what was likely to be taking place, hoping for any allusion to foreign service. Until recently, all that had ever been referred to were changes in rations and what items must be carried in his pack. Now, suddenly, on this bright April morning in 1892 he was presented with a list of those being drafted to the 2nd Battalion for foreign service, and to his overwhelming joy he saw his name upon it. He was going to South Africa!

Eagerly scanning the list for information on his companions, he hared off to let them know, all returning to gather round the list for confirmation of the news, and breaking into loud whoops of excitement.

There was much to be discussed then. Lieutenant Fitzroy, lately promoted captain, had also been posted to the 2nd Battalion. Probyn was glad of this continued association, not from any spurious assumption of friendship but because under Fitzroy, who liked him, there was a chance to further his own career. A not so cheery piece of information was that they were to remain encumbered by Wedlock who, having failed his sergeant's course, was even more malevolent of late. Melody might claim to be upset but, Probyn said, it was doubly disappointing for him who had hoped that the corporal's promotion would leave a vacancy.

Nevertheless, the bestowal of embarkation leave was reason enough to put the smile back on one's face. Given fourteen days, Probyn, Mick and their comrades spurted off to Dublin where they bided for a few days at the Soldiers' Home, Probyn remarking upon hearing the roar of the lions at the zoo in Phoenix Park that they would soon be witnessing this noise in the wild!

Unfortunately, their visit coinciding with Easter, they were to regret that they had not escaped Dublin earlier, for, trapped here on Good Friday amid a surge of religious fervour, the only activity on the streets being a performance of the Stations of the Cross and a blaring megaphone telling the crowds they would burn in hell, the next few hours proved acutely depressing.

Finally underway and arrived in England, Probyn said goodbye to the others and went first to York and Aunt Kit's where he felt most at home and where he spent a week, helping with the agricultural work. Following this he passed a few days at Meredith's in Huddersfield, using the latter part of his furlough for a brief stay at Ralph Royd.

His father appeared happy to see him when he arrived that evening, though relations between them were initially as stilted as on the previous occasion, Monty covering his awkwardness by launching into a diatribe about the impending strike. Things were looking pretty grim he told his son, the boom was over and the price of coal was falling. 'And we all know who'll bear the brunt of it don't we? Still you haven't come here to be bored with all that, you've probably read about it in the newspaper.'

'No, I don't get much time to read a paper.' Thinking that this made it sound as if his father had all the time in the world, Probyn added hurriedly, 'Not that I'd get the truth if I did!'

His father heartily agreed. 'No, it's always the miners to blame, as far as those editors are concerned.'

Having been affected by industrial violence in the past, the young soldier looked concerned. 'D'you think it'll be as bad as 'eighty-five?'

Monty shrugged. 'I pray not. We're in a lot stronger position these days, the masters can't push us around as much as they used to. The Federation's ordered a stop week so stocks can be cleared and they can hold the prices steady.'

Probyn knew when his father spoke of the Federation he referred to Uncle Owen but would never mention him by name. 'Well, at least if there is a strike it won't affect you so badly, this not being a colliery house.'

A sharp exclamation. 'They can't evict us but we got to eat!' At the look from his wife Monty bit his tongue.

The months of military training, the ability to withstand beastings like a man, all were suddenly expunged by the schoolboy blush. 'I meant to say last time I was here, if you want me to send money home –'

'You're not living here now.' Monty felt guilty the moment he had said it, especially under his wife's reproachful moue. 'What I mean is, son, there's little sense in you sending us money when you get no benefit.'

'I hardly need to spend anything, in fact I've opened a bank account. I'd like to help.' Probyn hoped his father would not prolong this debate.

But Monty had no wish to humiliate his son. 'Thank you, Probe, I shall bear that in mind if there is a strike.'

Grateful for this response, Probyn told his father and stepmother that they must write to him the moment there was any cause for alarm. 'Do act quickly 'cause I don't know how long it takes a letter to get to South Africa.'

'Africa!' Monty and Ann smiled at each other over this joint exclamation.

'Oh, didn't I mention I'm going next week?'

'*No*, Probe, you didn't!' Ann gave him a gentle cuff as she passed on her way to put the kettle on. 'And you've left it till bedtime to tell us, we'll never sleep for excitement!'

Probyn's own excitement was to make even this short stay at Ralph Royd a tedious, drawn out affair, eager as he was for foreign climes. Once all the information had been exchanged there was little else to do through the day apart from tending the family allotment while Monty was at work, and on an evening accompanying his father to bible class. But any such boredom was overruled by guilt that he had stopped an entire week at Kit's, and the thought that he might not see his father again for a long time compelled him to remain to the end.

On the day of his departure he rose at four and breakfasted with his parents. Then, saying goodbye to his stepmother, he accompanied Monty to the highway, the thud of his soldier's boots added to the noise of miners' clogs. Through the dinge anonymous shapes made their way to the pit. Glad that he was no longer amongst them, Probyn came to a halt at the end of Pit Lane and turned to issue a final note.

'Well, thank you for having me.'

'Our pleasure.' Monty seemed quite cheery for such an early hour. 'You're sure you've remembered to pack everything?'

'Certain.' Probyn held out his hand. 'Goodbye, Father.'

'Goodbye, son. Mind those black savages now, won't you? Don't go getting yourself killed.'

'I'll try not to.' With a last firm grip he severed the handshake with his father, hefted his bag and walked away.

Monty's eyes followed him nostalgically for a second, his mind awhirl with things unsaid. Then he turned aside and went to work.

Once returned to Crinkle there was a hectic few days ahead, packing up and saying goodbye to friends made during the year. Probyn had not anticipated feeling anything other than relief at leaving Ireland, but on the final evening at a packed village pub he was surprised to experience a twinge of emotion as a singer came amongst them, her ballad exhorting them to return to Erin, a sentiment that appeared genuinely expressed. It was all he could do to hold back the tears.

Until Rook put things into perspective, coming up with one of the snippets of information for which he had become known. 'It's not us they're sad to see the back of but our cash. I've heard the presence of a battalion can mean as much as sixty thousand quid a year to a town.'

Yet even recalling this cynical observation the next morning as he marched to the railway station behind the band, Probyn could not bring himself to believe that all those friendly faces who lined the route to wave him off had only his monetary value at heart. With few exceptions he had come to like the people of Birr and it was not without a tinge of sadness that he steamed away for more exotic shores.

During the temporary stop in England he and his pals were kitted out for Africa, had a medical inspection and were passed fit. All hale, they entrained for the docks and boarded a troop ship on which were drafts from other regiments, promising new friends and enjoyable competition in the weeks that would be spent on board.

Those first hours were sheer bedlam as attempts were made to bring organization to the ship. Probyn and his comrades were directed to their messes and hammock places and ordered to change into sea kit – blue serge jacket and trousers, blue jersey and stocking cap. When the ship sailed the following day all land clothing had been packed and stored and the men were detailed for various duties: ash parties, swabbers, mess orderlies, pickets. Probyn found himself posted sentry over one of two fresh water taps which were allowed to be used twice daily; hardly the role he had imagined for himself, but then, waste of water was a serious crime.

Initially the food was quite good, fresh meat being served on the first couple of days. But this happy state was soon to regress into the diet he had suffered as a raw recruit, soup as thin as dishwater, dry bread and porridge, and consequently there was endless queuing at the canteen. However, few were in a state to eat very much as the ship crossed the Bay of Biscay where the seas were incredibly rough, waves sweeping over the bulwarks drenching everyone and everything. Probyn had suffered this awful feeling before on his voyage with Kit to Spain, but had forgotten how bad it could be. Despite the rivalry between army and navy, at this moment he held nothing but admiration for those who endured such a life on the waves. Wet and miserable, wanting to vomit, he careened about the deck, trying to maintain his position. A passing sailor cheerfully advised him to put a cake of tobacco in his mouth and that would ease the nausea, but imagining this to be a trick he declined and thus continued to suffer.

During this squall, Melody fell badly and damaged his back, hence whilst Probyn and others slithered about the decks, attempting to stay upright and hang onto the meagre rations in their bellies, Mick was tucked up in the sick bay, somehow managing to remain there until the ship had left the Bay of Biscay and the decks were once again dry. As if this were not great enough cause for resentment, the news that he had acquired a kooshi job made him even more unpopular. By some quirk the ship's steward had taken a shine to him and asked for his assistance in selling biscuits, cheese and tinned goods in the canteen; only by promising to show favour did he escape his friends' wrath.

Boredom became the order of the day, especially if one were on guard duty with nothing more to do than watch the horizon go up and down for hours on end. Deeply grateful at being relieved after one such vigil, Probyn loped stiff and aching to the latrine in the hope of some blessed relief from his constipation caused by a poor diet and irregular hours. Had he been at home his stepmother would have been ready with the rhubarb and liquorice powder but there was none so affectionate here.

Sighing, he unbuttoned his trousers and prepared for a long sitting. The stench here was abominable and he probably wouldn't be able to escape it for ages. He had tried smoking a pipe to mask the foul odour but it had only made him bilious and so he was compelled to merely sit and think; thoughts of home, of his father and Aunt Kit and his sisters, of what lay ahead in South Africa, whether he would be required to fight, and how it would feel to kill a man.

A bugle percolated his reverie. There was an instant of confusion as it sounded Commence Fire, but soon he was to relax again; bugle calls had different meanings on board ship and this one was only instructing the troops they could begin smoking. For once it was welcome to his ears. They would start pouring in here in droves now, the clouds of their tobacco serving to cover the appalling reek.

Mick, as usual, was first to take advantage of the thrice daily occurrence, spotting Probyn and seating himself nearby. Forced to give up his cigarettes upon boarding in exchange for a pipe, he remained irritable at their loss. He whipped out his pipe, removed the compulsory metal disc that prevented sparks flying and began to cram the bowl with tobacco, desperate for a smoke and jabbering all the while about his new job. Obliged to sit there, Probyn was selective in what he listened to, occasionally drifting off into his own thoughts. As predicted the latrine was fast filling up with smokers, all of whom used the special lamps placed there for that purpose. Ready to light up, Mick found he had been talking too much and now found it impossible to gain access to a lamp.

'Jesus, it'll be time for Cease Fire before I get me smoke!' Highly frustrated to be restricted to three smokes a day, he swore and pulled out a box of matches.

At the sight of this contraband, Probyn immediately gave warning. 'What you doing with them? You'll have the bloody ship ablaze!'

'To hell with it I'm desperate!' Puffing frantically on the stem of his pipe, Mick sucked the smoke into his mouth and with a quick flourish extinguished the flame and made to slip the matches back into his pocket. Had not an infernal piece of bad luck caused a guard to poke his head in at that moment he would have got away with it.

Their eyes meeting through a pall of blue smoke, the guard ejected vitriol. 'How long have you had those bloody matches? You're supposed to hand them in!'

Mick tried to object that he was ignorant of this rule but it only landed him in deeper trouble. Providing amusement for rows of men with trousers round their ankles and pipes in their mouths, he was hauled away.

Knowing this would mean a term of imprisonment, Probyn sighed and straightened his back, his bare knees showing patches of red where he had leaned upon them so long. He was hoisting his trousers when the reality hit him. If Melody was indisposed who would help run the dry canteen? An enthusiastic grin came over his face. Finished in the latrine he rushed off to inform the ship's steward that his helper would not be back for some days and to volunteer his services for the post.

Though there was little glory to be had selling goods through a small hatch in the hold of the vessel, the conditions might be stifling and it might only be for an hour every day, to be rewarded by good food and a tidy little sum was very welcome indeed.

Mick, however, upon release, was most unimpressed by his friend's opportune move. 'Would ye be so quick to jump into me coffin?'

Probyn defended his action but looked suitably ambivalent. 'Sorry, but you could hardly do the job if you were in clink could you? If I hadn't grabbed it somebody else would.'

'Ah well, I suppose I should regard it as some sort o' favour then.' Mick gave an exaggerated nod, voicing no further lecture, except for the parting reproach. 'I'll be leaving you to examine your conscience.'

And though the job was to remain Probyn's for the rest of the voyage, it retained the taste of being acquired by doubtful means.

Following days of monotonous backdrop it was exhilarating to spot land, however insignificant a place. Upon the horizon appeared a dull red rock. As the ship grew ever closer, its colour intensified, contrasting sharply with the intense azure sea that lapped its flanks. St Vincent seemed to Probyn a barren place, with little vegetation apart from scrub, but anywhere was welcome after so long at sea and he was delighted that they were to stop here to take on coal and fresh water.

Even before it anchored the ship was encircled by swarms of natives in bumboats selling goods, calling out to the troops in unfamiliar tongue. Probyn was more interested in the women who, it was noted, did most of the fetching and carrying, the men being content to lounge and smoke.

'Look at the lazy hounds,' he objected to others. 'I'd take a blinking stick to them.'

Coaling took fourteen hours, during which a layer of black dust spread over everything, provoking ironic amusement amongst the ex-miners. Then, stocks replenished, they resumed their voyage to South Africa.

Life reverted to the humdrum. When Probyn had perused his map of the world before, even having travelled to Spain, the large expanses of blue hadn't meant much at all; only now did he begin to appreciate how vast were the oceans. Day after day there was nothing but endless sea. Apart from a couple of parades a day consisting of physical drill and kit inspection the troops were allowed to spend the time as they wished, through the daytime leaning over the side watching dolphins – which, after primary wonderment had now become commonplace – their evenings watching a concert or playing housey or other more illicit games.

The weather grew hot and muggy. A flurry of excitement was provided by the news that they were to cross the Equator but this turned out to be an anti-climax, for there was nothing at all to see.

Like hundreds of others, Probyn had taken to sleeping in the open air at night. Row upon row of cocooned moths, their low-slung hammocks filled the troop deck, rocking them gently to sleep. This evening, though, assigned as night picket, he could only envy those who slumbered thus, whilst he crawled beneath them on hands and knees, trying to negotiate a route to his post. And once there, he sighed again at the prospect of having to remain still all night long and the aching limbs that would ensue.

'That was a big sigh, Private.' A grizzled sergeant had appeared alongside him, his speech unusually soft for one of such rank. 'Bored are we?'

After an initial startled glance, Probyn remained looking straight ahead. 'No, Sarnt, I just wish we were there.'

The old sergeant murmured something he could not grasp, and seemed in no hurry to leave him, passing some moments gazing up at the starry sky. Finally, he asked, 'Do you know a cure for constipation?'

Dumbfounded to be consulted thus, Probyn replied, 'Liquorice powder usually works on me.' Then, the sergeant's glare informing him that he must have misheard, he blurted, 'Sorry, Sarnt, what was it you said?'

'I said, do you know your constellations?'

'Oh, a few!' Laughing inwardly, Probyn looked up at the heavenly formations, trying to pin a name on them. But the sky looked unfamiliar tonight.

Smiling at his confusion, the sergeant explained why. 'We're in a different hemisphere now, lad. See that there? That's the Southern Cross.'

Fascinated, Probyn continued to gaze at the firmament as the sergeant pointed out various other deviations. 'Even the man in the moon looks different down here.'

'You mean he's a black fellow?' Probyn grinned, then showed youthful contrition at the sergeant's narrow-eyed rebuke. 'Sorry, Sarnt.'

Giving him one more disparaging look, the sergeant moved on. Probyn raised his eyes once more to the heavens and sighed again. Please, Lord, move the land a little closer.

Land was eventually sighted, though he was not to set foot on it. Anchored only long enough off St Helena to transfer certain supplies to the boats that rowed out to meet them, they were soon on course again. Assuming to offer encouragement, a sailor informed Probyn that he had only five or six more days aboard, but to one unaccustomed to such voyages the news brought a wail of despair. Probyn had heard of men driven insane by the sea; was he to be one of them?

Then, early one morning before the stars had left the sky, he was awoken by an encouraging noise; the rattle of an anchor chain. The ship lay still! Instantly awake, he remained in his hammock with ears cocked for further evidence that they had at last arrived, hardly daring to risk a look for fear of being disappointed. Around him, men slept, their snores irritating him more than at any time during the voyage. Lashing out with his foot at various culprits, he almost tumbled from his hammock, beseeching them to be quiet. 'I think we're there!'

Disturbed from their slumbers, his drowsy comrades yawned and stretched, and, urged to listen, complained that they could hear nothing, only the gentle lapping of water.

'Exactly, we're not moving!' Gripping the edge of his hammock Probyn swung his feet onto the deck and began to crawl towards the side of the ship, only one or two of the others sufficiently interested to follow him. Now at the rail he squinted through the mist at what he at first assumed to be stars, then realized from the halo around each that these were artificial lights. Beyond that nebulous shroud must surely be land! Excitement rising, he cried, 'We're here!' But at the barrage of complaints, he was forced to lower his voice which was no less excited. 'It's South Africa!' And he wondered how others could continue to lie there with such a magical sight to be witnessed.

By reveille, though, all were alert and waiting for the sun to rise. With all the apprehension that accompanied a theatre concert, Probyn watched with bated breath as the curtain of mist began to lift, revealing first the harbour and its waterfront buildings, then the massive mountain wall behind; inch by inch in golden light, he watched the splendours of South Africa slowly reborn, gasped in surprise at the long flat top of the summit that appeared to have had its pinnacle lopped off. Then, too moved to speak, he simply stood and watched this beautiful land take form and for that one instant he knew what it was to be in love.

The sun rose higher, revealing Cape Town harbour in all its magnificence. So tantalizingly close, a beautiful woman with outstretched arms, the sea that lapped her ankles a deep inky blue, it was torment having to remain anchored in the roadstead, wanting to embrace her, but instead having to spend the whole day until evening in the preparation to disembark. Only the provision of fresh meat for the first time in weeks could dissuade mutiny.

Towards tea-time Probyn and Bumby, appointed mess orderlies, lined up at the galley with others to draw the tea. They were back in uniform now but still would not set foot on land until morning. The ship lying steady, Probyn cast yet another wistful glance across the calm waters at the remarkable flat-topped mountain, imagining what lay beyond it. Containers filled with steaming brew, he and Bumby were on the way back to their messing place when Bumby said, 'Oh, crumbs there's Wedlock reminiscing with Melody again.'

Probyn half smiled at Bumby's misuse of words, and groaned at the sight of Mick being tongue-lashed by Corporal Wedlock for some fresh crime. Shaking his head at the foul language, he was about to move nimbly past, when without warning the deck slowly but unnervingly began to shift beneath his feet, rolling further and further to one side. Amid shouts of alarm, men around him began to capsize, Probyn, too, trying to hang on to his container as he slid down the deck towards the rail, hot tea slopping dangerously about his feet, his arm shooting out, grappling wildly as he, Bumby and others tried to anchor themselves but failed and were pitched further towards the sea. A large boiler tipped up, spilling its scalding contents over the deck as the vessel continued to roll, its yard arm practically touching the water. He saw what was to happen but could do nothing to prevent it as they slithered and spiralled finally to a halt, men, officers and mess tins thrown unceremoniously together in a cacophonous writhing heap at the ship's side, saw Melody's foot make violent contact with Wedlock's face, smashing and grinding into his mouth as others fell on top of him to compound the injury, and as if this were not bad enough, the container that Probyn had been so valiantly trying to keep upright burst open, dousing Wedlock's groin in scalding hot tea, invoking an agonized yell and a flow of invective.

Within seconds the ship returned to an even keel. Quick to pick himself up, Probyn began to help others to their feet, calling for someone to throw cold water on the corporal's injury. Mick clambered upright too, the expression on his face one of horrified apprehension as he beheld the damage he had caused: where once had been Corporal Wedlock's upper front teeth was now a bloody gap through which poured forth violent curses.

When all returned to order it was discovered, miraculously, that there were few others injured, those that were contracting scalds or fractures. These, along with Corporal Wedlock, were packed off to hospital at the naval base of Simon's Town. Anticipating punishment, for who would believe that Wedlock's victim had not inflicted these damages on purpose, Mick was therefore relieved and surprised to be informed by his sergeant that none would be forthcoming, for this had been caused by elemental forces.

'They've got weird currents round these parts,' explained Sergeant Faulkner later to his platoon. 'One minute you're lying still, the next you're arse over tit.'

When his superior had gone, Mick held clasped hands to the sky and breathed his gratitude. 'Dear God in Heaven, thank You, thank You! Sure, I'll never sin again.'

'Neither will Wedlock wiv his scalded crutch,' joked Queen.

Probyn joined the uproarious laughter, rejoicing as the tale was repeated over and over again; the sight of Wedlock with his teeth smashed out was surely an act of God. But soon his mind was fixed on a far more relevant matter: with Wedlock incapacitated, could this be his own chance of promotion?

Reveille was precursored by the cawing of an unfamiliar bird. His enthusiasm robbing him of appetite, Probyn rushed his breakfast and prepared for disembarkation. As yet he had received no notification of who would take over from Wedlock, but this did not necessarily indicate bad news, and over there a whole new world awaited him!

One of the first to disembark, Probyn's excitement continued to burgeon as he stepped onto a wharf that was alive with natives, the few white faces standing out like spots on a domino, cape carts drawn by small wiry horses, trolleys piled with rickety wooden cages, one of which held several frightened chittering monkeys, wide-hipped grandmothers, bare-legged women with baskets on their heads, Africanders with skin like walnut, small boys in European clothing but with faces as black as coal. He could not take his eyes off them.

Fascination was suspended by the call to parade for inspection. There on the wharf amongst the mounds of cargo, great thick coils of rope, and notices in many different languages, each man was forced to unpack every item of kit to be displayed in the required regimental order at his feet, whilst the black tide eddied around them.

There was little time to form an impression of the town for, with the announcement through a loudspeaker, they were ordered to entrain – officers first, and lastly rank and file – Probyn's draft bound for Wynberg on the opposite side of Table Mountain. The trains were much smaller and less comfortable than at home, but with the journey only eight miles, the countryside most picturesque and the young soldiers agog with excitement there was nary a grumble to be heard.

Things continued to improve beyond all expectation, the incomers being greeted at the station by the band of their own battalion and also a large number of their new comrades, plus a host of the civil population, white, black and Creole. Wynberg itself was set amongst gardens and fruit trees with the atmosphere of an English country village and all the fiery colours of late autumn. Hardly what Probyn had been expecting from such a continent, but pleasant nevertheless. Marching into camp, he found this equally salubrious, situated amongst pine trees with the mountains as a background. Indeed, there were to be so many pleasures that those accustomed to hardship felt sure there must be some forfeit to be paid.

But no, throughout the day more luxuries were heaped upon them: a corking spread at the Regimental Institute, an informative and humorous speech of welcome from the colonel who warned them about the many pitfalls to health they were bound to meet and how to avoid these, and finally a concert performed by a fine orchestra, the effects of the latter persisting even as they emerged into the sunshine.

Probyn dashed away a sentimental tear, feigning to squint. 'By this sun doesn't half get your eyes. Good concert wasn't it?'

Mick didn't seem concerned about showing emotion. 'Oh, 'twas truly angelic!'

Rook gave a sage nod. 'I like Grieb.'

Others paid respect to his knowledge. 'Is that who wrote it?'

'Aye. *Fingal's Cave* they call the piece.'

Mick frowned and mopped his eyes. 'Em, I thought I heard someone say it was Mendelssohn.'

Rook shrugged. 'Well I could be wrong, but it sounded like Grieb to me. I went to see him in London in eighty-eight.'

Ignorant of either composer, Probyn showed appreciation. 'Well, he writes good stuff anyway.'

They were met then by a group of their new comrades who showed them around their quarters and gave advice on how to enjoy these unfamiliar surroundings, such as examining their boots before putting them on in case anything evil lurked within. But the discussion of scorpions and millipedes was to be interrupted by the arrival of Sergeant Faulkner.

'Private Kilmaster! Captain wants to see you now.'

Instantly alert, for this was the moment he had been awaiting – news of his promotion to corporal – Probyn dashed off after the sergeant to the officer's quarters.

'Ah, Private Kilmaster, I trust you enjoyed the spot of Mendelssohn?'

Enlightened, Probyn said he had.

'I shall not detain you long and you might find this to your advantage.'

He had been right! Probyn's heart soared, anticipating the proclamation.

'You will be aware that my valet, Private Coombes, was injured in yesterday's debacle aboard ship.'

Probyn had not been aware and was now slightly confused.

'Apparently his leg is broken and he will be incapacitated for some time, so I shall need a replacement, temporarily at least; Coombes is an admirable chap and I'd hate to deprive him of the post. Are you willing?'

A servant! Trying to conceal his crushing disappointment Probyn mustered an enthusiastic response. 'I'd be delighted, sir.'

'Good, Sergeant Faulkner will supply you with the details. Dismissed.'

Thank goodness, thought Probyn as he went back to convey the news to his friends, that he had not divulged his hopes to anyone. As it was, they were most impressed at his elevation in status, not to mention the extra one and sixpence per week he would earn. All were extremely envious.

On reconsideration of the matter, Probyn decided they were right, for how could any sane being mope for long enveloped by such wondrous nature? Even with the sinking of the sun its beauty was in no way diminished; against the violet-blue of the mountains the clear golden light of day becoming ever more golden, radiating into an extravagance of apricot, then orange, then flame, there seemed no limit to the Lord's palette.

Casting petty resentment aside, he experienced a flush of joy over the wonderful future that lay before him. Promotion would come eventually, he would not allow the lack of it to ruin this magnificent opportunity.

9

He adapted very quickly to life in the Cape Peninsula. Having imagined that South Africa would be insufferably hot he found that, on the contrary, the temperature was delightful, warm some days, cool on others, and with very little rain. What was impossible to acclimatize oneself to was that this was winter, for the month of May was as pleasant as he had experienced during an English summer – in fact, more so. True, the nights could be chilly, but compared to the rain and sleet and snow at home they were easy enough to endure, especially now in his comfortable quarters next to the captain's room. The only gripe he might make was induced by the persistent buzzing of flies – flies in winter! – that would insist on settling on him the moment he sat still and no amount of arm flapping could persuade them to leave. He doubted that he would ever grow used to these irritating passengers, but it was a small complaint amongst such bounteous living.

Initially the days were quite hard as the newcomers were drilled in the battalion's methods which differed slightly from those taught at home, but after that things settled down and as a servant Probyn was excused from further drills. With nothing much to do apart from clean the captain's uniform, lay it out on a morning and see to his general needs, he found himself with ample free time to enjoy a spell of fishing at the village to the rear of the camp, or to take the road to the fashionable suburb of Claremont for a day amongst the toffs. Life changed out of all recognition, he half expected some bombshell to ruin it, but no, not even Corporal Wedlock could impair this Arcadia, for upon recovery he was posted elsewhere, his replacement being much less tyrannical.

Inevitably, though, the captain's servant was restored to full health and Probyn was obliged to relinquish his post. The demotion was not so upsetting as it might have been for there was still much exploration to be made, the birdlife being spectacular, bee-eaters and rollers as abundant as sparrows at home, their iridescent plumage vying with exotic plants, the like of which he had only ever seen in books. Yet it was the people who captivated him most. Never having seen a black face except down a coal mine or at a minstrel show, his fascination with the natives remained as keen as ever and with each opportunity he made close study of them, especially the women.

'Have you noticed,' he said thoughtfully, as he sat on his day off with a group of his fellows in the evening sunlight, a bracing wind rippling female clothing, 'that African women's bums stick out like a shelf?'

Bumby who had been smoking contentedly now withdrew the pipestem from between his fat cheeks, interpreting the comment as a sign of sexual intent. 'Eh up, Pa's getting a taste for blackbird.'

Probyn was horrified. 'You must be joking, they stink! No, I'm just fascinated with the shape of them. I mean look at that little coolie lass over there, she's hardly got a bum at all.'

There was further discussion over the physical character-istics of the Africans who went about their business in varying degrees of black and contrasting attire – heathen women in flaming robes and beads, demure Christian girls in white blouses – but all with gleaming eyes and pouting lips.

Mick bashed his glengarry against his leg, removing the sand that had been deposited by the coastal wind. 'Well, there'll be no truckling with women of any sort for me. I'm staying pure till I find meself a wife.'

'Not much chance of finding one here,' sniffed Probyn but

it was not a genuine complaint, for he loved his army life and all that it currently offered.

'No, it'll be a good English wench for me,' pronounced Queen, responding to his urge to strip another length of flaking bark from the trunk of a red gum. 'Wonder how long we'll be here before they send us home.'

I don't care if they never send us back, thought Probyn. Though deeming it politic not to voice this, it was at that moment a genuine sentiment, his only reservation being that his family might not be enjoying so fine a life.

However, his qualms were ultimately removed by the arrival of a letter from home. His father was not one for writing but via Merry's report Probyn learned that things had settled down in the coalfields and the mine-owners hadn't after all demanded a reduction that year, so there was to be no strike. Added to this was the information that Meredith was expecting her first baby. Poor Wyn remained childless, Ethel was still unwed but doing well in the prison service, Rhoda had had a nasty shock last week when her husband was killed on his way home from work. Aunt Gwen had caused a stink at the funeral by talking out of turn. Apart from that everyone was well. But the most uplifting news was that Probyn's name was being mentioned again in the family circle. Now that Father had accepted him back into the fold the others had come round so Meredith wouldn't be surprised if their doors were open the next time he came home. When would that be by the way? Your guess is as good as mine, murmured Probyn. But when he folded the letter away he was smiling.

This inspiring news plus the consequent letters and gifts from Aunt Kit were all that he needed to make his life complete in these wonderful surroundings.

Despite any lack of promotion his contentment was to linger throughout the year, the one fluctuation being during annual manoeuvres at Constantia where his musketry skills proved yet again to be only adequate and forcing him to acknowledge that he would never be the company sharpshooter. Christmas, too, was a time of conflicting emotions for all the men, celebrating it as they were in brilliant sunshine while their families were thousands of miles away, though there was a spot of good cheer in the receipt of their first good conduct badges, and to coincide with this came the news that specific companies were to be moved to Natal and Probyn's was to be one of them. Hence, any despondency was cast aside as he and his friends packed up to embark on yet another adventure.

Their arrival at Durban on that late afternoon in January, the end of an eight-hundred-mile journey by sea, was signalled by a bold cliff swathed in evergreen forest that swept down to the water's edge, on the other side of the bay a low sandy spit. The city itself extended along the bay and inland to a range of low hills. Over everything hung a hot cloying mist. With much construction work taking place in the harbour, and their ship too big to cross the sand bar, the disembarkation had to be undertaken by lighters which ferried them between the dredgers to the wharves, unloading them amongst the rest of the general merchandise, watched by the unsettling deadpan eyes of a bobbing flotilla of pelicans.

How different to the region they had left, remarked Probyn, even before setting foot ashore, his uniform already sodden with sweat. It could have been another country altogether, for there was a definite oriental feel to the place, much of the work being undertaken by coolies, the background composed of dark glossy evergreens, gaudy sub-tropical flowers and palm trees. The pace of life was even slower than in the Cape, and no wonder, for the air was stifling and made him feel dirty even though he had enjoyed a wash before getting back into uniform, this sultry blanket seeming to emphasize the odour of the alien bodies around him.

It had started to drizzle though they gained no relief for the rain was warm, trickling from the brims of their white pith helmets and into their already waterlogged tunics. Glad to entrain immediately for Pietermaritzburg, the soldiers were able to grab only a fleeting impression of Durban, of Zulu houseboys in khaki shorts and tunics, warily respectful, hurrying home to beat the night-time curfew, of lacework balconies and limp bodies draped along the *stoep*, before the train at a painful rate of twelve miles an hour rattled out of the city heading inland.

Its occupants swaying and lurching as if on a switchback at the fairground, it forged its way through acres of sugar cane and pineapple, banana and paw-paw, ramshackle crushing mills and Indian shacks, a view which soon became monotonous. Warned of the seventy-one miles ahead of him, Probyn attempted to nap but was constantly jerked awake by the rolling of the train, whence he was compelled to stare at endless acres of lush crops.

But daylight was fading fast. The horizon had adopted that familiar violet tinge, the sky a deep rose, and soon there was only his own reflection in the carriage window. Eventually he drifted into erratic sleep.

Daylight broke. Whilst he had slept the country had become much wilder. Beyond the rich rolling pastures of white farmsteads came mimosa scrub, Zulu kraals, beehives of grass enclosed by fences of cactus, mealie crops and massive herds of humped red cattle that looked as if they had been etched from the earth. A small, almost naked herd boy ran alongside the train for a while as if trying to compete, then fell back with a final wave, teeth flashing. Waving in response, a smiling Probyn felt that only now had he glimpsed the real Africa, the one he had imagined in his daydreams, and was spellbound by the view. Where Ireland had been ancient, Africa was prehistoric. In the shadowy golden light of early morn, the cones and plateaux of the horizon assumed the guise of slumbering dinosaurs, stretched out across the tawny miles.

On its descent into a valley now, the train picked up speed, eventually steaming triumphantly back to civilization, the railway embankments of Pietermaritzburg afire with red-hot pokers and scarlet gladioli. It had obviously just stopped raining. Steam rose from the platforms, added to by the asthmatic gasps of the engine as the soldiers tumbled gratefully from the carriages and began to stretch their legs, remarking on the beauty of their environment. Barely had the compliment emerged when from exotic blooms came huge flying insects such as they had only ever seen in their nightmares, causing the brave adventurers to duck and run about in alarm until brought to order by their sergeants, and they were most keen to answer the command to move off.

They left the railway station, a most attractive building of red brick with cream stone and decorative cast-iron lacework, the latter a predominant feature throughout the town as Probyn was to find out during his march to the garrison. An utterly charming place, Pietermaritzburg bore not the slightest resemblance to any town at home, being laid out in the colonial style of blocks which to this Yorkshire lad made much more sense than crooked medieval lanes and made it easier to get one's bearings. Never had he seen such exquisite buildings, even the tiniest dwelling graced by a lace-adorned verandah, the town itself embraced by wooded hills and tranquil countryside. For a brief spell in these dignified surroundings he forgot how terribly humid it was, how damp and uncomfortable his uniform, and the terrifying insects, saw only the pristine streets devoid of coal dust, the sunshine and the colourful saris of the Indian women – for, as usual, wherever they went the local population was out to observe their march past. Here the crowd was a mixture of whites, kaffirs and Indians, their transport brought to a temporary halt for the occasion, although one rickshaw runner seemed determined not to lose his fare, the Zulu weaving his way in and out of the marching blocks of soldiers in an effort to be past them.

On arrival at Fort Napier on a hill overlooking the town they were given a hearty meal then allowed a few days to settle in, during which they explored their new territory. Back from a souvenir hunting expedition in the market square, Probyn imbibed a great chestful of the pine-scented air and declared to his fellows, 'I'm going to like it here.'

'Pity you're not stopping then,' said Sergeant Faulkner in passing.

'What, where we off, Sarnt?' A flabbergasted Probyn called after him.

Faulkner did not stop. 'Eshowe! A, D and H Companies to train in mounted infantry.'

With a look of horror at his pals, Mick exclaimed, 'Horses! God help us, I can't abide the bloody stupid creatures!' Running after the informant he tried to protest that he was not fitted to such duties but was sent packing, his only redress being to pour forth more grumbles to the others.

Rook said he did not like horses either. 'They frighten me.'

Probyn was more impressed, affecting to be an experienced horseman already through his work as a pony driver in the mine. 'Nay, you've just got to show 'em who's boss. I reckon it'll be a lark, get us out into the *real* Africa.'

Mick dealt him a grim nod. 'Aye, with lions and turkeys and things.'

'Turkeys?' giggled Queen.

'Those things with the red googly necks.' Mick shuddered. 'They make me want to puke.'

'Eshowe.' Probyn lifted his head as if suddenly recognizing the name. 'Wasn't that under siege during the Zulu War?'

Queen laughed at Mick's face. 'Oh blimey, don't put the wind up him any more than it is already.'

'Nay, nowt to worry about,' comforted Probyn in mature fashion. 'We sorted them out good and proper. It's the same as with horses. Long as you teach 'em who's boss they won't give you any trouble. Anyroad, I reckon it's the Dutchmen you have to look out for. I trust them a lot less than I trust the Zulus. I mean you expect the niggers to be uncivilized, they don't know any better, but white chaps?' He shook his head. 'I don't like the Boers at all. They're the one thing that spoils this place. They never crack their faces, do they? And you can feel their antagonism. I tell you, if I'd been in charge in eighty-one they wouldn't have their republics. They've had one go at us, I wouldn't put it past them to have another. I don't know, you only have to turn your back and if it's not them it's the Germans or the dagos nibbling away at bits of our Empire.' Suddenly aware that he sounded just like his father, he checked his flow, concluding that, 'Our grandfathers fought to build it, we owe it to them to maintain it.'

'My grandfather was a church organist,' admitted a sheepish Barnes.

'Well, I'm sure he played his part in building the Empire,' answered Probyn. 'I don't exactly come from a military background meself.'

Rook was looking thoughtful. 'My granddad once had an organ.'

'Well obviously or you wouldn't be here,' quipped Private Queen.

Chuckling despite his abhorrence of vulgarity, Probyn announced over the raucous laughter, 'I'm trying to be serious! I intend to hand on the Empire intact to my kids.'

'Kids, is it?' scoffed Mick, wafting at flies. 'And how are yese going to father them stuck out in the middle of nowhere?'

Probyn was unfazed. 'Stop wittering! We won't be in Africa forever you know. You should enjoy it while you can. I'm off to.'

It was a bold statement when he had no idea what Zululand might offer, and for one moment as he surveyed his new environment upon arrival he considered he might have been rash. Set high in the hills, surrounded by primeval forest and girded by mist, the village of Eshowe seemed on first appraisal an eerie place, the vapour lending a haunting quality to the birdsong.

But later with its veil lifted, the striking white turrets of Fort Nongqayi standing out against a cerulean sky, and a soft breeze whispering through the towering ironwoods, rippling palm fronds and shirt sleeves, it emerged as a much pleasanter venue than the lowlands.

The fact that it was to rain almost constantly throughout the following days detracted somewhat from the charm of the place, but between downpours with the hot sun to evaporate the moisture in their sodden tunics and native servants to attend their every comfort the soldiers considered themselves to be advantaged over their friends at HQ.

'They'll never believe me at home when I tell them I've got a servant.' Probyn grinned at his pals and thanked the young black boy Gideon for the dry tunic. He felt somewhat embarrassed to have another at his beck and call and preferred to keep his requests to a minimum. Naturally there were those who took liberties, kept Gideon forever on the run. Mick was one and Ingham another, both content to lie on their cots and let the youngster work himself into a frenzy, as they were doing now.

Probyn made scolding observance of this as he himself sat cleaning his rifle, the smell of gun oil helping to overpower that of male sweat. 'Of course there are always folk who'll take advantage. Tut! If the poor devil could go to the privy for you you'd have him doing that an' all.'

'What a splendiferous idea,' smirked the recumbent Mick.

'He's a little shit,' quothed Havron, flicking Gideon's rump with a towel as the boy travelled between the cots delivering items. 'That's all he's fit for.'

Stung by the blow, Gideon effected to skip past on the way back but Havron caught his arm and held it tightly.

Probyn squinted down the inside of his barrel, checking for cleanliness, but not too preoccupied to issue a warning. 'Leave him.'

Havron ignored him and continued to torment the boy, calling him a little heathen.

Greatly offended, Gideon objected, 'Sir, you wound me! I am as good a Christian as yourself!'

'What – comparing yourself to a white man?' Havron shook the prisoner vigorously, knocking him off his feet. 'I'll show you what for!'

Setting aside his rifle, Probyn jumped up and approached Havron. 'And I'll show thee an' all, now let him go, you bully!'

Others joined the protest. 'Aye let him go, Havron, he's nobbut a bairn! Stop being so bloody mean!'

With everyone ganging up on him Havron was forced to release the child. 'I weren't serious! Bloody hell you'd think I were going to murder him.' And he rubbed a rough palm over Gideon's tightly curled head before shoving him away.

Holding his arm, Gideon was about to walk away when Mick called, 'Before ye go, sonny, would ye fetch me a –'

'Fetch it your blasted self!' chastised Probyn, signalling for the boy to go. 'You lazy article. Poor little devil's run off his feet.'

Mick heaved a sigh. 'What's the point of having him here if not to work?'

'I'm sure the captain holds that same sentiment when he looks at thee,' came the sarcastic response from Probyn, who went back to cleaning his rifle, to the accompaniment of outraged exclamations from his pal.

To Mick's further chagrin their induction to mounted infantry was to begin almost immediately. For one who could barely drag himself out of bed in the morning it came as extra burden to look after a horse too, and to tuck it up at the end of the day even before he had attended his own needs. Though mocking these grumbles, Probyn was suffering in silence. Riding a horse was not as easy as it looked and, after hours in the saddle, his thigh and buttock muscles were screaming for relief, and they had not yet even ridden beyond the confines of the forest. On foot, this would have been a pleasant jaunt beneath the canopy of giant trees, through dappled glades where orchids peeped, a kaleidoscope of birdlife presenting itself for their entertainment. Atop a horse possessed of more endurance than its rider, with chafing thighs and paralysed rump and under constant deluge, it was anguish. Try as he might to imagine himself in an English wood on one of Aunt Kit's picnics, his tortured muscles dragged him back to reality, his only desire being to fall upon his bed and snuggle up against the icy cold nights.

In due time, though, his body became attuned to the contours of his mount and he was able to endure longer periods in the saddle, then the treks began to stretch further afield in the great undulating spaciousness that was Zululand. Under skies that went on forever, splashing through rivers whose banks grew thick with yellow flags and mallow and forget-me-not, an escarpment of sugar loaves and plateaux turned violet by the setting sun, he began to enjoy every moment.

'But what's the point of it all?' demanded Mick, still at odds with his equine partner after two hours in the saddle on yet another early morning trek. 'I'd like to be able to tell my arse that there's good reason for the calluses it's collecting. All we seem to do is drift aimlessly about the countryside.'

Rook had the answer. 'I suppose it's like a dog what goes round pissing up trees, we're marking our territory, letting the niggers know who's in charge.'

Sergeant Faulkner, moving past them to catch up with the captain, overheard the conversation. 'Very good, Private Rook, I couldn't have put it so eloquently myself.'

'Eh, look at that whatsit over there!' Alert for wildlife, Probyn had spotted a dog-like animal balancing on its hind legs atop a termite mound, and now gave an amused laugh. 'It's stood up like a little man. Eh, Sergeant, what is it?'

Sergeant Faulkner turned in the saddle as the little tawny sentinel alerted others of its kind to the presence of intruders and all gathered to watch the soldiers' passing, quivering excitedly. 'Meerkats,' came his answer.

Intrigued by the little watchers, the soldiers were pleased

to respond to the order to stop and rest the horses, swinging down from the saddle and arching their backs.

One of the meerkats was bolder than the rest, with tail erect it came right up to where they stood. Probyn broke into his rations and, squatting, threw it a morsel of bully beef. To his and others' delight it ran up almost to his feet and snatched the offering, not in the least afraid. The soldiers gathered round to watch as more bully beef was imparted, trying to coax the rest of the meerkats to join their companion. Gideon, here along with other native bearers, moved closer to watch the proceedings. The meerkat seemed to take great exception to this and, in a skittering rush, nipped the boy's toe, drawing blood and causing him to dance about in pain. The soldiers thought this a huge joke.

'Ooh, he doesn't like thee, Gid!' cackled Ingham and tried to shove Gideon forward for the meerkat to have another bite.

Gideon was having none of it, rushing away hoppity skip, leaving other native servants to be tormented by the soldiers who tried to provoke the little animal into biting them until the scrimmage grew too much for it and it ran off to join its companions.

Still grinning over this happy interlude, their horses rested, they continued on their trek.

For once the rain held off and they were to see more wildlife that morning: a band of monkeys with long stiff tails and, a while later, a long-limbed spotted cat which pelted away across the savannah before they could draw their rifles. Towards midday they headed for a group of trees under which to eat their lunch and came upon a dozing leopard, its limbs straddling one of the branches. Disturbed, the startled animal leapt down from the tree and began to run. With quick response, the captain drew his rifle and brought the cat down. As native bearers ran to retrieve the kill, an excited Probyn and others galloped ahead to view it, making envious comments on the accuracy of Fitzroy's musketry.

The captain ordered the animal to be skinned. It would make handsome decoration for his quarters.

After dinner they moved off again into the hot afternoon, the air shrill with cicadas. Not long afterwards they were to see, atop a grassy hill overlooking a valley, a Zulu village and made their way there. Probyn felt a sense of excitement that he was to come amongst these renowned warriors, though there was little hint of warring today, the scene a pastoral one. Outside the kraal grew native maize and sorghum, and in the valley a large herd of cattle grazed, white egrets at their feet.

Probyn tensed as a Zulu came to meet them, remaining in awe as the coal-black figure, a handsome and respectful man with noble bearing, saluted the visitors, his hand and arm lifted above his head. Captain Fitzroy dismounted and, to Probyn's admiration, returned the greeting in the same language, accepting the invitation for them to enter.

Leaving their horses to be tended by the bearers, the soldiers followed their officer into the kraal. 'I wonder how Fizzer knows their language,' muttered Probyn with obvious veneration.

'Maybe got a touch of the tarbrush himself,' sneered Havron.

'Going the right way to find yourself on a charge, soldier!' Sergeant Faulkner had overheard. He then explained to Probyn that most self-respecting Zulus would speak no language other than their own.

Probyn decided that he must emulate the captain's linguistic skills and listened carefully, though it was very hard to decipher what was being said. Besides which, it felt rather intimidating to be surrounded by tribesmen.

Inside the enclosure were the distinctive beehives with round roofs of straw that extended to the ground, exquisitely made. Probyn was murmuring his respect for this craftsmanship to his fellows, when a young woman came by carrying a pitcher on her head, her body decorated with beads and brass ornaments and little else save for a leather apron. Jaw agape, he immediately blushed scarlet and turned away, yet his eyes were constantly dragged back to her magnificent breasts. A glance at his fellows revealed delighted expressions as they watched her move past, and when she had crawled on hands and knees into a hut there were smirks and the odd lascivious comment until Captain Fitzroy noticed and called, 'Enough!'

There were to be more such sights, of native women brewing beer, their dark gleaming eyes darting shy looks at the soldiers. Trying hard not to stare, Probyn turned his attention to an emaciated dog who fawned and cringed around the visitors, bending down to pat it, but even whilst he did so taking furtive peeps at the barely-clad women. When he straightened he found himself the object of others' curiosity, inquisitive children coming to gather wide-eyed around him, their clothing little more than a leather thong or a fringe of beads. Here was a very different breed to the African with whom he had dealt in Cape Town. Beside them even Gideon appeared most civilized in his khaki outfit.

The women appeared to be enjoying some banter, one of them looking at Probyn as she spoke, her mouth splitting like a ripe purple plum as she burst into laughter. Sensing that he was the butt of their hilarity he blushed again, hoping the ruddy tan would hide his embarrassment, but the woman came towards him extending a bowl of beer. Examining the muddy brew he shook his head quickly but was told by the sergeant not to give offence and so he took a tentative drink, getting a heady whiff before passing the bowl to the next man who knocked it back without complaint. Still disquieted under the unwavering gaze of the young Zulus, for something to do he whipped off his pith helmet and planted it on the nearest child. On such a tiny head it came right down almost to the shoulders, causing the other children to scream with laughter and dance around, all trying to grab the helmet and take their turn with it, others jabbing their fingers at Probyn's auburn hair which against his rubicund face appeared as a beacon. Marvelling that these savages could enjoy the same humour as the white man, and feeling safer now that he had discovered common ground, Probyn and his young friends began to relax.

Provided with more beer, they were invited to sit down and be entertained with a war dance. This was a most exciting affair, the participants dressed in baldrics of spotted catskin, with white fur rings around their knees, ankles and wrists, ebony torsos gleaming with gold and silver wire, drumming on shields with sticks festooned with white feathers, stamping feet coated in ochre dust, drumming and stamping faster and faster still, infecting the native bearers and causing them to leap and join in, only Gideon maintaining reserve until inevitably he too was helpless to suppress the urge and sprang up to join the dancers, their frenzied display reaching a crescendo and finally ending with a unified roar as everyone fell flat on the ground to a loud burst of applause.

Thanking the headman for his hospitality, the captain said they must now be moving on. Slightly tipsy from the native beer, their bearers still under the influence of the dance, the soldiers remounted and moved off in much cheerier mood towards the valley.

Just before dark, their high spirits somewhat doused now by many hours in the saddle, they were told to encamp near a drift. They were to spend their first night under canvas.

Off-saddling was always a tiresome business, unloading packs and unharnessing horses, especially when accompanied by Melody's grumblings. Probyn attempted to steer his mind elsewhere, recalling the Zulu dance and more pertinently the women. Upon setting foot upon this continent he had been instilled by a sense of wonderment that had never left him. He was incessantly surprised, each venture into new territory bringing the announcement that *this* was the true Africa, yet each day he made fresh discovery as to what this meant and in consequence it was impossible to tell which was the *real* Africa. Tonight, though, as darkness came – if one could call it darkness, thought Probyn, for to him darkness was the colour of the pit, not this wondrous coverlet of indigo with its shimmering stars – tonight was when the true wildness of the country really hit him. The daytime quietude of the veld had undergone a startling change, a chorus of whoops and howls and roars from beasts unseen, the very air pulsating with the chirrup of crickets and the soft boom of frogs from the river.

Huddled in the tent against the bitter cold, its flap left open until its occupants were ready to sleep, Probyn scratched at mosquito bites, gazing in awe at the sky that seemed to be a living creature, shivering and twinkling with stars, and below it the deep violet outline of the escarpment. From a neighbouring tent came Bumby's breath of wonderment, 'Have you ever seen anything as lovely? Just like velvet covered in sequences.'

Exchanging a chuckle with his tent-mates, Probyn turned back to gaze out for a while longer, his breath coming as a cloud on the air as the temperature fell. It was hard to shut out this view but eventually he did so, pulling down the flap and burrowing under his blankets, and apart from an occasional disturbance by the pig-like snuffling of an aardvark, he enjoyed a good night's sleep.

He awoke before the bugler to the melodic twittering of birds and the harsh *kek-kek* of a monkey, but for which the veld was once more imbued with its usual serenity. Being appointed tent orderly, he dared not doze and pushed aside his blanket. Stepping between his mates he clambered from his tent, standing for a moment, squinting and beating his arms about himself against the cool air. There was a heavy dew on the grass, the flowers still tightly refusing to meet the day. The far bank was lined with antelope which, startled by the human form, veered away, leaving only wading ibis and red-legged storks to witness his ablutions.

Cupping his hands, Probyn splashed the tingling cold water over his face, shaking his head at the shock of it and smoothing back his hair. The sandy banks were peppered with holes, in and out of which darted bee-eaters, tiny mosaics of blue, green, turquoise, russet and yellow. He stood and watched for a while, then went back to where breakfast was being prepared.

When Gideon wished him good morning, he decided to try out his smattering of Zulu. 'Sawubona, Baba.'

There was a stunned hiatus, followed by gales of laughter from the other natives who were almost convulsed as they pointed derogatory fingers at their small companion, sharing the joke in their own language. 'He must be suffering from devils in the head!'

Aware that he had made some faux pas, Probyn looked for explanation to Gideon who had adopted a bad-tempered scowl. With the rest of his comrades up now and looking to see what the laughter was about he demanded an explanation.

Gideon rushed off in a huff and it was left to one of the other natives to explain. 'Oh I am truly sorry for laughing, master, but it is just that Gideon deserves no such respect. You have just addressed him as Father!' Encouraged by their white overlords, the congregation broke into renewed laughter. Probyn, feeling foolish, tried to dismiss the matter and grabbed a cauldron to receive coffee which along with the bread ration he hurried to his tent-mates' mess tins, deciding that from now on he would confine his attempts at linguistics to his letters home.

With the sun out and flowers beginning to unfurl, the small column resaddled and struck out for Eshowe. Hating being made a fool of, Probyn said little on the journey back to the fort, yet nothing could deter the teasing of his fellows, which was to continue intermittently all the way. Gideon too was bearing the brunt of Probyn's error, for occasionally Probyn would hear a native refer to the boy as Baba, when all would burst out laughing, and Gideon would glare in defiance.

'I'm sorry, son,' he said later that day when they stopped to rest the horses and Gideon handed him some coffee, 'I wasn't trying to make a fool of you I just got the wrong word.'

For a moment Gideon beheld the speaker as if he were mad. A white man issuing apology! Then he shook his head and said with dignity, 'That is quite all right, boss. It is they who are idiots to laugh at such things.' He indicated his fellow bearers.

'Yes, some people don't know when to stop do they?' agreed Probyn looking at his own friends.

Sharing a rare moment of kinship, Gideon bared his white teeth, then reverting to his role, rushed off to answer another demand.

The teasing was to continue even after they arrived back at the fort and indeed for days afterwards, every time Gideon entered the room someone, usually Havron, would shout, 'Here's your dad, Pa!' whence the jokes would fly thick and fast, until finally Mick made a joke at Havron's expense singling him out for his comrades' mockery for a change.

But then in the next instant it ceased to matter, for Sergeant Faulkner brought the news that Coombes had gone down with malaria and once again Kilmaster was required to stand in as the captain's valet, this time permanently. Wasting no time in removing himself from his tormentors, Probyn issued a smiling insult as he transferred his kit to more desirable quarters.

There was somewhat more to do this time. Apart from rousing the captain in the morning, setting his table for breakfast with real linen napkins and silver cutlery, boiled eggs and buttered toast, and laying out his uniform, there was also the horse to attend to. But still, if this job kept him in the captain's sights it was time well spent. Surely by now he must qualify for promotion? Undoubtedly the two got on well. By paying close attention Probyn had acquired a talent for anticipating just what the captain needed at any given moment, thus drawing forth praise.

'You really are a capital fellow, Private Kilmaster!' would come his exclamation upon being handed the relevant article even before having asked for it, and Probyn would respond with the nonchalant answer that he was glad to be of use, secretly bursting with pride over the compliment from such a gentleman.

And in return for Kilmaster's loyal service, the captain taught him many things, different things to those he had learned in the ranks but no less valuable. Taught him more than his own father even, so that Probyn came to look upon him as more than just an officer, became truly fond of him. Others in the platoon might refer to Captain Fitzroy as a real toff, but Probyn felt a much closer affinity, and viewed it as an act of love to make his superior's life as comfortable as possible during their long treks into the wilderness.

As the rains became less frequent and the water levels began to fall, so their treks were to extend further and further afield, the company splitting in half and each taking their separate course, communicating by heliograph. On such protracted journeys, it became necessary to take supplies, drawn by oxen, but that was not to say that the troops were well fed for, if they failed to spot any game, as often happened, they were required to exist for days on bully beef and biscuits.

'And ye still insist this is fun?' Mick would issue sardonically on such occasions.

Day after day, oblivious of time but for the misty golden dawn and the violet sunset, they travelled through wild and lonely country, pushed through wide rivers and open veld spiked with cactus, climbed lush hills and strove for the mountains beyond, to what end they did not know, conscious only of the order to follow.

Today, clinging to his superior's flank should there be any service to fulfil, Probyn wondered when they would again glimpse humanity. By his calculations they must have trekked a hundred miles or more in the last ten days without meeting a soul, their only encounters being with herds of gnu and zebra which scattered before their rifles with a thunderous zig-zag of plump striped buttocks and a panicked braying. His amazement at these encounters and at the vastness of this continent was invariably renewed, never more so than when looking at a map, for what seemed like gargantuan travels were in truth confined to just a tiny portion of the region. Reports had filtered in about trouble in the north; the telegraph wire between Salisbury and Cape Town had been cut. Both Matabele and Shona could be responsible, either to take wire for ornaments or simply to cause mischief. Either way, such news failed to assume much import for Probyn who at last understood that it was too far away for him to become involved, besides which he was travelling westwards towards Basutoland. He wondered vaguely if he would ever get to see any action.

Previously it had been quite hot but in this high country the temperature could be very erratic and now, as they came over the brow of a hill, the wind came as a sabre-slash. It would be spring at home. In reply to the letter he had sent his father he had recently learned that the coalmasters were demanding a twenty-five per cent reduction in wages due to the slump in prices. Characteristically, they had tried to undermine the solidarity of the Federation where it was weakest in the smaller coalfields of the Midlands but this had not worked and the consequent refusal had led to a lock-out. The Midland Federation had then been forced to ask their stronger colleagues for assistance for their locked-out members. This had resulted in a national strike. For once, wrote his father, public sympathy appeared to be high, but for how long the miners could enjoy this with coal prices rocketing he did not know. However, it was a matter of principle that the Federation must defend its members' right to a living wage. *Though as you well know principle doesn't put food on the table*, Monty had written, but, he hastened to add, Probe must not take this as a personal request for money, because even if they were to concede a reduction they would still be much better off than they'd been five years ago. Notwithstanding his father's last comment, Probyn had sent some money anyway. After the initial excitement of having cash at his personal disposal he had become an avid saver and, during the two and a quarter years he had been in the army, his abstemious habits and the extra one and sixpence a week plus tips he earned as a servant had accrued an enormous amount of money – over sixteen pounds – and this was even after deducting the amount he had sent his father. Where could one spend it in this wilderness?

Nervous of falling off, he held tightly to the pommel as his bay horse now descended the steep, rocky incline.

'Loosen your reins and let the horse make his own way down.' The captain must have noticed his white knuckles. 'Trust him, he won't fail you.'

Trying hard to do as instructed, Probyn ached from tensing against such precipitous slopes and his spirits soared when, in the late afternoon, a native village came into view, signalling an encounter with other human life.

My, but they were a dour lot! No one came to pay respects as at the kraal of the Zulu, merely watched the soldiers with little interest as the captain approached, though when asked for rations they provided it, at their own pace.

Things became a little more cordial after Captain Fitzroy had talked to the induna and it was decided to camp here for the night before turning for home in the morning. Gideon was sent to ask the headman for some dung to light a fire, for there was no wood to be had on this treeless stretch of veld. It was decided, also, to recruit more native bearers, one having died along the way and another having absconded.

Gideon returned with three volunteers, two of them tiny creatures no more than eight years old.

'And what am I supposed to do with those?' demanded the captain, arms akimbo.

'The induna says they are good workers, sir.' Gideon was keen to have someone younger than himself to boss around. 'And the boys have agreed to come.'

'Very well, but they can be your responsibility,' the captain told him, which was just what Gideon wanted to hear.

He wasted no time in showing his authority. 'Light a fire and be quick about it!'

Proving their worth, the little boys soon had the dung ignited, though the smoke it produced was most offensive.

They were also involved in the setting up of the field kitchen, plus a good many chores besides, throughout which Gideon drove them mercilessly. During the rest of the evening his despotic rule was to provide amusement for the soldiers, until Probyn had to intervene and instruct Gideon not to overstep his role.

The two little boys were allowed to sit down then, though they chose to hunker apart from the rest, speaking together in their own language.

'Tell them to come by the fire,' Probyn instructed Gideon.

Shaking his head in bewilderment, Gideon nevertheless went to pass on the message.

But the boys declined. 'We prefer to remain here. How can you bear to sit near the white man when he smells like rotting flesh?' They made faces at each other and giggled, white teeth intruding upon the night.

'Wretched hyenas! How dare you insult the Queen's uniform?' Gideon flew into a rage, dealing each a series of kicks until Probyn called a halt.

'I've told you! Leave them lads alone.'

'But sir, you do not understand, they are being most insulting!' Gideon kicked the nearest boy again.

'You deserve insulting,' rallied Probyn crossly. 'Now leave them alone and go to bed!'

The following morning Probyn rose to more trouble from Gideon, though this time it was the latter who was the victim. Bringing water to the captain's tent, he doubled over in obvious agony. 'Those wicked boys have put a spell on me, sir! They have put a snake in my belly whilst I slept!' And he cried out in pain before dashing off.

The captain seemed unconcerned, sighing to his valet, 'Go see what ails him, Kilmaster.'

Upon finding Gideon, Probyn reeled backwards at the awful

stench of diarrhoea. It was only as he caught sight of Havron laughing that he sensed it was not the native boys who had committed foul play, and went to confront the real culprit.

'You've slipped summat in his food haven't you?'

'I was only having a laugh,' complained Havron. 'Stop being such an old woman.'

Probyn was annoyed. 'Don't you realize, you twerp, that because of your stupidity, we're not going to get any work out of Gideon for the next few days?'

'It were only senna pods,' objected Havron. 'You'd think it were strychnine the way you're carrying on.'

'What's this . . . adulterating somebody's food?' Sergeant Faulkner had a habit of creeping up on one.

'It's nowt, Sarnt.' Probyn tried to make light of the affair. 'Just Gideon with bellyache.' And with a grim look at Havron he went back to the captain's tent.

'I've got my eye on you, Private Havron,' warned the sergeant before moving off himself.

Gripped by the painful squeezing in his abdomen, Gideon was not to be of much use for the rest of the morning, hitching a ride on the supply wagon as the column set off for home, though his incapacity failed to deter him from bullying his tiny subordinates who remained at his constant beck and call all day long.

So tyrannical was their master that by nightfall the boys had had enough. Under cover of darkness they stole away.

In the morning, when Gideon was late in making his appearance with water for the captain's ablutions, an annoyed Probyn had to go and fetch it himself, having no time to seek out the miscreant yet for there was the officer's breakfast to serve and his tent to dismantle. When he returned from his own rushed meal the captain had not finished and so his valet pottered around the tent, shaking dust and insects out of things and packing what articles he could. Handling a compass, he dallied for a while, trying to make sense of its magnetic needle.

'I don't think you're quite up to that yet, laddie!' Sergeant Faulkner materialized as if from nowhere, making the other jump. 'Put it away and leave it to the gentleman.'

'What have we here?' Captain Fitzroy now came upon them, mopping his lips with a napkin.

'Private Kilmaster's getting above his station, sir. I've told him he hasn't the brain.'

Fitzroy berated the speaker cheerfully, 'Oh, I think you malign him, Sergeant,' and to Faulkner's disdain he passed a few moments showing his valet how to use the compass. 'Though I do not think that we shall trust him yet to find our way home.'

'Very wise, sir.' Sergeant Faulkner now voiced his reason for being at the captain's tent. 'I was just wondering if the boy Gideon was here, sir. He appears to have done a bunk.'

As Fitzroy shook his head in exasperation Probyn looked alert. 'I think I've just seen him. Permission to go and collar him, sir!' This granted, he dashed off, wanting to get his own back on Gideon for having to do the other's job as well as his own.

Sneaking up on the culprit behind a wagon, he pounced. 'Come here, you! Where've you been, and what's that you're scoffing?'

The boy jumped and pulled the article away from his mouth, looking guilty.

'Come on, give us a look!' Probyn snatched his hand, out of which fell the most putrid morsel of flesh and hair. With a cry of disgust he let it lay on the ground. 'No wonder you've been ill, eating such muck!'

Gideon protested, 'Oh no, boss, it is medicine!' And he explained that he had got it from the witch-doctor before leaving the village yesterday.

Kicking it away Probyn gave another sound of disgust. 'You know the rules! If you need medicine you go to the surgeon. You wouldn't look so guilty if you didn't think you were in the wrong.' But intuition warned him that this was not the true cause of Gideon's look of guilt. It was then that he noted the absence of the two boys and demanded to know where they were. Informed of their escape, and of the full extent of the problem, he groaned and went back to tell the captain.

Fitzroy was rinsing his hands and face.

'Pardon me for intruding upon your ablutions, sir.'

'Ah! What news of the feckless Gideon?'

Withholding the bad news for a moment, Probyn handed his superior a towel, informing him of the witch-doctor's charm. 'You've never seen owt so putrid, sir! I were nearly sick meself. I can't believe he thought it would cure him.'

Fitzroy did not seem surprised. 'Yes, well, don't be misled by the fact that they go to church on Sunday. You'll come to learn that it's never far below the surface, innate barbarism.'

After a moment's thought, Probyn conveyed his news. 'I have to tell you also, sir, that the piccaninnies have run away in the night, and they've taken a load of stuff with them.'

The captain stopped drying his face, his cheerful air evaporating. 'Damn! What sort of stuff?'

'Couple of blankets and a bag of mealie and . . . I'm afraid they took a rifle, sir.'

The captain was furious. This meant that yesterday's ten-mile trek would now have to be retaken. 'Well, they shan't get away with it. Go fetch Sergeant Faulkner then saddle my horse!'

At first there was amusement from the men at the news of the boys' abscondment, but when Sergeant Faulkner began to choose a dozen 'volunteers', telling them they would be required to go after the escapees, the mood was not so convivial.

Whilst the rest remained at the camp to enjoy a leisurely breakfast, the captain, Privates Kilmaster, Melody, Ingham, Havron and nine others retraced the track they had made twenty-four hours ago.

With the sun at full strength the day became hot and dry and dusty, and was made even more unpleasant by the captain's urgency to get this done. The miscreants could have been gone twelve hours; even on horseback it would be difficult to catch up with them before they reached the village. They did not stop for some miles, not even for the benefit of the horses, the captain saying they could enjoy an overnight rest when this was taken care of. There was one brief pause at a muddy waterhole, for the water wagon had been left behind in camp, but with an eye on the green scum on its surface the captain warned that it was fit only for animals and told them not to partake, they would have to eke out what was left in their bottles. When the horses had supped the soldiers remounted.

'Permission to fall out and have a slash, sir!' called Ingham, hanging back, Melody joining his plea.

Leaving the two, Probyn set off with the rest, but something caused him to turn and he saw Ingham and Melody scooping handfuls of foul water to their lips. Realizing they had been spotted they quickly mounted and trotted after the group.

Probyn launched a tirade at Mick for his imbecility, though he kept his voice low, hissing through his teeth.

'Ingham forgot to fill his water bottle before we left camp,' explained Mick. 'So I've been sharing mine with him but now it's all gone.'

'So thanks to big daft Ingham you've probably got a bellyful of worms!'

'It tasted all right. Me throat's parched I couldn't –'

But Probyn kicked his horse and trotted away up the column to ride beside the captain.

'Righteous bugger,' growled Ingham. 'It's worse than having your bloomin' mother with you.'

Mick was torn between agreement and loyalty to his friend. 'Ah, maybe, but his heart is true.'

They were to make good time and reached the village well before nightfall, enabling them to perform a thorough search. Despite the protest of the induna that the boys had not returned, Captain Fitzroy demanded to know in which huts they lived and upon answer sent Kilmaster in to search one and Havron the other. The women who lived there stood by watching.

Crouching, Probyn entered the windowless dwelling and looked around. There was no furniture to move, only a blanket and a few personal items: beads and feathers and the like. The interior was black with smoke and there was a hint of cow dung, but its floor had been polished to a high degree and it was a tidy dwelling. He was about to turn and leave when, after a quick decision to lift the blanket, he found the stolen rifle. With a cry of triumph he emerged into the daylight.

'Found this, sir!'

'So, they haven't been here?' The captain beheld the induna with scepticism, as Havron came forth bearing army blankets. 'I shall ask you again. Where are the boys?'

'I have not seen them.'

'Presumably these are their mothers.' Fitzroy indicated the two women, then directed a final question at them. 'Where are your sons?'

At the negative response the officer looked grim. 'Very well, we will take those.' He pointed at two young goats which were small enough to be carried over the saddle. 'And your houses will be burnt. Private Ingham, Private Barnes, do the honours.'

Ingham looked round for a stick to shove into the fire, but was forced to ignite a rag and threw it atop the thatched roof which was soon ablaze, the other similarly dealt with. Upon seeing what was to happen the two women dashed into their homes to rescue their few belongings, then emerged to stand and watch as the blaze took hold.

Satisfied that justice had been meted out, the captain gave the order to remount and the soldiers went on their way, taking the goats.

Whilst admiring the captain for his firmness, Probyn could not help feeling sorry for the mothers, who had done no wrong,

248

and was later to voice his misgivings to his friends when they camped for the night.

'It was hardly Buckingham Palace,' scoffed Havron, trying to turn his biscuit to a more edible mush, 'just dried mud clagged together with cow shit. They'll rebuild them in no time.'

'Yes, but however humble, if it were your home –'

'You're too soft.' Ingham added his opinion.

Probyn laughed then. 'Not soft in t'head though! It weren't me who forgot to fill me water bottle.' Having noticed that neither Ingham nor Melody were partaking of the dry biscuits he understood the reason. Turning to Mick he enquired, 'How much have you got left?'

'Enough to wet me whistle,' lied Mick whose throat felt like sandpaper.

'Here!' Probyn handed over his own water bottle.

'Ah no.'

'I'll have a swig!' Ingham lunged forth.

But Probyn held it away, insisting that Mick drink first. 'Go on, we'll be back at camp in the morning.'

Mick accepted gratefully, and afterwards Probyn allowed Ingham to sup too, though he wiped the neck of the bottle afterwards, conscious of the other's slovenly eating habits.

After this it was heads down till dawn.

Somewhat dehydrated, they were most thankful to reach the camp by mid-morning and, after slaking their thirst, were even more heartened when the captain ordered one of the goats to be slaughtered to provide dinner.

They were to remain there until the following day when, fully rested, the homewards trek continued.

Four days passed, days that varied little in their aridness. But Probyn rarely gave in to despondency, as others might.

'Don't you ever get sick of it?' grumbled Mick, looking decidedly under the weather and seemingly irked by his friend's capacity for remaining cheerful under such conditions – even the tough native horses were looking jaded.

Probyn admitted with a weary, dust-laden smile that he did. 'Well, aye, I suppose sometimes I fancy just being able to go down t'chip 'oile for one of each or a bottle o' pop or see me Aunt Kit.' But in truth no amount of hardship could quell the sheer joy of being amongst his fellows, his family, under skies that stretched to infinity. For him, nothing would ever be so grim as working down a black hole in the ground.

In the late afternoon they made camp and, after setting the captain's table with Huntley & Palmers and pouring him an aperitif, he filled an idle moment by composing a letter to his father. He was eager to tell those at home about the piccaninnies, and tried to include the native words he had learned, having to write them as they sounded for he was not about to tempt ridicule by asking anyone how to spell them.

Later there was another goat stew to enjoy, yet he noticed that Melody and Ingham barely touched it, taking to their beds much earlier than their fellows. Concerned, he shouted after them, ignored by Ingham but receiving the answer from Mick that he had a headache. He was about to question them further when the captain called for service, although he made a mental note to keep an eye on their welfare. With the captain relaxing over an after dinner whisky, Probyn stood outside his tent to watch the last remnants of the sunset, never failing to be moved by its magnificent colours. Smelling tobacco smoke, he turned to find the officer at his side and came to attention but was told to relax.

Whisky in one hand, cigarette in the other, Captain Fitzroy seemed to be enjoying the sunset as much as he. 'Just think, Private Kilmaster,' he murmured, a note of wonder in his voice, 'of this same sun setting at home in hours to come, and across the Atlantic to the West Indies and Canada, then to New Zealand and Australia, and Hong Kong, and on all her Majesty's territories around the world, until it finally returns here to entertain us tomorrow evening. What a truly enviable role we share in upholding that Empire. Don't you agree?'

'Oh, I surely do, sir!' Probyn's heart soared that the captain had chosen to share this intimate thought with him. They might be on different levels but on this point, as subjects of the glorious British Empire, they met as equals. 'It's a wonderful life. I wouldn't change it for the world.'

The captain emitted a soft laugh. 'But you already have the world.'

And when Probyn thought about it he realized that he had. And he could not have been happier.

At reveille Ingham and Melody had to be forcibly roused from their beds. This was not unusual, but it was apparent to Probyn who kept his eye on them all day that their state of health was not all it should be, and at the first opportunity he demanded to know what ailed them.

Mick, looking none too happy, fobbed him off. 'Just a dose of the runs, don't concern yourself.'

'I'll bet it's that mucky water hole!' accused Probyn.

'Shurrup!' warned Ingham, similarly afflicted. 'You'll get us done.'

'You should go and see Mr Bryant.' The surgeon had accompanied them on the trek.

'And get put on a charge for disobeying an order?' scowled Ingham. 'Just keep your neb out.' And with that he rushed off, clutching his abdomen.

Mick was close to follow, remaining only long enough to beg Probyn, 'Keep it to yourself, Pa. We'll be fine in a couple o' days.'

As the soldiers came closer to home their spirits became higher, all talking of what they were going to do when back at Eshowe. Probyn, however, remained concerned about Ingham and Melody who had grown more and more lethargic, neither eating, both obviously very ill, at every opportunity laying on the ground in the shade of their horses. He fought with his conscience: should he inform Sergeant Faulkner or remain loyal to his friends?

In the end it was not for him to choose. Melody became so seriously dehydrated that he fell into unconsciousness and toppled from his saddle. Even as others rushed to attend him, Ingham followed suit, plummeting head first into a cloud of dust. Probyn finally had to convey his worries about the pair to Sergeant Faulkner. 'They've had bad guts for days, Sergeant. I thought maybe it was that goat stew.'

The sergeant narrowed his eyes then and, remembering the incident with Gideon and the senna pods, turned to Havron. 'Have you been up to your tricks again?'

Havron looked insulted. 'No, Sergeant! I wouldn't do that to me mates.'

Knowing full well that this was the result of the infected water, Probyn declined to speak out; the pair were suffering enough. Instead he asked, 'Shall I fetch Mr Bryant to have a look at them, Sarnt?' At the sergeant's nod, Probyn remounted and galloped along the column to inform the captain what was amiss. When it was seen how grievously ill were the pair, a tent was hastily erected and they were carried inside.

Roused to semi-consciousness, the invalids were questioned, the surgeon coming straight to the point. 'What are your motions like?'

Even in this stupor Mick was hesitant to open his cracked lips, but Ingham with his usual delicacy groaned, 'Pea soup, sir.'

Bryant turned to the sergeant, obviously annoyed. 'Didn't anyone spot them becoming listless?'

'Who'd notice the difference?' Queen muttered jokingly.

Probyn shot him a look of rebuke. At any other time he would have made the joke himself but this was a grave matter.

The sergeant accepted the blame. 'It's enteric, isn't it, sir? I should have noticed.'

'We'll have to get them back as soon as possible. Put them in the wagon!'

With a canopy erected over the infected men, the column set off again, their pace more urgent in the need to get to hospital. The days suddenly seemed much longer. Soldiers took it in turns to jolt about with Melody and Ingham in the wagon, draping wet rags on their foreheads to try and quell their raging temperature. Now added to their symptoms a crop of rose-coloured spots crept over their perspiring bodies.

It was therefore of great relief to all when they arrived back at Fort Nongqayi and the invalids were immediately conveyed to hospital, though it did little to stem Probyn's guilt over keeping quiet for so long, thereby endangering his friends, and this preoccupation was to offend his superior who, after the long trek, was looking forward to luncheon at the mess and intelligent conversation with his peers.

The captain gave a yell as scalding water was added to his bath. 'Aagh! I said a *little* more hot! What the devil's wrong with you, Private, you almost ruined my manhood!'

Probyn was mortified. 'I'm very sorry, sir!' And he rushed to compensate with a jug of cold water. 'I was just wondering how my pals are!'

'A lot better than I am, I sincerely hope!' But the captain was joking now, and dipped his shoulders under the water in a luxuriating manner. 'Don't worry, I'm sure they'll be fine.'

'Yes, sir.' Probyn became more attentive to the task in hand, pouring the captain a glass of sherry which he periodically handed to him as he bathed.

Once dried and dressed, Captain Fitzroy asked to be informed by Lieutenant Percy about any reports that had come in during his absence. It transpired that there had been further Matabele raids on the Shona, but more seriously there had been incidents against European settlers.

As always Probyn eavesdropped on these conversations and, though it was impertinent, could not resist asking the captain later if there was a chance of war.

Refreshed from his bath and anticipating a hearty luncheon, Fitzroy was congenial. 'Highly unlikely. Personally there's nothing I'd like better than to see some action, but we're not permitted to declare war unless British subjects are threatened. This ruction between the Mats and Shonas is nothing new.' He became pleasantly thoughtful. 'Nevertheless I think we shall have to get the men to improve their laagering skills. Three minutes is far too slow. Remind me to have a word with Sergeant Faulkner. Now, I shall repair to the mess. And you, my good fellow, may have the afternoon to do as you please.'

Thanking him, Probyn went to find out whether there had been any news of Mick and Ingham, but no one had heard.

There was no word the following morning either. After dutifully serving the captain all day, after tea Probyn asked if he might go and check on the invalids' progress. It seemed absurd to him that his friends should be at death's door after one sip of water whilst here was Gideon in the rudest of health even after nibbling on putrid flesh.

There was still no news of Mick but the others seemed not so concerned, too busy catching up with their mail that had arrived that morning and which they had only just had time to open. Probyn, too, found a letter to brighten his life. Forgetting about Mick for the present, he sat down on the step to open it, a ripple of happiness touching his heart in this pleasant evening. To a background of whirring crickets, the noisy twittering of birds from the forest as they jostled to find a roost for the night, and the pine-scented breeze rustling the palm fronds outside the turreted wall, he unfolded the letter and began to read.

After wishing him a happy twentieth birthday, Meredith's letter opened with the news that, following the birth of her son last year, she had just had a little girl. *Well, I say little*, wrote Merry, *she was a ten and a half pounder. I wonder if I'm going to match Rhoda and Alice in having one boy and three girls. Still, I think I'll wait a while to find out!* Smiling, Probyn's eyes moved on. He had barely reached halfway down the page before emitting a violent exclamation. 'The bloody swine!'

'Eh, steady on, Pa!' There was a combined outlet of mock

horror, but his face remained deadly serious and his anger was all too apparent.

'A bunch of strikers have been round to me dad's house and roughed him up. He's had an apoplexy!'

They were all ears then, wanting to know more as his horrified gaze raced over the letter, reading aloud as he went. 'My God, this was written over a month ago, he could be dead!' So contented had he become amongst his army pals, it came as a jolt that he still had a blood family who might be in urgent need of him. Swamped by guilt that he had not been there to protect his father he stood there completely stunned as others tried to rally him.

'He might just be paralysed,' said Rook. 'Me grandma lived for years after she had hers.'

Probyn remained dazed, unsure what an apoplexy involved. Could his father see or hear anything? Even if he were to send a letter he wouldn't know what to say, how to comfort him. His army training had not equipped him with such skills. One thing was certain: 'I'll have to ask for leave.'

The others were doubtful that this would be granted. Probyn too held misgivings, but said he had no option but to try. It would soon be time to go and attend the captain's bath. Folding the letter he marched away, rehearsing what he must say.

He was still pondering how to voice his request for leave some time later as he ordered Gideon and another black servant to take away the bath water and he himself helped the captain to dress. In the event it was Fitzroy who gave him the opportunity to broach the subject.

Indicating his own stack of letters and parcels, Captain Fitzroy asked idly, 'Any news from home, Private Kilmaster?'

Probyn took a deep breath. 'Yes, sir. Bad news, I'm afraid.'

Showing concern, Captain Fitzroy remembered that Kilmaster was from a mining family and, kept up to date with news-papers sent from home, exclaimed, 'Ah! The coal strike is taking its toll I presume?' He paused to allow his servant to expand.

'In more ways than one, sir.' Probyn outlined the situation in the mining community and of his father's stroke, ending with the plaintive comment, 'They don't know how long he'll survive.'

'That is most unfortunate.' The captain shook his head in woe. 'You must extend my sympathies to your mother.'

'Thank you, sir, but my mother's dead.' Probyn wanted his superior to know how vital it was that he be allowed home to see his only parent.

However, Captain Fitzroy did not immediately sense this, merely shaking his head and tutting, whilst proceeding with his dressing.

'I was wondering, sir, if there's any possibility of my being allowed home to visit my father, considering the gravity of his condition.'

The captain's mildly stunned expression told him this was out of the question. 'I commiserate with you entirely, Private Kilmaster, but in all seriousness you cannot expect me to grant such a request. It would take you the best part of a month to get there and a month to get back.'

'I wouldn't expect to receive pay, sir.'

'I'm most gratified to hear it but your request is still beyond reason. I could not possibly spare you for so long. Besides, we may be needed to help quell this trouble in the north.'

Desperation made Probyn rash. 'But you said yourself, sir, that you don't really set much store by all this talk of war –'

'Are you arguing with me, Private?' The captain's attitude completely changed.

'No, sir! I meant no offence, but I'm so worried that my father might die before –'

'If your father dies, then you must take it like a man, as must the rest of us. If the army were to grant leave to every bereaved infantryman we should soon be in a lamentable state. Now, I have given my verdict, let there be an end to it.'

'Yes, sir.' Knowing it was fruitless to continue, Probyn resumed his task of helping the captain to dress, handing over various accoutrements, performing each move with dignity though underneath his heart railed at the lack of compassion.

Fitzroy settled into a chair, extended his legs over the leopardskin rug and, after a few sips of whisky, reverted to his amiable mood. 'Be a good chap, stop sulking and pass me that will you?' He indicated a jigsaw sent from home by his mother who, aware of his fondness for such pastimes, despatched them regularly.

Quietly seething, Probyn set a table in front of the captain before going to fetch the jigsaw, then, in a small act of malevolence, deftly slipped his hand inside it and removed one of the pieces before handing it to the captain. 'Will that be all, sir?'

'For now, thank you, Private Kilmaster.' Without looking at his servant, Fitzroy took the lid from the box and tipped its contents on to the table, thereby dismissing the other.

Going about his business in the room next door, Probyn racked his brain for a solution, for he must make an effort to see his father, find out the true severity of his plight and help him. He *must*. A wave of guilt swept over him for the way he had bestowed Captain Fitzroy with the mantle of surrogate father. What had Fitzroy ever really done for him? Yes, he had contributed much to his military education, but did he truly care? No. He had not made sacrifice for him, worried over him, could not love him like a real father.

A glance into the captain's room saw Fitzroy concentrating over the jigsaw in total abandonment of his servant's sad dilemma.

Never had Probyn committed an imprisonable offence, but he seriously contemplated it now. To stow away, go without permission, would jeopardize his entire career, perhaps even bring a charge of desertion, but at this desperate moment it seemed his only alternative.

'Private Kilmaster, another whisky if you please!'

Jerked from his mutinous machinations, Probyn hurried to comply with the demand, at the same time abandoning his previous idea; however dire the situation he could not bring himself to risk a court martial.

The captain was well into his jigsaw. Replenishing the empty glass, his servant enjoyed a moment of vengeful pleasure, anticipating the irritation that one missing piece would cause. Damn him!

Over the following hour, as he cleaned the captain's spurs and laid out his apparel for morning, Probyn rummaged his brain for a better answer, casting the occasional surreptitious glance to check on Fitzroy's progress. Piece by piece the jigsaw took shape, until finally there were only half a dozen fragments left to insert.

His hand moving quickly and confidently now, the captain reached out triumphantly for the final piece then frowned and looked about him, peering to right and left, lifting the box to search beneath it, and even groping under his chair.

A smug grin twitched Probyn's lips over this small act of revenge, though soon it was washed away again as he himself continued to hunt for a solution whilst the captain searched high and low for the missing piece of jigsaw, then in a final act of frustration swiped the entire puzzle from the table and strode off to the officers' mess.

Left to pick up the pieces from the leopardskin rug, a grim-faced Probyn came to the only possible conclusion. The thought was heart-rending, made him feel physically ill, but much as he loved his regiment he could not stand idly by whilst the means to help his father was in his pocket. He must buy himself out.

10

The discovery that it would take the massive sum of eighteen pounds to purchase his discharge might have proved an insurmountable barrier to some, but was no obstacle to the determined Private Kilmaster. With his mind made up and sixteen pounds already saved he set about collecting the rest by selling the possessions he had acquired over the years, beginning with a copy of *Treasure Island*.

'Rookie, you're a reader, do you want to buy this?'

Lying supine on his bed, Rook cast a bird-like eye at the visitor's offering. 'Read it.'

'There's no law says you can't read a book twice.'

'What's the point if you know the ending?' Rook slapped at a mosquito.

'What about you, Queenie?'

'Never read a book in me life,' came the proud reply.

A slightly exasperated Probyn addressed them en masse. 'Anybody else want it – only two bob?'

Havron scoffed. 'Two bob? I could get slewed for a week on that.'

'How about a cleaning rod then?' Throwing the book aside, Probyn started to display the spare pieces of kit he had accumulated.

'Now you're talking.' Havron came over to inspect the items for sale.

Probyn continued to peddle, displaying Felix Lennon's battered footwear. 'Bumby, you're the same size as me.'

Queen sensed a frantic edge to Probyn's attempts at disposal. 'Never thought I'd see you short o' cash, Pa. Got a woman in trouble?'

'No, I've got to buy meself out,' said Probyn bluntly. Having gained their full attention, he explained the situation. 'Fizzer's refused to give me leave so I've no other option. Me father might be dead by now for all I know but I'll never be able to live with meself if I don't go and see.'

There was a combined murmur of sympathy for their friend and exclamations of disgust for the hard-hearted captain.

'You poor sod,' uttered Bumby. Of all his comrades Kilmaster was the most attached to military life. 'Will you rejoin later?'

'Maybe,' muttered Probyn. 'I haven't thought that far ahead, I just have to get home, quickly. I've got most of the money saved, I only need a couple of quid to make up the eighteen.'

Barnes's big barn door of a face fell ajar. 'You've got sixteen quid saved? Christ, you old miser!'

'Never mind that!' Bumby elbowed him out of the way and tried on the boots. 'I'll have these, Pa. How much?'

With various generosity to follow, Probyn very quickly found himself in possession of the required amount. He thanked them gruffly. 'I appreciate it . . . and . . . well, I'll be sorry to go but . . . well, you know . . .'

Rook clapped him on the back, looking embarrassed. Everyone else stood about looking similarly awkward.

Probyn manufactured a cheery farewell. 'I'd better get back, the captain'll be after my guts. Give my regards to Melody and Ingham when they come out of hospital.'

The mood altered yet again. 'Ingham's had it,' Havron informed him. 'Sarge told us last night.'

Probyn was shocked. 'What about Mick?' Despite having other things on his mind he was genuinely concerned.

The others shrugged. 'He's right poorly by all accounts,' muttered Bumby.

After a thoughtful interlude, Probyn murmured, 'Well, give him my regards if you see him.' Then, to calls of good luck from his friends, he returned to the captain's quarters to await his master.

At first, Captain Fitzroy took his servant's announcement with no great seriousness, continuing his ablutions in preparation of an evening at the mess. 'Purchase your discharge? I don't think you've fully considered the extent of what that entails, Private Kilmaster.'

'I know it costs eighteen pounds, sir, and I have that amount.' He revealed his savings.

At this confident response Fitzroy became annoyed, snatching the towel from his servant and mopping irately at his face. 'And what of the inconvenience you will cause to others?'

Probyn looked baffled.

'Dammit, man, I shall have to train a new servant!' Fitzroy hurled the towel back.

Probyn caught it, trying to remain calm. 'I'm very sorry, sir, but I have to see how my father is and if I'm refused leave –'

'Then you'll petulantly take it upon yourself to go!'

'It gives me no enjoyment, sir.' Probyn's face was grim. 'I love the army. It's my life. But I have a duty to go.'

'You have a duty to your regiment, you swore an oath of allegiance! It obviously meant nothing.' Deliberately turning his back on the young infantryman, the captain leaned over a table drumming his fingers upon it.

'I beg your pardon, sir, it meant everything. I'd gladly give my life if it were asked of me, but I could never hold my head up again if I failed my own father.'

The captain tried a different tack. 'Kilmaster, I regard you as one of my most trustworthy soldiers. The major, who shares my view, will be astounded when I inform him of your decision to waste over two years of training. Are you absolutely certain you wish to throw it all away?'

'I'm compelled by circumstance to do it, sir.'

'You stubborn –!' After much snorting, the captain finally recognized that his valet was not to be moved. 'Very well, I shall put your application forward.'

'Thank you, sir.' Probyn tried to sound grateful. 'Could you say how long it will be before –'

'I shall speak to the major this evening. The matter is obviously of great urgency to you.' Suddenly abandoning his terse manner, Captain Fitzroy looked Probyn full in the face, his eyes commiserating. 'I do understand your dilemma, Private Kilmaster, I really do, but might I just lay this scenario before you: what if after all your expenditure, your sacrifice, you arrive home to find that your father has already passed away? It will all have been for nothing.'

Did the man think him incapable of such coherence, wondered Probyn? 'That has been a worry to me, sir. It will be sad, but at least I can take solace that I made the effort.'

Defeated, the captain gave a final nod. 'Very well, I will do what I can.'

His application travelling up the chain of command, Probyn found himself the next day in front of the major, the latter making even more effort than Captain Fitzroy to try and talk him out of it. Private Kilmaster refused to budge.

Back in the captain's office later in the day, Probyn was informed of the outcome by Fitzroy. 'Now, Private Kilmaster, I must inform you at once that your request to purchase your discharge has been denied.'

Probyn started. 'But it's my fundamental right, sir!'

Captain Fitzroy looked stern. 'Before you get yourself into deeper water, Kilmaster, let me say that the major has submitted your request to HQ and spoken on your behalf. Neither of us has any wish to waste the two and a half years that has been spent on turning you into a soldier. A good soldier, all things considered. Therefore, presented with the gravity of the situation, and though he takes a very dim view of being blackmailed into such a position, the colonel has granted permission for you to proceed to England and attend your father's bedside.'

Probyn's look of outrage turned to astonishment. He was unable to speak.

'Naturally it will be without pay,' was the clipped addition. 'You will stay only until there is a return voyage, which means that after a journey of twenty-eight days you will have approximately one week on English soil, but that should be sufficient to your needs.'

Probyn breathed a sigh of relief and gratitude. 'Oh, it will, sir! I just need to see him in case – well it might be the last time. I can't thank you enough, sir.'

'I shall be sorry to lose you as a valet, but you do understand that I cannot hold the position open.'

'I fully understand, sir, and thank you again. I've enjoyed serving you.'

With a curt nod the captain provided written authorization for him to travel and told him to report to the depot at Pontefract where he would be given further instruction concerning his return to South Africa. 'And may I also offer a last piece of advice. If you intend to make a life in the army, you must learn the meaning of commitment.'

'Yes, sir,' came the quiet reply.

Before dismissing him, Captain Fitzroy made the unexpected move of shaking his hand. 'Good luck, Private Kilmaster. I hope you will find that your father's situation is not too dire.'

'Thank you, sir!' Stamping to attention, Probyn issued a last salute. His exit from the office marked a sorry end to an enjoyable association.

The voyage home was even worse than he had anticipated, the dawning of each tedious day bringing fresh fear that he would arrive too late. July became August, the weather becoming gradually cooler. It was September before he eventually arrived.

Even once on English soil his torment was not over for he was faced with a long train excursion from the coast, each hour sucking him further into desperation. The change in climate was even more depressing. Whilst other inhabitants had not yet reached for winter coats he himself shivered to keep warm.

To relieve his journey he bought a wad of newspapers, catching up with news of the national coal strike, but hard print could not convey the whole story and he was unprepared for the great distress that met him on his arrival hours later at Pontefract. Having been ordered to report to the depot before anything else, this is what he did, on his way there witnessing many signs of deprivation. Miners and their families were openly begging on the streets. With plenty of funds at his disposal he made several acts of generosity, but the entreaties became so frequent that he exhausted all his loose change and was left with only his precious banknotes and two sovereigns and was forced to tell them he had no more. Some of them became threatening then, called him names, even spat on his uniform. Shocked and upset, fearing that he would be robbed, he quickened his pace to the garrison, anxious to escape the spirit of bad feeling which pervaded the whole town.

Safe inside the depot he was informed of the enormity of the problem. Starvation was rife amongst the miners. Soup kitchens had been set up and efforts made to raise funds but that would only solve the immediate hunger. The hardship was creeping insidiously to other workers; the shops from whom the miners normally bought their supplies; the liquorice manufactories, the staple trade of the town, would soon be forced into idleness unless a supply of coal was forthcoming; the flood of degradation seeped ever wider.

Having acted out his orders and equipped with the date of his sailing in a week's time, Probyn was now free to execute the real reason for his coming here. In the hope of getting to his destination more swiftly, he returned to the railway station, treading warily to avoid beggars. However, after waiting what seemed like an age for a train, his healthy sunburned face a stark contrast to the mawkish creatures who glared contemptuously at his uniform, he decided it would be quicker on foot. Hurrying from the station, he struck out for Ralph Royd.

He arrived there to an atmosphere of gloom and general ill-feeling. The family cottage held no more welcome, one of its windows broken and boarded over. His stepmother, though, made amends for all this, her face lighting up with a warm smile as she answered his tentative tap.

'Oh, Probe, my goodness I thought it was a Red Indian come to scalp me! My, I can hardly recognize you! Come in, come in, your father'll be that glad to see you!'

Whipping off his glengarry, Probyn threw back his head and gave a cry of relief, all the pent-up anxiety rushing forth in his exclamation. 'He's still here then? Oh, I can't tell you . . . I thought . . . by, I'm that relieved!' Clamping the glengarry over his mouth, he followed his stepmother inside, unable for the moment to say more for fear of shedding tears.

'Yes, he's still with us, thank the Lord.' Ann's smile held sadness. 'But I have to warn you he's not the same as he was. He's managing to drag himself around but he can't speak.' She lowered her voice. 'Well, he tries but he gets the wrong words and he ends up so frustrated . . . anyway, you'll see for yourself.'

Happier now, Probyn was about to follow her into the parlour when someone made a swift exit. 'Oh, hello, Wyn! Don't feel you have to leave on my account.'

'I was going anyway.' Wyn did not appear in the least bit pleased to see him, donning her coat and brushing past, but not without an accusative whisper. 'You're the son, you should have been here to protect him!'

Probyn cast a look of dismay at her departing form. So much for Merry's opinion that they spoke more kindly of their brother these days. He turned to his stepmother who merely gave an uncomfortable shrug and escorted him onwards.

Though relieved to find his father alive it was a great shock to see him like this, one side of his body looking as if it belonged to someone else as he dragged himself out of his chair and came shuffling to meet his son. 'Ooh, don't exert yourself now, Father!' Probyn hurried to assist the invalid back to his chair, helping him to get comfortable. 'Are you all right? Doest want this cushion behind thee?'

Monty allowed himself to be fussed over for a moment, then gave an irritated flick of his hand ordering Probyn to sit down.

'I'll put the kettle on,' said Ann. 'Well now this is a grand surprise, Probe – I can't get over how sunburned you are! I'll bet this weather takes some getting used to.'

'Aye, I can't get warm!' Out of relief and sheer nervousness Probyn was abnormally talkative, though he directed his comments to his stepmother, unable to look upon his father both out of discomfort and also consideration of Monty's feelings. 'By rights I shouldn't even be here, but when I got Merry's letter I had to come and see how Father was. I asked for leave but was turned down so the only solution was for me to buy meself out.'

'That must have cost you a fortune!' Ann looked aghast.

'It would've done. The captain tried to talk me out of it but I wasn't having any of it, I couldn't sit by not knowing what had happened to Father so, as I said, I offered to buy my discharge but they decided they didn't want to lose a good soldier so they gave me leave after all and here I am!'

'And we're glad of it, aren't we, Father?' Ann grinned at her husband. 'Did you hear that? They think Probe's a good soldier.'

Monty gave a lopsided smile and nodded.

'I couldn't believe how bad things were in Ponty,' continued Probyn, hoping to bring the subject gently round to the attack on his father. 'Folk begging, getting really nasty when I ran out of summat to give them. I waited ages for a train but in the end I decided to walk.'

Stirring the teapot, Ann explained that the lack of transport was due to the strike. 'They've knocked lots of trains off altogether, and the railway workers are on short time.'

Probyn nodded. 'Bringing foreign coal in too by the look of it. I noticed a lot of unfamiliar wagons at the railway yards.'

Ann glanced at Monty. 'Yes, they started bringing it in from Durham, caused dreadful riots at Barnsley so we've heard. Mindst, we've had our moments here, haven't we, Father?'

At last Probyn was able to confront the matter. 'Merry said in her letter a mob attacked you –'

'Oh, they didn't lay a finger on either of us,' said Ann, 'but they might as well have done for the damage they've caused. Bloomin' bullies, trying to force your father to go with them and smash up blacklegs' homes. Well, he got so angry something exploded in his head.'

Over the next few minutes she related the course of Monty's affliction to his son. 'I thought we were going to lose him, didn't regain consciousness until the next day and even then he was still dangerously ill. It's been a miracle that he's managed to get himself walking again.'

Monty tried to contribute, wagging a trembling finger at his wife, but his words were slurred.

'Yes, I've been massaging your leg, dear, haven't I? It seems to help,' she added to Probyn.

'Toe, toe . . .' slurred Monty, one flaccid cheek puffing in and out.

Ann rose and assisted him with his teacup, but seemed only to frustrate him and eventually after several attempts to communicate he dashed her hand away, slopping hot tea everywhere. Without comment, she calmly went to fetch a cloth whilst Probyn looked away, deeply embarrassed.

'Did the police do owt?' he mumbled.

'Oh, we didn't want that lot involved.' Ann shivered. The tea mopped up, she sat down again, diverting the topic to a more general one. 'Anyway, at least the Welsh strike's over,' she said to her stepson. 'It's a start. I was hoping our lads would follow but the union's just voted unanimously again to hold out against any reduction. Undoubtedly they've got a cause and I fully agree with the strike but I don't like the way some of them are going about it. They've had to bring the military out to deal with them in some parts.'

That explained the looks of hatred directed at Probyn when he arrived.

'Who was it that came round here?' he asked and duly received a list of names that were familiar. 'Judson! That thug, he doesn't care about unions or causes he just wants a good excuse to punch somebody or commit vandalism. Right, I'm off to sort him out!' About to rise, he was prevented from doing so by his father's slurred command.

'Echo!' The flaccid side of Monty's face puffed out in exertion. 'Echo, echo!'

'Sorry, Father, I didn't catch that.' Probyn bent to listen, straining to understand, pretending it was his own deafness that was the hurdle, but after several embarrassing moments his only reward was a swift cuff to his head.

Snapping himself upright, he looked helplessly to his step-mother for assistance and Ann came to try and calm the frustrated invalid. 'I think your father's trying to tell you not to go round to Judson's, weren't you, dear?' In apparent relief, Monty flopped back in his chair, nodding exhaustedly.

'I'm not having him pushing my father about,' began Probyn, but was stopped by the sight of his father's renewed agitation. His stepmother, too, intervened.

'And your father doesn't want to see you pushed about or worse. You know what Judson and his cronies are like. Leave it be, Probe. You came to see your father didn't you, not to make war? Even if you do manage to give him a hiding we're the ones who have to live with him. Now, come sit down and tell us more about what you've been doing in South Africa. Eh, we could hardly believe the things you wrote in your letters!'

Reluctantly, he fell back into his seat, and began to recount his adventures. But the sight of his father's dribbling mouth, the look of torment on his twisted face when his wife or son misinterpreted some request, all made for a very uncomfortable afternoon. Tortured by helplessness over his father's plight, forbidden even to punish the culprit, Probyn wished he had not come here, would much prefer to be at Aunt Kit's or indeed anywhere else where he did not have to witness this suffering. But he had come here to see his father and would not desert him.

That five days, declared Probyn to himself at the end of his stay, must surely be the most exacting he had ever spent. For one who had undergone military training it was not issued lightly. To sit there, be forced to watch a once upright man drag himself around, slobbering and struggling to get out his words, constantly raging at the idiocy of those who could not understand him, berating his wife when she offered tokens of love . . . if Probyn had brought his gun he would surely have fired a bullet into his father's head and put an end to his suffering.

No one visited. It was obvious Wyn had broadcast his presence. Apparently Father had received plenty of visitors before, but not this week.

Finally, mercifully, it was time for him to return to the depot. Riddled with guilt at his relief to be going, he cornered his stepmother in the kitchen and handed over his entire savings, whispering instructions for her not to tell his father until he had gone for this would perhaps make him angry, and promising to send a regular amount when he got back to Africa.

Her thanks was uneffusive but genuine. 'How much longer will you be there, Probe?'

'I'm not sure. You'll write and keep me abreast of father's health?'

She promised to do so.

'Will he ever be completely better?'

Ann sighed. 'Well, the doctor says he could be mended, but it involves him having to be taught to speak properly again and when you try he accuses you of treating him like a baby.' Her eyes filled with tears but she quickly dashed them away. 'Anyway, I'm sure your visit did him the power of good.'

Probyn wished he could believe that. 'I'd stay longer if I could but . . . duty calls and all that. Anyway, now that I'm gone the girls will feel able to start visiting him again. Have you heard anything from Uncle Owen?'

'Not a word. You surely didn't expect it?'

Probyn shrugged, then wandered over to the doorway, secretly observing his father who was staring vacantly into space. Monty had obviously been out in the sunshine, freckles and a healthy glow taking the place of his usual coal miner's pallor.

Ann folded the banknotes and made to put them and the sovereigns in a tin, then had a sudden thought. 'Have you left yourself enough money to get to the ship?' When her stepson said he did not need it she took out some silver. 'Here, have this couple of bob.'

'Aye go on then, I might see if I can get a train back to Ponty.' Feeling deeply sorry for his stepmother, he dashed a quick kiss to her cheek, the first he had ever given her. 'Right, I'd best be off.' Turning away from her astonished face he moved into the parlour and sat down beside Monty, trying to sound both regretful and cheery at the same time.

'Well, Father, I'm afraid I must fly with the birdies.'

Monty donated an unsymmetrical smile, and issued a few words.

Not even pretending to understand, Probyn merely nodded and smiled in return. 'I'm right glad to find you on the road to recovery. I can confess now I were a bit worried. Should've known they make 'em tough round here. Next time I come I expect to see you leaping about like a good un.'

'You're a good lad really,' slurred Monty, but it came out as something completely different.

Though not comprehending, Probyn grinned and nodded, and sat for a moment in pensive silence. Then, rising suddenly, he scooped Monty's useless right hand from his lap and held it firmly, held it for a few seconds longer than was required from a normal handshake, before placing it gently back on his father's lap. 'Goodbye, Father, I'll write as soon as I get back. Hope the strike's soon over.'

'Toe,' slurred Monty and issued a little wave and a smile as his son departed.

He was glad to leave the village, for the atmosphere was not a pleasant one, though he did pause to stroke his old pit pony who, with others, was enjoying a greener existence due to the strike, their shaggy heads lining the fence expectant of some titbit, snorting and nuzzling his clothes. Just as he was imagining these to be the only friendly faces, along came Peggo Wilcox who shared a few sympathetic words about his father before relaying the information that a train was due in half an hour. Thanking him, Probyn hurried to the station in the next village and was just in time to catch the train, avoiding a six mile hike to the depot.

On his journey he was to have more evidence of the miners' strike, sidings that were blocked with vast accumulations of wagons bearing unfamiliar names, pathetic figures groping their way over slag heaps in the hunt for fuel, the dullness of the sky casting even more gloom upon the scene. At one point from his carriage window he saw a party of railway navvies who had been filling coal wagons scatter in panic as a mob of men and women descended on them wielding lumps of wood, they in turn were quickly routed by police accompanied by soldiers.

Nearing his destination, Probyn became apprehensive as to what his own reception might be, and was therefore gratified to find another train had arrived before his and was disgorging scores of soldiers, the platform awash with red.

However, as if in response to this, groups of miners had

begun to gather, their numbers swelling quickly as the news was broadcast and others came trickling in from the streets.

A good-natured jeer went up from a group of strikers as the lone figure alighted from the train. 'Eh up, here's reinforcements!'

Ignoring this jibe, Probyn began to make his way through the crowd to the exit. But when some small missile hit him on the back of the head he turned sharply to confront the culprit. Faced with nonchalant stares he was compelled to proceed, clenching his jaw at the mocking laughter that followed him. Almost to the exit, he was accosted by a sergeant of the South Staffordshire Regiment.

'Hold there, Private! Where do you think you're going?'

Probyn began to explain that he was not part of this unit, but the sergeant quickly dismissed his claim. 'Never mind that! We need every man we can get. You stay here till you're told you can leave.'

'But I don't have a rifle, Sergeant!'

His objection was quickly stilled. 'I'll find you one!'

It had been bad enough re-acclimatizing himself to England after eighteen months in the sub-tropics, but to be thrust into the middle of an imminent riot . . . Probyn turned to the soldier nearby, his bewildered face pleading for enlightenment.

'Don't ask me, chum.' The private of the South Staffordshire Regiment shook his head. 'We've been rushing about like loonies all day, chasing these buggers about from one place to another. First we're told to go to Bradford, when we get there the bloody strikers have gone somewhere else to smash up a brewery . . . looks like they've had a skinful while they were at it as well. Now we've been told to go to Garbrough Colliery, probably another wild goose chase.'

'Oh crumbs, that's where my uncle works,' breathed Probyn, dismayed, but at this point a rifle was thrust into his hands.

'Don't use it till you're told!'

Aghast at the prospect of having to quell a riot – he didn't join the army to shoot his friends and relations! – Probyn gripped his weapon, looking anxiously about him as the number of demonstrators continued to grow. To be here in itself was bad enough, but to be without his fellows, those he had come to know and trust . . . He was overcome by a feeling of utter isolation.

Under the watchful eyes of others, the soldiers were ordered to form up and march to the colliery some miles away.

The mob followed.

Upon arrival in the colliery yard it became clear that this was no wild goose chase. Hordes of men and women were swarming over the railway wagons and tipping out the contents whilst a small posse of constabulary stood watching helplessly. Now, joined by those newly arrived, the number of demonstrators swelled to threatening proportions. The roar that went up from them as they challenged the soldiers was alarming, although no violence was offered and the catcalls were good-natured as yet. Involved in previous lock-outs, Probyn knew how quickly the mood could alter. Feeling his hair stand on end, he glanced anxiously about him for a sight of Uncle Owen, but amongst such a mass it was impossible. Besides, it was now four o'clock and the light was failing. Surely they would have to quell the disturbance before dark.

A relieved police inspector greeted the captain of the South Staffordshire Regiment. 'Thank God you're here! We haven't been able to do so much as rap a knuckle, we're waiting for somebody to come and read the Riot Act.'

Captain Baker reassured him. 'I was informed by your superintendent in Bradford that a magistrate would be on the train to follow ours so he shouldn't be long now. Just as well.' He surveyed the mob. 'We weren't anticipating such numbers.'

Watching him deploy his troops, the inspector wished him luck, but voiced doubt that they would be any more effective than the police in quashing the disorder.

He was right. All efforts earned only contemptuous laughter. Worse still, news of the soldiers' arrival had spread to other collieries with the result that numbers continued to swell and by dusk had reached massive dimensions.

As night descended Probyn found himself enveloped by a mob of some ten thousand bearing banners, the majority of them already armed with bludgeons and others quickly arming themselves from a stack of timber in the yard, though no blow had as yet been struck.

'Why don't they give us the order to fire?' hissed the nervous youngster to Probyn's right flank. 'If we'd shot a few earlier it wouldn't have got to this!'

It's all right for you, thought Probyn, the most frightened he had been in all his life, they're not your people, you haven't lived and worked amongst them as I have. But like a good soldier he kept his opinion to himself, his body tense, eyes darting all around him, and was most relieved when the order was shouted to retreat to the comparative safety of the engine house.

Crammed inside, whilst the rioters cheered and shouted for them to withdraw, the same question rippled through their ranks. Why were they standing here helpless with weapons at their disposal?

The captain directed an oblique glance at the police officers amongst them. 'Perhaps you'd like to answer that, Inspector? I was assured by your superintendent there'd be a magistrate here to read the Riot Act. That was several hours ago.'

The inspector responded with an enquiry. 'Is there a telephone in here?'

'One in this office over here, sir!' called a voice, at which the inspector struggled through the mass of tunics.

'I'll try and get a message through to Pontefract!'

However, his endeavour at communication failed and before any further attempt could be made a stone crashed through the window showering everyone with glass, followed by another and another. 'Soldiers out! Soldiers out!'

The mood outside became increasingly frenzied. Someone had set fire to piles of timber and, as it took hold, fed the flames with barrels of oil. Amidst all this was the constant sound of breakage.

There was more banging on the door of the engine house and inducements for the soldiers to leave. 'Come out now and you won't be harmed!'

His nervous troops looking to him for instruction, a reluctant Captain Baker turned to the police inspector. 'I'm afraid I'm going to have to do as they ask.'

'You can't leave us here, we'll be massacred!'

'Then you must leave under our protection. The whole situation is ridiculous! I refuse to be held prisoner whilst a magistrate decides whether to give us leave to fire our guns, and I will not subject my men to further humiliation. We shall withdraw and send for reinforcements.'

Shouting to the rioters that they were coming out, Captain Baker relayed orders for his men to fall in ready to march, then unbolted the door. Warily, the troops began to emerge. A great cheer went up and the crowd parted to make way for them, dancing and singing and waving their banners in triumph. No sooner had the soldiers left the engine house than the mob took over, smashing and wrecking, looting workmen's toolboxes for anything of value, whilst those who had been sent to quell them were forced to slink from the colliery yard, feeling totally powerless and dishonoured.

Outside the gates, the captain called for his men to halt, then selected a messenger to go to Pontefract barracks for reinforcements. Stepping in with the offer of his pony and trap the inspector also despatched a man to find out what was keeping the magistrate. Those left behind could only stand in a pitiable state of helplessness and watch the orgy of wanton destruction as the blaze from the timber yard spread to an inferno, engulfing everything in its path, shooting flames and sparks hundreds of feet into the air and illuminating the district for miles around. It was, thought Probyn, like a scene from hell. With every corf derailed and hurled down the pit shaft, every window smashed, the mob then attacked the manager's house, smashing furniture, plates, chandeliers, anything they could lay their hands on came flying through the windows, whilst its owner and his terrified family fled towards the protection of the soldiers.

Drawn by the raging beacon, the fire brigade and steamer arrived, its men making valiant efforts to douse the blaze but coming under an immediate hail of missiles. Police and soldiers who tried to assist them were also pelted with stones, some seriously injured. Probyn fell back, staunching a cut to his cheek. He became angry then. From the manager's house came the discordant clamour of a piano in its death throes, books, clothes and family photographs were tossed into the garden and set alight, plants ripped from the greenhouse, every pane of glass smashed. Finally, only half sated, the perpetrators emerged with armfuls of food and beer which they began to consume with impunity, taunting the soldiers with chicken legs before cramming them into their own mouths.

'Where the devil is that blasted magistrate?' yelled Captain Baker, helping to deal with the injured.

As if in response at that precise moment a pony and trap arrived bearing a Justice of the Peace.

'Where in God's name have you been, man?' demanded Captain Baker. 'We've been waiting six hours for you!'

The other took offence. 'I beg your pardon, sir, but it was not myself you were awaiting. I only learned of the situation some minutes ago and might I say I have forfeited a pleasant evening to –'

'Never mind the twaddle!' Captain Baker shoved him forward. 'Just get on with it!'

Confronted with the hellish scene the magistrate paled and tried to hold back but was firmly escorted to within earshot of the rioters. The flames reflected in the whites of his eyes, he called for attention and began to recite the Riot Act, ducking frequently to avoid the hail of missiles but attracting several hits before his mission was accomplished and he was allowed to dash for safety.

At last they were permitted to fight back! The soldiers' spirits soared and were even more bolstered with the sudden arrival of reinforcements, not only military but police armed with cutlasses. Was Probyn the only one amongst them who struggled with his conscience?

'Fix bayonets!' A succession of clicks rippled through the night.

It was then that Probyn saw his Uncle Owen carrying a banner, on the other end of which was his Aunt Meg. He balked in horror and tried to hold back but was perforce swept forward by the mass of bodies behind him as the order was bawled.

'Charge!'

Run! Run! he begged the rioters and mercifully they did as the company of scarlet thrust across the colliery yard sweeping back the violent tide that retreated before them. Previously helpless, the fire brigade were now at liberty to fight the blaze and rushed in with their steamer. But the mob were only driven back so far before regrouping to approach again with stones which they hurled in accompaniment to screams of malice, roaring with laughter as the soldiers unsuccessfully tried to duck and dodge the shower of missiles, lashing out with vicious clogs at those who had tripped and fallen, and managing to push their opponents back, blood flowing from both sides.

The bayonet attack having achieved little, Captain Baker gave the order to fire a volley over the attackers' heads.

'This is more like it!' yelled the crazy-eyed soldier to Probyn's left, cocking his weapon with relish.

Completely at odds with this sentiment, Probyn nevertheless raised his own rifle, took aim with the others and fired into the air.

That had the effect of checking them, but only for a second, and they came on as strong as ever, furious now in their missile throwing.

Looking grim, the captain barked another order, one that

Probyn had been dreading and which froze his blood. 'Fire two volleys into the crowd!'

Once more Probyn shouldered his rifle, repelled by the thought of firing upon unarmed people. It was then that he recognized that the person in his sights was Clarence Judson. In that split second all misgivings about his presence here were eclipsed by the anger he felt for the perpetrator of his father's misfortune. Mercifully there was no time to think about whether he should shoot to wound or to kill for in a trice the order was shouted and carried out. There was the crack of rifle fire, the toppling of banners, the sudden collapse of several bodies, and a pall fell over the throng, all suspended by shock.

His ears filled with the crackling of burning timber, the smell of cordite tweaking his nostrils, Probyn stood there breathing heavily, the blood pulsing through his veins as he awaited the backlash, noting to his dismay that Judson was unharmed.

For a second it appeared that the rioters were defeated for they remained stock still, gaping at their fallen comrades, some half-dozen of them. Then, helped by his distraught wife and comrades, one of the wounded staggered to his feet. One hand gripping his banner, the other clutching his thigh, his face contorted in pain, he limped forward, urging the others to follow which they did in a rush, pressing around him to lend their support as he stood toe to toe with the front rank of soldiers and displayed the bloody rent in his trousers, haranguing those responsible.

So blinded by fury was Owen that at first he did not see that the soldier upon whom he poured his vitriol was his nephew. When he did, a look of sheer contempt took over his face, his black eyes gleaming with fanaticism. 'You, you bugger! Well, we don't have to ask whose side you're on do we? So this is what you joined the army for – to shoot your own relatives! You traitor! You're worse than your bloody father, sitting pretty in his own house, no need to kow-tow to the master for a roof over his head!'

'My father's lying half-dead 'cause of your bloody union!' Embroiled by conflicting emotions of fury and shame and guilt and frustration, Probyn lost his temper, slammed his musket across his uncle's chest and screamed at him. 'Aye, you didn't bloody know that did you?' he yelled at the sudden change in Owen's expression. 'Your mates came round and roughed him up in his own house! Not that you give a damn, all you're bothered about is your blasted union!'

Owen recovered from his shock quickly. 'Away then, maister, shoot me!' he goaded, and with others jostling around him, pressed his body to the weapon. 'Do the boss's dirty work!'

At this precise moment Judson reappeared, springing like a hobgoblin out of the baying mob, lashing out with an iron bar and smashing it across a soldier's ear, waiting only to see the blood spurt before vanishing into the crowd.

Hampered by the squash of bodies, Probyn roared further frustration at his uncle. 'You'd side with an animal like that over your own brother!' He was given no chance to say more for with the rioters crowding dangerously in on them Captain Baker gave his soldiers leave to fire at will and they did so with gusto, scattering the miners once more, several of them falling in the panicked retreat.

Demented by anger, Probyn unleashed round after round, uncaring where the bullets landed, thinking only to avenge his father. He did not see Owen or Meg again.

For another hour the firing continued apace, succeeding in dispersing the mob but only as far as the wooden bridge over the road which they proceeded to set on fire. At the same time as this some eighty men and four officers arrived from Pontefract Barracks, shouldering their way amongst their beleaguered comrades and immediately coming under a hail of stones. Not until a distant clock struck midnight did the crowd finally begin to diminish, only a few militant batches remaining to taunt and jeer, though the flames still roared high into the night.

Consumed by a sudden weariness, Probyn heaved a sigh and flopped to the ground, others dropping all around him, exhaustion setting in. They had been battling for eight hours.

A bunch of raw recruits came pelting into the yard then, eager for action but finding only the aftermath.

'Trust the bloody KOYLIs to arrive when it's all over,' Probyn heard a Staffordshire man grumble, but was too tired to defend his fellow Yorkshiremen. Try as he might he could not rid himself of Uncle Owen's snarling face, his words. How dare the man accuse him of being a traitor! He had joined the army to defend his country, could hardly be blamed if he was called to uphold the law of that same country.

He closed his eyes, but there was to be no sleep that night, he and others remaining as sentries protecting the colliery premises, or what was left of them.

To his great dismay, the next morning amid a pall of fog and smoke the strikers reassembled, though mercifully did not attack, their violence restricted to black looks and foul words. Replaced by fresh troops he was finally allowed to limp back to the depot, witnessing on his way the great outrages that had been perpetrated throughout the district, shops and pubs stormed, crops pillaged, the homes of scabs wrecked. Standing true and firm, the red-turreted walls of the garrison received him, whence, weary and faded, he threw himself onto his cot and slept through every bugle call until tea-time.

Later, when the Staffordshire Regiment entrained for other regions, he departed with them, a state of tension remaining in his wake. Never had he been so glad to leave Yorkshire.

What had been the point of it? Probyn asked himself many times on his way back to the Cape. If the aim had been to put his mind at rest then it had been a total waste of time for he was as worried and uninformed as ever over his father's condition. He had thought – it was a terrible admission, but he had envisaged the scene many times and in many different forms but all with the same outcome, the same sense of finality – he had expected to be returning to South Africa with some kind of relief, knowing one way or another if his father was going to survive, but he felt just as bad as on the way over, worse even, after his awful involvement with his uncle. Neither was there any bodily comfort to be had on board, for without cash he had to rely on basic rations, his only recourse being to peel potatoes in the galley to earn himself a little extra food.

After an exacting voyage the ship anchored at Cape Town in early October. The gardens were vibrant, exotic blossom dripping from wide-pillared verandahs, the air sweet with its fragrance, enormous cream and carmine globes bursting into petal, pastel walls bright and clean against the vivid blue of the sky, the sands of the peninsula white as snow. Even the busy cobbled squares were in total contrast to the hellish crisis at home, all nationalities intermingling – English ladies parading the latest spring fashions, berobed Malays in red tasselled hats, brawny Dutchmen, slender-limbed Indians, plus the usual heaving mass of blacks. Eschewing the chance to become part of its tapestry, his body weaved in and out and onwards towards the garrison where he would receive orders on how to get back to Natal, anxious to be amongst his comrades.

No one seemed sure what to do with him at first. Told by a corporal to stand outside an office and wait, he drifted back into the pensive mood that had enslaved him throughout the voyage, and was glad when the sound of boots jerked him out of this unaccustomed melancholia.

The newcomer who came to stand beside him was of similar build and age to himself but, wearing an ill-tempered scowl, appeared unapproachable. Probyn merely offered a wary nod then looked away. However, he had noticed that upon his wiry light brown hair the other's glengarry sported the badge of his own regiment and he could not withhold his curiosity.

'Are you with the Eighty-fourth?' He used the 2nd Battalion's old infantry number.

Retaining the bad-tempered glower, his unusually pale hazel eyes staring directly ahead, the other did not answer. Thinking he had not heard, Probyn was about to repeat his query when the answer was delivered in absent-minded drawl.

'Aye.'

'So am I! What company?'

Another elongated pause, the other seemingly miles away. 'D. You're in C aren't you?'

'Aye!' Probyn frowned. 'But I don't recall seeing you.' The other sported a much deeper tan than his own, suggesting that he had been here a long time.

Another hiatus. 'No, well . . . I don't stand out like thee. That ginger hair.'

'I'm Kilmaster.' Probyn glanced approvingly at the other's shiny boots and dapper appearance.

'Greatrix.' The voice was very deep, almost a growl.

'I thought your lot were in Maritzburg?' Probyn awaited the response. The other was still scowling but it did not appear to represent any threat, was probably only a natural feature. It would be effective, though, thought Probyn, in deterring any would-be attacker.

Eventually came the answer. 'I were . . . but then I got made servant to the colonel and he had to come back down here for summat or other.' Another pause for thought, during which he nibbled on one of his fingernails which Probyn noticed were bitten down to the quick. 'He brought me with him but then I got injured during manoeuvres and had to go to hospital so that's my kooshi job up the spout.'

Probyn sympathized, telling Greatrix of his own similar misfortune, including his father's apoplexy. But the mention of hospital had evoked thoughts of Mick. 'Don't suppose you heard what happened to Melody?'

Greatrix pondered for what seemed like an age, before finally growling, 'Can't say I know him.'

Difficult though it was, Probyn upheld the conversation and discovered that Greatrix had joined only shortly before himself and had been born not a stone's throw away from Ralph Royd. This sparked not only fellowship but the need to relate the dire situation at home.

'Have you got relatives in the coal industry?'

A long gap. 'Haven't got any relatives at all. I were left in a back lane as a babby and raised in an orphanage. Took the name of the bloke who saved me from freezing to death.'

Probyn felt instantly humbled. Here he was grumbling about his family difficulties to a poor chap who had no one at all. 'Bloomin' heck, it makes my troubles look nowt. You should have shut me up when I were yammering on about me dad . . .'

Greatrix shrugged. 'Not your fault.'

Merely to fill the uncomfortable lull, Probyn began to recount the episode of the strike.

In return Greatrix informed him that the spot of trouble in Matabeleland had escalated into a war. In his role of batman to the colonel he had overheard all sorts of information and now relayed it to his new friend, though at a painfully slow rate.

They were disturbed then by the corporal who told them to entrain for Wynberg, there to await orders.

Whilst not averse to a short sojourn at this pleasant venue, Probyn was confused. He had expected to return to his unit immediately. Faced with the prospect of being amongst strangers he was quite glad of Greatrix's company, for already, despite the superficial belligerence, he had recognized a fellow traveller. Neither foul-mouthed nor a braggart, nor a defamer of womenfolk, a bastion of the regiment if his spruce appearance were anything to go by, apart from his terrible fingernails, Greatrix would make a worthy pal.

He was even more glad of this back-up when, immediately upon entering their temporary barrack room, one of its inmates came swaggering up and announced, 'I don't like people with ginger hair.'

Responding with a penetrating stare, Probyn was about to turn away but was surprised by Greatrix's contribution.

'I don't like people with stooped posture.'

The antagonist frowned. 'I haven't got –' He broke off with a gasp as a fist took him full in the stomach.

'You have now,' drawled Greatrix.

Uproarious laughter from others showed the newcomers they would face no further conflict, at least not from their roommates.

The drill sergeant was not to be so accepting. After two months' absence from the ranks Probyn found it tough to get back into routine, especially now as the temperature was rising. Greatrix was in an even more pitiable state, his long stay in hospital having drained his stamina, and both were relieved at the end of the week when they were summoned to the adjutant's office, expectant of a return to their units.

The lieutenant issued thanks to the sergeant who had brought them in, then addressed them dually. 'Stand easy.

Now, Private Kilmaster, Private Greatrix, I am led to believe you have both done a stint at mounted infantry.'

Both answered in the affirmative.

'Excellent. I have received orders that you are to go up to Mafeking and report to Major Grey of the Bechuanaland Border Police, to whose force you will be attached.'

Probyn's jaw dropped. After a swift glance at Greatrix who was equally stunned, he returned his eyes to the speaker.

'You will be supplied with travel warrants and will leave tomorrow.'

'But sir, we were expecting to go back to our units in Natal!' Probyn felt the sergeant's eyes upon him for such impudence.

The officer seemed not to mind, treating the outburst as a joke. 'What? You'd miss out on the chance of a skirmish with the Mats? Most young soldiers would give their eyeteeth for such an opportunity.'

'Oh, I'm not jibbing, sir! I just don't want my commanding officer thinking I've absconded. I was only given –'

'Your commanding officer will be fully apprised of the matter,' butted in the lieutenant firmly. 'Now, you're not going to funk this are you?'

Both young men responded. 'No sir.'

'Glad to hear it. There'll be extra pay for you at the end of it. Dismissed!'

Both Probyn and Greatrix stamped to attention then were marched out of the office, immediately to be upbraided by the sergeant. 'You do not argue with an officer!'

'Sorry, Sarnt.' Probyn was contrite but still preoccupied with the news. He didn't want to be with a bunch of strangers, he wanted to be with his comrades!

'If he gives you an order to do something you do it!'

'Yes, Sarnt.' Still Probyn did not pay full heed.

'Corporal Bennett!' The sergeant beckoned another. 'That coal what wants shifting, these are your men!'

At which Probyn, now made fully conversant with the

extent of his misdemeanour, and his unfortunate associate were, for the next couple of hours, forced to shovel coal from one place to another under the hot sun.

Greatrix was unimpressed at being involved in what was Kilmaster's offence and as the corporal turned his back momentarily to talk to another, he was given the opportunity to vent his displeasure, leaning on his shovel, breathing heavily and wafting at flies. 'I'm not being funny mind, but if you want to give lip to an officer in future can you make sure I'm out of the room first?'

Probyn stopped work too, wiping the back of his hand across his perspiring cheek and smearing it with coal dust. 'Well, you don't want to go either do you?'

'Since when has the army given tuppence for what I want?'

Probyn looked apologetic. 'Aye . . . sorry. I don't know why I bothered opening me mouth.'

Greatrix offered a packet of cigarettes. Not wanting to offend, Probyn had accepted before today, deciding after the first eye-watering puff that he quite enjoyed it, and now accepted again.

There was a long pause whilst both employed the corporal's absence as a chance to relax. Probyn found amusement in his occupation. 'I'd hoped to get shut of anything to do with coal after the time I had in England, and what do I find meself doing?'

Greatrix was scowling, which the other had come to recognize as merely an indication that his friend was deep in thought. 'I'm in two minds about it really. I want to get back to me mates, but you have to admit it'll be an adventure.'

Of like mind, Probyn smiled and nodded. This would be *real* soldiering, against a proper enemy, would give him a chance to release his frustration over not being able to do anything about Judson. 'I wonder if we'll have to shoot any of these Mats.'

Greatrix shuddered and spent the usual time in responding.

'I'm not bothered as long as I don't have to use me bayonet. It makes me feel sick even to jab it in a sack.' He hesitated before asking his next question. 'Have you ever killed owt?'

'Only pigs,' replied Probyn, then looked away. 'Well . . . one pig. But I expect it'll be a bit different to that. Still, we'll have to do it if we're asked.'

Greatrix nodded through a cloud of smoke. 'And rather them than us. The thought of one of them assegais coming at me . . .'

Probyn grimaced in agreement, then spoke to one of the brightly-coloured birds that flittered in abundance round the camp. 'And you needn't sound so bloomin' happy!'

They stood and watched the jewelled creature for a while, Greatrix finally observing, 'Bird-watcher's paradise isn't it? I used to do a bit when I were a lad.'

'Me dad loves birds. Well, canaries and the like.' Probyn tilted his head back and narrowed his eyes against the sun, wondering over the state of his father's health, picturing Owen's wounded leg. A small predator scythed the firmament. He pointed to it. 'Kestrel up there.'

Greatrix squinted, pulling on the cigarette. 'S'not a kestrel, it's a hobby.'

Probyn bowed to the superior knowledge. 'You mean he only does it in his spare time?'

Greatrix threw back his head to issue a laugh of appreciation, only no sound emerged, his humour manifesting itself as little more than a throaty hiss, his whole face transformed by mirth. Silent or no, the corporal detected merriment and came charging back to deliver retribution. 'I didn't tell you to bloody stop!' And it was back to shovelling coal for the rest of the afternoon.

En route to Mafeking, aboard a clattering train, Probyn was to discover that Greatrix's knowledge extended way beyond birdlife. Hitherto, the Matabele had been a distant enemy, but now about to come face to face with them Probyn wanted to find out more and Greatrix was the one to tell him. Apparently, the Matabele, or Ndebele as some people called them, had never recognized the borders laid down by the white man and regularly breached them to attack the Shonas as they had always done, saying they had a right to kill these people because they belonged to them.

'Have you heard anything like it?' asked Greatrix, amazement in his voice. With only the two of them in the carriage at present he felt free to talk. 'From what I gather in listening to the colonel, they treat them a bit like grouse, only bagging them in season then allowing them to build up their numbers before killing any more. But now they've really overstepped the mark: been stealing cattle from white settlers who're demanding compensation from Lobengula, that's the king of the Mats, but he won't pay till they give up his slaves that ran to the white folk for protection during the attacks . . .'

Swaying with the movement of the train, Greatrix's unhurried growl almost sending him to sleep, Probyn forced himself to listen whilst the other continued to reveal his vast knowledge, gleaned whilst eavesdropping on the colonel's discussions and from his letters and telegrams.

Dr Jameson – 'Him what runs the British South Africa Company' – wanted to teach these black insurgents a lesson and had set about preparing columns to march on the king's kraal at Bulawayo. 'There was hell to pay down here when they heard,' drawled Greatrix. 'Sir Henry Loch, he's the High Commissioner and Governor of the Cape, he wanted to treat with Lobengula. He's managed to hold Dr Jim off until he got a column of his own together, but it's anybody's guess who'll get to Bulawayo first . . . are you listening?'

Probyn jerked himself awake. 'Aye! I'm just a bit confused as to why it's vital we get to Bulawayo before the representative of the Charter Company.' Wasn't the Cape's prime minister, Cecil Rhodes, in charge of this same company? And wasn't it his intention to paint the whole of South Africa red, just as was the aim of every British patriot? 'Surely, the map'll still be red whichever of us gets there first?'

'If only every man were as noble as you,' said Greatrix. Though he, too, was mainly ignorant of Cape politics, he knew the gist of this affair. 'They're all after their own ends. Whoever takes Matabeleland gets control. That's why we have to get to the king before the Charter Company or they'll have more clout than ever. I don't know where this Major Grey comes in 'cause I had to go to hospital then.'

Probyn made a small contribution, telling his friend that Major Grey had returned from leave on the same ship as himself.

Greatrix offered a packet of cigarettes. Probyn took one, being struck at the same time by a realization. 'Eh, you know how the railway line only goes as far as Mafeking? I wonder if we're expected to go the rest of the way on horseback. It must be about five hundred miles!'

A horrified groan emerged on a mouthful of smoke, his companion admitting that he had not done much training in mounted infantry at all. Probyn made sympathetic noises. If he, a veteran of the saddle, was daunted by the thought of this trek, how would a novice perform? He vouched to help all he could.

At this point the train stopped to take on more passengers which tended to inhibit their conversation.

Thereafter they smoked in silence as the engine went clattering over the Karoo, staggering over stony plains, dragging itself up hills and mountains and down the other side.

Throughout the day there were more stops, sometimes for food, the only items of interest being the folk who got on and off, for there was little else to fascinate in this barren landscape. Nor was there much life along the line. Apart from the yellow patches of sweet-thorn that somewhat resembled the gorse bushes of home, the only other spot of colour was in the violet sunset at the end of the day. Night was even worse, with no real beds, just a turned down seat upon which, even with hired blankets, it was nigh impossible to sleep with the train rocking about on its narrow gauge.

Stony plain gave way to grass veld, still the only feature being the sparsely dotted flat-topped thorn bush and an occasional windmill. Sometimes a cow or a sheep strayed onto the line, the train hitting it without stopping. To those trapped within its confines the other occupants of the carriage became of paramount interest, each trying to gain entry to another's dialogue. Conscious of their uniform, Probyn and Greatrix had hitherto managed to remain aloof, muttering in low murmurs to each other between necessary catnaps, but it seemed inevitable as another day ended that they would be drawn into discussion.

By their third day on board the young soldiers' uniforms were badly in need of an uplift, as were their aching buttocks and sinking spirits. The carriage was rank with stale body odour and tobacco smoke, everyone and everything coated in dust. Previously they had invented little games to while away the hours, such as trying to guess the nationalities of their fellow travellers, but these had soon been exhausted and now they merely slumped in their seats praying for deliverance. Besides, it had been all too easy to pick out the Britons in the carriage, mostly well-dressed and reserved. Another couple were obviously Dutch; the man had skin like tanned leather, his body lean, his face sly and shrewd beneath the broad-brimmed hat that Probyn secretly envied, whilst his wife was big and hard-faced with a red complexion. What surprised him was that their daughter was quite attractive. Probyn had responded to her polite smile when she had joined the train yesterday but had quickly put aside any amorous intention upon looking at her mother. No one on the train was black, though occasionally from the window they would see a native man, his bundle under his arm, making his way to work at the diamond mine.

Signs that the harrowing journey was nearing its end began to materialize in the form of mineheads, miles of them, as they approached Kimberley, a town of tin houses, mounds of refuse, wild and tough looking diggers and a filthy refreshment room.

Preferring to stretch their legs and reluctant to purchase anything from such an insalubrious venue, Probyn and Greatrix remained hungry, wandering up and down along the hot, dusty platform. Eventually it appeared that the others could no longer stand the refreshment room either and came out to brave the claustrophobic heat where the train sat breathing heavily from its exertions, waiting to be fed and watered. At the ticket office a spotty clerk with a superior manner was trying to throw his weight about with a passenger. Losing the argument he stalked off and began haranguing a small black boy, ending his tirade with a blow to the head that sent the youngster tumbling.

'There's no call for that,' muttered Probyn. Looking round and seeing that no one else seemed interested enough to intervene, he turned to Greatrix. The latter in agreement, both made to approach the offender; but he was already marching quickly away down the platform, and it became obvious he was about to trounce another victim.

A young dog had sought out a pool of shade and had just nicely stretched his body out when the clerk kicked him in the abdomen.

'Right, that's it!' said Greatrix. Having barely set the black boy on his feet he moved upon the perpetrator, but before he could act the Dutchman had grabbed the clerk by the scruff of the neck and dealt him two sharp slaps around his face before casting him aside like a piece of litter.

Smirking at each other, the soldiers were left without a cause, and instead bent down to comfort the ill-treated dog, little more than a puppy, who set up a grateful fawning. The train was ready to go again. The animal's prominent ribs advertising that it was a stray, Greatrix grabbed the dust-laden creature and took it on board, stowing it under his legs and tacitly defying anyone to object. No one did. This time when the train set in motion the young infantrymen were included in the conversation.

A man from England with salt stains under the arms of his creased suit asked where they were going.

Probyn told him. 'Mafeking first then on to Bulawayo.'

'Ah, to put those blasted niggers in their place! Good for you. Ten years I've been here and I still can't stand them.' And he ranted on about them being an untrustworthy lot.

A well-dressed young farmer begged to differ. 'I rather like the jolly old nigs myself.' Following an expressive sneer from the burgher, he added, 'I'd be lost without mine, they're a pretty good bunch.'

A debate ensued then, in which Probyn and Greatrix took no part, chatting merely to each other or to the pup whom they had named Boney.

'I'm not being funny, but isn't it about time you got your fags out?' prompted Greatrix. 'I've none left.'

'Sorry, I don't smoke.' Probyn looked awkward.

The hazel eyes showed amused outrage. 'You've been taking my fags for a week and now you tell me you don't smoke!?'

'I were just being sociable.'

'If that's your idea of being sociable I wouldn't care to be somebody you don't like!' Whilst Greatrix was rifling his pockets for a doff, the young farmer extended a packet. The recipient lit up gratefully.

The narrow-eyed Boer had been taking in Probyn's accent and now announced, 'You are from Glasgow. My friend he comes from there, he sounds just like you.'

At first amused, Probyn replied cordially, 'Actually we're both from Yorkshire.'

'Yes, that is near Glasgow,' came the assured response.

Though unwilling to give offence, Probyn was determined not to let the man get away with this. 'Glasgow's in Scotland, Yorkshire's in England.'

To the Boer five hundred miles was a mere stone's throw.

'So close it makes no difference.' Then he went on to tell them all about their own country, although it was obvious he had never set foot there.

Realizing that to argue was pointless, Probyn turned away and ignored the man, speaking instead to Greatrix who was equally annoyed and, when the Boer family got out at Vryburg, shook his head in exasperation.

The man from England joined their grievance. 'You can't tell a Dutchman anything. He knows it all. I hate them almost as much as the blacks. They're filthy and disagreeable, would cheat you as soon as look at you.'

Though this was one of the few Dutchmen he had encountered, Probyn nodded in agreement. To him the two Boer republics were as warts upon the fair face of South Africa, most of which lay in the reliable hands of the Empire.

However, the Englishman's carping about black and Boer became too much and the soldiers pretended to take a nap, leaving the young farmer to put up with it, all heartily sick of this uncomfortable ride.

After sixty exhausting hours of travel they finally juddered into Mafeking, an ugly town of corrugated iron shacks a few miles outside the Transvaal border. The station consisted of a little tin house and a goods shed. Beyond this was a street and a market square of similarly low-roofed houses. The people had a rough and ready appearance, mirrored in their attitude.

The army camp being close to the station, Probyn and Greatrix went straight there, rubbing their buttocks to remove the painful tingling, the wary young dog at their heels.

Once refreshed they were inducted to their new posting. It transpired that the detachment they were to join was made up of men from the Cape Mounted Rifles, and others seconded from various Imperial regiments, including two sergeants and a private from their own battalion, though none were familiar faces. Added to these were some natives, plus a large band of walnut-tanned volunteers in broad-brimmed hats and corduroy breeches with bandoleers across their chests and pistols on their hips, most of whom appeared to be drunks and ruffians and the friends gave these a wide berth for now.

Fearing that perhaps there might be an order against taking dogs on the journey, they chose not to ask and no one appeared to object to Boney's presence.

During preparations for the trek they were equipped with horses and were to learn the basis of Major Grey's involvement, a version that differed slightly from the one Greatrix had heard. It was untrue that the British Protectorate of Bechuanaland was under threat of invasion from Lobengula, but in order to get permission to declare war on him, Governor Loch, unable to restrain Cecil Rhodes, had wired Britain with news to the contrary. It had done the trick. A southern column led by Lieutenant-Colonel Goold-Adams and supported by Chief Khama of Bechuanaland with four thousand warriors was now well on the way north. Grey's troops were to act as reinforcements. Bolstered by the knowledge that the reputation of the British Army depended on them, Probyn and his new friend displayed an eagerness to be off.

On the twenty-seventh of October 1893 Major Grey and his force of three hundred men set forth on the race for Bulawayo.

From Mafeking their route skirted the eastern border of Bechuanaland, to their west lay the Kalahari Desert. The land they trekked was largely bare yet there was much to be avoided – clumps of tall coarse grass and the treacherous white-thorned mimosa, holes dug by aardvark and meerkat – and it made for tedious travel, especially for those steering the wagons and Maxims, wheels banging and jolting over ruts and stones, the going being even rougher for an amateur like Greatrix. Even after only a few miles his suffering was obvious to Probyn who rode beside him, trying to keep him in conversation to take his mind off it.

When finally they outspanned to boil a kettle and rest the

horses and change the oxen, it was with a little prayer of thanks that Greatrix slid painfully from his saddle, his equally exhausted dog flopping to the ground.

'Oh, Lord have mercy, I think me hip joints are about to pop out of their sockets!' It was the first complaint he had uttered, though his face and movements told all as he took a few tentative steps.

Holding both pairs of reins, Probyn tried to coax a smile. 'You look like you've cacked your strides.'

'Some pal you are!' The choking cloud of dust kicked up by horse and wagon was just beginning to settle. Thoroughly coated in it and having a perpetual need to clear his throat, Greatrix ran a hand over his dry lips. 'Oh Lord, I'm gagging for a cup o' char. I don't know if I'm going to be able to stick this.'

'Don't worry, it'll get better,' comforted Probyn, wiping the dust from his own sweating face. 'Lig down, I'll see to the hosses then get us some tea.'

Greatrix kept bending and unbending his painful limbs for a moment longer, then lay down, using his horse as shade, his helmet balanced on his chest, whilst the dog sniffed at him anxiously, and from the parched earth brown grasshoppers flicked themselves on and off his recumbent form.

Eventually he was forced to sit up again in order to drink the tea that his friend had provided, though they remained quietly pensive. Having drained his water bowl, the dog collapsed beside them, nose dry with dust, tongue lolling, snapping occasionally at a grasshopper or a buzzing fly, then finally capsizing into sleep.

Greatrix was reconsidering the wisdom of bringing him along. 'Poor little devil. How old d'you reckon he is, Kil?'

Probyn lifted a hand to tilt his helmet, revealing a dark patch of sweat under his arm, and studied the canine's white coat that was now loaded with ochre. 'About nine months.'

Greatrix sighed and lit the pipe that had taken the place of his cigarettes for this long journey. 'Only a babby. Don't know how he'll manage the rest of the way. It were cruel to bring him.' Puffing, he glanced away, distracted by a twinkling daylight star on a far-off hilltop, which informed them of Colonel Goold-Adams's position. Its distant glimmer appeared only to taunt the sufferer, especially with the accompanying order to remount. 'Oh blessed Lord, I'll look like bandy Bertha before we catch up with him!'

A sympathetic Probyn grabbed the other's mug, then helped him stand. 'Away Trixie, it won't be so bad tomorrow.'

'Trixie? Do you mind, you make me sound like a music hall tart!'

Laughing, Probyn assisted his friend into the saddle, then took to his own stirrups. The dog seemed reluctant to move. After several urgings Greatrix jammed the pipestem between his teeth and was forced to dismount, slinging the animal over his saddle. 'A good job you're not a Saint Bernard!' scolded its master.

A cloud of dust marked the progress of the column as it wound its way across an arid plain. The pace was hard and would have been harder were it not for the fact that the oxen needed regular rest. Major Grey, a veteran of the Zulu War and a strict disciplinarian, was rigid in his determination that an Imperial force would be first into Bulawayo and it was well after dark before they off-saddled, by which time Greatrix was almost weeping in agony.

Again Probyn bade him take the easier chores whilst he hobbled and fed the horses and brought his friend a meal, answering the other's argument by saying that when Greatrix became accustomed to the strenuous life he could return the favour. The devotion he showed was a mark of how close the two had become. That he had known Greatrix less than a month had no bearing, for in the first few moments in which they had met this young man had inspired genuine affection. It was the sort of friendship he had craved since joining the army and he was determined to nurture it. What was more, Greatrix had taken his mind off his father, for which he was doubly grateful. There was nothing he could do about the situation at home, so why continue to worry? It was not a callous thought, just a desperate need to get on with his life, and Greatrix was responsible for helping him in this.

The punishment was to continue for the best part of a week, during which Boney, having grown footsore, was to spend as much time in the saddle as his master. Striking out at daybreak, following the route of the twinkling heliograph, making camp to the whirring of crickets and the eerie call of a night bird, they pursued their goal over parched open veld, dry and stony river beds, under scorching sun and freezing nights. The oxen became ever weaker due to lack of water; consequently the troops were permitted to outspan more often, which was of vast relief to Greatrix whose muscles were only now becoming attuned to the torture.

Alas, when one torment ceased another began, this one shared by all. The rains broke. From being parched the veld suddenly became a quagmire, wagons, oxen and horses all becoming bogged down in the waterlogged sand and delaying the column to a chronic pace. At least, opined Greatrix, rain dripping from his pith helmet, they could be glad of one thing: the twinkling star of the north no longer beckoned, the heliograph being ineffective in cloudy weather. With no idea of how much further there was to go they could just settle down and get on with things at their own pace.

But the instant the sun came out to mop up the deluge the major was urging them on again.

New life began to burst its way through the yellow matted grass, the veld slowly turning a brilliant green. As difficult to manoeuvre as the rains had made it, they had also brought benefit in that the water wagons were constantly full and there was now no need to scrabble about to win a capful of water from a dried-up hole.

On the eighth day after starting out they reached Gaberones, a big kraal with many hundreds of inhabitants. They had come just over eighty miles.

Told of this and congratulated by Probyn for his endurance, Greatrix admitted that he was rather pleased with himself. 'You know, I'd never have envisaged a week ago that I'd grow so used to life in the saddle.'

'See, it's as I told you,' replied Probyn. 'You come to regard the horse as a mere extension of yourself, don't you?'

Greatrix readily agreed. 'Aye. Like a huge wart on your arse.'

Forced to laugh, Probyn admitted that he too was relieved to be stopping here for a couple of nights, especially as they had been received with much hospitality from the natives.

The headman sent enough sheep to the camp to provide a delicious meal for all plus other offerings in beautifully woven baskets, though there was no alcohol, for the King of Bechuanaland strictly forbade its sale even amongst white men.

They were to receive other visitors besides the natives. A missionary couple named Gower and their son and daughter were to join the column when it resumed its quest for Bulawayo. The arrival of a young white woman caused quite a stir amongst the soldiers, all eager to engage her in conversation and though she and her family were to prefer the company of Major Grey, Probyn was to make her acquaintance later when he and Greatrix volunteered to return the baskets to their owners, this in itself being an excuse to glimpse female nakedness.

As the young soldiers wandered to the kraal chatting, a male voice accosted them, the missionary and his family coming alongside on their way back to their own quarters.

'My! That's a grand Yorkshire accent.' The man of God mimicked their intonation although when he spoke again it was with a less abrasive tongue. 'Where are you two young men from?' Upon being told, Gower showed affinity. 'We hail from Bradford! Though many years ago.'

They spoke nostalgically about their shared birthplace for a while. His friend no conversationalist, Probyn did most of the talking, showing admiration for their intrepidness. 'But are you not afraid to live amongst so many savages, Mr Gower?'

'Oh, there may still be savages amongst them,' agreed the missionary, 'but many are good Christians now. Take Simon here.' He indicated the man who accompanied them.

Probyn glanced at the slender, reddish-brown, half-naked figure and considered him to be walking far too close to the young woman for his liking. What normal father would willingly expose his daughter to such attentions? Greatrix's face showed he was of similar opinion. Both made no comment.

Simon spoke for himself, a dignified address in English. 'I wish to thank you, sirs, for coming to my country to save us from the privations of our enemy.'

'You mean the Matabele?' said Probyn, secretly eyeing the movement of the young woman's legs beneath the dress, a sight which spurred longing and which he tried to fight. Apart from a tanned face she was quite attractive, a skein of fair hair protruding from the nape of her straw bonnet.

'Simon is referring to the Boers,' corrected Miss Gower, 'who, given an opportunity, would make slaves of these people. Their republics must never be allowed to grow.'

Simon confirmed this. 'I do not like them. They treat the Ngwato as if we are not human and would steal our land if we allowed it. My king is loyal to the British, he wishes for his people to remain within your protection. I myself love Her Majesty the Queen. I should very much like to put myself at your disposal during your journey to the land of the Ndebele.'

Impressed by the man's loyalty, Probyn said they would be pleased for Simon to accompany them. Nevertheless, he found it hard to come to grips with the way that this so-called Christian shamelessly paraded his nakedness before white women, though with so much hospitality and such kind words he kept his disapproval to himself.

Parting company with the others, he whispered to Greatrix, 'She's quite a looker, isn't she? Her dad can't have much about him. I wouldn't have my daughter anent savages.'

Greatrix agreeing, the pair wandered into the kraal with the baskets, keeping their eyes peeled for a glimpse of nubile womanhood. But in this village the female occupants were shielded by a fence of reeds, behind which they could grind their mealies and cook and take care of their babies in privacy.

Later, however, their disappointment was to be assuaged. The induna came to say that his people would like to give the visitors a dance, his announcement closely followed by the arrival of around fifty villagers. Bare-chested men armed with clubs and spears, with tufts of horsehair and feathers on their heads and bunches of lambs' tails dangling behind, formed a crescent in readiness. But it was those who took up the rear which caught Probyn's interest. Women with nought but a fringed girdle to protect their modesty, heads shaved except for a tuft on the crown that was daubed with earth and adorned with beads, red and bronze limbs encircled with bracelets of copper, iron and brass. Nudging Greatrix who needed no encouragement to stare, a grinning Probyn made himself comfortable for the show, glancing only occasionally at the men who put everything they had into the dance and made tremendous leaps into the air, preferring to ogle those curvier forms on the outer edge who accompanied the rhythm with a shrill chittering, breasts and buttocks a-quiver as they shuffled to the intoxicating beat of the drum.

The soldiers were silently rapt, only one member of the audience appearing not to approve the display. Frightened by the deep booming shouts of the men, Greatrix's dog leapt at them barking and snapping at every movement, hackles bristling.

'Boney!' Annoyed and alarmed, Greatrix tried to bring it to heel but, intent on protecting its master, it continued to press its attack.

'You'd better keep that dog under tighter control when we get to Matabeleland,' warned a sergeant. 'Or we'll have to shoot it.'

Aiding his friend, Probyn tried to coax Boney back to the audience too but his voice was drowned by the natives' chanting.

The dog leapt again and fell to earth with a yelp under a blow from a dancer's club. There was much raucous laughter. Infuriated, Greatrix would have launched himself at the culprit had not Probyn and the sergeant held him back and ordered him to sit still. Fortunately the dog was merely stunned and, looking bewildered, crept back to him, whimpering, its owner keeping a tight hold on him henceforth.

As the audience watched with bated breath, excitement churning every core, the dance became more frenzied and warlike, the dancers making vicious stabbing motions with their spears, attacking invisible enemies, felling and skewering them where they lay. Unable to tear his eyes away, Probyn imagined himself pitted against these savages and a thrill of danger ran through him. Wilder still became the dance, the warriors singing and stamping and chanting and stabbing until with a great unified roar that signified triumph, that all their foes were vanquished, they came to a sudden climax, and the audience rose as one to applaud.

It had been, all agreed, a splendid end to the day.

As the company of dancers broke up and loped back to their kraal, another member of the outside world simultaneously came to visit the army camp, a wizened-looking individual, obviously accustomed to living out of doors for his skin was as tanned as his clothes were bleached. He introduced himself to the major as Ronald Williams.

Within earshot Probyn and Greatrix lingered to eavesdrop on the conversation.

'Please sit with us, Mr Williams!' Major Grey, normally a strict disciplinarian, was in great spirits and called for refreshments for the visitor. 'And where are you come from?'

'Salisbury,' came the answer, along with thanks for the provision of food.

'Surely you have not travelled so far alone?' The major was confounded.

'Never do otherwise.' The weather-beaten man seemed unconcerned by the other's exclamation and took a sip of hot tea.

'But you are at terrible risk of attack, sir!'

'Not down here.' Another sip of tea. 'Besides, Lobengula's flown.'

Major Grey's attitude changed, the men around him becoming similarly keen. 'And what of Bulawayo? Have you news of Colonel Goold-Adams?'

'Oh yes, I passed him a while back. He's camped on the border.'

The major was astounded. 'Of Matabeleland? But a runner brought us news of that position several days ago, he must be further on by now surely!'

Williams shrugged.

Struck by the obvious conclusion, Major Grey spat bitterly, 'Then Jameson must have taken Bulawayo.'

'That's what I heard,' said Williams.

Probyn and Greatrix looked at each other in dismay. All their hardship had been for nothing! Won in conquest, the whole of Matabeleland now belonged to the British South Africa Company and Cecil Rhodes.

Major Grey had immediately ordered someone to wire for confirmation. The news that had come back was disheartening. Whilst Colonel Goold-Adams still dithered at the border, too afraid to cross, Jameson had indeed stolen the Empire's glory.

In a short speech to his troops the following day, the major confirmed the rumours, expressing commiseration that they had come so far and so hard for no gain. 'But all is not totally lost,' he added. 'Lobengula is still at large and he is a prize to be won at all costs. Therefore we are to proceed with our journey.'

It was hardly news designed to encourage them. King or no, Lobengula was a poor substitute for his landholdings and four hundred miles was a long way to go to capture him. But the column set off once again, the missionaries and Simon with them.

With Matabeleland still a long way off, shooting posed no danger and they were able to bag plenty of game along the way to supplement their rations. There was, too, a burst of excitement when a pride of lions was spotted under a tree, the first Probyn had ever seen, and in open-mouthed wonder he watched the competition to bag them, four of the animals stopped by a hail of bullets, the fifth allowed the sporting chance to escape. It was such a terrific thrill to gaze upon these fierce creatures at close hand, to run one's hand over the tawny flanks that one had only ever seen in picture books, to ruffle the thick manes and smell the musky odour. Acknowledging the congratulations of their men, the sharpshooting officers ordered a series of photographs to be taken, after which the lions were strung on poles by natives, and the column went on its way.

Such jolly interval was to be rare, more often it was frequent cloudbursts that interrupted their passage, clogging hoof and wheel and boot, and being enough to dispirit even the most stalwart of men. Their clothes rotted by sun and rain, flesh and fabric torn by spikes of cactus, the soldiers were beginning to look like vagabonds.

Travelling through bush country, where at least there was plenty of game to stave off hunger, it took five days to reach another town. Boney's pads were by now cracked and causing pain and in need of expert care. Greatrix had consulted a farrier who, apart from offering liniment, was only able to suggest smearing the pads with fat, which Greatrix had already applied and which was little use. Bandages were chewed off in seconds.

'He needs some sort of little boots,' said Probyn, picking off the ticks that hung from his horse's belly like clusters of blackcurrants then stamping on them contemptuously. 'If we can get hold of a bit of leather we could fashion some.'

Greatrix nipped a tick from his arm, and pronounced it a good idea, suggesting that they ask the local natives for material.

But the Bantus they approached did not understand their gestures. Returning with Simon who translated their request, they were soon able to trade, a few rounds of ammunition for a piece of kidskin. Cut into four and bound with strips of hide around Boney's fetlocks, the soft leather provided splendid boots and also much amusement for the rest of the troops.

Probyn laughed and dealt the dog an affectionate tap as Boney patrolled up and down before them as if showing off his footwear. 'We should make him a little hat and coat to go with them.'

Greatrix delivered a rare expletive. 'You're a sentimental old bugger!'

'You can talk!' laughed his friend.

'Nay, I'm hard as nails, me,' replied Greatrix. 'I'm not allowing him to wear them all the time, tha knows, only for best.'

Still, despite the merriment, Boney remained too lame to walk far and was to travel more often than not in the saddle, his owner keen to get him veterinary care as soon as possible.

Three weeks and two hundred and fifty miles on from their starting point, they reached Palapye at dusk. The land here was little more than scrub and the sky above them not so spectacular tonight, in muted tones of pale-gold and shell-pink, but they were too tired to care. For Greatrix the priority, next to sleep, was to get help for his dog whose pads, despite the boots, were still cracked and raw.

Fortunately, next to the little tin house of a police officer was a Dutch veterinary surgeon who turned out to be a kind and modest chap, showing the young soldiers another side of the Boer to the one they had experienced on the train. After chuckling at the dog's boots, the vet gave its owner a potion with which to bathe the affected pads and also some ointment. Whilst waiting for this to be dispensed, Probyn glanced at a calendar on the wall. It was the seventeenth of November. My goodness, he thought, another month and it would be Christmas. For a moment he imagined himself at one of Aunt Kit's grandiose tea parties, wondering too how his father was. It felt like an age since they had seen each other though it had been little over two months. But then, came the sobering thought, that invalid had not really been the Father he knew.

Jerked from his meditation, the consultation over, he replaced his pith helmet and accompanied Greatrix out into the hot, cloudy morning. Going back to the camp they set about bathing the dog's paws, smearing them with ointment and replacing his boots.

Meanwhile, Major Grey had received a telegraph message, the content of which was related to the troops. A large impi had been spotted at Motloutse and he was to send fifty men in search of it. The rest of the column was to go via Tati towards Mangwe and be ready to assist Colonel Goold-Adams who had finally arrived at Bulawayo and, along with Dr Jameson, was part of a large force that had been sent out after Lobengula.

Upon hearing the news Probyn and Greatrix shared enthusiastic grins, both hearts soaring, for, attached to either section, they would undoubtedly see some action at last.

Despite the promise of battle, there nevertheless remained a daunting trek ahead for those bound for Mangwe. A sea of green veld stretched out before them, upon which they were to encounter storm after storm, the land becoming so waterlogged that the oxen could not pull the wagons.

Twenty miles from Tati, by the ruins of a prehistoric stone fort, they were faced with a river that marked the border of

Matabeleland. It was still teeming with rain. Thanks to the ointment the little dog's feet were much better now, though his face was a picture of misery, reflecting the mood of his master as red droplets of rain dripped from his fur. There was a short rest whilst natives were sent to cut down the banks and form a drift, and then it was on again, half an hour being spent in transporting Maxim guns, wagons, men, horses and oxen to the other side, the rushing brown waters making all attempts to wash the intruders away.

Palms blistered from hauling on ropes, the two friends rode in silence, trying to keep their minds alert for they were now within the enemy's territory. The deluge petered out. Anxious to take advantage of this Major Grey chose not to stop the moment darkness fell, telling his men that there was little danger of attack for the Matabele were known to be further north. Even so, the order was given that all pipes be extinguished.

Greatrix was most indignant. 'It's me one bit of pleasure!'

The sergeant spoke kindly. 'Oh well, we'd hate to see you discommoded. Perhaps you'd like us to have the band play as well, just to make sure the Mats know we're here?'

Greatrix understood now that the pipes would act as little beacons across the dark veld, and nodded grudging acceptance. Lacking such comforts, it was a miserable ride through the darkness, harried as they were by swarms of mosquitoes.

Of the enemy they were to have no sighting save for their deserted kraals. After great hardship, many of the men succumbing to malaria, they finally reached Tati, a mining town with the type of rough inhabitant that Probyn had witnessed at Kimberley. Here they laagered, thick thorn fences plugging the gaps and, surrounded by pickets, enjoyed a decent night's sleep for the first time in ages.

They were to stay here a few days, giving Probyn and Greatrix a chance to repair their tattered uniforms, and to spruce themselves up, though the little mirrors they carried for shaving purposes gave a horrifying reflection.

For this reason, amongst others, Probyn was greatly admiring of the missionary's daughter who managed to appear as presentable now as when she had set off and this after travelling through all manner of terrain, through crocodile-infested rivers and thornbush and thunderstorm. He was, though, far too embarrassed at his own appearance to convey his esteem, and besides they had not spoken since their introduction weeks ago.

However, in passing the two young Yorkshiremen that day Miss Gower was to recognize them and paused to chat, thereby lending Probyn the opportunity to impart his admiration for the way she had survived the floods. 'There are not many young ladies so determined,' he told her.

'But they do not have the word of God for inspiration as do I,' she smiled. 'Father is holding a service of thanksgiving for our deliverance this evening. I hope you will both attend.'

His eyes flickering over her dress, Probyn said he would. Then, in a moment of awkwardness, bent down to pat Boney, this inviting comment from Miss Gower.

'How are the poor creature's feet?' She bent to stroke the dog, her hand coming into contact with Probyn's, causing him to draw away.

With Greatrix too long in responding Probyn said that they were a lot better, then voiced his puzzlement over another matter. 'Tell me, Miss Gower, the large number of blacks that have been trickling in since we arrived –'

'They are Chief Khama's men,' explained Miss Gower.

'But aren't they meant to be with Colonel Goold-Adams?' Probyn frowned at Greatrix.

'I believe they were,' said Miss Gower, still patting the dog. 'But they were obliged to come home to attend their ploughing.'

'You mean they deserted.' Probyn shared a disgusted look with his friend.

Miss Gower gave the dog a final pat and straightened, becoming rather cool. 'Private Kilmaster, do not condemn them without knowing the reason. Delay in planting their crops would be disastrous for them.'

'We could all claim to have better things to do at home!' argued Probyn. 'But we can't all just drop everything and clear off.'

'I think that you do not fully appreciate the situation. These people cannot go and buy their food at the shop as one might in England. Failure to plant would spell famine next year.'

Probyn was only half convinced. 'But from what I've seen it's the women who do most of the field work. They didn't need the men here.'

'Are they strong enough to fend off an enemy?' enquired the missionary's daughter. 'There is always the danger that a neighbouring chief might seize their lands if their husbands stayed away much longer.'

Probyn was exasperated. 'So they leave it all to us? I reckon it's the least they could do to stand firm after we've trailed all the way up here to rid them of their foes.'

'Oh come, Private Kilmaster!' Miss Gower gave an ironical laugh. 'You are here to secure Matabeleland for the Crown.'

Probyn did not care for her tone. 'And what's wrong with that?' he demanded. 'If by doing so we offer the natives protection.'

'You are misguided if you think that your superiors, or anyone else for that matter, cares about the African people,' she told him gently.

Probyn was growing annoyed. 'Better us than the Boers, you said that yourself! And didn't that Simon chap profess his loyalty to the Crown?'

She looked him in the eye. 'I fear that his loyalty may be misplaced.'

Probyn took this as gross insult. 'I'd like to see how these black devils got on if we weren't here at all, miss!'

Greatrix was abnormally quick to agree. 'They'd be at each other's throats sooner than you could blink. You only have to look at Lobengula for example.'

'On the contrary,' said Miss Gower, remaining calm. 'It is my understanding that Lobengula has no wish to fight. He has done all in his power to keep his indunas in check. It is the invasion of his land that has caused the problem.'

'Excuse me,' said Greatrix firmly, 'but didn't he grab the Shonas' land?'

One who had come through such inhospitable terrain, threatened by drought and tempest and poisonous reptiles, was not easily ruffled. 'I will grant that there have been many centuries of internecine struggle among the numerous tribes here, but that is no excuse for the white man, be it Mr Rhodes or your good selves, to rob them of their land by trickery or violence, simply because there happens to be gold and diamonds therein.' She pursed her lips. 'You have absolutely no idea of how the Africans feel have you? How they have been used and lied to time and time again. Perhaps when you have acquired some insight into these people whom you so denigrate, we shall be able to discuss this more rationally.'

Probyn bowed his head to hide his anger, saying nothing, and in time she walked away, leaving him to vent his annoyance on Greatrix. 'Bloody bluestocking! If it weren't for us there'd be no roads or railways –'

'No medicine,' chipped in Greatrix.

'No bridges, no telegraph, no . . . nowt.' His list exhausted, Probyn added, 'Well, I don't care what she says, you just can't trust them, can you?'

Greatrix shook his head vehemently as his friend continued.

'I wonder how the colonel will manage without these Khama blokes. I mean, there were a few thousand of them, weren't there?'

'I suppose that's why they want us up there,' replied Greatrix, stroking the dog, who licked him. 'Wonder when we'll be off? No chance of getting back to Natal for Christmas now, is there?'

Probyn was still annoyed over the exchange with Miss

Gower, all attraction having vanished. 'No. It'd be good to see me old platoon again – not that I don't enjoy your company, Trix. I wonder if poor Melody recovered from his enteric?' He had never thought to miss an Irishman but, as annoying as he could be, Mick was a good chap and the thought of his demise was a sobering one, and he offered up a little prayer for his survival.

Still dogged by rain, Major Grey's divided force set out again heading for Mangwe where most of them were to remain, the major going on to Bulawayo to find out what was happening and taking a small section with him, the missionaries, Probyn and Greatrix in tow. Ahead lay the Matopos, the great granite barrier that protected the capital, black and polished as ebony from a recent shower.

'Not far to go now.' Probyn spoke as a father to his child, trying to remove the look of despondency from Greatrix's face.

The other merely delivered a grim nod, his eyes fixed on the range of glistening pudding-like hills.

Probyn tried to raise his spirits. 'What plans have you got for the future, Trix?'

There was no immediate answer.

After several seconds Probyn gave an exasperated laugh. 'Bloomin' heck, Trix, I hope you respond a bit sharper if the Mats launch an attack!'

Greatrix dealt him a bewildered glance, pretending to be offended. 'Well, it takes some thinking about! I haven't decided yet whether to go for colonel or general.'

Probyn smiled. 'I'm hoping to make sergeant-major meself.'

Greatrix nodded. 'I used to hold that wish an' all. But right at this minute it seems a long way off.'

Probyn sighed in agreement. ''Specially when we haven't even made corporal yet. I'll be drawing me pension before I get promotion.'

A battle-scarred old colour-sergeant riding along the column overheard their conversation. 'Give it time, lad, you're too young to know yourself yet.'

With three years' military experience under his belt, Probyn was slightly insulted. 'I don't know what you mean, Colour-Sergeant.'

'Exactly! When you're old enough to know what I'm talking about you won't need to ask.' The colour-sergeant kicked his horse onwards.

Bemused and angry, a red-faced Probyn muttered, 'What's the soft old duffer gabbling about, *know* meself?'

Equally mystified, Greatrix shrugged and, trying to alleviate his friend's upset, asked, with little interest in his tone, 'What you going to do when we get back from here?'

Probyn scratched his chest. 'Have a bath, put me feet up, probably read a book . . .'

'Me an' all. After all this excitement I need to take it easy.'

Though still ruffled, Probyn shared his friend's sardonic smile, and enquired what sort of book Greatrix enjoyed, the discussion of this helping to while away a few hundred yards.

'Ever heard of Homer's *Iliad*?' asked Probyn.

Greatrix's reply was delivered in the customary uninterested drawl. 'Picked it up once in the library. Put it down again though. Iliad must be Greek for rubbish.'

Probyn nodded. 'Virgil wrote one of them iliad things an' all, didn't he?'

Greatrix yawned. 'Aye. I didn't bother reading that one either.'

They came, then, to the Mangwe Pass where the erstwhile careless mood was to alter. The road ahead of them wound through a tract of rocky hills and kopjes from which the enemy could launch a surprise attack. The route was ten miles long.

The old colour-sergeant, catching Probyn's nervous glance at his friend, sought to allay their fears as they embarked on the dangerous stretch, steering his bay horse alongside them. 'Keep your wits about you, boys, and you have naught to fear. I'm reliably informed that the Mats are demoralized by our harrying and they've been decimated by smallpox, many of them have already surrendered. It's only the very best regiments who remain with Lobengula and they're known to be retreating. I know you lads were probably weaned on tales of Rorke's Drift,' he smiled at their tense response, 'but bear in mind that the Mats are far inferior to their Zulu cousins. Remember your training, and you'll be fine.'

The column made its tentative approach. Probyn's heart had begun to thud. Had this been a normal outing the scenery would have made a stunning backdrop – mountains of piled-up granite boulders spattered with platelets of jade, long grass and bushy glades – as it was, he saw only places for his enemy to hide.

Eyes darting into every cranny, body poised for action, for ten miles his nervous state persisted, almost to the point where he could have lashed his horse and beat a retreat. Others felt the same, he could feel and smell their tension, the horses felt it too, dancing skittishly from side to side.

When the kopjes gave way to open downs a combined sigh of relief emerged, and the rest of the journey was completed in relative calm. That was until they came to the missionary station whence Miss Gower and her mother voiced little moans of horror.

What had been their home was now an empty shell, blackened by smoke. Ripped clothes, broken furniture and pictures were strewn across the veld. Books lay open and pulped by constant rain. As the stricken young woman and her family wandered about the ruins, sombrely observed by their protectors, Greatrix murmured an opinion, his words genuinely meant. 'I feel right sorry for 'em, but what else can you expect from savages?'

Probyn nodded woefully, yet he could not help recalling that night in Pontefract when houses blazed and pianos were smashed and books were torn asunder. And it came to him then that the savage was not exclusive to Africa.

Their house totally uninhabitable, the Gowers salvaged what they could, a pitiful amount, then climbed back into their carriage and proceeded with the soldiers. Moving his horse alongside the wagon, Probyn tried to catch the young woman's eye, wanting to convey his sympathy despite their difference of opinion, but she turned neither to right nor left, though she must be aware of his attendance. Did she imagine that he wished to gloat, thought Probyn, to demand of her which of them now had been misguided? He would never be so cruel.

Such thoughts were unproductive. She was never to speak to him again.

Finally they reached Bulawayo, its outlying blocks a scattering of houses in the red earth. It seemed to those who had strived so hard to get here an unprepossessing place, a town of bottle shops and dry goods stores and mining syndicate offices all undergoing refurbishment after the damage done by Lobengula, and the ruins of a royal kraal burnt by its king as he fled. A Union Jack had been hoisted. For much of the time it hung limp on this sultry day, but occasionally it would give a triumphant flutter, thereby displaying the Rhodesian lion at its heart, a sight to goad those who had ridden long and hard.

Discovering that Colonel Goold-Adams and Dr Jameson were returned from their expedition, Major Grey went to receive orders. Acrimonious words were to be heard concerning who was to blame for letting Jameson reach Bulawayo first, Goold-Adams saying he had been forced to wait for Grey's help, this argument filtering through to the ranks and the men becoming angry at being made scapegoats.

Whilst each of the volunteers was rewarded with a share of Lobengula's rich country on which to build a farm, it appeared that there was to be little compensation for those who had been expecting a battle. The uprising was virtually over. Beaten by the heavy rains and smallpox, great numbers of Matabele had begun to filter back to their villages. Lobengula was still at large though rumour had it that he was very sick. The volunteers had begun to disband, the Imperial force was to be withdrawn. And though there was deep concern over a Major Wilson whose men had become separated from the main force and had so far failed to return, overall the mood was one of finality.

'So we just turn around and go back do we?' a disgusted Greatrix asked Probyn, who could only shrug. 'Well, God rest ye merry bloody gentlemen!'

Blocked in by swollen rivers, it was weeks before they could make a move anywhere, the interim being spent playing rugby in between downpours. It was the most boring Christmas Probyn had ever spent. Whilst others made their fun with prostitutes, he and Greatrix passed the time cleaning rifles or grumbling about what they would be doing if they were in England, or simply relating information about themselves, by the end of the period knowing just about everything there was to know about each other, and forming an even closer bond.

In January 1894, with the rains less frequent and the waters beginning to subside, Major Grey collected his troops and began to wend his way back south. Despite their sojourn the troops were soon once again in a lamentable condition, dirty and verminous, their clothes in tatters, and their boots falling to pieces from being constantly wet. To a pair as fastidious as Probyn and his friend it was anathema.

Added to these hardships there were Maxims to manhandle across soggy terrain, rivers to ford and as if this were not enough they had been ordered, on their way south, to capture the Mlimo or invisible god who had great influence and could incite the natives to fresh revolt.

'I might be a bit slow,' began Greatrix to his pal, rocking side by side on horses as ill-kempt as themselves, across a grassy plain dotted with mimosa trees, 'but how do we catch a bloke who's invisible?'

Probyn gave a half-hearted chuckle. 'I think he has three priests what do his bidding.'

'Mumbo bloody jumbo,' sniffed Greatrix. 'Gimme dat old time religion.'

Probyn was thoughtful. 'I can't remember the last time I went to chapel.'

Greatrix was silent for a while, frowning over some idea before putting voice to it. 'Something's always puzzled me. You know how John the Baptist was Jesus's cousin? Well that'd make him God's nephew wouldn't it? That would mean God had a brother or sister. He might have relations all over the place.'

'I think you're verging on blasphemy there, Trix,' warned Probyn, though amused.

'Interesting thought though,' finished Greatrix. Then he became alert. 'Eh up, looks like a village ahead.'

Probyn matched his attentiveness as a kraal appeared over the crest of a hill. Their orders were to raid such villages and capture arms. This was the first they had come across and it was a tense time as they made their way towards its boundary.

The huts here were not so aesthetically pleasing, crude dwellings plastered with cow dung. The major's demands were met by a wall of surliness, the defeated natives complaining that they had already yielded their weapons.

Saying he did not believe them, Major Grey despatched a posse of men to search the huts, knowing as he did so that it was futile; the weapons would be buried elsewhere. Nevertheless he was obliged to go through the motions.

When the hunt proved fruitless, orders were given for cattle to be confiscated, leaving only enough to prevent the natives from starvation, and the village to be set alight.

Watched by a sullen enemy, Probyn joined his comrades in setting fire to the huts, though he took no pleasure in it, and as he galloped from the burning kraal he voiced distaste for his incendiary work.

Greatrix admitted to similar weakness. 'But all said and done, Kil, the Mats have done dreadful things. They deserve a bit of their own medicine.'

Probyn saw the truth in this. 'I suppose so. It's like me Uncle Owen says about coal mining; it's a nasty job but somebody has to do it.' Even so, if only on this point he had to agree with Miss Gower: white men were meant to set an example and under the bewildered, accusing gaze of a little girl, the flames of her burning home reflected in her wide brown eyes, he felt most disturbed.

There were to be other such forays along the way, all as disagreeable and unproductive, and the two friends shared the opinion that they would be glad to put Matabeleland behind them.

Thankfully the rains that had hampered their progress for months finally dwindled, with only an occasional thunderstorm to annoy.

Today had been one such annoyance, finally halting their progress, and the major had given the order to camp early for the night, his troops now tucked up under dripping canvas, though no less wet.

To the sound of raindrops beating down upon their tents, the cry of some fatally wounded animal, the rasping roar of a big cat and the gibbering whoop of hyenas, the men fell into an exhausted sleep.

Some time before dawn, Probyn woke to find that the rain had stopped. Not a drip to be heard. For a moment as he lay there half dazed he imagined that he heard whispering, then realized that a breeze had sprung up and was rustling the long grass. He was about to turn over when he heard a deep throaty growl. Instantly awake, he cocked his ears and heard the growl again, this time more menacing. It was Trix's dog. Before he could react the dog had burst into a frantic barking and all hell broke loose, horses squealing in terror, men giving cries of alarm – 'Attack!' – and he bounded from his tent, rifle in hand.

Outside pandemonium reigned. Silhouetted against the night sky devilish figures were leaping and thrusting, inflicting terrible violence, the air rent by unearthly shrieks from the hobbled horses as assegais were plunged into their bellies. In a panic and just emerged from sleep, the soldiers opened fire, taking no aim but discharging their bullets willy-nilly as the figures vanished into the night, but it was not over, for, as the soldiers came to order and took up positions behind the wagons they were met by a volley of rifle fire.

Side by side with Greatrix, Probyn levelled his Martini-Henry and fired blindly into the void, unable to see his attackers but knowing where they were from the little flashes in the grass all around, from the amount of which it appeared they were surrounded. Time stood still as round after round of ammunition was directed at an invisible enemy, shoulders aching from constant harsh recoil, fingers seared by hot barrels, men around them swearing and slapping and whacking as cartridge cases became jammed in the breech. Then suddenly the heavens opened, the initial pitter patter soon becoming a torrent with great claps of thunder and flashes of lightning sporadically illuminating the scene. In an instant it became clear that to continue was futile, both sides unable to make out a thing beyond the deluge of rain, and firing ceased as quickly as it had begun.

Drenched to the skin, the soldiers remained vigilant for some time, guns levelled in readiness, eyes squinting against the lashing needles of rain, but when it became clear that their enemy had melted away, they finally dropped their guard, and made attempts to ascertain the damage.

Rain streamed down Probyn's face. He began to tremble and, through the teeming curtain, tried to gauge his friend's mood, wondering if Greatrix was experiencing the same sense of exhilaration, fear and loathing that threatened to burst from his own chest. Above the hiss of rain came the bloodcurdling screams of wounded horses that thrashed about in their hobbles. Already, jackals and hyenas had smelt the blood and were beginning to gather. He jumped, immediately alert at the sound of rifle fire, but realizing that it was of a merciful nature, he sank back to his heels.

Thankfully there were few human casualties other than those who had been outside the laager on picket duty, the discovery of their butchered corpses bringing a thrill of horror to Probyn's lips. Pitying the victims, but thankful not to count them as friends, he went back to the tent to reflect on this his first combat.

As if sent for a purpose, now that the fighting was over the rain began to ease. By dawn there was nary a cloud in the sky . . . nor a cow to be seen; the Matabele had retrieved their confiscated herd and spirited it away. A search party was sent out to try and recoup the cattle and to punish the attackers but they were to remain as elusive as the infamous Mlimo. Amongst the searchers, Probyn and Greatrix shared humiliation over the loss, the bluest of skies unable to lift their mood.

Longing for the opportunity to teach their enemy a lesson, they were to spend the morning drying out their equipment, the veld taking on the appearance of a laundry with damp vests and tunics spread upon rocks and branches, steaming under the grilling sun.

When the column set off again the sun travelled with them and they were to have no more rain that day. Moreover, there came the chance for them to wreak vengeance for the attack as they came upon a kraal, this time Probyn setting fire to the huts without compunction, and obtaining a large herd of cattle to boot.

Thus, the day ended well.

With a good supply of beef at their disposal and the risk of attack lessening as they came within days of the border, the mood of the men was to become more cheerful, knowing that they were on the way back to civilization. After so much rain the sunlit veld was a picture, the long, lush grass shimmering with flowers and butterflies.

Gradually the horizon began to take on its violet tinge, an orange disc of sun suspended above it, the sky marbled with gold. Shabby of aspect but in genial mood, Probyn and Greatrix mopped up the last of their beef stew and left the laager, preparing to take up their duties as night picket.

Before setting up, Probyn relieved himself upon a little clump of blue lobelia, then all buttoned up, picked up his rifle and adopted his role of sentinel.

Some yards away Greatrix held similar pose, his faithful dog by his side, other men posted at intervals surrounding the camp.

There came a whispering in the grass. Even before Boney started to growl Probyn knew instinctively what it was and shouted – 'Attack!' Simultaneous to the bugler's call a horde of Matabele warriors rose out of the long grass and, beating on their dappled ox-hide shields, began to charge, those with rifles firing as they came.

Probyn fell to one knee and fired back several times before retreating a few paces then firing again, attempting to get back to the safety of the laager. Amid the gunfire there came the sound of manic barking as the dog went bounding through the long grass for the intruders, Greatrix calling him back, calling and firing frantically as the enemy pressed their attack.

The ring of pickets retreated, taking a few running steps then falling to one knee and delivering another short burst before retreating again. They were still outside the safety of the laager, from which covering fire continued apace. Natives fell like ninepins, no white man hit as yet, but there were many of them and despite their losses they came on with rifle and assegai. Probyn made another rearwards dash and managed to find cover behind an ant hill, from whence he got his first opportunity to check on Greatrix's position. His friend was still exposed and, between firing and reloading, calling to his dog who totally ignored him and continued to bark from somewhere in the long grass.

Still the warriors came, jousting bullets with their shields. One after another in his sights Probyn unleashed round after round, some thudding into flesh, downing his foe, others whizzing uselessly through the grass, whilst enemy bullets hummed over his head like a flight of bees. His shoulder was throbbing from the constant recoil, his finger burnt and blistered from the barrel, and then suddenly nothing happened! He had a native in his sights, had squeezed the trigger and there was no response. Slapping frantically at the rifle he tried to dislodge the cartridge that had jammed it. The Matabele warrior was coming at him with assegai upraised. Probyn slapped and punched and bashed the rifle against the ant hill, terror bristling his scalp as the warrior noted his dilemma and with a triumphant booming cry closed in for the kill. Seizing his last chance Probyn levelled his bayonet and lunged for the oncoming native but the warrior took the blow upon his shield where, embedded, the rifle was jousted aside and ripped from its owner's hands. Left with nothing to defend himself, Probyn raised his hands in self-protection, began to lower himself on one knee; the warrior was poised above him, assegai ready to impale; he made a grab for the white oxtail that dangled from the warrior's arm in an attempt to deflect his aim, and then to a crack of rifle fire his attacker suddenly careened to his left and lay moaning. Without hesitation Probyn scrambled to retrieve his rifle from the long grass, aimed its bayonet and skewered the assassin, pulling it from the flesh to brandish it as another foe came running at him.

'Whoa!' Greatrix stalled in his dash, then, at the look of recognition from his friend, knelt down beside him and started firing again. 'Get back to the laager. I'll cover you!'

Realizing that it had been his friend's bullet which had

saved him, Probyn grasped the other's shoulder, hesitant to leave.

'Go!' shouted Greatrix, unleashing another hail of bullets at the enemy and downing one after another. 'And take that bloody stupid mutt with you!'

Probyn quickly wiped the bloodstained bayonet on the grass, vouching, 'Soon as I get another rifle I'll be back!'

'Don't bother, we've nearly got 'em all!' Greatrix felled yet another warrior. 'The silly buggers are firing too high!'

Probyn took a frantic glance around him. None of the pickets appeared to have been hit, most of them now within a few dashes of the laager. Even as their dead piled up the bold Matabele came onwards, leaping over their fallen comrades with a terrifying whoop. Answering Greatrix's demands, Probyn called to the dog and made a dash for the safety of the wagons, crouching low so as to avoid being shot by his own side, the excited dog bounding after him.

Now there was only Greatrix outside the laager.

Throwing himself to the ground and rolling under a wagon, Probyn found sanctuary and immediately looked for a rifle with which to return his friend's favour. But by the time he had found one Greatrix was at his side, both he and the dog unscathed, and the decimated impi in retreat.

With a gasp of satisfaction Probyn let loose half a dozen more shots at the fleeing enemy, then heaved another relieved sigh and projected a look of gratitude at his friend for saving his life. 'I knew I'd find a use for you one day.' At Greatrix's scandalized laugh he added, 'Thanks, me old chum. I hope I'm around to return the favour when you're in a spot.'

Greatrix brushed this off with a joke. 'You? Crackshot Kilmaster? You couldn't hit the side of our house!'

'You cheeky monkey!' A grinning Probyn dealt him a shove, and there was much jesting to follow.

But in truth the incident had terrified the life out of him, and later in the darkness of his tent he was to contemplate his own acts of brutality, envisaging the warrior's blood upon his bayonet, desperate to erase it from his mind but unable to do so, enacting the scene over and over again. It had not been the same at all as killing a pig.

Yet, above all, he was to ponder how nearly had his own blood been spilt, and the thought of Greatrix saving his life brought him close to tears.

12

Once they had crossed the river there were no further incidents, only hundreds of miles of humdrum trekking.

Back at Mafeking, they underwent a delousing, a luxurious bath, a haircut and a change of clothing before being packed off to Cape Town. It was almost the end of February when they arrived. The startling whiteness of the colonial buildings, the flame trees and proteas, the cerise robes of bougainvillaea, almost took their breath away after months on an open and featureless veld.

Despatched to Wynberg, they were told that there was little point in sending them back to Natal for the battalion would itself be returning to the Cape in September. Perhaps to go home! With this splendid thought, the close friends settled in to enjoy the last of their time together. Probyn would miss his chum when the moment came to rejoin his company and urged Greatrix to keep in touch which he promised to do whenever he could.

But there were others whom Probyn was keen to see too, and he wondered again if Mick had survived his bout of enteric and would be on that boat from Durban.

With thoughts also for his father's health he was pleased to receive two letters, one from Aunt Kit and one from Meredith, both of which informed him that the coal strike was all but over. The miners were claiming a victory. Their Federation had been forced to concede a small reduction in wages but had triumphed in securing a new principle of wage fixing and things were steadily getting back to normal. Naturally his father would not be going back to work, but in health was much the same as when Probyn had visited.

He had little time to ponder on whether this was a good or a bad thing, for he was called before the adjutant and, to his great surprise, asked if he would like to be employed as an orderly room clerk for his remaining time here.

Why they had chosen him, Probyn could not say, maybe it was his attention to detail in his turnout, but he was happy to accept, and in the months that followed discovered that he had an aptitude for clerical work. Moreover, the access to other soldiers' records provided an interesting diversion, and he was at liberty to find intimate details about whomsoever he chose, with which to entertain Greatrix on their days off.

Towards September, however, the friends were to be temporarily parted, for Probyn was required to spend a fortnight at Simon's Town, to check the records of a company stationed there. It was not a venue he relished, for at the naval base sailors far outnumbered landlubbers and he feared his red tunic might be singled out for violent sport. Telling Greatrix he would bring him a fish, he bade his friend farewell.

Simon's Town consisted of little more than a single street which wandered without design along a curving spit of land that formed a natural harbour, yet the declivitous hill behind it garnished with spring flowers drew one's eye from its plainness and Probyn found it an enjoyable sojourn, especially with the opportunities for fishing. The days were leisurely, this afternoon his only task being to wander up to the hospital and collect some records. Furnished with directions, he strolled down a long avenue, breathing in the scent of sun-warmed eucalyptus, sometimes looking out across the glittering bay, simply enjoying the peace, until he came to a whitewashed building, more like a cottage than a hospital, and he stood appraising it for a moment, dazzled by the sun that bounced from its walls.

Entering by a door marked Surgery, he adjusted his eyes to the gloom.

'As I live and breathe – Pa!' came an astounded exclamation.

Still temporarily blinded he was seized by the hand which was shaken boisterously and there stood Michael Melody in the blue and red uniform of a medical orderly, his pillbox hat at a jaunty angle.

'Mick!' Hardly able to believe his eyes, Probyn uttered many more gasps of surprise before managing to blurt, 'What are you doing here?'

Mick was beaming. During the long absence he had added a little weight to his nineteen-year-old frame, but he remained the self-conscious youngster Probyn had known, jabbering to cover his shyness. 'Well, you know me! I was never out o' the place and someone sarcastically suggested I take up permanent residence, don't know why I never considered it before, so I transferred to the Medical Staff Corps, and here I am!'

Probyn laughed aloud, shaking his head and saying he could hardly believe it. 'When poor Ingham died of enteric I thought . . . well never mind, I'm right pleased to see you're recovered!'

'I am, though it took three months in hospital, had dreadful gastritis afterwards, and now here's good old Pa come to offer himself as me patient!' Mick pretended to help the other out of his clothes.

'Not a chance!' Probyn reeled away still laughing. 'I'm only here to collect some records.'

'Ah, pity!' Mick heaved a sigh. 'Sure, I'd kill for a live patient to practise me skills on. The hours of training, ye wouldn't believe it, anatomy and stretcher drill and all that stuff, and all I ever get to do here is cut up dead men. For post mortem purposes y'understand.' He was soon beaming again. 'Now, come tell me, what sort o' divilment have you been up to since last we met?'

'Oh, let me think where to start.' His helmet under his arm,

Probyn clutched his forehead, still bowled over by the shock of finding Mick here.

'That much, eh? Then I'd better get you a drink to wet your whistle.' The young Irishman started to back away, talking as he went. 'I think we've a couple of English beers tucked away for celebratory purposes. We usually just sup the Dutch home-brew ourselves, 'tis cheaper.'

'We?'

'The sergeant, meself and another orderly!' Mick's disembodied voice emerged from a cupboard. 'They're out fishing for the day.'

'What about the patients?'

Mick reappeared with two uncapped bottles and glasses. 'I told ye, there's none here 'cept dead men to cut up. Did ye know that when you saw the top of a man's skull off it comes away with a pop?' He poured the beer.

'That bit of information should come in useful some day.' Probyn reached for a wooden chair.

'Fascinating is it not? D'ye want to sit inside or out?' When the other said he did not mind, Mick said, 'Out, I think, in the sunshine,' and he bade his friend drag the chairs onto the cobblestones just outside the door. 'Here, get that down ye and give me the crack, then later I'll take you on a guided tour.' Sitting with his back to the stuccoed wall, he raised his glass to the man beside him. 'Slainte!'

'Your very good health.' Examining the glass, Probyn took a long grateful pull, gasped in pleasure, then took another gulp before setting the glass on the floor.

'Ah, Jesus, don't put it down there! There's red ants all over the place, they'll knock it back quicker than Felix Lennon.' Mick ripped off his pillbox hat and set it on his lap, enjoying a good rake of his curls.

Nursing their beers, they shared reminiscences then, Probyn telling Mick all that had happened to him, including his father's stroke, the trip home and the trek up to Bulawayo. 'I fear it isn't yet over with the Mats though. We couldn't find half their weapons. Did you hear about poor Major Wilson's patrol being massacred? Felix Lennon was right what he said about the blacks, they're brutes all right, but at least the Mats are quiet for now and their king's dead.'

Mick was astounded. 'And here's me stuck here with nought to do!'

'I would've thought that's just up your street,' teased his friend.

Mick grinned. 'And so it is. Here's to ye.' He drained his glass.

'Are we having another?' asked Probyn, smacking his lips.

'Not at a shilling a bottle you're not! And you purporting to be a teetotaller.'

After a couple more beers, this time home-brewed, Mick showed his friend round the hospital. The ward had only four beds, which were rarely full, said Mick, being unequipped to deal with serious casualties, the infectious cases going to Wynberg. Between the ward and the dispensary was Mick's tiny two-bunk room which he shared with another. 'And that's about the extent of it.'

'You keep it very clean,' complimented Probyn, once they were back on their chairs.

'Thanks, but sure I have to do something to earn me bread.' Mick laughed, then shuffled into a reclining position, closing his eyes and tilting his head back so that it touched the wall. 'Apart from that there's only the shopping to do at the general store and medical supplies to check. After that the time's me own.'

'So what do you do with it?' Probyn leaned his own head back against the wall, causing his pith helmet to tip up and down like a lid.

'Sometimes I go fishing –'

'Oh, we'll have to have a trip before I return to Wynberg,' cut in Probyn.

Mick said he'd like that. 'But mainly I just read. I've taught meself algebra and all sorts since being here.'

'To what end?' asked Probyn.

Mick opened one eye and gave him a vacant look. 'Does there have to be a reason?'

'Well, I thought you meant you were doing it so's you could get a better job.' He had his own career mapped out.

Mick guffawed. 'What better job can there be than this? The greatest loaf known to man!'

'But why bother to educate yourself if you don't intend to do anything with your qualifications?'

'Can't a man do anything for his own enjoyment? What do I want to go getting promotion for?'

Probyn felt a twinge of annoyance that someone with such talents could waste them so blithely; if possessed of similar gifts he would make it his business to fly through the ranks in no time. But then that was Mick for you.

An unexpected arrival was to suspend their conversation.

'Looks as if you've got a patient,' observed Probyn, watching two soldiers helping another up the avenue of eucalyptus, the man between them appearing to have an injured ankle.

'Sure, what are they bringing him here for?' frowned Mick, then donned his hat, slipped the strap under his chin, jumped up and went to meet them. 'Don't let the ants get me beer. I'll be back!'

Probyn sat there for a while longer, watching a stick insect perform its unhurried movement along a twig, enjoying his ale and listening to the voices inside. Then, seeking a change, he moved his chair to the dim interior and sat back to watch Mick in action, admiring the way his idleness was transformed when tending the sick. Having expertly checked the ankle to announce that there were no broken bones, Mick said with kind authority that he would keep the man here anyway, just for a rest, then helped the patient into bed, treating him with compassion.

'Can I be getting ye anything to eat now?' Mick was heard to ask.

Probyn could not make out the mumbled reply, but saw

the patient handing over a watch which was examined by the orderly.

More mumbling occurred. Then came a loud objection. 'But it's worth five pounds!'

Mick gave a pleasant laugh. 'Sure where would a medical orderly get that amount o' brass? I can give ye twenty-five bob for it, if I starve meself for a week.'

After much grumbling the man nodded and Mick emerged from the ward to grab a sip of beer.

'Sorry for deserting ye, Pa! I'll be back just as soon as I get your man something to eat.' He pocketed the watch and went off to the kitchen, returning some time later with a plate of bread and some meat.

Probyn watched the man's face as he examined the butterless bread and reluctantly handed over some of the money Mick had just given him in order to purchase a knob of butter.

On his return to the kitchen, Mick paused to ask if his friend required any sustenance. Probyn declined with a cynical laugh.

'Don't worry, Pa, I won't charge you for it.'

Shaking his head at the audacity, Probyn said he was fine with the beer. 'Tell you what, I'll just grab those records if you tell me where they are, then I'll come back this evening when you're not so busy.'

He was to return many more times during his stay, either to go fishing or simply to chat over a beer, for there was no entertainment here other than brothels and saloons. Delighted to renew this friendship, Mick voiced disappointment when the fortnight came to an end and he implored Pa to keep in regular touch.

They were to see each other sooner than expected, for with the arrival of the rest of his battalion from Durban that same week a grand reunion was proposed.

Probyn was overjoyed to see his friends again, joining his excited voice with theirs as they rushed to gather around him,

Barnes, Bumby, Queen, Rook and the rest obviously as pleased to see him as he was them, clapping him on the back and asking where he had been.

'We weren't sure what had happened to you when you didn't come back!' cried Queen. 'Thought you'd deserted.'

'Eh!' Probyn aimed a jocular swipe. 'While you lot've been sat on your bums I've been scrapping with the Mats.'

They were all agog then, demanding to hear about his exploits.

'Oh, I'll tell you later.' Fending them off, he introduced Greatrix. 'This is the bloke you have to thank for me being here. Trix saved me from getting an assegai in me gizzard.'

The morose-looking young man with the dog issued only a shrug and, as usual, chose not to contribute much to the dialogue that followed, merely nodding or grunting at the appropriate moment.

Asking about Captain Fitzroy, Probyn was told he had gone down with rheumatic fever. A new man was in charge.

'So how's your old dad, then, Pa?' asked Queen. 'Did you get there in time?'

Probyn dealt a relieved nod. 'He's still with us, though a bit wonky – but thereby hangs another tale, and it'll have to be told over a beer.' Counting heads, he sensed someone was missing. 'By the way, where's Havron?'

'Cut hisself on a sword palm,' explained Rook. 'Got blood poisoning.'

Probyn gave a subdued murmur and said it was rotten luck to die by such error.

To lighten the mood Barnes underwent a quick change of hat and exclaimed, 'What do you reckon to these new field caps, Pa?' The glengarry had recently been taken out of service.

Probyn surveyed the big barn door face. 'Never mind field caps, they should be giving us decent rifles! It's all very well firing at a bull's eye but when you've got the real thing coming at you it'd be nice if the blasted thing didn't jam.'

'We've got new uns, Lee-Metfords,' said Barnes.

'Jammy blighters!' Probyn said he would have to see about getting one. 'Eh, talking about jammy blighters, did you know Mick's alive and well and working as a hospital orderly?'

This caused great mirth, the others saying they must invite him on the coming night out. Probyn said he would organize this.

'You'll have to get in touch with him quick,' warned Bumby. ''Cause we won't be stopping long.'

Probyn had been unaware of this. 'Aw pity, I've right enjoyed being here.' This was an understatement: in truth he had acquired a deep love for Africa the moment he laid eyes on her. 'Still, I'll be glad to see the folk at home.'

Rook frowned. 'How come you're off home and we're not?'

Probyn frowned back. 'Well, I just assumed that they'd sent you back down here 'cause we're all going home.'

Queen laughingly advised him. 'Never assume anything in the army, Pa! No, we're off to St Helena.'

It had been something of a shock to say the least, and only now after several days on the choppy open sea was the news beginning to sink in.

The night out that had been organized as a reunion turned out to be a farewell party, farewell not just to Mick, but to his close friend Greatrix, and it was with hollow heart that Probyn had left the rest of the battalion at the Cape, embarked with his company for St Helena, buffeted and battered on a rust-stained craft, and was now heading for a lump of volcanic rock in the South Atlantic Ocean, with no idea how long he would be there.

St Helena first appeared as a dot on the grey horizon, taking shape at a painfully slow rate, stretching into a flat nobbly worm, then to a mountainous slab of rock. The closer they came the more inhospitable it seemed to Probyn, its steep walls a cold steely blue against the overcast sky, offering no harbour, rising sheer out of an inky sea, completely lacking in vegetation and not an inch of beach to be seen.

With soldiers lining its rails, the ship gradually came around, seeking a place to land. The island was indented with coves, though none offered hospitality, jagged teeth holding the interloper at bay. At closer inspection the giant boulder took on a pinkish hue, its surface formed into rugged folds by volcanic excretions frozen in time. A road could faintly be seen snaking dangerously along the sides of a valley and, amazingly, there were cottages balanced precariously atop the cliffs. Paradise, it was not.

He saw now that there were trees after all, and could make out the tiny settlement of Jamestown nestling in the cleft of huge basalt walls. The harbour was crowded with fishing vessels. Seabirds arose from the crags to flock above the ship, yelping and mewing and diving at the three gulls which had accompanied the vessel since Cape Town. Added to this was the noisy rattle of the anchor chain, the shouts of the master to his crew, the apprehensive murmur of the soldiers who were to live here.

The Union Jack was run up the halyard. Then, to the soldiers' wonderment, an old Russian gunboat, adorned in gold paint, steamed out into the roadstead where she dropped anchor and her guns fired a salute to the British flag. Wincing and covering their ears as their own batteries returned the salute, the bangs reverberating from the mountains, Probyn and his friends watched a fleet of small steam pinnaces and row-boats put out from shore, some conveying officials, another bearing soldiers from the detachment who were about to leave the island and seemed very happy about it.

Ferried ashore, the newcomers prepared to make the hazardous landing, the bumboats at the mercy of the swell. Up and down, up and down, each awaited his chance to disembark, the waves washing over the landing steps. Attempting to keep his balance, Probyn grabbed an assisting hand and made a leap for the wharf, skidded on the slimy step, but managed to right himself just in time. Once secure, he looked around him in bemusement. It seemed that not only the resident soldiers and officials but every single inhabitant of the island had come to meet them, and every one of them displaying warm welcome, lining the stone walls of the quayside the entire way along the seafront. There was no noisy cheering, the people graceful and polite, the women in sedate hats and gloves, but all smiling. Some were darker skinned than others, some were coffee-coloured, some almost white, most had luxuriant wavy dark hair and more European features than Probyn had been used to seeing in the Cape, though there were one or two Africans amongst them.

There was a short handing-over ceremony between the departing commanding officer and the new incumbent, Captain Galindo. Then the soldiers, still wobbly on their legs, were marched along the quay, over the narrow bridge that spanned a dry moat and through a portcullis gate into a bygone age.

In the square was a castle with whitewashed stone walls and a coat of arms and close by an old-fashioned police station, on the other side a church. Looking further uphill he glimpsed colourful rows of Regency buildings, pastel yellow and peppermint and bright blue, some with verandahs, and balconies on their upper storeys. It was like being in a fairy tale where time stood still, thought Probyn, somewhat disorientated but much taken with the place nevertheless. Under a pair of lovely big shady trees was tethered a small pack donkey whose lazy flicking of tail signified the relaxed pace of life here. He was still mesmerized by his surroundings when the troops were called to a halt.

The captain had obviously been here before, speaking genially to another. 'Right, Colour-Sergeant! Shall we make them suffer the two-mile hike or allow them to take the short cut?'

Colour-Sergeant White cocked his head. 'Oh, I should hate for them to suffer, sir!'

'Jacob's Ladder it is then!' said Captain Galindo brightly.

Ordered to wheel to their right the troops found that the street ended abruptly in a mountainous wall, a flight of steps cut into it and an iron handrail to either side.

Probyn could hardly believe his eyes, craning his neck right back to try and see where the steps might take him but they were so numerous and went so high, way, way beyond the rooftops, that they became a single line upon the rugged cliff that seemed to vanish into the clouds. It was not just that there were so many of them but that they were so incredibly steep, almost like a vertical ladder, seeming even to bulge out at one point.

Daunted, even before setting one foot on the stairway, Probyn was nevertheless obliged to climb after his commanding officer who led the way with a sprightly air. To take his mind off the ordeal, he began to enumerate, but had not even gone half way when a look down onto the tiny iron rooftops, a threadlike maze of lanes and the white postage stamp that was the castle way below and the ocean all around them, caused him to flinch and lose count. Thereafter, he tried to concentrate on putting one foot in front of the other, upwards ever upwards, the steepness increasing with every step – it must be forty-five degrees here – muscles aching, lungs panting, brows oozing sweat until they eventually came to the barracks at the top.

Congratulating his perspiring troops, the amused captain went off with his lieutenants and the colour-sergeant, leaving their sergeants and corporals to direct them to their barrack rooms.

'What d'you think to this then, Pa?' asked Bumby, throwing his valise on his cot and studying his antiquated surroundings.

Probyn looked unsure. 'I think it might get a bit claustrophobic.'

'What's that mean?'

'Well, like prison,' explained Probyn.

'I wouldn't know, I haven't been in clink.' Bumby tested the mattress.

'Neither have I, you cheeky blighter!' Probyn upbraided him.

'Yes, you have,' Queen reminded him, 'for insulting that red cap.'

'Oh aye, I'd forgotten about him.' Probyn looked gloomy. 'But that was only for one night. I wonder how long we'll be stuck here?'

'A long, long time if I have my way.'

All eyes turned to the doorway, their hearts falling as the speaker made his entrance, a strutting bantam cockerel with a large gap where his front teeth had once been.

'And I'm gonna make your bleeding lives a misery,' sneered Corporal Wedlock.

It transpired that the hated corporal had only been on the island a matter of months, posted here to replace a time-expired soldier, and now transferred to this unfortunate detachment. It also emerged that Wedlock had a long memory, and Probyn, for his role in scalding the corporal's groin two years ago, was now to come in for harsh treatment, being sent down and up Jacob's Ladder several times a day for no feasible purpose. He could now state with certainty that there were seven hundred steps.

It seemed unjust, after all his brave deeds in Matabeleland, to be reduced to the role of corporal's plaything. But if that awful trek had taught him anything it was endurance, and he bore Wedlock's petty atrocities without a murmur. If Napoleon Bonaparte could withstand such exile then surely an English soldier could.

What was truly unfair was the non-fraternization rule which Wedlock enforced with zeal. The island existence might not have been so bad had Probyn been allowed access to one of the beautiful girls there, but Wedlock made sure there was to be no such fun. This injustice was compounded by the fact that Dinizulu, the king they were guarding who had been sent here for rebelling against the British, was furnished with a tutor, had been taught to play the piano, and had all manner of home comforts, including two wives who had during his stay provided him with a number of children! How ironic, thought Probyn, that the captive was allowed such human pleasures whilst he, the guardian, was not even permitted to exchange niceties with a girl. Would he ever find a wife?

It seemed likely that he would be spending yet another Christmas under the sun. Often, as he carried out Wedlock's idiotic orders on this isolated rock, he wondered what his family would be doing at home. The islanders were a warm and closely-knit people, every weekend large family groups gathering after church to picnic together, to play with their children, to fish or to swim, making this onlooker all the more conscious of his loneliness. Every day since his ominous convergence with the corporal he had looked out over the glistening ocean for a sign of the ship that would bring news of Aunty Kit or Merry, anything that might brighten this prison-like existence.

Finally, at last there came a sighting.

At his shout, Barnes, Bumby, Rook and Queen came pelting from the barracks in eager anticipation.

Balanced at the top of the mountainous ladder, high above the ocean, Probyn made a daredevil challenge. 'I'm going to do it!' Others before him had devised an ingenious way of descending the steps, but until now the very thought of this had produced tremors.

'Two bob says you don't!' Queen had won this way before.

'Right!' Closing his eyes to the perilous drop, Probyn took a deep breath, braced himself, then gingerly hooked his ankles over one rail, and edged his shoulders over the other, spreading his arms along the iron bar and clinging on for all he was worth whilst below lay certain death.

Waiting for him to make his move, the white knuckles advertising his dread, Queen laughed at the others. 'Told you he wouldn't!'

With that, Probyn released his grip and immediately began

to slide down the rails, drawing whoops of admiration from his pals as he gathered speed. Down, down he went, slithering over the rails, accelerating at an alarming rate, the rooftops growing bigger and the ground hurtling towards him.

'He's going too fast!'

Probyn heard Barnes's faint yell from above as he plummeted towards the ground and, at the last minute using his arms as a brake, landed on his feet unscathed, laughing triumphantly up at his friends, his heart thumping. 'Come on you sissies! You owe me two bob!'

One by one they came careering down then to join him, apprehensive faces growing nearer and nearer until he caught them at the bottom, all offering each other congratulations for their intrepid descent before running to join the townsfolk in their excited rush to meet the ship.

After all that, there was no mail for Private Kilmaster. Bitterly disappointed, he was forced to make do with snippets from his roommates' letters, afterwards mooching despondently from chore to chore for the rest of the day.

'Private Kilmaster!'

Probyn closed his eyes at Wedlock's loud demand, but turned to answer it with cool detachment. 'Yes, Corp?'

'Captain's office, now!'

Deducing from this tone that he was in trouble, Probyn wondered over the reason. Perhaps it was his foolhardy descent of the steps, though with others similarly guilty it could not be that. Accompanied by Wedlock, he went to find out.

'Stand easy, Lance-Corporal Kilmaster,' murmured the captain, looking down at the record sheet in front of him.

Probyn relaxed, then frowned.

The captain glanced up, smiling. 'No, your ears did not deceive you, I'm about to authorize your promotion.'

'Thank you, sir!' Thrilled, Probyn could not help a glance at Wedlock, but the other betrayed no emotion.

'Not at all, it's thoroughly deserved,' replied Captain

Galindo, putting his signature to the record sheet. 'I hope you will continue to maintain such efficiency.'

'Yes, sir!' Probyn could hardly wait to get out of the office, racing to broadcast his good luck to all who would listen, before rushing off a letter to inform his father, and also scribbling excitedly to Aunt Kit and to Meredith.

After this, his exhilarated mood preventing him from sitting still, he continued to bore his roommates. 'I wonder which squad I'll get put in charge of?'

'I'd have thought there'd be a more pressing matter on your mind,' said Queen.

'How so?' In the act of sewing on his stripe, he barely looked up.

'Well, you'll be messing with your little pal Wedlock, won't you?'

With a loud groan, Probyn fell back on his mattress to contemplate this double-edged sword.

Prior to taking up his role, the new lance-corporal was granted a day off and, eager for the world to behold his new status, decided to go for a walk around the town, travelling first down one side of the main street, then up the other, trying to catch a glimpse of his reflection in even the smallest of windows. Eyes to the right, seeking another window in which to admire himself, he almost barged into a post, but stepped aside just in time and threw an embarrassed grin at the group of islanders seated on the post office steps observing him. Returning his smile, their brown treacle eyes followed him up the slope, in fact everyone seemed to be smiling over his well-turned-out appearance. With a grin of pride, he returned to barracks. It was not until he visited the latrine that he realized his trousers were already unbuttoned.

Anxious not to repeat this same mistake in front of his new charges, he spent much time the next morning in checking his buttons before going to introduce himself to the small squad of youngsters who had only recently come from England. It was obvious from their deferential treatment that he had created a good impression. Keen to make his mark as a non-commissioned officer, one who was not simply there to make life as miserable as possible for the young infantrymen, but would share his experience, Probyn began his introduction by saying that he wanted to be proud of them and therefore would allow no foul language nor drunkenness. Other than this, his attitude displayed him as a kindly master, one devoted to sharing the benefit of his knowledge with those less able, for to his mind kindness always won respect.

'Eh lad, you're making a right pig's ear of that,' he told one of the youngsters who was applying his pipeclay in much the same manner as he himself had once done. 'How long have you been in the army?'

'Eighteen months, Corp.' The speaker seemed apprehensive.

'Eighteen months, and nobody's ever taken the time to show thee where you're going wrong? Here, let me. There's always an easy way if you care to look for it,' he found himself quoting Felix Lennon's words, and cocked his head in sage-like manner. 'Consider this, you're locked in a cell, its walls are twelve inches thick, there's a window but it has iron bars on it, the only items are a stone slab for your bed, and a bucket. How do you escape?'

Muttering amongst themselves, the youngsters failed to come up with a solution.

Probyn spread his arms and smirked. 'Why don't you just use the door?'

The youths exchanged glances, one of them daring to say, 'But you said it was locked, Corp.'

'No I didn't.' Realizing his mistake, Probyn flushed and made blustering attempts to get out of it. 'Anyway, lads, I think I've showed you enough! Just you remember what I told you, no swearing, keep yourselves dapper and we'll get along fine!' He turned and beat a hasty retreat, almost colliding with Wedlock in the doorway. It became obvious then that the boys' deferential treatment had not been for Probyn at all, but for Wedlock of whom they were terrified and who had been standing there all along, smirking.

'Knocking them into shape are we?' Wedlock was most amused.

'They're doing all right.' With the other blocking his exit Probyn was compelled to remain at the source of his embarrassment. He felt an utter fool.

'Call this heap of shit all right?' Wedlock patrolled the room, tossing clothing and equipment hither and thither, swearing and even hitting one youth across the face.

Probyn had been humiliated enough for one day. He held the bully with glittering blue-grey eyes. 'It was good enough until somebody started throwing it around!' It was a rash exclamation and not the done thing to have this exchange in front of underlings, but if he was to maintain what little authority he had he needed them to witness his stand.

Immediately Wedlock abandoned his victim and marched from the room, signalling with a crooked finger for Probyn to exit too.

Outside the door, he asked the other, 'You wouldn't be arguing with me would you?'

'I meant no disrespect, but if the captain thinks I'm proficient enough to look after a squad I'd like to be able to do it in my own way.'

'Without me interfering?' Wedlock put his face nearer, challenge in his voice. 'Come on don't mince words, say what's on your mind.'

'I don't want to fight –'

'Good, 'cause you'd end up worst off.'

Probyn knew this well enough, but the cause exceeded the risk. 'I don't think us brawling would be a very good example to set young uns, would it?' he asked calmly, his eyes continuing to penetrate the other's. 'Corporal Wedlock, I'm beholden to you for saving me from a thumping all those years ago but don't expect me to stand by and let you walk all over me.'

'I told you at the time,' said Wedlock, 'it wasn't done for you but to defend the uniform.'

'Well, I share your pride in the regiment,' replied Probyn, 'and I respect you as a fellow soldier.' In spite of disliking Wedlock on a personal level he knew such a man could be relied upon in battle. 'But you have your methods and I have mine –'

'How long have you had that stripe, a few days isn't it? Think it spoils the line of your sleeve do you? Because we can always arrange to have it ripped off.'

Probyn's heart sank, but he managed to uphold his level gaze as he formed his rejoinder. 'And what reason will you give the CO for having me reverted? I wasn't the one who struck a soldier.'

Wedlock was not slow to grasp the threat, and nodded knowingly, answering with a snorting laugh. 'You expect that little shit in there to make a complaint against me? It'd be your word against mine.' However, his attitude seemed to undergo a conversion then. 'Ah, don't worry! I've decided to let matters lie for now, but just remember that's one stripe not three, it qualifies you for supervising shit-shovelling and little else. Got it?'

13

Surprisingly, despite the threat to remove his stripe, it seemed that Probyn's attempt to make a stand had had the desired effect. Following their altercation, Wedlock left him alone to do the job and, with renewed confidence, he was able to set about moulding the little squad under his command into the kind of soldiers of whom he could be proud.

Yet the life of a non-commissioned officer was turning out to be a lonely one. No longer allowed to socialize with his friends, and less popular with them for having to dole out orders, he began to feel more isolated than ever. Though it was true that there was great advantage in not having to do fatigues, the very act of having to associate with Wedlock was punishment enough, and it was all he could do to share two words with the man. And though the other corporals might be less offensive, they were not the type with whom he would choose to spend his free time.

To add gravitas to his role, he decided to grow a moustache and, after only a few weeks of effort, was pleased with the result, waxing and cultivating the red-blond whiskers at every opportunity, and wondering how long it would be before he had the chance to show it off to those at home. He had finally heard from his stepmother who must obviously have written before receiving news of his promotion for there was no congratulations, but she told him that his father was managing well, and that the area was beginning to recover after the strike. Though she had seen nothing of Owen, reportedly his injury had not been too serious and the Earl had responded to his workers' violence against him with charity, though certain masters had been less forgiving and many had been sacked. There had also been a dreadful storm in Pontefract which had blown down the massive barracks gates and thrown tiles about like confetti. Never had Probyn thought to feel such homesickness for that colliery town, but, imprisoned by an ocean, month after month, the novelty of his stripe was beginning to wear off.

To stave off boredom he had written to everyone he could think of, including Greatrix who, in his reply, had stated that he too had been promoted, so at least they would still be able to associate whenever they might be granted the opportunity.

He had also applied for the second-class certificate needed to become sergeant, and studying for this helped to take up some time, buffing up on his arithmetic, reciting poetry to himself and balancing the accounts of the mess.

It was a great achievement when he passed. But with no more studying to do for the time being, his only other means of escape was to go for long walks around the island, for, within the desolate cliffs that imprisoned him and the cannons that dotted the rocks, he had discovered rich green meadows, tilled over the centuries by English immigrants to resemble their motherland, with cattle, sheep and rabbits and even the troublesome briars that grew in the hedgerows of home.

Yet rounding the corner into the next valley, one would be presented with a grandeur one could never find in England: dramatic escarpments of pink basalt, swathes of pine and eucalyptus, cactus and aloe and sunbursts of hibiscus, banana fronds and bougainvillaea, and acres of New Zealand flax, its spiky ten-foot clumps towering above him, all abetting to remove the fantasy that he was at home.

The youngsters under his supervision were also growing restless, and beginning to fight amongst themselves. To prevent the list of defaulters from becoming too long, he set them the task of reproducing the regimental colours in patchwork and embroidery, which had the desired effect for a time, although the stock of material was now becoming low. He would have to find more from somewhere.

One summer's evening, whilst supervising two members of his squad through the town, he paused outside the tiny gaol next to the church to share a few words with a colonial policeman who was enjoying the last rays of sunshine. He had come to know and like many of the inhabitants and loved to hear their accent, the strangest he had ever heard, a kind of mixture of Cockney, West Country and African and all manner of other nationalities thrown in, yet far removed from being mongrel, its inflection rather genteel. Asked a question, the policeman obligingly entertained him with that engaging lilt, the pair of them quickly becoming hemmed in by a flock of mynah birds who waddled and pecked around their feet.

A brown-skinned woman was wending her leisurely way across the square, her knees alternately displacing the folds of her long pink cotton dress to reveal a froth of white petticoat around her ankles. Finding his eyes naturally drawn to the female shape, Probyn examined her for a moment, but seeing that she was thirty-five or maybe more, soon lost interest and was about to look away when all at once the bottom appeared to drop out of her basket and from it tumbled a host of vegetables which started to bounce and roll away from her.

Deeming it beneath his dignity to chase them himself, but responding to his instinct to help, Probyn alerted the two young guards who pelted off and made sporadic grabs at the vegetables until all were gathered and safely returned to their owner.

Treating both soldiers and their corporal to a gracious smile, the woman seemed in no hurry to get away. 'Tank you, you saved me a werry long walk, Corporal . . . ?'

'Kilmaster,' he answered her unspoken question, having to raise his eyes for she was slightly taller than himself. 'And it was our pleasure, madam.' He was standing alone in the dappled light now, the policeman's attention having been distracted by someone else.

She inclined her straw hat in dignified pose. 'Miss Emily Hercules.'

He made no comment on the unusual name, nor on the lack of marital title for one so aged. His eyes flickered over her, admiring her shape, though he did not find in her face the delicacy he so admired in a woman, her jaw being on the heavy side and crammed with long teeth, albeit gleaming white. However, her brown eyes were velvety soft, betraying a compassionate nature. Here was a woman who would do one a good turn.

'I'd like to repay you –' she began rapidly.

Ever the opportunist, he jumped in. 'There's no need but if I might impose on you, there is a way you can help us.' He hurried to explain that the soldiers were in dire need of scraps of material for their patchwork. 'If you don't think it rude could you ask your friends too? Anything that might otherwise be put to waste.'

'Most certainly,' she smiled at him, her eyes brimming with a friendly intelligence. 'I shall do it straight away.'

'Oh, I wasn't implying that it was urgent!'

'It be no trouble at all,' she reassured him, her gloved hand changing the heavy basket to her other arm. 'If you would care to call at my house tomorrow I shall have it ready.'

Informed of where she lived, Probyn thanked her and said he would come at the end of the day.

Walking along a steep valley path the following evening he followed the woman's directions to her stone cabin that stood alone in a hollow scooped out of the hillside. She had been waiting for his coming. The door was thrown open before he had even reached her verandah.

'Come in! I have it ready.' From behind Emily Hercules's skirts peeped three small, barefooted children.

Taken aback by their presence, he hesitated, affecting to look at the damage to her woodwork, great chunks of it chavelled away.

She followed his eyes, seemingly embarrassed. 'White ants, such appetites, dey had almost eaten the place from under me before I noticed. What must you think of me? I keep telling myself to repair it –'

'I could have a word with the captain and ask if I can send some of the boys up. It's no trouble,' he stalled her objection, 'they're lost for things to do.'

'Hence de patchwork,' she flashed a smile and nodded. 'Well, plenty material here for dem to be going on with. Please come in.'

Finally responding to her gracious invitation, he entered awkwardly but ignored her request to sit down, fixing his eyes on a picture of the Queen. The children, exquisite little creatures, seemed mesmerized by him.

'You must forgive my nephew and nieces staring,' said Miss Hercules, bending suddenly to tickle the infants and set them all a-giggle.

Probyn was careless in his reply. 'Oh, they're not yours then? I mean –' he felt the colour rush to his cheeks.

She seemed unabashed. 'No, I remain unblessed.' Maternal hands stroked the trio of curly heads. It was obvious she doted on them. 'Dey are my sister's. I have the privilege to care for dem whilst she is at work.'

She smiled at her nephew's close interest in the visitor. 'Young George, he wants very much to be a soldier.'

Probyn smiled at the youngster. 'I hope he'll face less opposition than I did.'

'Do sit yourself down,' bade Miss Hercules for the second time.

Noting the teapot and cups, he looked uncomfortable. 'I hope you don't think I'm being rude but I mustn't stay too long, I have to escort the guard.'

'Oh, den I must not keep you.' With the slightest flicker of disappointment she turned away to fetch a large bag, revealing the scraps of material therein.

He peered into the bag, exclaiming his delight. 'That's awfully generous!'

'I should like to see de end result when it be finished,' she told him.

'You shall,' he said and took the bag, then, sensing her loneliness but not daring to flout regulations, he apologized again for being unable to stay, saying he hoped he had not put her to too much trouble, before making his escape.

Whilst thankful to the woman for supplying his platoon with enough material to last all year, Lance-Corporal Kilmaster found that his encounter with her had stirred up thoughts of his own female relatives and he was to become even more homesick than ever. The letters and parcels which arrived sporadically over the following months were no substitute for the real thing, though had it not been for them he felt he would sometimes go mad, and if, after all the ritual that went into greeting a ship, he found that it was not carrying a message for him, the gloom he experienced caused him seriously to consider buying himself out.

But there was no such despondency on this May morning as he and everyone else slithered down Jacob's Ladder to greet the vessel which had stopped here to take on coal. Not only did it carry letters but a draft of his own regiment. To great ceremony, the old gunboat firing a salute, the men were ferried ashore to engage in a cricket match. Leaving his letter unopened for now in order to relish it later, Probyn took up the wicket on the only level piece of grass on the island. Surrounded by deep ravines on all sides, there followed a precarious game which the local side won, the afternoon ending with a splendid feast and fun all round.

Only after the visitors had returned to their ship did he open his letter, settling down in the corporals' mess with a cup of tea, intent on savouring the contents.

'Dear Brother,' wrote Merry, 'I am sorry to have to tell you . . .' His heart lurched. Even before he read the next line he knew that his father had died.

'You look as if you lost a quid and found a clod.' Noisily stirring his tea, Wedlock remarked on his companion's grief-stricken expression.

Not divulging his loss, fearing that he might cry and needing to get completely away from Wedlock, Probyn shot from his chair and left the room, continued past the gates of the fortress and into the countryside beyond, the only place where he could truly be alone.

Surrounded by open fields, no witness save a distant man-sion and the sinking sun, he dropped to his hunkers and gave vent to his emotions, sobbing into his palms. He had known it would come eventually, why was it such a tremen-dous shock?

When finally he managed to control his tears, he pulled out the letter and read it in full, seeking a line that would tell him his father had been proud to learn of his son's promotion before he died; but it was non-existent. Maybe he would never know.

He folded the letter away and sat there for a while gazing red-eyed into space, listening to the distant whine of a flax mill, the yelping of gulls and the low rumble of the sea against the rocks. He would have liked to sit there much longer, but shadows were beginning to creep across the valley. Having managed to check his grief, he coughed twice, blew his nose, then replaced his helmet and began to make his way back to barracks, in no hurry to arrive.

Leaden with bereavement, he hoped to meet no one, and was devastated to see a woman coming towards him along the valley path, and even more so when he recognized it to be Emily Hercules. With no way of avoiding her, he braced himself to offer a courteous greeting, intent on hurrying by. But her toothy smile and the fact that she stood in his way made it impossible to do anything other than tarry.

He prayed the failing light would hide his torment, but the immediate change in Miss Hercules' demeanour told that she had interpreted his red eyes. 'Why, Corporal Kilmaster, whatever be the matter? You are deeply distressed I tink.'

He had not anticipated such open comment. But he might as well tell her the truth. 'I've just received news that my father's died.' At her look of genuine compassion, fresh tears sprang to his eyes but he fought them valiantly. 'So if you'll excuse me –' He tried to get by her. The pain was dreadful.

'I cannot let you go like this!' She laid a brown hand upon his arm. 'I know how badly you must feel, my father is dead also. Come, let me make you a cup of tea.' She made as if to lead him.

'I should get back to the barracks –'

'And so you shall when you are feeling better but a barracks full of men is not the place to be when one needs comfort and my house is just over dere.' Without further ado she ushered him towards the white cabin, murmuring condolences.

Small fat wire-birds pecked amongst the long shadows that led to her door. They went unseen by his grief-stricken eyes, though the sight of the ant-ravaged verandah brought forth a shamefaced apology. 'I'm sorry, I promised to do something about that.'

'Never mind, you have more important tings to tink 'bout.' In motherly fashion she urged him inside and began to stoke the fire, then put a kettle on to boil.

He placed his white helmet on the table and sat down, watching her miserably, feeling he should say something. 'You're not looking after your nephews and nieces today?'

'No, I don't have dem every day, only on certain days when I'm not at work myself. My sister and I take it in turns to have the pleasure of their company.' Her eyes simmered with affection.

Head throbbing, he asked where she worked and received the reply that both women were employed by the post office.

'Does your sister's husband work there too?' He was not interested, merely trying to take his mind off his grief.

'Elizabeth is unwed.'

'Oh.' Used to his aunt's colourful past, he was not as scandalized as some might have been at the news of three illegitimate offspring. In fact this woman here reminded him somewhat of his Aunt Kit, not in appearance but certainly with her deep fondness of children and her inherent kindness. 'So they're all called Hercules too. It's a nice name, unusual.'

'It's a slave name,' she told him without any trace of rancour, pouring boiling water into a teapot and giving it a stir. 'My grandfather was rescued by the Navy whilst on the way to America. He was liberated and brought to St Helena where he married my grandmother. Her family have been here for centuries. Dey had six children and so did my parents.'

Immediately he thought of his own family, but pushed the image aside. 'Have you ever left the island, Miss Hercules?'

She shook her head and placed a cup and saucer before him, smiling. 'No, but I should werry much like to see the Mother Country before I die.'

'I don't know how you can bear to live in such isolation.' He stared dolefully into his empty cup. 'Knowing the rest of the world is out there.'

'But that is what I love 'bout it!' exclaimed Miss Hercules, sitting next to him at the table to pour the tea. 'This is the only world I know.' She looked into his eyes, saw how young he was. 'Of course, I understand that it is different for you. There must be people whom you miss.'

Watching the beverage flow into his cup, he heaved a sigh. 'There's just Aunt Kit left now, and my sister Meredith. Since I joined the army the rest of them don't speak to me. Not that I care.' The latter was issued with boyish conviction.

Without asking she dropped a spoonful of sugar into his cup and tinkled the spoon around it, her nut brown face showing disbelief. 'I would be proud if my brother defended the Flag.'

The steam from the kettle and the heat of the fire had made his nose run. Excusing himself he pulled out a damp handkerchief and trumpeted into it, then dabbed assiduously at his moustache before shoving the rag away. 'Did you never want to marry?' He would not normally be so blunt but her attitude invited intimacy.

'I would like to, yes.' She lifted her cup. 'But in thirty-six years nobody ever asked me and time flies so quick now.'

He sought to lend a glimmer of hope. 'My aunt was almost as old as you when she got married, so don't give up yet. But I know what you mean about the years flying past. Why, I'm almost twenty-two myself! I were barely nineteen when I left home.'

Her eyes gazed into his, delving beyond the attempt at maturity, then with a little smile she proceeded to sip her tea.

Mention of home had brought the hurt flooding back. He drank quickly to stave off the tears, scalding his throat. 'I should be going.'

Miss Hercules bade him take his time. 'You have not far to go. Bide a while.'

Reluctant to face Wedlock's questioning, he nodded and took his tea more slowly. Neither of them spoke for some moments. The light was fading quickly now, though she made no effort to ignite a lamp.

'When I was young,' Miss Hercules had adopted a distant stare, the light of the flames dancing over her brown features, 'I boasted that I would have ten children, and here I am alone.'

'But you might not always be,' murmured Probyn throatily.

'Few men would take a wife who cannot bear a child.' Her voice had the merest quiver of pain.

'But how can you be sure? I mean . . .' He coughed, trying to dislodge the lump of grief that clogged his throat, 'I don't want to be indelicate but if you've never been wed how can you be sure you can't have children?'

She studied his innocent face, pityingly. 'Because I have a defect of the womb.'

He looked stricken. 'I'm sorry, I never meant to pry!' And his eyes fell away quickly.

'You did not pry. You asked, I told you. Just as you told me 'bout your sadness.'

At the compassion in her voice, tears sprang to his eyes, he could not hold them back. 'Lord, I feel so stupid!' He dashed an angry hand to his face.

'You must not.' She rose quickly and put her arms around his shoulders, pulling him to her, cradling his head in her bosom, rocking him.

He dared not move but sat there hypnotized, seeing from the corner of his eye a brown hand stroking his cheek, the digits rough against his skin, rough and comforting and loving. Tilting his face, he was presented by a look of such tenderness that he had never known, not even from his mother.

A sudden sense of danger welled, causing the half-hearted protestation, 'I shouldn't –'

But she stifled his objection with quick warm lips, her eyes so full of desire that he could not resist. 'There's nothing to be afeared of,' she whispered, and pulled him gently to his feet, and kissed him, thenceforth introducing him to such overwhelming feelings, such indescribable passion, as he had never experienced in his life.

Laying alongside her afterwards on the fireside rug, caressing the brown limbs that had only moments ago been locked around him, pulling him into her very core and draining him of everything, he could scarcely believe that life could change so drastically within so short a span, and yet perversely it had also seemed like an eternity that they had spiralled together in mid air, suspended in time, deaf and blind to all outside influence, conscious only of each other. It was all totally beyond any fantasy he could have conjured.

And then under the disapproving gaze of the Queen's

bulging eyes came guilt. How could he do such a thing with his father lying dead and buried? And he shed tears of remorse and loss, wept into Emily's shoulder whilst she held him, issuing naught but maternal whispers of adoration.

And then they made love again, she to lead and he to follow, but this time the path was a familiar one and he took it with confidence, anticipating its twists and turns, mischievously racing her towards a distant paradise, but never overtaking her, content to let her dance along just one step ahead, gazing with rapture into her face as she lost all reason and finally came back to him, to beckon him onwards to heights of renewed bliss.

It was dark outside now. Sated, and adhered by perspiration to the womanly form beside him, he gave a smiling wince and eased himself away but only in order to face her. 'I must go, Emily, and I mean it this time.'

Nodding, she kissed him and allowed him to stand, helping him to dress in the firelight, handing over his soldier's accoutrements one after another.

There was a hint of anxiety as she saw him to the door, a reluctance to let him leave, but she did not voice her fears and kissed him warmly as he promised to call again the moment he could.

However, he sensed her mood. 'Have I done something wrong?'

Emily wrapped a shawl about her against the cold evening and shook her head, smiling.

'Then what is it?' He embraced her quickly.

'I'm afeared that you might be too embarrassed to call on me again.'

'Embarrassed?' He was thoroughly perplexed.

'Because I have witnessed your tears. Some men might not like being reminded –'

'I'm not like that!' He squeezed her taller form. 'Emily, you're the best thing that ever happened to me. I can't wait for us to meet again.' Before tonight he had assumed that he knew the extent of sexual matters, but the ecstasy that he had enjoyed in this woman's arms bore not the slightest resemblance to that first sordid coupling with the girl in York. He kissed her fervently, and Emily returned his passion.

'Now, I really must dash!'

She laughed and bestowed a gentle shove. 'Go then, Corporal Dasher.'

Assuming this was an accusation he again felt guilty. 'I meant it about coming back!'

'And I believe you.' She continued to smile. 'It was just a nickname – everybody on the island has a nickname.'

He had heard of this. 'And what's yours, Emily?'

'Aunty, even to those who are no relation.'

He understood why, but chose not to use it, for to him it only emphasized the difference in their ages. 'I prefer Emily,' he told her, then, with one last kiss and a wave over his shoulder he dashed off towards the fort, still reeling from the predicaments of life and death that had assailed him this past couple of hours.

Upon serious thought, it occurred to him that Emily had been uncannily intuitive. He *was* embarrassed at revealing such emotion before her and had it been anyone else he would have wiped them from his memory. But Emily was not so easily extinguished. Dear, warm, passionate Emily had suddenly become the focus of his entire life, lingering in his mind much longer than the image of his father. Even after his grief began to wane and he was no longer in need of comfort his visits did not lessen, for he was now totally besotted with this woman who mothered and pampered and loved him, and he in return finally mended her ravaged verandah and other things about the home. For indeed, he did feel at home with this generous being.

Aware that he would be in serious trouble if they were found together he made no mention of his trysts to others, least of all to Wedlock who would immediately stamp on such pleasure. To all intents and purposes his evening and weekend jaunts around the valley were just a form of release from this prison-like existence, an escape shared by many others in the fort and so invited no suspicion as long as he was back in time for lights out.

Throughout the remainder of the year, in sunshine, wind and torrential rain, through the mist that swirled over the flax-covered hills, his boots followed the well-trodden path to her cottage, therein to enjoy another evening of ecstasy, before army commitments wrenched the lovers apart.

'Can you not stay just one night, Dasher?' she begged him as he made ready to leave yet again. 'Maybe for Christmas . . .' Another festive season would be upon them in a few days. Despite her many siblings Emily cherished the hope that her lover would share the occasion too.

'You know I can't.' Smiling apology, he allowed himself to be dragged back into her arms for one last embrace. 'If I don't turn up they'll think I've fallen down a ravine and send out a search party. They mustn't find out about us, Em, or we're done for.' And so would be his army career.

'I long to wake and find you still at my side.' Her fingers performed exquisite torture, to which he immediately succumbed, wrapping himself around her in abandon.

'Just one night,' she begged.

Aroused, he fought his better judgement. 'There might be a way . . .' If he could find the right mark, one of his fellow corporals who might cover for his absence, maybe he could spend a night here. 'If I can get someone to look in on my squad, to explain my empty bed if anyone should ask . . .'

This idea was to occupy him for the next couple of days, great thought being paid to which of the corporals he should ask. None of them were entirely trustworthy but one was more approachable than the rest and had been the only one to show commiseration when Probyn had told them his father had died.

On Christmas Eve, before heading off to see Emily, he braced himself to ask.

'Goody, can I beg a favour?'

'Depends what it is and what it's worth.' But Goodwill seemed amiable as he pinned decorations to the wall of the corporals' mess.

'I'm off to see a friend and might not get back in time for lights out. Can you look in on my lot and explain my absence in the mess if anybody asks? I'll be back in time for reveille.'

'Woman is it?'

Probyn hesitated, but when Goodwill did not seem concerned, he nodded. 'I'd like to keep it between ourselves.'

Goodwill pressed another drawing pin through a loop of paper chain. 'Is this where you've been going all these months when you're supposed to be bird-watching?'

'Not all the time,' lied Probyn. 'I just thought, seeing as it's Christmas and all that . . .'

Goodwill was thoughtful, then said, 'A quid should do it.'

Concealing his disgust, Probyn handed over a sovereign. At this exorbitant rate his nights with Emily would be restricted to once in a blue moon.

However, the look of joy on her beloved face when he informed her he would be staying was worth every penny, and the night that followed was possibly the best of his life. Even the fact that he had to rise before dawn on Christmas Day to be back in time for reveille had its compensations, for he and Emily were to witness the most magnificent sunrise. It was as if God Himself had endorsed their union. With such approval how could any earthly power object? Aching to shout his love to the rest of the island, the errant lance-corporal was wiser than to do so. Sufficing with a whisper to the breeze, he pressed his ardent lips to hers, ran his hands about her body, squeezed her, kneaded and embraced her one last time, then stole a furtive passage back to the garrison.

How could he ever have hoped to conceal his absence from Wedlock? He had barely set foot in the room when his adversary uttered comment.

'Noticed your bed hasn't been slept in.'

Though shocked, Probyn barely faltered and launched into his breakfast. 'I was up early.'

'Ballocks!' A wet morsel of bread was projected from Wedlock's lips along with the nasty laugh. 'You've been out all night – I hope you haven't been shagging the niggers.'

Probyn felt as if he had been stabbed. A quick look at Goodwill provided a discreet shake of the head. It had just been a lucky guess but the sordid comment had totally demolished any magic. He was appalled to have Emily referred to like this. 'Don't talk rot!' he told Wedlock.

'Only joking,' said Wedlock blithely, continuing with his meal. 'A man'd have to be puggled to risk getting himself reduced for a bibbi.'

It was a definite threat. Warning himself to be more careful, Probyn took his frustration out on a lump of bread, tearing into it with his teeth, and deciding there and then that he must not see Emily for a while until the gossip had died down.

It had been done for her benefit as much as his but the moment he set eyes on her he chastised himself for not putting himself in her stead, for not realizing what must have been going through her mind.

'I thought you had deserted me!' Emily was distraught, the tears streaming down her cheeks as he tried to explain. 'A week! A whole week, Dasher, and not a word. What was I supposed to think?'

'Oh, Em, dear Em, I was just trying to protect you!' He pressed her streaming face to his shoulder, rocking her in the same manner that she had comforted him. 'There's been talk, nothing specific but Wedlock keeps making these sarky comments, I think he suspects and I didn't want to give him any proof so I thought if I kept away –'

'I felt that my heart was torn out!' wept Emily.

'I know, I know, I missed you dreadfully too!' He crushed her even more tightly. 'I couldn't bear to keep away any longer,

357

but truly we must be careful, I mustn't stay long.' And with this he launched an impulsive, passionate assault upon her body, the two of them lost to all reason, all words of caution evaporating in the heat of desire.

On return to barracks Probyn slipped into the corporals' mess and, trying to appear nonchalant, calmly took up his embroidery.

'Been to see Topsy again?' Goodwill barely looked up from his knitting.

'Don't call her that!' God but it was sickening, having one's fellows know one inside out, or claim that they did, having one's life constantly held up for inspection. His annoyed reaction had jerked the thread out of the needle; trying to reinsert it, he asked, 'Where's Wedlock?'

'Dunno.' Finishing another row, Goodwill turned his knitting around and began to purl.

Needle threaded, Probyn stabbed it through the pieces of cloth, all the while thinking of Emily.

Wedlock entered then. There was no untoward remark, in fact no comment of any kind, but Probyn had the distinct feeling that he was enjoying some private joke, and after several irritating seconds was compelled to ask, 'What's up with you?'

Wedlock glanced at him in surprise. 'Nowt. In fact I'm very happy. I've just had orders that we're leaving at the end of the month.'

Probyn's heart lurched. How long had he yearned to be off this wretched island and now just when he had every reason to want to stay they were ordering him to leave!

He must go see Emily, right away. He had left her earlier than usual, there would just be time for him to return and pass on the information and get back to barracks before dark.

Inserting his needle into cloth, he rose and wandered leisurely to the door. 'There's still a bit of sunlight left, I think I'll just go and enjoy it while I can.'

Wedlock nodded, then buried his face in a book. 'Aye, best make the most of it.'

Probyn maintained his casual attitude until he was out of the garrison, then broke into an urgent trot, making for Emily's cottage.

At first she was surprised and delighted to see him again, but upon examining his worried face she in turn became anxious, especially when he told her what brought him back.

'I've just heard we're to leave the island!'

She moaned and almost fainted.

'Don't worry, everything's going to be all right.' On his way here he had come to a decision; there was only one way that the lovers could be assured a future. 'I've come to ask you to marry me!'

She was disbelieving, but plumbing his gaze saw that he was deadly serious, and cried out, 'Yes, yes, my dearest!'

He gasped a laugh at his own audacity. 'I'm supposed to ask permission, but there's no point, they won't grant it.'

'But why not, are we both not British?'

'Yes, but . . .' He could not bring himself to tell this lovely woman that the colour of her skin was the handicap. 'People have been turned down before for no good reason, I daren't risk losing you. Once we're wed they can't do anything about it. I'll apply to have you put on the strength and then I'll be able to take you with me wherever I go.' He hoped fervently that this would be the case, and that he was not about to jeopardize his career. But he had risked it all before and won. He was a good soldier, they would not want to lose him for such a mean-spirited rule.

Emily was overjoyed and threw herself into his arms. The short time they had together was spent making hectic plans for their clandestine marriage, for both agreed that it must take place as quickly as possible. They arranged to meet at her own little chapel the following Sunday after Church Parade, Probyn saying he would have to get a licence and a ring, Emily replying that she would speak to the minister and organize all that had to be organized, it would be easier for her, everything would be ready and waiting for them, her beloved must put his mind at rest.

Deeming it too risky to meet her in the interim, Probyn vowed that there would be endless nights of love after their marriage and, dealing her a long lingering kiss, rushed back to barracks.

He did not notice in his excited dash that he had been followed.

Naturally the week crawled by. Even with all the preparations to be made for the coming embarkation he was still left with too much time to think of Emily and how much he missed her. He wondered if she would like Mauritius, for that was where his company would be heading. It had been a shock at the time, but upon hearing the additional good news that Wedlock would be alighting at the Cape to rejoin the rest of the battalion it was turning out to be cause for celebration.

Sunday came at last. Everything went as usual; the mad rush to turn his men out in review order for Church Parade, then back for dinner. In the afternoon, tingling with nerves and arrayed in his scarlet regalia, Lance-Corporal Kilmaster prepared for his nuptials, checking over and over again that both ring and licence were safe. It was sad that none of his family would be present to witness his happiness, but then everything paled into insignificance when compared to spending the rest of his life with Emily. A moment of heart-warming reverie, a last check of his appearance, a deep breath, and he set off.

'Going somewhere nice?' asked Wedlock as they passed in the sunshine.

'Just out for a stroll.' Probyn did not falter.

'Sure about that?' Wedlock called after him, a note of warning in his voice.

Probyn stopped and turned, held the other with glittering eyes, defying Wedlock to try and stop him. 'Quite sure.'

Wedlock set his mouth, and turned aside, leaving Probyn to go on his way.

He thought as he journeyed through the tranquil countryside to the chapel what a quiet affair it would be. Emily had wanted to share the news with her family and have them present; she had been quite devastated when he had warned her they must tell no one and was only pacified when he swore they could reveal it to the world once the deed was irretractable. The very fact that they required two witnesses had proved unnerving, but as one of them was the policeman with whom he had become very friendly, the other an upstanding but romantically minded official, he was not unduly worried about the army getting to hear of it prematurely.

He arrived at the little stone chapel. There would be no more services until eventide, the building was quiet and empty except for those few attending the wedding. Probyn's boots echoed dangerously loud as he hurried to Emily's side, beaming in self-consciousness and love. Oh, how he wanted it all to be over and done with so that he could spirit her away to the little white cabin and make love to her.

The shuffling and clearing of throats petering into silence, the ceremony began, the words booming around the empty church. 'Dearly beloved . . .'

When it came to his turn to make his vows he spoke up calm and clear, Emily's vows coming as little more than a whisper but her eyes laden with so much love that there could be no mistaking the sincerity of it.

The ceremony was almost over, the minister about to declare them husband and wife, when the door opened and more footsteps echoed down the aisle.

A look of gravity came over the minister's face. Probyn froze, and then turned to meet the new arrival, knowing even before he set eyes on it who this would be.

'I must advise you, sir, to stop this mockery at once,' Corporal Wedlock told the minister.

'It is too late!' replied the bewildered man. 'The vows have already been sworn.'

Wedlock was unmoved, though his breathing was quite rapid after hurrying to catch up with his quarry whom he had followed at a distance. 'That is impossible, sir, it has no legal basis –'

'But Corporal Kilmaster has acquired a licence.'

'The British Army would never countenance such a partnership! Lance-Corporal Kilmaster is well aware that he is in breach of regulations even to be in this woman's presence.'

'This *woman* is my wife!' Probyn's eyes were shot with passion as he gripped Emily's arm.

Wedlock did not flinch. 'Then I have no alternative but to report this matter to the commanding officer. Unless you agree to accompany me voluntarily I shall fetch the guard and have you put under arrest!'

Emily clung to her husband. 'Dasher, can you really be arrested? Is it true, is it so?' Her question was flung wildly at the policeman witness who shrugged unhelpfully, saying this was a military matter of which he had no knowledge.

'He's bluffing!' said Probyn, but his self-assurance was draining fast. In the face of such opposition it was coming home to him now just how futile this attempt at marriage had been.

'Would you care to put me to the test?' The vicious little bantam thrust his nose closer to that of his victim. 'Somebody has to save you from yourself, Kilmaster. You're not a bad soldier, all things considered, that's why I've given you ample opportunity to admit the error of your ways. But you've chosen to ignore all attempts to help you and this is your last chance. If you leave this church now and come with me I'll say nothing, I'll even allow you to keep your stripe, but if you choose to go ahead with your stupid plan and bring the regiment into disrepute I'll have no qualm in having you court martialled.'

Probyn rallied, drew Emily into his side and clutched her tightly. 'The captain wouldn't be so petty!'

Wedlock spat contempt. 'You call it petty to debase this fine regiment's reputation by marrying the likes of her?'

'I just want to marry the woman I love!' raged Probyn.

'You'll marry who the army says you can marry! Now, this is your last chance. Come back to barracks now or I'll fetch the guard!'

'Dasher, my dearest!' Thinking that he was about to strike his adversary, Emily grabbed his arm and held onto it. 'Go with him, do!'

Tearing his furious eyes away from Wedlock, Probyn stared into her anguished face.

'I can't see you ruined.' The crack in her voice showed that her heart was breaking but she managed to retain her dignity, did not weep and rail but uttered calmly, 'Go with him, we are man and wife, we can –'

'You are not man and wife!' contradicted Wedlock. 'This wedding is invalid.'

Emily ignored him, speaking only to the man she called her husband, behaving with great composure. 'When the time is right we will be together. No matter where you are in the world I will find you and come to you.'

Burdened with responsibility both to his wife and to the regiment, Probyn clamped his hands to the sides of his head, moaning in despair.

Seeing that he was winning, Wedlock addressed himself to the minister and to the witnesses. 'None of this must be recorded –'

The minister tried to assert himself. 'But as I said, the ceremony has been completed, Corporal Kilmaster produced a licence!'

'Let me see it if you please!' demanded Wedlock. When the dubious minister complied, the recipient tore the licence in half.

'There will be a copy,' pointed out the minister.

Wedlock was grave. 'If you write one word in that register, if any of you breathes so much as a word, you'll put this man in gaol.'

'Well, I have no wish to be responsible . . .' The minister exchanged uneasy glances with the witnesses, both of whom hung their heads in discomfort.

Emily was finding it harder to sustain her air of dignified calm, and urged Probyn, 'Go with him, dear one!'

'But what about you, Em?' he wailed.

She closed her eyes, fighting off tears. 'I will be all right. I beg you, don't make this sacrifice.'

With one last anguished cry he hugged her, almost smothering her with the ferocity of his embrace. Then, with one angry movement he wrenched himself from her arms and stormed out of the church, such agony in his heart that it felt as if he had lost his mother all over again.

14

Never had there been pain like this.

True to his word, Wedlock had restricted the matter to the corporals' mess. There had been no hint of gossip from the ranks nor from their superiors, his stripe was still on his arm and his career safe, but it made not an ounce of difference to the one afflicted. Nothing could remove this terrible, gnawing, constant ache.

In return for keeping silent Wedlock had extracted the pledge that Lance-Corporal Kilmaster would make no attempt to see Emily. And he had not. Not so much as a note, nor a wave of goodbye as he left the island, nor even a backwards look to see if she was there amongst the crowd. For he did not know how to cope with his betrayal of her.

Even now on the ship that took him to Cape Town he just could not believe that he would never see her again. How could he, when the smell of her skin remained in his senses, his body still reacted to her absent embrace.

Only by virtue of self-discipline and regimentation could he maintain the role that was demanded of him. To the callow youths in his platoon he behaved as normal, if perhaps a little testier of late, a little less forgiving, but compared to Wedlock's malevolent rule his conduct provoked few grumbles.

That his pain went unnoticed made it no less severe. The very act of eating was an ordeal, every morsel transformed to a boulder, choking and sickening him.

Another week was to pass and he felt no better. Whilst

others disembarked, Probyn's company remained on board to be joined by four companies of the Black Watch bound for Mauritius. Greatrix's company was also amongst those headed for the Indian Ocean. Probyn had spotted him on the quay waiting to come aboard, but even his best friend's presence was no salve for this weeping abscess.

Still, it helped to be rid of one thorn in his side, the one who constantly reminded him of his misfortune and, indeed, who was responsible for it. Wedlock was now lining up his section to disembark, squawking and pecking like the vicious gamecock he was. Good riddance, came the thought.

His men now marching to order, Wedlock caught Probyn's sullen glare and delayed his leaving to offer comment. 'Well, you'll no doubt be happy to see the back of me.'

Probyn merely curled his lip and looked away. It was all he could do to prevent his hands closing round the other's throat.

Wedlock manufactured a friendly tone, tapping Probyn on the breast. 'A word of advice for when you get to Mauritius. Don't go tupping any more nig –'

The sentence had barely emerged when Probyn's knuckles slammed into his face, the swiftness of it taking the other completely by surprise. There was a mad rush then to avert any further violence before an officer got wind of it, Goodwill and another struggling to prevent Wedlock from retaliating, others holding Probyn back, both men riving and twisting to be at each other until Wedlock was bundled off the ship by his friends.

Released, Probyn dismissed the congratulations on his lucky punch, his heart thumping with anger. It had been a long time coming, but the small satisfaction it gave was inadequate compensation for his loss.

However, diversion came aboard then in the form of Greatrix and once the ranks were settled and the ship was underway there was much catching up to do in the corporals' mess.

'You still owe me a letter, maister,' complained Greatrix.

Probyn apologized. 'There wasn't much to write about.' In truth, he had been somewhat remiss with his letter-writing since meeting Emily.

'Blimey, there is here,' replied Greatrix. 'Suppose you've heard about Dr Jim?'

Probyn shook his head. 'We never heard anything on St Helena.'

Greatrix then relayed the latest news from Rhodesia, Probyn affecting to listen with interest. His friend was unusually animated, announcing that Dr Jameson had invaded the Transvaal creating an international incident. Apparently it was based on President Kruger's refusal to allow the Uitlanders the right to vote when their wealth contributed the greater part to the Transvaal coffers and they had plotted revolt aided by Jameson. But the conspiracy had gone badly wrong, Dr Jameson and his raiders had been arrested and the Uitlanders holding Johannesburg had given in. 'What puzzles me,' said a bright-eyed Greatrix, 'is how an upright soldier like Major Grey was part of it. He wouldn't have been involved if he thought there was something fishy – anyway, whatever the cause, there's been hell to pay with the Boers, they've really got it in for us now, even the ones in the Cape – the Prime Minister's had to resign and everything! And just for good measure the German Kaiser's stuck his two pennorth in as well, siding with old Kruger . . .'

There came a passing remark from another. 'I hope you're not talking shop.'

Greatrix sat back and took a sip of tea. 'No, just giving my friend the basic details of the Raid, but that's enough of me droning on. I should hate to get him too excited.' His companion had yawned frequently throughout.

Probyn was immediately repentant. 'Sorry, I haven't been sleeping well since I learned me dad died.'

Greatrix displayed suitable remorse, nodding gravely. 'I thought you looked a bit miserable.'

If only you knew the real reason, thought Probyn, but he felt totally unable to broach the matter even with his friend.

'Me dog's snuffed it too,' said Greatrix dispassionately. 'Puff adder got him.'

Probyn made no comment, just sat there looking glum, examining the red knuckles damaged by Wedlock's cheekbone. 'I never knew we'd be away this long,' he breathed eventually. 'Apart from those few days I spent with me dad I haven't been home in four years. I'm very grateful, truly I am, for all the wonders I've seen, things that other people can only dream about, but I just want to go home.'

Greatrix admitted that he was homesick too, raising the question of whether to extend his service with the colours to twelve years or enter the reserve. 'So, are you still going for your pontoon, then?'

Probyn hesitated, but it was not really a serious decision for one who loved army life, it was just the dejection over Emily that caused this ambivalence. 'I suppose so.'

Greatrix nodded, chewing on a nail. 'Me an' all. But I know what you mean, I'd just like to be back in mucky old England once in a while, and see white faces again. I've nowt against darkies but I'm getting a bit sick of them.'

If he had been unable to ventilate his pain before, there was no chance of him doing so now. Merely dealing his friend a grim nod, Probyn gazed into mid air as the ship carried him towards yet another lump of volcanic rock surrounded by ocean, yearning for Emily's dear brown face.

The voyage lasted over a week but for most of those aboard it was an enjoyable trip with concerts, sports and games, the band playing nightly. Not given to maudlin, Probyn joined in too, though he derived little joy.

On the tenth day a picturesque island materialized against a hazy sky, a grand outline of lofty hills, magnificent terraced mountains, their jagged summits tangled with angel hair, beaches of white ground coral, casuarinas and palm trees and the lush damp greenness of cane fields.

The dockside at Port Louis was a seething mass of different races, Creole, Arab, Indian, Chinese, interspersed with a few maggoty faces of the newly arrived from England. Here, the two friends were again to part company, Greatrix marching through a city of white colonial buildings and soaring palms to Fort Adelaide, Probyn's company, band and drums and the rest of HQ entraining for Curepipe eight miles inland.

The railway system was abysmal, transporting them at five monotonous miles per hour through acres and acres of sugar cane, across a network of bridges spanning deep ravines and pockets of mist to the highest point on the island. Things were no better when they eventually arrived at the barracks, these being situated close to the mouth of an inactive volcano, the crater clothed in dense forest with a lake in its basin. The atmosphere was heavily laden with moisture and there was an overlying smell of mould in their living quarters, these being raised on struts. The body of Black Watch whom they were here to relieve seemed ecstatic to be leaving.

After smoothing the commotion that took place at finding a python in their hut, the men refusing to go to bed until he had one of the natives remove it, Probyn finally managed to settle them down, then peeled off his own damp clothes and hung them in a drying shed that reeked of stale sweat. Then after automatically checking his cot for scorpions and snakes, he fell upon it, the sheets immediately clinging to him. He kicked them off bad-temperedly and tried to sleep. Pray God tomorrow things would improve.

They did not. If anything, he felt even worse as the week wore on, his clothes constantly damp, the atmosphere laden with moisture, rain or mist occurring every day, food rotting within hours, rats scurrying about – and there was so little to occupy, parades being over before the sun got too intense, thereby lending him ample time in which to brood.

Once, he would have been interested in the bird life, the green parakeets with red beaks that came to perch at his window in hope of food, birds of scarlet and yellow and other gaudy apparel. None of them provided any novelty now, he had seen them all before. Nor did he care for the chittering monkeys who performed acrobatics upon the roof for they had too many attributes of people, regarding both species as a nuisance.

Attempting to shake off his despondency and to remove the staid image he was creating amongst his peers, on Saturday evening he accepted the invitation from his fellow corporals who had arranged to travel to a village and attend a sega, the hip-wriggling dance performed by Creoles. The sight of a woman dancing had never failed to excite, perhaps it was just the tonic he needed.

After tea and a refreshing plunge in the bathing pond they set off for the village. Clubbing together, they went first to see the headman and offered to pay for wine and rum to get the party going. Baskets of exotic fruit were placed before the visitors, bananas, mangoes, pineapples, though these invoked little relish, the soldiers having become accustomed to such fare, and were neglected in favour of alcohol.

Faking enthusiasm, Probyn rubbed his hands together glee-fully, but, unobserved, his expression was quick to fade into its sombre mask. Taking the occasional sparing sip of rum, trying not to think of Emily, he gazed around him waiting for the show to begin, his eyes falling on a dog chained in the dark shadows beneath the velvety spread of a tree and causing him to think instead of Greatrix and their trek to Bulawayo. The area, too, reminded him of Africa with thorn trees and grassy plains, wild flowering creepers with bright red flowers growing amongst the village huts from which peeped wide-eyed children. Emily had loved children . . .

'Try one of these, they taste like apple and custard!'

Feeling a nudge, Probyn wrenched his mind from Emily and took the apple-like fruit that was thrust at him. At first bite he found it disgusting, and spat out the mush discreetly. The light was fading rapidly now, the noise of a thousand parrots squabbling for a roost in the surrounding trees almost drowning out his friends' high spirits. With firelight providing the illumination, the music began, if music one could call it, the instruments being tin cooking pots and spoons, hand clapping, seeds shaken in a tin and a gourd with strings. Probyn tried to look intent as the dancers appeared. They moved slowly at first, snaking their hips in accompaniment to the drumbeat, the villagers congregating around them, singing in Creole. Gradually, the pace increased, building into a frenetic beat, the musicians eventually becoming overworked and others leaping in to take their place, but the dancers seemed inexhaustible, one of them coming to stand over Probyn thrusting her hips provocatively into his face. It was all too much. Angry and frustrated over his lost love, he leapt to his feet and stormed off into the darkness.

'Miserable sod,' commented one of his fellows, then paying Kilmaster no more thought, returned his focus to the erotic dance.

Breaking into a trot, Probyn tried to run out his anger, ran and ran and ran. A sambhur crashed out of the undergrowth and leapt across his path, making him jump and cry out in alarm. The deer vanished into the night. He sagged with fatigue, resting his hands on his knees and panting his lungs out. Would this wretchedness never cease? Damn her! Why had she started it all? All he had asked of her were some bits of material for his patchwork, why oh why had she insisted on taking it further? She was old enough to know better, had taken advantage of his grief – and his father could shoulder some of the blame too! If he had died when he had been meant to die three years ago instead of hanging on none of this would have happened.

Fuming and sweating, he lashed out at a bush, scattering

leaves and bark, alarming the roosting parrots who set up a jarring din. No better for this display of rage, he made his miserable way back to barracks.

Over the following weeks the atmosphere, already heavily laden with humidity, became unbearable, finally culminating in a cyclone. Pre-warned of its coming, the day turning black as night, the soldiers rushed around securing all doors and windows. Once barricaded inside, no one was allowed to leave except when on duty.

'But don't think this means you're getting out of gym!' Probyn warned his squad, trying to make a joke of it for some of the youngsters were frightened by the strength of the wind which at times felt as if it were capable of blowing the hut away and them with it. 'I've got some nice little physical jerks to keep you occupied!' And he set them to jumping and running on the spot, dripping with perspiration, whilst outside the powerful wind and rain set up a terrific noise, howling and wrecking all within its path.

With no supplies able to get through it was good old bully beef and biscuits for every meal, those who consumed it staring miserably out of the window, though it was impossible to see anything beyond the deluge except occasionally when the wind swept aside the curtain of water one could see palm trees being buffeted and bent to mimic inside-out umbrellas.

In the evening whilst the cyclone raged around them, for want of anything better to do Lance-Corporal Kilmaster set his men on the regimental patchwork they had begun on St Helena, attending also to the one of his own, though it dredged up sad memories and before long he had tossed it aside, lying on his moist bed to watch a gecko scamper around the walls, for it was impossible to sleep with this fearful racket going on.

The cyclone raged for four days. With the deluge finally evaporating into a cloud of steam in the brilliant sunshine, the prisoners emerged from their huts to survey the damage. Whilst others gasped over the wreckage, Probyn reflected instead upon his mood, amazed to find that the tempest had acted as a catharsis, completely purging him of grief. Thank God, it was over.

Feeling oddly cheerful, he became slightly bombastic towards his underlings. 'Right, you wasters, you've done nowt for too long. Get all this debris cleared up! Privates Johnson, Williams, get them fallen branches out of the road. Adams, shift that broken glass. Roberts, go see what's happened to that goat, and if you see any dodos on the way bring them to me, the government's offering a reward for every one sighted.'

Roberts beheld him slack-jawed. 'I thought they were extinct, Corp?'

'And most of them are! But they say there could still be the odd one hopping about and the government's keen to find it, so keep your eyes peeled and I might share the reward with you.' Normally one who defended less intelligent beings, Probyn could not help this streak of impishness today, chuckling with others as the hapless Roberts dashed away on his futile quest.

The cyclone that had marked a turning point in his life had a beneficial effect on the humidity too; from then on the weather becoming much more bearable. For a time the soldiers remained short of fresh food, the railway having been damaged by torrents of water rushing down the ravines and dislodging the foundations, but eventually things were mended and life became not so bad. Things were also improved by the arrival of new khaki uniforms, far more comfortable than red serge.

More complimentary, too, for one accursed by auburn hair, thought Probyn as he stepped out in his own new attire this afternoon, casting an eye around the camp to check that all was in order.

'Roberts! Where's your ruddy headgear?'

About to come down the steps of his hut, the dullard paused. 'I'm only off to the lat, Corp.'

'Don't argue! You're puggled enough without the sun baking your brain. Get it on or you'll be on a charge.'

'By, you're turning into a right little tyrant, you are!'

At the gruff drawl, Probyn wheeled around to see his friend Greatrix and immediately lost his frown to rush forth and greet him. It was the first time they had seen each other in two months.

Greatrix explained that he had escorted some men up from Port Louis. He wouldn't be here for long but it was good to see his friend. 'You lucky blighter, you've a cooler billet than I have.'

'You're joking!' Probyn indicated the sodden patches on his uniform.

'You don't know you're born!' Greatrix raked at the large red blotches of prickly heat on his neck that made life a misery. 'I'd swap with you any time.'

Wandering away from the camp, the two strolled through tropical greenery, discussing the terrible news that had filtered from South Africa. In the wake of Dr Jameson's disastrous foray into the Transvaal and the subsequent arrest of his troops which had left Rhodesia unprotected, the Matabele had seized the chance to get their land back. Not one white settler remained alive outside the four main towns in which the survivors had barricaded themselves. Men, women and children slaughtered without mercy by household servants.

Probyn reacted with disgust. 'I just knew the Mats weren't finished!'

'Little babbies though!' breathed Greatrix with disbelief. 'I mean, how could anyone do such atrocities on them?' And he detailed some of these atrocious acts until his friend begged him to desist. 'Decent white women murdered by the people they gave hospitality to. I wonder what our pompous Miss Gower thinks about them now?'

Probyn was less judgemental towards the missionary. 'That poor lass might be one of their victims an' all.'

'True enough,' Greatrix delivered a thoughtful nod. 'I'll tell you what, it's just as well the brutes have no tactical strength. We've given them a good hammering by all accounts. I just hope we sort them out good and proper this time. Shall us sit down here and have a fag?'

They had come to a waterway, its banks lined with native women. Saris hitched around their knees, the females beat and scrubbed the clothes then laid them out to dry on plant spikes. Selecting a flat slab of rock, Greatrix and Probyn sat down to enjoy a cigarette and the view.

Probyn had heard enough of barbarity. 'All's peaceful here at any rate.' He marvelled at the women's appearance. 'It beats me how they manage to look so crisp and clean in this sticky heat.'

Greatrix took his usual time in answering. 'I love that long, black glossy hair.'

Probyn nodded. Emily had had nice hair, not dead straight like these dusky beauties but attractive all the same, thick and wavy. It was good that he was able to think of her without pain now. He singled out a girl for approval. 'Now that one, she's the sort of woman I like, not red and freckly like me sisters.'

'Aye, they're lovely to look at,' agreed Greatrix, drawing on his cigarette, 'but not for weddin'.'

After maintaining privacy for so long, not simply because of what his friend might think but because it was hurtful to speak of it, Probyn finally revealed his secret. 'I already have.'

A delay. 'Have what?'

'Married a dark lass.'

Greatrix was stunned and merely gawked at him. For a moment there was only the sound of rushing water and women's voices.

'Not here,' murmured Probyn, flicking ash from his cigarette, 'on St Helena.' And he related the full story then, telling his friend all about his beloved Emily, knowing that Greatrix would not laugh or gossip to others, otherwise he would not have entrusted him. 'She were lovely, Trix. I hated having to leave her.'

His friend's deep voice held sympathy. 'I don't know what to say, Kil.'

'Not much you can say.'

'So is it legal?'

Probyn shrugged. 'Wedlock said not, and I don't think there'll be any record of it.' Taking a last draw on the cigarette he ground the butt into the river bank, then rubbed his glistening face. 'Anyway, there's nowt I can do about it. Right, maister, do you want to wander back now and have a cup o' char?'

Greatrix nodded, trying to think of some way to make his friend smile. 'Aye, and you can provide the bloody cigs this time.'

The sharing of his secret helping to remove the last dregs of misery, Probyn accepted his friend's invitation to come to Port Louis on his next leave, and even agreed to Greatrix's suggestion that they find themselves some women.

Having grumbled about his own environment, he was quick to change his opinion on sampling the dry tropical heat of Port Louis, expressing gladness that he did not have to live in these hot narrow streets where the climate was foul and the oppressive heat seemingly trapped by its surrounding mountains. The fort might give excellent views over the city and of the coral reef and the islands beyond dotted around the turquoise sea like jewels, but he was far better off in the wooded slopes of the uplands.

The evening of his arrival was spent in a very good saloon, dancing and sharing a pint of claret with two very attractive young white women, and though no intimacy took place it felt good to be in legitimate female company once again. Feeling less sensitive over Emily, he even began to seek answers. Was he married or not? What if he met someone else, how would it affect him legally? He even entertained a certain amount of regret at his decision to marry so hastily. Oh, he had loved Emily . . . but had he really? For if that were true how would he even be able to contemplate marriage to another?

On the second day of their leave, the young lance-corporals arranged to visit a beach, Probyn suggesting they purchase some tea and sandwiches from the canteen of the Citadel to take with them.

'No chance,' growled his friend. 'They only serve beer and tinned stuff. You can buy something on the way if you want, I'm not hungry.'

With the exchange of seventy-five cents for a pint of lemonade, they departed for a fishing village where they found a shady spot beneath a group of casuarinas and fell down on the white sand to slake their thirst, taking turns from the bottle. After this they removed boots and stockings, rolled up their sleeves and reclined beneath the pendulous tassels to enjoy their bohemian existence. Over the years Probyn's fair skin had lost its angry glow and he was now deeply tanned, his hair and moustache more blond than red, the fuzz on his arms glistening like gold.

A cloud of butterflies fluttering around them, they talked about what they would do when they got home. Fixing his eyes on the elaborate tattoos on his friend's arms, Probyn spoke without enthusiasm. 'I should go to Ralph Royd and see me stepmother, but I won't stay. There's nowt for me there now that Father's gone.' Remembering that Greatrix had no one at all, he made guilt-ridden apology. 'Sorry, Trix, you must get sick of me moaning. Eh, why don't you come and spend some time at Aunt Kit's with me? She always said my pals are welcome. She serves lovely grub.'

'Aye, but is she as tight with the baccy as her nephew?' enquired Greatrix.

'Oh, is it my turn?' Probyn brought out a squashed packet. 'Sorry, I forgot. I only ever smoke when I'm with thee.'

'I'd never have guessed.' Greatrix examined the deformed cigarette before lighting it.

Sharing a smile, the two sat and smoked for a while, then

Probyn murmured, 'Our Merry's asked me if I'll get her some seashells. I suppose I better had, seeing as how she's the only one good enough to write to me.'

'You'd best do it now,' observed Greatrix, squinting through the branches. 'It's turning overcast.' Scrambling to his feet, he took a last drag of the cigarette then dropped it and ground it into the sand, letting out a yell as he did so. 'Christ! I forgot I didn't have me boots on.'

'You noodle!' Probyn laughed as his friend hobbled to the water's edge and dabbled his injured sole. 'What's up with you? You've been in a trance all day.'

Then, knotting the laces of their boots and draping them around their necks, they wandered along the warm sand, Probyn looking for shells, his companion limping and grumbling. Further along the beach a group of native fishermen sat amongst their boats unravelling nets. Glimpsing the wanderers, several children came rushing to sell food which a scowling Greatrix refused but Probyn bought and ate as they meandered along, alternately snatching a bite then bending to pick up a conch or a cowrie, his knapsack slowly filling.

After walking for quite a while, a tired-looking Greatrix paused to lean against a large black rock and suggested they make their way back. The sky was a deep shade of purple now, the ocean in contrast pale jade. 'I feel a bit groggy, I think I've had too much sun.'

Retracing their steps, Probyn continued to drop shells into his bag, though voicing dubiety at how they would survive in the post. 'Ooh, there's a good un!' He made a darting grab, but immediately let it fall with an exclamation of pain. 'Damn! I've cut me blasted finger.'

Greatrix was concerned. 'It isn't one of them cone shells is it?'

'Dunno, why?' Probyn sucked his injury.

'Well, I don't want to worry you,' drawled Greatrix, 'but they're deadly poisonous.'

Probyn was aghast. 'Bloody hell, we'd better get to hospital right away!'

The fevered rush back to the garrison was extremely stressful, Probyn sucking constantly at the wound in an attempt to remove any poison.

But when they finally arrived at the military hospital and he breathlessly conveyed his fears, they were met with mockery.

'Cone shell?' scoffed the orderly. 'You'd be dead long before now if it had been. That's just a scratch, but I don't like the look of your friend.' Dismissing the cut finger he frowned at Greatrix who appeared to be on the point of collapse, sweating more profusely than was normal.

Relieved that he was in no danger himself, Probyn lent support to his friend. 'He said he wasn't feeling too well, too much sun.'

'I think it's more than sunstroke. Poke your tongue out.' Exclaiming over the yellow fur on the protuberance, the orderly took Greatrix by the arm and began to lead him away. 'Looks like enteric to me. We're rife with it at the moment. I'll get the doctor to see him.'

Alarmed, Probyn called after them, 'What shall I do?'

'Stay there in case you're infected!'

Probyn fell onto a chair and rubbed his hands over his sweating face. Enteric! Ingham had died of it. God forbid that Trix would suffer the same fate. Worried and impatient, he sat there for a while, then jumped up, unable to bear the suspense, and began to walk up and down the corridor.

Hearing footsteps other than his own he looked up expecting to see the same orderly but instead was presented by a more familiar face.

Mick's face creased into his self-conscious grin. 'They can't seem to keep us apart can they?'

'Seems not.' Probyn grinned and shook Mick's hand, though remained somewhat preoccupied with Trix's fate. 'Another kooshi posting is it, Mick?'

'Ah, I'd no choice in the matter, but 'tis acceptable, and not so lonely as me last billet.' Mick stood admiring the other's khaki uniform for a moment. 'Any more luck attracting the women in the new rig-out, or perhaps you're even married?'

'Not me,' lied Probyn. 'How about you?'

'No, no. I'm sure there's a saint out there that'll put up with me but I've yet to find her.' Mick beamed. 'So, what brings you into my clutches, Pa?'

Probyn revealed Greatrix's predicament.

'Chroist not another,' groaned Mick. 'We've got enteric cases coming out of our arse, so to speak. Had to call for volunteer orderlies to sit with them.'

Probyn immediately offered his services. 'I'll sit with him!'

''Tis a shitty job, ye'd have to be awful fond of someone unless you were being paid for it, and will ye not be needed elsewhere, you being a lance-corporal and all?'

'Stuff that! I'm not deserting Trix, he saved me life!' And Greatrix was facing a deadly situation now. 'Anyway I'm on leave. I just wish I could do something more positive to help him.'

'Ah, he'll be fine, we caught it early.' Mick steered him to the relevant ward. 'Come on, if you're intent on sitting with him I'll show ye how to help. And won't you be in the right place if you go down with it yourself.'

The Irishman had been right, it would require great devotion to sit with his friend, for the ward where he and numerous others lay reeked of diarrhoea. Mick was obviously not inured to it either and began to throw open the windows.

The orderly who was settling Greatrix into bed voiced objection. 'They're not meant to be in a draught.'

'Sure the bloody stench is more likely to kill them than a puff of air,' said Mick, using a helmet shell to prop the door wide open and circulate a current. 'It's like a blessed farmyard in here.'

He took over from the objector, telling him that Probyn had volunteered. With a perfunctory hello to Greatrix he shoved a thermometer in his mouth before the other had time to reply, then took his pulse. Whilst Probyn stood by impotently, Mick asked the patient a series of questions then drew back the sheet and laid a hand on his belly, at which a gurgling emerged.

'I'll have to run!' Greatrix began to climb out of bed.

'You're running nowhere. Your friend will fetch you a bedpan. Well ye might as well start as ye mean to go on,' Mick told Probyn, to the embarrassment of both. 'Come on, I'll show ye where to find everything.'

The bedpan was only the first in a series of intimate services he was to provide for his friend over the days that ensued. From being slightly raised, Greatrix's temperature proceeded to soar, robbing him of any coherent chat he might have enjoyed with the friend who looked after him, leaving only a gurgling listless form on sweat-soaked sheets. Weakened by constant diarrhoea, he was in no state to object to any indignity performed upon him.

Every morning and evening Mick would come round with a pill and an enema of starch and water and opium to limit the violent bowel actions, and in between these times a deeply concerned Probyn would sit by his friend's side, sponging his body with cold water in an effort to lower his raging temperature, cradling his head to offer sips of water, trying to coax him into taking a glass of milk to keep his strength up, whilst thoroughly neglecting his own welfare.

'You should get some proper rest,' Mick had warned Probyn on the first evening at the sight of him about to spend the night at Greatrix's bedside. 'You'll be no good to man or beast without sleep.' And he had thrown down a mattress in his own room.

But after only a few hours' nap, whilst it was still dark, Probyn had crept back to his friend's bedside, afraid that Greatrix might die in his absence. No matter that Mick swore he was going to be fine, he could not bring himself to trust the Irishman's word, for others on the ward had died as he watched them, and he could not allow that to happen to the friend who had saved his life.

This loyal vigil was to be maintained throughout the week, Probyn snatching just short naps before returning to his tender ministrations, his wrecked appearance drawing forth acid comment from Mick.

'You'll soon be lying in the next bed to Greatrix if you're not careful.'

Exhausted, Probyn said nothing, just automatically sponged his friend's brow.

Mick brought over a glass of milk. On being told that Greatrix was asleep he replied, 'It's for you. Get it down ye.' He stood and watched as Probyn complied. 'When are ye back on duty?'

Probyn could not even think what day it was. 'A few more days I think. It doesn't matter, I'm not going till he's better.'

'He might not look it but he's doing fine,' said Mick, testing Greatrix's brow with the back of his hand. 'Got away lightly, I'd say. Why, I was bad for three months when I had it.'

'So you told me,' muttered Probyn.

'It's ironic ye know, I haven't suffered a day's illness since I joined the Medical Staff.' Mick stood for a while, stroking his chin, one finger moving underneath to rub thoughtfully at his neck. 'I'm just a bit concerned about this. Have a dekko, does it look like a lump to you?' Tilting his head he invited Probyn to feel his flesh.

Irritated that Mick could be so self-absorbed whilst another was genuinely ill, Probyn declined to feel it. 'Can't see anything.' His eyes remained focused on Greatrix who had once more begun to effuse beads of sweat. 'Punkah wallah!' A native came hurrying with a fan.

'I'm sure there's something,' said Mick rubbing worriedly at his neck.

Probyn felt he might strangle him. 'Have you got a needle and thread?' A button had come off Greatrix's tunic whilst he had been cleaning and pressing it.

'Taking up surgery are we?' At the angry expression Mick threw up his hands. 'All right, don't chew me head off! I'll go fetch ye one.'

He returned in more subdued fashion with a tin of assorted haberdashery. Raking through it, Probyn came up with a tiny bell, bits of wire and all sorts of other things, laying them on the bedside locker before finding what he wanted. Then he sat quietly stitching the button back into place. Whilst he sewed, birds wandered in and out of the open door, amongst them a black crow whose strutting arrogance began to grate. The punkah wallah made comment that it was bad juju, and several times Probyn got up to chase it off fearing that it was a bad omen too, but it kept coming back.

The button finally attached, he hung up Greatrix's uniform, stroking it reverently into place before attending to his friend's bodily needs.

'Want some water, Trix?' He held the glass to the patient's lips.

Barely awake, his hazel eyes half concealed beneath drowsy lids, Greatrix supped gratefully. 'Wouldn't mind a beefsteak.'

Probyn grinned. 'Oh, the man was right, you are getting better!'

'Well, I can fart without messing the bed at any rate,' mumbled Greatrix.

'I'm gratified to hear it, but please there's no need to give us a demonstration.' Much relieved that his friend was on the road to recovery, Probyn sent a native servant to go and ask Mick for some food.

The latter duly arrived at the bedside, but only to say, 'Sorry, no solid food until your temperature's been normal for a week, maybe some softly scrambled eggs.'

'Can I at least dispense with the bloody bedpan?' pleaded Greatrix.

'I'm afraid ye won't be allowed up for another couple of weeks,' said Mick.

'But he's definitely over the worst?' queried Probyn.

'He is, so will ye please go home to bed?' begged Mick.

Allowing himself an elated smile, Probyn replied, 'I'll just have a cup of tea with my mate first, then I will.'

'Sit there. I'll fetch it.' Mick went off.

A few moments later, assisting Greatrix to drink his milky tea, Probyn admitted, 'I've been right worried about thee. There's been three snuffed it while I've sat here.'

Displaying little interest, Greatrix snatched another gulp of tea then fell back on his pillow. 'Have you been here all the time?'

Probyn nodded.

Greatrix nodded too, signifying thanks.

Nothing was said for some while, Greatrix undergoing much ponderance before speaking again. 'How could any mother abandon her baby on a doorstep?' It came completely out of the blue, the tone of his voice and his expression suggesting that it was a complete mystery.

At last Probyn was bestowed with insight as to what occupied Greatrix's thoughts during those long silences. The poor wretch must think of it all the time. But it would take a wiser man than Probyn to furnish the answer.

Weary and emotional, he fought for something with which to lighten both their moods, making comment on the crow that hopped insolently from bed to bed whilst the occupants lay comatose and unable to object. 'I'm going to have that beggar!' Surreptitiously he took a blanket from the next bed and, as the crow came past again, he hurled the blanket over it, after a short struggle taking it captive.

'See how you like this!' Whilst Greatrix watched with a tired smile, he took a piece of wire from the haberdashery box and proceeded to thread it through the holes in the crow's beak, attaching the little bell as ornament.

Released, the bird flapped away, but they could hear it outside the window jingling.

'That'll teach him!' announced Probyn, then addressing his

friend's sick countenance added, 'Well, I'd better be off or the police'll come looking for me. I'll come and see you whenever I can, Trix!' With a cheery goodbye he made to escape from the foul ward, but upon afterthought he skipped back and warned his friend not to divulge any intimacy to Mick. 'Eh, and if you've any secrets keep them to yourself. Tell that blabbermouth nowt or it'll be all over the camp before you know it!' Thus saying he returned to barracks for a bath and some much needed rest.

15

A month later, Greatrix was still in hospital but almost fully convalesced and deeply frustrated at being kept there. Seated outside on the verandah, partaking of his beef tea, he bewailed his incapacity to his visitor. 'They say if I'm allowed up before I'm fully recuperated it'll do more harm than good, but I'm going to kill somebody if I'm stuck here much longer. Has that mate of yours got any influence?'

Probyn raised his eyebrows. 'Mick?'

'Aye! Can't you talk him into getting me out?'

'I don't want to be responsible for you having a relapse.'

'I don't want to be responsible for your death but I'll flamin' well murder you if you don't help me get out of here. Suppose you've heard the latest?'

'About the Shonas?' Probyn nodded. A new disaster had hit Rhodesia, the Shona too had risen in revolt, adopting the same grisly methods as the Matabele. More British regulars were required.

'And who are they going to call for?' demanded Greatrix. 'Mounted infantry. We've got to be in on it, Kil.'

Probyn displayed similar eagerness to revisit Africa. 'I'd love to get stuck in, but are you sure you're fit enough?'

'I will be if I'm allowed to get out of this dump and get some good grub down me. Now will you talk to Mick and have him persuade the doctor to let me out?'

Though dubious at being involved in Greatrix's premature exit from hospital, Probyn could not bring himself to let his friend down and so went to persuade Mick who in turn spoke to the doctor.

Hence, within weeks of that conversation, the pals were to find their dreams answered. Along with all those others who could ride, they were packed up and ready to leave Mauritius.

The cane harvest was in full swing. Now instead of lush green fields the train rattled through vast acres of stubble, the sky black with kites and birds of prey who circled the burnt fields, awaiting the quivering mammals and reptiles that would be there for the taking, the air heavy with the sickly sweet smell of burning sugar.

Aboard the ship bound for Africa there was a mood of enthusiasm, an urgent desire to finish the Mats once and for all, and to avenge their white victims.

Once arrived, though, and patrolling familiar territory around Bulawayo attached to Colonel Plumer's column, Probyn and Greatrix voiced disbelief at the change that had overtaken this lovely country since they had last been here. Plague after plague of drought and locust and now rinderpest, had wreaked havoc. The air was rank with death. At every turn of the way rotting carcasses of oxen lined the roads, not just one or two but thousand upon thousand. Moreover, the rich rolling pastures of white farmsteads were littered with broken down wagons, left behind in the hasty rush to escape, the crops going to seed, the farmhouses looted and burnt whilst their Dutch and English owners laagered in Bulawayo.

The town itself was considerably expanded since last they had been here over two years ago. Its broad streets were now lined with red brick hotels and banks, there were golf and cricket clubs and even a theatrical hall, though under this sham veneer of respectability it was still at heart a frontier town.

Apart from the other ruffians, it was also disturbing to find Matabele included in the native levies. How could one trust such people after the butchery inflicted by their tribesmen? However they conceded that it was useful to have guides who knew the enemy's devious ways, though neither Probyn nor Greatrix would be turning their back on them.

All things considered, both agreed that it was good to have the opportunity to rectify this terrible state of affairs, indeed good just to be back in Africa. It was remarkable how easily one fell back into the life, the veld for one's bed, a saddle for one's pillow, the shimmering, star-spangled sky as a canopy and, perhaps not so thrilling, bully and biscuits for dinner.

If rations out on patrol were poor they were no better in town, for with so few oxen to pull the wagons there was great difficulty in obtaining supplies, hence prices had rocketed. Averse to having something in his mess-tin that might have died from rinderpest, Probyn and his friend stayed clear of all but tinned meat, existing mostly on bread, for there were no vegetables. Badly in need of sustenance, before the week was out their hunger had taken them to the general store where they asked for a dozen eggs between them.

'That will be thirty-two shillings,' said the shopkeeper.

Probyn stared in amazement. 'I don't want them gilded! The ordinary sort will do.' With the price still thirty-two shillings he and Greatrix were forced to change their request to half a dozen, and left with the disgruntled comment, 'By 'eck, now I know where they got the story about the goose that laid the golden eggs.' And to add insult to injury two of them turned out to be bad.

With beer at a florin a glass there was little chance of drowning one's sorrows either. But despite the hardships, the young soldiers found it exhilarating to be out on active service again, and showed much eagerness in responding to reports of impis being seen in the vicinity of Bulawayo, deriving great fun in routing the rebels and holding competitions as to who could bag the most. The three columns that were based in Bulawayo had been involved in regular sweeps across the country to the effect that most of the insurgents of the northern region had been broken and dispersed in all directions, except at one spot near Inyati some fifty miles north-east from town.

Today Colonel Plumer's eight hundred strong column, to which the men of the York and Lancaster Regiment were attached, were to rectify this; after a night march they surprised the enemy at dawn, stormed their stronghold in the hills, killed a hundred and fifty of them with few losses of their own and took six hundred prisoners.

Meeting his fellow lance-corporal again after the battle, an exhilarated Greatrix voiced his opinion of the Cape Boys, remarking that he was most impressed by their pluckiness. 'Did you see Janny?' A splendid guide, a fearless fighter and a similar sense of humour to their own, the latter had become a particular companion of theirs lately. 'He took his boots off to get a better foothold on the rocks –'

'Lord weren't they a devil to climb?' butted in Probyn, bright-eyed from the chase. 'I thought I were going to fall on me bum once or twice.'

'– he shinned over the ridge like a monkey and knocked down half a dozen Mats while I were still on the first rung! He's a fantastic bloke, as good as any white man. In fact a lot better than some.'

'Well, he had a good teacher.' Probyn indicated their own Major Kershaw who had been responsible for moulding the Cape Boys into the doughty fighting force they had become.

'Oh, talk of the devil.' Greatrix indicated the wiry, khaki-shorted figure who loped from rock to rock, rounding up stray rebels – men, women and children.

Catching their observation of him, Janny threw them a grin, holding his rifle aloft and shaking it in triumph. Later, while others buried the dead or rounded up the captive cattle, he came to join his lance-corporal friends in a search of the stronghold kopjes. It had, all agreed, been a splendid battle, a massive blow that must surely finish the enemy as far as the north was concerned, although, Janny informed them, Mqwati the local priest of the Mlimo and Mtini his induna, both important men, had escaped. 'They say the Mlimo's cave is somewhere hereabouts.'

'Oh not that invisible bloke again,' complained Greatrix, wandering through the maze of chambers with his usual indifference, in the next instant startling Probyn with an echoing cry, 'Look out, Kil, he's behind you!'

Probyn twirled round, gun at the ready, then seeing that his friend was joking dealt him a thump, rather annoyed that Greatrix should do this in front of the men. 'You soft 'a'porth!'

'I were just trying to aid your constipation.' Winking at Janny, Greatrix turned his head at a shout, all going to investigate the find. From every nook and cranny men came scurrying, the scene resembling a termite mound. Within one of the large dry caves was a massive cache of grain: grass baskets containing mealies, dried melons, monkey-nuts and rice, much of it obviously looted from white stores. Along with these were found pots and calabashes, assegais and knobkerries, and little clay models, one of which Greatrix picked up, pronouncing his disgust. 'Bloody heathen thing. Look it hasn't got no head! I wonder if it's supposed to be an effigy of us, some sort of black magic.'

Janny laughed heartily. 'It is only a child's doll.'

At first sheepish, Greatrix examined the model further. 'No this one's definitely modelled on Lance-Corporal Kilmaster. Look at its short legs.'

'I'm warning thee!' Probyn dealt his friend another whack, observing as he did that Greatrix's skin was darker than Janny's and wondering whether to use this as retaliation but decided against it and continued to move through the labyrinth.

At the next cavern, Janny was first to investigate but seemed reluctant to go further. Asked what was amiss, he said, 'It's the Mlimo's cave.' The Cape Boy who had shown such courage in battle seemed slightly unnerved at being here but, at Greatrix's demand for explanation, remained long enough to convey how he knew this. This part, he told them, was a kind of waiting room. The priest would leave the supplicants here and enter that narrow cleft which would take him deep into the rock wherein lived the Mlimo.

Greatrix was mildly sarcastic. 'How does he know he's there? I mean, this Mlimo's invisible.'

Janny ignored the flippancy. 'He does not see him, merely makes his request through a crack in the rock.'

'And the Mlimo grants his wish?' Greatrix pretended to be impressed. 'Reckon we should try this bloke out, Kil.' Whilst Janny made his retreat and others looked on, Greatrix approached the fissure and cleared his throat. 'Er, cod and chips and a bottle of dandelion and burdock please.'

Laughter echoed around the cave. Then another voice, 'Eh, Corp, can you get me a couple of scallops, some mushy peas and –'

'That's enough, Watson!' Transformed by the arrival of those in his squad, Greatrix abandoned the leisurely jaunt with his friend and began doling out orders, whereby Probyn became more authoritative too, the friends not seeing each other again until the column was on its way back to Bulawayo.

With a sullen mob of prisoners and eight hundred head of cattle in tow, they had laagered for the night and were partaking of the usual cold meal, no fires being permitted for fear of attracting rebels. With no pipes allowed either, Greatrix was in a less jovial mood than he had been this afternoon, a curmudgeonly look upon his face as he sat huddled with his friend during the hiatus before bed time. From the darkness came the whoops and barks of animals unseen.

Trying to cheer himself up as much as to rally the other, Probyn maintained the conversation, his breath white on the bitterly cold air. 'Wonder how long this'll last?'

Greatrix underwent a seemingly interminable pause. 'Dunno.'

'We must surely have them smashed by now.'

Another overlong pause. 'Probably.'

At a loss as to what to say next, Probyn gave a sigh. 'All right, Trix, just one last question, now I don't want you to answer too impulsively!' He made a dramatic gesture. 'Take your time, don't put any exertion on your brain . . . Shall we get our heads down?'

'Yes,' said Greatrix emphatically.

'You mad impetuous fool!' Smiling, Probyn dealt him a pat to the back and settled down for the night.

He awoke to an alarm call from one of the pickets, springing into action before his eyes were fully open, Greatrix and everyone else equally alert.

In the cold early morning mist all remained tense as the subject of the commotion was half dragged, half carried into the laager, a woman in a desperate state, her clothes ripped and heavily stained with blood, her hair awry and her eyes haunted. Probyn felt he would never forget that look as long as he lived.

So horrific had been her experience, so obviously terrified was she still, that she could not speak at first, but eventually was able to reveal the source of her dishevelment. Her father, having steadfastly refused to be driven from the farm for which he had worked so hard, had finally been compelled to dash for the safety of a nearby fort when the rebels overran his land. But the strain of living under siege and the constant guerrilla attacks had proved too stressful and he had decided yesterday afternoon to make a dash for Bulawayo with his family. They had been driving here when the rebels had caught them. Her father and elder brother had, whilst trying to protect their women, been hacked down immediately, the females had been maltreated then left for dead. She did not know whether her mother or sister had survived, had dared not look but had instinctively sought to save herself, first crawling amongst some rocks to hide, then travelling once it was dark.

'Yesterday afternoon you say,' murmured the captain to whom she spoke. 'Then you cannot have travelled far.'

'I feel it is a thousand miles,' came her haunted whisper.

Concluding that the scene of the attack could not be far away and worried that there might be more survivors, the captain deemed it worth the risk of attempting a rescue mission and gave the order for a sergeant to elect riders. Hugging herself within an army blanket, having told her story the young woman watched with lifeless eyes, rocking back and forth where she sat, as there were calls from eager volunteers.

Probyn and Greatrix, as angry as the next man over this abomination, immediately offered their services and were accepted, picking several good men from their respective platoons to accompany them, all saddling up and finally riding out of the laager behind the officer, apprehensive as to what they would find.

What they found, only a couple of miles away, was a scene of such butchery that each one wished he had not come, for never would he be able to erase it from his memory. The hyenas had been at work overnight and had exacerbated the outrage, but enough of the carcasses remained to show what had happened. It was bad enough that the mules had been disembowelled, that men had been hacked and mutilated in similar fashion, their faces beyond recognition, that fine English women lay with their limbs exposed and contorted, their breasts disfigured for sport and their black female servant treated likewise . . . but the sight of two small children, the survivor had not mentioned them and Probyn knew full well why, two little white children with the life smashed out of them . . . it was one horror too much.

He had never known that such rage was within him. From his very boots it surged up in a volcanic eruption, travelling with suffocating intensity through his chest and into his skull from which there was no outlet, whirling and churning and burning, around and around until he thought he was about to lose his mind.

From a distance, an order was being barked. Jerked back to sensibility, he automatically obeyed, instructing his equally horrified young platoon members to excavate graves, into which the bodies were finally laid.

'The fiends,' Greatrix kept muttering as he supervised the digging, his hands clenched with futile anger. 'The evil black devils.'

But mainly there was no comment. Nothing could be said that would encapsulate the horror.

After burying the victims they made their way back to camp, later resuming their march to Bulawayo where the lone survivor was handed into the care of the nuns at the hospital.

The prisoners captured at Inyati were grilled for information as to the whereabouts of their chiefs, Greatrix commenting that he would dearly love to be in on the interrogation. Neither he nor Probyn, nor any of the others they suspected, had lost any of their anger over the current atrocity, indeed it had been exacerbated by the circulars that had greeted their return and which were to be posted about the district, offering leniency to those who surrendered.

'Proclamation of Clemency, which idiot thought this up?' asked Greatrix. 'Some office wallah in London who's no idea of how things are here. Clemency? These people don't even understand the word!' He clutched one of the offending posters in his fist and brandished it at Probyn, his face almost puce with fury. 'There's only one thing these murdering swine understand and I'll be more than happy to give it to them.' He ripped the poster to shreds. Then, after an angry pause he added gruffly, 'I hope we don't get many more like last night, Kil, it were really distraughting . . . dis . . . I can't remember the damn word but you know what I mean.'

They had not talked about it before, Probyn did not know how Greatrix could even bring himself to make this small reference to it now. Signifying his reluctance to dwell on this subject he gave a curt nod, saying quickly, 'Well, better get some rest before we have to go out for another pop at them.' The campaign on the Matopos was fast being organized.

Greatrix showed unusual zeal. 'And I can't wait, me old pal, I can't wait!'

At last, halfway through that July of 1896 the campaign seemed about to take off, each of the columns encamped near the Matopos awaiting the final order.

Lance-Corporal Kilmaster, his friend Greatrix and eight hundred others were bivouacked near the central hills. Atop a great dome-shaped lump of granite was a burnt-out farm, from which wafted the sun-warmed perfume of blue gums. To either side a barrier of rugged kopjes which fortified the valley beyond, in which the enemy were hiding.

It was all so much more nerve-racking having to wait than to actively seek them out. But great preparation had gone into making this the final smash and it could not be hurried.

They realized something was about to happen with the arrival that night of Colonel Baden-Powell, for he was to act as guide, knowing the country extremely well. Probyn had much admiration for him, as indeed he did for his own company commander Major Kershaw, a cool, brave, energetic officer. In such good hands he felt confident of the outcome and was eager to make a start.

But Baden-Powell was to ride out again soon afterwards, dampening the mood of enthusiasm and bringing a sense of anti-climax to the camp, the occupants settling down to another evening of boredom. With no smoking allowed and no fires upon which even to boil a billy, nerves were stretched beyond endurance. A dog yapped. Immediately a lieutenant sought out the owner and upbraided him furiously though restraining his volume. 'The order was no dogs!'

'Sorry, sir, he's not usually any trouble,' came the murmur.

'He won't be again!' The lieutenant summoned one of the friendly natives.

In the time it took Probyn to blink the dog had been despatched with an assegai. Disliking such summary violence, he ordered his men to get their heads down and himself did likewise.

Four tense days went by; days of dew-soaked blankets, days of near starvation under a grilling noonday sun, and bitter nights.

At last the order came. That morning, the men were told to bake two loaves of bread and to get as much sleep as they could in the afternoon.

At the time they would normally be going to bed the whole column paraded without noise or trumpet call and at ten-thirty moved off into the moonlit Matopos. Marching in a large square ready against attack, they had now been joined by other celebrities, Sir Frederick Carrington, Lord Grey and Cecil Rhodes. There was also a detachment under Sir Frederick Frankland whose members had volunteered for the fun of it.

Navigating his horse around a thick patch of bush, Probyn wondered if these distinguished men shared the great pride and excitement that beat within his own heart. He could certainly tell that those around him did even though they were forbidden to voice it, the only sound an occasional cough or a soft Yorkshire warning from the man in front, ''Ware 'oile!' to signal a dip in the ground.

Soon after midnight they were within a mile of their goal. The square halted and in the bitter cold each man lay down to sleep where he stood. An hour before dawn they were up and moving towards the pass amongst the kopjes which led to the enemy's valley. Here, just as dawn was rising, they formed ready for attack.

First came an advance force comprising the two corps of Cape Boys, two hundred friendly Matabele, twenty mounted white scouts, a Hotchkiss and two Maxims. Then came two mountain battery guns and the main body of white troops under Colonel Plumer, amongst which was Probyn. His blood was pounding through his veins as they advanced in growing daylight into the broken bushy valley, surrounded on every side by rocky crags and kopjes, from which might spring the enemy, the fresh spoors they came across showed just how many they were up against. As yet, though, they had seen no life, except for small mammals darting about the rocks.

Then, making use of his telescope, Major Kershaw informed his men that there was a large camp ahead. The guns were brought up to the front and were soon shelling. Atop the surrounding kopjes warriors began to materialize.

A youngster in Probyn's platoon turned to him in consternation, 'Why haven't we been ordered to fire, Corp?'

Probyn spoke calmly. 'Don't worry, lad, it's a good sign, the darkies showing themselves. It means we're too strong for them to attack. Still,' he made ready his rifle, 'won't harm to take a few pot shots.'

As the order was given there came a volley of enthusiastic firing, returned only half-heartedly by the rebels who appeared to take more pleasure in performing their war dance along the kopjes and shouting insults at those far below, before finally vanishing as if into thin air.

To those prepared for all-out battle, it was most frustrating, especially as this state of affairs of pot shots and insults was to continue for several days.

After more reconnoitring, mapping of ground and pin-pointing the enemy's position to the Chabez Gorge some fifteen miles east of camp, Baden-Powell returned to say that the way was impassable for wagons. It was therefore necessary to order some pack transport to take them to the Chabez stronghold and afterwards by the Umzingwani valley, towards the stronghold of the eastern end of Matopos. Once here they would be on the Tuli–Bulawayo road where the wagons, having gone round by Hope Fountain or by Bulawayo, could rejoin them.

Meantime, Major Kershaw took out a strong patrol for further reconnaissance of the Chabez position, Probyn and Greatrix amongst the riders. It was a nasty bit of country, with plenty of places for the rebels to hide, but they reached their destination without encountering any.

Grappling their way onto a high rocky ridge, Probyn and the others found themselves overlooking an enormous river gorge, the terrain a most difficult one to negotiate, with kopje and bush and deep ravines leading down to the river. From the thick jungle bush along the banks could be heard a distant lowing, evidence that cattle were hidden there. The soldiers were also given an excellent view of the numerous caves which formed the rebels' hideaway, and out of them now poured a good number of Matabele, disporting themselves on the various kopjes to show that they knew of their enemy's presence, though not inclined to attack.

It was the general consensus that the soldiers should make themselves scarce. Happy with this splendid piece of reconnaissance, they descended and made their return to camp.

On the return march, Probyn was riding some distance ahead of the main patrol alongside Major Kershaw and a handful of others when suddenly his sharp eyes spotted a large party of enemy, some way off but heading towards them. Given this information, the major quickly steered his horse behind a tangle of rocks and euphorbia, the others close at heel, where they spied through the chinks as the danger came almost within touching distance.

Heart in mouth, throat parched with dust, hardly daring to breathe, Probyn crouched beside his superiors and watched the large impi pass by in their white war ornaments – a ball of clipped feathers at each brow, white oxtails, kilts of catskin and monkeys' tails, assegais and knobkerries, ox-hide shields and bodies like polished bronze. They had rifles too: Lee-Metfords, Martinis, Winchesters, blunderbusses and elephant guns. It seemed the column would never end, so quiet the padding of their feet that Probyn felt they must surely hear him breathing.

The danger passed, but not the frustration. With the memory still fresh of those massacred innocents, it was hell to be so near to the perpetrators yet not strong enough to attack. But, came his grim thought, they now knew where to find them.

The rest of the patrol, being too large for the rebels to attack, came galloping up some time later. Greatrix, amongst them, had been most fearful that his friend had been killed and was delighted to find him unharmed.

On return to camp there was much activity, the wagons taking a detour by a less rocky route, a train of packhorses carrying four days' supply accompanying the column which that evening started its eastwards march to the Chabez. Before dawn they were formed ready for attack against the high ground overlooking the river gorge.

Major Kershaw, being familiar with the territory, was detailed to command the assault. Positioning his squad, Lance-Corporal Kilmaster glanced at each to check on their mood but need not have feared for all were keen to be at the enemy, having awaited this moment for days. His own state was like that of the night he had first partaken of ale – not that befuddled condition one experienced after a surfeit, but just enough to lift him to the point where nothing in the world seemed to matter. Far from being drunk his wits were considerably sharpened by the thought of what was to come and what was expected of him, his one fear being that he would let down those who were depending on him. He had no fear of death.

Whilst others were sent around to have a look in at the back of the position and see whether a second attack could effectively be made, Major Kershaw's party made its assault on the steep cliffs, and once on the move all doubt vanished. Despite the lack of food and sleep and other privations all fatigue was miraculously washed away, Probyn's mind as clear as a bell and eyes in the back of his head. Rallying his squad ever upwards towards the skyline, he was soon atop the ridge and ordering them to lie down and fire as the enemy came swarming out of their caves to meet them, their alarm cries echoing around the heights. Soon, added to the rifle fire, two seven-pounders were hauled onto the summit and joined the action. Shells started to fly, exploding above the heads of the rebels and scattering them, whence a huge cheer went up from the ranks. 'Run, you buggers, run!' laughingly exhorted the man to Probyn's right whilst he, equally thirsty for blood, took aim at one after another, damning each to hell.

More heavy firing resounded from the artillery, the next three shrapnel bursts scattering the main force of rebels and driving them down into the river gorge where they came to brief blows with their adversaries before finally fleeing to a rousing cheer from the British.

The contest thus ended, an exhilarated Probyn made his way down to a breakfast of water and biscuits with Greatrix.

But the day was only just begun. Leaving the dismounted men and baggage, the mounted troops embarked on a raid towards the cattle valley near Ingyanda's stronghold, moving along the open valley close under the foot of the Matopos for four or five miles until they came on some cattle paths leading from the grazing grounds into the hills. Here another successful skirmish was fought, again the rebels being driven back, as they were to be on the next occasion, and the next. Soon it would be time for a final stand-off.

During one of Baden-Powell's reconnaissances, he had captured an elderly woman, which resulted in pleasing information which Janny the Cape Boy relayed to his friends when next he saw them, saying that she was a charming old lady of high birth.

'Oh yes, very charming,' Greatrix could not help the sarcasm. 'They cut our people to ribbons then sing like birds when they're caught themselves. I wouldn't put it past any of this lot to be playing on both sides either.' He indicated the friendly Matabele who travelled with them.

Janny went on. 'She says Umlugulu has joined the other impis and they are not far from here.'

'That makes five,' nodded Probyn, seemingly unworried by this news. 'Still it's good to have them all in one place.'

'The rebels are much disheartened by the heavy blows we have dealt them,' continued Janny. 'Many of them would like to give in but their chiefs will not let them.'

'How are they off for food?' asked Greatrix, having become obsessed with the lack of it.

'They have plenty of meat and ammunition but are tired of war. It keeps them from sowing next year's crop and they are losing faith in the Mlimo who promised that all the whites would die of rinderpest.'

'Oh, not him again!'

Probyn smiled at his friend's outburst and tapped Greatrix's knee as a gesture of encouragement. 'Won't be long now, pal!'

On the morning of the fifth of August whilst it was still dark, at half past four the column paraded, then moved off silently, close under the heights occupied by enemy lookouts. Having first to pass through two outer ranges of hills and through a wooded pass into a semi-circular valley, two sides of which were occupied by rebel impis, at sunrise they found themselves in the pass that led to another valley, and in this one they were completely sheltered from view by bush. The back of the valley was formed by a single high ridge of smooth granite and from it five offshoots ran down into the valley like fingers. At the top of these fingers rose rocky peaks amongst the bush jungle of the lower valley, these peaks forming the strongholds of the individual impis. Forced to remain concealed for the moment, Probyn surveyed the scene. One did not have to be a general to see that if the guns could be got onto a particular ridge they could effectively fire on each impi in turn. A pleased smile twitched his lips as this was indeed carried out, Colonel Plumer ordering the guns with a strong escort of a hundred and thirty men under Captain Beresford to gain a position on the high ridge.

Whilst waiting, Major Kershaw took a peek through his

telescope, reporting on Beresford's progress up the rocky incline, reporting too that on almost every hill he could see natives who were completely unaware of their presence. The troops enjoyed a grin.

But it was not long before the glint of Beresford's party attracted the rebels and alarm spread. There was no noise nor shouting but the kopjes were suddenly alive with activity.

Major Kershaw had just looked at his watch to report that Beresford had been gone an hour when there came the rattle of shots, followed closely by the roar of volleys and rapid sustained fire, this reverberating around the hills and developing into a continuous roar which was added to by the roll of the Maxims and big guns.

'By Jove!' announced a surprised Major Kershaw to his lieutenant, 'I didn't expect to hear that sound so early in the day! The Mats must be more wide awake than we'd imagined.'

A moment later a panting messenger arrived with the news that Captain Beresford had been attacked on all three sides at once but had formed his small party into a square on a plateau though he remained hotly engaged. 'But they're managing to hold the niggers at bay, sir!'

Recognizing that serious fighting was afoot, Colonel Plumer ordered the immediate advance of the main body.

Major Kershaw held his whistle at the ready.

Each platoon commander addressed his men, Probyn's lieutenant announcing, 'This is the big one, chaps! Score as many as you can, I've a large wager riding on us getting a higher bag than the West Ridings.'

The whistle blew. This was what Probyn had been waiting for! With a warrior's cry he galloped into attack, cheering his men on as he rode. Reaching the foot of the ridge the conquering horde dismounted, left their horses under cover of rocks and began to clamber up the hill, firing as they went. The rebels fired back but with little accuracy, the only casualty being Private White who was shot in the buttock by one of his friends below. As the soldiers clambered nearer and nearer to the summit the rebels suddenly appeared to lose heart and fell back to another ridge, thus making victory seem almost effortless. However, this was soon to be disproved. Some of the enemy had lodged themselves in rocks and were pluckily determined to hold their own, giving impressively accurate fire. Lieutenant Hervey made a valiant dash to dislodge them but fell mortally wounded, his sergeant-major shot dead. In the few seconds he had to take stock Probyn was to witness other such scenes of valour: the enemy making a mad dash to take a vacated Maxim, an officer acting alone jumping forth and beating them to it, jumping into the saddle and spraying the fleeing blacks with lead; a lone Matabele rushing out to perform his war dance, dodging the machine gun bullets for a good few seconds before he was cut down. The native muleteers showed courage too, assisting with their carbines, though apart from one or two the so-called friendly natives who had been employed in carrying Maxims and Hotchkiss showed a marked lack of loyalty; as Greatrix had foretold, the moment the enemy got close they merged into their ranks.

Flat on his belly, awaiting the order to move, Probyn glanced quickly about him concerned for his friend, but there was Greatrix, unscathed, firing like a man possessed. With only a second in which to feel gratified, Probyn was up again and driving forward with the squadron to take the main cave, but just as they reached the entrance Major Kershaw went down! And even as Probyn answered the reflex to stoop by his officer and examine the two bullet holes in his tunic he knew it was useless, at the same time a sergeant falling nearby with a shot through the head. Self-preservation had him up and running again.

The two sides collided in a violent tangle of stabbing, feet skidding on the gory rocks, blood spurting in fountains, skulls stove in, flesh and bone and brain spilling onto the rocks, guts and skin and hair, on and on and on and then in the midst of that brutal carnage that seemed as if it would never end, a war rocket soared into life, exploding in a firework display over the bloodstained hills with such deafening intensity that both sides were shocked into a momentary truce.

Distracted, his bayonet poised for more slaughter, Probyn lifted his eyes from the abyss to watch the rocket's path. When he lowered them again the enemy was on the retreat and another weird sound was reverberating amongst the hills; the siren-like wail of a war horn calling up reinforcements.

But for the Matabele the battle was over. By now the Cape Boys had worked their way round to the enemy's right as far as the third and fourth ridges. Crazed by bloodlust, Probyn and his squad raced in hot pursuit, whilst Beresford's 7th Hussars directed shell after shell at the high ridge to the rear over which the impis retreated, dispersing them into long black strings, like shattered ebony necklaces.

'Most excellent pig-sticking!' Probyn heard the observation of one bright-eyed young officer to another as he himself bent over to recapture his breath.

By turns exhilarated and revolted by his own deeds, he stood for a moment resting on his knees, before raising his panting face to check on the casualties. Sad though they were, the British losses appeared to be minuscule in comparison to the number of black corpses littering the scene, almost two or three thousand he estimated.

In time, Colonel Plumer came by congratulating the men, though he was obviously most sad at the loss of his friend and right-hand man Major Kershaw.

Searching for his own close friend, Probyn could not at first find Greatrix and was to feel great concern until a deep voice behind him growled, 'Eh you'll never guess what time it is!' And he wheeled around to see his pal.

'Three o'clock!' Greatrix projected amazement. 'Doesn't time fly when you're enjoying yourself?' But despite the flippancy his expression concealed a nightmare of images, and there were spatters of dried blood upon his face.

'Well, I'm right glad to see you're unscathed, Trix!'

'Unscathed? I nearly had me arse blown off!' And he attempted to show Probyn the massive bruise where the stone wrapped in lead from a large bore gun had hit him.

'I'll take your word for it! Did you lose any lads?'

'No, all intact thank the Lord.'

Probyn, too, voiced gratitude that none of his platoon were amongst the dead, and few wounded. 'Janny's still in one piece too. He's indestructible that one.'

They were not to talk for long as the columns were then re-formed for marching back to camp, the fifteen wounded being taken on stretchers by the Cape Boys.

As they moved slowly, burning everything as they went in the way of huts and long grass, they could see small parties of enemy going about the field picking up their dead and wounded. However, they were not prepared for the large impi that appeared on the horizon just as they were leaving the hills, an impi obviously uninvolved in the previous fighting for their demeanour was too fresh, too energetic, knobkerries banging their shields in warlike defiance.

A worried murmur rippled through the ranks, until it became obvious that the only things to be thrown were jeers.

'Go home and sow your crops you lazy dogs!' A rebel voice bounced from rock to rock.

'We're not sowing!' retaliated a British voice. 'We're harvesting – your blokes!'

Another yelled from the ranks. 'Why don't you come and *konza*, make peace and save your skins while it's not too late?'

Greatrix added his own insult. 'Where've you been, lads? You're too tardy, the war's over!'

'You think it is over? We shall show you who is the victor!' And the impi followed them, dancing along the ridge and slinging more insults.

But there was no attempt to attack and, dealt a parting long-range volley, they hurriedly dispersed leaving the victors to proceed to the safety of the open veld and, in time, to the twinkling campfires of their base.

Welcomed by the loud cheers from those left behind to act as guards, they rode in singing heartily, 'The Man Who Broke the Bank at Monte Carlo', ending the day with a delicious mug of cocoa.

And as he laid his weary head down, Probyn was to marvel yet again, what an enviable role it was to be part of this mighty Empire.

During the weeks that followed, apart from sporadic attacks by individual groups of rebels, it became evident that the war was indeed almost over. The old lady who had previously been captured, being of high status, was sent into the hills to draw the chiefs into peace negotiations. Towards the end of August, under a white flag, a meeting was arranged in the Matopos between the rebel leaders and Cecil Rhodes, though as yet no treaty had been made.

For Probyn, life had slipped back into dusty boredom and he watched enviously as Greatrix prepared to take out a patrol this bright sunny morning. 'Jammy blighter.'

'Now now, no sulking.' Bouncing into the saddle, Greatrix called his men into formation, then moved off, dealing Probyn a cheery wave as he left town. 'I'll bring you back a stick of rock!'

Hours later, at the call from the lookout on Eiffel Tower – 'Patrol coming in!' – Probyn went expectantly to meet his friend.

But the patrol came in unsupervised. 'Sorry, Sergeant!' One of its number made swift apology in response to the sergeant's query. 'Lance-Corporal Greatrix just didn't come back.'

'What do you mean, not come back?' Probyn elbowed his way through the knot of men.

The young soldier explained. 'Private Welburn's hat blew off as we were crossing a drift and went sailing off around the bend. Lance-Corporal Greatrix went with him to find it, but Welburn said they parted company for a second or two and when he turned round Lance-Corporal Greatrix had just disappeared. We searched high and low for him but –'

'You shouldn't have come back without him!' With a curse, Probyn turned to the sergeant, asking to be part of the search party.

This quickly organized, he rode out of Bulawayo fully expecting to see his comrade's disgruntled face coming down the road to meet him, and onwards to a distance of ten miles, but at no point along it did he see any sign.

The drift was little more than a muddy trickle at this time of year. There was no chance that Greatrix and his horse could have drowned. An exhaustive search of every kopje along its banks produced nothing more than a startled old warthog who made a half-hearted squealing charge at the group before running off. No matter how desperately Probyn urged his horse into every cranny, how keen his eyes, Greatrix had indeed vanished into thin air.

Reluctantly, the lieutenant who led the patrol ordered a return to the garrison.

'Please, sir,' Probyn begged his superior, 'we can't just leave him.'

'Then where do you suggest we look?' demanded the lieutenant. 'We've searched every damned inch of – hang on!' He became alert and stood in his stirrups. 'I saw movement over there.'

Hardly had he uttered this than Probyn was splashing across the muddy trickle, forcing his horse up the steep bank and galloping across the rocky outcrop to a tangle of euphorbias to where the lieutenant had pointed.

But when he arrived there was no sign of anything. When the others galloped up he had dismounted and was lashing about furiously in the bushes.

The lieutenant admitted his mistake. 'It must have been a dassie. Come along, we can't waste any more time.'

Probyn's horse had wandered off. With a last desperate whack at the bushes, he took a few forlorn steps towards retrieving it when the ground beneath him suddenly disappeared and he found himself sliding into a donga. In a cloud of dust and rock he came to rest on his buttocks, grunting in pain, and then gave a yell of alarm as he laid eyes on the two surprised men that were staring back at him.

His disappointment that these were only natives was put aside as they made a hasty scramble to escape. They might be responsible for his friend's disappearance! The fact that they were armed giving credence to this, he lunged for them. Trapped, the natives raised their rifles but were immediately encircled by a dozen gun barrels as more soldiers jumped down into the donga, and were forced eventually to lay down their weapons, though they did so with great surliness.

'Show me your tickets!' barked the lieutenant.

'We not need tickets, we soldiers.' There was a hostile edge to the reply.

'To whom are you attached?'

'We are at Bulawayo –'

'You're lying. Corporal, take them in!' With no further ado the natives were seized and had their hands bound.

'Sir, maybe they can tell us where Lance-Corporal Greatrix is!' Probyn reminded him.

The lieutenant addressed the captives again. 'Tell us what you know.'

A casual shrug. 'We know nothing, maybe a lion got him.'

'Come! You are to be hanged anyway.'

Their facade was immediately replaced by defiance. 'Your friend will not be planting his crops again!'

Probyn gasped, then flew at the speaker. 'Where is he? You black devil, I'll kill you!'

'Desist!' The lieutenant ordered him.

'But it was them, sir! They've admitted it!'

'And they'll hang,' said the lieutenant firmly, looking for an adequate branch but finding none.

'But we can't just leave him!' came the plea.

'Lance-Corporal Kilmaster!' berated the hot and bothered

officer. 'Your friend is dead, we must accept that. There is nothing more we can do except bring his murderers to justice.' And with that he ordered his men to remount and, dragging the two prisoners, the patrol set off for Bulawayo.

Driven almost insane by the most awful images, Probyn was compelled to mount and follow, as he rode seeing over and over again the cheery wave that Greatrix had dealt him as he'd left that morning, knowing that he would never be able to strike it from his memory. Nor would he ever be able to stamp out the guilt over his absence at his friend's time of need.

16

Poor Greatrix. His demise was a reflection of his whole pathetic life: no one knew where he'd come from; no one knew where he'd gone.

It took a long time to accept that his friend was dead. With few to mourn, Probyn took Greatrix's death upon his own shoulders, the magnitude of his guilt driving him deeper than he had ever been before. Even seeing the murderers dangle at the end of a rope made not an ounce of difference to his mood. Who had been the one to persuade them to let Trix out of hospital? Who had waved him off to his death? First his father, then Emily, now his best friend. How many more losses could a man take? When the year finally came to an end he was thoroughly glad to see the back of it.

Mercifully, the new year was to unfold on a more optimistic note. Lance-Corporal Kilmaster was to be transferred to the 1st Battalion and, whilst others went on to India, Probyn sailed home to an English spring.

It was a wonderful but confusing time, the air pungent with cherry blossom and lilac, every sense assailed by the strange familiarity of it, sweet and spumy hawthorn hedgerows adorning the fields with bridal wreaths, blinding acres of golden rape that filled his nostrils with a stench like ammonia, huge and ancient polls of copper beech shimmering like his sisters' hair, outspread arms of horse chestnut weighed down with pink candles, earth the colour of rich chocolate, grass like thickly-piled velvet, a gentler sun that did not burn but threw him into quandary with its position. It would take him a long time to reacclimatize himself to the northern hemisphere.

Landing in Dover, and shortly promoted to full corporal, he was to be stationed in the south for six months during which time he wrote to inform his stepmother that he was home, also sending letters to Aunt Kit and Meredith. It would have been easy enough to catch a train up to Yorkshire and he could not explain his own reluctance to do so. Had he not been wanting to go home for years?

Finally, though, he was precipitated into making the move when the battalion was ordered north.

Kit was tidying her autumn garden when she saw a man with a moustache coming along the dirt track that led to her gate. He raised an arm in greeting, causing her to frown long and hard before realizing that it was her nephew.

'Why, it's our Probe!' Calling for her little son to follow, she hurried to the gate, hardly able to believe that this was the youngster she had last seen five years ago. He had not altered greatly in stature, but the face was no longer that of a boy. 'I saw this man with a tash coming towards me and wondered who on earth it could be!' As they came together she touched his blond moustache in fond amusement, hugged him, then held him at arms' length again to exclaim, 'I can't believe how you've changed!'

Whatever the extent of his aunt's shock it could not be as great as the one Probyn received. From being voluptuous, Kit had grown incredibly fat, even her once nimble fingers bulging out like little cushions on either side of her wedding ring.

There came teasing accusation from his aunt. 'Well, fancy waiting to come home until now. You've missed all the fun!'

Momentarily whisked back to the savagery, Probyn wondered if he would ever have fun again, but he continued to smile as his aunt announced:

'We had a lovely Jubilee party, didn't we, Tobe?'

Unused to strangers, the little boy hid behind his mother's vast bulk, though chanced a smiling peep at the soldier who winked at him.

'I went one better, saw the Queen herself,' Probyn affected to don airs and graces, telling them his battalion had been chosen to line the streets for the parade.

Kit showed suitable admiration, then bent to instruct her son. 'Well, you'd better go fetch your father. Tell him there's a soldier come to – oh no, don't tell him that, he might think we're under attack. Just tell him Probe's home!'

Toby rushed off in the direction of the stable, then tripped, scattering hens and causing Kit to rush over and pick him up to smother him in kisses. When the child seemed unhurt, she set him on his way, watching fondly for a second. She and Worthy had hoped for more children but they had just never happened. Toby had become the centre of their world. Yet no matter how precious her son, there were always two empty spaces in Kit's life where her little girls should be.

Emerging from her reverie, she whirled back to the visitor, still extraordinarily agile for one so huge. 'Come on inside then, Probe!'

He uttered a grateful laugh. 'I thought you'd never ask. I can't seem to get warm since I got back.'

'Have you seen anybody else yet?'

'No I thought I'd come and visit my favourite aunt first.' Probyn followed her into the kitchen, quite amazed by the enormous width of her hips.

'Eh, always the flanneler!' The kettle on, Kit began to pile buns on a plate, corsets creaking with every darting move. 'We were a bit worried till we got your letter. We thought you might have been aboard that ship that went down.'

'The *Warren Hastings*?' Probyn shook his head. 'No, thank the Lord. That was on its way to India. The only things that were lost were folks' possessions and the regimental silver. Bad enough, but at least none of the lads drowned. That's the most important thing.'

'It certainly is.' Her whalebones still groaning, Kit made the tea and thrust the plate of buns at her nephew.

Toby came dashing in then followed by Worthy, at which there was much joking over Probyn's moustache, all of it good-humoured.

Waiting for his tea to cool, Probyn spoke to the youngster who, after initial shyness, was now hovering by him like a shadow. 'By you've grown a big lad, Toby! How old are you now?'

'Seven!' The little boy looked delighted to be addressed.

Probyn shook his head in disbelief.

Kit voiced her own incredulity. 'It doesn't seem five minutes to me since you were his age, Probe. How old are you now, is it twenty-four?'

He had to think about this himself, never marking time by birthdays, only by events. 'Aye, almost a pensioner.'

'So, are you home for good now?' asked Kit and answered her own question. 'I suppose it depends if the natives behave themselves. We had one of their kings over here you know, his picture was in the newspaper, wasn't it, Worthy? I didn't know they dressed like us.'

Probyn smiled benignly. 'Most of them don't. That'd be King Khama one of the friendly ones.' He shoved aside the nightmare vision of stabbing blades, and said, 'I think I'll be home for a while now. They've moved us to Strensall so I'll be able to visit you more regular.'

'Oh, grand!' A chicken had wandered in through the open door, Kit chased it out amid an indignant cackling. 'Your stepmother will be pleased to see you too.'

Probyn became subdued, and sat for a while gazing into his tea. The longer he left it the harder it would be to visit his father's grave. 'I'll maybe go next Sunday.'

'Are you planning to see anybody else?'

'Only Merry. Not much point trailing miles to have the door shut in me face.'

'Oh, I don't think they'd do that to you now.' Kit spoke with confidence. 'A lot of water's flowed under the bridge.'

'Well, maybe . . .'

Kind-hearted as ever, she offered encouragement. 'I was thinking of inviting everyone over for a big reunion at Christmas. Now that your father's not with us any more I feel as if it's my duty to keep the family together. Don't worry I'm not inviting Aunt Gwen. My charity doesn't stretch that far. Will you join us?'

He did not have to think about this. 'Miss one of your dinners, Aunt? Never!'

There were nerves, of course, at the thought of meeting them again. It was no good telling himself that it was ridiculous to feel like this after the terrible ordeals he had been through, nothing could erase the fact that he was, and always would be, the youngest child.

Yet in the event it was not such a test as he had feared. His stepmother was absent, preferring to spend Christmas with her own offspring. The rest of them were all very nice, very welcoming, as if they had parted the best of friends. Christmas dinner was scrumptious as ever, and with Aunt Kit to break the ice everyone, including Probyn, was soon laughing and taking turns to relate family anecdotes. Indeed, after the initial tentative greeting there was never an awkward moment, with so many children to meet, the ones who had been born in his absence.

'Haven't any of you noticed this?' Kit finally demanded of the gathering, pointing at her nephew's moustache.

Ethel gave a straight-faced laugh. 'We'd noticed but we daren't say anything. What exactly is it?' There was jocular comment from the others, some of his sisters coming over to tug at his facial embellishment.

'Some sort of fungus he picked up in Africa,' smirked Wyn.

Kit scolded her. 'Aw! I think it lends him an air of nobility meself.'

'Listen to you lot!' Probyn remained good-humoured, knowing their teasing was not malicious. 'I've never seen so many wrinkles except on an elephant.' All his sisters were in their thirties now, in fact Ethel must only be a few years off forty.

'Ooh, he's still the cheeky little monkey! A lot of good the army's done him!'

Asked to relate his adventures with elephants, Probyn was forced to admit he had only ever seen one in captivity. Then, with the laughter dying down, he took the opportunity to convey his regrets to Rhoda over the death of her husband, commenting that he had been a nice chap. 'It must have been a dreadful shock.'

'It was, but it's been five years now,' sighed Rhoda. 'But thank you for your kind words, Probe.' She patted his hand.

'Have you been to see Father's grave?' asked Ethel.

'Not yet. I've been meaning to go for months.' He glanced at his eldest sister, hoping she would understand. He felt guilty enough without her schoolmarmish accusal. Ethel had been thirteen when he had been born, and had always seemed like an adult to him, never impish or silly like Meredith.

'I'm sure Mother would appreciate a visit.' Alice had sidled up.

Probyn tendered a characteristic nod that told them he would make up his own mind. Chancing a look around at his siblings, he felt that none of them understood why he could not bring himself to go. Despite all the laughter, all the warmth, he could not help feeling out of place after the things that had happened to him.

Starting to feel trapped, he sought a way out. 'Let me do the washing-up, Aunt!' Kit and Meredith were clearing the table.

Brushing aside the array of eyebrows that were arched in derision, he carried a stack of crockery into the kitchen. There was a mountain of dirty pots and pans everywhere but despite this chaos it was much quieter in here.

'Get your pinny on then!' Merry threw one at him as a joke.

Reciprocating the silliness, he donned it with effeminate manner, then noticed the initials GOB embroidered on its breast and exclaimed, 'Who the heck is GOB?'

Tipping hot water into the sink, Kit laughed. 'Oh, it belongs to Grace, Mrs O'Brien's niece. She's doing the washing for me; her aunt's bedridden with white-leg. She must've dropped her pinny when she was here last week. Nice little lass.' She nudged him, and grinned. 'Don't let that lot in there know I've an Irish girl working for me or I'll never hear the last of it.' Observing his grim nod, she told him, 'You've done really well to put up with your sisters, Probe.'

'Oh thank you,' Merry chuckled.

'I didn't mean you,' scolded Kit. 'You're not like them.'

'I can tell they think I'm odd not wanting to visit Father's grave,' muttered Probyn, tea towel in hand. 'I know I'll have to go some time but –'

'You'll go when you're ready,' his aunt reassured him kindly.

He nodded and began to dry the pots. But in truth he did not know whether he would ever be able to go.

As had happened to him time and time again, events were to rob Probyn of choice. Three months into another new year Wyn's husband died of kidney failure. Attending his funeral Probyn was finally brought into contact with his stepmother who was so kind, offering not the slightest recrimination that he had not been to see her, and extending such warm invitation for him to spend a few days at Ralph Royd that he had no alternative but to accept.

On his next spot of leave he duly presented himself at her door, fully intending to stay for at least two days. But as nice as she was, his stepmother was no substitute for real kin, and even within the first hour he was itching to escape his father's ghost.

However, he managed to stay the course, and on Saturday morning as he took his leave promised that he would not lose touch with Ann.

But there was one thing more to be done before he left the colliery village. Leaving by way of Ann's back garden, he climbed over the fence into the allotment, and wandered between the rows of vegetables and pigeon lofts in the direction of the graveyard.

'Murdering bastard.'

It came not as a shout, but as if the speaker were merely expressing comment on the weather.

Looking round, Probyn saw a man with whom he was not acquainted tending his cabbage patch, moving calmly between the rows with his hoe. Disbelieving, he enquired, 'I beg your pardon?'

The dour, coal-scarred face did not look up, its owner continuing to hoe.

Probyn walked on, only to hear another bitter comment. 'Remember 'ninety-three.'

Again he stalled, abruptly transported to a night four and a half years ago when the world had gone mad and he had been forced to loose his bullets on men whom he had once regarded as comrades. Sick at heart, he quickened his step towards the graveyard, the accusations following him on the balmy spring air.

'Aye that's right, sling your hook, soldier boy! We don't want your sort round here.'

Entering through a door in the wall that enclosed the church and its weathered tombstones, Probyn closed it behind him and stood for a while mulling over the insults and taking his bearings. Clumps of daffodils adorned the hallowed ground, capering in the strong breeze. From this elevated position he could see the pit where he had once toiled, as most of those buried here had done. Most, but not all. Moving between the blackened headstones he sought out those of his mother and sister, hoping that his father would lie close by.

In Memory of Montague Kilmaster, beloved husband of Ann, passed away 20th March 1895. Such empty words, he thought, incapable of conveying the full tragedy: more truthfully, the one who laid here had been harried to an early grave by those he had called friend. As he stood pondering the memorial to his father he heard the door scrape across the gravel. Not wanting to speak to anyone, he remained head down, presenting his back to the intruder.

The door scraped again. Frowning, Probyn turned to see someone going out; his presence had obviously been as irksome to them.

He lingered amongst the daffodils for only a moment, not wanting to tarry long for fear of bumping into old workmates. Deciding to call at Aunt Kit's on the way back to barracks, he said a quiet goodbye to those who could never do likewise and left the graveyard.

From the corner of his eye he detected a figure to his right, leaning further along the wall, but he did not look at them and made his way down the slope. Suddenly, two men came bounding over the allotment fence and launched themselves at him.

The prickle of apprehension that he experienced on seeing Judson was almost immediately transformed to fury and he braced himself for the onslaught, using Judson's own momentum to hurl him aside and butting the other attacker full in the face before either of them could get a punch in. This was not the time for gentlemanly tactics. Quick to rise, Judson aimed a blow which Probyn only half managed to dodge before returning one of his own, and from then it was a mass of flailing arms and fists and boots until Probyn's knuckles made contact, downing his attacker like a pole-axed beast, the other still unconscious from the head blow.

'I was coming to help, but you obviously don't need it.'

Fist still upraised, blue-grey eyes glittering with fury,

Probyn span around and was met by a laconic pipe-smoker. 'Uncle Owen . . . what brings you around here?'

'Just wandering. Been laid off for a while with me leg. Get bad rheumatism in it ever since somebody shot me.' Pipestem clamped between his teeth, Owen glanced down at Judson. 'Doesn't pay to tangle with soldiers.'

Allowing his breath to emerge in a noisy rush, Probyn stood rubbing his knuckles and observing his handiwork. 'That was a long time coming.'

Owen's billy-goat face was impassive as he sucked on his pipe, taking note of the group of flat-capped allotment holders that had gathered to watch. 'You might like to make yourself scarce. There's others round here'd like to do the same to thee.'

'You being one of them?' Probyn's anger was quick to re-ignite.

'Nay, I reckon being in the army is punishment enough for a lad with conscience, having to go against your mates –'

'He's not a mate!' Probyn made a derisive gesture at the unconscious Judson. 'He were one of them that helped kill me dad. 'Course I don't expect you to understand that, you and your blasted union martyrs.'

'You arrogant little sod!' A bark of disdain shot from Owen's lips, procured by the implication that he had no feelings for his dead brother. 'If it weren't for us union martyrs as you call us you'd have hungered to death at the masters' hands before you could even entertain t'idea of being a big brave soldier.'

'Aye . . . well.' Though still angry, Probyn showed a hint of contrition. 'I didn't mean to slander, I know well enough what you've done for us and I'm grateful. It's just that I can't for the life of me understand how you can defend scum like him!'

'I wouldn't give him the ash off me pipe!' Owen dismissed Judson in a trice. 'I'm talking about upright lads who were shot in cold blood when all they were trying to do was to defend the principle that the working man is worthy of his hire, to win themselves and their comrades, your father included, a living wage.'

'But there was no need for them to suffer, Uncle!' Probyn's face still displayed incomprehension, feeling additional anger that these men of whom his uncle spoke had forced him into an act he had no wish to commit, had put a stain on his brilliant career. 'I side with you wholeheartedly in your argument with the masters, their demands weren't fair at all, but surely the lads could have made their point without resorting to such wanton wreckage? I never knew you to be on the side of violence.' Veiled threats and intimidation maybe, but never outright violence.

'I weren't, till I nearly died at the hands of one of your fellow swaddies, Meg too! I ask you, what threat did we represent with nowt more than a banner in our hands?'

Probyn fought his uncle's attempt to shame him. 'None, but there were others present who were intent on waving more than banners. Don't try and tell me there weren't for I witnessed them myself, could have been killed too in that madhouse. They started the violence first, what else were we to do but try and contain it? I'm sorry you were hurt, Uncle Owen, I hated to be party to it whatever you might believe, but don't ask me to condone such rabble-rousing as I saw that night, there was no justification for it.'

'Then let the Lord be thy judge,' said Owen, adding a grim observance of the gathering crowd. 'And with such views to air I wouldn't hang about any longer if I were thee.'

'I don't intend to. Goodbye to you, Uncle Owen.' Spinning on his heel, Probyn walked away.

Taking a few calm puffs of his pipe, Owen remained to watch his nephew march down the slope until he disappeared around the corner. Then he himself shoved open the door into the churchyard and went to pay respects to his brother's grave.

*　　*　　*

Thoroughly fed up, Probyn was disappointed upon arriving at Kit's to find the house empty apart from a few impudent pullets that ran into the scullery at the sight of him. Throwing down his knapsack and his field cap, he was on his way to make himself a cup of tea when there came a female exclamation.

'Oh, shite!'

Knowing his Aunt Kit would never utter such filth, he frowned and went quickly to investigate, seeing now that the door to the back garden was open which was obviously how the pullets had got in. He poked his head around it to see a girl. The crude vociferation had obviously been invoked by an item of clean washing that had fallen on the soil. Much as he had grown used to soldiers' profanity and knew it had no bearing on a man's true character he could not help being offended at hearing it from female lips.

The girl saw him and screamed. 'I've no money!'

'I don't want your money,' retorted Probyn coolly. 'I'm here to see my aunt.'

She was all apologetic then, telling him Kit and Worthy had taken the old hens to market. 'What on earth must you think of me? I don't normally use words like that. 'S'just that I've spent ages washing the wretched thing and then to drop it in the mud –'

'I didn't hear anything, I've only this minute arrived.' Why on earth did he feel the need to excuse her? If there was one thing he detested more than foul-mouthed men it was vulgar women. However, this one did not totally adhere to that category. She was clean and presentable and looked most abashed.

'Did you not? Oh, thank goodness! Oh well, I'd best wash it again.' Laying the soiled garment to one side she continued pegging out the rest.

Probyn realized then that this must be Grace O'Brien. He had expected an Irish accent but there was no trace. Despite the first impression of vulgarity, he was rather taken by her youth and innocence after all the recent horrors, and remained in the sunshine to watch her. Beneath the poor quality woollen dress was a good figure. That she was of a lesser height than himself was also in her favour. Her wavy brown hair was drawn back from her face and held with a comb, although tendrils of it had come loose and curled around her fair cheekbones. Her eyes, and what eyes, thought Probyn, were dark-blue and heavy-lidded, these and the shapely bow of her lips forming a seductive expression, though her overall air was not one of seduction at all; it was gentle and rather vague.

Grace moved along the line, inserting pegs, casting the odd worried glance at the bruises on the visitor's face and thinking he must be a rough kind of fellow. Soldiers were noted for their roughness. Her brother Fred was talking about joining the army but so far had been dissuaded; he wasn't the type. Not normally a shy person, she was assailed by a flutter of self-consciousness under the glittering gaze that followed her every movement.

Probyn sensed her apprehension and, realizing what a bad impression his bruises must create, strived to put her at ease. 'So, you must be Gob, are you?'

'I beg your pardon?' she said half offended, half laughing.

He laughed too and told her about finding the pinafore bearing her initials.

'Well I must admit it does look a bit odd,' smiled Grace, fingering the embroidered letters on her breast. 'What are yours then?'

'My initials? PMK. Nothing funny there I'm afraid.'

'Mm, pity, I was hoping to get my own back.'

'Sorry, I didn't mean to be rude,' smiled Probyn, feeling more and more attracted by the second.

'You're forgiven.' Her primary concern over the bruises had gradually been overcome. There was warmth in her eye. Looking into his tanned face and blue-grey eyes she saw no threat, only kindness. The waxed blond moustache was somewhat severe but this was offset by the little curl at his forehead which she found enormously endearing. 'What does the PMK stand for?'

He told her, explaining that Mrs Treasure had been a Kilmaster before her marriage. They found themselves chatting very easily after this, Grace informing him as she hung out the washing that she had taken over from her aunt whose illness had been a stroke of luck for her out-of-work niece. 'I used to work at Rowntrees but got sacked for bad time-keeping.'

Thinking of Michael Melody, Probyn decided laziness must be an inherent fault of the Irish, until the girl went on to explain:

'It's a wonder I ever managed to get there at all, having to get me brother up and give him his breakfast, all me sisters are away in service d'you see, then prepare dinner and do the cleaning and the washing before I go off to work, so's there's not so much to do when I get in. Anyway, I'm hoping to get another job soon, but this'll tide me over nicely till I do.'

'So, there's only you and your brother at home?'

A peg clamped in her mouth, Grace moved along the line, nodding sadly. 'Father died of heart disease a few years back. Mother died last year, consumption.'

Noticing that her eyes had misted over, Probyn felt immediate empathy. 'My mother too.'

'My eldest brother died from it as well,' said Grace, blinking furiously and pegging another item.

'And my eldest sister!' He wanted to hug her.

Grace paused to commiserate. 'What a terrible death it is to be sure.'

Pegging the last item on the line she went to retrieve the soiled garment and disappeared for a moment to rinse it in the trough, rubbing and sloshing to try and get rid of the mud, tutting away to herself. When she came back out into the sunshine the soldier was still where she had left him.

She put the item through the mangle, telling him to stand back as water gushed forth. 'So Mr Kilmaster –'

'Nay, don't call me mister, I'll be getting ideas above

me station! Mister is for officers, I'm only a humble corporal.'

Corrected, she nodded. 'I can't help noticing you're very sunburned.' When he told her where the tan had been acquired she became excited. 'Oh Africa. Tell me all about it!'

'Well what would you like to know?' He hoped she wouldn't ask about the fighting.

'Start with the flowers,' she instructed, forgetting all about her task for the moment.

He looked awkward, not unappreciative of the exotic blooms, just unsure how to describe them. 'Well, it depends whereabouts in Africa you are, it can seem like several different countries. In the Cape there are these ones called proteas and, depending what colour they are 'cause they come in all sorts of shades, but there are these dark red and white ones and before they're opened, when they're all curled up tightly they look like bloodshot eyeballs.'

'Oh that's very poetic I must say!' Grace ejaculated mirth. 'Trust a man to come up with that!'

Captivated by her laughing face, his own mirrored her amusement. 'Well! You can't expect a soldier to be expert on such things.'

'I suppose not,' she smiled, and asked him to go on about Africa which he did for a while.

But wanting to know more about her he changed the subject and observed, 'You don't sound very Irish.'

'I've never even been to Ireland. My grandparents came here years ago.'

He wanted to know everything about her. 'So, does all your family live in York?'

'What there is of them, yes.'

'Are your grandparents still alive?' He had always envied people who had a grandfather.

'No – though I've a great aunt who's ancient. She'll probably outlive us all.'

'And how many sisters have you got?'

'Three.'

'And are they all as pretty as you?' He hoped he didn't sound smarmy.

She turned pink at his compliment. 'Oh . . . well, they're much better looking I think.'

'Must be stunners then.'

'You're very kind.' Rushing on, she told him, 'I've a brother, too, Fred. They're all older than me.'

'I'm the youngest as well!' marvelled Probe. 'What a lot we have in common. You haven't by any chance got an Aunt Kit, have you? Now that's something everyone should have.'

Grace smiled and replied in the negative.

Probyn spoke warmly. 'She's lovely, Aunt Kit, don't you think?'

'She is,' said Grace, though only out of politeness. She found Mrs Treasure rather a daunting mistress.

Wanting to keep the conversation going, he asked, 'So, how does working for her compare to chocolate bashing?'

'There's no free chocolates here,' smiled Grace.

He gave a soft laugh. 'What exactly did you do?'

'Put the chocolates into boxes. I was chosen for my cool hands. Mine are always like ice even in summer.' She displayed her fingers.

Probyn looked at them, imagining those cool digits sliding down the front of his trousers.

The sound of cartwheels heralded the family's return then. 'Well, I've enjoyed our chat, Grace . . .' He seemed reluctant to leave her. 'Er, tell me, what days do you work for Aunt Kit?' When she told him he smiled to show he was pleased. 'Then we'll no doubt be bumping into each other again.' With a final grin, he wrenched himself away and went to meet his aunt.

The novelty of English weather already beginning to pall, one minute warm, the next freezing cold, and badly in need of love after his heavy losses, Probyn looked forward to having the gentle Grace brighten his life again and was quick to repeat the experience, many times. It had turned out that her aunt's illness was more debilitating than had been expected and Grace had taken on the job permanently, an arrangement which suited everyone.

Delighted at the regular visits from her nephew, Kit did not realize what was happening at first, until one afternoon as she was making a pot of tea for Probyn, who had ostensibly gone to answer the call of nature, she overheard his voice in the laundry, addressing the O'Brien girl.

'Sorry, Gobbie, I didn't mean to make you jump!' He excused himself as he emerged through clouds of steam. 'I'm supposed to be on my way to the farleymelow.'

Gobbie? He must know the girl well to apply a nickname! Curious as to what was being said, his aunt moved nearer in order to listen.

She heard Grace laugh. 'What or where on earth is a farleymelow?'

He explained that it was a family word for the privy, though he was ignorant as to how it had come into existence. He seemed in no rush to go there. 'Actually, I wanted to ask if you'd come out with me on Saturday night?'

Shaken, Kit covered her mouth and awaited the Irish girl's response.

There was no coyness. 'I'd love to, Probe, but my brother wouldn't allow me to go with a man on my own. However, I've a good friend called Charlotte. Perhaps if you've a friend to keep her company . . . ?' Grace saw the flicker of pain cross his features and immediately asked, 'Have I said something wrong?'

Probyn tore his mind from Greatrix. 'No, no! I was just wondering if your friend is as bonny as you, I wouldn't want to let her down with one of the ugly mugs I know.'

She laughed teasingly. 'You're saying you're an oil paint-ing?'

The cheeky little madam! Kit set her mouth in an angry line.

Then, just in case her remark had hurt him, Grace added quickly, 'Only kidding! You're quite presentable.'

'Don't get too carried away,' advised Probyn, tongue in cheek.

'No, I mean it,' insisted Grace, oblivious to the sarcasm. 'I'm very choosy myself, but Charlotte's not, I'm sure whoever you pick to accompany her will be suitable.'

'So you'll come?' Probyn sounded happy.

Kit almost collapsed as the two arranged to meet in town on Saturday night. What could she do? This would take serious thought. She didn't want to have to sack Grace but she would if necessary.

Anxious not to be caught eavesdropping, she was pouring the tea when Probyn came back into the kitchen.

'I was about to send out a search party,' she told him, eyes darting over his face for signs of guilt.

But there was only happiness. 'Sorry, Aunt, I was just talking to Grace.'

At least he was being open about it, thought Kit. 'I wouldn't have thought you two had much in common.'

'Oh, you'd be wrong there, Aunt. I've asked her to come out with me on Saturday.' The moment he said it Probyn knew it was a mistake. Aunt Kit's expression made it obvious she did not want him rubbing shoulders with her Irish servant. He had assumed her to be over such prejudice. He would have to tread carefully here. 'But then, she wasn't sure if she'd be allowed so it'll probably come to nowt – eh, did I tell you I got my Master Cook's certificate? I'll be able to cook dinner for you now!'

Kit smiled and projected interest, though silently wondering what on earth to do about this. But for now there was nothing she could do, merely keep it to herself and hope it would fizzle out.

Since the death of his best friend, Probyn had not formed a bond with any other soldier and doubted that he ever would again. However, he got on well enough with his fellow corporals and on returning to barracks set about persuading one of them, Dawson, into escorting Grace's friend.

Meeting in Exhibition Square that Saturday night, the two couples went first to a café for tea and then to the theatre. He had purchased the tickets beforehand to make sure he would not be embarrassed by being turned away. Nothing could be allowed to ruin this relationship, for even after only a few months and without even kissing her he knew that this joyful personality was the one to whom he would give his name. Grace was everything a soldier's wife should be: of upright character, clean, tidy, honest, a good listener, not to mention enormously desirable. He did not know how he managed to keep his hands off her.

She was a good conversationalist too, able to discuss anything under the sun, whether knowledgeable on the subject or not, honestly admitting to this lack of experience and willing to learn from her much-travelled sweetheart.

Tonight, their time together disappeared as if by magic and already he was walking her home. How he wished the others would vanish too, though perhaps their presence was a good thing for without a chaperone he could not trust himself to respect Grace's chastity. Never had he been so physically attracted to anyone. And from the way she looked at him, it appeared that Grace shared this fascination.

Arm in arm, they strolled along the decrepit Walmgate, the summery light not yet completely faded though it was ten o'clock. The discourse had remained constant since they had left the theatre. 'And what do you think of us women getting the vote?'

'I think you should have it,' came the immediate response. 'The black fellows in the Cape have it and if they're even so much as contemplating extending it to those in other colonies I think it's an insult not to give it to British women. The country would collapse without you.'

Grace was pleased he shared her own view, then asked his opinion on the enfranchisement of the Africans.

For a second, Probyn was plunged back into savage war, saw Greatrix wave goodbye, and was only half successful in ridding himself of the image, saying cautiously, 'Well, I've met some genuinely nice people among them, kind and thoughtful. There's good and bad in every race – there are one or two white men to whom I wouldn't give the vote either – but in general I don't think they can be trusted. It doesn't take much for them to revert to their tribal ways and they need to be protected from each other, ruled with a rod of iron.'

They walked a few steps in silence. Then Grace said, 'I suppose you must have had lots of lady friends on your travels?' And she leaned her body inwards slightly, nudging him, though her eyes looked anywhere but at him, as if the question made her self-conscious.

'Oh, not really.' He turned his head to smile at her.

Still she did not meet his eye. 'So you've never met anyone special?'

'Not until now.' He felt no guilt at saying it. Over the two and a half years since he'd last seen Emily he had come to understand that their affair had been a pipe-dream. Had it been true love he could never have got over her so quickly. She had just been there in a vulnerable moment and in his youthfulness he had mistaken his feelings for love. He hardly ever thought about her at all now except in moments of sexual frustration, treasuring her only as a sweet passionate memory. Whereas this young woman filled his mind constantly. 'I'm surprised nobody's snapped you up, though,' he told Grace fondly.

She responded with a smile, clinging to his arm affectionately.

'Could we make Saturday night a regular thing?'

Grace beamed into the face she had come quickly to love, nodded eagerly, then cast a glance over her shoulder at the other couple and whispered, 'The only thing is, Charlotte confided that she doesn't think much to your friend.'

Probyn steered her around a party of drunkards, using his body to shield her. 'I thought you said she wasn't fussy?'

'That was before I knew you were bringing a gargoyle.'

Probyn chuckled and played with his moustache. He had selected Corporal Dawson as not bad-looking. 'I thought you women usually admired wavy hair?'

Grace scolded herself. 'Oh, I'm being cruel, I suppose he's not bad, but he's got mucky eyes.'

Glancing at Dawson, he still did not know what she meant. It would never fail to mystify him what attracted a woman to a man. He could have said that Charlotte with her big square face and tiny eyes and mouth was not the sort that could be choosy, but Grace's friend had a lovely nature and had been very nice to him and so he offered, 'I could see if anyone else –'

'It's all right,' interrupted Grace with an impish grin. 'I've coaxed her into pretending I'm out with her if my brother asks. I'm sure we don't want anyone else along with us cramping our style, do we?' At his smiling shake of head she confirmed her own keenness. 'So, next Saturday then?'

'And the Saturday after that, and every day of the week if I had my wish,' said Probyn, eyes gleaming.

Grace looked flustered but pleased and said that she would like this too.

She drew him to a halt then, saying reluctantly, 'We'd better part company here, just in case our Fred's lurking.'

He showed concern. 'I don't like leaving you with all these roughs about.'

Grace smiled. 'I went to school with most of them. They won't hurt me. Thank you for a lovely time, Probe. I really enjoyed myself.'

Saying the pleasure had all been his, Probyn caught a glimpse of Charlotte beating off an attempt to kiss her and wondered whether he too would be repulsed. But looking into Grace's desirous blue eyes he thought it safe to risk a quick peck.

As he made his goodbye and walked away he threw a glance over his shoulder and saw that Grace had laid her fingers over the spot on her cheek, as if wanting to retain the kiss forever.

Kit had been on tenterhooks for days, waiting to find out if her nephew had kept his date with Grace. The shock of finding out that he had was enormous, but this was to be salved by his casual addition that he did not know if he would be seeing her again. Though not wholly convinced by his nonchalant attitude, Kit had wanted very much to believe him and, with his visits becoming less frequent over the next six months and his interest in Grace apparently dwindling, she came to be reassured, seeing this as confirmation of her strategy to let the infatuation run its own course. It was natural that he would tire of one who was so much younger.

Had she but known that Probyn was meeting Grace in town on his days off, in fact courting her at every opportunity, Kit would have been horrified, and even more so had she known that her own past was one of the topics under discussion.

'You know, I feel that I can say anything to you, Grace.' He had already spoken about the death of his parents, related some if not all of his terrible time in Rhodesia and the death of his close friend Trix. Now on this autumn evening, seated on a bench by the river, his arm around her, Probyn had just finished informing her of Aunt Kit's tragic loss of two illegitimate children.

Though inwardly scandalized, Grace passed no judgement for she knew how close Probyn was to his aunt. 'Ah well, don't all families have their secrets?' And she in turn aired family skeletons, though they were in no way as lurid as his.

'So now we know all about each other,' smiled Probyn, hugging her into his side, his breath white on the cold riverside air.

Yet there was one name that would never pass his lips; what would be the point in telling her about Emily? It would only hurt her and besides, he would rather forget. Would rather. Why, then, was it Emily's face he saw when he bent to kiss Grace now? He should try and tell her, he really should. What if Wedlock's intervention had been too late and his marriage to Emily was valid? That would make what he was about to do illegal. He was old enough to know that problems could not be made to vanish simply by not thinking about them. But the strength of feeling he held for Grace made him afraid of losing her, and as his lips settled on her own sweet mouth the image of Emily completely vanished.

They kissed and cuddled for some moments, Probyn becoming so aroused that he slipped his hand inside her coat.

Immediately Grace slapped him. 'There'll be none of that!'

'Sorry!' Afraid that she seemed ready to jump up and leave he begged her to remain, holding onto her gloved hand. 'I just couldn't help meself! I promise I'll be good.'

'You will, or else!' But, reassured, she melted into his side. 'It's not that I don't love you, Probe, I do.'

'Do you?' He seemed somewhat amazed.

She laughed. 'Of course I do! I'm not in the habit of giving my kisses away to every man I meet.'

'They're lovely kisses.' He risked another, trying to keep it chaste, but she made it dreadfully difficult for him, giving her lips quite willingly, if nothing else.

Eventually pausing for breath, he asked, 'Gobbie, will you marry me? Of course I'll have to get permission from my commanding officer, but if he says yes, will you?'

Grace tilted her chin, projecting thoughtfulness. 'I suppose I could . . . though I'll have to get permission from Father Murphy.'

He looked offended.

'Well, what sort of a proposal is that?' she scolded, though lovingly.

'I'm sorry, I didn't mean it to come out like that. I truly want to marry you, Grace. Will you have me?'

'I will!' Laughingly, she embraced him, injecting it with every ounce of love.

'I did mean it about having to get permission though,' he warned her.

'Oh, so did I,' Grace replied lightly, resting her head against his tunic. 'They won't allow me to marry a Protestant.'

'You mean I might have to convert?' He looked doubtful.

'I should say so.' She seemed unduly confident that this would prove no obstacle; to Grace there was only one true church.

Even though his religion had never meant a great deal to him, Probyn was driven by conscience to wonder what his parents would have said; but to Grace he smiled and murmured, 'Oh well, I'd do anything for you, dear.'

Noting her pensive air, he kissed the tip of her nose and asked what was amiss.

'I was just thinking what my family will say. I suppose I'd better take you to meet them. We get together on Sunday afternoons. Would that be convenient for you?'

He nodded. 'Do they know we've been courting?'

'No. Aren't they in for a shock?'

It took him aback that the Irish could harbour such prejudices too.

Grace hugged him, her eyes brimming with desire. 'But no matter what anybody says, I think you're wonderful.'

At their Sunday afternoon meeting outside York Minster, Probyn asked Grace to come inside with him for a moment, for he wanted to see the memorial that had been erected to his officers killed in the Matabele uprising.

Even though he had shown her his campaign medal, it was only then as she stood in the magnificent cathedral looking at the names of the dead that Grace realized what life was going to be like married to a soldier. 'Is that the business you were involved in?' she enquired softly. At his nod she fell silent.

Probyn was thinking about Greatrix – no memorial for him, nor even a proper grave – when he heard Grace sniff and noticed she was crying. Immediately he pulled out his handkerchief which she used to blow into then to wipe her eyes.

'Sorry, I was just thinking it could be your name on there.'

He tried to reassure her with a smile. 'I doubt it, I'm not important enough.'

'You know what I mean.' She was gently scolding. 'I don't know what I'd do without you, Probe. I've never loved anyone quite so mu –' Her face crumpled.

He laid his hand over her mouth, would have liked to use his lips but a church was not the place for such a show. 'I know, dear,' he told her. 'I feel the same, that's why I'm making it my business to take extra special care of myself.' It was true; he recognized his responsibilities towards her. 'But don't let things that might never happen cloud today's happiness.'

Nodding, a tearful Grace blew her pink nose and asked if she could keep the handkerchief.

They were to leave the Minster then for a much smaller venue, St George's Church, where Grace had prearranged for him to be interviewed by the priest, to whose officious questioning Probyn took great umbrage. Nevertheless, he remained cordial for Grace's sake. He had told her he'd do anything for her and so he would. After answering all queries politely, it was arranged that he would meet regular appointments at the church to take Catholic instruction.

From there it was on to the O'Brien household, perhaps an even bigger ordeal. However, he was to receive a lot fairer treatment than he suspected Grace would get from his family.

'Well now, let me tell you, Probyn,' said her eldest sister, Lizzie, at the outset. 'Millie and Ellen and meself were not very pleased to learn that our sister was courting a soldier, neither is Fred here, even though he wants to be a soldier too, but we're fond of her and we can tell you make her happy. Why, look at her face, God love her, it'd light up the room!' She squeezed her youngest sister's cheeks, causing Grace no end of embarrassment, before going on, 'And we can see you're serious by the fact that you're willing to take instruction. So when all is said and done you have our blessing.'

Inclining his head in gratitude, Probyn said he would do his best to maintain Grace's happiness.

'Right, now that's out of the way can me and this poor lad have our bloody tea?' begged Fred, telling Probyn he had been forced to sit here in his stiff collar all afternoon.

Lizzie clipped him, but there was a lot of affection in the gesture and Probyn could honestly say as he sat down amongst them that he liked the O'Brien clan, especially Fred whom he had expected to be the main hurdle but had in fact proved most amenable, although he was quick to recognize that this alliance was motivated by self-interest, Fred having secretly enquired if Probyn would help persuade his sisters to allow him into the army.

'Well, that went better than I could have hoped,' Probyn told Grace as they kicked their way through a brown blanket of sycamore leaves to the end of the street some hours later. 'I only hope I have the same success with my lot.'

'When will you tell them?' She clung to his arm, gazing up at him fondly.

'Well, I shall only want to do it once, so I need to have them all in one place. Aunt Kit's invited everyone over for Christmas again –'

'But that's nigh on a month off!'

'And it's still too soon for me,' said Probyn grimly. 'You don't know what they're like.' He kissed her pink nose. 'But I promise, I'll do it then.'

Deciding it would be less rash to test the ground with Kit first, the next time Probyn visited his aunt he made to broach the subject, making sure it was an afternoon when his beloved was not here laundering.

'Are you coming out to help us milk the coos, Probe?' asked little Toby, about to accompany his father to the shippon.

'I'll just finish me cup of tea,' smiled his cousin. 'And be with you anon.'

Knowing him well, Kit sensed that he had something to discuss but could not think what it might be. However, she was soon to learn once they were alone.

'It's about me and Grace –'

At the mention of that name Kit felt as if he had smote her. No it could not be!

'We're getting married.' By his aunt's horrified reaction he knew straight away how badly the rest would take it. Smile fading, he offered quiet reproof. 'I thought you'd be pleased for me, Aunt.'

'No you didn't or you wouldn't have kept it a secret!' she countered accusingly.

'It wasn't a secret! You knew I was taking Grace out.'

'*Once!* You've obviously seen a lot more of her since then.' Kit's heart was pounding.

He gave no reply.

'She's only seventeen, Probe, and you're twenty-five!'

'Age makes no difference when you feel as we do about each other. Besides, we both know that's not the real cause of your objection. For heaven's sake, Grace has never even been to Ireland.'

'That doesn't make her any less Catholic.'

He voiced exasperation. 'Bloomin' heck, Aunt, I don't know what sort of fuss you'd be making if she were a black woman!'

'Now you're just being plain daft!' sounded Kit.

If only you knew, thought Probyn. If it had been an unconscious attempt to tell all, to confide in his worldly aunt who might be educated enough in these matters to inform him if his marriage to Emily was valid or not, then he would certainly not be confiding in her after that unmistakable outburst. But whatever her prejudices his aunt was fundamentally kind at heart and it was upon this trait that he made a foray now. 'I was relying on you to help me coax

436

the others into accepting her. If Grace is invited to Christmas dinner –'

'Not in a million years!'

He had never known his aunt to be so vicious. It saddened and offended him. 'Then I won't come either.'

Kit bared her teeth in frustration. 'Ooh, you know just how to get my back up you little demon! Have you stopped to think what your mother or father would have said?'

It was Probyn's turn to accuse. 'That's not fair, Aunt! Don't go using them, it's your objections we're talking about here.'

'Not just mine! How are you going to explain this to your sisters – light the blue touch paper and stand well back? Oh yes, it'll be fireworks all right. Your Aunt Gwen'll have to be told too.'

'Be that as it may, I don't see what you've got against her, Aunt. I mean, you employ the lass.'

'Employ her, yes! I wouldn't turn a needy person away, Irish or no, and she's a good little worker, but I'd hoped for someone –' Kit had been about to say, someone better for my favourite nephew, but at the look on Probyn's face she could not bring herself to inflict further hurt. 'Well, it's your life I suppose,' she finished tightly. 'I hope you'll be very happy.'

'Well, that were very sincere, I must say.'

Kit's buxom body sagged. 'Oh, I do mean it, Probe! I really do hope you'll be happy, you've just given me an awful shock that's all. It'll take some getting used to.'

'And will you start getting used to it by inviting Grace to your party?' He sounded determined.

Kit grimaced, and issued a reluctant nod, but thought silently what a dreadful event it was going to be.

'Thank you.' Looking calmly triumphant, Probyn said he would go out and help his uncle with the milking now.

In his absence Kit shed a few tears, and later when he had gone back to barracks she was quick to gain a sympathetic ear.

But Worthy was pragmatic, saying there was little she could

437

do. 'You wouldn't have let anyone come between us would you, Katherine? And neither would I.'

It was easy to counter this. 'You're not an Irish Catholic!'

'Is that the only thing you've got against her?' asked her husband.

'Isn't that enough?' Kit's indignant expression faded into woe. 'And apart from anything else she's such a . . . such a *brown* person!'

'Anybody would be beside you.' Worthy had never been one to mince words.

'Cheek! You're as bad as our Gwen. Eh, I dread to think what grief she's going to cause the lad!'

'All the more reason why he needs our support then.' Worthy stood firm. 'What's done is done, if Probe loves the lass who are we to say he can't marry her?'

For once Kit could not be persuaded to see beyond her own prejudice, in answer wailing, 'But how am I going to make the transition from her being my laundress to a member of the family? I just can't, Worthy. It's the way I was brought up. It was drummed into us over and over that we didn't mix with Catholics, I can't throw it all aside as easy as changing the sheets.' She heaved a sigh. 'But . . . you're right on one count, I must give him all the support I can, even if I don't like it. I don't like it one bit.'

It was most unsettling, thought Kit, having them arrive in clusters, introducing each of them to Grace O'Brien, seeing them eye her up and down and reading their unspoken question: why was she here?

Naturally it was Gwen who voiced it, no sooner handing over her old-fashioned camphor-reeking bonnet than demanding in a loud whisper to Kit, 'Since when have you been given to entertaining the Irish?'

But this was quickly brushed over, Kit maintaining her happy banter and keeping them all entertained as she showed

438

them to the table, talking incessantly so as not to give Gwen another chance to ask.

For Probyn and his bride-to-be the meal was less than wholesome, knowing the ordeal that was to come at the end of it. But Corporal Kilmaster was not a man to shirk his duty and after the flaming Christmas pudding had been devoured he stood resolutely, glass in hand. 'I'd like to propose a toast to Aunt Kit for giving us this superb dinner!'

'Hear, hear!' Everyone raised their glasses, Kit smiled and nodded but looked as if she would like the earth to swallow her up, and was deeply grateful to Worthy for the supportive grip on her hand.

Probyn remained on his feet. Stomach gurgling, he blurted, 'Now, you've probably guessed that Grace and I have an announcement to make, so I'll not make any long speeches. We're getting married next summer.'

A deathly hush fell over the table, each face as shocked as the next.

Rhoda was the first to recover, a note of horror in her exclamation. 'But you can't! She's a . . . well, she must be, with a name like O'Brien!'

'A Catholic?' said Probyn lightly, concealing his impatience. 'Yes, and so am I now. I've been taking instruction.'

Everyone looked accusingly at Kit who held up her hands and retorted, 'Nay don't look at me, it's none of my doing!'

Whereupon they launched into a full attack on their brother, even Meredith. 'How could you do this Probe? How could you do it to Mother's memory?'

'I'd better go.' Head down, young Grace pushed herself from the table.

'Not before you've had an apology,' Probyn told her, glaring at the assembly.

But everyone remained tight-lipped and looked away, except Kit.

Her voice was softly apologetic. 'I'm sorry. Grace, I really am, you're a nice lass and we've nothing against you but, well,

Probyn's mother and father believed in like marrying like and we've been brought up to believe the same. Under any other circumstances –'

But Grace was already on her way to the door, with the parting shot that Mrs Treasure could find herself another laundress.

Probyn remaining only long enough to tell his relatives what he thought of them. 'You're a bunch of blasted bigots!'

17

After the distressing time Grace had suffered at the hands of Probyn's family, his commanding officer was lenient in comparison, taking great pains to welcome her and put her at ease, although he did stress that she was the fortunate one for landing a soldier for a husband.

Nevertheless, she was grateful for his kindness, for she had anticipated a much loftier attitude and, with the confirmation that living quarters would be made available for the future Mrs Kilmaster, Grace was now at liberty to make plans for their wedding.

Though, 'It's going to be a very one-sided affair with only my relatives present,' she told Probyn. 'Are you sure you wouldn't like to invite yours?'

'They've made their feelings plain,' he said firmly.

'Not even Meredith, or your Aunt Kit?'

Her husband-to-be was quiet. They were sitting in the front room of the O'Brien house, the only one that held hospitality to the pair. He had not been to see Kit since their last exchange several months ago, nor had he heard from her. His feelings towards her were mixed. She had always supported him in the past and he had great affection for her, but there was also great hypocrisy in her stance: having borne two illegitimate children she was hardly the one to throw stones. And to speak in such a manner to the woman he loved had reduced her considerably in his eyes.

Young as she was, Grace understood his reasons. 'Don't deprive yourself of their company for my sake.'

Probyn grasped her hand and held it lovingly. 'By, you're an unselfish soul, Gobbie. I'm sure I wouldn't be so charitable if the boot was on the other foot.'

'Well, your aunt said it all, did she not? It's the way they were brought up, you can't really blame them.'

'I was brought up the same way –'

'But you've taken off your blinkers.' Grace coaxed him with a gentle nudge. 'Go on, invite them to our wedding.'

'Well . . . all right.' His reluctance overcome, he kissed her. 'I might invite Aunt Kit and Merry – but I'm definitely not inviting the others!'

With the marriage arranged for July, two extra invitations were hurriedly despatched. Alas, one of them turned out to be a waste of time. Meredith regretted that it was too far to travel from Huddersfield for one day and, besides, she could not possibly attend a wedding if none of her sisters were included, but thanked Probyn and Grace for their thoughtful gesture and wished them every happiness. That the sentiment was genuine Probyn did not doubt, but her biased refusal left him with a very nasty taste and he resolved never to contact her or any of his sisters again.

The same might have applied to Aunt Kit, had she and her husband and small son not turned up at the church as requested. Yet, although relieved and glad to see her, Probyn knew now where his loyalties must lie. Things would never be quite the same again between them.

It was a small affair, with only a handful of fellow soldiers to balance Grace's family on the other side of the aisle. It was difficult not to be reminded of another time, another chapel, far away. But upon seeing his bride in her virginal dress all memory of Emily evaporated. This was his right and true marriage.

They made a handsome couple, everybody was quick to agree as the wedding party made its way back to the O'Brien household for tea and sandwiches. Even Aunt Kit paid compliment, though the bride and groom could not fail to be aware of how uncomfortable she felt and it was obvious she was only here because of her husband's tacit insistence. Grace's relatives found Probyn and his guests odd in their reserve, and in turn Probyn's kin found them overpowering. Much as Kit had enjoyed dancing in her youth they were too much even for her, and she was the first to voice intention to leave.

Sad though he was, Probyn refused to allow this to blight his special day. Besides, there were more important things on his mind. Longing in his eyes, he whispered to Grace after everyone else save those who lived here had departed, 'We should be making a move too.'

Returning his affectionate gaze, she began to collect her belongings and soon both were at the door.

'What about me shirt for tomorrow morning?' asked Fred.

'There's a clean one in the top drawer,' Grace told him. 'I'll be round on Friday to collect your washing.'

'Who's going to get me tea ready?'

'Mrs Onions said she'll feed you during the week.'

Fred demurred the support of his neighbour. 'I don't like her gravy, she serves it by the slice.'

'Ah well, you can come to us on Saturday and Sunday,' promised Grace.

'Isn't there a tram that runs from Fulford in the afternoons? You could do my tea and still get back in time to do Probe's. I don't mind it being kept warm on the stove till I come in, rather that than get indigestion.'

Having always looked after him, Grace was torn. 'Well, I'll see what I can do. Take care now.' And she left for her new home.

'Why can't he do it himself?' asked her husband as they made their way down the dingy street.

'Fred cook a dinner?' Grace laughed. 'He's a man isn't he?'

'So am I but I can take care of meself. He wouldn't last five minutes in the army.'

Grace changed the subject, gasping, 'Oh look, a motor car!' And Probyn broke off his condemnation of her brother to watch in admiration as the glossy vehicle chugged down the street with half a dozen ragged boys galloping excitedly behind.

But this rare spectacle had not deterred him as she had hoped and once it had disappeared around the corner he continued, 'You won't be able to run around after Fred once we've got a family. I'm not sure I like you doing it now.'

'I don't mind.' Grace hugged his arm, thinking how marvellous he looked in his scarlet dress uniform, how proud she was to be Mrs Kilmaster.

'Lazy article. Oh my goodness and here's another!' Probyn's face lit up as he almost collided with the man who had just emerged from a side street. 'Mick! How are you? How long have you been back in England?'

'Pa!' Mick shook him strenuously by the hand, his ruddy face wearing that familiar welcoming beam. 'I was coming over to the barracks to look you up. I'm just off to see me aunty first.'

Probyn jumped in. 'Did you just see that motor car?'

'Aye! Great, wasn't it? Well, as I live and breathe, fancy bumping into yese!' After severing the lusty handshake Mick turned expectantly to the young woman.

'Ah, this is my wife Grace,' said Probyn with a fond smile. 'Grace, this is an old army pal Mick.'

Mick looked delighted. 'Oh, God love ye! How long have ye been married?'

Probyn affected to look at his watch. 'Ooh . . . just over an hour.' Then he laughed and pointed down the road at the Roman Catholic church.

Mick enjoyed a sly laugh. 'Ach, so you're one of us now?'

Probyn gave a self-conscious chuckle. 'I suppose I am.'

'Well, 'tis delighted I am to meet ye, Mrs Pa!' Mick told the attractive young bride, shaking her by the hand, though less vigorously than he had her spouse's.

Probyn quickly explained to Grace that this had once been his nickname. 'If I'd known you were in York I'd have invited you to the wedding, Mick.'

'Ah don't you worry yourself! I'm happy just to wish ye both luck.' The broad smile was genuine.

'How about you?' asked Probyn. 'Married yet?' The other shook his head vehemently. 'And are you still with the Medical Staff Corps?'

'I am, but they don't call us that any more, 'tis the RAMC.'

Probyn nodded. 'Well, it's good to see you. I hate to rush off but –'

'Oh I thoroughly understand.' Mick gave a rather bashful look at Grace. 'And I'll postpone my intended visit for a while, let the both o' yese get settled in – and may a thousand candles shine upon your marriage. Goodbye to ye now, Mrs Pa!' And with a final handshake they parted company.

'What does RAMC stand for?' asked Grace as, arm in arm, she and Probyn made their way towards town.

Probyn smirked, remembering the way Mick had taken the patient's watch in exchange for food. 'I can only guess that the R has summat to do with robbery.'

'He's a villain then?' Grace turned anxious.

'Nay,' her husband's smile was warm, 'Mick's a good-hearted lad, really. You'd like him. He's an easy person to get to know, though there's not much more to him than what you've just seen on the surface. He joined on the same day as me, but he wasn't cut out for it so he transferred to the hospital corps. We've never been really close pals, I find him rather shallow, but he's great company. Anyway that's enough about him! Let's go get that cab, Mrs Kilmaster.'

Mick never did come to visit, not that Probyn was in the least bit concerned, when not performing his role of corporal, acting out his marital duties and loving every minute, Grace taking to her role with equal enthusiasm.

445

Even after a month of making love every single day it took a supreme effort for him to leave her on a morning, and it did not take much to coax him back into bed.

Not this morning though. After delivering a lingering kiss he begged to be granted leave. 'Aw, Gobbie, I can't! All this friction's given me a blister.'

She giggled and allowed him to rise. 'Don't be so indelicate, and I never thought to hear you complain.'

He rolled onto the edge of the mattress and sat there rubbing his face. 'I'm not, I just need a little break then I'll be good as new.' He added a teasing quip. 'It's just as well there's this South African business to take me away for a while.'

Her frivolity faded. Outside the bugler called, lending the moment a plaintive atmosphere. 'So you think you'll be off then?'

'My lads are hoping so,' answered Probyn, reaching for his trousers and pulling them on. 'They're that excited at the prospect of a scrimmage.' From a personal point of view it would be exhilarating to visit the Cape again after two and a half years of English weather, though rather a wrench to leave Grace.

His wife frowned thoughtfully. 'What caused it?'

'I wrote to President Kruger and said can you create a diversion? I need a break from my wife who won't leave me alone.'

She leapt onto his back pretending to strangle him. 'Oh, you're so mean! Anybody would think I had to tie you to the bed.' They wrestled for a while, then, flopping back against her pillows, Grace became thoughtful again. 'But seriously, will you have to go – and what's it really all about?' Busy looking after house and husband, not to mention her brother, she rarely had time to digest a newspaper these days.

Still only half-dressed, an affectionate Probyn shifted on the edge of the bed and began to stroke her thigh over the sheet. 'Well, this bad feeling between us and the Dutch has been going on for years but it got a darned sight worse after

446

Dr Jameson upset old Kruger. It started out as an issue about the enfranchisement of the Uitlanders, they're the people of British stock who live in the Transvaal and Kruger won't give them the vote, but now it's more about who's running the show in South Africa. The Boers have been spoiling for a fight for years, hankering to replace the Union Jack with their own flag, and there's a real danger now they might invade Natal. I can't stand them meself, real arrogant devils.'

Grace shoved out her lower lip. 'I hope you don't have to go.'

He scolded her softly. 'Now you knew what you were getting when you married a soldier.'

'I know,' she projected contrition, gripping his arm as she did so. 'I'm just terrified of anything happening to you.'

He made light of this. 'Me, a British soldier, the best in the world? And didn't I promise to take extra special care of meself? It won't take us five minutes to sort them out, and it'll give me the greatest pleasure, I can tell you.'

Comforted by his enthusiasm, Grace smiled upon him fondly. 'You really love the army don't you?'

Probyn beheld her as if she had spoken the obvious. 'It's my life.'

And, kissing her, he rose and left the bedroom with the promise of breakfast in bed, totally unaware that he had broken his young wife's heart.

On the eighth of September reinforcements were sent to the Cape. It seemed a war was now unavoidable. A month later, the full might of the Empire was unleashed on President Kruger and his impudent frontiersmen. The largest force ever dispatched since the Crimea steamed away from British and colonial shores heading for South Africa. As yet, Probyn had received no order to join the mobilization, though it seemed inevitable that he would.

'But don't fret,' he comforted his anxious wife with the phrase coined by the newspapers. 'It'll all be over by tea-time.'

Grace looked satisfied. 'Good, because there's not only me you have to worry about now.'

He stared at her for a second, then grinned widely. 'You mean, we're having a babby?'

'We are!' Thrilled with his response she abandoned her casual air to fling her arms around him. 'I haven't been to the doctor but I'm sure, I've been waiting to tell you all day!'

'I knew you were hiding something!' He lifted her off her feet, then set her down gently. 'Ooh, I'm right chuffed – eh, it's just as well I've got promotion if there's another mouth to feed!' At her squeal he introduced himself, 'Lance-Sergeant Kilmaster at your service, madam.'

'Ooh, you call me secretive!'

'Nay I only just learned this afternoon. Must be a red letter day for both of us.'

With Grace sitting on his knee, each patting and stroking the other, they discussed then what the baby would be called. Probyn voiced indifference, saying only that he was too pleased to be able to think of anything and that his wife could name all their children if she so wished.

Excited though she was, Grace showed a lack of confidence, hooking a forefinger over her lower lip. 'I've no idea what to do now. I mean where do I find a midwife?'

The masculine hand that was laying on her abdomen dealt a gently protective pat. 'Nay, you don't have to bother your head about a thing, you'll be going into hospital.'

She turned her blue eyes to him, afraid. 'But people only go into hospital to die!'

'Not here they don't!' He squeezed her gently. 'The army looks after its own.'

'What, even women?' Reassured by her husband's laughter, Grace became excited again. 'I can hardly wait to tell me sisters. I'll drop them a line tonight. Will you tell yours?'

'Oh, I don't think so.' His happy smile became fixed. 'To tell you the truth I couldn't care less if I never see them again.'

'Aw, don't say that.' Grace was genuinely concerned. 'You shouldn't lose touch with your family.'

'It's not me who's cut them off!'

'I know, but won't you give them another chance?' She bumped him with her head in the persuasive manner of a cat. 'I hate to see families fall out.'

Arms around her, Probyn squeezed her thoughtfully. 'I suppose we could tell Aunt Kit.'

'And the others,' she was gently insistent.

He gave in to her kittenish wheedling. 'Eh, you're a bully you are, Gobbie Kilmaster! Go on then, we'll pop over to Aunt Kit's this Saturday and see how the land lies.' And as he kissed his darling wife he could not for the life of him understand how anyone could not love Grace as much as he did.

Kit wasn't in. Leaving her a note they instead trailed all the way back to the railway station and caught a train to Leeds, for, being so close to her own family Grace was eager to reunite her husband with his and insisted they did not waste the day. Surely news of the baby must sway their aversion?

Though wanting to keep his wife happy, Probyn had misgivings. Even as he knocked at Ethel's door he wondered whether it would remain closed to him. But his spinster sister was braver than Wyn or Rhoda and even after a peek from behind the curtain had revealed the identity of her visitors she came to confront them face to face.

'Hello, Ethel,' said her brother warily. 'I thought I'd just come and see you before I went away to war, and tell you our bit of news.'

Ethel offered no invitation to enter, neither did she give him the chance to reveal his news. 'Well, I'm sorry you've come all this way, Probyn,' she told him, not even looking at Grace. 'But I thought I'd already made it perfectly plain that I don't approve of this marriage, nor that my brother has chosen to desert his own religion, and in respect for our dead mother I can't countenance it by inviting you in.'

Without further ado, even before Ethel had time to shut the door, an angry Probyn wheeled away, taking his wife by the arm and hurrying her back to the railway station and home. 'That's it! That's their last chance! I shan't ever contact them again – and don't you try and persuade me!'

'I won't,' murmured Grace sadly, gripping his arm, deeply piteous of her loved one's hurt.

'I never want to hear from any of them again!'

In fact he was to hear from one family member again, though only by letter. Responding to his note, Kit congratulated him on the news that he was to be a father and said she would come to visit as soon as she could. So far she had not appeared and it seemed unlikely that they would meet again before the war in South Africa was over, but Probyn showed little concern. Having successfully negotiated his sergeant's course during the latter weeks his promotion was now fully endorsed and for him this overruled all.

For Grace, too, the Kilmaster family squabbles were to lose all importance. On Friday the first of December a farewell service was held in York Minster for the regiment. Faced with the awful prospect of being parted from her husband, she clung to him at every opportunity.

'It won't be for long, dear,' Probyn tried to comfort. 'Don't just take my word for it. The general himself said it might all be over before we reach South Africa.' He had personal doubts about this. Knowing the stubborn arrogance of the Boer it could extend till spring.

'But even if you turn straight round and come back you won't be here in time to see the new century in with me.' Desolate, she laid her head against his uniformed chest where he stroked it.

'True, but I'm bound to be here when little Tommy's born next summer.'

'Oh, God, I'll miss you!' She burst into tears, then immediately berated herself, flapping at her eyes as if to banish the salt water. 'Oh, I'm sorry for making it worse. I swear I'll be good when I come to wave you off.'

Probyn lovingly dissuaded her. 'I can't have you trailing all the way to Liverpool in your condition.'

She blew her nose. 'I'm coming.'

He wagged a finger. 'No, Grace, I'm ordering you not to.'

She bridled. 'I'm not one of your men. You can order all you bloody well like, but I'm coming.'

He admired her spirit and her devotion and hugged her. 'By, you're a forceful little thing for one so young.'

Grace wished he did not sound so patronizing – eighteen or no, she was a married woman with responsibilities and a child on the way – but she made no complaint. It was not the time. They might never see each other again.

Having galvanized herself for the separation, her reaction upon being told a few hours later that the departure had been delayed was a mixture of devastation and relief.

When it happened yet again she voiced anger that the army could be so cruel. 'Isn't it enough that they're taking my husband away without extending the misery?'

Probyn felt similar frustration but for different reasons. Geared up for a fight, the men in his platoon were growing quarrelsome and insubordinate, fearful that the war would be over before they arrived.

Finally though, on the thirteenth of December, the 1st Battalion departed York for Liverpool.

The day was bitterly cold but this had not deterred friends and family from seeing them off and amongst all the army paraphernalia, the black tin trunks and polo sticks of the officers, a flag-waving crowd thronged the quay. Grace was amongst the singing, swaying mass, standing there for hours, refusing his entreaties to go home, all girlish and pink-cheeked and frizzy-haired, pinning her eyes to him as he boarded, and trying her best not to cry.

It was always an awful time, thought Probyn as he leaned on the rail, both soldiers and crowd waiting for the ship to depart, occasionally waving, singing, fluttering flags but generally just waiting, waiting, waiting. Today, with his young wife on the quay it was twice as difficult, and it was with almost a sense of gratitude that he blew her a final kiss as the aptly-named *Majestic* sounded its fog-horn and pulled away from the dock to a roar and a frenzied hurling of streamers.

Once the ship was on its way to Durban things settled down into the usual routine, a daily parade for an hour when the officers and men did gym; beyond this, and an occasional fire alarm or practising their shooting at crates in the water, there was little to do but wait and ponder what lay ahead. Probyn was glad to be reunited with a few of his old platoon mates, Queen and Bumby, both corporals now who had also been posted to the 1st Battalion, and therefore much of his boredom was eaten up by catching up with their news, a good deal of laughter being shared.

But there was other more serious news to contemplate. Whilst at Liverpool a disturbing rumour had reached them: their western army had suffered a reverse at Magersfontein on its way to relieve Kimberley. Perhaps there would be more for them to do after all – the boys in his platoon were certainly hoping so.

Despite the grumbles from those who had never been overseas that the ship was moving too slowly, the *Majestic* reached the coaling station of St Vincent in remarkable time. Berthed alongside was the SS *Britannic*, homewards bound with sick and wounded, the presence of which had the effect of quieting the grousing from those not yet involved. Seeking confirmation of the rumoured defeat, Probyn cupped his hand to his mouth and called out, 'What's the news, sir?'

'Afraid we can't tell you!' came an officer's cool reply.

'Stuffy ass,' muttered Probyn, and marched along the ship's rail in search of a friendlier face.

Eventually one of his own officers managed to evince a response but it did not make pleasant listening. His informant on the *Britannic* revealed a situation much worse than that rumoured. Their troops had in fact met with three reverses: besides the one at Magersfontein there had also been that at Stormberg to their central army guarding the line into the Free State, and one at Colenso to their eastern army searching for the key to Ladysmith.

This news left Probyn deeply thoughtful. The Boers might not be such easy nuts to crack as had been assumed. It would be most disappointing if he was not home in time for the birth of his first child.

Upon leaving St Vincent the troops were prepared for inoculation against enteric fever. Having made acquaintances amongst one of the other regiments who were treated first, Probyn's platoon had discovered that the effects could be quite uncomfortable, the site becoming stiff and sore, and none of them were keen to undergo the experience themselves. To quell murmurs of insurrection, the captain suggested to his fellow officers that they should line up first to encourage the men, but this was sadly ineffective.

'Will it protect me from the Boer bullets?' an obviously frightened Private Juggins demanded of Sergeant Kilmaster who was attempting to coerce him. 'Then I'll do without it if you don't mind, I'd rather put up with a dose of the runs.'

Probyn dispensed with all niceties. 'That dose of the runs could be fatal, Juggins! They're not jabbing needles in you for the fun of it. I've seen men suffer such a death and it's not noble – and I don't just mean weeds like you but big strong men, good friends amongst them. So if some doctor is clever enough to invent a prophylactic we're not going to insult his genius by turning it down. Now roll up your sleeve!'

With their sergeant taking the needle without flinching, the rest of his platoon were to follow his example, which was to him a fine comment on his leadership and gave great satisfaction, especially when there were plenty on board who still refused.

He chose not to mention later that he was beginning to regret his own participation, for his arm became so rigid that

453

he could scarcely use it, and the fact that there was little to do gave one time to dwell on the discomfort. To stave off self-pity, he concentrated instead on Grace, who had never been far from his thoughts and was especially present on Christmas Day as he sat listening to the band playing carols and hymns.

But another was to creep into his mind as they passed St Helena, and he wondered what Emily was doing, whether she too had found anyone else. Had Wedlock's intervention truly prevented the marriage from being legal? It was best to believe it had for if not then he was now a bigamist. Assailed by a prickle of shame and guilt, he drove her from his thoughts, glad that he would not be landing there.

Being vastly superior to others that had made this voyage, the ship took only twenty days to reach Durban, arriving on the first day of January 1900, although an extra three days were spent in having to unload everything onto lighters, the ship being too large to cross the harbour bar.

Durban was packed with refugees from the Transvaal, its wharves crowded with transport and soldiers, horses and wagon wheels and crates of arms. Cramped amongst all this, the new arrivals were ordered to spread out their kit for inspection. Then it was time for a march through cheering crowds of English patriots and the usual heaving mass of blacks in every manner of dress – shabby European suits, gaudy blankets, knitted helmets – all delighted to see the soldiers before they entrained for Natal.

Packed into open trucks, they spent thirteen hours at the mercy of flies and fleas and mosquitoes, dust and grilling heat, the train whistling and grunting its way up the steep winding mountain railway of the garden colony, alarming large apes that scrambled away from the iron monster and bounded onto rocky ledges. It was much hotter than Probyn remembered, but such discomforts were tempered by the knots of smiling, grateful people who waited at every stopping place with gifts of tea and fruit and cigarettes. It was marvellous to be so feted.

Early on Thursday morning they arrived at Estcourt, once a

mere village, now a vast city, the plains around its old sandstone fort lost in a sea of white bell-tents. Here they were met by Lieutenant-General Sir Charles Warren and their Brigade Major, Captain Vertue, and welcomed as the last regiment to complete the 5th Division. There had recently come the news that General Buller had been replaced as commander-in-chief by General Roberts though Buller retained command of the Natal army. Probyn was glad of the latter, having great admiration and faith in General Buller despite the recent setback.

From then on, the next five days were spent in practising a new scheme of attack in extended order – the folly of advancing in close formation having been learned at Colenso – and camouflaging the light-coloured parts of their uniforms with earth from ant hills. With the officers being required to exchange their Sam Brownes, swords and revolvers for the buff belts and rifles of the rank and file, it was hard to distinguish them and frequent insults occurred, tempers exacerbated by the climate.

Three years had passed since Probyn had last been in Africa and this time he found it difficult to readapt. The current heatwave had turned the waterways to little more than muddy runnels, the shortage forcing him to go unshaven and unwashed which he detested, and even worse was the choking cloud of dust stirred up by manoeuvres.

But within days came a refreshing breeze signalling that rain could not be far away, and his affection for Natal was rekindled. In this lovely country with its clear golden light, the fluid birdsong and the soothing chant of African labourers in the fields, it would have been difficult to imagine the enemy was just beyond the terrace of hills, had it not been for the distinct sound of bombardment that periodically ruined his idyll.

'Hang on, Ladysmith, the Young and Lovelies will soon be there to rescue you,' he announced cheerily for the benefit of his platoon who had grown increasingly frustrated at being kept from the fighting.

Though he was not so jaunty a few hours later as he saw a sheet of blackness looming towards the camp, turning day to night, and rain came lashing through the line of bell-tents, the ensuing deluge almost washing them away.

From being smothered in dust, the soldiers were now up to their ankles in mud. Yet at least there was to be no sitting around in it for the order came to strike tents and with it a great surge of enthusiasm. Regiment by regiment, the 5th Division began to move off towards the Tugela, a fifteen-mile-long column of heavy artillery, thousand upon thousand of white troops, native levies, turbaned stretcher-bearers, ambulances, great spans of mule- and ox-wagons, and it was with a confident air that Sergeant Kilmaster and the rest of the 11th Brigade answered the bugler's call to join the convoy at four o'clock on that January morning, each man having great faith in his leaders, and relegating General Buller's initial failure to relieve Ladysmith to a mere aberration.

Heavy rain made that first day's march an arduous one, the meandering road extremely slippery, wagons being delayed for hours in trying to cross the swollen spruits, the constant yells from the Zulu drivers and the cracking of their bamboo whips as the poor beleaguered oxen became bogged down time after time, rain streaming over their ebony flanks, it was a most dreary trek. It was not until nine-thirty in the evening that they eventually squelched into Frere and pitched tents, by which time Probyn was exhausted, his previous role of mounted infantry and his lack of footwork in England leaving him ill-prepared for such ordeals.

But the army did not make concessions. Under orders to move off at noon on the following day, this diligent sergeant ensured that all was packed and ready by then, he and his men eager to respond to the shells they could see erupting from the garrison at Ladysmith, which made it all the more galling to be told they would now not be moving until evening. Left to the mercy of the broiling sun without any form of shade, Probyn could only order his frustrated zealots to be calm. Thenceforth, he and they were compelled to sit and examine their surroundings now that the tents were packed, all that was left being the stationmaster's house bearing scars of a Boer raid, a Union Jack on a pole, three corrugated iron buildings, and the usual detritus of an army on the march, acres of churned up mud littered with empty cans.

Night clouds brought relief, but this feeling was short-lived for with the march came sheets of rain, men constantly slipping and jumping aside to avoid obstacles, sometimes falling into an unseen donga. Moreover, the wet season had given birth to a variety of insects.

'I'd forgotten what a joy this was,' muttered Probyn to Corporal Queen who marched nearby, both caked in mud.

A miserable Queen agreed. 'What I want to know is, why hasn't our stint at mounted infantry been put to use?'

Probyn did not know the answer, saying only, 'Ours not to reason why.' Then, coming to another swollen spruit, he advised his men, 'Take hold of the rifle of the man in front and keep your eyes on the officer with the lamp!' A staff officer stood on the far side of the rushing stream with a lantern to pinpoint where it was shallower to cross. In the shaft of light termites danced like strips of silver.

Forming his men into a chain linked by rifles, Probyn embarked on the route indicated – only to find himself completely submerged. Helped by a laughing Corporal Queen and another, he shook the water from his head, retrieved his helmet and waded forcefully towards the other bank as if nothing had happened, urging them to follow, whilst privately furious at being made to look an idiot in front of those under his care, cursing the staff officer and his ilk.

At two in the morning they were called to a halt, whence they lay down at the side of the road and slept, despite the rain and the rumbling, whip-cracking din of ox-wagons passing within a few feet of them.

Oblivion reigned for a few blissful hours, and then it was on again.

For countless miles they were to suffer similar privations: torrents of rain both hot and cold, alternating with oppressive heat, rheumatism giving way to sunstroke; more and more was to be heard the call from a debilitated man – 'Permission to fall out, sir!' – hundreds collapsing along the roadside. Oh, what rejoicing was to be heard upon reaching Springfield and in the quiet breathing space that followed, their tents being returned to them along with the opportunity to dry their clothes and to enjoy a bath in the Little Tugela, whilst they pondered the task that lay ahead.

Though far from happy with his limp moustache, it was a refreshed Sergeant Kilmaster who organized his men for Church Parade that Sunday and in the evening, to the sound of a Zulu concertina and the croak of frog and toad, he took out his violet pencil and wrote a letter to his wife.

> *My dearest Grace,*
>
> *I trust this letter finds you in good health and hope you are enjoying better weather than we have suffered of late. It has been one long quagmire this week, except when the sun comes out then the mud sets like cement. Still, mustn't grumble, we managed to get in a game of cricket today and as I write the sky is such a palette of colour as you would never imagine – peach, pink, oyster and gold against the violet mountains. I wish you were here to share the beauty of it with me. I sit here contemplating those poor beleaguered souls in Ladysmith who are depending on us, under siege and starving, yet gallantly holding the town and keeping at bay the thousands of Boers who encompass them. Those Boers surely don't know what they have started. I cannot begin to describe the magnificence of our own force. Suffice to say we are certain to turn the tables and wipe Magersfontein and Colenso off the slate. I know you will have read of these setbacks in the newspaper but I cannot impress upon you strongly enough that you have nothing to be concerned about. I myself have every faith in our great General Buller.*

Once we are over that ridge it will be downhill all the way to Ladysmith.

Well, I had better get my head down now. You are always with me, Grace. I look forward to hearing from you.

Your loving husband, Probyn.

Spirits renewed, it was time to meet the great struggle for the line of hills commanding Ladysmith, to throw themselves at the fortresses which the Boers had built for protection and defence along the heights. To Probyn and the men under General Warren fell the task of attacking the Rangeworthy Hills. Departing Springfield, the column of ten and a half thousand infantry, two thousand mounted troops and thirty-six guns embarked on another gruelling ten-hour march, finally coming at two in the morning to Ennersdale south of the Tugela. En route they had been afflicted by yet another thunderstorm, but this one was pronounced a godsend for, afraid of being cut off by the rising water level, the Boers had evacuated the south bank, leaving the way clear for pontoons to be laid at Trichardt's Drift. Intelligence reported that there were no more than six hundred guarding the hills for which General Warren was heading. It was all very encouraging.

In preparation of the battle, the regiments were drawn up in lines, the South Lancashires being first, then the Lancashire Fusiliers and behind them the York and Lancasters. Then followed a four-hour wait in the cold wet night without greatcoat or blanket, their only comfort being the knowledge that their hardship was contributing to defeat the enemy.

Huddled against the icy shards of rain, his ears filled with the river's roar, Probyn grew nervous, as indeed he always did at such a critical time. He tried to remind himself that once battle was in motion, like an actor taking to the stage, all his jim-jams would disperse, boosting himself with the thought of those under siege who were relying on him, his main desire being that he would not let anyone down, might even distinguish himself.

459

Darkness began to filter from the sky, the early morning cooing of doves suddenly shattered by the boom of big guns. Shells from his own artillery began whizzing in a great arc to explode upon the opposite bank, churning up huge colonnades of red earth and rock. The noise was tremendous, black clouds of lyddite turning the air acrid. Holding his men at the ready, Probyn tensed, awaiting the order to move, contemplating the great red ramparts that arose from the northern bank. As the bugle gave voice so did he, yelling encouragement to his men, urging them towards the boats and pontoons, and the armed multitude began to cross the brown, fast-flowing water.

Upon reaching the northern bank, he and his company scrambled on for two miles to take possession of the foothills, whilst behind them the long caravan of men and horses, wagons and guns proceeded to trundle with excruciating slowness across the wooden planks of the bridge.

For two whole days they came, days of baking sun, throughout which Probyn and his men, with nothing to eat other than the rum and biscuits which he served out for breakfast, lay spread-eagled on their kopje, grumbling about General Warren's lack of urgency and surveying the fortress of hills over which they would have to cross once the advance began. Overhead in the bright sky hung a war balloon, its silken skin shimmering like a giant silver onion. Probyn did not need such a lofty observation point to tell which way things were going. Yesterday upon arrival they had seen atop the opposing ridges a small number of their enemy digging trenches and fortifications. Over the hours the number of Boers had swelled considerably, and all Probyn and his fellows could do was watch, itching to be at them.

At last the final wagon was hauled onto the northern bank, all save one unfortunate man having arrived intact. A relieved Probyn was removed from his oven-like kopje, if only to suffer another long march in fearful heat. But at least by the time he bivouacked that evening below the heights called Venter's Spruit Hills he was equipped with the information upon which he had been waiting. Tomorrow, the battle would really begin.

They were up and under arms at two-thirty, the stars still twinkling when their guns began to shell the enemy trenches. Stomach taut with nerves and hunger, Probyn watched and waited for the order to advance, offering reassurances to the young men who looked to him for guidance. There had been no breakfast, the only waterhole being at a distance and that was bad. It looked like it was going to be another hot day but he tried not to think of this, fixing his mind on the task ahead. The ground which they were poised to attack was like a huge open hand with an unremarkable mound called Spion Kop being the thumb and the main Boer position a wrist. Probyn's battalion was to aim for the spurs which formed the third and fourth fingers, long ridges of rough ground with deep valleys running up between them and all converging onto the plain which sloped up to the enemy's location. He had engaged such a hand before in the Matopos, and had every confidence that they could loosen the Boer's grip. Still, it was a nervous wait.

As yet there was no hint of movement. Probyn had learnt enough to know that, safe in his bombproof shelters, the wily foe would not make himself seen until it was time to defend his trenches against the attacking infantry. The artillery were having similar difficulty in locating their target, though they pounded the hillsides relentlessly, setting the grass ablaze.

After massive bombardment of the enemy's supposed position, thick smoke rising like a wall before them, the infantry finally moved off at six o'clock. With the spur on their left being attacked by the Devons and West Yorkshires, the Young and Lovelies moved off in attack formation, their advance slow but determined, intent on pushing the Boers back across the succession of crest lines.

Hours passed. Advancing gradually across the kopjes towards the Boer position, Probyn finally scrambled into position, deployed his men along a slab of rock and conveyed the officer's order. 'Lay down and fire at the skyline!'

'But I can't see anything to aim at, Sergeant!' objected Private Juggins.

'You will do. Just keep firing, it'll vex the tripe out of them and draw them out from behind the hill, then you'll have something to shoot at.' Cool and calm now, Probyn lay down alongside and began to fire at the ridge.

Though this had the desired effect, it also brought them under fire themselves, and with the Mauser's smokeless powder making it impossible to see where the Boers were hidden, it was a hair-raising time, in addition to which the sun was rising higher and it had become ferociously hot.

With more hours passing and no order to press forward, the question was bound to arise.

'Are we going to sit here all day, Sergeant?' fretted a scarlet-faced Juggins.

'The poor blighters in Ladysmith have sat there for weeks,' replied Probyn. 'If it was that easy to break through somebody would have done it by now. These things can't be rushed.'

But he too was growing impatient and fought to suppress a sigh that would infect the men. Lying on this slab of rock, being baked to a biscuit, his puttees set like drainpipes around his calves, he looked to his leader for any hint that they might press forward, but none came. And there he and his men waited, getting hotter and hotter, under attack not only from bullets but from hordes of mosquitoes who seemed unusually voracious today. Dealing one an irritated puff to dislodge it from his lip, he risked a quick look around him. Through the stinging trickles of perspiration he glimpsed a swarm of locusts moving over the countryside, settling in a white blanket, before rising again as a cloud to devour a fresh patch of crops. Wishing he was at home, he shifted from his uncomfortable position, sucking in his breath upon receiving a burn from the exposed rock. Where had all the fun of soldiering gone, the rush and thrust and swift capture of a savage enemy? All he seemed to do nowadays was lie about doing nothing, at the mercy of the elements.

For a few brief seconds came diversion in the shape of a young lizard, barely an inch long from nose to tail but exquisitely striped with bronze, its tiny feet skittering across the lump of rock under Probyn's nose where it rested to imbibe the sun. Keeping perfectly still, he marvelled at its minuteness. Only when he reached out a finger did it scurry into a crack, leaving him at the mercy of boredom and the relentless heat.

The sun was almost at its zenith now, those around him gasping for breath, their faces glowing and vexed. Just when it seemed they had been forgotten, the order finally came to advance. All discomfort was shrugged aside in an instant. Probyn urged his men up the rugged kopje; they responded eagerly, scrambling towards the skyline – but the moment they became visible they drew heavy crossfire. Extending the line outwards, his rifle at the ready, the captain increased the pace and led his section onwards and over the crest of the kopje, maintaining this rapid pace whilst descending the slope for they were especial targets here, the *pft pft* of Boer bullets throwing up little spurts of earth or, worse, flesh and bone.

A man fell to Probyn's left. Barely stopping, he grabbed a handful of tunic and ran for his life, dragging the unfortunate fellow after him down the slope, bashing and bumping the wounded body over rock and shingle until he reached safety. Depositing his burden, he made an urgent check to see that most were still following him, then grabbed and shoved one after the other of them up the ascending kopje, launching himself with them after the captain. Once more under cover, he was able to retrieve a little of his breath whilst he climbed, running for all he was worth as he pelted over the top and down the other side.

Working in this fashion across a series of kopjes, they got into position in the early afternoon with only two casualties.

And here the sweating soldiers were delayed again, fortifying their hard-won ground whilst awaiting reinforcements.

Fresh troops arrived, and a drummer came amongst them distributing ammunition. Their stock of bullets replenished, the force advanced to the kopje beyond and set about fortifying that.

But this hillock was turning out to be inadequate for such a large body of men who were packed six deep in places, providing a larger target for the Boers who now gave them special attention.

Firing blindly at the hill from whence the enemy bullets seemed to come and which the British guns were shelling in the hope that it was the right one, Probyn wished he could be as invisible as his enemy, and consoled those around him who had less confidence in themselves by telling them, 'We're as good as theirs any day. Give 'em humpty, lads!'

Throughout that day they lay firing from that kopje, under hot shell and rifle-burst without food or water, only too thankful to maintain the action so that they could forget the pangs of hunger in their bellies, their throats clogged with dust and smoke, the sweat that dripped and sizzled on their gun barrels and the desiccating heat of the rocks below, the blazing sun above.

At last the merciful order was received to push on. With an apprehensive glance at the open plain before him, Probyn responded to his captain's order, giving his men a word of encouragement and leading them from their place of refuge.

A hail of fire erupted. Before they had gone eight hundred yards too many men had been wounded to go further.

'Take what cover you can!' yelled the captain, hurling himself face down. 'We'll have to wait for reinforcements.'

Trying to blend himself against the khaki grass that afforded little asylum except its colour, Probyn risked a quick examination of the situation, but immediately ducked as a bullet thudded into his pith helmet. However, in his brief inspection he had seen that other British troops had occupied the kopjes they had just left, removing all hope of retreat. They must remain exposed between the two lines of fire. All around him men were groaning, crying pitifully. Amongst them he recognized poor Juggins. The latter within reach, Probyn stretched out his arm along the hard ground until his fingertips made contact with the other's, feeling the stickiness of blood.

'Don't worry, Jugsy, we'll soon have you out of here!'

But help was slow to come. Pinned down under that merciless sun, bullets coming frighteningly close, those wounded around him becoming weaker and weaker through loss of blood, the flies an added torment. Probyn held on to the hope that God would not let him die before he had seen his child. The hand to which he had reached out clung to him like a vice for an hour. So effectively had it blocked his circulation that he did not at first notice that the grip had become looser. Only with the return of blood to his veins and the accompanying sear of pain did he realize that Juggins had died.

Then towards late afternoon, either in answer to his prayers or the distressed cries of the wounded, the sun was obscured by cloud, a precursor to heavy showers. The vultures and kites that had been patiently circling overhead were now forced to abandon their hope of a meal as a sheet of darkness moved across the battlefield. Veiled by rain and darkness, the stricken warriors were at last able to regroup and bivouac, those uninjured giving what succour they could to their comrades, though it was a bitterly cold night for those already weak from lack of blood, and with only a sip of rum for food and drink it was not surprising that some perished before help finally came. The regiment lost that day eight killed and seventy-four wounded.

During the next two days, whilst the wounded faced a trying journey of seven hours to Springfield, Probyn and the rest of his regiment made no advance, perched like hapless sea birds on the edge of the plateau, their ranks enfiladed by invisible Mausers and showered with shrapnel from their own guns that had been captured at Colenso. Four howitzers had arrived from General Buller but seemed incapable of dealing with the enemy's pom-pom, its aggressive barrage resulting in yet more casualties.

Hardened to the barbarity of war, Probyn remained impassive whilst others were physically sick at the sight of a living being suddenly exploded to pulp, he himself being more revolted by the looting of the dead performed by the kaffirs whose kraals littered the veld. And yet he gradually came to accept even this, for given the chance his own comrades would rifle a dead Boer's pockets too in the hope of a shiny Kruger rand, and who would condemn them for seizing these small comforts, faced with such hardship themselves? Certainly not the dead. Even so, he sought no personal loot, preferring to cling to the thin veneer that separated himself, a civilized man, from the savage.

When night fell there came a warning to expect firing on their right as the decision had been made to attack Spion Kop. An excited murmur rippled through the ranks, this news being all that was needed to bolster flagging spirits after another day of starvation.

How cruel then to be told later that the attack had been postponed.

'Oh ballocks, I'm sick o' this,' grumbled Corporal Bumby. 'What's stopping us now?'

Probyn had come to realize that swear words meant nothing when it came to a man's true character; what mattered was his ability to stand firm in battle and defend the pals who relied on him, and he could rely on Bumby. 'Seems they haven't done enough reconnaissance.'

'Well we have only been here four days,' said their friend Queen sarcastically.

Bumby thumped the ground, dislodging a cricket that somersaulted into the air. 'It's so frucking frustrating!'

Probyn thought so too. Above the whirring chorus of the crickets could be heard the humming of Dutch Psalms, drifting across the cold night air from Spion Kop. It was at that moment he began to wonder whose side God was on.

However, the following day his faith was to be restored. It had started badly, the battalion being in reserve in the valley but by no means at rest, having to undergo half an hour's drill before the fiery Irishman Major-General Hart as though they were at home on the barrack square, the rest of the day being spent in trying to construct shelters with what few tools they had on the very exposed piece of ground, all attempts failing.

But the sight of General Buller riding into camp on his charger was enough to raise spirits. His heavily-moustached bulldog face, naturally quite red, was today livid, forecasting a rough time for Lieutenant-General Warren.

'Now you'll see an end to the shilly-shallying,' Probyn promised those under him.

And indeed they did. News soon came that Warren was finally to launch an attack on Spion Kop.

It was a very wet evening, but nothing could douse the expectant mood of those who waited in the wings, ready to support General Woodgate in his attempt to take the plateau. In readiness of his night attack, the General moved off into the blackness, two thousand men, a few picks and shovels for the sappers to entrench, and a string of ammunition mules in tow. It was not until midnight that they began to make their ascent.

For those left behind it was hard to snatch anything more than a catnap, waiting to hear above the hiss of the rain a sign that they were needed, yet appreciative of the quietude after the barrage of the day, the only intrusion being the rustle of a meerkat on the hunt or the bumbling jaunt of a porcupine.

By the early hours a thick mist covered the peaks. Still they waited.

And then a human sound. The sound of cheering. 'They've done it!' laughed Probyn to whoops of jubilation from his own ranks. 'They've taken the ridge!'

Such magnificent tidings after all their setbacks – and there was to be further joy when a message came down later to say that General Woodgate had seized one half of the end plateau of Spion Kop ridge and was now firmly entrenched. Ordered to open heavy fire and hold the Boer right as the attack was pressed home, the men of the York and Lancaster Regiment gladly settled themselves into position, rifles at the ready, to await the signal. Then it came, and the ghostly call of a night bird was immediately suffocated in an eruption of shellfire directed at another of the enemy strongholds and setting up a colossal reverberation from the hills. Kilmaster, Queen and Bumby launched their men into action, they themselves directing their own heavy fire at the mist-covered ridge. Again it was impossible to see a target, but with thoughts that the door to Ladysmith was about to be unlocked, Probyn and his comrades gave furious fire, all anticipating an end to this drawn-out affair.

Hour after hour the valiants worked, unable to hear anything save the shrill hissing and horrendous bangs, fingers throbbing with the strain of pulling the trigger, eyes blurred by smoke and lack of sleep, spitting out dust from a nearby shell-burst, until the flush of daylight began to creep across the sky and, finally, exhausted, they were relieved by the Dublin Fusiliers, and fell back into reserve to a more sheltered place behind a spur of the hill.

Belly in spasm from lack of food or drink, limbs aching, Probyn lay smoking one of Queen's cigarettes as the mist began to clear from the hills, whence it became possible to attain a better view of what he had been firing at. General Woodgate's attack on Spion Kop appeared to be developing at a splendid rate, seemingly unhindered by the Boer shells that were dropping all over the hills, sending great columns of earth and rock into the air. He ducked himself as another shell came too close for comfort, exploding amongst his own ranks and sending flesh and earth and bone all mingling together in a plume of destruction. Peppered with morsels of men and rock, he was relieved to find himself unharmed, and upon checking that all under his care were unscathed too, he resumed his cigarette and his observation of the battle. In the lull he even heard a skylark trilling its heart out. It was going to be a hot morning.

Some hours later an old black man came by with a can of water, into which Probyn scooped a mug and drank long and deep even though the water was lukewarm, gasping afterwards to the donor, 'Oh you don't know how good that tasted, thank you! And pass my thanks to whoever sent you.'

The reply was polite but without the obsequiousness that Probyn had come to expect from the natives, although the speaker did accord the white man his expected title. 'No one sent me, boss.'

Ever since Greatrix had been slain by the Matabele, Probyn had lost what small regard he had possessed for any black man, whatever the tribe. He did not treat them as animals like some, nevertheless he could not wipe away the fact that their countrymen had killed his best friend and regarded them as not to be trusted. Now he observed this one with genuine respect. 'Then double thanks for your own kindness. I really appreciate it.'

Feeling the sentiment was authentic, the old man raised a smile then, not the flashing white grin of youth, nor the artificial one from those who feared the jambok, but a slower, more dignified response. 'It is my pleasure, boss. Would you like another drink before I go?'

Saying he had better make the most of it, Probyn supped again.

Waiting for him to finish, the old man chanced a remark. 'The battle for N'Taba N'Yama is going well, boss.'

Probyn's face came out of the mug, frowning, then made an assumption. 'That's what you call Spion Kop?' All the hills had several names, it could be very confusing.

'We black men named those mountains first, long, long

before the Boers took them from us.' There was no air of bitterness, simply resignation.

Probyn supped again, more thoughtfully. Even when the Boers were defeated the black men would not have their Tabanyama or whatever he had called it, but at least they would be treated better than by the tyrannical Dutchmen. 'You know, it puzzles me, in all the time I've spent here I've never set eyes on an elephant. I've seen all sorts of other animals, but I'd give anything to see one elephant.'

The old man shook his head. 'You will not see one around here, boss. Your British gentlemen are such good shots. They shoot things then expect them to grow again on trees. I have not seen an elephant myself for many a year.'

Probyn gave a wistful sigh, then handed back the mug, leaving the old black man to go on his way.

Throughout the day the air was filled with the sound of guns plastering the hillsides with shrapnel, the thunder of bomb-bursts and the crack of rifle fire. Secreted amongst the wooded slopes of another hill, Botha's guns constantly deafened. Probyn sought shade under a group of mimosa trees, one of which had a huge branch half severed by the machines of war. Miraculously above the noise came a high-pitched peep of a bird and he looked up to see the tiny creature hopping about just over his head. Smiling, he watched it for a while, happily pondering the morning's success, though occasionally his optimistic eyes would stray beyond it to the crest of Spion Kop, seeking the glint of the heliograph that would signal victory. There had been no new message for hours now.

Night came quickly in the southern hemisphere. Darkness fell upon them at seven, the crash of artillery fading into silence with just the infrequent sputter of rifle fire. Probyn slept.

The moon was still in the sky when he was awoken by a sense of unease. Forbidden the luxury of coming-to gradually as he might at home, he was awake in an instant and on his feet when the rumour reached him.

'Captain Vertue's dead!' said a devastated Corporal Queen.

'He can't be!' said Probyn. Their brigade major had been party to yesterday's success.

'He is. General Woodgate's copped it too!'

'Dead?'

'Near as damn it! And they're not the only ones. There's been a bloody massacre up there, the Boers have taken it back!'

'But it was going sailingly! I watched our lads stream up that hill –'

'Well, they're streaming down again now! The Boer sneaked up the other bloody side, just about wiped them out. They say we're going to have to retire.'

Probyn grabbed his arm as men began to gather round. 'They? Who's they? Who's told you this, Queenie?'

'It's all over the –'

'Yes, but is it right?' Probyn was angry. 'I don't want you spouting such dangerous twaddle in front of the lads, where are your facts?'

'Go ask the captain, then,' advised Corporal Queen, his face projecting woe and irritation.

'I will!' Probyn went off to investigate.

But what he heard brought the cold fingers of defeat to clutch at his heart, and as dawn crept over those inpenetrable hills there was to be the evidence of his own eyes. The transport parked some miles to the rear was on the move to the pontoons at Trichardt's Drift.

With a heartfelt groan, he steeled himself to meet the men, wondering how on earth they were going to take this repugnant news. For four drawn-out days his brave lads had endured continuous exposure to shell and rifle fire, had fought stoically with little more than a burning nip of rum in their bellies, their one saving glory being the thought of winning a way through to Ladysmith. Now it seemed inevitable that they would be told to retire.

Tragically, as the morning wore on, this proved to be the case. Whilst the medical officers and burial parties performed their hideous duty on the summit, transferring the lacerated bodies to stretchers and those beyond help to the trench that had failed to protect them, headless torsos, ragged fly-infested limbs, General Buller gave his army the order to withdraw.

After a terrible march through a morass of slime, of hissing rain and pitch blackness, having to dig roads and take their turn in the firing line as they went, the weary and disconsolate troops finally came to the pontoons, though their torment was not over by far. For two days and a night in cold so intense that it reached one's very bones they struggled to transfer the immense convoy of ox and mule transport, the heavy guns, a thousand wounded in ambulance wagons and on stretchers, back across the Tugela, whilst in no danger of enemy fire now, assailed by the bitterness of defeat. And for many the blame lay with the man on the charger who supervised the whole affair.

As the General's horse sloshed alongside the tramping caravan of men and machines with his entourage, Corporal Bumby lifted his head into the driving rain, but only to mutter insolence. 'There goes Sir Reverse Buller.' Others echoed his derisive comment.

Probyn made a move to stifle the grousing. 'Buck up, lads!' His body racked for the first time with ague, he tried his best to rally those around him. 'Just look at this as a chance to have a wash and brush-up before we're at them again.' Yet his own confidence had been badly shaken. The Boers, with the benefit of their smokeless weapons and their ability to blend into the hillside, were proving a much tougher enemy than the savage ever had.

'You like traipsing back and forth across this bleedin' river then do you?' Corporal Queen had come from the rear and fell in beside them. 'Think it's a lark to risk your life taking these bleedin' hills only to be told to give 'em up again?' For miles ahead he could see soldiers tramping into the distance, and for miles behind, a great ragged muddy column of disgruntled manhood.

'That's not General Buller's fault.' Probyn retained his faith in his superiors and was a particular admirer of Buller, regarding him as everything a general should be, brave and bold, yet not so proud that he lost sight of his men's needs.

'Whose fault is it then?' demanded Bumby. 'He's in charge isn't he? He wants to get his wife out here and see if she can do any better.'

'There's no call for that,' growled Probyn. After all he had gone through, those big buttock cheeks and that mean puckered little mouth were enough to almost make him lose his temper. 'Keep your stupid ideas to yourself.'

''Snot my idea,' sniffed Bumby. 'The captain's saying the same thing.'

'I should've known. You never had an original thought in your head.' Probyn regarded such gossip as odious, especially from an officer.

'I heard him tell Lieutenant Swift he couldn't understand how old Buller had ever given that duffer Warren command of his army,' finished Bumby.

'Course you'd know just what it takes to run an army, wouldn't you?' sniped Probyn.

And on they tramped through mud and rain, until the last wagon had arrived on the south side of the Tugela. When the pontoon was rolled up, the roadway planks were so worn that they could barely last another half an hour.

Demoralized, disheartened, filthy and ravenous with hunger, the men were in no mood to be paraded for a speech, and even less so from the man whom some considered to have let them down.

But when the bronzed, burly figure began to speak, almost shyly for such a great man it seemed to Probyn, there were few who could retain their opposition for long.

General Buller cleared his throat, his eyes moving over the sullen army before him, resting occasionally on an individual face, his eyes and voice trying to convey the depth of his feeling. 'I have called you together today to expressly thank you for your gallant conduct during the last ten days, whether it was before the enemy, or at work in a drift or pulling wagons, every man did his best. No other army in the world could have done as well.' His emotive words echoed from the kopjes, reaching every patriotic heart and dissolving cynicism, Probyn himself fighting tears. 'I want you to thoroughly understand that all your hard work and great sacrifice has not been in vain. I can confidently predict that we have got a short road to Ladysmith. There may be some hard fighting on the way but I am sure you will overcome it.' The tone of his voice imparting his deep faith in them, he paused a moment to let this sink in, then announced, 'I should like now to read you a telegram from the Queen,' and he conveyed the monarch's admiration for the conduct of the troops during the past trying week, before rounding off his own address. 'Once again, I thank you all from the bottom of my heart. By your courage you have given me the key to Ladysmith. We shall be there within the week.'

18

After a bivouac of several hours, the York and Lancaster Regiment was marched eight miles to be stationed in rest camp, the first day spent enjoying a decent meal, burning the lice out of their uniforms and patching up the rents as best they could.

Somehow a sack of mail managed to get through, and though the envelope from Grace was smeared with mud, and water had soaked right through to the letter, causing the ink to run in places, the mere sight of it served to lift Probyn's mood.

Escaping from the heavy rain into his tent, he was about to read it when a dog sneaked under the flap. They stared at each other for a few seconds, until Probyn asked, 'Who are you?'

The emaciated dog wagged its tail and came to sniff at him, obviously liking what it smelled for it immediately curled up on the mackintosh beside him.

'Make yourself at home!'

At the loud tone, the dog ducked its head, fearing that it was about to be ejected. But Probyn merely smiled, thinking of Boney and Greatrix, and allowed it to stay. It was a filthy, lice-ridden creature, but then so was he. With the warmth of its body helping to relieve his ague, he went back to his letter, managing to fill in the gaps caused by the rain.

My own dear husband,
Every day seems like a week without you . . .

Probyn groaned, his wife's lament bringing his own sense

of emptiness to the fore. Flicking a gold-green beetle from his leg, he read on.

I try to keep busy but your dear face keeps intruding on whatever chore I am doing. Every morning I go to Mass and pray that you'll soon be home, and I often light a candle for you and try to imagine that you feel its little warm flame in your heart. Dearest, I love you so much the very thought of it makes me cry . . .

He wondered then whether the smudged writing had actually been caused by rain or tears, and at the thought of his little wife sobbing he paused to trumpet into his handkerchief, then fought to contain his emotions as a fellow sergeant entered the tent. A few seconds were taken up discussing the dog, then, with the other man not seeming to mind, Probyn returned to his letter. Fortunately it went on to tell of more mundane things now: the weather at home, the rush of recruitment, the support of her friend Charlotte who made constant visits and knitted clothes for the expected baby, the hasty marriage of her sister Ellen, the enlistment of brother Fred in the West Ridings.

If you should bump into him, please look after him. Well, I must go now. Oh, I haven't answered the question you asked in your letter to me. Yes, I am in very good health. My sisters say I look blooming – blooming awful! Take care of yourself, dearest. Sorry this letter is so short but I am really just sending it to tell you that a parcel is on its way and a longer letter is in with that. Your loving wife, Grace.

The rain drummed down on his tent, so heavily that drips began to seep through the canvas. After reading his wife's letter a couple of times he replied to it in violet pencil, gently preparing Grace for the worst, though without mentioning the slaughter, saying only, 'It might take a bit longer than we thought, but you know my heart is with you.'

The hiss of rain ceased abruptly. The dog uncurled itself, stretched, wagged its tail and left.

'Call again,' he said as it went.

And so it was to do, though its frequent visits did not mean that it had chosen him as its owner, for almost everyone in the camp gave it bits of food if they had any, in times of paucity the animal relying on rats or insects. And had there been any misapprehension about it hanging round purely for selfish reasons, the dog was to refute this, seeming to consider itself part of the regiment to the point where it began to attend parades, quickly earning itself the honorary title of Private Mutt and a regimental number.

The antics of the dog, the arrival of his wife's parcel crammed with chocolate and socks plus other home comforts and a long letter helped to balance the misery of the dreadful stinging insects and the rain. But this was only the first of his fortunes, for Corporal Bumby stumbled across a wild peach tree and came back tunic bulging with the succulent fruits on which the deprived comrades gorged, the juice dripping down their chins. And to cap it all, over the next few days a strong wind sprang up, and this unusual occurrence blew in a procession of Boer farmers and their families wanting to surrender, finally removing all gloom induced by the previous setback. As the mimosa began to blossom so Probyn began to recoup his fighting spirit. When the third attempt to relieve Ladysmith was announced, he was ready for it.

The battalion moved off from Hastings Farm in the early hours of the third of February, Private Mutt attending parade then moving off with them. They crossed the Tugela at Potgieters Drift half an hour before noon. The road down to the river was very steep and from the top of the hill, the sides of which were covered in mimosa scrub and aloes and flaming red lilies, Probyn was given a magnificent view of the battle arena. The plain stretched before him with Spion Kop on the left, in front of him Brak Fontein and Vaal Krantz, and to his right the wooded slopes of Mount Alice.

On crossing the river the regiment took up positions on three kopjes, where they were to remain throughout that day and the next. Probyn found himself once more in company with the dog who this time was not so welcome, the position being very cramped and very hot, the sight of its lolling tongue and incessant panting reminding him of his own thirst and making for an irksome time.

Early on Monday morning their big guns roared into voice and, under cover of this brisk fire the infantry moved into action again, the York and Lancasters and South Lancashires forming the first line and supported by the Royal Lancasters, advancing stalwartly on Braksfontein to a medley of northern voices.

Once upon the ridge Probyn relayed the order. 'Lie down, but on no account fire unless you have a proper target!'

Even as he said it it seemed futile, for in spite of being so close to the Boers there was no sign of life along the entire length of the ridge. Within reach, a low shrub sprouted from the rock. Spotting a lone white berry he plucked it quickly and popped it into his mouth, savouring the taste of strawberry.

Three hours later they were still here, lying in the grass whilst their big guns bombarded the hill in front of them.

At midday there was still no sign of the enemy.

The dog had fallen asleep. 'All right for some,' muttered Probyn to the soldier nearby.

The middle-aged Private Snowball wiped the sweat from his eyes and peered across at the ridge. 'I think them buggers over there must have fallen asleep an' all.' A heavy smoker, he let forth a tremendous cough, causing his sergeant to avert his ear in discomfort.

'Blimey, they won't be after that.' Probyn cringed. 'That'd drown out Long Tom that would.'

Snowball emitted a rattling laugh, but his look of boredom soon returned. 'What's the name again of this hill we're supposed to be taking?'

Probyn wondered how the other could so easily have forgotten. 'Why, Spion Kop, you daft pizzock.'

'Spion Kop,' muttered Snowball with a bitter nod. 'I'd rather Mount Alice.' Then he gave his raucous catarrhal laugh, making his sergeant aware that he had been used to set up a joke.

'Less of that vulgar –' Probyn had no time to finish, for at that instant the Boer guns exploded in a clamorous fusillade. Everyone ducked, apart from the dog who, jolted awake, leapt up and began to dart up and down the ridge barking and snapping and leaping at the shells and bullets.

Corporal Bumby had developed hiccups through laughing at Snowball's joke. 'Where the *hic* hell's it coming from?' he yelled to his sergeant, glancing all around him but unable to detect so much as a glimpse of the enemy.

But Probyn could not enlighten him, could only keep his head down under the perfect storm of fire that ensued, the whole plain soon becoming obscured by smoke and dust.

'Christ that *hic* bloody dog!' a complaint spat from Bumby's round cheeks. 'As if there isn't enough racket without *hic* him!' The dog, miraculously unharmed, was twirling about in a frenzy of yapping, trying to catch the Mauser bullets that whizzed around his ears like troublesome bees. 'Will somebody get rid of the bloody voiceterous thing before I shoot it meself. *Hic*!'

The dog was still leaping around like a dervish when the sudden order came to retire.

'Oh not *again*!' Private Snowball thumped the ground in frustration. 'If God meant us to keep retreating why didn't He make us with feet that point in the other direction?'

'The day's not yet lost,' Probyn told him, and ordering the rest to move calmly and steadily, he himself began to withdraw. 'With a bit of luck we've done what we came to do.'

'What's that, get our arses shot off?' muttered another out of hearing.

And indeed it did seem a foolhardy thing to retire so leisurely under such heavy fire. Probyn rushed forward to support the colour-sergeant who had just gone down with a bullet in his leg, he and another dragging him down the slope to find cover.

479

But before they had gone two more steps his words were to bear fruit. With the wave of British infantry in apparent retreat, the Boers now came out of their hiding places to take advantage and so betraying their position.

'That's it, Dutchy, keep shooting.' Probyn enjoyed a defiant smile as he struggled to support the heavy wounded man. 'We'll be back to call on you tomorrow.'

Their feint attack having done all that it intended without firing a shot, the battalion fell back on the north side of the Tugela where they were to remain for the rest of that day and the next. Meanwhile, a battle was taking place for one of the other kopjes, Vaal Krantz. Having helped to locate the Boers' position, Probyn was keen to see the advantage pressed home and led the cheer as a hurricane of fire from their naval guns exploded the Boer magazine on Mount Alice. It was a truly magnificent spectacle, the sun beginning to descend, the sky adopting the colour of flame and molten gold against the violet-blue escarpment, on every kopje a Boer gun ejaculating puffs of smoke which became more conspicuous as dusk advanced, decorating the fiery mantle with woolly white pom-poms.

With Vaal Krantz won, he went to bed uplifted.

How utterly dispiriting then to receive the captain's order in the morning, 'Prepare the men to retire!'

With the constant boom of enemy guns, Probyn thought he had misheard. The other non-commissioned officers gathered there sharing his disbelief. 'Retire, sir?'

'Beastly, I know, Sergeant, but Vaal Krantz has proved somewhat smaller than was anticipated. It's impossible to haul the guns up its narrow ridge and so it's been evacuated, though it has not entirely been a wasted gesture and you must impress that upon the men.' The captain sought to uphold morale, 'the shellfire it attracted gave us an extra chance to gauge the position of the Boer guns. We shall soon have another pop at them.'

Clinging to this shred, a bitterly disappointed Sergeant

Kilmaster was once again forced to organize his men for a withdrawal, as he did so cursing the enemy guns, these same guns lobbing shells into the ranks of departing British and their casualties, as yet again the mighty Imperial juggernaut was compelled to retreat over the Tugela.

And still poor Ladysmith waited.

It was good that others were enjoying success elsewhere, the Boers suffering their own defeats and in some parts surrendering in droves. Alas, for Probyn and his friends the situation in this corner of Natal was to remain stalemate.

Back at Springfield digging trenches, there was some consolation to be had from fresh mutton, fresh bread for breakfast and the chance of an occasional bath in the river, though the water was fetid and the weather was to remain very trying with terrific thunderstorms, on one occasion the camp being flooded out. It was a miracle that such deprivation added to three failed attempts on Ladysmith did not demoralize the troops, but apart from the occasional criticism of those who led them, when the order came that there was to be another push every man in Sergeant Kilmaster's platoon seemed eager to try again, to face the enemy with a doggedness only equalled by his own.

This time they were to go via another route. To the north of the Tugela was a range of three hills. These formed a virtually impregnable fortress but, as the Boers there were reported to be disheartened, little opposition was expected. Hence, an attack was launched on Pieters Hill.

Again the Tugela was crossed.

This time the dog was left behind for its own safety. Tied to a tent peg, it pranced about in frustration on realizing it was not to take part.

Under shellfire Probyn deployed his men, scrambling into position and throwing himself down beside Corporal Queen with a thud of dust.

'Cop this!' An amazed Queen presented a lump of shrapnel

that had embedded itself in his helmet, almost slicing the top off so that his headgear resembled a boiled egg. 'I'm taking that home as a souvenir.'

'I'm waiting for a piece of Long Tom himself,' announced a wild-eyed Probyn, ducking as another shell burst among a group of mules blowing them to bits. 'If we ever get near enough that is.'

No sooner had he lifted his head than another shell burst, nearer this time, and another. It became evident that the hill was more stoutly defended than they had been led to believe, a storm of iron was unleashed upon them, ripping off limbs and heads, indiscriminate in its slaughter, stray shells landing on a kaffir's hut, blasting black and white together, man and mule.

Averse to another ignominious withdrawal, they tried to struggle on valiantly amid the stench of hot gun oil and cordite and blood but it was plain to see that the frontal attack was a calamitous error. Men were dying rapidly.

A bugle sounded Retire. This having seemed a regular occurrence over the past weeks, Corporal Bumby wasted no breath complaining this time and instead began to lead his squad from the cover of the rocks. They were immediately mown down, but as if unable to believe that they would meet the same fate others were to answer the bugler's call, all tumbling, their blood spurting over the red rocks, until an officer shouted to Probyn, 'Sergeant! Get the men back, it's a trick, the Boers have learned our bugle calls!' And Probyn tried to stop them but like the crazed mules who scattered over the kopje dragging their guts with them the men in his platoon refused to heed, anxious to respond to the sham call of Retire, their bodies amassing in a pile until at last the call to Retire was genuine and Probyn was free to lead what was left of them down the slope. Hopping alongside him amongst the decimated troops were Corporals Queen and Bumby, when another enormous boom threw up the earth in front of them, all were catapulted through the air, Probyn too, and for him everything went black.

He had only been unconscious for seconds, coming round to the screams of his friends. Bumby's arms were gone, one leg ripped off at the knee, he died before Probyn was only half conscious. But the screaming continued. A piece of the shrapnel that Queen had so recently pocketed as a souvenir had ripped through his thigh, but it wasn't him who was screaming, he just sat there staring back at Probyn with an amazed gawp on his face. The soldier who screamed was only a youngster. With others tending him, Probyn examined himself and found that his shirt had been completely ripped off his back, the shrapnel leaving nothing more than a long scratch across his shoulders that made him wince when he touched it. There was no time to ponder on his luck. Trying to organize those around him, to separate the walking wounded from the tangle of carnage splattered over the rocks, he hurried them to safety, back across the Tugela.

In the lull there came guilt. Until now, Probyn had managed to protect those under his care from harm but this time there were severe losses, men that he had come to know well. In the light of such carnage, to maintain his optimism would take a tremendous amount of faith.

On Sunday a partial armistice was agreed in order to bury the dead and remove the wounded, some of whom had lain there for two days and were a buzzing mass of flies. The ceasefire might lend credence that this was the Sabbath; once the wounded had been removed the silence was almost deafening, but there was little leisure to be had, most of their time taken up with digging graves.

As ever, it was the blacks who did most of the digging, Probyn supervising the excavation, watching impassively as one mutilated, fly-blown corpse after another was interred. Poor old Bumby was amongst them, but it did not pay to dwell on identities. There would doubtless be many more friends gone before the war was over. Whilst his natives dug, so the Boers instructed theirs likewise, both sides eyeing each other suspiciously, neither inclined to talk.

Later though, with the bodies underground, a British officer called a greeting to a gnarled old Boer, extending a leather wallet of tobacco, this encouraging other bitter foes to sidle closer, and eventually they came together in conversation.

They were an undisciplined lot, thought Probyn watching them, not yet ready to make the move himself, their clothes those of peasants rather than soldiers. Young or old they seemed to treat each other as equals, looking to no one for authority. At the sound of honking, Probyn lifted his eyes to see a skein of geese and watched them for a while, wishing he could fly away himself. It struck him suddenly that it was his father who had taught him how to identify geese from their V formation flight, this in turn sparking remembrance of other talents his father had conveyed. He thought of his own unborn child and wondered whether he would be around to teach it things.

'This is my family!' A filthy walnut-coloured hand interrupted his reverie, thrusting a photograph under his nose.

Startled, Probyn glanced at the speaker who was somewhat younger than himself, then his equally filthy fingers came out to hold the snap. 'Very nice. Your son? He's very like you.' He produced his own photograph of Grace and as the Boer looked at it, he took the opportunity to study his enemy at close quarters, envying his broad-brimmed headgear that was more suited to the climate than his own.

With the brim of the hat pinned up at one side, he could see that the young man's hair was the colour of straw, whilst his wispy beard was almost ginger. His eyes were deep-set and determined and his skin like soft kid leather.

'No children?' The slits of eyes looked up from the photograph.

'One on the way,' Probyn told him proudly. Grouped around him, Boer and British were sharing similar moments, eagerly filling pipes from an adversary's tobacco pouch. For the moment the enemy seemed not very different to himself.

But then came the reminder of why he disliked them so much. The tanned finger tapped Grace's photograph. 'She is pretty, but not so pretty as mine, I think.'

Insulted, Probyn retrieved the snap, wanting to tell the boaster that his wife had a head like a turnip, but had never been one to make such derogatory statement. 'She'll do for me,' he said, and turned away to seek a more pleasant conversation partner.

'They can't bloody help themselves, can they?' he muttered in an aside to Private Snowball. 'Always trying to out-do you.' But in fairness he had to admit that the British boys were doing their share of this, unlike him seeming to take great pleasure in the rivalry and insults.

'Why don't you just give up now so we can all go home?' asked an English voice, cheerfully impudent. 'We're bound to beat you.'

'We will never give up, *rooineck*,' came the answer.

Probyn feared this was not mere bravado. Despite not liking the Boers as a race he had been forced by events to admire their guile and courage. Spotting a youngster standing alone, he wandered across the grass to talk to him.

'Hello.'

The young man glanced up at him, a look of undiluted hatred in his eyes. 'God rot your teeth,' came the Irish mutter.

Taken aback, Probyn stared into the twisted face for a brief second, then wasted no further time and wheeled away.

Intending to make his way to his tent, he passed another who explained, 'The English shot his father.'

He paused and turned to the speaker. 'You're not Dutch.'

'How very perspicacious,' replied the British Uitlander.

Probyn was still angry over the Irishman. 'Then what are you doing with this lot?'

'Because I hate the meddlers in Downing Street who tell us how to run our country and have never been here.'

'But old Kruger won't even grant you the vote!' scoffed Probyn. 'That's what we're fighting for, to get you it.'

'But then you'd give it to the kaffirs too,' came the reply.

Probyn was too tired to argue, and merely shook his head. 'I don't understand you people.'

The other smiled, not in any way mocking. 'And that, my friend, is why we are at war.'

Probyn sighed and nodded and stood there for a while, saying nothing, whilst the other smoked his pipe. The crickets had begun to chirp. The sky was mottled with rose and the breeze carried the fragrance of mimosa. It must surely be time for the armistice to end, and indeed it soon appeared to be so, for the Boers began casually to withdraw into the dusk.

Saying goodbye to the Uitlander, Probyn moved off too, as he did so catching sight of the one to whom he had originally spoken.

'Good luck,' called the young Boer as he departed for his lair.

'Thanks but we don't need it,' volleyed Probyn, his voice joined by cheers.

The tanned face creased in an arrogant smile, his eyes had a fanatical shine to them like two bright blue sapphires. 'Remember Majuba, Khakis, it is almost the anniversary!' And so saying the rag-tag army withdrew to their lair on the hill.

The artillery began again at ten o'clock that evening, from when recommenced the battle for Pieters Hill.

But Probyn was to be informed that there would be an altered plan of attack to the one which had decimated his ranks. On the following night the pontoon was taken up and relaid at a new site and it was here at the end of a five and a half hour march that the York and Lancasters crossed the Tugela yet again at midday on Tuesday and bivouacked with the 11th Brigade at the foot of the high and precipitous hills which rose abruptly from the river bank.

Before sending his troops into action, General Buller assembled them for a short address. After the last debacle they were warned to ignore all bugle calls to Retire or Cease Fire and also white flags which the Boers had employed as trickery. There would be no withdrawal this time and no quarter given. There was then a more poignant note. 'Now as most of you will be acutely aware, today is the anniversary of Majuba . . .'

Amongst the apprehensive khaki mass, Probyn looked briefly at his boots, not wanting to be reminded of this infamous defeat, especially after suffering so many of his own these last two months.

'But that was a long, long time ago, and I must urge you to put it from your minds. For those of you who find that too hard a task, then I have a piece of news which should help to raise your spirits considerably: I have just heard that General Piet Cronje has surrendered with his army of eleven hundred men at Paardeberg.'

An enormous cheer arose, echoing around the kopjes, the mood at once transformed, Private Mutt lending his bark to the din then whizzing around and around after his own tail.

'That's right, let the Boers hear it!' rallied the General to even louder cheers.

And Probyn raised his voice to the heavens too, his heart soaring with it, but for him the rest of the general's speech was a blur, that one sentence imprinted on his heart and helping to restore his enthusiasm for the crucial task ahead. When the order came to advance he was carried forth on a wave of renewed determination.

In companies the regiment moved off, the left half being under Lieutenant-Colonel Kirkpatrick, the right under Major Lousada whom Probyn had known and respected since his arrival as a raw recruit at the depot almost ten years ago. Under cover of heavy artillery fire which pounded and churned the slopes ahead, he and the rest followed their commander in single file along the edge of the river, through a thicket of aloes and jagged red boulders where butterflies abounded, a gradual ascent being made over rocks and scree until they had almost reached the railway line. Here the major crouched to take stock.

There was a party of Boers strongly entrenched on a small kopje some five hundred yards away, with an open stretch of ground between them. The major blew his whistle and with a tremendous cheer the first company spilt over the crest, immediately coming in for heavy fire and many of them went down, but their places were to be taken by others, in their hundreds they came like a stone wall towards the enemy trench. Ignoring the *zippp* of bullets that peppered the ground all around them and filled the air with a huge hornet whine, Probyn and his comrades went streaming across the trampled grass, yelling their intention as they launched themselves upon the enemy, overrunning his lines with bayonets, jabbing and slaying, wreaking vengeance for the slaughter at Spion Kop, until the panicked Boers came tumbling out of their trenches waving white flags and the kopje was taken. There was to be no stopping now, no disheartening turning back. Almost opposite Pieters Hill, Probyn and his comrades wasted no time in scaling the heights, raked by sharp fire and shells bursting all around them, the air a choking cloud of gunsmoke, but on they pushed, wave after wave the long lines of infantry went shinning up the hill, calling to the Boer in their north country burr – 'Majuba! Majuba!' – and racing for the summit, finally, gloriously, to take Pieters Hill.

There were ten wounded but to an exhilarated Probyn the victory was worth it. All his faith in General Buller had been repaid. No more would they be sent splashing back across the Tugela: the key to Ladysmith was well and truly won, now to be endorsed by a triumphant announcement from their commander. 'Not Majuba Day, boys – Ladysmith Day!' And a rousing cheer went up, ricocheting off the towering red crags to deal the retreating Boer a parting shot.

Such cries of victory were to be heard throughout that day and on into the next, surpassed by even louder cheers when the news came across the mimosa flats that General Buller had entered Ladysmith. But the eclipsing moment was yet to come, that moment for which every man had strived so long: the triumphal march through town. The fact that it was a miserable looking town could not detract from the ideal for which they had fought and suffered, represented in the hordes that came out to salute them. Between battered rows of tin-roofed houses marched the victorious parade to an eruption of wild cheering from the delirious throng, those courageous defenders with set, dogged faces, heroes every one, even the wounded coming out of hospital to applaud their general, and once more Probyn felt tingling through his soldier's heart the rush of pride that had suffered so many blows of late. No more the laughing stock of lesser beings, he and his doughty Young and Lovelies had helped to restore the honour of the glorious British Empire.

19

After three days at Ladysmith the regiment entrained for Pietermaritzburg, but were to be there less than three weeks. Though the siege had been raised the contest for South Africa was by no means over and with reports of renewed Boer aggression around Ladysmith orders came for Probyn and his fellows to strike tents, pack kit and return immediately.

Yet when they did it transpired that there was to be little action other than trench-digging that first week, the Boers, as was their talent, having disappeared into thin air. There was, however, still much to contemplate. Along with the boxes of chocolates from the Queen they were presented with the sombre news that General Woodgate had finally died from his wounds at Mooi River. To Sergeant Kilmaster the general's demise came to symbolize the whole drawn-out nature of the war. It was, he feared, to be a long, lingering affair.

That first week, camped at Surprise Hill to the north of Ladysmith, was to pass quietly. From the top of the hill was a superb view looking south and west over Spion Kop right across to the Drakensberg and north as far as the Biggarsberg Mountains, reminding him of what he loved about South Africa.

But there were other things he did not love: the Australian troops who were tall and tanned and undisciplined, whose idea of a joke was to gallop their horses through the British camp knocking down tents and causing general mayhem; the constant moving about from place to place, responding to commando raids upon the native population whose kraals were burned and looted in retaliation for helping the British; the march, march, marching over rough grassland, soft sand, shingle, rock, up hills and over spruits while an army of vermin crawled over them; the clothes that were falling apart; the Boer shell that would unexpectedly land in the middle of parade, sending them all scattering to unpeg tents that had only just been erected, the flies that crawled over one's food, the tepid water, the long days and cold nights that brought on aches and pains, the dread of enteric that was rife; the murmur of the wind over the mealie fields that had them leaping for their rifles thinking there was to be an attack . . . he just wanted to go home.

And yet for all this he could not help but admire the enemy who kept him here. Self-reliant, formidable, brave, cunning, excellent horsemen, and with no officer to accuse them of desertion they could leave off the fighting for a while to go and plant their crops. Even with their leaders capitulating the stubborn Boers held on. After the surrender of General Cronje, an offer had come from Presidents Kruger and Steyn to make peace, though only on terms of keeping their independence. This was anathema to the British government which had stated its intention to annex the former republics to the Empire. Such news was music to Probyn's ears. Even so, the Boers were to continue the struggle in guerrilla fashion.

Came the first nip of African frost and still there was no hint that the war was nearing an end, though the British were making great progress and had now forced their way into the Transvaal.

The summit of the Drakensberg wore a mantle of snow. June passed and then July. The letters from home became more urgent. Had he not promised he would be here to see his child born? asked Grace.

Well, there was no chance of that, even if he were to go now.

How much longer would it go on? she asked also. As if he could tell her.

He missed Grace dreadfully, not just because he loved her but the sheer physical ache produced by the absence of sexual contact. For some, celibacy proved no hardship; Sergeant Kilmaster was not of that ilk. Such nagging emptiness began to remind him of his time on St Helena. But there would not be another Emily here. As the man responsible for sending out a patrol every night to prevent Tommies consorting with the native women for fear it would lower their dignity in the eyes of the Dutch, he could not be so hypocritical as to submit to his own weakness. But, dear Lord, the thought of it almost drove him mad.

By the end of August with his child now surely born, he himself remained atop an isolated hill, the only thing to look forward to being the next delivery of tinned rations and biscuits. Such lack of food was now exacerbated by the numerous surrenders from outlying districts, those giving themselves up half-starved, their horses bags of bones for all the grass was dry and burnt up. Presented with such pitiful spectres what could one do but share the meagre rations with them.

That the receivers' attitude had not been one of total appreciation, rankled with the giver. 'You people should be grateful we give you anything at all!' Probyn was goaded into retorting to a Boer farmer who bitterly complained about the meanness of his family's ration.

'Grateful?' The man turned on him, outrage in his blue eyes. 'You are not the only one to count himself a loyal subject of the Crown.' And from the cart containing all his worldly goods he tugged a picture of the Queen which he brandished under the sergeant's nose.

Thus, rendered momentarily dumb, Probyn was given time to digest this salutary lesson: the distinct enmities that had been present in his mind at the outbreak of hostilities now becoming blurred. There were no clear-cut lines in this war. Dutch, British and African, the horrors were equally distributed.

The misery went on, dust storms filling the tents with grit, driving mist and cold winds. Probyn's moustache through lack of wax hung limp and walrus-like, his clothes and boots in tatters – which made it all the more fantastic to receive the order to entrain for Durban with an outgoing draft of those whose time had almost expired; he was to go home!

But the best news of all was almost to elude the delighted sergeant as he prepared to march off to the station. A backlog of mail arrived, amongst it the letter he had been awaiting for weeks. Ripping it open, his fingers fumbling with excitement, he read that his wife had given birth to a son in July, a few days short of his own birthday.

Thence, all the hardships merged into nothing as he bestowed those around him with a wide grin, his announcement quiet but proud. 'Eh, I'm a dad!'

And a little cheer went up to mark the occasion, sending him on his way with a buoyant heart.

By the time he arrived home his child was almost three months old. Fascinated by the tiny auburn-fuzzed creature, Probyn was hardly able to take his eyes off him in those first few days, voicing regret to Grace that he had missed his entry to the world.

'Never mind.' She smiled up at him happily from the fireside rug where she sat bathing the infant, including the baby in their conversation. 'At least we've got you here for the christening, haven't we, Clemmie? I thought he might be frightened of his father when the two of you finally met but he never batted an eyelid did he?'

'Ah well, he's the son of a soldier,' came the proud reply. 'He's got backbone.'

'Whoops! A wobbly backbone,' laughed Grace as the baby's buttocks slipped from under him in the bath.

Momentarily, Probyn removed his attention from the baby to look at his wife, under that heavy-lidded seductive gaze becoming instantly aroused. She was if anything even lovelier since the birth of their child. Upon homecoming, his first instinct after inspecting the baby had been to seize her and take her up to bed. He had done so many times since and wanted to do it again now, but she was otherwise involved. Turning his eyes back to the baby, he smiled. 'I like the names you've chosen.' She had called him Clement Michael, the second being after her father. 'Would it be too much if I added another?'

'Of course not!' cried Grace, adoration in her eyes. It was obvious that having a baby had displaced none of her bridal feelings for Probyn. 'I only named him because you weren't here.'

'Does Clement Michael Buller sound all right?' His eyes glanced at her swollen breasts.

'Very noble!' Out of love for her husband Grace hid her aversion well, knowing how Probyn admired his famous general.

Lifting the baby from the bath she proceeded to dry him, singing to him as she dabbed and dusted. 'Ta-ra-ra-boom-de-ay! Ta-ra-ra-boom-de-ay! He likes that one, don't you, Clemmie?' She sang again, every time she came to the *boom* planting a kiss on the baby's bottom which he appeared to delight in.

Probyn delighted too in watching the tender scene.

'Feel his little heart!' Grace held out the tiny body, instructing Probyn to lay his palm against its chest.

Doing so, the father voiced his wonderment. 'Ooh aye, it's pumping away there like a little piston! Better wrap him up now though or he'll get cold.' It was teeming with rain outside. 'Does Aunt Kit know he's born? I didn't receive a word from her while I was in Africa.'

Grace shook her head, presenting a carefree air but underneath quite hurt. 'Me neither. Not a word nor a visit. So I assumed she wasn't interested in hearing about Clemmie and didn't bother informing her.'

Probyn felt hurt too. 'Aye, blow her if she's going to be like that.'

A knock came at the door.

'Oh, who's this come to disturb us?' Grace asked the red-headed baby, then passed him to her husband. 'Here, hold Clemmie!' She went to admit the caller.

Balancing his tiny son on his knee, the proud father jiggled him up and down, showing no awkwardness and obviously enjoying himself, which drew comment as the visitor was admitted.

'Eh, I see you've got him trained!' exclaimed the neighbour, another sergeant's wife. Then at Probyn's cool smile she realized she might be interrupting his homecoming and said hurriedly to Grace, 'Sorry to bother you both, I just wondered if you've been able to –'

'It's done, love!' Grace rushed off and returned with a parcel, handing it to the visitor with a broad smile.

'Eh, you're a good lass!' The recipient beamed. 'How much do I owe you?'

'Oh not a thing – no, I wouldn't dream of it!' Grace refused all offers.

'By, I hope you know what a good un you've got here, Sergeant Kilmaster!' called the woman to Probyn as she left.

'I do,' he answered, though much bemused.

''Twas just some mending I did for her,' explained Grace. About to close the door she let out a cry of ecstasy. 'Oh, come and look at the rainbow! Bring the baby. Oh look, look! Isn't it gorgeous?'

And, carrying his son, a smiling Probyn came to look, sharing Grace's love of simple things and thinking that his dear wife's face was a picture in itself and how lucky he was to have her.

Now that his father was safely home the baby's christening was arranged for that Sunday afternoon, attended by Grace's relatives, her friend Charlotte who was to be godmother and a few soldiers. Probyn chose not to invite Kit, remembering the distaste she had shown at his wedding upon having to enter a Catholic church. Though he himself had converted to his wife's religion it had only been done for her sake, and it was with some self-consciousness that he marched to Mass at Church Parade and later to the baptism. He doubted that he would ever make a good Catholic, but if all this embarrassing genuflection kept Grace happy then he would have achieved his aim.

The absence of his own relatives was of little consequence to him, for he had replaced his sisters with Grace's who were much kinder to him, as was Charlotte who was indeed like another sister to his wife and in the short time they had been acquainted he had come to share Grace's affection for her. As for his stepmother, he had not been in contact with her since the day he had met Grace, and though he sometimes thought about her, intending to write and check on her health, this invariably slipped his memory.

On prolonged leave after his spell on the war front, he spent the first week of it helping his wife about the house, for Grace seemed to find it hard to adjust in having him here, her attendance of the baby often causing her to be late in the serving of meals – not to mention that soldiers' wives kept popping in to beg a favour from this charitable body.

'Tell you what, why don't I cook dinner this week?' he said watching her hurry about trying to answer both his needs and the crying babe's. 'Seems daft me having a Master Cook's certificate and not putting it to good use. You see to the lad, I'll see to us.'

'I can see to all of us.' Though her face did not show it Grace was profoundly insulted, taking his comment as a slur on her abilities.

But he was insistent on helping. 'I can't sit here and watch while the bairn runs you ragged. No more arguing, I'm doing it.' And he began by peeling the potatoes, leaving his deeply hurt wife with no option but to smile.

The fortnight that followed was to pass similarly, Probyn taking it upon himself to do all the cooking and Grace having to pass compliments on his prowess when she really felt like screaming. It was all she could do to persuade him to leave the house for an hour with the excuse that he should be out enjoying his leave before winter set in.

'Then come with me!' he bade her, reaching for her coat. 'We'll go into York, have a walk round the walls.'

Grace stalled him. 'I can't be out that long, Clemmie will want feeding in a while, but you go. Go on!' She gave him an affectionate push. 'Enjoy yourself. I'll still be here when you get back.' And she gave a sigh of relief as he finally complied.

It was odd, thought Probyn, as he wandered around the leaf-strewn city walls in the autumn sunshine, how accustomed one became to the noise of battle and how deathly quiet was England in comparison. Odd, too, that despite the horrors he still occasionally found himself homesick for Africa. That was the trouble with furlough. It gave one too much time to think.

Reaching the end of this stretch of wall he came down the worn stone staircase and, missing Grace and Clemmie, made his way back to the hansom cab rank.

A street sweeper was brushing up the leaves and tipping them into a cart. He was halfway past the man when he realized who it was.

'Felix?'

Matching the speaker's frown, the sweeper looked long and hard at him before breaking into a rapid response. 'AchiftisntyoungPa!' And his hand shot out to grasp the other's. 'Whdefecknhellreyedoinhere?'

'More to the point, what are you doing here?' asked Probyn, marvelling at his own interpretative skills.

'Ah sure, I left Ponty a while back. Answered an advert for a job here, but lost that and now I'm doing this. Listen, d'ye remember when ...?' And this sparked a flurry of reminiscences with the battered seashell of a face hardly drawing breath, obviously eager to relive his army days, his old cot-mate being forced to stand there and grin and nod as each instance was excitedly recounted, gaining no enjoyment but embarrassed and sad for this pathetic display and deeming it a sorry ending for an old soldier.

After ten minutes or so, Felix's attitude suddenly changed and he faltered mid-stream, a strange look coming into his eye. 'Ah well now, I'd better not be keeping you, nor must I be shirking my task. It's been good seeing you, Pa.' And he made ready his broom.

He knows, thought Probyn with a jolt, he can tell what I'm thinking, and his own cheeks were momentarily overtaken by the kind of burning display he had not suffered since boyhood. Trying to convey pleasure at having run into his old friend, he patted the other's shoulder then backed away. 'Yes, we'll have to have a drink together some time. Look after yourself, Felix!' And with that he turned his back and hurried home.

Thankful for the few hours respite, and fully restored to cheeriness, Grace had begun to feel almost guilty at wanting to be rid of the man she loved and had ached to be with for the past nine months. When Probyn came through the door she launched herself at him, hugging and kissing him as if he had been away another nine months instead of just an afternoon.

Laughing, he asked what he had done to deserve this.

'Oh, I just feel so lucky to have you!' Face gleaming like a beacon, Grace squashed his cheeks between her cool hands then led him to a chair. 'You've spent all your holiday doing work that should by rights be mine. Sit there and I'll cook you a nice tea. No arguing!' She forestalled him. 'Clemmie's asleep, I've nothing else to see to.'

Obeying, he sat back to watch, a beneficent smile under his moustache.

However, she appeared to be having difficulty in finding something. 'Where's the blessed potato peeler?' She was opening and shutting drawers and frowning.

'Ah, I forgot to say!' Probyn shoved himself from the armchair. 'While I've been doing the cooking this week I've shifted everything round.' He began to point out the different utensils. 'See, if you put that here it makes more sense than where you used to have it, then it's nearer to hand. Felix Lennon taught me there was always an easy way, always a way you could save time and shoe leather. Much better now isn't it?'

'Oh yes,' agreed Grace brightly, wondering how she could sound so convincing, only the fact that she loved him so much barring her from screaming in frustration. He looked so delighted with himself.

'Then when I go back on duty life'll be a lot easier for you!'

In more ways than one, sighed Grace to herself.

Having become rather edgy towards the end of his furlough, Probyn was glad to return to soldiering, though he felt sorry for Grace who would miss his help around the home. Still, his assistance during those few weeks had provided her with a good foundation and he could happily leave her knowing she would no longer be torn between tending the baby and getting her husband's dinner ready on time.

With plenty of new recruits to knock into shape for South Africa, he himself had enough to concern him throughout the autumn months and by the time Christmas drew near he was rather looking forward to another rest.

However, there were sorrowful elements to it. 'This is the first Christmas I haven't had an invitation,' he told Grace upon receipt of a letter from Aunt Kit who explained that if she invited him the others would not come and so it would not be very festive – but perhaps another time, she added. He treated the news with indifference. 'Can't say I'm bothered. I must be getting old.' He smiled at Grace. 'Eh dear, another two and a half years and I'll be thirty.'

Grace smiled back, but wished he would not keep reminding her of the difference in their ages. She herself was not even twenty. 'Never mind, our Ellen's invited us to eat with them.'

'Has she?' He became enthusiastic. 'I shall look forward to that.'

Never had Probyn been made to realize how austere his own Christmases had been until he witnessed its celebration in an Irish household. Oh, they might none of them have ever been to Ireland but that did not put a cork on Celtic emotions. Being amongst them made Aunt Kit's parties seem like life in a closed order. After the meal came roisterous singing in which he was forced to participate, then followed a fight between two of Grace's cousins, a no punches pulled hammer and tongs of a ding-dong in which blood was drawn before the antagonists were finally made to kiss and make up and all parted the best of friends at the end of the afternoon as if nothing had happened. Amazed at how such violence could be so brushed aside and normally hating such displays of abandon, a dazed Probyn conveyed his admiration none the less, wishing that his own relatives could be so forgiving.

1901 did not start well, being only three weeks old when the Queen died, prompting an interval of mourning not only in the populace but the regiment too.

To add to the awful weather, heavy snowstorms marking the first three months of the year, there was further despondency on the war front. Peace talks in South Africa had failed to end hostilities. The Boer still continued his dirty method of fighting, refusing to make war like a gentleman, his audacious guerrilla raids even taking him into Cape Colony, though this was more of a nuisance than an invasion, Probyn told his wife. Somewhat removed from the war, he had taken to following its progress by means of a map from the *Daily Mail*, every week moving the lines of little Union Jacks to show the British position and including Clement in his routine, even though the child was less than a year old.

Grace tried to show an interest over these sessions too, though her concern was more at the result of South African weather on her husband. Since he had come home Probyn had suffered from rheumatism in his legs, especially in the cold damp slush that followed the regular snowstorms. He hardly ever complained but she could see the discomfort in his face.

'Look at you sitting there squirming and saying not a word,' she reproved him this evening. 'Swivel round in your chair, let me rub your legs.'

'I won't argue.' Clemmie still on his knee, he put the map aside and shuffled around to give Grace access. Whereby she unwrapped his puttees, tugged up his trousers and began to massage his stocky calves, her hands gentle and loving.

He closed his eyes as if in ecstasy. 'Eh, this is luxury, Clemmie. Make sure you find yourself a wife like your dear mother.' A knock interrupted his enjoyment then. 'Oh, pizzle-pozzle!'

Grace left off to answer the door, whence a lot of whispering ensued. When his wife temporarily came back into the room and seized her purse, Probyn looked at her questioningly, though she did not immediately explain. Only after effusive thanks were given and the door closed did she come back to say, 'It was just Private Rowland's wife. The poor soul, her mother's died and they're running a bit short what with the funeral –'

'So you lent her some.' During the past year Probyn had seen frequent examples of his wife's generosity.

'She'll give me it back!' A slight note of reproof for his lack of charity, but a ruffle of his hair to show she did not mean it. 'I couldn't see them struggle. Now, where was I?' Grace sat down at his feet and began to knead his aching muscles again. 'You know, I've been thinking –'

'That's dangerous, Clemmie,' he joked to the baby.

'You haven't seen your Aunt Kit for ages and the two of you used to be so close. Maybe we should invite her for dinner one Sunday, once all this slush has gone.'

'If you want.' Eyes closed in rapture at the massage, Probyn hardly seemed to care; for him there was sufficient family here.

Grace smiled. 'I'll drop her a line.'

'But I don't want you making lots of work for yourself. She's my aunt, I'll cook the dinner.'

Piqued, Grace faltered in her rubbing and kneading. But when Probyn opened one eye to investigate why she had stopped, she merely gave a tight smile and continued her ministrations. But it did not stop her thinking. Something must be done about this.

In fact Grace did not send her invitation for another month, until she was certain there would be no further snowfall and the bulbs had started to push their heads through the sodden earth. Expecting to receive some excuse from Kit to say she could not come, Probyn was therefore surprised upon receipt of her acceptance.

It was even nicer when Kit turned up in the flesh with her gigantic husband and fast-growing son, ostentatiously dressed as ever, behaving the same as he had always known her, making a beeline for Clemmie and taking him on her lap as she had done with Probyn in his infancy.

'Oh, little gingernut!' she hugged the little boy who did not seem to be overwhelmed by the fuss and smiled obligingly. 'Just like his father.'

The child's mother issued a gracious smile, knowing there was no malignancy in the remark. Besides, Clemmie was like his father.

'And look at you!' Kit turned to Probyn who was still dressed the way he had been for church, her eyes flitting over the scarlet tunic with its gleaming white cuffs and piping, its white stand-up collar on either side of which was a shiny brass badge of a tiger and a rose, brass Y's and L's on his white shoulder epaulettes, but her eyes drawn most of all to the three lace chevrons on his arm. 'Sergeant Kilmaster!'

Laughing, her nephew displayed suitable modesty, whereupon Kit finally deigned to address his wife, taking in the plain white blouse and brown skirt. 'You're looking well, Grace.'

'I am, thank you. And yourself?'

'Oh yes, we're all fine, aren't we, Worthy?' Kit smiled up at her ox of a husband.

'By heck I nearly didn't recognize Toby!' Probyn was examining the eleven-year-old with amazement. 'He's as tall as me. A few more years and we'll make a cracking soldier of you.'

'You will not!' exclaimed Kit, half laughing, half serious. 'He's not going in the firing line, he's all I've got. Grace knows what I mean, don't you?' The two women shared a mother's smile.

Grace, though, did not feel totally relaxed and in the moments that followed, said awkwardly, 'Well, I'll just go see to the dinner.'

'No you won't!' But she had gone to the kitchen before Probyn could stop her. 'I'm doing the cooking,' he told his guests. 'Sit yourselves at the table, it's almost ready.' And he too dashed off.

'May I help?' Kit handed over Clemmie to his great-uncle and followed her nephew into the hectic atmosphere of the kitchen.

Grace was opening and shutting drawers as if searching for something. Pans bubbled and steamed on the range.

'No, everything's in hand, Aunt!' Probyn was trying to remove a joint of beef from the oven. 'Grace, shift your bum, love, you're in me way!'

'I'm looking for the masher,' came the low reply.

'I've told you, I'll do everything! Go and sit down with our guests.'

Inwardly furious at being ejected from her own kitchen, but

not wanting to cause a scene, Grace forced herself to smile and went with Kit back to the parlour where the meal was duly served.

'Eh, you're a lucky lass to have such a husband!' Kit told Grace, before wading in with her knife and fork, the other guests showing similar relish.

And Grace returned a smiling nod of agreement, wishing that she had never invited them.

After dinner, she tried to escape by washing the pots but Probyn told her to leave them in the sink and he would do them after Aunt Kit and her family had gone. 'Come and sit down, Gobbie, enjoy yourself. It's not often we have guests.'

'I'll just rinse them off so the gravy doesn't stick.' Grace hurried away with a stack of plates.

Kit transported a gravy boat to the kitchen. 'Where shall I put this?'

I know where I'd like you to put it, thought Grace, with her back to the guest, but she threw Kit a smile and said, 'Just leave it there, thank you,' before returning her attention to the sink.

Kit's lips parted in surprise. There had been the glint of tears in Grace's eye, she was sure of it. Taken aback, she was momentarily lost for words and cast her mind back over the last hour, wondering what could have caused such distress. Had it been her fault? She hadn't really wanted to come but Worthy had talked her into it. Perhaps her reluctance had shown on her face. Much as she detested the marriage, she had tried to be civil. Obviously she had failed. Pricked by conscience, she wandered over to stand at Grace's shoulder, wondering how to approach this.

Grace sensed the huge flouncily-clad presence at her side, felt dwarfed by it and wished Kit would go away. Saying nothing, she continued to rinse the plates.

Kit folded her arms under her colossal silken bosom. 'Our Probe seems very happy.'

Grace cleared her throat and stacked the rinsed plates

on the draining board, trying to sound cheerful. 'Yes, he does.'

'Well, I'm not surprised. Who wouldn't be with a nice little family like he's got?' Kit tried to crane her neck to see if she had been mistaken about the tears but Grace kept her face averted.

Only when the diminutive figure snatched a handkerchief from her apron and blew her nose did Kit suspect she had been right. 'Are you crying?'

'It's nothing! I've just got a cold.' Grace dashed her eyes and put the handkerchief away.

A bolt of guilt assailed Kit. 'I'm right sorry if I wasn't very welcoming to you, I've regretted –'

'It's not you,' rushed Grace.

'Then what is it – oh, lass, what's wrong?' Kit saw the tears well up again and her heart went out to the young wife.

Grace was angry with herself for airing her marital troubles before an outsider. 'I'm just being silly. I'm sure nobody else would object if their husband helped around the house.'

A look of understanding flooded Kit's face as she recalled the previous scene in the kitchen. 'Ah, but he's taking too much upon himself? I thought he was a bit bossy, being a sergeant's gone to his head.'

'You mustn't say anything!' Grace wiped her eyes one last time, making certain that all tears were dried. 'He'd be dreadfully hurt.'

'I won't say a word,' promised Kit. 'But you wouldn't object if I make a few hints surely?'

Grace managed to issue a damp chuckle. 'Then I hope you'll have more luck than me. Probe doesn't get hints. Anyway, thanks for listening, I'm sure I'll get over it. Go sit down and I'll fetch us all a cup of tea.'

Kit pressed Grace's arm, a genuine gesture, then returned to the parlour.

'What's that wife of mine doing in there?' asked Probyn happily, jiggling Clemmie on his lap. 'I hope she hasn't started the washing-up. She puts all the do-dahs in the wrong place.'

'She's just making a pot of tea.' Kit sat down and smoothed her silken lap.

'I'll go do that!'

She grabbed his sleeve, preventing him from rising. 'Leave the lass something to do! You've been whizzing around like a bluebottle since we arrived.'

'I don't mind!' Probyn handed the baby to his aunt and rose.

'I know what you're doing,' said Kit, taking possession of Clemmie. 'You don't want to be like your father who did nothing at all.'

Stopped in his tracks, he marvelled at Kit's insight.

'But nobody expects you to drive yourself into the ground,' added his aunt. 'Least of all your wife. I'm sure she can't appreciate all the interference.'

Probyn gave a breezy smile. 'Nay, Gobbie doesn't mind!' And he went off to the kitchen, blind to all hints.

'Well, I tried,' sighed Kit to her bemused husband.

Later, she was to whisper the same thing to Grace as the two men brought the cart around to the door. Grace brushed the matter aside and said it didn't matter, somewhat guilty now that she had complained.

'Well, it's nice that we're friends at least,' murmured Kit, gripping the other's hand. 'We are friends, aren't we?'

'Oh surely,' smiled Grace and returned the fond grip, though she still found the huge woman daunting.

Probyn's aunt made her way to the cart. 'Say goodbye to Clemmie for me.' The child was having an afternoon nap.

It took both men to get the overweight Kit into the vehicle, Probyn and Toby to push from the rear, Worthy to pull from his driving seat. Then it was all waves and smiles as they rolled out of the barrack gates.

It was a lovely, crisp, sunny afternoon and even after the

visitors had disappeared onto the main road Probyn and Grace remained for a moment to enjoy it.

As often happened due to his long terms in the southern hemisphere, the position of the sun in the sky still confused Probyn. He held his face to its light, closed his eyes and soaked up the warmth.

Grace too was enjoying the moment. 'Spring's in the air,' she murmured.

'Aye, almost September,' came the absent reply.

She laughed. 'No it's April. My birthday next week remember?'

'Oh sorry!' he laughed. 'I was back in Africa for a moment.'

Yes, you're always far away, thought Grace wistfully, and was first to turn indoors.

He followed her, tweaking his moustache and sounding cheerful. 'Aunt Kit seemed a lot more well-disposed towards you.'

Grace went to the kitchen. 'Yes, we appear to have come to an understanding.'

'Oh, that's good!' He steered her away from the sink. 'I'll do that, you go and sit down in the parlour.'

Sighing, Grace did as she was told and picked up some sewing.

Later, the washing-up done, Probyn fell into the chair opposite and watched her for a while, smiling in contentment, before he realized that the garment she worked upon was very tiny and said expectantly, 'Eh, you're not smittled again are you?'

She returned his smile, but there was sadness in it. 'No it's a shroud for Sergeant Atkinson's little girl.'

He lost some of his verve, expressing sorrow. But soon he was smiling again. 'Oh well, I don't suppose it'll be long before Clemmie has a brother or sister.'

She looked up briefly from her sewing to share his fond grin.

Those hooded eyes could always stir him. Enjoying a

moment's imaginary passion, Probyn then picked up the Sunday newspaper he had not had time to finish that morning.

'It was nice Clemmie being born with the new century,' said Grace. 'He'll always feel special.'

Probyn spoke without taking his eye from the page. 'Some folk are still arguing that the new century didn't begin till this year. Daft beggars, nothing better to do.' He read for a while longer before exploding, 'And if I see *fin de siècle* mentioned in this blessed newspaper one more time I'll rip it to shreds! Blinking journalists, once they latch onto a word or phrase they can't write a paragraph without using it.'

Grace laughed. Then both fell silent, she to sew and he to read.

He had not realized he had fallen asleep until a noise woke him. Grace's chair was empty. Stretching, he was about to go and see where she was when she poked her head around the door. 'Sorry, I dropped a pan. Hope it didn't make you jump?'

'What are you doing in there?' Ever keen to be in her presence, he went to join her in the kitchen.

'Just getting things done while Clemmie's asleep, sorting the washing out for tomorrow.' She was separating clothes into piles.

Probyn stood to watch her, then, noticing that a utensil was not where he had hung it, began to change things around, straightening and tidying. Grace held her tongue.

A knock came at the door. Probyn went to answer it, returning to say rather tersely, 'It's for you – another one wanting your services.'

Grace went off, returning a few moments later.

'What did she want?' asked Probyn, still rearranging articles in the kitchen.

'Oh, I promised to lend a hand with –'

'Another hand! How many hands do those swaddies' wives think you've got?'

'I don't mind,' said Grace tightly.

'Well, I do!' he complained. 'I'm not having it, Grace. Things have got to change around here.'

'You're damned right they have!'

Startled, he fixed his eyes on the potato peeler that Grace had grabbed and was now directing at him with menace.

Her expression was furious – almost maniacal. 'I'm sick to death of this house being run like a military operation! *That's* your area out there!' She wagged the utensil at the parade ground, then made a stabbing gesture at the kitchen floor. 'In here is my domain and I'll be the one who says what goes!'

Gasping at the audacity of this, he finally found his tongue. 'I'm only trying to look after you!'

'I don't need looking after!' she raged at him. 'I'm not a child!'

'I didn't say you were! If this is all the thanks I get for –' he broke off as she seized a potato and aimed it at his head.

Ducking quickly, he swore at her, 'You're bloody mad!' And he marched out, his own face as red with fury as her own, hearing as he went another potato hit the woodwork.

Breast rising and falling under the crisp white pinafore, Grace swore too, hoping that the din had not woken the baby. How stupid of her to let it build up like this! What if he didn't come back?

Probyn had no intention of coming back, marching directly to the sergeants' mess. Here, he glanced into the carpeted sitting room, seeking out an armchair, but all were taken. The billiard table was occupied too. He stood there indecisively for a moment, clenching and unclenching his fists and looking at the military pictures on the wall. Then, catching sight of his angry face in the mirror over the fireplace, he made his way to one of the small tables, calling for the waiter to fetch him a cup of tea and a Sunday newspaper, behind which he was to sulk for the next half an hour until he realized that he had not digested a word and slapped the paper down with a sigh.

The ungrateful . . . ! What woman in her right mind would turn down the offer of help from her husband? Not many, he'd be bound. There weren't that many men who would put themselves out in such a fashion. His mind racing with angry thoughts, he tried eventually to put these aside, to see it from Grace's point of view, but he couldn't. Try as he might, he just could not understand her.

'Mind if I join you?' He looked up as another sergeant presented himself at the table.

Shaking his head, he indicated for the man to sit down. 'Have this if you like.' He pushed the newspaper across the tablecloth in the hope that the other would leave him alone.

'Thanks, I've read it.' His fellow sergeant obviously preferred to talk, for he was to bend Probyn's ear for the next fifteen minutes, during which the recipient hardly heard a word, consumed by his own dilemma.

He had shot himself in the foot by walking out, would have to go home some time, but was damned if he was going to be the one to say sorry.

The man who had been speaking to him was mumbling something. 'Major's here.'

Glancing up, Probyn noticed that the RSM had entered the mess and upon this sight he swiftly rectified his tardiness, joining the others on their feet to evince respect for this absolute master, before sitting down again to brood.

As the man beside him droned on, he simply nodding, Probyn finally began to see the situation more clearly. He had totally forgotten in all this that, despite being a wife and a mother, Grace was still very young. One could not expect her to view this with the same maturity as did he. He must put aside his own hurt and behave like the disciplined individual he was . . . besides anything else, he could not stay here all afternoon.

Excusing himself to his tablemate, he went home.

An hour had passed since he had stormed out. Grace had gone back to the parlour and resumed her sewing in an attempt to calm herself down, but only succeeding in pricking her thumb and sat there trying to fend off the sporadic bouts of tears.

She had pricked her thumb yet again and was sucking this and wallowing in self-pity when a subdued, disembodied voice asked, 'Is there any more danger of flying spuds?'

She whipped her thumb from her mouth. 'I'm not laughing!'

Fighting his own pride, Probyn entered sheepishly and analysed her angry stance for a moment before muttering, 'I just don't like to see generous bodies like you being put on. I wasn't trying to throw my weight about.'

Grace had not finished scolding. In fact after being compliant for so long she seemed to have acquired a relish for rebellion, stalking up to place her trembling little body before him, her face flushed and upset and her dark blue eyes swimming with moisture. 'It's not just what you said! It's what you've been doing ever since you got home, taking my job away from me. You make me feel inadequate!'

He projected shock. 'I never intended to! Believe me, I wouldn't hurt you for the world!' He wanted to hug her but daren't. 'It's just that I always promised myself I'd never treat my wife like a slave as my father did. Even when Mother was at death's door he expected her to run around after him. It's not right!'

Taking her heavy sigh as a sign of mellowing, he made a tentative attempt to hug her which she accepted, though her spine remained unyielding. 'I'm sorry, Grace.'

Grace became more pliant then and melted into his embrace. 'No, no, I'm sorry, Probe. I shouldn't have been so touchy, I know you were only trying to help and I'm glad of it really, it was just –'

'The way I went at it like a bull in a china shop.' Glad that she had admitted it was not wholly his fault he could be magnanimous now, and hugged her more tightly, kissing her and breathing in the scent of her hair. 'Oh, Gobbie, I hate to see you so upset. I swear I won't do it again. To think you've been suffering in silence all these months . . . Well you must never put up with it again! If anything I do makes you angry you must always tell me.'

Blowing her nose, she promised. 'And vice versa.'

'Well, now you come to mention it –' he broke off with a laugh to show he was joking.

They stood hugging for a long time before he made another pacific gesture. 'From now on, you'll be the one to give me orders and I'll carry them out.'

Restored to happiness, Grace turned impish, lifting her tear-mottled but gleeful face to his. 'Right then, Sergeant Kilmaster, I'm ordering you to get up them stairs!'

He was not slow to get her meaning, one blink of those hooded eyes inciting him to press himself against her. 'What about Clemmie? We might wake him up.'

'Then we'll just have to be quiet about it, won't we?' And with that Grace laughingly drove him up to bed.

20

From then on things were much improved between the couple, each being clear as to where their own boundaries lay. Over the following months they continued to learn about each other, for in the two years they had been married they had spent much of it apart. Although acutely aware that her husband had another life besides the one he shared with her and their child, Grace was not prepared for the things he told her in the dark haven of their bed, wanted to cry as, stage by stage, he divulged things she could never have imagined, the true awfulness of battle, the human losses, the guilt over his own barbarity. Yet even more difficult to fathom was his attitude the following morning when, as if all this were forgotten, he embarked with gusto on the life he loved.

Unable to erase such horrors from her mind, and with Probyn's time about to expire at the end of that year, Grace hoped that perhaps he might leave the army and allow them both to have a normal life. Some wives might envy her the good pay and the free accommodation but for Grace this was far outweighed by the risk of her dear husband having to go to war again. Her experience of being parted from him during those nine months had been so miserable, and his feelings appearing to sympathize with her own, she hoped never to repeat such a separation.

But when Probyn did not raise the subject of his exit from the army, she began to fear the worst.

'Might we soon have to find another place to live?' she asked somewhat tentatively as she knelt at his feet trying to rub the ache from his legs after a long day on the parade ground.

'Oh no, I shan't be leaving!' He patted the top of her brown head. 'I've asked permission to complete my service with the colours. So, you're guaranteed a roof for another ten years if that's what you were worried about.'

And Grace smiled as if thankful, though her heart plummeted at the thought of having to share her husband with the army for another decade, the prospect of being parted from him to some foreign war, or even losing him altogether. But never would she ask him to reconsider. Had he not said the army was his life?

The war dragged on throughout 1901, a year that saw Probyn's favourite general, Buller, discredited and sacked for indiscipline, and vilified by the press. General Lord Kitchener, who had succeeded Lord Roberts as commander-in-chief in South Africa, had undergone peace talks with Botha but these had not borne fruit. Nothing, it seemed, could bring the war to an end. Despite the blockhouses and barbed wire the Boer would not be tamed.

The newspapers told of strong agitation from the Cape Dutch on behalf of the annexed republics, told also of concentration camps into which women and children were herded in an attempt to force their menfolk to give in.

Reading such reports, Grace was incredulous. 'This can't surely be true?' Probyn had warned her about the dirty tricks employed by unpatriotic journalists to make out that the British soldier was more brutish than his enemy. 'Could little children really be dying in these places? Can our soldiers really be killing their animals as ruthlessly as they say?'

Probyn admitted he did not like this calculated elimination of anything that might give the Boers succour, but then, 'War is a dirty business, Gobbie, and if they won't give in you've got to do something. And as for us starving them, well, there were many times when me and my lads didn't eat at all either so the Boers don't have it very different to us.'

Grace wondered what she would feel like if it were she and her child who were imprisoned through her husband's deeds, but said nothing, for it would only sound disloyal, though if the situation was true then it was indeed horrible.

Not wanting to think of the children who may be dying, she wondered instead if this year would see an addition to her own family. Now that she had stopped nursing Clemmie the chance had increased that she would fall with another, though so far no happy event had occurred.

Again there was no Yuletide invitation to Kit's but Probyn and his wife saw the reasoning behind it and were not offended. Besides, there was a plethora of O'Briens with whom to spend the festivities and many colourful events at the barracks.

The year turned, this one starting on a more tuneful note than the last, for during the first quarter there came a breakthrough in the war. By the end of May the Boers, giving up all hope that one of the sympathetic foreign powers would come to their aid, finally surrendered.

'I thought you'd be glad!' said Grace, puzzled at her husband's air of thoughtfulness over the news that was plastered across every billboard and newspaper.

'Oh I am!' He gripped her hand. 'It's just . . .' With the signing of peace had come amnesty for the rebel leaders. The republicans were vanquished but the promise of self-government for the Boers loomed large in the peace agreement. How could he begin to explain the way he felt about this, his fear that the rot had begun to creep in, that the Empire for which he fought so hard was starting to be eroded? Yes, the Union Jack might be fluttering over the whole of South Africa, except for a few tiny foreign possessions, but despite being the overall victor British pride had taken a huge pounding during that long affray. 'The Boers have been defeated, Grace, they shouldn't be allowed a say in anything, otherwise it's all been for nothing. All those pals who laid down their lives, all the times we tramped back and forth across that wretched Tugela, being shot at but wouldn't let them get the better of us, and now . . .' He gave a despairing gesture.

Then he looked at her young face, just come of age, and saw that she did not understand, would never understand, and he laughed off his own despondency. 'Listen to me, of course it's a good thing it's over! Far be it from me to put a damper on all the fun there's going to be.'

And there certainly was fun: triumphant marches through the streets, bunting and celebration, Union Jacks everywhere in evidence, soldiers home from the war all tanned and cheerful, arriving in their droves at barracks throughout the country, and to follow this the Coronation of the new King. It certainly was a dynamic year.

Only in the final month was it spoiled by the news that with the war over the 1st Battalion would be going to India, thereby invoking terror in Grace's heart.

'But I've never been out of York!' she told Probyn upon his announcement during tea-time. 'How will I manage?'

'Nay! You don't have to worry.' He suddenly frowned over his bacon sandwich. 'This hasn't got any butter on it.'

Looking vague and anxious, Grace swapped their plates over. 'I knew one of us took butter I just couldn't remember which one – what do you mean I don't have to worry? Of course I'm worried.'

With a smiling shake of head for her absent-mindedness, he explained, 'I mean you don't need to worry because we won't be going. Each time the battalion I'm in gets sent to India I get transferred to the other battalion. It happens every single time. You and me are off to Dover.'

'Nearly as bad!' complained Grace, though not quite so fearful. 'What about my family, and Charlotte? I'll never see any of them.'

'We can come up for visits, it's not the end of the world.'

* * *

Grace seemed to think it was and poured out her heart to Charlotte who luckily chose that weekend to call. Probyn had taken Clemmie to watch a parade, leaving his wife free to air her emotions.

'I suppose I should count myself lucky we've been allowed to remain at York so long, but I don't want to leave everybody, Lottie! I really don't.'

'But do you have to?' Charlotte seemed equally anxious over the parting, her big square face full of woe.

'What choice do I have?' asked Grace helplessly.

'Well, the army might tell Probe where to go but they don't have the right to give you orders. I mean if he were only to be in Dover a short time you could stay up here and . . .'

'Oh, I couldn't do that!' Grace looked shocked at the very suggestion. 'He could be posted there for years and I can't even stand to be away from him for two days.'

Charlotte smiled sadly and nodded, knowing how deep was her friend's love for her husband.

Grace issued a sigh of resignation. 'No, I have to go where Probe goes and he doesn't seem to regard it as that far away. I suppose it isn't to him who's been all over the world.'

Charlotte tutted. 'He's lovely is Probe but I do think he's a bit selfish expecting you to up sticks and move away from everyone you know.'

Grace defended her husband now. 'Well, he can't really help it can he? He has to go where the army tell him to go.'

'No, but he didn't have to sign on for another ten years did he?'

'Oh, I couldn't ask him to give it up, Lottie. The army's his whole life.'

'He's lucky having you,' declared Charlotte. 'I couldn't stand being uprooted like that. Oh, I'm going to miss you!' And she leaned forward to embrace her friend.

'I'm going to miss you too.' Grace fought tears. 'Oh God, and I've got to go through all this again when I break the news to my sisters.'

As feared, it was hard to broach the subject of her imminent departure when she and Probyn gathered with the O'Brien clan at Christmas, to inform them it would be their last for who knew how long.

Grace held off telling her relatives until the end of the afternoon, allowing others to enjoy their Christmas dinner and the afternoon games, before finally taking a deep breath and divulging, 'I've got some news. Me and Probe are off to the Infidel Barracks at Dover –'

'The Citadel!' Probyn laughingly corrected her. 'Mindst it does house a load of infidels I must admit.' But his amusement was lost amid an outpouring of grief as each took their leave of Grace, of such a magnitude that one would think there had been a bereavement.

And indeed for Grace, so close to her sisters, it was a kind of bereavement, over which she was privately to weep many times when her husband was not looking.

Conversely, for Probyn there was to be reunion almost the moment he moved in at Dover. Having seen Grace and the baby settled, he was answering her request to take himself from under her feet and was strolling over to the sergeants' mess when an officer came by, returning his salute but also making friendly announcement.

'Why, Sergeant Kilmaster!' The officer took quick stock of the chevrons before greeting his old servant, 'How jolly to see you!'

'And you too, Major Fitzroy!' Probyn had heard that his old captain was to be commander of his company, and showed pleasure as they now shook hands. 'I heard that you were home from India, sir, and been looking forward to making your acquaintance again.'

'Splendid, splendid!' No mention was made that they had

not parted on the best of terms. 'I wish I could say the same about this dreary weather. I miss India dreadfully.'

Probyn looked up at the grey sky. 'Yes, I rather miss the sunshine too, sir.' Whilst his own tan had faded to a healthy glow, the major looked like a kaffir.

Fitzroy then enquired about Probyn's movements since last they had met, envying his role in the Matabele Relief Force but particularly in the war against the Boers. 'I was awfully disappointed to have been excluded from the show.'

Probyn nodded thoughtfully. 'It was a lot different to fighting the blacks, I can tell you, sir. Yes, a hard job we had.'

'But we British did it,' came Fitzroy's encouraging response.

'Yes, sir, we did.' Probyn was quietly proud.

'And I shall look forward to having you work alongside me, Sergeant.' Fitzroy seemed genuine in his proclamation. 'I'm delighted that you have fulfilled all my expectations of you.'

'Thank you, sir.'

The major seemed about to go.

Probyn was respectful but friendly. 'Sir, I was just going over to the mess, would you do me the honour of being my guest?'

'I should be delighted to accept your invitation, Sergeant.' Major Fitzroy smiled broadly. 'But we had better dispense with all this shop talk before we get there.' The two contrasting figures moved off side by side, Fitzroy tall and still athletic of build despite being middle-aged, his sergeant much shorter but more thickly-set. 'Tell me, is there anyone at home awaiting you?'

'Yes, sir, I have a wife and a son.'

The major, unmarried, pretended to be disappointed. 'Ah, so we shall have to share you.'

'Oh no, sir.' Probyn quickly disabused him of this notion. 'Mrs Kilmaster is as loyal to the army as am I, she's devoted her life to it.'

'A most noble woman,' praised Major Fitzroy.

'She is, sir, she is,' Probyn told him fondly.

And later he was to relate this conversation to Grace, hoping that the major's praise would help to rouse her from her misery over her faraway relatives, telling her too how much he himself valued her assistance in working towards his goal of regimental sergeant-major, for he could not do it without her.

Thenceforth, his loving wife was to put aside her own loneliness and with typically generous heart consign herself to making the best of her new home.

With such good deeds that had made her so popular in York, it was not long before Grace had endeared herself to her neighbours at Dover too. This was fortuitous, for within months a new baby was on the way and it could have been a time of intense loneliness had the army wives not rallied round to reciprocate her acts of kindness, their attendance going some way to replacing absent family.

Named after the month in which she was born, Augusta was a good baby, totally lacking in the demanding habits of her elder brother, this giving Grace plenty of time for the letter-writing which maintained the link with her loved ones. Though not going so far as to include Aunt Kit in this category, Grace nevertheless did feel obliged to inform her of the new arrival.

Kit had today responded with a hand-stitched gown for Augusta, the accompanying congratulatory letter also containing a piece of news that she hoped would amuse the parents.

'You'll never guess,' she wrote. 'After all the fuss that Wyn made about you two getting married she's gone and married a Catholic herself! Naturally, she tried to keep it secret, but Ethel managed to wheedle it out of her so now she's the one being ostracized! I just thought it would bring a smile to your lips that she's getting a taste of her own medicine . . .'

'Aye, and I'll bet she never comes to say sorry to us!' declared an annoyed Probyn on reading this news at the end of the day.

Grace found it more entertaining. 'Never mind, we don't need their sorries, do we, Gus?' She changed the baby to her other breast, watching in amusement as Probyn went to the wall and straightened a picture. Sergeant Kilmaster was a stickler for having everything in its place. 'What's that you've brought home?' Finished with the picture, he was setting out books on the table.

'I'm taking the plunge with my first class certificate,' he announced with a look of enthusiasm. 'Are you any good with algebra?'

'Afraid not.'

The enthusiasm paled somewhat. 'Neither am I. I was hoping you'd help me. Oh well, if Mick Melody can teach himself so can I. Wonder what he's doing these days?' He had not seen Mick for years.

The baby had fallen asleep at the breast. Grace stroked the little cheek to wake her and the rosebud mouth started working again. 'Will this make you a colour-sergeant? What else do you need to do?'

'Maths, English Literature, geography, history . . .' He groaned. 'I'm almost put off before I start.'

Grace smiled encouragement. 'I've every faith that you can do it, dear.'

And it was for this reason over the following months that she was to put up with his text books and soldier's paraphernalia all over the house, knowing how much it meant to him, and wanting to help him in his ultimate ambition of being sergeant-major of the regiment.

Alas, it was a much more difficult examination than Probyn had feared, and the first class certificate was to remain elusive that year and also the next. By nineteen hundred and four he had begun to despair that his cherished goal might also evade him, for in recent years time had simply flown. Why, it had only seemed like the blinking of an eye since he was bemoaning the approach of his thirtieth birthday, and now he was thirty-one! If he did not make colour-sergeant soon there would be no hope of winning the supreme accolade.

An air of desperation crept into his efforts. With Clemmie ready for school, Sergeant Kilmaster sought his commanding officer's permission to enrol too, thus instead of having to confine his studies to an evening he could swot at every opportunity. What with this and the bouts of annual training and visits to the School of Musketry to improve his chances of promotion, Grace was hardly to see him, but she unselfishly set aside her own needs, happy just to sit there sewing on an evening after the children had gone to bed whilst their father pored over his books, and to contemplate how it would feel to be the wife of the regimental sergeant-major.

Yet despite her popularity in the garrison, Grace still could not prevent a feeling of loneliness from welling up at times, and it therefore came as such a marvellous surprise when in the new year her husband brought home the news that he was to be posted to the 3rd Battalion, which meant they would be moving to Pontefract. At least there she would be nearer her kin.

Having hoped that Probyn would share her view, and that once back in Yorkshire he would vary his studies with trips to see their relatives, Grace was to be disappointed. Blind to anyone else's needs, his lust for promotion becoming no less energetic, Probyn could waste none of his valuable time in taking her visiting, and it was rare that she had the opportunity to go on her own. Occasionally Charlotte would visit but, still unmarried and with work to go to, she could not come often enough for her friend. With no more children born, Clemmie at school and Augusta so undemanding, Grace found herself at a loose end and volunteered to take on the officers' laundry, finding some solace in the laughter shared in the wash house amongst other military wives and comforting herself with the thought that the extra money would help.

But this was not to say that life was all drudgery, for there were regimental dances and garden parties, plus a Royal visit to the north and all the pageantry that entailed. It was wonderful to watch her husband line the route of the procession in his scarlet regalia, to point out this splendid figure to her children and tell them, 'That's your father!' And it was at times like this, despite all the enforced absences, Grace truly was proud that her husband was a protector of the realm and swore to do her utmost to help him achieve his dream.

Others in the world were realizing their own dream. In America the new-fangled flying machine called an aeroplane was maintaining its flight for longer periods and higher altitudes.

Probyn could not fail to be impressed. 'The US authorities say it won't be of military use but I'll tell you what, Grace, I wish we'd had one when we were fighting the Boers. Why, you could just sit there lobbing bombs to your heart's content! We'd have had them beat in half the time. Come the next war and it'll be the side who has the aeroplanes that's the winner.'

Grace objected to his pessimistic forecast. 'Oh, don't talk about war! There's enough of it in the papers.' All over the world there seemed to be political unrest, if not outright war then some kind of revolution. Russia had been in a state of open revolt for months, vast crowds marching behind red flags to petition the Czar for better conditions, five hundred of them, not just men but women and children, having been shot down in cold blood. Nearer to home, further outrage had been committed by Russian battleships who, whilst heading for Japan with whom they had been at war for the last twenty months, had sunk two Hull trawlers off Dogger Bank, claiming that they were torpedo boats and refusing to apologize. Recently had come the news that their forces, both military and naval, had been crushed by their opponent.

'I'm glad the Japanese beat them,' said Grace. 'It serves them right for sinking those poor fishermen – and they still haven't apologized.'

Such turbulent times seemed destined to continue, the years ahead beset with a series of political upheavals. The resignation of the Prime Minister Arthur Balfour over tariff reform occasioned a general election in which not only did the Liberals enjoy a landslide victory but the Labour Party made remarkable gains, trebling its share of the vote. 'That'll please Uncle Owen,' declared Probyn, whilst for him the most significant outcome of this was the new Prime Minister Sir Henry Campbell-Bannerman's announcement that annexation of the Boer republics had been unlawful.

'So is he going to give them their independence back?' Grace responded to her husband's anger as he read aloud from the newspaper.

'As good as!' spluttered Probyn. 'He's granted them self-government!'

And soon added to this was the galling news that an amnesty act had given seven thousand ex-rebels readmittance to the franchise. 'Well there you are!' Probyn dealt the offending newspaper an angry rap with the back of his hand and threw it aside. 'You might as well hoist the Dutch flag for them. They couldn't defeat us with bullets but they'll do it with the ballot box, mark my words.'

Grace stooped to pick up the paper. 'At least the Zulus are starting to surrender.' She had been afraid that her husband would be called upon to quell the bloody uprising that had arisen over taxes, and was relieved to find he would not.

The reply was grim. 'They'll wonder what they had to complain about when the Boers take charge.'

It was issued satirically, but to his horror as the months wore on Probyn's statement began to adopt an ominous portent. In February 1907 an election was held in the Transvaal and General Louis Botha was appointed Premier with Mr Smuts as Colonial Secretary; moreover, the new cabinet voiced optimism on the eventual federation of South Africa. 'What did I tell you?' came Probyn's bitter sigh to his wife. 'It doesn't matter whether the map is pink or navy blue now the Dutch have got a foothold. They'll take over the whole country.'

And as the months progressed it appeared that his prophecy might come true, for in the Orange River election the Dutch were to triumph again.

Whilst 1907 may have been a bad year politically, on a personal front there was much cause for joy. For Grace came the deliverance of another son, Joseph Fitzroy; for Probyn a reward for all his hard struggle, the achievement of his first-class certificate.

How he celebrated, could hardly keep still while relaying the news to his wife, pacing up and down excitedly, stopping to straighten a picture, before pacing again.

'Oh Lord, I can't tell you how glad I am to see the back of that classroom!' he cried to her. 'And that snooty bloomin' schoolmaster.'

'I thought you were taught by a sergeant?' With her husband's back turned, a mischievous Grace tilted the picture he had just straightened.

'He might have three stripes but he's not a soldier! Just a jumped-up clerk in uniform!' Frowning over the crooked picture Probyn came back to straighten it again, then bent to address his four-year-old daughter excitedly. 'Isn't your dad clever?'

Lifting his smiling eyes from her, he frowned. 'That dratted thing keeps going crooked!' And he went to straighten the picture yet again.

'It was Mother,' divulged Clement, sniggering behind his hand.

'Ooh you little tell-tale!' Grace shrieked as Probyn made a grab for her as if to tickle, and the room erupted in the joyous laughter of children and adults.

But even this moment was to be surpassed in terms of pride and happiness upon his consequent promotion, and at the Church Parade which followed, when, dressed in all their finery, Grace took her children to watch Probyn march to his place of worship to the sound of band and drums, and pointed him out to them loudly so that all in earshot might know his worth: 'There's your father – the guardian of the Colours!'

The year was to close with serious rioting in India, the Labour leader Keir Hardie being held to blame for the tone of his speeches which claimed that the British ran India like the Czar ran Russia. Though fulminations of disgust at this attack on the Empire were to be heard in the Kilmaster household, as the year turned there were to be fewer outbursts from Probyn, for his new administrative chores and his desire to be fully efficient in all the regimental duties that would elect him to the eminence he sought were to take him away from home even more. Added to these responsibilities, a new Territorial Army was formed, merged from the Yeomanry and the Volunteers. Having been concerned over events in the Balkans, Probyn acclaimed the move, saying, 'The more the merrier. Who knows what the Kaiser's got up his sleeve?' Upset by the German leader's insult of Britain in a recent interview, he added, 'I won't forget that he sided with the Boers.'

Grace agreed – 'He's got mad eyes' – before saying goodbye to her dear one yet again and waving him off to his manoeuvres.

Though missing him, Grace reminded herself how lucky she was that her husband had such a high position that provided a regular wage, for the amount of industrial unrest that year was frightening. The country was racked by disputes, in ship-building and engineering and the cotton trade, each of them stemming from a reduction in wages. Yes, she should surely consider herself fortunate to know where her next loaf of bread was coming from when others were starving, especially as she had quickly fallen pregnant again, giving birth in November.

'I shall have to call you Mrs Fruitful,' teased Probyn, visiting his wife's bedside to greet the new arrival and wondering what his men would say if they could see their stern and respected colour-sergeant indulging in such tender moments.

Having been accustomed to having only Clem and Augusta for so long, Grace was now overwhelmed to find herself with four beautiful offspring. 'And what shall we call this one?' She smiled down at the crumpled little face in her arms. 'I thought Emily would be nice, Emily Madeleine.' She noticed a look of panic flicker over his face. It was as if she had slapped him. 'What on earth's wrong?'

Trying desperately to recover from the shock, Probyn merely succeeded in making a fool of himself, opening and shutting his mouth like a fish, his heart beating at a tremendous pace. Staring down at his daughter he saw not a babe but Emily's smiling brown face. Struggling to rid himself of it, he finally blurted, 'Oh nothing! I, er, sorry, I just had an awful thought that I'd forgotten to carry out an order.' He stared down at the baby as if mesmerized. 'Er . . . I'd hoped we might call this one after my mother Sarah.' It had been the last thing on his mind – he did not even particularly care for the name, but it was the first thing that jumped into the gap.

'Oh, of course!' Grace looked chastised and reached out to him gently. 'How selfish of me.'

'You're never selfish!' He grabbed the hand she offered.

'I didn't mean to take over, Probe.' She looked most concerned. 'It's just that you've never been really bothered before what we call them.'

'No, it's me being daft!' He shook her hand in reassuring manner. 'Call her what you will.'

'No, Sarah it is,' Grace insisted.

'We'll compromise: Madeleine Sarah.' He could hardly look his wife in the eye. Emily: how could the mere sound of her name shake him so? He was quivering like a jelly.

'Are you sure there's nothing the matter?' asked Grace. 'You look as if you're in pain.'

'As a matter of fact I have got this dreadful earache.' Probyn raised his hand to the side of his head. It was not a lie. His ear had been throbbing for hours.

She sighed. 'I wish you wouldn't be such a martyr!'

'Oh, thanks!' He managed to laugh.

'Well, you wouldn't have said anything if I hadn't asked – would you now?'

He admitted this was the case. 'I shall have it seen to once you're back on your feet.'

'Get it seen to now!' instructed Grace. 'Never mind the children, Mrs Mackenzie will look after them.'

'I won't argue.' The pain was becoming so bad that it almost took his mind off his previous shock. 'I'll go across and see the doctor now.' He kissed her and left.

The result of his following examination was not good. Probyn was admitted to hospital where he was to spend twelve days waiting for an operation, only to be told at the end of that period that it could not be done in Pontefract and he would have to go to York.

In the time it took to arrange this, Grace was back on her feet and able to cope, and the pain in his ear had become agonizing. Transferred to York, he was told that the operation could not be done today and he was sent back to Pontefract where he was to wait for another month, during which time the pain became all consuming and the ear had set up a discharge.

Shuttled off once more to York, today he sat once again in the waiting area of the hospital, holding a handkerchief to his throbbing pus-filled ear, head to one side in an attitude of misery, when a voice sent volts of fresh pain through him. 'Pa!'

He hardly dared turn for the discomfort it caused him. 'Mick, I was just thinking of you, I had this terrible pain . . .'

'Oh charming!' Mick seized his hand and shook it.

Wincing, Probyn looked him up and down, thinking how youthful he looked to say he was over thirty. 'So, you're working here?'

'No! I'm here as a patient.' Mick rubbed his neck. 'They keep saying there's nothing wrong with me and I know full well there is.' Without warning he knelt before Probyn and opened his mouth wide. 'Just look at the back of me throat and tell me if ye see a lumpy thing.'

'I'm not a doctor.' Consumed by his own agony, Probyn was disinclined to take part in Melody's hypochondria.

Mick was still kneeling, mouth agape. 'But ye've got eyes, haven't ye?'

Probyn's brow had an impatient frown. He made a snap decision to tell this picture of health what he wanted to hear. 'Yes, I think I can see something.'

Mick blanched. He sat back on his heels looking stricken. 'Oh, God! I knew it.'

'You'll have housemaid's knee too if you keep kneeling on that floor,' said Probyn with little sympathy. In such a mode Mick was always an irritation but even more so when the recipient of his paranoia was in agony.

As if in a trance, Mick slowly rose and transferred his buttocks to the bench.

Probyn felt he ought to say something, if only to take his mind off his pain. 'Are you married yet?'

Mick stared at him, blue eyes filled with thoughts of his own mortality. 'No . . . just as well isn't it?'

'You'll be all right,' muttered Probyn – then looked up as his name was called and gladly departed for the examination room. 'See you again, Mick.'

Petrified, Mick raised a half-hearted salute, saying nothing.

Completely forgetting about the other, Probyn gave himself up to the medical officer's expertise, making no argument when this resulted in him being readmitted to a hospital ward, for at least it would mean an end to the continual pain.

Thirteen days later, though, still engulfed by the awful throbbing, he begged an orderly to tell him when this might be relieved.

'Has nobody told you?' came the careless reply. 'We haven't

the instruments here so you're being transferred to Millbank.'

Condemned, or so it seemed, to spend the rest of his life as a human shuttlecock, Probyn collapsed against his pillow, despair driving him to issue a rare four-letter word and to rave at the orderly over this inefficiency.

But it was not to do him the slightest good. Not until three months after it first erupted was his terrible pain finally assuaged.

Upon coming home that Friday and entering the house to the smell of fish, he found his wife crawling about on all fours giving rides to the children.

But Grace jumped up as soon as she saw him, her face joyous, making out that he was the most important person in the house. 'Oh, Father's home!'

Returning her warm embrace, Probyn gestured at the demolished meal on the table, plates littered with fish bones. 'Looks as if the cavalry have been through here.'

'You should have warned us what time you'd be coming,' said Grace. 'We'd have waited. Never mind I've got a lovely bit of smoked haddock in the pantry for you, it won't take a minute to cook.'

'Is your lug better, Father?' asked Clem.

'What's that?' Probyn feigned deafness and laughed when his son repeated the query. 'I'm only kidding. Eh, it's grand to be home!' Making a grab, he planted a child on each knee.

Cooking the fish, Grace warned the children not to tire their father out, and spent the rest of the afternoon pampering him.

For once he was content to sit back and let her do so, telling her how lovely it was to see her after so long and to hear all that had been going on at the barracks in his absence; although Grace was a dreadful storyteller, constantly having to stop and insert bits – 'Oh hang on I forget to say' – so often, that the listener became frustrated and bored to tears with her vague commentary, though somehow he managed to sit through it, shaking his head and smiling upon her fondly, his heart filled with love.

Unrestrained by such emotion, the rest of the world seemed intent on killing each other. In India Moslems and Hindus committed mutual outrage, the situation mirrored in the Balkans where Austria had sent troops to the Serbian frontier. With atrocities in danger of spilling into full-blown war again, the European powers converged to bring about a solution, urging Serbia to drop its claim to Bosnia and Herzegovina.

Envisaging her husband being called away to foreign lands, Grace was vastly relieved when the crisis was defused. 'Thank God,' she breathed to Probyn. 'I had visions of the whole world being at each other's throats.'

His reply, delivered lightly, was somewhat cynical. 'Oh, they don't need to fight wars these days, Grace, when countries can be won more easily by the ballot box.' What he had long feared now looked set to come to reality: the Cape, Natal, Transvaal and Orange River colonies were to be united under one government. Under the British crown or no, he knew which race would eventually emerge supreme. 'Our scrap with the Boers was all for nothing. And there's one thing for sure, the poor wretched blacks will be treated a lot worse under the Dutch. It wouldn't surprise me if they take away the Cape niggers' vote once they get in charge. They won't even let their own blacks walk on the pavement.'

Grace diversified the topic. 'Did you see there's been two more lynchings and burnings in America?' Such outrages had almost become commonplace. Her face showed revulsion. 'I can't believe any human could burn another alive, can you?'

Equally disgusted, Probyn shook his head. 'It's bestial. I agree with Mr Balfour that giving the vote to blacks would threaten civilization but there's ways of keeping people in line without such cruelty.' He reached out to her, fondly. 'Anyway, we shouldn't be discussing this before bed, especially as we won't be seeing each other for twenty days.' Tomorrow he would be off to Whitley Bay for annual training. Taking her hand he pulled her onto his knee and planted a seductive kiss behind her ear, murmuring, 'Away let's to bed and have a cuddle.'

The next morning, though rather pleased at the change of venue, Probyn voiced further regret that the trip to Whitley Bay would take him away from his dear wife for so long. 'But I'll bring you back a stick of rock,' he promised as he made ready to leave, then his smile suddenly vanished upon remembering that these had been Greatrix's last words.

Sensitive over their parting, Grace went to him and put her arm around him in concern. Over the years she had witnessed such looks of indescribable sadness come over Probyn's face and, after once receiving explanation, had no need to ask what was wrong now; he was thinking of his dead friends, or some abomination of war.

He gripped her arm in thanks of this unspoken support, then finished winding his puttee up his calf. 'I'm all right, s'just somebody walking over my grave.' Finishing at the knee, he secured the puttee and folded the upper part of his khaki trouser leg over it.

A knock at the door revealed his batman, come to deliver items of blancoed webbing and other items of kit.

With everything in order, Probyn made to be off. 'Look after your mother,' he offered cheery instruction to young Clem on the way out.

'Will you play draughts with me when you get back, Father?' asked the boy.

Grace chuckled and patted him. 'Your father's an important man, he hasn't time to play.'

'We'll see what we can do.' Probyn winked at his son and finally left.

Looking forward to having his father's attention, Clem spent the next few hours running to the window at any sound of marching boots, though after countless reminders from his mother that his father would be ages yet, he had by the end of the week abandoned the process.

Now though, almost three weeks later, he was once more happily running to the window at every sound.

'Oh, do come back to the table, you little scallywag!' begged Grace, trying to give the children their tea in order to have them all ready for bed by the time their father came in and so avoid the current commotion. 'Why are boys never still?' she asked her daughters with a sigh.

Clem finally came to stand at the table, allowing the meal to get underway. For a time things were quiet. Then a knock came at the door.

The spoon delivering milky rusks to nine-month-old Madeleine poised in mid air, leaving the baby open-mouthed like a nestling awaiting its worm. Grace issued an even heavier sigh.

'Is it Father?' Nine-year-old Clem demanded with an expectant smile, ready to make a dash.

'Stay where you are!' said his mother with a scolding laugh. 'He wouldn't knock on his own door. Gussie dear, if you've finished your tea go answer it.' The baby on her lap, she inserted another spoonful of rusk into its gaping maw.

Six-year-old Augusta left the table and ran to the door, auburn plaits flapping around her shoulders, returning to say, 'It's a brown lady.'

'I wouldn't have thought a gypsy would get past the gate.' Puzzled, Grace plonked the baby on a cushion and went to check for herself, seeing not a gypsy but a well-dressed, middle-aged woman wearing an apologetic smile.

'I am so sorry,' began Emily in a tentative whisper. 'I told dem at the gate I am looking for Lance-Corporal Kilmaster. Dey said there was a Colour-Sergeant Kilmaster at this house but I fear he might not be the person I seek.' But as her eyes went once again to the small red-haired girl who stood clutching the edge of her mother's apron, she knew in her heart that she was at the right address and a well of foreboding had begun to bubble up from the pit of her stomach.

Grace took in the row of large white teeth, then returned

the woman's smile, captivated by the strange but endearing accent. 'Well, this is Colour-Sergeant Kilmaster's house –'

'Would his name be Probyn?' enquired Emily.

Still smiling, Grace gave a puzzled frown. 'Yes, do you know my husband, Mrs –'

'Kilmaster,' said the woman with the large teeth. 'I am Emily Kilmaster. And I think that your husband may be my husband too.'

Grace's hand shot out and grabbed the jamb, the other flying up to cover her mouth.

Suddenly afraid, Augusta lifted wide blue eyes to her mother. Grace did not respond, completely stunned into silence.

'I am sorry,' whispered Emily, not knowing what else to say, her own heart thudding with shock and disappointment.

Fearing that if she opened her mouth to speak she would vomit, a trembling Grace indicated for the woman to come in. When the visitor moved past her she remained clinging to the jamb for a second, then pushed herself from it and followed her into the living room, still too dumb to comment, but her eyes took quick stock. Now on a similar level, it became evident that the other woman was much taller than herself. Clad in a summery printed dress and white gloves, a navy fitted jacket and a straw hat laden with full-blown roses and ribbons, a handbag over her arm, she looked so very English . . . yet at the same time so very foreign.

Faced with the enquiring glances of three more red-headed youngsters, Emily smiled at them though her heart was breaking, then turned anxiously to the other Mrs Kilmaster.

Realizing that her children were looking to her for explanation, Grace found her voice. 'Gus, take Maddie upstairs and change her nappy, Clem, Joe, go up to your room till I call you.'

Without argument, the children did as they were told.

'You have excellently behaved children,' commented Emily when there were only the two women left in the room.

Grace went to close the door, every nerve tingling.

Half way up the stairs carrying the baby, a worried Augusta turned around and sneaked back to sit on the bottom step, trying to hear what her mother was saying. Clem and Joe scampered down to squeeze beside her.

'Who is that old brown woman?' Clem demanded of his sister.

Looking anxious, Augusta cuddled the baby who played with her sister's plaits. 'She said she's married to Father.'

Exchanging worried glances, the children strained to listen.

From outside could be heard the tramp of marching boots on the parade ground, the yell of a sergeant's instruction, and birdsong. In here was deathly silence.

Pacing about the carpet, Grace took a long time to voice her anguish, and only then muttering abstractedly, 'Oh God, I can't believe this. I can't believe it.'

It was left to Emily to explain. 'Please, may I sit down?' With Grace's nod, she perched on the edge of a brown leatherette sofa, looking grave, and began to relate the details of her marriage, telling the other where she came from, how she and Probyn had met and how they had been forced apart on their wedding day. Grace remained standing throughout, hardly daring to breathe until Emily came to her soft conclusion. 'I promised that I would find him somehow . . . I did not know it would take so long . . . nor that he would have found someone else.'

Still Grace clung to a shred of hope, studying the other and gauging from the amount of grey in her wavy hair that she was surely over fifty. 'Are you certain that they share an identity? Why, the man you refer to must be considerably older than my husband.'

Though anguished, Emily emitted a self-conscious chuckle. 'I know how old I must appear to you –'

'I didn't mean to be rude but –'

'Probyn was much younger than I.' To bring matters to a close, Emily furnished the other with his date of birth.

535

Grace was left in no doubt now. They were both married to the same man.

'Oh God! What will I do? What will I do?' The children heard their mother wail.

'I am so, *so* sorry,' whispered Emily, tears in her eyes.

Through a blur of salt water Grace stared back at her. Had Emily been a tart it would have been so much easier to rant, to condemn her as a slut and throw her from the house, but she wasn't. She was lovely, serene and gentle. Finding herself in this situation must almost be as hard as it was for Grace; but not quite, for there were others to consider in this dreadful fiasco.

'If you and Probyn were parted on your wedding day,' distressed though she was, Grace thought how ridiculous it sounded discussing her husband's wedding day, 'I don't suppose you'd have time for children?'

Emily was looking increasingly miserable. 'No.'

'Then the marriage wasn't –' Grace forced herself to say the word, 'consummated?'

Emily beheld the other wearily, seeing the flicker of hope upon the face much younger than her own and feeling wretched at having to douse it. 'Perhaps not *after* the ceremony, but we were lovers long before den.'

Grace blushed furiously at such detail.

'Unfortunately I am unable to bear children,' finished Emily.

'Make way for the infantry!' Both heads turned quickly to the door as Probyn came through the hall to make his cheery entrance. Emily shot to her feet.

Tired and sweaty, but exhilarated from manoeuvres, a smiling Probyn whipped off his field cap and strode into the room, preparing to dole out kisses to wife and children but stopping dead upon sight of the visitor.

For a second he stood there staring into that lovely tanned face that he had thought never to see again, recalling the way he had felt about her, the passion that she had aroused in him.

Emily smiled back, watching the damp curl at his forehead slowly unfold from being compressed beneath his hat. 'You still look the same, Dasher.'

'Save for being ... fifteen years older,' he murmured. *Fifteen years!* This was like being in a dream.

Riveted by the look that passed between the former lovers, Grace fought her horror to issue tightly, 'So you do know each other then?'

Stunned, he wrenched his eyes away from Emily to look upon his wife, or the one he regarded as his wife, but could not immediately recognize her, for Grace's eyes held a coldness that he had never witnessed before. He knew then that Emily had revealed everything. 'Grace, I never told you because I didn't see the point. It would only have hurt you!'

Grace issued an outraged gasp. 'You were right there! I might just have had second thoughts on becoming Mrs Kilmaster had I known there was another lurking about in your seedy past!' Fresh tears welled.

Frantic now, he took a step towards her but stopped upon seeing that he was to be rebuffed. 'No, you don't understand! I meant what would have been the point of telling you when it wasn't a proper marriage?' He caught the look of distress on Emily's face and quickly apologized, 'I'm sorry, Em, but you know as well as I that it was hopeless. It wasn't legal.'

'To me it was, and you believed the same then.' Emily was deeply hurt, though she did not disport it in the same near hysterical manner of Grace who moaned and paced about, chewing her knuckles.

Probyn bowed his head and sighed. 'Yes, I did, I have to admit that, Grace – I'm sorry!' he cried as she turned away in despair. 'But I can't discount what I felt for Emily or it would make me a bounder. I was attached to her, otherwise I wouldn't have asked her to marry me.' Looking back at Emily, he made a lame gesture with his hands. 'But you must understand, Em. I never expected you to turn up after all these years.'

'Did I not promise I would find you wherever you might be, no matter how long it took?' Emily reminded him.

'You did,' he confirmed softly, feeling himself suffocating in the brown pools of agony that were her eyes. 'I can't tell you how deeply I regret having let you down.'

Watching this exchange, it became obvious to Grace that her husband held strong affection for this woman and suddenly she became more afraid than angry. This was not just a case of a brief infidelity, Probyn had loved Emily enough to marry her – perhaps he would go back to her now! Her heart began to thud even more quickly, setting up a pounding in her head and a lump to her throat, she wanted to vomit, felt herself on the point of collapse.

'So,' Emily took a deep breath, 'what are we to do about the situation?' The question was not a plea for him to choose; he had already chosen. 'How does one undo an inconvenient marriage?'

Looking at the two women, both equally certain that they were his wife, Probyn felt tormented. He had loved Emily deeply, the pain he had felt upon losing her had been horrendous. Even though he no longer felt that way, had he been free there would be no question that he would do his duty by her.

But he was not free. He looked at little Grace and saw absolute terror in her eyes, terror that he was about to leave her, and at that point more than any other in their marriage he was made aware of the overwhelming love he had for her. How could she think he would abandon her and the children? He felt desperate to put his arms around her, but knew she would not suffer his attentions until he had voiced his decision.

'I'm sorry, Emily,' was all he had to contribute. 'I can only reiterate that the authorities didn't look upon our marriage as valid and that was sufficient for me. Of course, if you want to pursue it legally . . .' Even dreading that she might take him up on the offer, he had to appear fair. However, he felt anything but fair upon looking at the expression he had created; he felt an out and out blackguard.

With barely a hint of the devastation she was feeling, Emily merely shook her head, lips pressed together not in anger but to contain her sadness. Without another word, and holding herself with the great dignity he had witnessed so many times before, she inserted a gloved hand through the handle of her bag, and made for the door.

'At least let me escort you back to – where was it you landed in England?' Even the offer of help sounded callous, as if he couldn't wait to get her back on the boat.

Emily obviously thought so too, turning to look deep in his eyes. 'No. I have been a long time on my own. I will not die for want of a companion.'

There was the air of a survivor about her exit, but it was no consolation to Probyn. For a moment after she had gone, neither he nor Grace said a word, the former merely rubbing a hand over his face, his wife staring at the door through which the woman had passed. But Emily still impregnated the room, the smell of cooking from her clothes, the coconut oil upon her skin.

Grace spoke first. 'My God, this is rich,' she breathed. 'All that rot about black people not being fit to vote and here you are married to one!'

He reacted with disbelief that she could equate the lovely Emily with the savages who killed Greatrix. But the colour of one's skin was not the main issue here. Coming up to his wife he attempted to touch her arm. 'Don't you want to hear my side?'

She pulled away. 'It might have been nice to hear it before you inflicted four illegitimate children on me!'

'Don't be daft, they're not –'

'Don't you *dare* call me daft!' In the confidence that he was not going to leave her Grace's anger had been slowly building again and now it emerged in full fury. She punched him again and again in the chest.

Never had he seen any woman so angry, not even his mother, who had possessed the most foul temper. He staggered under her blows. 'I only meant to say that our marriage is legal!'

'How can it be legal when you were already married to another?' screamed Grace.

'But it was that marriage which wasn't legal! Wedlock stopped it before anything was signed –'

'But you went through the full ceremony, she said so!'

'Yes, but there was nothing written down, nobody else knows about –'

'*I* know!' shrieked Grace. 'I know that for ten years I've been living a life of sin! I'm not even legally entitled to be in married quarters! And what's the Colonel going to say when he finds out you're a bigamist?'

He experienced a thrill of alarm that this was going to ruin his army career when the prize of RSM was just within his grasp.

'Grace, listen to me!' He tried to take her by the arms but she kept struggling. 'It was not bigamy! I've told you I didn't have permission to marry Emily that's why it was stopped. Please don't mention it to anybody, the army takes a very dim view of such matters.'

Grace was momentarily pulled up by the utter thoughtlessness of this remark, before yelling, 'Wives take a very dim view of such things too!' And she laid into him again, her clenched fist hammering and thumping at his khaki uniform, lashing out at his head, slapping and screeching in absolute abandon. 'No wonder you didn't want me to call our daughter Emily! You pig, you bloody shite!'

Lurching away from him she began to seize things, ornaments, cups, plates, pictures, anything that came to hand, hurling them one after another at him whilst he ducked and swerved and did his best to dodge them though one or two found their mark and drew blood.

The door burst open and in ran Clem. 'Stop hurting my

mother!' And he too began to flail at Probyn, whilst Augusta, Joe and the baby simply wailed.

'I'm not hurting your mam, Clemmie, I'm not!' Probyn tried to cuddle his son but the little boy had a temper on him too.

Unable to stem the disturbance, Probyn had no option but to remove himself from the room. Hoping that his absence would halt the violence, he opened the outer door, intending to call upon his neighbour for help but there stood Aunt Kit looking most bemused at all the noise.

He gasped. 'Oh Aunt, I'm that glad to see thee!'

Probyn had no sooner spoken than his neighbour Sergeant Mackenzie and his wife emerged. 'We were just coming to see what all the racket was about!'

Urging both women to enter, he asked breathlessly, 'Can you do owt with our Grace? She's gone doolally with me – I deserved it mindst – but the kids are upset and I'm frightened she might damage herself. I don't know what the hell to do!'

'Eh, dear, men!' Kit signalled for him to come out of the way. 'Come out and let me past!'

'Take him into our house,' Mrs Mackenzie told her husband, then flew after Kit.

Almost demented himself, Probyn gave a helpless shrug at his Uncle Worthy who looked equally at a loss, then both went into the house next door with Sergeant Mackenzie where they were to remain for the next few minutes, waiting until the noise died down.

Only when told to do so by Mrs Mackenzie did Probyn attempt to gain re-entry to his home, though he paused on the threshold to enquire tentatively, 'Did Grace tell you what all that was about?'

Mrs Mackenzie nodded her disapproval. 'Another woman.'

'It was a long, long time ago when I were only a lad,' said Probyn quickly. 'Years before I was married to Grace. I'd be much obliged if you didn't broadcast it.'

Mrs Mackenzie gave a sharp laugh. 'I doubt there's anyone on the camp who didn't hear that commotion.' But on seeing the seriousness of Probyn's face she added, 'No, I won't say anything. Grace didn't give me the details anyway.'

He nodded relief. 'Thanks.'

'I'd go to her now if I were you. The lass is still right upset. Your aunt's making her a pot of tea.'

'Is it safe for me to go an' all?' enquired Worthy, and was granted permission.

Upon entering, the men found Grace cuddling her children, who were somewhat recovered now, though Clem beheld his father sullenly.

'Are you all right, love?' asked Probyn.

There was no answer.

Kit came out of the scullery bearing a tea pot. 'Yes, she's all right, aren't you, lass?'

'I don't know if I'll ever be all right,' replied Grace. So saying, she hefted the baby onto the crook of her arm and bade the children follow her. 'In fact I don't feel well at all. Don't pour a cup for me, Aunt Kit, the children and I are going to bed. You'll be all right to fend for yourself?'

'Course I will!' Feeling utterly wretched, Probyn watched her leave the room.

'Don't worry I'll see to him,' vouched Kit, though she sensed Grace did not care and, when there was only her husband and nephew in the room, she added, 'Poor little lass, I didn't have the heart to tell her she hasn't got any cups, smashed the lot.' She had swept up most of the mess, but the room was in a sorry state, broken pictures lying on the sideboard.

'I'll go borrow some from Mrs Mackenzie.' Probyn was gone for little over a minute.

When he set out the borrowed cups, Kit poured tea into them, saying, 'Tell me to mind my own business –'

'No, I know you're only trying to help, Aunt, and you might be able to tell me how to make things up to her.' And, sitting down, he began to relate to her and Worthy every detail.

'By heck,' breathed Kit when he had done. 'And I thought

I'd had a colourful life.' Though deeply shocked and feeling great sympathy for the wronged wife, she tried not to sound judgemental, for it was the last thing Probyn needed. To cover her discomfiture she took a sip of tea, trying to envisage her nephew in a torrid embrace with some black woman; to her he would always be the three-year-old who had presented a dead chaffinch to wear on her hat. 'I don't know what to suggest, Probe. I don't really know Grace that well.' She rather regretted her laxity in this field now.

The soldier raised his eyebrows as if in disbelief. 'Neither do I, at least not the Grace I've just witnessed. She was like a ... like a little savage. If you hadn't come I think she might have killed me. I don't know where to start in making it up to her.'

Kit put down her cup and began to rise. 'Well, you'd better make some sort of effort and you'll not get much done with us here.'

He discerned a hint of censure. 'I know how you must feel but please don't think badly of me, I was only a lad when –'

'Nay! I'm not one to cast stones ... well, maybe I've chucked a few pebbles in the past, haven't we all?' She smiled to reassure him that they were not leaving for the reason he thought. 'No, this was only intended as a flying visit. We've been to Doncaster and we thought as we'd be coming right past your door we might as well pop in.' In spite of her disapproval of his behaviour she made a joke of it, nudging her nephew as she put on her coat. 'Good job we did or you might have been mincemeat.'

Somehow she managed to sound amused.

'Toby's looking after the farm and we don't like to leave him too long.'

Probyn raised a smile. 'For a second I got the image of this little lad being left in charge but he must be ... what, nineteen now?'

'Aye, he'll be the next to marry,' laughed Kit.

Worthy winked at Probyn. 'She'll never let him marry, wants to keep him at home all to herself!'

Probyn saw them to the door and waved them off. Once alone in the room he discarded his manufactured smile, flopped into a chair and unwound his puttees, then sat rubbing his calves for a moment, before finally bracing himself and venturing upstairs.

Lying fully clothed on the bed, Grace heard him open the door but kept her back to him.

Probyn came and sat on the edge of the mattress. 'I'm sorry, dear, I really am. I wouldn't hurt you for the world.'

Grace said nothing.

Tentatively, he stroked her hair. 'Can I get you anything?'

'Can you legitimize our children?'

He moaned. 'They are legitimate! I've told you, you won't find another marriage certificate with my name on it.'

She sat up suddenly. Probyn shrank back in alarm. 'Don't worry!' scoffed Grace, 'I'm not going to start again.' Instead, she leaned against the bedhead, hugging her knees, forming a barrier between them. 'I may not find a certificate no, but I've had all the evidence I need.'

He leaned over to cup her face. 'Grace, if I could turn back the clock I would!'

'But you can't,' she said. Then, utterly betrayed, she wept again.

21

He was awake an hour before the bugle sounded. In fact he had barely slept at all. Turning his weary face, he examined the back of Grace's head for a few seconds, wondering if she had been similarly afflicted. Odd, how the back of someone's head could be so expressive. She said not a word and he knew better than to speak to her, had been surprised that she had let him into their bed at all. Causing as little disruption as possible, he rolled onto the edge of the mattress and straight onto his feet, then crept from the room.

Downstairs, he lit a fire and got everything ready as for a normal morning, wondering if life would ever be normal again.

Should he take Grace a cup of tea or let her lie? Deciding to leave the gesture until it was time for him to depart for duty, he instead got the children up and gave them breakfast.

Clem bit into his bread and marmalade. 'Where's Mother?'

'She's having a lie-in,' replied his father smartly. 'She's a bit poorly.'

Clem looked at his six-year-old sister who sat with wide eyes, saying nothing as she fed Maddie her rusks.

'So!' Their father showed them a list he had compiled. 'I think you're old enough now to help her around the house. Every morning you'll find one of these lists pinned to the wall. That's Battalion Orders and it will tell you what jobs you have to do before you go to school. Clem, today yours is to clean the range, Gussie, you wash the window sills and the front step.' The other children were dealt only a smile. 'I think Joe and Maddie are a bit young yet, but they'll take their turn in time.'

He pinned the list at a suitably low point on the wall. 'Don't forget now, every day before you've done anything else.' He turned back to them. 'Now, I'll just take your mother a cup of tea then I'm going on duty. When you've got yourselves ready for school take Joseph and Madeleine next door and ask Mrs Mackenzie if she'd mind looking after them today as your mother is ill. Think you can remember that?' At their nods he buttered some bread for his wife, poured her a cup of tea, then somewhat apprehensively went upstairs.

She hardly responded when he placed the offering on the bedside table, nor when he told her that he had organized everything and she need not worry about the children. Only when he bent to kiss her did she come alive, the look in her eyes telling him not to try that again.

'I'll be off then.' Miserably, he left her and went off to perform his duties.

It was a substantial relief that no soldier questioned him as to the identity of the black woman who had presented herself at the gate yesterday. He had been ready for it, having concocted a story that Emily was looking for a mutual acquaintance, but no one asked. Naturally, his subordinates would not dare, but neither had there been query from an officer. Nor did there appear to be any gossip nor any telling looks. Thinking about it, he was reassured by the fact that those who knew the story, Wedlock and John Goodwill, were somewhere far away. There was little danger from that quarter. However, Grace was another matter.

When he came home that lunch time to see how she was he found her still in bed, the bread and butter untouched, though she had taken a few sips from the teacup. His offer to make her a sandwich rebuffed, he removed the cup and the plate of stale bread and replaced it with freshly made tea, then went back to his duties.

The evening found her much the same, except that by now the room stank of urine. Discovering a chamberpot that was full to the brim, he emptied it first before taking her food. Again it was ignored.

'Grace, you've got to eat,' he begged the despondent figure.

'Why?' Her pale heartbroken face looked up from the pillow.

'Well . . .' He spread helpless hands.

'I don't want anything. Leave me alone,' she told him.

So he did.

Collecting his two younger children from next door, he asked if Mrs Mackenzie would mind looking after them indefinitely.

'I'd do anything for Grace,' came the rather accusing answer. 'They can sleep here if you like.'

'Thank you but I think they'll be happier coming home and seeing their mother for a while. It's just the daytime I need help.' Granted this, he thanked Mrs Mackenzie and returned to his own house.

Things were all right whilst they were eating tea, but afterwards there was a hiatus before bedtime and to avoid awkward questions from the older ones he set them more tasks. 'I thought we'd make Mother a rug for when she's better. I'll map out a pattern for it but first what I want you to do is cut up these old garments into strips. Here, like this.' Taking up some scissors he showed them what size to make the pieces. Satisfied that this would keep them busy for ages, he got the two younger ones ready for bed.

Later, congratulating Clem and Augusta for their little pile of colourful strips, he sent them to bed too, remaining downstairs himself to get things ready for morning and to have a mug of cocoa.

Reluctant to go to bed, he did everything possible to keep

him from it. Taking his dress tunic, he slid his button stick behind one of the brass buttons and proceeded to apply polish. It was madness. He had a servant to do this, a servant who had already cleaned it perfectly well. He was just making excuses. Sighing, he abandoned the task and finally turned out the lights.

It was horrible getting into a bed that had not been properly made, even more so when the other person in it emitted such mute hostility.

As if the domestic situation was not enough, he could not get to sleep for worrying that news of this was going to reach higher order, that it was going to blight his dream. After the hiccups of those early years he had managed to control his boyish streak, had acquired the exemplary character that was mandatory for the role he prized. Was one youthful misdemeanour destined to ruin everything?

For days the anxiety was to continue, days in which Grace hardly set foot out of bed apart from to answer the call of nature, receiving no visitors except for her children who came to bestow kisses at morning and night.

After almost a week in which she neglected her health to a dangerous level, taking nothing except cups of tea and looking like a scarecrow, Probyn was forced to bring in the doctor.

But, faced with a mystifying complaint, the doctor could only prescribe a tonic, give her powders to help her sleep and tell her to get plenty of fresh air, advice that both Grace and Probyn knew would not bring about a cure.

Racking his brain for who to go to for advice, he did think about writing to Charlotte, but dreading her condemnation of his behaviour he postponed it. However, as if she had received a mental telegram, Charlotte turned up that Saturday afternoon.

At first her big square face beheld him gladly, tiny eyes scrunched up even smaller within her friendly beam. But when he told her Grace was ill, she went straightaway upstairs.

Upon seeing her Grace immediately burst into sobs. Rushing to her, thinking her friend was in the grip of some dreadful life-threatening malady, Charlotte was perhaps even more horrified to learn the true cause. She covered her mouth and said nothing until a tearful Grace had related the whole sordid episode, listening aghast until at the end of it she enfolded her friend in a supportive hug.

'Oh, I could kill him for hurting you – I never thought Probe capable of such a thing!'

'That poor bloody woman, Lottie!' Grace wiped her eyes and took a deep shuddering breath. 'I can still see the look on her face.' Her own face mirrored the grief she had witnessed on Emily's. 'I hate her for being his wife, for landing us in this mess, but it wasn't really her fault was it?'

Charlotte was still stricken with disbelief, her tiny emerald eyes poring over the other's tear-stained face searching for answers. 'What happened to her? Where did she go?'

Grace shook her head. 'I don't know. Probyn offered to take her –'

'He *didn't!* Talk about rubbing your nose in it!'

'Oh well, I suppose he felt obliged. She didn't accept, just went. I was just so relieved to see the back of her . . . but I can't rid myself of her face.'

Holding onto Grace's hand and stroking it, Charlotte frowned. 'I hate to ask, I know how dreadfully hurt you are already, but . . . does this mean you're not legally married?'

Grace bit her lip which was blood-red from constant chewing. 'I don't know that either! I'm too frightened to ask officially. If he's really married to her, where would that leave me and the children? No, I can't risk anyone finding out, Lottie. I'd rather not know.'

Charlotte nodded in agreement. 'But what are you going to do about Probyn, dear?' she asked gently.

Again came the anguished wail. 'I don't know. I just don't know.'

'Well I know what I'd do!' said an angry Charlotte, 'I'd go and tell his commanding officer, get him a dressing down.'

'No you wouldn't.' Grace shook her head.

'No, you're right I wouldn't.' All vindictiveness banished, Charlotte laughed softly at herself. 'I'm as daft as you.'

'Oh, it's not that I mind him getting into trouble, I just don't want anybody to know what he's done.'

'But you've nothing to be ashamed of, dear.'

Grace's bloodshot eyes looked away. 'I would if the truth came out; my children might be illegitimate.'

Unmarried, Charlotte had been slow to comprehend and now put her hand to her cheek. 'Oh, God! Oh, if only I could change things for you, Grace. It shouldn't happen to somebody as sweet as you, after the way you've devoted your life to him, followed him all over the country.' Toying with one of the frizzy dark-blonde curls that framed her face, she asked thoughtfully, 'So what will you do, carry on as if it hadn't happened?'

'It *has* happened hasn't it? Sweet God in heaven, I feel as if it's sending me mad!' Grace clutched her head, rubbing hard as if to drive away the torturous thought. 'That bloody song keeps going round and round in my head – you know, the one,' she gave an angry rendition, her voice emerging as a thin pathetic warble, '*Can't get away to marry you today, my wife won't let me!* I don't know if I can ever forgive him, Lottie.' Grace would have cried again, but she had no more tears to give.

Charlotte stayed for as long as she could, tending her stricken friend as best she was able, brushing her hair, washing her face, plumping her pillows to make her more comfortable. 'I don't like leaving you. I'm going to ask for an afternoon off during the week so I can come and see you again.'

The fact that Probyn was thoughtful enough to bring up a tray of tea and jam sandwiches for them did not sufficiently raise him in her esteem, and upon leaving she gave him a piece of her mind.

He did not retaliate nor try to give excuse, merely hanging his head when she asked what he had to say for himself.

'No, you can't say anything can you!' demanded Charlotte, quietly so as not to upset the children, but forcefully enough for her message to get through. 'You've broken that girl's heart. God help you if her sisters find out.'

He felt sick. 'Are you going to tell them?'

'No! But not for your sake. That's up to Grace.' She hooked her bag over her wrist and made for the door. 'I'll be back next week to see how she is. Make sure you take better care of her!'

Unable to get an afternoon off, Charlotte was to return on an evening a few days later to check on her friend's health, and finding Grace still in bed, suggested that she might feel better if she got up.

Instead of being tearful, Grace had plunged into lethargy now, replying that she might later, but privately thinking that there was nothing to get up for. And although she enjoyed Charlotte's visit, when her friend went downstairs she curled up into a ball and pulled the sheets over her head.

About to leave, Charlotte spoke to Probyn more civilly, telling him how worried she was about Grace. 'We can't allow her to go on neglecting herself.'

'Short of dragging her out of bed, I can't force her to get up. I've tried telling her how sorry I am but . . .' he shrugged helplessly.

Charlotte set her prim little mouth in a decisive line, then turned on her heel and instead of leaving went back upstairs. Grace was surprised to see her, but was not appreciative of the scolding that followed.

'I know you've been deeply hurt, Grace,' Charlotte, normally as gentle a soul as her friend, tried to sound firm. 'But it isn't going to do you any good at all wasting away up here. Even if you feel angry at Probyn, and quite rightly, you shouldn't neglect your children.' Knowing it would not have any effect telling Grace to look after her own health she chose to rouse her with guilt. 'They're only little, they need you and they haven't done anything wrong.'

Grace was offended to be so accused. She opened her mouth to retort . . . but then she saw that Charlotte was quite right, and she closed it again, merely nodding in answer, tears in her eyes.

Equally emotional, Charlotte came and pressed an affectionate kiss to her cheek then. 'I know you'd never hurt them. Goodbye, dear. I'll come again when I can.'

Not expecting much to come of Charlotte's parting declaration that she had talked some sense into Grace, Probyn closed the door on her and went back to seat himself amongst his children.

By cutting up old garments for over a week they had a large pile of strips and were now shown how to insert them into the piece of hessian that their father had stretched onto a frame, using sharp pegs of iron. And as Probyn shoved the peg in and out he remembered that it had been his father who had taught him how to do this, and thoughts of Monty led him to think of Emily, wondering what had happened to her. Despite her rebuttal he should have insisted on helping her get home, if only from simple courtesy; his father had always taught him to be courteous. From having two wives it appeared that he had no marriage of any kind now, might not even have a future in the army either.

'Look what I've done, Mother,' said Clem, proudly displaying his section of the rug.

Probyn's eyes shot up to see Grace's bedraggled, nightgowned figure in the doorway. Immediately he rose. 'Come and sit down. Can I get you anything to eat?'

'No, but a cup of cocoa would be nice.' The children had obviously had theirs, each mouth encircled with brown. Grace smiled but this loving gesture was restricted to her children and now she looked concerned. 'They shouldn't be using those sharp pegs.'

Probyn had not thought of this. 'They're being careful.'

Coming to stand beside them Grace praised her offspring's efforts with the rug.

'Yes, they're making a lovely job of it,' agreed Probyn, 'but it's time for bed now. Fold it all away.'

Without argument they spent a few moments with their mother, then went off to bed, taking the little ones with them.

Grace was still ignoring him, sitting and staring into the fire. She looked gaunt and corpse-like; a twenty-eight-year-old crone.

'We had a letter from Aunt Kit this morning.' He took it from behind the mantel clock and held it to her. When she showed no interest, he told her the content. 'She's asked if we want to go for a little holiday at the farm.' Still Grace did not respond. 'I could request leave . . .'

Grace remained abstracted.

Assuming he was wasting his breath, Probyn tucked the letter back behind the clock, then sat down, not knowing what else to do.

An age seemed to pass. He sat rubbing at the blue coal scar between his thumb and forefinger.

Finally Grace's lips parted. 'You say you weren't legally married . . .'

He came alive, eager to keep up the dialogue. 'That was what I was told. This corporal threatened to report me, said it was against regulations.'

'And you believed that to be the case?' An edge of doubt competed with the need to believe him. 'That you weren't really married to her?'

'I swear it, Grace.' It was injected with the utmost integrity.

Not that this seemed to sway her. 'I don't suppose we'll ever really know one way or the other, will we?' She glanced at him then. Her eyes were filled with betrayal. Then she took a deep breath. 'So I've got to make my mind up whether or not I want to stay with you.'

'I want you to,' he told her softly.

'But I'm not sure if I do,' she responded, her hooded eyes more lizard than seductress. 'I've thought and thought about it, and thought again, I've thought of what it would do to the children, where would we live . . . I just don't feel married to you any more. It's as if I'm living with somebody else's husband.'

Probyn clasped his hands, wrung them in quiet despair, bowed his head and stared at the floor between his khaki-clad knees. 'I can only say again how sorry I am and that I never meant to deceive you. I genuinely thought you were my only wife – you *are* my only wife.'

She nodded slowly, as if accepting what he said.

Her attitude ignited hope. 'Will you come with me to Aunt Kit's?'

She spent a few moments deciding, staring into the embers, before nodding again.

He looked relieved. It was premature.

'But I still don't know if I can ever feel married to you again,' Grace added ominously.

Telling his superiors only that he had family health problems, Colour-Sergeant Kilmaster acquired two weeks' leave and scribbled off a letter to warn his aunt of their coming.

Reassured by the presence of their mother in the kitchen once again, the children were even more delighted to be told of the holiday.

'Who's Great-Aunt Kit?' asked Clem.

'She was here the other week,' Probyn told him, hoping the child would not connect it with the violent scene.

'The big fat lady?'

'Don't be rude!' His father looked stern. 'Or you'll be made to sleep with the animals.'

Augusta wanted to know, 'What sort of animals are they?'

'I'll tell you on the way,' said Probyn, seizing a suitcase and ushering his wife and children from the house. 'Now jump to it or we'll miss the train.'

The train journey in itself was exciting enough, although the two eldest had travelled this way before, it had been a long time ago.

They could hardly believe their eyes upon being shown around the farm, small as it might be, and in the days that followed were to spend much of their time following Worthy and Toby from byre to sty to field, so lending their parents the time they needed to try and restore their ailing marriage. Kit, too, did all in her power to give Probyn and Grace the chance to be on their own, and was gratified to see towards the end of the first week the colour beginning to return to Grace's cheeks.

But, 'That brown does nowt for her,' she complained to Worthy as they lay in bed that night. 'She's a pretty lass, I don't know why she wears such drab stuff. I'm going to make her a dress. I'm sure it'd help.'

'I don't think it's her dress that's the problem,' came the low murmur from the large mound beside her in the dark.

Kit grimaced, trying to imagine what was occurring on the other side of the wall. 'No, I suppose not, but it'd make her feel better in herself surely? Poor souls. I wonder how they're going on.' Wanting to ensure that everything ran smoothly, she had checked that the bed her visitors were in did not creak. 'I know it's nosy —'

'Yes, it is.' Worthy rolled his massive bulk towards her. 'Instead of wondering, why don't we just put our time to better use?'

In the room next door, Probyn heard Kit giggle and, recognizing the tone of it, was rather embarrassed to witness his aged aunt's sexuality, but wondered too if he would ever again hear such laughter from his own wife. He and Grace were in the same bed but might as well be miles apart. He had not attempted to touch her, awaiting first the sign that would announce his forgiveness. But he was not sure if it would ever come.

*   *   *

Plied with good food and country air, Grace's recovery was to continue into the second week, though it was evident that her mind was still in turmoil. Still, she was cogent enough now to volunteer help in the kitchen, even if Kit did refuse.

'I feel awful leaving you with all this washing-up,' objected Grace after another generous breakfast. 'You've looked after six extra people all week, I should –'

'I've told you,' interrupted a smiling Kit. 'I enjoy having the company. Just go for a walk with your husband. It's a lovely morning. We'll keep an eye on the children.'

Grace nodded thoughtfully. Last night, hearing Kit giggle, she had faced the truth. It was no good trying to soldier on in this half-hearted fashion, she must make her mind up one way or another. Did she want this marriage or not?

Probyn entered the kitchen then, asking if he, too, could help. Kit laughed and repeated the instruction she had given Grace. Whilst his wife momentarily disappeared, Probyn sought answer to that which had been troubling him. 'Aunt, you haven't told anyone else about . . . ?'

'No! I haven't told a soul,' Kit lied effortlessly, her clear-blue eyes projecting the look of utter honesty that she had perfected in girlhood. But in truth this piece of family gossip was too momentous to keep to herself and she had disclosed it in a letter to her sister Amelia, telling her not to broadcast it further.

Probyn gave quiet thanks, then turned at Grace's reappearance. Now wearing a navy cardigan over her high-necked blouse, she signalled to him and he joined her eagerly, both setting off along a path across the field towards distant woods.

As they walked she slipped her arm through his. He did not know whether to be encouraged or whether she had acted simply on reflex. But the birds were singing and the sky was blue, and the last week had seen a vast improvement in his wife's health. It was enough to content him for the moment.

Grace lifted her face to the sky, showing a spark of her old self. 'What a day. As clear as a baby's eyes.'

After he had smilingly agreed, she said as if plucking it from the blue firmament, 'If we're to continue, Probe, then we have to get married again.'

He was deliriously happy that she had decided to give him a second chance, but, 'We already are legally married, we don't need –'

'*I* need,' interrupted Grace.

'I'm not sure it's possible to go through the ceremony twice.' The look she gave him told Probyn what a stupid thing that had been to say. His military bearing was shattered as he hung his head. 'Sorry.'

'It's not just the legality of it all,' explained Grace, strolling onwards, the hem of her gored navy skirt dappled with dew. 'What I want is to *feel* married. I'll only be able to do that if we have God's blessing.'

'If a blessing is what you want you shall have it,' murmured Probyn, and gripped her hand.

'Right, then we'll go to see Father Murphy today,' she nodded resolutely. 'He's an obliging soul. He might do it straightaway.'

And arm in arm they continued into the bright morning.

After lunch, without divulging their intentions to Kit, they went to church, arriving to find confession in process.

'I think I'll go in too,' whispered Grace. Apart from Charlotte she had not confided her troubles to anyone else, not even her sisters. But now she felt the need to talk.

Probyn sensed a question in her eyes. 'I can't, love,' he murmured guiltily. 'I know I should, but I can't. I'm not made that way. I just don't want anyone else knowing –'

'It's all right.' She seemed to understand that what came as second nature to her was alien to him; no amount of Catholic instruction could make it otherwise. Her eyes recognized his guilt and sorrow, bestowing him with a merciful smile.

Whilst his wife was closeted with the priest, Probyn could not help a certain amount of anxiety, wondering what secrets she was divulging.

But when Father Murphy offered no recrimination and agreed to perform a blessing, he knew that his bigamous past remained a secret.

Absolved, blessed, and a great deal happier than he had seen her in weeks, Grace accompanied her husband back to Aunt Kit's where, all smiles, they shyly announced what had occurred and were given a celebratory tea by a delighted Kit, the children not fully understanding anything other than their parents were laughing again.

And that night when they went to bed Grace allowed him to make love to her, and though the act might not have been infused with passion, it was at least a start.

22

An endorsement of her parents' reconciliation, Beata Honoria Kilmaster was born the following summer, her birth doubly welcome after the period of mourning which marked the old King's demise, the lengthy industrial disputes of miners and boilermakers and the news that the Boer nationalists had won the first parliamentary elections in the Union of South Africa.

Compared to his personal traumas, the latter was of insignificance to Probyn these days, his only dream being that life would get back to normal, and indeed with Beata's arrival it seemed that this had come to pass, the one sticky moment coming when he was forced to absent himself for annual training, this coinciding with the anniversary of Emily's visit, and though it was never mentioned it did tend to cast a shadow for several days afterwards.

But all in all, Probyn felt confident that their troubles were behind them and so was able to concentrate on his army career, about which he was not nearly so assured. Having to wait for the rank of RSM to become vacant was like waiting for a blue moon. As each month passed the odds against him achieving his aim grew steeper. When 1910 came to an end, taking him into the final stretch of his term, he began to fear that it would ever come about.

Grace had fears of her own. Their marriage back on an even keel, Probyn had resumed his healthy appetite, this and the onset of middle age settling a great deal of weight around his middle. He was more easily exerted, his face assuming a ruddy glow at the least effort, and he had developed varicose veins that caused him great discomfort. Even though he was not called upon to do the twenty-mile marches of his youth he had still to keep up to a certain extent with the recruits and she worried that one day he might collapse under the strain of yelling at them.

'I wish you'd go and see the doctor,' she begged him as, yet again tonight he enlisted Augusta's help in rubbing the ache from his calves. 'He might be able to give you something.'

'Nay, all they need is a good rub.' Under his daughter's ministrations, he uttered a groan of pleasure. 'Oh, that's lovely, Gus!'

'It wouldn't harm to have an examination,' pressed a worried Grace.

Yes it would, thought Probyn. The last thing he wanted was a doctor telling him he was unfit to continue, not when he had come so far.

Her husband's only response being one of those slow, deliberate nods that she had come to recognize as a sign that the debate was ended, Grace saw that it was hopeless to use his own deteriorating health as a reason to persuade him to give up the army. No matter how she pleaded, no matter the lack of argument on his part, she knew that Probe would dig in his heels and do as he liked

'Eh, you're a stubborn devil!' Thank goodness, thought Grace, that his twenty-one years was almost served and he would have to leave, even if it would be a great wrench for him to abandon the life he loved and a challenge to find another job. With seven to support, it would also be hard for Grace to make ends meet for there were few jobs which came with free accommodation, and she was not the most economical housekeeper at the best of times. But if Probyn could get a desk job, perhaps in York near to her family, without having to be at the army's beck and call, they would at last be able to call life their own.

Removed from public life, those in the Kilmaster household continued their comfortable existence in the barracks while those outside the garrison walls were to suffer the consequences of the perpetual violent unrest that marred the Coronation year. A constitutional crisis had produced a dead heat in last December's general election. The Liberals remained in government but only with the help of Labour and the Irish Nationalists. There were strikes by seamen and transport workers, disputes on the railways and in the cotton mills, fifty thousand armed troops being prepared to quell the nationwide unrest that had brought the country to a standstill. Grown mightier in recent years, the Trades Union Congress condemned the use of troops against fellow citizens, a sentiment with which Probyn wholeheartedly agreed for he dreaded a repetition of his involvement in the strike of 'ninety-three. And as if all these things were not sufficient to concern one, there was speculation over the Kaiser's motives in sending a gunboat to Morocco; rumour had it that the Germans were seeking a naval base there.

Notwithstanding this, most of the population managed to find cause for celebration during the summer, much of which was taken up with parties in honour of the King, not only at the barracks but also one at Aunt Kit's which they were forced to miss as Probyn was involved with annual training.

But during August, to make it up to Grace he took her to celebrate with her sisters and brother. It was as they and their tribe were on the way home from here that they bumped into a familiar personage.

'Mick!' Recalling their last meeting at the hospital, Probyn felt rather guilty now at having told his friend he could see a lump when he in fact could see nothing. 'I'm glad to see you're still alive.'

'I am, and in glorious spirits!' Whipping off his cap, Mick turned to the extremely pretty woman whose arm was threaded possessively through his, gazing upon her fondly. 'May I present Mrs Mick.'

Probyn bared his own head to the semi-tropical sunshine and grinned at the woman with the heart-shaped face. 'Oh, somebody's finally took him in hand. Congratulations to you both!'

Grace offered her own best wishes, taking her turn to shake hands with the pair, and noting that Mrs Mick was heavily pregnant, her face glowing not just with happiness but from the current ninety-degree heatwave.

'We were married last year.' Mick was beaming at his spouse, and she at him; it was quite obvious they were devoted to each other. 'Got a house just off Walmgate. You're welcome to call at any time. I'm a civilian now, ye know.'

'So I see!' Probyn examined the smart navy-blue suit and gleaming white collar, the air of fulfilment. Without an ounce of fat, not a grey hair in sight, Mick was a man in his prime. The Irishman found it hard not to remark on the change in his friend in only a couple of years. From being a stocky youth Pa now cut a bullish figure, with barrelled chest and wide shoulders, his determined jaw quite florid. But Mick kept this to himself and instead poured admiration upon the Colour-Sergeant's insignia and asked teasingly, 'And will it be RSM the next time we meet?'

'I think I might have left it too late.' Using a handkerchief to mop his brow, Probyn gave a regretful smile. 'I've only a short time left.'

'Ah, get away with yese! An ambitious sort like yourself will have a field-marshal's baton under your arm before the year's out – though I hardly know where you find the time, God love us, are all these yours?' He was looking with amazement at Probyn's children who stood in their Coronation attire, a Union Jack in every hand. 'Sure, we'll have a lot of catching up to do, Louie.' And at this he passed his wife a fond grin.

Wafting her face, Louisa made a contribution, saying it did not take much guessing to tell that the family had been to a Coronation party and asking the rather frazzled children if they had enjoyed themselves, before saying to Grace, 'That's a very pretty dress you're wearing.'

'Probyn's aunt made it.' Grace smiled self-consciously, her gloved hand displaying the folds of the kingfisher blue silk. 'I don't get chance to wear it very often.'

More compliments were passed on the dress, a good fifteen minutes being spent in Mick's company, the children growing more hot and bored whilst the adults shared each other's news and commented on the abnormal temperature and the amount of people who had died from it, which finally led Probyn to say, 'Well, we'd better not keep your good lady standing here in this heat.'

Glad to be off, the children perked up and began to move.

'Ah well, 'twas great to see ye, Pa!' cried Mick, doffing his hat to Mrs Pa. 'God Save the King! Don't forget where we live now.'

'I won't!' And with that the two couples parted.

But the sight of Mick's face seemed to have struck a chord in Probyn's mind and even after they had long been home he was to make comment on it. 'I can't get over how happy he looked.'

Grace was changing the baby ready for bed, napkins and ointment and safety pins spread out on the red chenille tablecloth, whilst Augusta got the others ready. 'His wife too. I envy her – oh, not for her husband!' she hastened to explain – things were quite good between herself and Probyn again and though she doubted they would ever enjoy the passion they had shared in the earlier days she could not complain. 'But because she's only married to the one man, not an entire army.'

Probyn offered gentle reproof. 'Nay, a man couldn't ask for a finer career, you've got a nice house, regular pay.'

'Yes, well, we won't have that much longer will we?' murmured Grace, pulling Beata's nightgown over her renewed napkin and picking her up off the table. 'Would it not be better to start looking for work now rather than leaving it till the last minute?' To date he had made no mention of his termination in December, possibly because it was a sensitive subject. She did not wish to upset him now but the matter had to be discussed.

'I've been meaning to talk to you about that,' tendered Probyn, stooping to retrieve a woollen bootee that the baby had kicked off. 'We have to be realistic, I'm not going to achieve RSM in the time that's left to me, so I'm going to ask permission to stay on.'

Grace could not believe what she was hearing, was crushed by disappointment. Knowing it was useless to hold up his own poor health as reason not to stay in the army, she saw that she would have to raise her own selfish needs.

Probyn saw that she did not share his confidence. 'I don't imagine there'll be any problem.'

There came a gasp. 'Not with your blessed officers maybe!'

Still holding the bootee, he looked at her askance.

Hot and exasperated, Grace hugged the baby, whose blue eyes were round with apprehension at her mother's raised voice. 'Don't you ever consider what army life is like for your wife and children, not seeing you for weeks on end, not knowing whether we're going to be uprooted or whether you're going to be sent to war? I've spent my whole married life at the army's whim. For God's sake, when are you going to put me first? You just seem to regard this marriage as a . . . as a sideline!'

'No, I don't!' He was grossly affronted.

'Yes, you do! Just look at your children, each one of those boys is named after an officer. It's a wonder you haven't called the girls after officers too! The army's your proper family, not us.'

So flabbergasted was he by this that it took a few heart-searching moments to recognize the fundamental truth of what she said, and he was thenceforth compelled to examine his motives: had he not joined the army because he wanted a family? But did he not have a family right here? Fingering the bootee, his stricken gaze fell on the perspiring row of little red-haired watchers. Only a fool could have been so blind.

He came then swiftly to examine other truths, saw that talented though he might be at interpreting the moods of men, could spot the malingerer trying to wangle his way out of Church Parade, could tell at a glance whether a man would make a good soldier or let the side down, he was totally inept at penetrating the female mind – could not even understand his own wife. Having always assumed that because she had not complained Grace loved being part of the army as much as he did, yet here she was telling him that not only did she not like it, but that she would stand for it not a moment longer.

He stared into her blue eyes, seeing in them the awful challenge: me, or the army.

Faced with losing his happy family, there seemed little choice. She had forgiven him over Emily, had let him have his own way during their entire married life, now he must consider Grace's needs. 'Well . . . if you want me to quit . . .' he paused, playing with the woollen bootee, allowing himself the chance of reprieve.

But none was to come, forcing him to conclude, 'Then, all right, I will.'

'Thank you,' said Grace firmly but with relief and gratitude in her eyes, and her attitude softened as she reached out to take the bootee, her fingers issuing an intimate squeeze as she took it. 'Besides anything else, it's not doing you any good at your age all this marching. Maybe you could get an office job, I mean you were clever enough to pass all those exams. It'll be a nice change for you to sit down instead of tramping about, won't it, Bea?' She kissed the baby reassuringly, smoothing a lock of hair from its sweaty little brow.

He gave a nod, trying to look bright but feeling wretched, and to hide this he wandered over to stand by the open window. The heat seemed even more oppressive now, the curtains hanging as limp as his spirits.

Reading his disappointment, Grace felt selfish that she had

been the instigator, but even if she could have tolerated another ten years in the army, it would not do Probyn any favours. She formed a sympathetic smile. 'We'll discuss it further when the children have gone to bed.'

And so it ended, thought Probyn dismally as he presented his somewhat stunned cheek for the children's goodnight kiss: his illustrious career plucked in half bloom, to wilt and wither before his eyes.

Though a competent clerk, Probyn was soon to dispense with all thoughts of office work upon discovering the pittance he would earn. Generous though his army pension might be, it would not keep the seven of them in the manner they had been used to, he must find better paid work. But what could he do? His only occupation before joining the army was mining and he was strongly indisposed to the dangers of underground labour again – there had been two big pit disasters in recent years. Perhaps there would be work on the surface. One thing was certain: any job would have to come with accommodation. With Grace's benevolence to others there had been no money put by for such an emergency.

'What about being a cook?' asked Grace. 'You've got your certificate.'

He contorted his mouth. 'I don't mind cooking at home but I don't know if I'd be any good doing it for a living. Still I could try.'

But once again he discovered that the wage was not commensurate with his needs. He could have been a cook in the army, but then Grace wanted to have nothing further to do with the army.

Other job interviews yielded the same disappointing results. Only the coal industry, it seemed, would pay the bonuses needed to provide for a family of seven. But with his sole experience being in pony driving it was inevitable that others more skilled would fill the vacant posts.

The months wore on but even with the commendations of

his officers he could find no suitable position. The date of his expiry loomed dangerously close, and still in between looking for work there were his regimental duties to attend. Moreover it looked as if he might be involved in military action, for Italy had declared war on the Turks and the Balkans had exploded into violence again; the British army could be required to quell the situation. Life became almost as tense as when Emily had dropped her bombshell.

'I told you there'd be a military use for aeroplanes,' Probyn commented on the news that aviators had dropped bombs on Tripoli. 'It must have been a nasty shock for the Turks.'

Grace, fearing that he was making excuses so that she would let him stay in the army, began to accuse him. 'Yes, well, it's nothing to do with you any more, you'll be leaving it all behind in a month or so – and if you don't find something soon we're going to be homeless!' This was all going wrong. Her main concern had been for her husband's constitution but there had been panic on finding out that a desk job was too badly paid. Now, that same panic caused her to envisage them being destitute, she just wanted him to find anything.

'I've tried!' His voice begged her to understand. 'I've been to just about every mine in the area. I'd go to Ralph Royd if I thought I stood a chance but my involvement in the strike of 'ninety-three has put paid to that. There's only two things that have longer memories than an elephant – an Irishman and a Yorkshire miner. I'd just be a target for violence.'

'Well, you have to do something!' Grace spread her hands in despair. The ideal of moving closer to her family had now been displaced by expediency. 'What's the name of that pit where your uncle works? Your face isn't known there, is it?'

'No, but it wouldn't take long for word to get round.'

'But couldn't your uncle help you?' asked Grace who had enlisted her own relatives' help in finding Probyn a job, as yet to no avail.

'My family isn't the same as yours,' he told her gently. 'Once they've made up their minds that they've cut you off, that's it, forever. And Owen's the worst of them.'

'God, your lot are stupid!' Grace was angry, and nothing he could say would make her otherwise.

In fact, she was to become even more distraught, for the search was to continue right into the third week of December, causing Grace to fall ill and take to her bed.

Deeply concerned himself, and feeling something of a failure, Probyn was finally compelled to swallow his pride. 'I don't suppose it'll do the least bit of good,' he told her, seated at her bedside, 'but I will go and see Owen. He can only throw me out. I can't think of anything else to do.'

Even the wearing of mufti could not conceal his soldier's bearing, and he was to receive inquisitive looks from a couple of housewives on his arrival at the colliery village. Apart from these, the streets of Garborough Junction were strangely deserted, but then it always was quiet whilst the men were down the pit.

But the moment he knocked at Owen's door he knew that the sense of desertion was more than just an illusion. There were no curtains at the window. A quick look through the pane showed that the house was completely empty. He now noticed that most of the others in the street were uninhabited too.

Shocked, he went back to the main street and entered the post office. The post office was also a general store though its shelves were depleted. The woman behind the counter was looking bored until he came in. Now she brightened at the thought of a sale.

With little from which to choose he bought some cigarettes. He had been smoking more recently. 'You're quiet today.'

'Quiet every day,' came the disgruntled reply. 'Since His Lordship closed the pit. It's worked out, or that's the excuse he's given. Myself I think he's just got fed up and washed his hands of it. He's selling the land.'

Probyn showed genuine concern, and not just for himself.

Such closure was a death knell for the whole area. 'How long's it been closed?' He could not recall having seen anything in the newspaper.

'Oh, months.' Handing over the cigarettes she folded her arms under her pinafored bosom and looked him up and down. 'Why, come for a job? You don't look much like a collier to me.' His fingers were too finely-tapered.

Putting one of the cigarettes between his lips and lighting it, Probyn shook his head woefully, the lie emerging on a cloud of smoke. 'No, I've just come to see my uncle, Owen Kilmaster, do you know him?'

The woman nodded. 'Aye, Owen's moved to Denaby Main so I believe.'

Probyn's heart fell even further and he drew deeply on the cigarette. The Denaby Main branch of the union had a reputation for militancy against a ruthless owner, with a record of major strikes and lock-outs. He had no wish to become embroiled in this. Still, he had no choice.

'Oh, you wouldn't believe it!' The woman's voice made him jump. 'I've just seen one of his grandbairns pass the door. Go catch him, he'll tell you.'

Thanking her, Probyn hurried from the shop and, seeing only one figure loping down the street, called to him. 'Hold on, lad!'

The young man, about fourteen, turned to wait for the other to catch up.

Probyn approached him in friendly manner. The lad was as tall as himself, though several stones lighter. 'Is your granddad called Owen Kilmaster?'

The other's brown eyes remained wary. 'Aye, what of it?'

'I don't think you and I've met.' Since the brothers' rift their families had not associated much. 'But your granddad is my uncle.' Swapping the cigarette to his other hand, Probyn extended his right.

The lad relaxed somewhat, nodding, and engaged in a handshake. 'I'm Roy.'

'Probyn.'

There was a slight change of expression on Roy's face. 'The sodjer?'

Probyn's gaze remained steady. 'Aye, but not for much longer. I've come to see your granddad but they tell me he's moved to Denaby. Do you have his address?'

The young man hesitated. 'I don't think he'll want to see thee.'

'It's important,' said Probyn firmly, using the gimlet gaze that had unnerved many a soldier.

Only through feeling intimidated by the man's strong character did the boy finally give him the information he sought.

Thanking him, Probyn wasted no further time and went to catch a train to Denaby.

His arrival coincided with the end of the six-to-two shift. His uncle was still in his pit clothes and came with bare arms and braces dangling to answer the knock, though he had undergone a wash and still held the grey towel in his mutilated hand as he opened the door.

Owen had grown even more goat-like in his sixty-second year, the lines that led from his nose to his small pointy chin deeply engrained with coal. Only the black astrakhan eyebrows remained unaltered, a strange combination when everything else about him was grey. Except for these Probyn would hardly have recognized the wizened old man who peered suspiciously round the edge of the door.

But seeing past the extra weight Owen recognized him and a look of disdain accompanied his words. 'By heck, you're taking your life in your hands.'

Unafraid, Probyn held the other's face, to which bits of lint adhered. 'Hello, Uncle Owen. Can I come in?'

After a moment's shaking of head for his nephew's audacity in coming here, Owen finally admitted him.

Probyn entered the parlour to be greeted coolly by his Aunt

Meg. 'By, you've put weight on; you'd make three of your uncle. Not in the army now?'

Not being invited to sit, Probyn remained standing but took off his cap. 'I'm nearing the end of my time. That's partly why I'm here.'

Age had not atrophied Owen's brain. Guessing the motive, he gasped and cried out to his wife, 'He's only got the nerve to come and ask if I'll help him get a job!'

Humbled, Probyn sought to explain. 'I wouldn't be here if I wasn't desperate, Uncle.'

'Oh, that makes it so much better!' Owen's stick-like body marched across the room and seized a newspaper over which he pored for a moment before folding it noisily and presenting it to his nephew, striking the relevant page with the back of his hand. 'There's a job at Cadeby that'll suit thee!'

Taking hold of the paper, Probyn read the advertisement for a master's weighman; the most detested position in the colliery.

'Thou bloody hypocrite,' muttered Owen, shrugging himself back into his braces.

Hypocrite? Yes, Probyn supposed he was. But, 'If it's a choice between hypocrisy and making sure my family don't starve, I'll choose the former.' He studied the twisted face for a moment longer, then said, 'Thank you, Uncle. I'll go and apply now.'

No one stopped him from leaving.

He had gone several paces before he realized that he did not know the location of the manager's house and had to ask a passer-by. Going there, he first offered his apologies to the manager for disturbing him, adding that he had come many miles to apply for the job.

The official seemed influenced by his military bearing and manners, sufficiently so to invite him in. Discovering that Probyn was a colour-sergeant he looked even more impressed.

'Why, you're just the kind we want, know how to get

the best out of the men! The job is yours if you want it.'

No he did not really want it. He would be a hated man among strangers. But at least it would save him from going underground, and it would be good news for his wife.

Enquiring over remuneration and inspecting the house that went with the post, he made his acceptance, agreeing to start after Christmas when the pit reopened. Then he went home to tell Grace.

Naturally his wife was overcome with relief and happiness, having envisaged them out on the street the moment the Christmas festivities were over. Now she could start to eat again, could relax and enjoy all the dances and parties, knowing that they marked the beginning of a new life, whilst for Probyn it was perhaps the worst Christmas he had ever encountered, including all those spent flooded out in South Africa.

Certainly it was marvellous for him and Grace to be invited into the colonel's office, where all the officers had gathered to show how much he was valued and to present him with a handsome gold ring.

'For your energetic devotion to duty,' announced the colonel to applause, afterwards presenting Mrs Kilmaster with a bouquet of flowers for her excellent work with the officers' laundry.

There were, too, accolades from the parade ground, the men sending up three rousing cheers for their respected colour-sergeant, even men from whom he had heard the private grumble that they hated his guts.

A final enthusiastic flurry of handshaking . . . and that was that, came his desolate thought.

All that was left was to supervise the loading of his family's belongings on a wagon and catch a train. No more the bold soldier but a colliery employee. Denaby Main was a company town, its houses, shops, the parish church, the public house and even the school built and owned by the coal masters, just as they now owned him. A company man.

Arriving before the furniture, Grace could not believe her luck upon being shown around her new house, delighted that even if the outside walls were grimy with coal inside it was clean and she could see green fields from its windows.

She examined each of its rooms, only two of them being bedrooms but these were very large, a ducket lavatory and a shed filled with gleaming coal that would never run out, eventually exclaiming, 'Oh it's lovely!' And she hugged him, both for the house and his sacrifice. 'But the best thing of all is that you've not been forced underground. I had awful visions, felt really guilty that I'd made you leave, but you've got a safe job, a sitting down job, an *important* job.' She squeezed him reassuringly. 'This is surely going to make your changeover from the army a lot smoother, Probe.'

And Probyn returned the hug, agreeing with her, though in truth he felt that nothing could fill his empty heart.

He was to see little of his uncle. Owen lived only in the next street but worked at the Denaby pit which, though amalgamated to the same company as Cadeby, was almost a mile apart from it. The few times they did pass in the street Owen's only acknowledgement was a nod and Probyn expected nothing more.

Grace's own transition was much easier, her kindness and pleasant personality endearing her to her new neighbours straightaway and making up too for the fact that her husband was a weighman, and most showed a willingness to help the Kilmasters settle in. The parish priest, Father Flanagan, became a regular caller and a good friend. With a fire in every room, including the bedrooms, the house was as warm as toast, and the atmosphere too, the children being as adaptable as their mother.

Probyn wondered if he was the only one not to have settled in. Seated in the dark little office that he shared with the check weighman day after day, watching a procession of tubs rumble past his window, having to weigh each one . . . he tried to project enthusiasm, he really did, but it took every ounce of willpower to look cheery as he set off for work on a morning, especially now that winter had really set in with heavy snowstorms blighting his passage. There had been a spark of excitement upon receipt of the letter that had gone out to all reservists, telling him to hold himself in readiness for mobilization. A cheque had accompanied the letter, to be cashed if he was called up, enabling him to pay for the train to the depot, and giving rise to the idea that some matter of great import was pending – there had been concern over Germany's naval build-up for some time. Quivering with excitement he had held himself in readiness for days, but nothing had happened. He was still sitting here watching his tubs. At least the colliers had come to know that if he reprimanded a miner it was because his tub was genuinely underweight and not done out of pettiness, and with his fines being not so punitive as they might have been he did not have to bear any more resentment than that which usually went with the job.

But occasionally, when his wife took the children to Sunday Mass, he would demur, saying his legs were troubling him and preferring to remain in bed. Then, once alone, he would take his dress uniform from the wardrobe and polish its buttons, reverently pick off each speck of lint, and gaze upon it longingly, thinking of battles and comrades long dead, before reluctantly restoring it to its hanger.

That mining was a precarious existence, he had always been aware; but a few weeks after he had started work Probyn was given a stark reminder. A sudden outpouring of men from the shaft signalled that something was wrong, for the shift was not yet over. Their frightened faces confirming his worries, he came out of the office into a snow-covered yard to investigate.

Eyes narrowed against the cold driving flakes, he saw that a few of the men had signs of injury, and hence took immediate charge, telling a boy, 'Get me a first-aid box!'

But the under manager was to countermand him – 'Go back to your office, I'll see to this!' – giving rude reminder that he was no longer in the army.

Feeling belittled, he stood there for a moment in the bitter cold, whilst others gave expert management, then asked one of those who had come out what had occurred.

'Gas in t'old one-twenty-one's stall,' explained the informant, hunched against the weather. 'We were working a hundred and fifty yards away and felt t'blast. Lucky they weren't more badly burned. There were a gob fire back in November, I reckon this were in t'same place, though there's allus one somewheer. She's a fiery owd pit.'

Nodding, Probyn watched for a moment longer, snow settling on his cap and shoulders, before the cold drove him back to the comparative comfort of his dingy office.

Before long, the fire was brought under control, the men persuaded to go back down and work resumed.

However, the dangers of explosion were not the only hazards in the mining industry and Probyn was shortly to find his new employment threatened from a different angle. He was aware of the Federation rumblings over a minimum wage that had been in motion previous to his appointment as Owen and others argued that no man working underground should receive less than five shillings per shift, the boys no less than two shillings. Probyn agreed with the principle. It was not fair that those working where the seam was thin were unable to earn the recognized minimum wage for the district. Nevertheless, if the miners were to strike, without union membership himself he could expect no financial backing, and he dreaded the outcome.

Some agreement had been reached, but not enough for the Federation. A ballot was taken on the question of handing in notices to establish the principle. A large many were in favour and, to Probyn's dismay, notices were handed in to terminate at the end of February. From the first of March the pit was on strike, as were those over the entire country.

He feared that Grace would take it out on him. She had been very unpredictable since 'the visit'; it didn't take much to disturb her equilibrium and at the slightest upset she would begin to neglect herself, which would make her prone to any transient infection, which usually precipitated another bout of bed rest.

However, upon his news she did not fly into a panic, but sympathized and said, 'You can't be blamed, dear. We'll manage somehow.'

Though relieved at her response, it was hard to see how they would manage for, during the weeks that followed, no amount of negotiation could bring about an end to the national deadlock involving three-quarters of a million men. Foreseeing that the situation would become dire if no intervention occurred, the Prime Minister wasted no time in calling each of the sides to meet him in conference. Yet with such bitter opponents even he had no sway, the dispute extending from one month into the next and spreading financial distress over the nation.

With no wages, the debts began to build. The level of coal in the shed fell dangerously low, having to be eked out by anything else that might burn. Food had to be purchased on credit.

'The others in my class have breakfast at the Big Drum,' announced Clem over his bread and butter one morning during the long drawn out boycott. 'They have these nice tea-cakes. They get their dinner there too. Why can't we go?'

Teapot in hand, Grace looked questioningly at Probyn, who told his son, 'Because their fathers are in the union and your father's not. If the union didn't pay for their food they'd starve.'

Anxiety filled Madeleine's big blue eyes. 'Will we starve?' Whilst her elder siblings had seats, she and the younger ones must stand at the table, there being insufficient chairs.

Probyn smiled reassuringly. 'No, we have money from the army to live on.'

Little Joseph chipped in. 'The army's good, isn't it, Father?'

Probyn gave a wistful smile and nodded.

Grace offered no argument, for once grateful to the military and adopting all blame for landing them in this situation.

'There's a German spy in my class,' announced Augusta, nibbling the corner of her bread.

Grace threw an amused glance at Probyn. 'Really, dear? What's his name?'

'Ruth Kaiser – she's a girl.'

'Oh, she must be Mr Kaiser's daughter, the man who has the butcher's shop.' Grace prevented the gossip from spreading further. 'They're not spies, they're lovely people. Well, Mr Kaiser is.' She murmured now to Probyn in a confidential tone, though it was easy for the children to overhear, 'I hear his wife was involved with that violent suffragist demonstration in London. Much as I'm a great believer in votes for women and don't hold with the treatment they're getting, being imprisoned and force-fed, I detest wanton destruction. What good do they expect that to do? It just drags us all down. As if there isn't enough violence in the world. They'd set better example by putting forth intelligent argument rather than behaving like vandals.' She handed another slice of bread to the youngest child. 'And nine times out of ten it's the posh folk who are in the thick of it, pretending they're representing the poor downtrodden women like me. What the devil do they know about how we're forced to cope, what with servants at their beck and call? I don't need them to speak for me, I can speak for myself thank you very much.'

'We can see that,' teased her husband.

Grace laughed.

'Why aren't you in the union, Father?' asked Clem.

Probyn was slow in responding. 'It's a bit too complicated for you to understand.'

'What's complicated?'

Grace ignored the question, telling Madeleine, 'Stand still whilst you're eating, and don't lean on the table.'

'Can I be in the army when I grow up?' asked Joseph.

Probyn glanced at his wife, saw her purse her lips. 'We'll see. Now, no more talking at the table. By Jove, if my father were alive I don't know what he'd have to say. I were never allowed half the freedom you are. Let's just finish our breakfast in peace.'

'Finished it,' said Clem, looking down rather miserably at his empty plate.

Grace tore her own piece of bread in half. 'Here, gutsy!'

Probyn shook his head in reproof. His wife often shared her portion with the children.

'Well, he's a growing lad,' came Grace's excuse as she dribbled the last drop of tea into her cup.

'Aye, he's growing at his mother's expense – you're looking right scrawny.'

'You cheeky 'a'porth!' Grace flicked him with the back of her hand, though she was laughing. 'That's the pot calling the kettle black. If this strike goes on any longer we can always eat you!'

But it was really no laughing matter with this austerity seemed set to continue for many more days. Only when a bill was put before Parliament, and the Royal Assent given, did the miners' long struggle for a minimum wage finally appear to be won. Yet stubborn to the end, they were to drag the strike into another week before taking the ballot that would signal a return to work.

To a flourish of banners and brass bands the pit reopened in April. Though making a less boisterous entry to his workplace, Probyn was relieved to be back here too, and felt rather proud of himself for being able to exist on his army pension without having to cross the picket line, which made his return to work a lot less hostile than it might have been. Bad as things were, he was fortunate enough to have a job at all, for some of the collieries were never to reopen.

With the pit in bad condition, it took another week for normal work to be resumed, thereby extending the financial misery. Added to this came another report that a flash had been seen in the district of the last explosion, though nothing was found and officials placated fears by saying that the fire had been put out.

'There's going to be trouble down there if some bugger doesn't sort it out,' Probyn was informed by the check weighman, a quite elderly chap with fifty years' experience at the face. 'I warned them last year about fire in that seam but they wouldn't pay any heed. That's why I decided to pack it in and come up here. There's going to be a big un if they don't fettle it, mark my words.'

Whilst Probyn could only claim ignorance, others were in agreement with the old fellow. But then in a few weeks a disaster at sea overcame all talk of fires and strikes as the whole country expressed its horror at the calamitous sinking of the ship *Titanic*.

'My Aunt Flora's married to a fellow on the White Star Line!' exclaimed Probyn, aghast at the newspaper report of the disaster. 'I hope he's all right. I shall have to ask Kit.'

'How dreadful it must have been! I'm sure it was that eclipse of the sun that had something to do with it,' said Grace, close to tears. 'It felt really eerie when it went all dark, as if something wasn't right in the world.' She shivered. 'I keep imagining the icy water closing over my head, those poor women having to leave their husbands behind, watching them perish . . . ooh, it doesn't bear thinking about!'

And though she could ill afford it with their debts not yet settled, and feared that Probyn would be annoyed, she contributed secretly to the *Titanic* Relief fund that was set up, and helped to put on concerts in aid of those lost souls.

* * *

With the blooming of May came yet another Home Rule bill for Ireland spawning more grumbles from Probyn over the attempted carve-up of the Empire. In England the great industrial conflict that had marred previous years was to repeat itself, this time amongst the dock and transport workers.

But in summer came excellent news for those in Yorkshire. 'The King and Queen are coming to visit!' Grace told Probyn when she and little Beata came to fetch his dinner to the office that noon.

'What, us personally? You'd better get t'house cleaned up then.' He winked at the check weighman.

She hit him on the head with the newspaper. 'I've brought this so you can read it yourself but we'll take it back if you're being cheeky, won't we, Bea?'

Smiling his apologies, he thanked her for this kindness and, wiping his coal-smeared fingers on a rag, poked about in the basket to see what she had brought him for dinner. Satisfied with the contents, he bit into the thick sandwich, waved her and Beata off, then spent his break reading the newspaper report. Besides visiting the manufacturing centres of the county, the King was to review the National Reserve of the West Riding. Probyn's heart soared. A chance to get out his uniform!

With this exciting prospect under his belt he could scarcely wait to get home to Grace that evening and tell her his intentions. He would have to take the day off, but she was not to worry for everyone else was talking of doing the same for the visit had created great excitement in the village, and he would go to Wentworth Woodhouse to parade before the King. She and the children did not have to go so far, for their Majesties would be driving right through Conisborough on their way to be entertained by Earl Fitzwilliam. It would be a grand day out for all of them!

Happy for this burst of enthusiasm from one whose life had been all drudgery of late, Grace laughed and clapped and hugged him to show that she too was thrilled. Dear Probe, he deserved a treat.

On the day of the visit the weather was glorious. The Royal couple would not be arriving at Doncaster until almost four o'clock but Probyn had to leave early in order to report to his military commanders. Grace, too, voiced her intention to set off in plenty of time so that she and the children could get a good place along the route. They could take a picnic lunch with them.

Leaving his wife to get the children ready and to make sure the boys did not slope off to climb trees in their best clothes and the girls' pinafores stayed clean and their hair ribbons intact, he himself went to put on his uniform. Last night he had polished his boots until they gleamed like patent, the brass buttons on his tunic equally bright. With great care and reverence, he took it from the wardrobe and suspended its hanger from a hook. The July sunlight streamed through the window, setting the buttons a-glint.

Having waited to shave until now, he stood before the mirror and lathered his chin, the reflected eyes twinkling back at him as he dipped his razor into the bowl of water and began to scrape off his whiskers. Once shaved and washed, his moustache faultlessly trimmed and waxed, he finally put on his uniform, complete with medals, donned his helmet and made a last-minute inspection in the wardrobe mirror. Then, for old times' sake, he saluted himself, before going downstairs.

Having heard his boots thud against the floorboards as he performed his salute, Grace alerted the children that their father was ready to go – 'I thought he was going to come through the ceiling!' – and by the time he got down they were at the open door, Grace in her kingfisher gown and white gloves, with feathered hat, his offspring equally smart, not a hair out of place on each auburn head and pink cheeks aglow with excitement. Union Jacks in hand, they set off for their appointment with the King and Queen.

Whilst Probyn went off to catch a train, there were hours to wait for Grace who, along with other excited families, seated her own by the roadside along which the King would travel, all squashed onto a rug to spare their best clothes from grass stains. Having to cope with much fidgeting over the following hours, and constant questions from the children who demanded to know when, oh when, was the King going to come, she was forced to open the picnic hamper early and by noon everything in it was devoured.

By the time their Majesties' motor car drove through more than four hours later the children were once again complaining about their hunger, pinafores had acquired wrinkles and satin hair-ribbons had slipped from their neat bows, but this was all wiped away in an instant as the King and Queen dealt regal waves to right and left and the welcoming crowd of miners and their families erupted into a frenzy of cheers and flag-waving. Nothing mattered but that they were here.

And as the Royal motor car made its way through the village and onwards, eventually to arrive at Wentworth Woodhouse, nothing else mattered to Probyn either.

Proud and erect amongst the host of veterans, he marched behind the regimental band, his boots and his heart marking time to the big bass drum that without fail made the hairs on the back of his neck stand on end, his whole body throbbing with happiness as he saluted the Monarch. It might only be for one day, but he was a soldier again.

With such wonderful moments to share with his family upon meeting them again that evening, Probyn's excitement was to be maintained for hours, the happy and dishevelled children eager to tell their father what they had seen, until, all replete with fish and chips, they tumbled into bed.

Only in the morning did anti-climax come when Probyn awoke expecting to hear the bugler, but heard instead only the clip of miners' boots as those on the night shift made their way home.

Light seeped through the curtains which were billowing under the summery breeze from the open window. Grace rose and dressed, telling him to have a lie in. He did so, listening to the sounds of the children as one by one they were roused from their beds. Not due at work for a while, he closed his eyes, reliving the splendour of yesterday, dreading the thought of being trapped in his dingy office.

Telling himself it would do no good to lie here moping, he kicked his limbs together and sat on the edge of the bed, rubbing his face, then began to dress.

He was in the act of buttoning his trousers when he heard a commotion outside, a wail that signalled catastrophe. He stood stock still for a moment, images flying through his head, then rushed to the window, pulled back the curtains and stuck his head through the open sash.

Men, women and children with puffy eyes and tousled hair, some only half-dressed, were streaming out of their houses, appearing from every direction and coming together like a flock of starlings, swirling and weaving down the street and around the corner towards the pit.

Without calling to any of them, he rushed to the staircase and thudded down it to meet his wife's startled face.

'What on earth is all the din?' Grace clasped her breast, shock in her voice.

He pulled his dangling braces up over his shoulders and hurried to put on his boots. 'Summat's happened at the pit – I'll have to go and help!' And without wasting further time he rushed out into the street, his wife and children after him, all joining the torrent of panicked humanity that surged down the slope to Cadeby Colliery, over the river and the railway, hundreds of feet thudding across the long wooden gantries.

Running for almost a mile, by the time they arrived at the colliery gates Grace was clutching her side, her husband's face bright pink. 'Slow down, Probe!' She reached out to grab at his sleeve, pretending it was for her benefit. 'I've got a stitch.'

At his wife's behest Probyn stopped, panting heavily, but seeing that Clement had got ahead of him and was shoving his way through the herd, gave a loud command, 'Clem!

Come back, you'll only get in the way.' Then, still breathless, he continued with his wife to the pit-head that had been besieged by a distraught throng, men arguing as to what should be done, women clutching shawls over hair that was still tangled from bed, crying that their husbands and sons were down there.

Accustomed to being in control, to guiding men and having them obey him, Probyn felt the desperate urge to take charge, but was compelled by inexperience to stand and wait whilst others gave command, feeling like a duck out of water.

'What's happened, Father?' He felt little Joseph tug on his sleeve.

'I don't know, son. There's been some sort of accident.' Probyn cast his worried eyes around the crowd, searching for enlightenment.

There was a moment's awkwardness as he found himself standing right beside his uncle, both men reticent in their greeting.

Probyn spoke first. 'Do you know what's happened?'

Owen's face was grim. 'There's been an explosion on fourteen level. Gob fire so they say. Started in t'early hours.'

'How many's down there?' asked Probyn.

Owen did not know. 'The wick uns who came out said they saw a load of tubs blown about and a couple of bodies. They're just getting t'rescue team together.'

As he spoke, a grim-faced rescue team emerged from the enquiry office with Mr Bury the manager, equipped with breathing apparatus and spare oxygen cylinders, and all descended the pit.

A few moments later the crowd parted as a motor car swept into the yard bearing men from the Wath Rescue Station who also descended. Following this, the onlookers were left to wait in anxious ignorance.

Ignorant, too, as to the whereabouts of his uncle's family, for they had not spoken in years, Probyn felt he should ask. 'Are any of yours down there?'

Owen shook his grizzled head. 'Nay, thank the Lord. I've just come to see if I can do owt.'

The atmosphere uncomfortable between the two men, plus the general tense attitude of the crowd, nothing much was said for the next hour. The waiting was terrible.

Probyn dared not look at his watch for fear of upsetting someone. He guessed it must be about seven when Mr Witty the agent arrived, immediately to be engulfed by a crowd of women wanting to know what he was going to do to get their men out. Fearing that her smaller children were going to be knocked over with the crowd's rush, Grace grabbed them close to her, listening anxiously.

Tactfully removing himself from the grasp of supplicating hands, Witty accosted a deputy and asked to be apprised of the situation.

The informant looked tired and worried. 'Mr Bury and Mr Cusworth are already down there, sir, and the ventilation's been restored.' At the latter information there was a slight sigh of relief. But at his next statement concern was resurrected. 'Bodies have been located but Mr Bury has telephoned to say they need help in getting them out.'

'Is there any alive?' asked Witty.

'None found sir.'

A combined moan went up. Feeling desperately sorry for the woman who stood beside her weeping, Grace extended a comforting arm.

Mr Witty, looking pained but remaining in control, said to the informant, 'Right, then we'll need somewhere to put them. Get the pay shed ready, we'll use that. We'll need stretchers too, and volunteers,' he embraced the crowd in his next words. 'I'll need twenty of you to start with.'

There was an immediate and positive response.

'Are you going, Father?' asked twelve-year-old Clem.

Owen, about to step forward himself, paused to behold his nephew, a cynical look on his face.

Though his uncle made no comment, Probyn set his jaw

into a resolute slant as he answered his son. 'No, lad, I'm not. If there were any alive down there I might do, but I'm not trained and I won't risk my life for dead bodies. Not with a family to think about.'

Retaining his cynical expression, Owen went off to collect his lamp, leaving his worried wife to wait. Grace reached out a tentative hand to Meg, though it was barely acknowledged.

At the supposed cowardice from his father, the big bold soldier, Clem hung his head.

Sensing accusation in this pose, Probyn recalled the time when the scales had dropped from his own eyes and he too had made the discovery of his father's failings, seeing Monty not as an invincible hero but as the vulnerable human being he was. That knowledge should have provided comfort to him now. It did not. Too wounded to offer explanation, he remained silent.

But Grace understood her husband's motives, and rested a hand on her son's shoulder. 'Sometimes, Clem, it's braver to say no.'

Wondering what on earth he was doing here if not to assist, Probyn made a sudden announcement. 'I'm off to see if they want anybody to supervise the mortuary. You go home, dear, there'll be grim hours ahead.'

But Grace refused. 'I'll wait a while, there might be some way I can help.'

They separated then.

Hours were to pass. Hours of waiting in which the silent crowd hung around the pit-head with terror-stricken faces, their numbers constantly accumulating so that every foot-bridge over the railway and river, every road leading to the pit yard became clogged with people. Newspaper reporters came barging from the railway station, breathless and eager, pads and pencils at the ready. Others came to offer succour, clerics of every denomination bestowing prayers amongst the flock. Through a sea of dreary garb that was incongruous under the brilliant sunshine – black stockings, plaid shawls, woollen caps

– the stark white pinafore of a nurse shone out in bright relief as her bicycle carved a passage, come to aid the injured.

But there were no injured. The bodies started to come out then, emerging in stages; at first just a few, then eighteen in a row, transported reverently out of the pit mouth and into the sunshine. And every time another came the crowd would close around it, anxious to see if it were a relative or friend and a horrible keening would go up from a bereaved wife or mother. Whilst her husband rearranged the contorted limbs of the dead, Grace could only offer sympathy.

At mid-morning the Mines Inspectors arrived and went immediately down the shaft. Others were to arrive some time later but delayed going down and instead studied a plan of the district.

Guarding his roomful of corpses, Probyn sneaked a look at his watch, discovering it was after ten. No bodies had been unearthed for a while, and another hour was to pass without news.

In the enquiry office a telephone rang. Those standing near the office surged closer, hoping to learn something. Mr Witty frowned, straining to hear what was being said at the other end above the buzz of anxious queries. 'Yes, Captain Brook . . . yes, I'll pass that on to Mr Pickering straight away!' Settling the receiver back on its hook he went to a different telephone and made contact with those at the pit-bottom.

The voice from below must have said something devastating, for Witty's face turned ashen and he said, 'Oh my God . . .'

Harried for news by those who crowded round his door, his dazed face observed them. 'It's gone off again.'

A heartrending wail went up. Hearing it, Probyn came to the door of the makeshift mortuary. Dear God, Owen!

The commotion seemed to shake Mr Witty from his trance for he rushed to the cage, taking another man with him.

Feeling utterly inept over his lack of underground training,

Probyn could only employ his eyes to telegraph sympathy to his Aunt Meg, but she did not look at him, just stood there with her black shawl over her head, totally devastated, whilst Grace made every effort to support her. Not for a long time had he felt so isolated.

When Mr Witty eventually emerged the full horror of the situation was writ large upon his face. Only four live men were to exit from the shaft with him, and even these were to be borne on stretchers; one of them, though barely conscious, kept moving his legs like pistons, as if trying to run away from the horrors he had seen. Two hundred tons of roof had come down, instantly annihilating many of the rescuers, the rest trapped behind it and succumbing to gas.

Preparing himself to be inundated by another round of corpses, seared by anguish over the death of his uncle, Probyn's heart raged for those brave men. Poor, poor Owen, but worse for his wife left to grieve.

The sun rose to its zenith. The waiting crowd grew more distressed. With the younger children beginning to whine Grace whispered to Augusta to take them home and give them something to eat. She herself stayed to lend her arms to the grave-faced womenfolk, to watch and to wait for hours as one after another the corpses of the brave rescuers were brought out into the hot afternoon, some identifiable, others not, but all evoking an emission of grief from the crowd.

The desperate work was to continue throughout the day, the last of the bodies eventually brought up by evening and the order given that no one else was to go down until stoppings had been built and the pit made safe.

'Close to eighty by the look of it,' murmured Probyn with a sad shake of head for the lifeless occupants crammed into the mortuary, one of them his uncle. 'What a waste, what a terrible shameful waste.'

Stretching his tired, aching back, he wondered if Grace was still out there waiting, and stepped from the pay shed to check on her whereabouts, narrowing his eyes against the still bright sun. Running his gaze over the crowd, he allowed it to settle occasionally, but was swift to tear his eyes away, for each face resembled a tragic gargoyle. Unable to see his wife and assuming she had gone home, he went back to his thankless task of guarding the dead.

The coroner arrived to open the inquest and, with his jury appointed, the grim identification of the bodies began, death certificates filled out for those able to be recognized.

Only then did Probyn beg leave to go home. After the gruelling day, the ghastly task of identifying his uncle, he was glad for others to take charge of the dead, who were to remain here all night. A heavy stone within his chest, he made his weary passage through the crowd. Its numbers had begun to thin now, though hundreds remained to keep their vigil, for many of them had no reason to go home.

Pausing only to scan the messages of condolence that had arrived throughout the day and had been posted on some railings – amongst them words of sympathy from the Home Secretary, the Archbishop of York and from the King and Queen – he finally left the place of disaster.

Arriving home, he found Father Flanagan there. In the middle of telling the children a story, the priest broke off to say in concerned tone, 'Good evening to you, Probe, and how's yourself? It's a grave day and no mistake.'

'It is that, Father.' There were six extra children in Probyn's kitchen, their stark, tear-stained faces advertising that their fathers were among the dead.

Grace came immediately to her husband, providing comfort and food, whispering, 'I said we'd look after them for a day or two. Their mothers have enough to see to. You don't mind do you?'

Probyn sank gratefully onto a chair, saying quietly, 'Of course I don't. They can stay as long as they like.' Exhausted and hungry, he ate his meal in silence whilst Father Flanagan gathered the children about him and resumed the tale that had been interrupted, only emerging from his trance to ask what had happened to Meg.

Told that she had rejected Grace's offer of help and had gone home, Probyn fell back into silence, maintaining his reflective air for a good while after he had finished eating.

After half an hour or so, Father Flanagan left saying he had better tend the rest of his poor bereft flock, but had not been gone a minute before he reappeared with word that the King and Queen had made a surprise return to Cadeby to offer solace to the people who had cheered them so warmly yesterday, and were down at the colliery.

Once again Probyn and his family went out to gather in the warm sunny evening to pay their respects. But this time there was no cheering, only expressions of sorrow from their Majesties as they went amongst the depressed crowd in the colliery yard, shaking hands and extending condolence.

'I wish he'd got his crown on instead of just an 'at,' grumbled Joseph, having passed disapproving comment on the King's bowler yesterday.

'It would look a bit out of place, dear,' reproved his mother softly.

Probyn wondered if the King felt as out of place as he did himself amongst the bereaved crowd of miners; an impostor, a man apart. And as the royal couple approached the place where he was standing he moved a step back, detaching himself from those who had suffered and melting into the background so that he might not steal their moment, for he had done nothing to deserve it.

On Wednesday morning, leaving the blinds closed as were those in the rest of the terrace, Probyn went back to the pit, not to work but to help transfer the bodies to coffins. Grave as the death toll might be, it was a miracle there had not been more, for news emerged that the men who had spent the night building stoppings to make the pit safe had also been forced to run for their lives as a third explosion occurred, injuring two of them.

Throughout that day the mean, blackened streets thronged with various dignitaries eager to pay their condolences, aristocracy by the carriage load, the Archbishop of York who held a service at the pit-head before visiting bereaved relatives. The humble pit village had never seen such distinguished visitors en masse.

But once the flow of sentiment dried up, a pall began to settle over the neighbourhood as reality sank in and the villagers were left to bury their menfolk.

During the weeks after the disaster the funerals of eighty-eight men took place, those bereaved coming together in a spirit of community and, as was the way of things in a mining village, helping each other to get on with their lives.

Probyn felt guilty for feeling as miserable as he did. The last horse-drawn hearse had departed weeks ago. He had lost no one, at least no one really close, why should he harbour such emotion? Despite all that had happened here, even maybe because of it, he still did not feel part of the colliery village; part of anything.

Grace sensed her husband's misery and hoped that her news this Sunday evening might lift him. 'I've either been eating too much pastry, or baby number six is on his way.'

'Aw, that's grand.' Probyn hoped he sounded pleased, for he was.

'Which officer are you going to name him after this time?' teased his wife, smiling.

Taking a last drag on his cigarette, he ground it into the ashtray. 'Oh, I'll leave the names to you.' Despite the warmth in his eyes he sounded despondent. 'Besides, it might be a lassie.'

Feeling for him, Grace came through the grey pall of cigarette smoke to sit on the arm of his chair, snaking her hand around the back of his neck to rest on his broad shoulders. With all the weight he had put on, he looked older than thirty-nine. 'You really miss your pals, don't you?'

He shrugged as if uncaring, then admitted, 'Well, it is a bit lonely being a hated man.'

'Aw, you're not hated!' She kissed the top of his sandy head. 'Me and the children love you.'

He patted her knee and chuckled thoughtfully. 'I know, I meant hated by the chaps whose tubs have stones in them.'

'Well, I can't do much about them but I can help in another matter. The pit's playing tomorrow.' It was August Bank Holiday. 'Why don't you go and visit the boys at the depot?'

'Ooh, it's a fair way to go . . .'

'Then set off early,' advised Grace, shaking him gently by the shoulders. 'There'll be a train running. Didn't the colonel tell you to call in at any time?'

He was beginning to perk up. 'But didn't you mention you'd like to take the children for an excursion?'

'I can still take them for a walk to Ivanhoe castle. Go on, Probe, treat yourself!' And she lovingly chivvied him until he complied.

So, the next morning, washed and spruced, boots polished, moustache waxed to perfection, he caught a train to Pontefract, intending to seek out his old army pals.

His heart was lighter than it had been for some time at the thought of being part of it all again, already he could hear the sound of marching, of orders being bawled across the parade ground . . .

But when he came to the barrack gates, he just could not go in. Fixed to the spot, he just stood there looking at the sentry from a distance, the latter eyeing him back suspiciously.

What prevented him from entering he could not say. It was just the most overwhelming feeling of awfulness, so awful that he had to turn away and march briskly down the hill.

Plunged back to his former gloom, he wandered around the ancient streets of Pontefract, racking his brain as to what it was that had forbidden him to enter those gates. Then quite by chance he came to the Buttercross under whose stone arches a group of old soldiers were gathered in their uniforms, reminiscing about old times, trying to behave as though they were still part of the army. Was this all that was left to him? Pausing a moment to watch them, he considered how pathetic they were, no longer part of the family, but unable to admit it.

And that was the crux of it. The revelation smote him in the breast as effectively as had the big bass drum of the regimental band, except that this time there was no joy, only anguish. He must learn to let go.

Overwhelmed by grief, he felt the tears prick his eyes, before damning himself for a sentimental fool. And, taking an imaginary sword from his belt, he dealt the umbilical cord a swift, irrevocable blow.

Nothing happened, no vital haemorrhage occurred, and yet when he looked at the old soldiers again it was as if a shaft of light had pierced his brain. No, *not* pathetic. Oh, so much wiser than he, those old warriors had learned that no matter how removed from the days of glory, no matter how weak of limb, how decrepit, how worthless to others or to themselves, the bond with their comrades could never be severed, and the blood of the regiment would always pump through their hearts, as surely as it would through his own.

Imbued with this vital truth, he had no need now to be amongst soldiers in order to feel that big bass drum raise the hairs on the back of his neck, for it happened even as he was standing here, that prickle of excitement and pride and belonging, and he knew then that he would carry it with him to the grave.

Still shaken by his almost miraculous conversion, he made not for the barracks but for the railway station and caught the next train home, with every mile his heart becoming lighter, so that by the time he eventually arrived at the end of the street he could almost admit to feeling happy.

And as he turned the corner and spotted Grace and the children coming along the terraced row towards him, caught the looks of surprised delight as their eyes alighted on him, he sensed even a moment of euphoria as his own little army came pelting down the street to greet him, the gladness on their faces serving to wipe away every last trace of loss.

EPILOGUE

September 1914

BATTLE OF THE MARNE. Fourteen-year-old Clem, just home from his new job as clerk in the pit manager's office, studied the newspaper headline for a moment before asking his mother, 'Where's Father?'

'Gone to do his duty,' came the vague reply.

'Well, I hope he isn't long in there 'cause I want to go.'

Grace looked up from her task of settling the younger ones at the tea table to see that her eldest son was joking. She lashed out playfully. 'You silly monkey, he's gone to Pontefract! How did work go?'

'All right.' Clem sounded unenthusiastic and flopped into a chair, loosening his tie and unbuttoning his starched collar. 'I'd rather be joining the mobilization.'

'You can get any such ideas out of your head right now!' His mother donned the kind of face that brooked no argument. 'One soldier in the house is enough.' Only the fact that her husband was in the Reserve and so compelled to answer the call of emergency had prevented an argument between them.

'I'll join when I'm old enough.' Clem was testing his manhood. 'No one can stop me.'

'No, but a bullet can, cleverclogs,' rebuked his mother. 'And you'd better get that collar buttoned before your father gets home too. Think yourself fortunate he got you that job so's you don't have to work down the mucky pit.'

'Will Father get killed?' Madeleine looked anxious.

'No! It'll all be over by Christmas.' Eleven-year-old Augusta, mindful of a little girl's fears, sought to allay them as she transferred the contents of her tray to the table.

'They said that about the last one,' replied Grace, 'and that went on for three years – but Father won't be harmed. Oh, I think I can hear him now! Is that you, Probe?'

'No, it's Jack the Ripper!' His merry reply bounced off the passage walls.

Whilst Clem hastily fastened his tie, Grace laughed and called back, 'How did it go?'

Still Probyn did not appear. 'Seems the powers that be have abolished the rank of colour-sergeant. So they had to give me summat else. Said it was a pity to put all my years of experience to waste.' Only now did he make his grand entrance.

Grace turned around inquisitively, her smile momentarily faltering before it curved into a great beaming crescent. There he stood in his old uniform, stretched to the limits by a girth much wider than at its last airing; yet it was not this which invoked her smile, for across that broad khaki expanse was strapped a Sam Browne belt.

Seven-year-old Joe gasped – 'Father's wearing a gun!' – and leapt from the table to come and examine the leather holster at his father's hip.

Grace clasped her hands together, overwhelmed with happiness for him so that tears sprang to her eyes. 'Oh, Probe, you've finally got it?'

'I've finally got it!' His own eyes glittered with pride and fulfilment. 'Regimental Sergeant-Major!'

Inspired by his mother's whoop of congratulation, Joe looked delighted too and gazed up into the noble beefy face, searching those blue-grey eyes and asking, 'What does a Regimental Sergeant-Major actually do, Father?'

'*Do*, lad?' boomed Probyn, his face a mixture of joy and achievement as his eyes twinkled down upon his son. 'Why, he just *is*!'

And more quietly. 'He just *is*.'

A Sense of Duty

Sheelagh Kelly

Flamboyant and fun-loving Kit Kilmaster rebels against the constraints of Victorian society and pursues her dreams. But, as Kit is to learn, there is a high price to pay for happiness . . .

While her brothers and sisters resign themselves to a life of drudgery, the voluptuous Katherine Kilmaster years for better things. Though her kin try to instil in her a sense of duty, Kit's cravings for the good things in life are too strong. And when her generous heart tempts her into dangerous situations with young men above her station, the family are scandalized by Kit's brazen attitude – although that doesn't prevent them accepting a share in the material rewards. For a time Kit revels in the life of a courtesan, launching herself upon London Society, until an unexpected consequence of her free-and-easy lifestyle stops her in her tracks.

Thrust back into claustrophobic village life, Kit falls prey to malicious gossip, and then to tragedy. Overwhelmed by events, she finally heeds the advice of her family, and is almost destroyed in the process. But then a chance encounter promises to deliver her the husband and children she has always wanted – provided her shameful secret is not revealed . . .

ISBN 0 00 651143 0

My Father, My Son

Sheelagh Kelly

From the author of the bestselling Feeney saga:

He survived the Boer war and the carnage of the First World War, but it was the bitter conflict on the home front that tore his life apart . . . .

After a year of fighting the Boer, Corporal Russ Hazlewood – missing his wife and tired of long, passionless nights on the veldt – seeks solace in the arms of an African woman. Only his friend Jack Daw knows of the relationship and the son who is born of it, and Russ's secret seems to be safe. He returns to his native York and builds a successful career in business, while he and his wife Rachel raise six daughters and a son.

But when the former comrades branch into local politics, rivalry breeds betrayal. Suddenly the past comes back to haunt Russ, threatening to destroy everything he cherishes, shattering the bonds between husband and wife, father and son.

Then, overshadowing all, comes the most dreadful war the world has ever seen. But when it is over, the greatest battle has still to be won – on the home front.

ISBN 0 00 651161 9